THE BLACKGOD

BY J. GREGORY KEYES
Published by Ballantine Books

CHOSEN OF THE CHANGELING

The Waterborn
The Blackgod

Chosen of the Changeling

BOOK TWO:

THE BLACKGOD

J. Gregory Keyes

Ballantine Books • New York

A Del Rey® Book
Published by Ballantine Books

Copyright © 1997 by J. Gregory Keyes
Illustrations copyright © 1997 by David A. Cherry
Endpaper map copyright © 1997 by Kirk Caldwell

Manufactured in the United States of America

For My Mother
Nancy Ridout Landrum

CONTENTS

Part Two: UPSTREAM PASSAGES

Part Three: THE GODS OF SHE'LENG

Acknowledgments

For Moral Support:
John Keyes, Tim Keyes, Earl Ridout, Helen Ridout
For Criticism:
Ken Carleton, Veronica Chapman, Gene Crawford, Tom Deitz,
Pat Duffy, Nell Keyes
And for Hard Work:
Christine Levis

PROLOGUE

Death

GHE plunged his steel into the pale man's belly, watched the alien gray eyes widen in shock, then narrow with terrible satisfaction. He yanked to withdraw his blade and, in that flicker of an instant, realized his mistake. The enemy edge, unimpressed by its wielder's impalement, swept down toward his exposed neck.

Li, think kindly of my ghost, he had time to think, before his head fell into the dirty water. Even then, for just a moment, he thought he saw something strange; a column of flame, leaping out of the muck, towering over Hezhi. Then something inexorable swallowed him up.

Death swallowed him and took him into her belly. Dark there, and wet, he swirled about, felt that last, bright blow like a line of ice laid through his neck flutter again and again and again, hummingbird-wings of pain. It was most of what remained of him, though not all. The little spaces between the memory of that blade stroke were like a doorway into nothing, opening and closing with greater and greater speed, and through that portal danced images, dreams, remembered pleasures—danced through and were gone. Soon all would gambol away like fickle ladies at a ball, and he would be complete again, just the memory of his death, and then not even that.

But then it seemed as if the sword shattered, raced up and down his spine like rivers of crystal shards; and the belly of death was no longer dark, but alive with light, charged with heat and lightning, burning, pouring in through that doorway. The light he recognized; he had seen its colors blossoming from the water as his head parted from his body. The doorway gaped and wrapped around him, bringing not darkness, not oblivion, but remembrance.

Remembrance carried hatred, bitterness, but most of all hunger. *Hunger.*

Ghe remembered also a word, as strands met and were torturously yanked into crude knots within him, tied hurriedly, without care.

No, he remembered. *Ah, no!*

No, and he fought to hands and knees he could suddenly feel again, though they felt like wood, though they jerked and quivered with unfamiliar weakness. He could see nothing but color, but he remembered where he wanted to go and had no need of vision. Down, he knew, and so he crawled, blind, whimpering, hungrier by the moment.

Down for he knew not how long, but after a time he fell, slid, fell again, and then plunged into water that scalded so terribly that it must have been *boiling.*

For a while, he could think of nothing but boiling water, for pain had returned to him, as well.

No. The pain went into him like a seed, grew, spread roots, sent limbs out through his eyes and mouth, shoots from his fingers, and then, very suddenly, ceased to be pain. He sighed, sank down into the water, which now enfolded him like a womb, utterly comforting and utterly without compassion; just a womb, a thing for him to grow in, but no mother or love wrapped around *that.* There he waited, content for a while, and after he was sure the pain was gone, he looked about for what had not blown through that dark doorway into nothingness—what remained of him.

He was Ghe, the Jik, one of the elite assassin-priests who served the River and the River's Children. Born in Southtown, the lowest of the low, he had risen—the memory stirred!—he had kissed a *princess*! Ghe clenched and unclenched his unseen hands as he felt the ghost of his lips brushing hers. He realized, dully, that he had kissed many women, but that the only actual, *particular* kiss he could remember was hers.

Why was that? Why Hezhi?

They had sent him to kill her, of course, because she was one of the Blessed. His task had been to kill her, and he had failed. Yet he had kissed her . . .

Abruptly his memory offered mirror-sharp images, a scene from his past—how long ago? But though his mind's sight was keen, the voices floated to him as if from far away, and though he saw through his own eyes, it was as if he watched strangers dance a dance to which he knew only a few steps.

He was in the Great Water Temple, in the interior chamber. Plastered white, the immense corbeled vault above him seemed to drink up the pale lamplight in the center of the room. More real, somehow, was the illumination washing down from the four corridors that met in the chamber, though it was dimmer still than the flame. He knew it for daylight, rippling through sheets of falling water that cascaded down the four sides of the ancient ziggurat in whose heart they stood, curtains of thunder concealing the doorways of the temple. In that coruscating aquamarine and the flickering of the lamp, the priest before him seemed less real than his many shadows, for they constantly moved as *he* stood still.

On his knees, Ghe yet remembered thinking of the priest standing over him, *You shall bow to me one day.*

"There are things you must know now," the priest told him, in his soft, little-boy voice; like all full priests, he had been castrated young.

"I listen for the fall of water," Ghe acknowledged.

"You know that our emperor and his family are descended from the River."

Ghe suppressed an urge to rise up and strike the fool down. *They think because I am from Southtown I know nothing, not even that. They think I am no more than a throat-slitter from the gutter, with the brains of a knife!* But he held that inside. To betray his feeling was to betray himself, and betraying himself would betray Li—Ghe-in-the-water wondered who *Li* was.

"Know," the priest went on, "that because they carry his water in their veins, the River is a part of them. He can live through them, if he chooses. The power of the Waterborn has but one source, and that is the River."

Then why do you hate them so? Ghe wondered. *Because they are part of the River, as you will never be? Because they need not have their balls cut off to serve him?*

The priest wandered over to a bench and sat down, taking his quivering shadows with him. He did not sign for Ghe to arise, and so he remained there, prostrate, listening.

"Some of the Waterborn are blessed with more," the man went on. "They are born with rather *more* of the River in them than others. Unfortunately, the Human body can contain only a certain amount of power. After that . . ."

The priest's voice dropped to a whisper, and Ghe suddenly realized that this was no mere rote litany any longer. This was something *real* to the priest, something that frightened him.

"After that," he went on, sounding like nothing so much as an eight-year-old boy confiding some terrible childhood discovery, "after that, they *change*."

"Change?" Ghe asked, from the floor. Here was something he did *not* know, at last.

"They are distorted by their blood, lose Human form. They become creatures wholly of the River."

"I don't understand," Ghe replied.

"You will. You will *see*," he answered, his voice rising to a firmer, more dissertative pitch. "When they change—the signs are discovered in childhood, usually by the age of thirteen—when they change, we take them to dwell below, in the ancient palace of our ancestors."

For a moment, Ghe wondered if this was some silly euphemism for murder, but then he remembered the maps of the palace, the dark underways beneath it, the chambers at the base of the Darkness Stair behind the throne. Ghe suddenly felt a chill. What *things* dwelt there, below his feet? What horror would disturb a priest merely to discuss it?

"Why?" Ghe asked cautiously. "If they are of the Blood Royal . . ."

"It is not only their shape that changes," the priest explained. He looked squarely at Ghe, his pale eyes lapis shards of the light shimmering down the facing hall. "Their minds change, become inhuman. And their power becomes great, without control. In times past, some River Blessed have passed unprotected; we have missed them. One was even crowned emperor before we knew he was Blessed. He destroyed most of Nhol in fire and flood."

The priest stood up and walked over to a brazier in which coals glowed dully. He nervously sprinkled a few shavings of incense on them, and a sharp scent quickly filled the room.

"Below," he whispered, "they are safe. And we are safe from them."

"And if they know their fate?" Ghe asked. "If they try to escape it?"

"We know what happens when the Blessed are not contained," the priest murmured. "If they cannot be bound beneath the city, then they must be given back to the River."

"Do you mean . . . ?" Ghe began.

The priest nearly hissed with the intensity of his reply. "The Jik were not created to carry on assassinations of enemies of the state, though you now serve that purpose well. Have you never wondered why the Jik answer to the priesthood and *not* the emperor directly?"

Ghe thought for only an instant before replying. "I see," he murmured. "We were created to stop the Blessed from running free."

"Indeed," the priest replied, his voice relaxing a bit. "Indeed. And more than a few have been killed by the Jik."

"I live only to serve the River," Ghe replied. And he meant *that*, with all of his heart, both of him; Ghe *then* and Ghe in the water.

But now he could see the lie, of course. The great lie that was the priesthood. They existed not to serve the River but to *keep him bound*. Those whom the River blessed were given their power for a purpose, so that he might walk the land rather than live torpidly within his banks—so that the god of the River might roam free. And the priests *bound* the River's children, though they pretended to worship him. If one worshipped a god, would not one help it realize its dreams? What matter to the River if a few buildings were crushed in the pangs of birth, a few Human Beings died? The River took in the souls of all when they died anyway; he drank them up. All belonged to him.

Far from worshippers, Ghe could see now, the priests were the *enemies* of the River. They had fought for centuries to keep the Royal Blood checked, diluted. That was why they had set him to kill Hezhi, the emperor's daughter—kill that beautiful, intelligent girl. And he would have done it, had not her strange barbarian guardian been unkillable! Ghe had stabbed him in the *heart* with a poisoned blade, and still he stood back up, chopped off Ghe's head—

He flinched away from that thought. *Not yet.*

However it had happened, it was fortunate that he had not slain Hezhi. Much depended upon her, he realized. The River had many enemies plotting against him, and now Ghe, the River's only true and loyal servant—now *he* had those enemies.

And he knew his task with a wonderful, radiant certainty. His task was to save Hezhi from *her* foes, for she was the River's daughter, and more. She was his hope, his weapon.

His flesh.

Soon enough, Ghe knew, he would open his eyes, would creep back up to the light, take up his weapons, and make his way where Rivers do not flow. A wrong would be righted, a god would be served, and perhaps, just perhaps, he would once again kiss a princess.

PART ONE

MANSIONS OF BONE

© Cherry '96

I

The Mang Wastes

Hezhi Yehd Cha'dune, once-princess of the empire of Nhol, yelped as what weight her small body possessed was suddenly stolen from her in an explosion of force and wind as the thief—her horse Dark—shook all four hooves free of the earth. For a moment they hung almost still above the uneven slope of shattered stone and snow, but Hezhi knew—knew in her belly—that when they struck back down the mare would just keep falling, tumbling head-over-tail down what seemed almost a sheer grade. She doubled her hands in Dark's mane and leaned against her neck, straining to hang on to the barrel-shaped torso with her legs, but when the horse's hooves were reunited with the ground—first front and then thunderously rear—she slapped back into the saddle with such force that one leg kicked unwillingly free of its stirrup. The surrounding landscape blurred into jolting white, gray, and blue nonsense as she ignored the free-flapping stirrup and just held on. Then, suddenly, the earth was flat again and Dark *really* ran, digging her head into the wind, hammering across the half-frozen ground like a four-limbed thunder god. The mare's flat-out run was so smooth, Hezhi's fear began to evaporate; she found the stirrup, caught the rhythm of the race, and her tightly held breath suddenly released itself in a rush that quickly became triumphant laughter. Never before had she completely given the Mang-bred horse her head, but now that she had, the chocolate-and-coffee-striped mare was gaining on the four riders ahead of her. When one of them—perhaps hearing her laughter—turned his head to look back, she was near enough to see the surprise register in his unusual gray eyes.

Thought you could leave me back farther than that, didn't you, Perkar? she thought, with more pride than anger. Her self-esteem doubled when the young man's expression of amazement became one of respect. She felt her own lips bow in glee and then promptly felt stupid for beaming so, like one of those useless creatures back in the palace or some brainless child. Still, it felt wonderful. Though she was only thirteen years of age, it had been many years since she felt anything at all like a child, good or bad. It couldn't hurt to smile and laugh if she *felt* like it, could it?

She clapped Dark's flanks harder and was rewarded by a burst of even greater speed from her steed—and was consequently nearly thrown over the mare's head when the animal quickly stamped to a halt to avoid crashing into Perkar and the others, who had stopped suddenly.

"What?" Hezhi sputtered. "Are you trying—"

"Hsst, Princess," Perkar stage-whispered, holding up a finger. "Yuu'han thinks our quarry is over the next rise."

"And?" she shot back, though lowering her voice, too.

"We should walk from here, or we may panic them," another man answered. Hezhi switched her regard to the second speaker, who was dismounting. He swung his right leg over his mount's head and let his thick, compact body slide to the ground; his boots crunched in the thin layer of snow. He was clothed in heavy breeks and an elkskin parka tanned white. In the hood, his face was paler than the coat, like bone, and his thick hair fell from one side in a milky braid. His eyes, on the other hand, were black, set deeply in his head beneath cavernous brows and a forehead that sloped back rather sharply from them, the legacy of his unhuman father.

"Thank you, Ngangata, for explaining *that*," she replied, "though I haven't the faintest idea what you are talking about."

"It's what we brought you to see," Perkar explained, also dismounting. His hood was down, his short chestnut hair in wind-combed disarray. He was slighter than Ngangata, narrower in every dimension though nearly as bleached looking to Hezhi's eyes, many shades fairer than her own sienna complexion. Lighter by far than their other two companions, Yuu'han and Raincaster, who were both Mang tribesmen, flesh burned copper brown by the fierce sun of their native deserts and plains.

"You brought me to see nothing!" Hezhi answered. "Indeed, you tried to leave me behind." She gestured back toward the hills they had just spilled down, where the highlands crumbled into the more gradually rolling plains the Mang called *huugau*. But even as she said this, she blushed; Perkar was grinning broadly and Ngangata not at all, but the two Mang were both studiously looking down and away from her. After half a year among the Mang, she knew what *that* meant. They were trying to keep her from seeing *their* smiles, which meant Perkar was telling the truth. They had intentionally goaded her into following and *let* her catch them.

She pursed her lips and made to wheel Dark about.

"No, wait!" Perkar shouted, forgetting his own admonition to silence. "We just wanted to see how well you can ride."

"You could have merely *asked*," she replied icily. But she was curious. "What did you decide?"

"That you have learned to ride as well in six months as even many Mang do not in six years," Raincaster answered, turning his youthful, aquiline features frankly on her. *That* startled her. The Mang *never* dissembled when they spoke of riding skill.

"I—" She frowned in frustration. Was she supposed to be angry or not?

She decided not, and dismounted. On the ground, her legs felt wobbly, and the snow immediately began leaking cold into her feet to match the numbness of her nose. "What am I supposed to be seeing, anyway?"

Perkar gestured in the direction they had been riding. Here the huugau was gently rolling, as if a sky god had pressed down on the hills with a great palm. The ridges and valleys were still there, but they were so gradual that one could be fooled into thinking their high places merely represented the distant horizon; this was especially true, Hezhi found, when they were blanketed with snow. "Over the ridge," Perkar explained, and the Mang nodded their slight but clear assurances.

"Very well," Hezhi said. "Let us go, then." And with that she marched past the men, striding quickly toward the ridge.

PERKAR stood rooted for an instant as Hezhi brushed past him, the hem of her long vermilion riding coat trailing imperiously behind her, short bob of obsidian hair bouncing with her stride. He looked to the other men, but Ngangata was fighting a grin while the Mang studied the earth.

"I'll watch the horses," Yuu'han assured them, and Perkar nodded, started at a jog to catch up with Hezhi. She heard him coming, though, and broke into a run.

"No, Princess!" He tried to whisper loud enough for her to hear him, but it sounded only like steam escaping a kettle—and she heeded it no more than that. But then she reached the crest of the hill, and her booted feet slowed. Perkar came alongside of her just as she halted completely.

"*By the River,*" she gasped, and Perkar had but to agree. In fact, the vista before them *reminded* him of the River, the Changeling, upon whose banks Hezhi had been born, a watercourse so wide one could scarcely see its far bank. But *this* river—the one before them—was of meat and bone, not water. It flowed brown and black, tinted reddish on the woolen crests of its waves, the humps where the great muscles of the beasts piled high behind their massive heads.

"*Akwoshat,*" Perkar breathed in his own tongue, despite himself. "Wild cattle. More cattle than all of the stars in heaven."

"I have never seen anything . . ." Hezhi trailed off, shaking her head. Her black eyes shimmered with wonder, and her mouth was pursed as if to say "oh!" She was very pretty, Perkar thought. One day she would be a beautiful woman.

"There's your Piraku, Perkar," Ngangata said softly, padding up behind them. "Drive a herd of those back to your pastures . . ."

Perkar nodded. "Would that it were possible. Look at them. They are the most magnificent beasts I have ever seen."

Raincaster had arrived, as well. "You would never tame them, Cattle-Man," he whispered. "They are like the Mang, untameable."

"I believe it," Perkar acknowledged. At this distance it was hard to comprehend the proportions of the individual animals, but they seemed to be at least half again the size of the cattle he knew, and the proud, sharp horns of the largest could probably fit his body between them. These were the cattle of giants, of gods, not of Human Beings. But they were beautiful to behold.

"You really brought me to see this?" Hezhi asked, and Perkar suddenly understood that she was speaking to *him*, not to all of them.

"Yes, Princess, I really did."

"I wish you wouldn't call me that," she said.

"Hezhi, then."

To his surprise, she reached over and squeezed his hand. "Thank you. I forgive you for trying to make me break my neck riding down from the hill. Although we could have seen this just as easily coming down here at a leisurely pace."

"That's true. But admit it—you love riding. I've watched you learn."

"I admit it," she said, releasing his hand.

They stood there silently for a time, watching the slow progress of the herd. Now and then one of the beasts would bellow, a proud, fierce trumpet that sent chills straight to Perkar's bones. The wind shifted in their direction, and the smell of the wild cattle

swirled about them, powerful and musky. He literally trembled
with homesickness then, with such a fierce desire to see his
father's damakuta and pastures—and the man himself—that he
nearly wept. Flexing and unflexing his hands to warm them, he
was only absently aware of the arrival of other riders behind
them, of the soft crunch of boots approaching.

"Ah, well," a reedy voice piped. "Look at this, Heen. My
nephew Raincaster has no more sense than to let our guests stray
onto the open plain."

Raincaster turned to the new arrival and shrugged. "As soon
hold the wind as this one," he replied, gesturing to Perkar.
"Yuu'han and I thought it best to go with them—keep them in
our sight."

"Heen," Perkar said, shaking himself from reverie to confront
Raincaster's accuser, "tell Brother Horse that I have no time to
travel at the pace of an old man."

Heen—a tired-looking spotted mutt—looked up when Perkar
said his name, wagged his tail slightly, and then sniffed at the
scent of cattle. If he conveyed Perkar's message to the old man
who stood beside him, Perkar did not notice. Nonetheless, the old
man—Brother Horse—glared at him. He was shorter than Perkar,
most of the difference in height coming in his bandy, bowed legs.
It was remarkable, Perkar thought, how the man's wide mouth
could be downturned and still somehow convey a sly grin. It was,
perhaps, the guileful twinkle in his dark eyes or, more likely still,
the memory of a thousand smiles etched into the brown leather of
his heavy square face.

"This pace has kept me alive much longer than yours is likely
to serve *you*," Brother Horse admonished. "And you, Granddaughter," he said, shaking a finger at Hezhi. "*You* should be
wise enough not to follow young men when they set out alone. I
have never known an instance in which they failed to find whatever accidents wait along the trail. Let them go *first*, flush out the
dangers. That is what young men are *for*."

"Oh," Hezhi replied, "I had no idea they had *any* use. Thank
you, *Shutsebe*, for the advice."

"Yes, *Shutsebe*," Perkar said, bowing, calling Brother Horse "grandfather," as well. Of course neither he nor Hezhi was actually related to the old man, but referring to someone—sixty years old? *eighty?*—thus was only common courtesy. "And see, we have found all your dangers for you."

"Have you? Have you indeed?"

Perkar shrugged. "You see them." He gestured at the cattle.

"*I* see them, but do you?"

Perkar frowned at the old man, puzzled.

"Raincaster?" Brother Horse asked.

The young Mang pointed with his lips, downslope and to their right. "Spotted Lion over there, crouched down, watching that straggling calf. She scents us, but she will stay away."

Brother Horse grinned at Perkar's gape of astonishment.

"A *lion*?" Hezhi asked. "A *lion* is near?"

Raincaster nodded. "That's why you shouldn't run off alone," he explained. "If the lioness had been watching the herd *here* rather than down *there* when you came running over . . ." He shrugged. Perkar felt himself blushing at his own stupidity. Of course where there were wild herds there would be wild hunters.

"Why didn't you say something?" Hezhi demanded.

"I would have—*later,*" Raincaster assured her. "When it would not be an embarrassment to speak it." The young man shot Brother Horse an admonishing glance.

Brother Horse only chuckled. "Raincaster, do not forget that they are like children in this land. We have to treat them that way." He stepped forward and clapped Perkar on the shoulder. "I don't mean that in a bad way, Perkar."

"I know that," Perkar replied. "And you are right, as usual."

"Everyone knows their own land the best," Ngangata put in. He had been silent throughout the whole exchange. "So I'm sure that Raincaster meant to mention the second lioness, downslope and on our *left* hand. Twenty paces." His voice, though a *very* faint whisper, got the attention of everyone. Even Brother Horse started a bit.

"Stand tall," the old man murmured. "Stand tall and walk back."

Perkar laid his hand on the hilt of his sword. "Harka?" he whispered.

"*Yes?*" his sword replied in a voice that was born just within the cup of his ear—a voice no one else could hear.

"This lioness . . ."

"*I was just noticing her. She may be a slight threat, but I sense no real intent to attack.*" Perkar suddenly felt his eyes move of their own accord, and a nearby jumble of rocks and scrubby bushes suddenly revealed, in their midst, a yellow eye and the darkened tip of a cat's muzzle.

"And the other? Why didn't you mention the other?"

"*She is no danger at all. My task is to keep you alive, not to prevent you from appearing foolish. It would take more enchantment than I possess to fulfill that obligation.*"

"What of Hezhi? *She* might have been in danger, when first she ran up there."

"*I can sense danger only to you, not to your friends,*" the sword replied.

And so the four of them walked backward until they reached their horses, where Perkar thought he heard Yuu'han—who, true to his word, had waited patiently for them—chuckle dryly.

THEY waited, mounted, while Raincaster went cautiously back to the ridge and made his offering to the god of the herd. Perkar could see the little wisp of smoke and hear the young man singing in a fine, clear voice. He feared that the lioness would choose to attack the lone warrior, but Raincaster went unmolested. Perkar understood the man's determination to make the offering; back home he and his family sacrificed daily to keep the good graces of the gods of their pasture—how much more important that must be here, where the land was untamed, where many of the gods must be like the lioness, seeing them only as potential prey. He shivered. It put what he and Ngangata were soon to do into a different perspective. And it had been foolish of him to so endanger Hezhi; though she had learned more than seemed possible in a few months, it was important to remember that she had been a captive in her father's palace for nearly her entire life. She did not even have the natural cautions *he* did, and his served him poorly in this treeless land. Inwardly he nodded. Any thoughts he had entertained of asking the young woman to join Ngangata and him on their journey vanished. She would be safe with Brother Horse; *he* knew the ways of this country, had survived them for many years.

The decision brought many kinds of relief with it. It was undeniable that he was developing some small sort of affection for Hezhi, though it would be impossible to articulate exactly what he felt. In her, pain and distrust were so tightly bound; he wished sometimes that he could draw her into his arms and somehow understand, soothe away some of that hurt. But she would detest such closeness; it would harden her. And at other times, he had no wish to touch Hezhi at all, much less hold her. There was still so much for him to forget, when it came to her . . .

As Raincaster sang, the remainder of the Mang hunting expedition came down out of the hills, slowed by the travois their horses carried, packed with meat, pine nuts, and skins for winter clothing. All told, they numbered some thirty men and women and fifty horses. The thin cry of an infant rose clearly from the approaching riders. For the past two months they had all camped in the hills, hunting, singing, and drinking. It had been a good time, and it had given him some chance to heal, to forget his crimes, to be merely a man of eighteen, hunting and riding with Ngangata, Yuu'han, and Raincaster. Now, however, it was time to shoulder his burdens once again.

Raincaster finished his song, and they mounted up and rode east, away from the herd. There had been some suggestion of trying to kill a straggling cow, but they were already burdened with too much food, and the older people—Brother Horse included—disdained hunting for sport. A few of the younger men wanted to ride off and engage in a sport known as Slapping, in which they would ride close to a bull and strike it with a wooden paddle, but Brother Horse forbade it, grumbling that he was too old to explain such foolish deaths to grieving parents. And so they left the incredible herd behind, in peace.

Hezhi rode beside Brother Horse, and Perkar trotted T'esh over to join them. Hezhi was enthusiastically remarking on the previous night's snowfall.

"It never snows in Nhol?" Perkar asked Hezhi, coming up beside her. T'esh whickered softly, and Dark responded with a like sound.

"Not that *I* know of," she replied. "It gets cold sometimes—I may have *heard* about it snowing there before, but I've never seen it." She gestured out at the landscape. "This is like riding upon the clouds," she offered.

"Eh?" Brother Horse grunted.

"Clouds. It's as if we ride above the clouds—on top of them."

Perkar nodded agreement. They could easily be on the back of an overcast sky; the land was gently rolling paleness, the highlands receding into a gray line to their right and behind. Above them, higher heaven was profound azure with no hint of white. It seemed almost reasonable that at any moment they might pass over a small rift or hole and, peering through it, regard the green, blue, and brown of landscape far, far below.

"Will this weather hinder the—" Perkar paused to try to get the word right. "—Bun-shin?"

"*Ben'cheen*," Brother Horse corrected. "*Ben'*, 'tent,' see? 'Swollen Tents.' "

Perkar nodded through his exasperation. "Will the snow hinder the Ben'cheen festival?"

"Not at all," Brother Horse said. "Our kinfolk from the high plains will be arriving already, and they'll have come through worse weather than this."

"How many people will attend this gathering?" Hezhi asked. "Duk and the other women talk as if it will be the whole world."

"To you they will seem few," Brother Horse admitted. "But

there will be many hundreds, perhaps a thousand, for at least a score of days."

"Why in wintertime?" Perkar asked.

"Why not?" Brother Horse grunted. "What else is there to do? And believe me, the winters here in the south are mild—it's really almost spring, and this the first, probably only, snow. It is our obligation to host the Ben'cheen for our less fortunate kinfolk, give them a warmer place to stay." He smiled ruefully. "Like birds, flying south," he offered. "Winter is the best time to tell stories, best time to find a woman—" He winked at Perkar. "—best for all of that. Summer is just work!" He reached over and clapped Perkar on the back. "The two of you will enjoy it. Meet new people. Perkar, you might even encounter some warriors from the northwestern bands and start talking to them about that truce you want to strike between them and your folk."

"Really more than a truce," Perkar said. "I hope to convince them to let us expand our pastures into some of their higher rangelands."

"It's not impossible," Brother Horse said. "Not with the right mediator."

Perkar shook his head. "Our people have been enemies for so long . . ."

Brother Horse spread five fingers in the wind. " 'Thus the tree grows,' " he quoted, " 'and each new branch, as a new tree. Nothing is unchanging, least of all the ways of people.' " He frowned a bit sternly. "But you have to *be* there, to have hope of accomplishing anything."

Perkar set his mouth. "I *will* be there," he promised. "According to your nephew, Yuu'han, my trip will only delay me for a few days."

Hezhi turned on him, eyes suddenly wide and angry. She seemed to fight down a sharp remark—so sharp that, by her face, it must have cut her throat to swallow.

"You *still* plan to go?"

"I must, Hezhi," Perkar explained. "If I am to set matters right, there are many things I must do, and this is one. Two days' ride north of here, no more; I must go."

"Then I should go with you," she snapped, all her earlier happiness and enthusiasm evaporated. "Unless you *still* don't trust me."

"I trust you," Perkar insisted. "I told you that. I hold *no* animosity toward you."

"So you say," Hezhi whispered, her voice carrying an odd mixture of anger and . . . something else. "But I see you looking at me sometimes. I see that look. And when you talk of 'setting things right,' I *know*—" She broke off angrily, seemed unsure whether to glare or look hurt. She was, he reminded himself, only thirteen.

Perkar puffed an exasperated breath, white steam in the frigid air. "Maybe. A little. But I know you did nothing purposely—not like *I* did."

"I thought you could—" she began, but again didn't finish. Her face clamped down in a determined frown, and she kneed her horse, laying the reins so that he turned.

"Go then," she said. "You owe nothing to me."

"Hezhi . . ." Perkar started, but found himself staring at her back. A moment ago they seemed friends, watching the wild cattle hand in hand. He wondered what it was about him that always led him to *do* the wrong things, *say* the wrong things.

"What was all that about?" the old man grunted.

Perkar cocked his head in puzzlement, then realized that his conversation with Hezhi had been in Nholish. He started to translate, but a second thought struck him; Brother Horse *knew* Nholish. When the Mang had spirited Hezhi and him out of Nhol, it had been Brother Horse who first comforted the girl. He was pretending—in typical Mang fashion—not to understand the argument out of politeness.

"Nothing," Perkar said. "She just doesn't want me to go."

"Well, it *isn't* wise," Brother Horse said.

"Ngangata will be with me."

"Yes, well, even *he* may not be able to keep you out of trouble. Nagemaa, the Horse Mother, gave birth to the Mang. She watches us, teaches us out here on the plain. Did you know that six races of Human Beings died out here in the Mang country before *we* came along? Among them were the Alwat."

"He saw the lion when you did not," Perkar reminded him.

"So he did. As a hunter and tracker, few can match him, I will grant that. But without the blood of horses in his veins, with no kin among the hooved gods, he must rely *only* on himself. That is a dangerous position to be in."

"He can rely on *me*, as I rely on him."

"Two blind men do not make a sighted one, my friend," the old man answered.

HEZHI tried to keep her face low, to hide it from the Mang women. If they saw her face, they would read the anger on it as easily as *she* might read a book. She didn't want anyone trying to guess what she was angry about, especially since her *own* ire puzzled and confused her—vexing her even further. Not for the first time, she wished she were back in the palace in Nhol, tucked away in some secret place, alone with her thoughts. Instead, she was surrounded by strangers, people watching her face, noting and questioning each quirk and quiver of her lip. People who wanted to know what she was thinking and were good at figuring it out. These Mang were *too* concerned about each other, she reflected. It was *everybody's* business how everybody else felt. Not because they were kindhearted, either; Duk had explained that. It was just that when you lived with the same few people most of your life, you had to know how they were feeling; there were stories of people going berserk or becoming cannibals because they hadn't been watched carefully enough, hadn't been caught before they lost their minds. All of the women told their children such stories—taught them a certain suspicion of everyone, even close relatives.

Well, she could understand knowing only a few people. Everyone here seemed to think that because she was from Nhol, the great city, she must have known *thousands* of people. But she had really known only a handful, a tiny few, and all of the others had just been shadows cast by the palace, less substantial than the ghosts that wandered its halls. Here, with the Mang, she had to deal on a daily basis with easily three times as many people as she ever had before—people who *watched* her.

It was wearing thin, and she wanted to go with Perkar and Ngangata. They were only two, and not as nosy.

Why wouldn't he take her? Did he think she didn't know where he was going—that she cared? She knew he was going to see the goddess he was in love with; she had heard Yuu'han tell him that her stream was only a short ride north. Did he think that she would be jealous, that she *loved* him in some silly, romantic way? If so, then he remained a stupid barbarian and had learned *nothing* of her since they met. She didn't care about the goddess; she just didn't want to be left alone with the Mang and their eyes. She didn't want Perkar to go off and be eaten by some snow-colored carnivore. Mostly, she wanted him to stop *blaming* her.

Or maybe he didn't really blame her for the twists his life had taken. Maybe she was just blaming herself. Maybe every time he made it clear how *guilty* he felt about everything, it only reminded her that it had been her silly, childish wish at the fountain that had brought him down the River to be her "savior" in the first place—that all of the horrible things that tasked him so were really *her* fault.

It had taken an instant of weakness at the fountain, that was all—one single moment in her life when she had thought it might be nice to have someone other than herself to trust and count on. Wasn't she even allowed that? She guessed not, not when the Blood Royal in her veins could make such wishes come true.

Maybe she was just mad at him because there was no one else suitable to be mad at. Not Tsem, faithful Tsem, waiting back at the Mang village recovering from near-fatal wounds he received saving *her*. But it was *someone's* fault that she was in the wilderness, with only the single book her old teacher Ghan had managed to send her; she had read it twice now. And it was surely someone's fault that she was doing boring things like scraping hides while Perkar and his friend Ngangata went hunting beasts and roaming across the plains like wild brothers.

Still fuming when they made camp, she rebuffed Perkar's single attempt to make amends, and, not knowing what else to do, she took out some of her precious paper, her pen and ink, and she began writing a letter to Ghan, the librarian.

She began:

Dear Ghan,

I think that I will never be Mang. I know this is a peculiar way to begin a letter, but I have never written a letter before, and the best thing I can think of is what I am thinking. I shall never be Mang, though I thought for a time I might. I have learned to cook and tan hides, to praise the men when they return from the hunt, to watch children when the married women—many my own age— are busy. None of these things are difficult or bad, once one learns to do them; it is just that they are not interesting. The Mang seem to lack curiosity, for the most part, seem to believe they under- stand the world as much as it can be understood. In this, they are no different from most people I knew in the palace. Wezh, for instance, my onetime paramour—how angry you were with me for humoring him, and for good reason—what does he care for knowl- edge? I think that people everywhere must generally be content without knowing very much.

Not that knowledge has ever made me content; it has always complicated my life. It is only in the action of discovery that it brings me any sense of satisfaction.

So I will never be Mang, any more than I could have been Nholish. I can only be Hezhi, and perhaps, someday, Ghan, for you are the only person I know who shares my disease, whose life I ever aspired to lead.

I am safe here, I believe, at least from the power of the River. As you suspected, the change in my body has ceased now that I have left the River behind—unnatural change, that is, though some of the "normal" changes I continue to face seem at least unholy. But whatever happens to me, whatever fate befalls me now, it will not be that dark hall beneath the Darkness Stair where the Blessed dwell, where my cousin D'en and my Uncle Lhekezh swim about like eels. It will not be that.

I should tell you a bit about the Mang, to correct some of the more fanciful accounts in The Mang Wastes, the book you sent along to me. For one thing, they do not beat their children to make them strong; on the contrary, they are perhaps too lenient with them. They also do not live entirely on horseback, sleeping and making love in the saddle—though both occur now and then, I hear. They live for most of the year in houses of timber and clay known as yekt. During certain seasons they move about in smaller groups, but even then they carry skin tents called ben' which they can erect in a few moments. The accounts of them living only upon the flesh of giant beasts with snakes for noses and long sabers of bone instead of teeth are partially true, however. I have yet to see such a beast—the Mang call them nunetuk—but I am told that they exist. Men hunt them on horseback with long lances, and it is very dangerous. More often, however, they hunt deer, bison, elk, rabbit, and so forth. (Today I saw dubechag, beasts like water oxen but much larger. They were unbelievable; they reminded me that there is wonder here.) Most of what they eat isn't hunted at all, as I should well know, for women spend days at a time picking berries and nuts, digging up roots, making bread (they trade for the flour) and so on. They also keep goats, some of them, for milk and meat. The food is filling but bland—they don't have much salt and seem careless of spices. I miss Qey's black bread, pomegranate syrup, coffee, and River rice! Please find some way of telling Qey so, but do not endanger yourself.

My light is fading; now I write by firelight, and the women are beginning to talk about me; I suppose I should do some chores. First I must tell you something important.

Our escape plans went wrong, as you know, and only Perkar and his sword enabled us to leave Nhol. We were betrayed, Ghan, by the one called Yen. I did not tell him anything—I would not have jeopardized your life so—but Yen was not, as he claimed, a young engineer. He was, I think, an assassin, a Jik. His real name is Ghe, or so he boasted. Perkar killed him, cut his head off, so he is no danger to you. But be careful, Ghan. He may have told others about the help you gave me; he observed us so closely, I think we *had no secrets from him. I am constantly surprised by the masks people wear. I trusted Yen, thought he liked me, and yet he was my worst enemy. I thought you hated me, and yet you were my most loyal friend. I miss you.*

Whoever takes this letter to you will be instructed not to give it to anyone else. I've written it in the Middle Hand so that even if someone else does intercept it, they will probably have to bring it to you for translation!

I'll write more later.

Hezhi sighed, sprinkled powder over the wet ink, then blew it off. She waited a bit, there by the fire, for the ink to dry, meanwhile taking over the chore of stirring the stew from Grumbling Woman, the oldest of the women on the trip.

Duk, Brother Horse's granddaughter, only a year or so younger than Hezhi, sidled over and squatted next to her, shot long, obvious glances at the paper.

"What were you doing?" she asked, when Hezhi did not readily offer any explanation in response to her nonvocal query.

"Writing," she answered, using the Nholish word. There was no such word in Mang.

"What's that?"

"Putting speech down so that someone else can see it."

"See speech?"

"Those marks stand for words," Hezhi explained. "Anyone who knows them can understand what I wrote."

"Oh. Magic then," Duk said.

For a moment, Hezhi considered explaining. But this was Duk, who was content to think that Nhol was at the very edge of the universe, that anyone sailing beyond on the River would plunge into an endless abyss.

"Yes," Hezhi agreed. "Magic." And she reflected that if she were ever a teacher, she would be a teacher like Ghan, accepting only the brightest. She had no patience for anyone else.

"Then you should be careful," Duk whispered. "There are already those who say you are a witch."

Hezhi snorted but then became more thoughtful. Being thought a witch was dangerous. It was the kind of thing that could get you killed in your sleep. She would have to think on this, certainly.

"I'm not a witch, Duk," she said, her best response for the moment.

"I know, Hezhi. You are just very strange. From *Nhol.*"

"Well, sugar candy and brass bells come from Nhol, too, and everyone *likes* them," Hezhi replied.

"*That's* true," Duk agreed. "Oh," she then went on. "Mother wants us to lace together those boots."

"Ah," Hezhi said. *That* was why Duk had wanted to know what she was doing; not because she really cared, but as an overture to conscripting her. She shrugged. "Very well."

MORNING rendered the snow-covered plain into beaten brass, and they rode straight into the glare of it. The novelty of snow was beginning to wear off for Hezhi; it was becoming the same nuisance to her that it was to everyone else.

Not long into the day, Perkar and Ngangata rode over to say their farewells. Perkar had that worried, put-upon look that she was coming to recognize instantly. Perhaps she *was* becoming Mang, at least in *that* way. In Nhol she had rarely paid much attention to what others might be thinking.

"I'll rejoin you in a few days," Perkar told her. "Give my regards to Tsem."

"I will," she replied, trying to keep her voice neutral, trying to be nice.

Perkar nodded, then leaned a bit closer. "When I return, we shall race, you and I. Practice your riding!"

His attempt to sound jovial failed, but she relented and smiled—just a little smile—to let him know she didn't hate him. It was the kind of smile she used to give Qey when the old woman was on the verge of tears. *Just enough, and no more.*

But Perkar, the dolt, replied with a big grin, certain that he had won some victory.

"Watch him, Ngangata," Hezhi told the half Alwa, "though by now you must be weary of *that* task."

Ngangata quirked his mouth evilly. "True enough. Perhaps I will do us all a favor and 'take him hunting.'"

Brother Horse, not far away, clipped out a little chuckle at the reference—the plot of half a dozen Mang stories in which an unwanted child was "taken hunting" in some faraway place and abandoned there.

Perkar, a bit slower than Hezhi when it came to learning Mang, looked merely puzzled by the remark and the reaction it evoked. Hezhi had to suppress an *actual* smile then: Perkar was at his most appealing when he looked perplexed.

Hezhi watched the two until they were black specks on the horizon, gone.

She kept to herself, after that, though Duk and Brother Horse both tried to start conversations. Hezhi, however, was thinking about her next letter to Ghan. She sorted through the things she had learned since leaving the city and lagged Dark back so that she could watch the motion of the hunting party. The Mang liked to laugh and play, but when it came time to do something, they did it. Not for the approval of some court, not to win the respect of others, but because their lives depended upon it. In the movement of the horses and their riders, little motion was wasted; packs were distributed evenly so that no one animal was burdened more than the others. Not that there were no lazy, selfish, or stupid Mang; but such persons learned to do what they must anyway, because even a mother would indulge her child only so far. What she had written to Ghan was true; children were not beaten. Their punishment consisted of being ignored, even to the point of not being fed when they were too willful. A Mang learned early that cooperation and hard work were the only secure route toward a full belly, something she herself was having a hard time adjusting to—in the palace there had never been any question about whether she would be *fed* or not. Still, despite the drudgery of the work, in peaceful moments it brought a subdued joy, like reading a well-written phrase, not flowery, not audacious, just saying what it should say clearly and perfectly.

She wondered what the Ben'cheen would be like, how interested Ghan might be in the goings-on there, and her heart lifted a bit more.

It will be good to see Tsem, too, she reflected, and decided that perhaps her anger at Perkar was, after all, inappropriate. She had never *needed* anyone before, never been annoyed at someone simply for not choosing to remain near her. What was the point in becoming too dependent on a barbarian she hardly knew?

Satisfied for the moment, she glanced out at the landscape once more. Up ahead—half of the horses had already passed it—she could see a little cairn of stones. As she watched, Brother Horse reined in his horse, dismounted, and added a stone from his pack to the pile. Hezhi thought to herself that she should remember to ask him why . . . and then she *saw* it.

Though "saw" could never describe the way her eyes were invaded, as if they were doors forced by soldiers storming a house. Images and sensations far removed from mere vision raced through those shattered portals and assaulted her mind. It was a shivering of the air, like the outline of a ghost, like her father conjuring, like the string of a lute vibrating, but it was something much more violent than that, a rape, and she shrieked at the unexpectedness of it, at the alien thoughts that suddenly filled her head like crawling worms and spider hairs. She gagged and turned away, only vaguely aware of a voice, shrieking—her own voice. She was as she had been by the River, growing, her power becoming greater as her *self* shrank away beneath a flood of motives that were no more hers than the distant stars. Then she lost that association, shuttered her eyes against the terror, but it was still there, in her head.

And then it was gone, leaving only a confused memory, a beast who crossed the trail and left only its stench.

Brother Horse was beside Dark, murmuring something soothing. He was dismounted, she saw, holding out his arms to her. She felt, for a moment, that she would not need his comfort, for she seemed not to feel anything at all besides confusion. Her body, however, knew better than her shocked mind, and as the first of many sobs heaved from her tiny chest, she slid from Dark into Brother Horse's arms, the scent of leather and smoke and old man. He stroked her hair and said nothing of consequence. Nothing, that is, save for one brief statement.

"I was afraid of this," he murmured. "I feared this would happen."

II

Rebirth

GHE awoke. Something was trying to eat him.

It was something massive, an impression of fish, snake, and scorpion all at once. It nuzzled against him, fine tentacles groping at the strands of power that held his life together. This he noticed only peripherally, without any real fear. All of his fear and emotion was consumed in a flame that racked his body with trembling need, a need so great he did not even begin to understand it, one that allowed no space for other concerns. Every fiber of him yearned, pleaded, begged. He gasped and pushed away from the monstrous nuisance, searching for whatever it was he needed so badly. He sucked in a breath and his lungs stung as if he had inhaled shards of glass, and he suddenly understood that he had not *breathed* in a great while . . .

The *thing* took hold of him with cables of living flesh, and Ghe snarled, turned on it, and lashed out with the edge of his palm and with all his objectless frustration. The blow glanced harmlessly from the armored skin of the thing, but at the same moment, the beast seemed to open up, become a fine webwork of lines, clustered about a knot of color so tantalizing, so very beautiful, that Ghe cried aloud. He recognized, in that instant, his need. It was *hunger* he felt, hunger magnified and distorted beyond all comprehension, but still hunger. Hunger for what he saw, for the light and life of this thing. Howling like a dog, he reached, tore at the rich heartstrands of the monster, snapped them like spiderweb. He understood that it was not his hands that did this—he could see them, motionless against the rubbery flesh—yet as the strings of light tore writhing apart they seemed to burrow into his palms, course like fiery new veins up his arms, into his chest, burning into the cavern where his hunger dwelt and filling it with substance. It was such a profound pleasure and agony that it threatened mindless delirium. The fish-thing struggled, tore at him with claw and stinger, but its life gave Ghe strength, and pain meant little in the face of his hunger. Soon enough, the beast lay still, the last feeble strands of its life drifting into the waist-deep water like shed hairs.

Only then did Ghe look about him. It was dark, pitch-dark, and yet he could see. He was beneath the vault of a great hall, majesty cloaked in darkness, drowned in water, smeared with filth. Water, cold and flat as lead, filled the place. Four hallways ran out from the great chamber, each blocked by a massive iron grille.

"Where am I?" he asked aloud of the darkness. "What place is this?" But it seemed to him that it was *his* place, *his* throne room. He could see the throne itself, carven alabaster waves lapping down from it to join the real water. Thoughtfully, he approached the magnificent chair, walking up the steps to it and out of the water. After a moment's reflection, he settled into it and surveyed his newfound kingdom once again.

Far off, down one of the halls, something moved, rippling the water. He could sense the flicker of its heartstrands. That stirred a faint hunger, but he was sated enough to be curious. Concentrating, he saw another, and another.

"You there," he grated, his voice harsh and clotted from long disuse. "You there," he repeated. "Who are you?"

For a long moment no reply came, but then slowly, with seeming reluctance, one of the swimmers approached. A semi-Human head arose from the water and peered at him through the grille.

"You killed Nu," the head accused.

"Did I? This Nu tried to eat me."

Gar-teeth flashed in the fishlike face; bulging eyes goggled at him. "Hezhi? Is that you? Hezhi, my niece?" the head asked.

Ghe narrowed his eyes. "What do you know of her?" he demanded.

"Ah, so it is *not* you, not Hezhi." The head sniffed. "Not of the Royal Blood at all, but *like* the Royal Blood. How did you kill Nu?"

"I ate him, I think."

"Her," the creature corrected pettishly.

"Her," Ghe amended. "Tell me, where am I?"

"Well," the thing answered, now swimming—or possibly pacing—back and forth at the grate. "Well. So many visitors lately."

"Answer me," Ghe commanded.

"So many visitors coming in the back door, not down the stair at all."

"The stair?" Ghe frowned. He remembered a stair, remembered himself and others carrying someone down it, long ago, down it into a black place. "The Darkness Stair? We are below the Darkness Stair?"

"The chambers of the Blessed." The thing in the water sneered. "Don't you feel blessed?"

"But I didn't come down the stair?"

"You *fell* in, through the duct, the one Hezhi crawled through. We thought you were dead, all except Nu. I think *she* thought you were her child, something stupid like that." The creature laughed. "Now I guess she doesn't think anything. Lucky Nu, eh?"

Ghe felt his annoyance growing. Still, he tried to keep hold of his anger, control it, as he always had. "How long? How long ago?"

The head suddenly burst into a gurgling parody of laughter.

That went on for some time, as Ghe gripped the armrest of the throne more and more tightly. When at last the creature lapsed into quiet sobs of mirth—or sorrow—it was difficult to tell—he repeated his question.

"I'm *sorry*," the creature said. "I'm afraid I lost track of the suns passing overhead, the phases of the moon. Careless of me, eh?"

"Long time? Short time?"

"All time is long," the thing returned, and retreated beneath the water.

GHE remained on the alabaster throne, ordering his thoughts, watching the distant swirl of the creatures. They were the Blessed, of course, the sort of things Hezhi would have become; creatures so filled with the River's power that they became distorted and inhuman. Here the priesthood trapped them, where their power was nullified by the essence of the River itself. The water in the hall was barely wet at all; it was *She'ned*, smokewater, a powerful, numbing substance.

Why am I alive? The thought bloomed like a black rose, always there, never fully opened before. He had thought and dreamed and remembered for what seemed like an eternity; but at the root of that dreaming was the blow to his neck, over and over again, his head falling into the muck, a weird glimpse of his own legs buckling, the fountain of iridescence rising. Now he was here, with the Blessed. Was he trapped, as they were?

Ghe blew out a long breath, steeled himself, and reached fingers up to his throat, stroking lightly from the base of his ear down. *There:* a raised ridge of flesh. He followed it around, found that it ringed him, a necklace of scar tissue.

"What does it mean?" he demanded, of no one in particular. But after a moment he nodded, answered himself. "I *know* what it means. The River remade me, put me back together, so that I might find his child and return her to him." He reached his hand out before him, marveling at the touch of his fingertips against one another. "Not dead," he whispered. "But not exactly alive either, I'll wager. Not exactly alive." And he remembered his hunger, like the hunger of fire for more wood, and he felt a little thrill of fright.

"I wish I knew more." But he wanted *more* than that. He wanted to *see* someone, *talk* to someone, prove to himself that he *was* alive and not in some lonely afterworld. He wanted to understand why he could open the doors to certain memories so easily, while other rooms in his mind were swept clean or drowned in chill, deep water.

It seemed that there was *someone*—an image came to him: an old woman, dark, hunched over a cloth, casting bone dice. But there was no name, no place, nothing. His mother? But no, that felt wrong.

Whom *did* he know? He remembered several priests, but even in this state he did not want to see them. No, he remembered only Hezhi very clearly, he remembered everything about her, he remembered her friends—the giant, Tsem; the old man, Ghan; and that little idiot, Wezh, who courted her.

Well, Hezhi was not in Nhol; that was why he was still alive. Tsem was probably dead, for Ghe remembered stabbing him— though, of course, he had stabbed the white demon swordsman and *he* had not died. But if Tsem wasn't dead, he was gone with Hezhi. Ghan . . .

He considered Ghan, the librarian. The old man had helped Hezhi escape; Ghe had followed him and divined his plans. But Ghan himself had not planned to leave Nhol. Furthermore, Ghe had never told the priesthood of Ghan's identity; he had been saving that for later, to tell the high priest himself so no lower-order theurg could claim to have discovered the traitors. That meant the priesthood might not know about him, might not have tortured him to death.

That pleased Ghe for more than one reason. He remembered, vaguely, that he admired the old man for his willingness to help the girl. He had considered never reporting him at all . . .

Ghe shook his thoughts back into line. Ghan might still be alive and well in the library. And Ghan knew him only in his disguise as Yen, a young engineer who engaged in harmless flirtation with Hezhi. If he were Yen, Ghan might speak to him. *He must speak to me,* he thought, again feeling the scar and wondering why there was no revulsion.

Yes, he could be Yen again, couldn't he?

Of course, first he had to leave the underpalace, and the only way out *he* knew was by the Darkness Stair. He was not yet ready to risk the stair and its guardians—who knew what effect the priestly wards might have on him? Yet the thing in the water seemed to intimate that there were other ways out, one way, in fact, that Hezhi herself had braved. Ghe smiled and shook his head at the thought. His estimation of Hezhi continued to rise. Certainly he had been a fool to try to kill her; she was worth the whole priesthood and the aristocracy, too. He imagined the sweetness of her lips once more, that warm forbidden thing.

Yes, she was a marvelous creature. If she should reduce Nhol to rubble when he brought her back, why should he care? He was now, in his own way, a child of the River, too.

But out, he reminded himself. He must have come down from the sewers, somehow. His memory of it was of no use: he had been blind, a worm crawling down, waterward. Now he was a man again, and so he would have to use his mind, his hands, his eyes—though his eyes were no longer human, nor, he suspected, were his mind and hands.

He used those eyes to find the water duct that emptied into the chamber, though no light at all existed to aid him. *Well,* he thought, *a place to begin.*

He rose up from the throne.

He made many false turns in the strange, twisted ways beneath the city, but eventually, he found a clean breath of air and followed it. Its source was a sewer grate, peering down at him from above, the air sweet, smelling of smoke and roasted meat. He shuddered in relief, for he had begun to suspect that his resurrection was merely some terrible joke played out by the River God, a punishment for failing—a curse to wander the beneath forever. But the air and its scents were real, because he could not have remembered them sharply enough to imagine them.

No light fell through the grate, and so he judged it to be night. This was fortuitous; he had no desire to emerge onto a crowded, daylit street. He realized that he had no idea what he looked like, though he knew his form was much as it had been. He was not, like the Blessed, a distorted monster. Still, it would be safer to see himself before another saw him—there might be surprises more evident than his scarred neck. He *knew* his clothes would attract attention, for they were rotted; they stank, though he only now took note of that. He would have to do something about them. As he thought this, he shook his head in wonder. *His clothes were rotted.* How long had he been beneath the city? Perhaps Ghan and everyone he knew was dead, Hezhi an old woman. There were old stories about such things, men thought drowned in the River who emerged after generations . . .

Best not to think about that anymore. Best to learn the truth, since it lay just above him. He found the foothold spikes in the stone wall and climbed up them. The grate, cast iron, shifted easily—too easily, and he began to wonder how different he was now. He could see in the dark, he was stronger, much stronger . . .

He was something like a ghost, but not a ghost. A memory tickled at him. There were stories of things like that, as well. He could hear the voice of an old woman talking, almost chanting. He could not see her face, nor could he remember the words, or again, her name.

He pulled himself out onto the street. A wind swept over him, channeled by the walls of the buildings on either side. Above, dense layers of smoke and perhaps clouds as well obscured the stars, but he could see a faint, pale luminescence seeping through them that might be the moon.

He was in a long, narrow courtyard. A fountain gurgled not far away. He could hear a baby crying.

This was, he realized, no street in Nhol. He had emerged, been reborn to the world, in the Chakunge's palace, the very heart of the empire.

As it should be, he thought. *As it should always have been.*

III

Snow Thunder

Perkar eyed the sky dubiously. "I wonder if we should make camp *now*," he muttered.

Ngangata surveyed the ominous black billows edging in from the western horizon. "All bluff," he opined. "It doesn't smell like a storm to me. Though . . ."

"Though what?" Perkar grunted.

"It has a strangeness about it."

"Oh." Perkar regarded the skyline once more, straining to sense whatever it was that Ngangata could feel. Nothing unusual came to him: the stormheads remained, to him, mere clouds.

"Sometimes I wonder if you say things like that just to be mysterious," he grumbled.

"No. Unfortunately, life is already mysterious without any help from me," Ngangata answered.

Sighing, Perkar leaned forward and patted his mount. "What do *you* think, T'esh?" The charcoal-and-gray-striped stallion spared him a laconic sidewise glance before returning his full attention to tearing at the clump of grass protruding through the slowly melting snow. As far as he could tell, T'esh had no opinion on the matter.

"I'll assume you agree with Ngangata," Perkar decided. "We'll push on."

He urged T'esh to a walk, and Ngangata, abreast, clucked to his own mount in the weird, unhuman language of his father's folk. An eerie banging punctuated whatever he said, like a god hammering a moon-size sheet of tin—but in a distant sky, the black one on the horizon. *Snow thunder,* Perkar's father called it—rare and unnatural. A sign that gods were playing games with the heavens. Perkar nearly remarked on the sound—to show that he knew at least *something* of such signs and portents—but they had both heard it, and it seemed silly to point out so obvious a thing to a hunter and tracker of Ngangata's skill. Instead, he listened alertly for further noises. The distance, however, was quiet thereafter, as if the heavens had only a single word to speak before returning to stubborn, sullen silence.

The quiet itched at Perkar. His lungs seemed crowded with the necessity of speaking. He cast about for something to say and finally settled upon the obvious. "It's good to have you along," he told Ngangata.

The halfling nodded. "I'm eager to meet this goddess, this maker of heroes," he answered.

Perkar wondered if he should take offense at that—he knew Ngangata's opinion of heroes—but when he glanced over at his companion, there was no hint of malice on the broad, pale face.

"I don't know that she will show herself to you. Or to me, for that matter," he said.

"Then we will have wasted a trip," Ngangata answered simply.

"No. No, whether she manifests or not, she will hear me. That is all I want, to tell her a few things. To apologize."

"In my experience," Ngangata remarked, "gods have little use for Human apologies."

"Perhaps," Perkar said. "But she will hear one from me."

Ngangata nodded as the wind gusted from the north, straight into their faces, numbing their lips into wooden clappers only vaguely capable of shaping speech. Perkar reached to lace his elk-skin hood tighter and draw a thick woolen kerchief over his nose, so that only his squinting eyes were visible.

"Something odd in those clouds," said a voice in his ear, just as his face was warming.

"So Ngangata tells me," Perkar mumbled.

"Eh?" Ngangata queried, catching his muffled speech.

"It's Harka," Perkar explained, and Ngangata pursed his lips and urged his mount on up ahead. He knew that Perkar disliked talking to his sword when others were near.

"Odd," Harka repeated. *"Too far away to see more."*

"Let me know when you can say something useful."

"Still bitter? At least you answered me this time. It is difficult for me to understand your attitude. One would think you would be grateful. I've saved your life many times."

"So you've told me before. And I should be, I admit. But my body remembers what has been done to it, knows that it has died several times now. There is a peculiar ache to that, Harka."

"An ache I can feel well enough," the sword answered. *"Find some way to free me, and both our problems will be solved."*

"If I can find a way to do so, I will," Perkar promised the blade. "If nothing else, I will return you to the Forest Lord."

"How far will you go to make amends, Perkar? The Forest Lord will snap you down like a toad swallowing a bug. As Ngangata said, gods have precious little use for Human sentiment. I should know."

"It doesn't matter to me what the gods do or do not value," Perkar remarked, very softly indeed. "I know what my father taught me: Piraku, the code of honor and glory. I have walked away from the path of my father for too long now."

"You always command such endearing platitudes," Harka replied. *"Don't you ever tire of them?"*

"Perhaps they are all I have," Perkar rejoined. "Now let me ride in peace, until such time as you sense danger."

"Very well," the voice in his ear conceded, and was thereafter silent.

The dark clouds boiled and spread eastward; Perkar could sense the sleet in their bellies, feel the cold sucking at him from that quarter of the world. Yet, as Ngangata predicted, they did not advance, and by the time evening came, the sky had nearly frozen clear, indigo veined with copper and crimson where a few high, attenuated clouds still clung. When the first star winked brightly at them, Perkar and Ngangata stopped to make camp. They worked silently at erecting the small horsehide tent Brother Horse had lent them. Perkar searched out a few scraps of withered wood in the dying light as his companion tightened the straps of their shelter.

When he returned, Ngangata was chanting over his bow, thanking the god of the tree from which it was made. Perkar considered following his example, but his sword, Harka, *was* a god, and as they had argued that day, it would be disingenuous to chant a song of thanks to him. Still, he had bragged that he was returning to the path of Piraku, and so after a few moments, he sang the one song that seemed appropriate, though it was alien. He chanted "Thanking the Horse Mother," what little he knew of it, to show proper respect to their tent, made as it was from the mortal remains of a stallion named Snakeskin. All Mang tents were made of horsehide, and so each had a name. The song he had learned by listening carefully to the Mang as they made and broke camp.

He and Ngangata finished their chanting at roughly the same time. They met back in front of the tent. In the ruddy remains of sunset, his companion's face seemed more alien than usual, stripped of its Human heritage. His dark sunken eyes and low, sloping forehead recalled the deep, awesome forest of Balat, where the Alwat dwelt. Perkar remembered the broken bodies of Digger and her family, the Alwat who perished because he offended the Forest Lord, and wondered what he could do for their kin, what solace he could offer, what apology?

"Ngangata," he asked, staring out at the darkening rim of the world, "did you know the names of those Alwat who died in Balat?"

"I know their names," Ngangata answered, and Perkar noticed, as he often did not, the faint burr in his voice that no Human Being had.

"I would like you to teach them to me someday."

"Someday," the other replied, "but only in Balat. Their names should be spoken only there."

"Ah." Perkar felt the cold eating into his legs, but he did not yet desire to enter the tent and start a fire. "The sky seems to drink me up here," he confided instead. He turned to take it all in, noticed the bone bow of the Pale Queen climbing in the east.

"I prefer more crowded land myself," Ngangata admitted. "Like you, my Human mother was kin to pasture, to hills, to mountains. Her blood was fast-running streams, red bulls, and snowmelt. The Alwat, my father's people, are kin to the trees; they despise to leave them. You and I will both lose our minds if we live long beneath this sort of sky." He gestured at the heavens with the blade of his hand and half grinned to show that he half joked.

"The Mang live here," Perkar pointed out. "Surely other men can do it."

"But the Mang have the blood of horses coursing in their veins. They *are* horses, in some ways. Without this sky, they would die of suffocation."

"So they say," Perkar acknowledged, recalling Brother Horse's similar claim.

"You seem very thoughtful tonight," Ngangata observed. "I believe you should take the first watch. Give yourself more time to think."

Perkar accepted that with a faint chuckle. "Fair enough," he replied.

Morning was still clear, and Perkar conceded, once again, that Ngangata understood the sky better than he. They rode out without much talking, though at one point Perkar attempted a song. It fell with the rising wind however, and Perkar glumly reflected that he missed Eruka, who would have sung right on into a gale. Eruka, whose voice and laughter were now bleached bones without even a proper burial.

So *much* to do.

Just past midday, Harka spoke to him again, and even as he did, Perkar caught himself scrutinizing a certain point on the horizon. He was unaware, at first, that his attention was a product of the strange power his sword had to compel him to "see" danger. But then Harka said, *"Comes something strong."*

"From the direction of the storm?"

"Where else?"

Perkar could make out a speck now. He pointed it out to Ngangata.

"Yes, I see," the half man said. "Your sword uses your eyes well."

It seemed a rather backhanded compliment to Perkar, but he knew it was the only sort he deserved. Ngangata would have seen the approaching stranger well before Perkar, all other things being equal.

Harka, however, made things decidedly *unequal*, protecting Perkar from much harm and healing even the most terrible wounds in a few days at most. It was difficult, therefore, for Perkar to conjure up any fear of a lone figure in the distance, despite Harka's concern. Harka, after all, would be concerned if a jay were diving at him, protecting its nest. Even such slight threats were considered worthy of the sword's attention. Still, a menace to him was also probably a threat to Ngangata, who *could* be killed rather easily. Perkar did not want that; enough of his friends were already ghosts.

It soon became apparent, however, that the rider—Ngangata said he could make that much out—was moving along the same course as they, rather than coming to meet them. This delayed any worries Perkar might have been tempted to invent, especially because he knew that they should be drawing near the stream where his goddess dwelt, and he was rehearsing what he would say to her. In fact, after some time, the rider ahead of them vanished, not over the horizon but presumably behind some nearer crease in the landscape, obscured by the white sameness of the plain. Perkar's heart quickened, for such a crease might also hide a stream valley.

Midway from noon to sundown, they breasted the lip of the valley. It was a gentle, gradual dale, nothing like the crevasse the Changeling had dug for himself. Indeed, the crest of the hill was scarcely noticeable as such. The stream was not directly visible, hidden by a stand of leafless cottonwoods and furry green juniper. But she was there; Perkar knew her instantly. He clapped T'esh's flanks, bringing the horse to a canter, but Ngangata hailed him down. Almost irritated, Perkar turned to his comrade, who was gesturing at the clean snow of the valley—gesturing at a line of hoofprints not their own.

"You make your peace with the goddess," Ngangata suggested. "I think I will find out who our stranger is."

"No," Perkar snapped. "No. Harka believes it to be dangerous. Leave it alone, whatever it is. Just keep your bow out and your eyes busy. I will not speak to her for long."

"Best not," Ngangata muttered. "I don't like not knowing where an enemy is."

"We don't know that it is an enemy," Perkar pointed out reasonably. Then, to Harka: "Do we?"

"No. But strong and strange, certainly. And dangerous, like a sleeping snake."

Perkar nodded, so that Ngangata would know he had been answered.

"But go cautiously," Ngangata said. "We should dismount and walk down. Do no good for you to break your neck now—it could take days for you to heal."

"Fine," Perkar said, though he would have rather galloped down, heedless.

How *old I look*, Perkar thought, staring at his reflection in a still edge of the stream. His hood down, he could see the new lines on his face, the unkempt brown hair, gray eyes that seemed rather dull to him, though he had once been proud of their flash and sparkle. He was struck, suddenly, by how much more he looked like his father, and that thought brought an almost dizzying recurrence of his earlier homesickness. Up this stream, far up it, his father's pasture lay. A leaf fallen there might pass now by his feet. The stream blurred, as tears rimmed his eyes.

"Always so sad," she said, rising from the water before him, "even from the first."

She looked older, too. Her skin still dazzled whiter than the snow on the hills around them, her eyes shone purest amber, and yet in the jet of her long hair lay wisps of silver, lines etched on a face that before had been smoothest ivory. She remained the loveliest woman Perkar had ever seen; the sight of her caught at his breath.

"Goddess," he said.

"The same, but not the same," she answered. "Farther downstream, more children. But I know you, Perkar, I remember your arms and kisses, your sweet silly promises."

She stepped up and out of the water, stretched a tapered finger out to stroke his chin. Her touch was warm, despite the chill wind. Her unclothed flesh was raised in goosebumps, but other than that she showed no discomfort.

"What have they done to you, my sweet thing?" she asked, moving her hand down, to the thick scar on his throat where a lance had passed through his neck; across his coat, beneath which hidden scars bunched like a nest of white caterpillars.

"I did it to myself," he muttered.

"You did it for me," she corrected.

"Yes, at least I thought I did."

She moved to embrace him, though his thick coat must have been rough against her. She pressed her cheek against his, and it was so warm it was nearly hot. "I tried to stop you," she reminded him. She stepped back, and he stood there, not knowing at all what to do.

"I tried to stop you," she repeated.

He shrugged uncomfortably. "I loved you. I did foolish things."

She nodded. "I have heard rumors, flying down from the mountain. *He* sang of you, where he eats me. Do you feel more a man now, Perkar? Do you feel more a match for a goddess?"

"No," he said, his voice small but firm. "No, you were always right."

"What do you want of me now?" she demanded, and her voice was a bit sharp. She had always been like that, hard and soft, comforting and angry, all at once.

"I only want for you to forgive me."

"Forgive you?" she asked, as if she were repeating words in a foreign language.

"Forgive me for killing in your name. Forgive me for . . ." He searched his brain, but despite his rehearsal, he could not find the words.

"Forgive you," she repeated. She shook her head slowly. "So many things men have done for me, over the years—so many stupid things. At first, you know, I did not try to stop them. They amused me. But the blood of this girl, this form you see, oh, it sleeps for long, but sometimes I am almost Human. I feel sorrow, feel ashamed, just as you might—though I hate it. And I feel love, Perkar. You can hurt me, I think. I was always afraid you would hurt yourself and add to my sorrow. And so you have."

"But I am alive," he told her. "Here I am."

"But so terribly hurt," she said, "so scarred. Can I forgive you for that, for scarring my sweet Perkar?" She shook her head, pursed her lips. "Take whatever you want," she said at last. "If you want my forgiveness, take that."

"You have to give it to me, I think," he replied.

She spread her arms wide, gesturing up and down the river, spreading her naked body before him. "Here is all that I am," she answered. "Upstream, downstream—anything in me is yours. If you can find forgiveness here, take it—I give it to you. But I cannot *find* it for you."

He nodded, unsure what to say next, and she gazed at him

long and thoughtfully before she said anything else. Then, with a little sigh, she approached him again and took his hand. Together they gazed into the water. "There *are* some things I can find for you," she confided. "Things that have come downstream to me."

"Yes?" he said hopefully.

"From your father's people. See, there—and there." She gestured at the flowing water, but he saw nothing noteworthy.

"What?"

"Blood," she said, gripping his hand tighter. "It is their blood."

PERKAR did not believe that any news could stun him now, and yet as he walked back up to where Ngangata waited, he felt numb, and not from the cold. The goddess had talked for some time, explained as much as she knew, then left him with a faint kiss on the lips to remind him of his first lesson in passion, so long ago. But even the kiss of a goddess dimmed next to what she had told him.

"Well?" Ngangata inquired, rising from his haunches and shouldering his laminated bone bow.

"War," Perkar mumbled. "My people are at war with the Mang."

"Your people are *always* at war with the Mang," Ngangata replied, though rather tentatively.

"No. The Mang have always raided us, and we have always repelled them. But now my people have invaded the Ekasagata Valley and established damakutat to defend what they have taken."

"Why haven't Brother Horse and his people heard of this?"

"Perhaps they *have*," Perkar said darkly.

"No, I don't believe that," Ngangata disagreed.

"Well, maybe they have heard rumors but assume it is the same sort of raiding that has always gone on. The border with my people is many hundreds of leagues away."

"True. And the Mang are not all one people. What troubles the

Mang of the western plains need not have any effect on the Mang of the South."

"Except," Perkar noted, "in times of war. Their confederacy exists for mutual protection and mutual raiding."

Ngangata shook his head unhappily. "This means trouble for us. Brother Horse may find it difficult to treat us with hospitality when the news arrives."

"Ngangata!" Perkar cried. "Hospitality! My people are dying, and it is *my* fault. You know that, you were there. The Forest Lord had agreed to give our king more land. Because of me, that offer was withdrawn and will never be made again. Now it seems, unable to expand west, my people have chosen to move into the Mang borderlands. My fault, all of it."

Ngangata regarded him for a moment. "Apad and Eruka—" he began.

"Are *dead*," Perkar finished. "I am the only one left to shoulder the blame. In any event, Apad and Eruka would have lacked the courage to *do* anything without me."

Ngangata's face was grim. "I know that," he replied. "I agree; much of the blame for this lies with you. But if I understand Piraku, you should be thinking of something to *do* about it, rather than blaming yourself over and over again—rather than telling *me* about your guilt yet again."

Perkar clenched his fist and shook it in Ngangata's face. "And just what is it I *can* do?" he shouted. "How is it that I can set *this* right, resurrect those already dead, my father perhaps among them?"

Ngangata watched the fist impassively. "If you don't intend to hit me," he growled, "unclench that."

For one awful, helpless moment, Perkar *did* want to hit the half man. But at last he let the fist drop, uncurling it. He was opening his mouth to apologize when his head yanked around of its own volition—or rather, Harka's.

"In the trees," he suddenly whispered, just as an arrow struck him in the shoulder. He gasped at the impact, surprised that there was no more pain. He had a confused glimpse of Ngangata in motion, heard the dull flat whine of his bow.

"Watch out!" Harka warned, as Perkar fumbled him out. The blade trailed out into the light, a sliver of aquamarine ice.

As he stumbled back to his feet, his gaze was again drawn to the trees; another shaft whirred from them, though not in his direction. Ngangata—the likely target—was nowhere to be seen. Of more immediate concern were the two horsemen churning through the snow toward him, both mounted on striped Mang horses. The men were Mang, too, multiple braids indicating that they were warriors of some rank, the red-dyed horsehair plumes on their leather helmets a sign that they *were* at war. Perkar had never seen Mang at war until now. They looked like wolves.

They bore down on him, one with a lance, the second with a short, curved sword. Perkar whooped at them, his father's battle cry, and waited, Harka held steady with both hands. The arrow, he now guessed, had not penetrated more deeply than his outer flesh, halted by the thick coat of elk hide and the light lacquered armor beneath.

He waited until they were nearly on him, and then he suddenly darted to his own right; both horsemen swerved, still hoping to catch him between them, but Perkar sank to one knee and cut through both front legs of the nearest horse. The animal shrieked piteously and pitched past him, into the snow, the rider sprawling over his mount's neck.

An absolute master of his steed, the second Mang had pulled in tight, but had to strike awkwardly to reach Perkar. Perkar avoided the blow entirely, stepped up, and slashed deeply into the warrior's leg. The man uttered no sound, but his face registered a vast surprise as the blade sliced through the heavy lacquered layers of wood, bone, and leather that protected his thigh.

Perkar turned back to his first opponent, who was rising to his feet, murder on his face. Unfortunately for him, his lance was too long to bring around effectively, and though he managed to graze Perkar's shoulder, he soon held only a wooden pole, the steel blade severed from it by a quick blow from Harka. The Mang shot one glance at his mutilated steed, snarled, and hurled himself weaponless at Perkar, though a knife flapped against his hip. Harka took him in the heart, yet the man remained on his feet for a few instants, the purest look of hatred Perkar had ever seen only reluctantly replaced by death's cold gaze.

The second man was lying on his horse's neck, teeth clenched; as Perkar watched, the blade dropped from his hand into the blood-spattered snow. The horse itself pranced nervously, as if unused to having no direction.

Another shaft sped past Perkar, but almost at the same moment, he heard a sharp cry from the direction of the trees. He crouched behind the quivering body of the downed horse, waiting for more attacks, but none came, and Harka remained still and quiet.

After a moment, Ngangata emerged, cautiously, from a clump of trees. "Are there more?" he asked, eyes nervously picking through the valley.

"I don't think so. Harka?"

"No more. But there is someone else."

"What?" Perkar turned to Ngangata. "Harka says no more Mang, but there is someone else."

Ngangata nodded. "Someone killed the archer."

"Ah. I thought *you* did that."

"No," Ngangata denied.

Perkar drew a deep breath. "Come out, if you are a friend. If not, ride on."

There was a pause, and then a stirring in the trees. The figure of a man emerged and began walking leisurely toward them.

"That," Harka informed him, *"is not Human."*

IV

The Godsight

SHE stood beneath a leaden sky, the vastness of the River stretched before her. Those waters seemed a perfect reflection of the obscure heavens—his substance seemed dense, as if it were really polished slate or beveled steel—and it radiated a cold strength that numbed and quickened her simultaneously.

She bent closer, touched her finger to the dark water, then gasped when she saw impressions upon the surface, as if invisible objects lay pressed upon the skin of the Rivergod. Nearest was a hollow shaped like a water scorpion, so clear that she could even make out the delicate patterning of its plated underbelly. There, a trumpet-cuttlefish, long tapering horn of its shell smooth, the tentacles and a single large eye pressed in relief. And there—she gasped and looked away from the detailed mold of her cousin D'en's face, as she had last seen it, with his eyes on stalks, like those of a crab.

Trembling, she turned from the River, but looking away, she felt less comfort than ever. Four masked priests strode toward her, grim-faced, swinging their water cans and spirit-brooms. In *front of them came Yen, the young engineer who had playfully courted her, only to reveal himself as a coldhearted assassin named Ghe. Behind those five figures were a hundred others, obscured by a veil of mist, but all threatening her, all intent on locking her away. As panic whetted keen in her breast, however, she felt something cross her toes; she looked down to see what it might be.*

It was a tiny snake, no bigger than a worm. It shimmered in iridescent colors, and something about it made her happy, promised to protect her from her enemies. She stooped and picked up the small reptile, and, on impulse, she swallowed it.

I have just swallowed a snake. She wondered, Now, why did I do that?

At that moment, the snake stirred in her belly. Then lightning seemed to course out into her arms. The gray waters rushed into her toes, and as she watched, the River began to drop in level, even as the worm in her grew and grew, as the greedy serpent heads that her toes had become drank and drank. The River was drying up, but it was entering her, and with a cold horror she felt the weight of his vast sentience crushing her own, squeezing her like a giant's fist. But part of her was delighted to at last have the power to destroy any who threatened her, who wished her harm . . .

The revulsion was stronger than the joy. Shrieking, she spit the snake out, and with it went her power, as the water flowed back into the River and returned it to its former level. But then she saw something else, a thing by a small stony cairn, and the horror began again . . .

Until she awoke, fingers balled into fists, wondering where she was. She sat thus for long, terrible moments as it all came back to her. *A dream, a dream, a dream,* she repeated to herself, but she knew it for more than that. It was really a distorted memory of what had actually happened scant months ago, when the River tried to manifest in her frail body and had very nearly succeeded. But she had escaped that, hadn't she? Escaped her curse?

She gradually understood that she was in a ben', one of the

horsehide tents the Mang used for camping. She was cold, except on her left side, where the dog, Heen, lay curled against her, snoring raspily. Nearby, Brother Horse snuffled out a harmony to the canine's tuneless song. Earlier, Hezhi had found these noises distracting; now they comforted her, for they were Human, mundane.

But she was in danger again, as certainly as Heen was a dog. And Brother Horse *knew* it. He had forced camp before they had gone half a league beyond the cairn where she *saw* . . .

Tomorrow he would explain. Tomorrow.

She lay back, her breathing growing calmer, but sleep did not return to her that night.

HEZHI drew her knees up beneath her chin as she watched the colorful riders enter the village, listened to their raucous shouts. The half Giant sitting next to her stirred restlessly, shifting a frame easily twice as massive as that of any Human as he braided and unbraided fingers like fat sausages into a double fist resting against his thick-featured face. The knotted hand hid a scowl, and she could imagine she heard his teeth grinding.

"Princess . . ." the Giant began, but Hezhi shook her head.

"Hush, Tsem," she said. "Watch the riders. I want to write Ghan about this."

"I've seen plenty of these barbarians enter the camp in the past few days," Tsem grumbled. "I've had little else to do."

"That isn't what Tiin tells me," Hezhi answered, glancing side-wise at the half Giant.

Tsem blushed almost purple. "One has to do something to pass the time," he mumbled. "I can't hunt, horses groan beneath my weight—"

"But at least you can entertain the unmarried women," Hezhi finished. "Just as in Nhol." She sharpened her glance. "*Unmarried*, Tsem. These people are not as forgiving in their policies toward adultery as those you are accustomed to."

Tsem scrunched his face in mock concern, bushy eyebrows

steepling like mountain ridges. "What might the penalty be?" he asked.

"You know Barks-Like-a-Dog?"

"The old man with no nose?"

"Exactly."

"Oh. *Oh!*" Tsem's face fell into lines of *real* dismay.

"So take care," she cautioned.

"I can do that," Tsem replied. "I'm glad you told me."

"This isn't Nhol, Tsem. Don't ever think it is. Nothing we know will serve us out here."

Tsem snorted. "People are people, Princess. *Much* of what I know serves me wherever I go."

Hezhi started at the bitterness in that. It was rare for Tsem to display such acrimony.

"What is troubling you, Tsem?"

As they spoke, thirty warriors thundered around the village, shrieking like demons. Each bore a long, colorful streamer knotted to a lance, and the result was breathtaking, barbaric, a cyclone of color. Unmarried girls dodged in and out among the surging mounts, snatching at the streamers, while younger children jostled alongside, jangling strings of bells and clapping wooden noise-makers together. The din was impressive.

Tsem was silent, pretending to watch the spectacle; Hezhi prodded him with her toe, then kicked him when he did not respond. He turned on her, flashing knuckle-size teeth in a dangerous-looking scowl, and she was again taken aback by the anger in his reply.

"You cannot ask me that," he snapped. "If you cannot tell me what troubles *you*, then I . . ." He trailed off into a growl and a glare.

"Tsem," Hezhi began, laying her small hand on the corded bulk of his arm. The muscles in his neck worked silently for a moment as he ground his teeth. Then he sighed and turned a milder gaze on her.

"What good am I out here, Princess?" he asked after a moment. "What good have I been to anyone since leaving Nhol? Since before that, even?"

"Tsem, you were *injured*."

"Yes, and stupidly so. And you have had to pay for my healing, pay by working like a common maid."

"That has nothing to do with you, Tsem. These people expect everyone to work. There are no princesses among the Mang."

"And what sort of work am I suited to? Now that I have healed, what will I do to show my worth?"

"Tiin said—"

Tsem dismissed that with a roll of his eyes. "Curiosity, Princess. Woman are *always* curious about me. Once. Novelty is a fleeting thing. The truth is, these people think I am worthless, and they are not far from the truth. I was raised to be the servant of a princess, and, as you say, there are no nobles here."

"No slaves, either," Hezhi reminded him. "Stop feeling sorry for yourself. There are things you can learn to do."

Tsem began to reply, but then his eyes bulged.

"You *did* it," he swore.

"What?"

"Made me tell you. Made me complain. The only thing I know how to do is serve you, and you won't even *talk* to me."

"We are talking," Hezhi noticed.

Tsem turned his eyes back to the riders. Some of the girls had managed to snatch pennants, and now the original bearers of those streamers were chasing *them*, trying to grab them up onto their horses.

"Something happened to you," he said. "Something bad. Are you going to tell me?" The bitterness had left his voice, but there was challenge there, as if she were withholding something she owed him.

"I don't know," she said at last. "I don't know what happened. Brother Horse tried to explain."

"But it has to do with your . . . nature."

She shrugged. "Brother Horse said that I saw a god. He saw it, too; just a little god, he said, the child of some spider goddess."

"Did you?"

"I saw *something*. No, it was more than seeing . . ."

She felt suddenly very close to tears. Her voice trembled as she said, "I thought I had escaped it, Tsem, but my blood is *doing* something. I thought I was *safe*."

Tsem gently drew her to him, and she relaxed, rested against his mammoth frame and took comfort in the familiar smell of him. She closed her eyes and imagined that they were in her mother's rooftop garden, hot sun bleaching the city white around them—before everything, before the whole nightmare began, when she was still just a little girl.

"I don't know about these things," Tsem soothed, "but Brother Horse says you will not change, will not become one of the Blessed. We are far and far from the River, Princess."

"Yes, so Brother Horse said. But Tsem—in Nhol there was only the River, the River and ghosts. Nothing else. Out here, there are gods everywhere. Every other rock, every creek. Everywhere. And if I am going to start *seeing* them, the way Brother Horse does, the way *I* did yesterday . . . if that happens, I will lose my mind."

Tsem patted her shoulder thoughtfully. "Does Brother Horse believe that this will happen, that you will keep seeing these gods?"

"Yes," Hezhi confirmed. "Yes, he thinks that I will."

"Oh," Tsem said. He turned his gaze thoughtfully back to the village perimeter, where the great chase was winding down; horsemen were beginning to dismount and clasp their relatives to them. The air was thick with the smell of roasted meat; soon the feasting would begin.

"While odd," Tsem began again, in an optimistic tone, "Brother Horse has not lost *his* mind, and you say he sees these gods. Perkar speaks of seeing gods, as well. It cannot be so terrible as you fear."

Hezhi nodded into the crook of his arm. "Brother Horse and Perkar are different. Perkar has seen gods, it is true, but they were clothed in flesh—they were manifest. I am told that anyone can see a god thus, and while their form might be disturbing, it is not the same as what Brother Horse and I see. We see the *essence* of the god, the unmanifested form. That is altogether different."

"How so?"

"They get in here," Hezhi said, tapping her head. "They worm through our eyes into our minds, the way the River did, when I almost lost myself." She paused. "I never told you, Tsem. It was after you fell down, when Perkar was fighting the Riverghost. I . . . I was filled up. The River filled me up, and I could have done almost *anything*: torn Nhol apart, killed Perkar, killed you. I wanted to do all of those things, because *I was not me*. That's what it will be like, every time I *see*. Thoughts and feelings and desires that have no place in me—yet they feel *right*, too, as if they have always been there." Her voice felt dull in her throat.

"Brother Horse must know how to live with it. He *must*," Tsem insisted. "I don't understand these things, but he must. He can help you."

"Yes," Hezhi murmured as, across the plaza, an oaken keg of beer was tapped to a general chorus of approving howls. "Yes, that is what he says. But . . ." She gazed up into Tsem's sympathetic eyes, at his thick harsh face and the kindness it yet contained. "I thought I had *escaped*," she whispered. "Won't I ever be free?"

"Hard to be free of what you *are*," Tsem said, and Hezhi knew that, at least to that extent, he understood.

Hezhi wrote later:

This is what they call the Ben'cheen. It is a winter gathering, in which many of the Mang tribes come together. They feast, play games, and make sacrifices to the gods. I expect it to be very interesting. So far it is noisy, this festival, barbaric. The newcomers look very strangely at Tsem and me but are generally not unfriendly. However, Brother Horse had to dissuade some of the young warriors from challenging Tsem to fight—they have legends of the Giants, who live to the northeast, and in their legends they are great fighters. A warrior who proves himself against them is considered very brave. Brother Horse tells them that Tsem is still recovering from injuries—which, of course, he is—and that it would thus be inhospitable to challenge him openly. Fighting is something Mang men love, on horseback or off. One of their sports is called bech'iinesh, *which I think just means "Slapping." What they slap each other with, however, are long-handled wooden paddles with just enough padding to keep them from always being lethal. They charge at each other on horseback and try to knock each other from the saddle. On foot, they like to wrestle and box. I believe that they would be sorry if they wrestled Tsem. He doesn't know the use of weapons, but I have seen him fight with bare hands, and it is difficult for me to believe that even one of these wild warriors would have a chance against him.*

In a few days they will hold their main festival, as I understand it. It is named the "Horse God Homesending," but other than that, I know nothing of it. I will write more afterward, when I do.

It seems my studies did not leave off when I left you. Brother Horse believes that I must learn something of being a gaan, *if I am to live with my godsight. These gaan are something like priests, using drums and singing to talk to their gods. Brother Horse became one, long ago, though now he rarely "sings." It sounds barbaric, superstitious, worse than the silly witchery of fishwives. It is difficult to adjust to how different the world is, away from the River, how different the truth of things is. That the world can be as full of gods as it is of rocks and trees seems ludicrous. Yet I know that what Brother Horse says is true—he knows these places, where the River does not hold sway, where he has not devoured all of the little gods these people know. I wish these Mang had books; I would rather go somewhere alone and read about these gods, about the ways of the gaan. Instead I must learn by listening to Brother Horse talk. Hearing people talk all of the time is tiring. I am not used to listening so much, as you may remember.*

One observation which may interest you: This word gaan—it reminds me of what I call you; Ghan, "teacher," and also of Ghun, "priest." Many of their words bear this sort of similarity to Nholish. I suspect that they learned to speak from our ancestors, but that being barbarians they learned everything wrong, pronounced the words incorrectly. For instance, when we say nuwege, they say nubege—and both mean "eye." I hope you will find this peculiar and interesting, for I intend to make a list of their words

*to send you. Perhaps you can find some evidence in the library that
the Mang learned to speak in Nhol—perhaps they were slaves who
escaped, long ago. Their legends say nothing of this, but they have
no books and so their histories cannot be very accurate.*

Hezhi looked thoughtfully at the paper, considered beginning
the list right away. There were other things she should be doing,
however, and she didn't want people to think she was shirking.
She blew on the ink. When it was dry, she would go find Duk and
help with the afternoon meal. She wondered, idly and with some
annoyance, where Perkar was. According to Yuu'han, he and
Ngangata should have returned by now. There had been no more
snow—in fact, the snow on the ground was melting—so bad
weather had not slowed them. Still, she was determined not to
worry. Perkar would return soon enough, and she could ask him
what he knew of this witchery she was supposed to learn about.
He would know something, after all his dealings with gods and
demons.

"There you are." Brother Horse's voice pulled her out of her
thoughts. She looked up, a bit startled to see the old man, who
had been busy constantly since their return to the village—
greeting strangers, settling minor disputes, arranging marriages.
He smiled down at her, gaudy in a long vermilion coat nearly covered with copper coins, gold-embroidered felt breeks, and a tiger-
pelt underjacket. In one hand he held an otterskin bag that bulged
around something round and flat. Behind him lolled Heen, dustier
than usual, ears twitching as if offended by the raucousness
around him. Hezhi tentatively returned the smile.

"I think you may have questions for me," he said. "I'm sorry
that I haven't been around to talk to you."

"I needed to think anyway," Hezhi replied.

"You think a lot. That is good, considering. And what have
you decided?"

"That I don't know enough to decide anything."

"Wise," he said, shaking his head. "I *never* waited until I knew
enough. Which makes it a miracle that I am an old man and not a

young ghost." He extended his hand. "Walk with me a bit, child."

Hezhi hesitated. "Now?"

Brother Horse nodded. "It's important."

Hezhi sighed. "I don't think I'm ready." She rubbed absently at the dully tingling scale on her arm, the one physical sign of her magic.

The old man grimaced. "I would give you more time if you had it. But soon—tomorrow—we will slay the Horse God and send him home. Without some preparation, if you *see* him—"

"I will go mad," Hezhi finished.

"Perhaps. Perhaps not."

"I see," she muttered. She checked to see that her ink was dry, and, assured that it was, carefully rolled up the paper and replaced it in its bone case.

They walked out from the village, pausing as riders thundered by on the racetrack that encircled the houses. Felt and horsehide tents crowded the landscape; the village scarcely resembled the one she had come to know—though it was nothing like a city, of course. The air was thick with smoke from burning wood and dung, half-charred meat, other scents she could not place. A pack of children—screaming and batting a ball along the ground with bent sticks—nearly ran over them, but when they saw Brother Horse, they parted and streamed around, like a school of fish effortlessly negotiating a snag in the River. Heen paused at the village edge—apparently disapproving of their direction of travel—but after it became apparent that they were ignoring his tacit advice, he followed regardless.

It seemed a long time before they were in the open desert, with the cries, laughter, and music of the Swollen Tents behind them. Patches of rusty sand glared through thawing white drifts. Here and there, muddy trails marked the paths in from elsewhere, from wherever the Mang tribes came.

"I'm sorry for your sake that I have to help you with this," Brother Horse stated. "It has been a long time since I was a singer. Years. I wish there was a younger one around who could help you, but Cedar went off into the mountains a month ago, and I trust none of the others with you." He paused for a few heartbeats and went on. "When it happened to me—the sight—I was a bit older than you. A warrior. It nearly ruined me; I was sick for days after my first sight of a god."

"I was sick."

"For a short time. You are very strong, Hezhi."

"Tell me more about yours," she appealed, "your first sight."

He seemed to consider that, and for a few tens of steps the only sound was that of their boots crunching through the melted and refrozen surface of the snow.

"I first saw Ch'egl, the god of a small spring. A very minor god indeed, much less imposing than he whom *you* saw."

"And?"

"It was after a raid. My companions and I scattered to divide the pursuit. We were to all meet at the water hole. I reached the place first, and I saw *Ch'egl*. They found me wandering in the desert, nearly dead of thirst, as mad as a shedding snake."

"But you recovered."

"Only after my friends took me to a gaan. He sang a curing song for me. But then he told me that if I wanted to live, I would have to apprentice to him."

"And so you did."

"No! I wanted to be a warrior. I felt certain I would never have such a vision again. But I did, of course. Fortunately, that time I had companions with me."

Hezhi glanced up at him. "What? What happened that time?"

"That time I saw *Tu Chunuleen*. The great god you call 'the River.' Perkar calls him the 'Changeling.' Your ancestor, Hezhi."

"Oh."

"He was asleep. He is almost always asleep. But he dreams, always. When I saw him—" He stopped, fumbled with the ties of his shirt. At first, Hezhi thought he was stopping his story to relieve himself—the Mang showed no hesitation or shame in doing such things. But he did not. Instead, he raised the shirt up so that she could see an ugly, jagged scar.

"I did that myself," he explained. "With my skinning knife. I nearly spilled my guts all over the ground, before my friends stopped me. I have never come closer to death. I did not *want* to live, not after seeing him. A gaan had to follow my soul halfway to the Ghost Mountain before he could save me."

As he spoke they reached a low line of red rock, a shelf where the land dropped down the height of a tall man. Part of the upper level hung over like a roof, and Hezhi could see a little hearth of stones on the floor of the natural shelter. Cold prickles ran up her back, and she had a sudden, vivid memory of the priests, back in Nhol, waiting for her that day. Though many months in the past, the pain and humiliation of that experience stained her like red wine.

"What are we doing?" she demanded. "What is this?"

Brother Horse laid a hand on her shoulder. "We are only talking, as of now. Only talking, little one, away from the madness of the town."

Despite the comforting words, Hezhi felt panic rise in her chest. They had tied her down, naked, drugged her—awakened that thing in her belly, in her blood. This seemed somehow like that, another trick, something thrust upon her. The similarity between *ghun* and *gaan* flashed once more through her mind. Priest, shaman, what was the difference to *her*?

"Wh-what will you do?" she stuttered.

"Nothing. Nothing without your leave. Indeed, Hezhi, there is nothing I *can* do. You must do it, though I can guide you, help you along the way."

"There must be something else," she insisted. "Some way to be rid of him forever."

They stepped beneath the slight natural roof, the enormous sky halved by the red stone. It was oddly comforting to Hezhi, making the world seem smaller, more manageable. Brother Horse motioned her toward a flat stone and lowered himself by degrees onto another, as if his joints were rusted metal. He placed his elbows on his knees, clasped his hands with thumbs together, and pointed skyward. He looked first at the cold stone and charcoal between them, but then raised his gaze frankly to meet hers.

"No way that I know of, child. My hope for you was that the ember in you would die away without the River nearby to strengthen it. But it has caught, you see? Even without him, it will burn inside of you. Not as the Changeling planned for it to; it will not transform you as you have told me it did your kin. Still, unless you bank it, bring it under your control, that little flame will yet consume you."

Hezhi considered that she *did* know one way; she could fling herself from a cliff, break her body, and release her curse with her spirit. But even that might not work; more likely she would become a monstrous ghost, the sort that had once attacked her in Nhol. The Mang spoke often of ghosts, as well. However different the lands beyond the River were, they were not so different that death was a certain escape.

"What then?" she asked. "What must I do?"

Brother Horse reached over to stroke her hair. "It may not be so bad as you think," he said. "But I won't promise you that it will be easy."

"Nothing is, for me, it seems," she replied dully.

"It may even make you happier," he went on. "I've watched you, these past months. You took to camp work pretty well. In time, I think you could even be good at it. But you would never *love* it, would you? The only things that I know you love—that I can *see* you love—are your paper and your ink, your book. The *thought* of books."

"What does this have to do with that?" she muttered.

"Mystery," he answered simply. And in that small word, Hezhi caught a glimmer of something. Hope, possibilities—something to fill the growing emptiness in her heart.

"Mystery," she repeated, a question really. Brother Horse nodded affirmation.

"That is what you find in your books, am I right? Questions that you had not thought of yourself? Visions you could not imagine unaided? I can offer you the same."

"It frightens me," she admitted. "What lives in me frightens me."

"It always will, unless you master it," he said. "And probably even then, if you have sense, which I believe you do. But did your books bring you only comfort?"

She quirked an insincere smile at that. "No, not comfort," she answered.

"Well, then," the old man said. "Why do you hesitate?"

"Because I'm *tired*," she snapped. "Weary of new things, of being frightened, of being sick, of losing what I know! Tired of these things happening to *me* . . ."

He waited until she was done, until she chewed down on her lip, panting, fury replacing fear.

"What then?" she asked again, this time sharply, insistently. "How do we start this?"

The old man hesitated, then reached into a pouch at his waist. He withdrew a small dagger, its blade keen and silver in the shadowed shelter.

"As always," Brother Horse replied. "With blood."

HEZHI turned the knife over and over in her hand, as if inspecting it would allay her fears. Instead, she only grew more nervous as Brother Horse kindled a small fire in the stone hearth.

She was distracted by the process of fire-making itself, which relied not upon matches—the only way she had ever seen fire "made"—but upon a dubiously simple device. He placed a flat piece of wood on the shelter floor; the wood had grooves cut along one side, and these shallow cuts terminated in blackened depressions. In one of these depressions he placed a stick, about the length of her forearm, and began to twirl it briskly with his palms, starting at the top of the stick and working quickly to its base, returning his palms to the top again, and so on. In moments a coil of smoke sought up from the juncture of the two pieces of wood. The smoke grew thicker and thicker until Brother Horse removed the stick and blew upon the hole he had been twirling it in. Astonished, Hezhi saw a small red coal there.

"Hello, Fire Goddess," Brother Horse said. "Welcome to my hearth. I will treat you well." He shook the coal onto a small wad of shredded dry material of some sort, held it delicately in his fingers, and breathed upon it. In an instant, he held flame between his fingers. With that small blossom, he ignited a pile of twigs leaning together like a little tent and, as they caught, added larger pieces of wood on top. Heen, sleeping with his head between his paws, opened a single eye halfway at the scent of smoke, then closed it once more, singularly unimpressed by the birth of a goddess.

"Can you teach me that?" she breathed.

"To waken the Fire Goddess? Of course. It is simply done. I'm surprised you haven't seen it happen."

"The women would never let me near, at the hunting camp; not when they made fire."

"Women have some odd taboos about the goddess," Brother Horse informed her, then added, "and about foreigners, as well."

"That I know." The wood crackled gleefully. Hezhi cocked her head and even smiled, despite the threatening edge of the knife in her hand, the nervous twitching in her belly. "I never thought of fire as a miracle before," she breathed.

"See her in there?" Brother Horse asked. "Look closely." He gestured with his lips, his gnarled brown fingers feeding bits of juniper twigs to the flame.

"No," Hezhi said, suddenly understanding what she was being asked to do. She averted her eyes from the little tongues of light.

"The Fire Goddess is different," Brother Horse reassured her gently. "She has lived with Human Beings for a long time—at least this aspect of her. Look, child. I will help you."

He reached over and took hold of her hand; trembling a bit, she turned her gaze back to the fire. The evergreen tang of juniper smoke wrapped her as the wind shifted, and her eyes squinted over the sting and tears. Brother Horse tightened his grip on her, and in that instant the fire seemed to rush up, open like the shutters of a window. As through a window, she could suddenly see through it, to another place.

Once again, alien thoughts crowded her mind, and the scale upon her arm pulsed madly. She gasped and jerked to release herself from Brother Horse, but he kept his grip, and when she turned her head it was to no avail; the goddess was still there.

But after the first instant, her beating heart began to slow. Seeing the god at the cairn had been terrible, like suddenly understanding that she had pushed her hands into a nest of stinging worms, the shock before the pain. There was nothing of her in that experience, only the promise of dread and power.

The Fire Goddess *was* different. Hezhi saw warmth and comfort, an offer of aid rather than of power, an acceptance of her will and self that she did not fear. The Cairn God had threatened to sweep her away, like the River. The Fire Goddess only filled her with light and hope. It was still uncomfortable, but it was not terrible, not unbearable.

"Oh," Hezhi murmured as comprehension waxed. She glanced at Brother Horse, to show him she understood, and her jaw dropped.

Brother Horse still sat watching her, but his body had gone gray, insubstantial, and within it, dark shapes swam about. She got the fleeting impression of fangs, of flickering yellow eyes, of hunger. There was also something there that reminded her of raw fish, of fish in the kitchen, just after Qey gutted them for steaming.

"What?" she gasped, and violently yanked her hand from his. She staggered to her feet, and, though Brother Horse called after her, she scrambled as quickly as she could out of the shelter and into the wide, bright eye of the sky. She did not stop running until she could no longer hear Brother Horse at all.

V

The Blackgod

Perkar watched the stranger advance, keeping his grip on Harka firm, despite his sword's assurance that the approaching god—or whatever it was—posed no immediate threat. Whoever it was seemed, at least, to be in no *hurry* to threaten them, ambling across the eighty or so paces separating them, pausing to examine the sky now and then.

As he watched this, Perkar caught a movement from the corner of his eye. He turned reluctantly and saw the Mang warrior whose leg he had injured crawling across the snow, a fierce determination shining through the glaze of pain over his eyes. Perkar started, wondered why Harka had not warned him. Stepping quickly back, he was able to put both the Mang and the approaching being in his field of vision, and then he understood Harka's lack of alarm. The injured man was not crawling toward *him*, or even Ngangata. He was clawing across the frozen ground toward his companion's downed horse, which, despite the fact that Perkar had severed both front legs at the knee, was still panting heavily.

As Perkar watched, the man collapsed, ending the crooked red trail he was painting in the snow an arm's reach from the stallion.

"Gods curse you, Perkar," Ngangata hissed. "How could you—*kill* him. Now!"

For a moment, it was the old Perkar, the old Ngangata. What was the half man jabbering about? Why kill an injured man? And who was Ngangata to curse *him*?

"The horse! For pity's sake, kill it!" Ngangata had his bow trained on the approaching figure. Perkar was nearest the suffering animal.

Of course. The Mang had been trying to reach the horse, put it out of its pain.

"Watch *him*, then," Perkar answered, waving at the stranger. He turned on the beast.

It was gazing up at him, flanks heaving but its eye steady, a pool of black incomprehension.

"Oh, no," Perkar whispered. "Harka, what did I do?"

"Bested two mounted men, I would say," his sword replied.

Perkar said nothing to that, but he swung the blade savagely down, cut through the handsome neck. The body heaved once as blood spurted, steaming, onto the snow, and then, mercifully, ceased to move.

Sickened almost to vomiting, Perkar turned as much of his attention as he could focus on the newcomer, who was by now only a score of paces away.

He had the appearance of a Mang man, though taller and rangier than most, features regular and handsome. His clothing was rich and spectacular; a long split coat of midnight-blue sable, ermine boots, a fringed elkhide shirt adorned with silver coins. Thick black hair, unbound, flowed from beneath a cylindrical felt hat, also banded with coins, both silver and gold.

"Huuzho," he said, uttering the typical Mang greeting in a sibilant, musical voice.

"Name yourself," Perkar snarled back, still fighting nausea. "Name yourself or come no closer. I have slain gods and will gladly do so again."

"Have you?" the man said, bowing politely. "How interesting. In that case—I have no wish to die—I name myself Yaizhbeen, and I present myself to you *most* humbly."

"Yaizhbeen?" Perkar looked blankly at Ngangata, who was more fluent in Mang. "Yai" meant a god of the sky, he remembered.

"Blackgod," Ngangata translated. Perkar caught his friend's peculiar tone.

"At your service," the man answered. "And so good to see you both again."

"Again?" Perkar asked, but already puzzlement was grading toward dismay.

"Blackgod," Ngangata said, without ever taking his eye from the man, "is one name that the Mang give Karak, the Raven."

PERKAR snapped Harka up, flicking thick drops of horse blood through the air. A bit of it splattered on the Crow God's cheek, but he did not blink, maintaining his somewhat condescending smirk.

"Karak," Perkar gritted, "if you have a weapon, I suggest you draw it."

"Perkar, this is useless," Harka's voice came in his ear.

Karak looked mildly surprised. "I fail to understand your mood," he remarked, his voice smooth, confident. "And let me remind you that I named myself Blackgod. *You* asked me for a name, and that is the one you were given. Please call me by it."

"I will call you as I please," Perkar retorted. "Find a weapon."

The Blackgod stepped forward until Harka was a fingerspan from his heart. His yellow eyes were steady on Perkar's. "What quarrel do you have with me, Perkar?" he demanded, though softly.

"Must I name them all? You tricked my friends and me into slaying an innocent woman. You yourself killed Apad. That is sufficient, I think."

"I see," the Blackgod replied. Perkar could feel the tension in Ngangata, but the halfling said nothing, though he surely wanted to. From the corner of his eye, Perkar could see that his friend's bow was still raised.

"Ngangata," Perkar said, "please leave us."

"Perkar—"

"Please. If you have come to care for me at all, if you have forgiven me at all, Ngangata, mount and ride from here. I could not stand it if you died now."

"This is sweet, but there is no need for anyone to die," Karak assured them reasonably.

"I believe otherwise."

"Then let me answer your charges, mortal man," the god said, a trace of anger showing at last. "For though I love carrion, I would prefer that you live for a time. Now, first, the woman. Who summoned my aid to enter the cavern and find the weapons she guarded?"

"We did not summon *you*."

"Does it matter whom you intended to summon? You wished a guide to take you precisely where I took you, true?"

"Don't play games with me."

Karak leaned into Harka until blood started on his skin. The blood was gold in color, dispelling any doubts Perkar had as to his identity. "True?" he repeated.

Perkar flattened his mouth into a grim line. "True."

"You wanted the weapons. They were bound to her blood, and *she* to the cave. The only way to take them was to kill her."

"I would not have chosen to do that."

"You *did* not. Your friend Apad did. Because *you* led him there, because he thought himself a coward and was proving himself to you. Apad got you what you wanted, Manchild."

"And you killed him."

"That was war. I obeyed my liege, the Forest Lord. I might remind you that *disobeying* your liege was what got you into that mess, by the way. Apad attacked me, and he died a warrior, rather than a coward or a murderer. He did considerable damage to the host of the Huntress before losing his ghost. What better death can a seeker of Piraku desire? How better to redeem himself?"

Perkar fought for words, but his tongue seemed thick and stupid beneath the weight of the Raven's verbal onslaught. "You are twisting this . . ." he began, but the Blackgod shook his head.

"Wait," he went on. "There are crimes you did *not* name. Let me name them for you. I allowed you to survive, after the Huntress wounded you. I left you among the dead so that Harka, there, could heal you. I gave you a boat to negotiate the waters of the Changeling, at risk to my own life and position both from the River God and from my own liege lord. I cajoled and bribed Brother Horse into aiding Ngangata, here, to *find* you, and I told them when and where to locate you. Just now I killed an archer who might have slain your friend. *Now*. For these crimes will you kill me, as well, or will you kill me and then thank me, in the order that I brought things to you?"

Karak narrowed his eyes, and in that moment, though he retained his Human form, he seemed very birdlike indeed. "And," he snapped, "if you have no interest in thanking me, do you not have even the slightest curiosity about my motives for following one lone, silly Human across half of the world to give him my aid? Do you not even wonder at that, Perkar? If not, you are a dolt. Push that sword into me, and we shall see who is the stronger, Harka or myself."

"*I know the answer to that already,*" Harka said. "*Sheathe me, you idiot.*"

Perkar ignored the blade. "Tell me then. Tell me *why* everything."

"Perhaps," the Crow God said, his voice again mild, "when you have lowered your weapon. Perhaps I will tell you how to set things right. Set *everything* right."

"The war with the Mang? My people?"

"Everything."

Grinding his teeth, Perkar slowly, reluctantly lowered Harka. He heard the creak of Ngangata's bow unflexing, as well.

"Make camp," Karak commanded. "I will retrieve my mount."

* * *

"You play dangerous games," Ngangata told him as the Blackgod walked back off the way he came.

"Not a game, Ngangata. You know that."

"I know."

"Don't forget your own advice, my friend," Perkar said.

"Which advice?"

"About heroes. My fights are not your fights. When I provoke my doom, you should walk away."

"That's true," Ngangata acknowledged. "I should. But until you provoke it again, why don't you gather some wood while I see if our friend, here, is still alive." He gestured at the crumpled figure of the Mang warrior.

"What will we do with him?" Perkar muttered.

"Depends. But we should learn why they attacked us."

"Perhaps they know my people and theirs are at war. Perhaps they merely wanted our skins as trophies for their yekts."

"Perhaps," Ngangata conceded. "But did you hear what they were yelling as they attacked?"

"I don't remember them yelling anything."

"They called us *shez*. Shez are demons who bring disease. This is not an ordinary sort of insult."

"Oh." Perkar watched Ngangata kneel by the side of the injured man. The warrior *was* still alive, though breathing shallowly. Perkar walked back toward the stream, searching for deadwood, trying to keep his feelings from crowding out reason. What could Karak—or Blackgod, or whatever his true name might be—what could he offer to "set everything right"? The Raven was glib and clever, had a way of making the absurd seem reasonable. Yet one thing he said rang powerfully true to Perkar. Why would Karak care about *him*? Karak had changed his whole destiny—or at least given him the means to change his *own* destiny and follow a certain path. Why would a god take such an intimate interest in him?

He glanced back, to see that the Raven was leading his mount to where Ngangata still knelt over the injured man. Perkar pushed a little farther into the thin trees, trying to remember what he could about Karak while also searching for firewood.

Ngangata had reminded him that Karak was an aspect of the Forest Lord. The Forest Lord had other aspects—the Huntress, for instance, and the great one-eyed beast who had carried on the actual negotiations with the Kapaka—but Karak seemed to be the most deviant, the most free-willed of those avatars. And Karak himself was said to be of ambiguous nature, the Crow and the Raven. The Crow was greedy, spiteful, a trickster who took pleasure in causing pain. Raven—the songs spoke of Raven as a loftier god, one who went about in the beginning times shaping the world into its present form. Some said that he had actually drawn the original mud from beneath the waters to create the world. Others claimed that he stole the sun from a mighty demon and brought it to light the heavens. Perkar had paid little attention to such stories; the faraway doings of gods distant in both time and space had never been as important to his people as the gods they *knew*, the ones who lived in pasture, field, forest—and, of course, stream.

Now he was camping with a god said to have created the world, and he could not remember which stories about him were supposed to be true and which were told merely to entertain children on dark winter evenings.

"Tell me about Karak, Harka," he said.

"About Karak or about the Blackgod?"

"They are the same, are they not?"

"Mostly. But different names always make a difference."

"Did he really create the world?"

"I wasn't there."

"Don't evade."

"No one created the world. But I think the Raven may well have created dry land."

"I can't believe that."

"Why is it important? What does this have to do with the present?"

Perkar sighed. "I don't know. I just . . . what does he want with me?"

"I think that he will tell you, soon enough," Harka replied. *"Just keep your wits about you. Listen to everything he says, so*

that you can go over and over it later. The Raven gets things done. He is the Forest Lord's wit, his cunning, his hand. He goes about making things and unmaking them. The Crow always tries to twist around what the Forest Lord commands, make it into something different, and even when the Crow and Raven are in accord, the Crow works through treachery, deceit, and chicanery. Still, they say, if you pay close attention—very close attention—you can hear the Raven telling you how to defeat the Crow."

"That doesn't make sense."

"It makes perfect sense. You've done it yourself—made excuses for doing things you knew you shouldn't do. Planning to check on the cattle because your father wanted you to, but finding just enough other things to keep you busy so that you didn't have time to."

"That doesn't seem like the same thing," Perkar answered doubtfully. "But I will think on it."

By now he had an armload of deadwood and so, with many misgivings, turned back toward Ngangata and Karak.

He got the fire started in silence, as Ngangata erected the tent. The Mang warrior had regained consciousness and regarded them with a mixture of bleary resignation and hostility. Karak merely sat, silent, watching them. Perkar decided that if the god was going to speak, it would be in his own time; he would not *beg* him to talk, certainly.

"What are you called?" he asked the warrior instead.

The man narrowed his eyes. "You are not my friend, and you are not kin to me."

"I didn't ask for your *name*," Perkar persisted. "Just something to call you."

The man regarded him sullenly for a moment more. "Give me a drink of water," he finally said, "and I will give you something to call me."

Wordlessly Perkar handed him a water skin. The warrior drank deeply.

"Does your leg hurt?" Perkar asked.

"It hurts." He took another drink of water, then threw the skin back at Perkar, who caught it deftly. "You may call me Good Thief."

"Good Thief," Perkar repeated. "Fine. Good Thief, why did you attack us?"

"To kill you." The warrior sneered. Across the fire, the Black-god chuckled in appreciation.

"Well, you failed in that," Perkar apprised him lightly.

"Yes. Because we did not believe," the man retorted bitterly. "We thought the gaan was exaggerating."

"A shaman?"

"He saw you in a vision. He said you were a disease upon the land. He said you brought the war with the Cattle People."

Perkar stared. "What?"

"Yes, but he said you were also demons, that only by singing and drumming could you be killed. Only by fighting you with gods." He turned to gaze at his companion's corpse, at the messy ruin of the horse. "We should have listened, but we wanted your skins. We were fools."

"You came after us, specifically after *us*?" Perkar pressed, frowning, poking at the fire with a branch, unwilling to meet the Mang's accusing eyes.

"The Brush-Man and the Cattle-Man, traveling together at the stream. The gaan saw you in a vision."

"Saw us in a vision," Perkar echoed dully.

The Blackgod sidled up to the fire, sat closer. Ngangata, finished with the tent, joined them, as well.

"You see," Blackgod said. "You have many enemies, Perkar. Enemies you don't even know about. You need my advice."

"What do you know about this?" Perkar demanded.

"In the west, there is a Mang shaman. He has been given a vision and seeks your death."

"Given a vision by whom? By what god? You?" Perkar snapped.

"Oh, no," Raven answered. "Sent by *another* friend of yours, the Changeling."

"The Changeling," Ngangata interjected placidly, "is not so sentient."

"Oh, well, certainly you know more about gods than *I* do. Certainly you know the Changeling better than *I*, his brother." Raven grinned evilly. "Listen to me. All you know is altered, for the years have moved. Once the Changeling was the most cunning of us all. Once he was stupider than a beast. Now—well, now he has awakened sufficiently to send dreams to a shaman. To do other things, as well."

"Why? And why does he provoke them to kill Ngangata and me?"

"That is simple enough," the Blackgod said, his voice laden with dark glee. "He knows that you have the means to destroy him."

VI

Old Friends

GHE stopped outside of the library door and fingered his neck again, felt the ridge of flesh beneath the high collar, hoping no one would find it suspicious. High collars came in and out of fashion in the palace. They were currently out, but then, he was supposed to be Yen, a merchant's boy who joined the engineer corps of the priesthood. Merchants' sons were known for ambitious but uninformed fashion sense.

He fingered through his memory, as well, retracing his fictional life as Yen, trying to remember all that he had done and said. It would be both embarrassing and dangerous if Ghan were to catch him in a lie. Fortunately, he had rarely spoken directly to Ghan, but instead to Hezhi. What he *didn't* know was how much Hezhi had told Ghan about Yen.

And so he continued to hesitate near the arching entrance to the library, peering around the dark places in his mind, re-creating Yen. Soft updock accent, each syllable of each word carefully pronounced. Different from his own Southtown accent with its clipped words and clattery consonants, but familiar enough to him, easy to imitate. His father was supposed to be an up-River trader, himself a lover of the exotic. The trace of a smile lightened his brooding features as he remembered the little Mang statuette he had given Hezhi, the story he fabricated about how his "father" obtained it. Hezhi had loved it—how well he recalled *that*. Surrounded by a palace full of riches and servants, her eyes had genuinely flown wide in delight at a stone's-weight of brass cast in the form of a horse with a woman's upper body. How would she have felt had she known he took it from the shelf of a petty noble from the Swamp Kingdoms, just after ending the man's overly ambitious career?

The hallway was beginning to become crowded as midmorning absolutions approached. Gaudily clad nobles, prim maidservants, bodyguards, and austere counselors all mingled through the arteries of the palace. Elsewhere they were pooling in fountain rooms, praying to the River where he erupted into the palace itself.

He should leave the hall, he knew. It would not do for someone—from the priesthood, for instance—to recognize him. Especially not now, when the Ahw'en arm of the priesthood— those who investigated mysterious goings-on—must surely be active, searching for some trace of a certain vanished nobleman— the man whose clothes Ghe was currently wearing. The Ahw'en were often Jik, like himself. No, best he avoid crowds.

Thus, although not certain he was prepared, he stepped into the library, where few in the palace ventured.

It was, as he remembered, daunting. Mahogany shelves suffused the illumination from thick-paned skylights, swirled it about the room like cream stirred into coffee. Ghe was struck by the illusion that walls were hung with tapestries woven from the bodies of enormous millipedes, each segment of their bony armor the spine of a book. Most of the books were black and brown, enhancing this impression. The few that stood out—here a deep yellow, burgundy, indigo—these only suggested, somehow, that the great worms were poisonous. The books curled thus around a carpeted area in which several low tables stood, surrounded by cushions for sitting. Beyond, the shelves wandered back into the deep, narrow labyrinth Hezhi had named the Tangle. He remembered how effortlessly Hezhi had glided through the endless shelves of books, selecting first this, then that one for "Yen." At first he had only pretended to pay attention to her talk of the "index" and the manner in which books were filed. Eventually, however, her enthusiasm proved infectious; knowledge was a weapon, and Hezhi had an arsenal at her command, one she seemed willing to share. He wondered now, belatedly, if she hadn't used that arsenal to defeat him; certainly she had used it to escape the city. But had she somehow found the pale stranger with his supernatural weapon in the pages of these books? Had she conjured him, like a demon, from some tome?

Ghan's desk was set apart, and behind it sat the old man himself, working at copying or annotating a bulky volume. He wore an umber robe, and his skin gleamed a peculiar parchment yellow, so that he seemed as much a part of the room as the ancient documents that filled it. His features were sharp—jagged, almost— harsh frown lines etched permanently in his flesh. Not a pleasant man, Ghe remembered. He had dreamed, on first meeting him, of slipping a knife into his heart. Later he had come to think of the scholar as brave—but he had never learned to like him.

Though Ghe was the only other visible person in the room, Ghan never raised his eyes to acknowledge him.

He approached Ghan timidly, as "Yen" might. The old man continued writing, obscure and beautiful characters licking from his pen onto the paper with astonishing speed. Ghe cleared his throat.

Ghan did look up then, his eyes hard pinpricks of annoyance beneath the wrapped black cloth that obscured his bald head.

"Yes?" he inquired testily.

"Ah," said Ghe, suddenly not certain that his reluctance was entirely feigned. "Master Ghan, you might remember me. I am—"

"I know who you are," Ghan snapped.

For a frozen instant, Ghe felt a stab of something like fear. Ghan's gaze seemed to tear away the brocaded collar and reveal his throat, his true nature. He was acutely aware of all of the things he had forgotten. Had Ghan ever known him to be a Jik?

"I'm sure you remember how to find your books on arches and sewers," Ghan went on. "There is no need to bother me."

Relief rushed from his feet, through his gut, up to the top of his head. Ghan was merely being himself, impatient and unhelpful. He still believed him to be Yen, the architect.

"Master Ghan," he rushed out as the old man threatened to return to his work. "It has been some time since I have been in the library."

"A few months," Ghan replied. "A fraction of a year. Is your head not capable of holding information longer than that?"

Ghe shifted uncomfortably. "Yes, Master Ghan, it is. I . . ."

"Don't waste my time," Ghan cautioned.

Ghe lowered his voice, willed his face into lines of distress. Inwardly he felt relief; he was now in complete control of the mask he wore, his worry evaporated into the stale air of the library. "Master Ghan," he whispered almost inaudibly. "Master Ghan, I have come to ask you about Hezhi."

Ghan stared at him for a moment, and something flashed behind his flat countenance, was mastered, and vanished. Ghe appreciated that; Ghan had a very well crafted mask, as well.

"*Hezhinata*," Ghan corrected, adding the suffix to denote someone a ghost.

"Hezhi," Ghe insisted softly.

Ghan trembled for an instant, and then the trembling reached his face and transfigured it, tightened it into fury.

"Darken your mouth!" he barked. "Don't speak of such things."

Ghe persisted, though adding even more reluctance to his manner. "I believe you cared for her," he said cautiously. "She was your student, and your pride in her was obvious. Master Ghan, I cared for her, too. We . . . she cared for me. Now she has gone, and everyone says she is a ghost. But I know better, do you understand? I have heard the rumors the priests whisper. I know she escaped the city, fled with her bodyguard."

Ghan ticked his pen against the white page; Ghe noticed that the heretofore flawless document now had several irregular splotches of ink upon it. *He knows!* Ghe thought exuberantly. *He knows where she has gone!*

Ghan glanced away and then stared back up at Ghe.

"Young man, I can only caution you against repeating such things," he said softly. "I know you cared for her. It was evident. But she is dead, do you understand? I'm sorry for you, but it is true. I myself am still in grief—I will be until the day I die. But Hezhinata is dead. She was laid in state with her ancestors in the vaults beneath the Water Temple."

He glanced down at the ruined page and crinkled his eyes in exasperation. "If you need to use the library," he said, "I will help you, as she would have. I will do that for her. If you do *not* want to use the library, then you must leave. I will call the guard if need be, and you will be embarrassed before your order. Do you understand?"

Ghan's eyes were mild now, but they were also inflexible. Ghe could think of no reply that might draw out more information.

"As you say," he finally relented. And then, defiantly: "But I *know*."

"Get out," Ghan said, his voice as brittle and dangerous as broken glass.

Ghe nodded, bowed in respect, and left the library.

HE retraced his steps through the narrow corridors, eyes alert, brow furrowed. Ghan was more obstinate than he had imagined; winning his help would be no easy task—and he *needed* Ghan's help.

It had, at least, been good to speak to someone, to further prove to himself that he was indeed alive. He had been living in the palace for two days now, but furtively, observing and trying not to be seen. His only real encounter with a person up until now had been—well, less than cordial.

His first day had been spent trying to find a place to stay; that had been, actually, his easiest task. The old wing of the palace had many uninhabited sections, and beneath that were the even less frequented spaces of the earlier palace that the present one was built upon. Hezhi had spent much time in those abandoned places, and Ghe had followed her, now and then, exploring them himself at other times. Finding a place where the guards never went was far from impossible, and he had done so rather easily.

Finding clothes to replace his own ruined ones had been more difficult and more dangerous. Worse, he had discovered something unpleasant about himself. The apartment he entered for the purpose of stealing garments was that of a young man attached to minor nobility. Ghe had chosen him from a number of drunken revelers in the Red Blossom Courtyard, favored by the young for its remoteness. The fellow had the right build, no bodyguard, and was so inebriated he would likely never notice Ghe's entry into his apartment. Nor did he; and yet when Ghe saw him, unconscious on his bed, hunger suddenly replaced his desire for clothing. Feeding on a monster beneath the city was one thing; killing a man in the palace who would be missed was another. Nevertheless, almost without his own knowledge, he had torn apart the strands of life in the sleeping man and devoured them, leaving a body as cold and bereft of life as a stone. It had seemed incautious to leave the body where it lay—the Ahw'en might have some method of determining how he died—and so now it rested beneath the palace, returning its substance to the River.

He wondered how often he would have to feed like that.

Indirect afternoon sunlight dazzled from stuccoed white walls as he stepped from the dark hall into a courtyard. He brushed past the fronds of a tree fern, savored the smell of bread baking and garlicky lamb singeing on skewers. The old woman cooking gave him a glance and then returned to her work, uninterested. Above, a second woman clucked something from her third-story window down to the cook, who merely waved indifferently up at her. He swept on through the small plaza, relieved when he gained the near darkness of the next hall, lit only obscurely by the blue patterns seeping through bricks of colored glass set in the roof.

He returned his thoughts to Ghan. He had learned at least three useful things from the old man. First, that he could still speak to other Human Beings in a normal fashion, something he had begun to doubt; not only normally, but as a Jik, concealing his true self—whatever that *was* now. Second, that Ghan did not, in fact, know his true identity. As far as Ghan was concerned, he was Yen, a young man infatuated with Hezhi. Finally, though denying it verbally, it was clear from various subtle signs—which he could still read—that the librarian knew that Hezhi was alive and probably knew where she could be found. That meant that he was on a productive trail, likely the *only* trail, since, as it turned out, he had lain in the depths of the palace for nearly five months. Hezhi must be far from Nhol, far from the River and his vision.

Ghe passed the entrance to the Hall of Moments, where light coruscated so brightly through colored glass that he had once believed the Waterborn had snared a rainbow to live there with them. He went by it quickly, head lowered as if in thought or deference, and hurried into the empty portions of the palace. It was there, some fifty paces down the Hall of Jade Efreets, that he noticed the man following him. Though startled, he gave no sign, instead continuing on as if nothing were odd. He took a few strange turns, leaving the traveled thoroughfares far behind, and eventually stopped to rest and wait in another of the palace's innumerable courtyards. This one—he did not know its name— was in a sad state of disrepair, yet, consequently, had a melancholy beauty. Small, open to the sky, it was sunken through three tiers of palace, overlooked by eight empty, cobwebbed balconies. The pallid winter sun draped a scraggly, ancient olive tree in saffron light, and a few grassy weeds clawed at the pitted limestone pavement. Ghe sat on a bench of antique design, a stone slab supported by leaping granite fish—though the latter were mostly obscured by moss and lichen. A thick, black thornbush of some sort twisted tortuously up the wall he faced to cling to a wrought-iron second-floor balcony. Ghe idly wondered if it were some sort of rose vine and if its blossoms would also be black.

A moment later, the man entered the court, and Ghe had his

first good look at the person's face. He nodded in gentle surprise; the face seemed familiar, and he *should* know the name that went with it. But he did not; it was fled into the darkness where so much of him had gone. For a moment, as he watched the recognition dawn on the other face, Ghe felt a profound bitterness, resentment even. Why should this man be whole, when he himself was not?

"Ghe?" the fellow asked.

Ghe managed a smile, though his anger continued to grow.

"I am Yen presently," he said. "*Watching,* you know."

"Where have you been?" He had boyish features, mouth a bit crooked. Ghe seemed to remember liking the man, or at least liking something about him.

"Just now? The library."

"I mean for the past several months. You disappeared, after that mess at the Ember Gate. We thought you were dead."

Ghe feigned puzzlement. "Dead? No, I was just reassigned. They sent me down to Yengat, in the Swamp Kingdoms, to alleviate a little problem. I've just returned, and they've assigned me to another . . . child."

"Oh," the man said. "I guess I just didn't hear. Things were in such chaos, afterward. All of those priests and soldiers, dead—I just assumed she got you, too."

"What happened to her?" Ghe asked. "I never heard."

"They caught her, finally, in the desert."

"Ah."

There was an awkward pause, and the man flashed Ghe an uncomfortable little smile. "Well," he said at last. "I thought I recognized you. I just wanted to make sure. Come around the compound, when you get a chance."

"They have me staying over here right now," Ghe replied. "But I will."

"Good." He turned to go. Ghe watched him walk ten paces, quickening slightly with each step. He sighed. "Wait," he called. The man took another step or two, then slowly turned around. "Come back. What did I say wrong?"

The soft face hardened, eyes narrowing; he snorted at Ghe. "Everything. Who are you, really?"

"Oh, I *am* Ghe. That part is true."

"Is it? One of the priests who survived saw your head cut off. And I've been promoted; I would know if you had been sent to the Swamp Kingdoms. So I ask again, who are you?"

"No one, if I am not Ghe," he answered, standing up and striding toward the young man, who nodded as Ghe approached— as if he had asked himself a question and then answered it.

Ten steps away, and the man's right hand struck out, an easy, casual, fantastically quick motion. Ghe was prepared, and when the mean, thin blade reached where he had been, *he* was a full step to the left, pivoting against the wall. The steel pinged against something behind him as Ghe pounced, landed lightly just beyond arm's reach. His opponent lashed out with a second blade, this one not made for throwing but for penetrating bone, for cutting heart and lung. The knife was wielded skillfully enough, but to Ghe it seemed pitifully slow, its arcing thrust utterly predictable. He stepped in, caught the wrist and elbow, just as the other Jik's left hand slammed into the cluster of nerves on the side of his head. A jangling pain rang though his skull, but Ghe's grip remained firm on the knife-arm until the other twisted strangely, dropping his knife in the process, and quickly stepped away, free of his grasp.

"Very good," Ghe softly commanded. "A trick I didn't know."

"You *are* Ghe," the man said. "Quicker, maybe, stronger. But his moves, his techniques. What happened to you?"

In answer, Ghe skipped forward, feinted with a lunging punch far short of its target, followed it with a rear foot sweep. Almost, but not quite, his enemy avoided the low, vicious kick to his ankle; but Ghe clipped a heel, and the other man grunted as he stumbled back, off balance. Ghe leapt forward, committing to a dangerous lunging kick, hoping that the man actually *was* off balance and not feigning. He was rewarded with a harsh gasp as the ball of his foot splintered the man's sternum. He fell heavily against the courtyard wall, glaring at Ghe and spitting flecks of blood.

Ghe paused, not quite knowing why. Had this man been his friend? Probably not; he felt that he had few friends. But he was certainly a Jik, and perhaps a fond acquaintance.

Though clearly injured, the other lashed out with the back of his hand, but Ghe knew it for a feint and so sidestepped the stronger punch from the opposing fist, cracked his own knuckles along the man's spine. The Jik dropped and did not move until Ghe retrieved the fallen knife; then he made one feeble attempt to sweep Ghe's feet. Ghe was never convinced his opponent was really unconscious, however, and easily avoided the attack. He finished him with a quick thrust under the jaw, up into the brain case, watched the eyes roll and then set themselves, senseless, to watching the sky.

"I wonder what your name was," Ghe whispered to the dead man, and panting, sat against the wall, hand still on the knife hilt.

He watched, fascinated, as the colored strands inside of the man began to unravel. He was not hungry, not at the moment, and so he just watched, curious to see how men died.

The strands fell away. The ones extending into limbs and organs withered, vanished, were sucked up by the dimming knot in the heart. The knot, untied into slender filaments, now braided into a thick strand, and as Ghe watched, it retied itself in a new pattern, dimming further still, until almost he could not see it. It lay there for a time and then stirred, like a feather touched by the merest breeze. Curious, Ghe reached to touch it, not with his hand but with the *something* he used when he fed. The little bundle shivered, fluttered, moved to him. Ghe took hold of it gently, felt its rhythmic pulse, like a bird's heartbeat.

What is this? it said. Just like a voice, but a voice that spoke in the hollows of his bones, in the beat of his own heart. *What has happened?*

It was the dead man. Qan Yazhwu, son of Wenli, the net-maker—images flickered in Ghe's mind: childhood, a woman, the first terrified moment when learning to swim . . .

Shuddering, he thrust it away, and the voice was gone. The ghost-seed tumbled away from him and then once again chose a direction, floating purposefully down the hall. When it met with a wall it passed on through it effortlessly. Ghe understood where it was going. Downstream, to the River.

"Farewell, Qan Yazhwunata," he whispered, and then turned back to the body, considering its disposal.

VII

Surrounded by Monsters

Hezhi leaned against the wind-smoothed stone, steadied herself, and caught her breath. Already the terror of what she had seen was fading, but the strangeness of it remained, the shock. Brother Horse had seemed to her, in the short time she had known him, the most Human of creatures: earthy, affectionate, and easygoing. He had comforted her from the first, from the moment they met, lifting her onto his horse, wrapping her tight in his arms as they thundered away from Nhol, from her birthplace and her doom.

But he was most certainly *not* Human, or at least not completely so. Human Beings did not have *creatures* living inside of them.

At least, she did not think they did.

"I can't trust anyone," she said aloud. "Only Tsem."

And perhaps Perkar. It was odd, that thought. She had known Perkar for no more than a day longer than she had known Brother Horse, and she had *seen* the ugliness *he* was capable of, the slaughtered bodies of her father's elite guard, the decapitation of Yen. But

Perkar and she were twisted together in some way, braided by their own desires—not for each other, perhaps, but bonded in some inextricable fashion. It was not love—she loved Tsem, she loved Ghan, loved Qey. What bound her and Perkar was not that, nor was it the awkward, restless desire that Yen had inspired. It was something less compelling but more powerful.

But that was her belly talking. Her brain was learning to trust itself, and it told her that even Perkar was not to be counted on.

The cliffs behind her soared as high as three-story buildings and were often as sheer as city walls. She had regarded them from afar, from the village, and they had seemed mysterious, intriguing. Like a city, yet not a city. Spires, walls, caverns like halls—she had imagined them all. Crinkling her brow, rebellious, she strode back into them, following a crooked canyon floor, trying not to think about the things in Brother Horse, the god of the cairn, about gods and demons *everywhere*, not even about the Fire Goddess.

She was suddenly struck by an odd memory. The stone rising about her seemed to form a vast hall, and save for the lack of buttresses and a real ceiling, she was suddenly, powerfully reminded of the Leng Court, where her father often held ceremonies and audiences. When last she had been in the court she had seen a drama, a representation of the legend of her family. It told of the People, surrounded on all sides by monsters, unable to save themselves, and of how Chakunge, the son of Gau—a chieftain's daughter—and the River destroyed them all.

Surrounded by monsters: that was what the Mang were, surrounded by monsters, in every stone—maybe more than surrounded, maybe even *penetrated*, if all were like Brother Horse. In Nhol, the River had changed *that*, at least, killed these things that infested the land the way termites infested wood or maggots old meat. Maybe that was what these cliffs were, a place where these "gods" had burrowed, like insects, through the land, tried in some crude fashion to form a city comparable to Nhol.

It dawned on her that her people might not have been all that different from the Mang at one time. The girl in the story, Gau:

she had been the daughter of a "chieftain"—a very old word, one not used anymore except to refer to the leaders of barbarian tribes. But Hezhi's own people had once had chieftains, very long ago. Before becoming a part of the River, before escaping from these *visions* . . .

The wind hummed and shuddered through the stone corridors, and Hezhi felt fright creeping back upon her. What if her "god-sight" came now, and she saw whatever thing made that noise? What if the cliffs suddenly came alive around her?

They could most easily enter her through her eyes, Brother Horse claimed. Despairing, she sank down to her knees, then sat, shut her eyes, and imagined a cool breeze across rooftops, Qey in the kitchen, fussing over an evening meal of braised chicken with garlic, black rice, and fish dumplings.

In Nhol she had learned to fear darkness; now she found solace in it.

I wish Perkar were here, she thought, clenching and unclenching fistfuls of the grainy sand. There was no snow here, though she had noticed drifts piled against the south canyon wall. Still, it was cold. It would get colder at night. Where would she go? Back to the camp, where Brother Horse and those creatures in him waited? Where everyone was a relative of the old man and no one trusted *her* at all?

Yes, she needed Perkar.

As she thought this a second time she suddenly realized what she was doing and snarled in sudden self-fury. Perkar was right not to trust her! Once she had called him from across the world, from his home and family, and for what? So that he could slaughter men in the streets of Nhol that *she* might escape her destiny. And now, here she was, in the midst of that *new* destiny he had sacrificed so much to help her create, and she was wishing for him to come save her again, to bring his bloody blade and make carrion of her problems.

No, not again. This time she would make her own way.

But what did that mean? Could she survive here, in the Mang Wastes, without the Mang or Perkar?

No, she could not.

Could she face Brother Horse again? She didn't know if she could do *that*, either.

Abruptly she realized that she might no longer have a choice. New sounds intruded upon the slow, terrible melodies of wind through stone. The muffled rhythm of hoofbeats, tinkle of brass bells, and human voices moving nearer with each moment. Reluctantly she opened her eyes and glanced quickly around. What would she do if it was Brother Horse? He must know that she had *seen* him. Had he intended that?

Well, she would face him. If she died, she died. She would not die weeping or cowering. She was Hezhi, daughter of the emperor of Nhol, once possessed of enough power to make the world quake beneath her feet. It would take more than an old man possessed by demons to make her cringe.

Still, she trembled a bit as she stood to face the hoofbeats.

Two horsemen had entered the canyon. Neither was Brother Horse. They were Mang, clothed in *bachgay*—long black coats split for riding—and flaring elkskin breeks. Rigid bands of lacquered armor showed beneath their coats. Both bore bows. It was plain, even to her, that they were following her tracks—and that they now saw her.

As they drew closer, she realized that she did not recognize them; they were not of Brother Horse's band. This was no surprise—since the Ben'cheen had begun, there were more strange faces than familiar ones. What was *more* disturbing was that these men also wore steel caps with plumes of red-dyed horsehair, and she remembered hearing that this signified being at war. She glanced around, wondering where she might hide, but there was nowhere; the cliffs were too sheer to scale—at least for *her* to scale—and there were no obvious caves or crevasses to crawl into. She could only watch them come, alert for any sign of their intentions on their faces.

When they drew nearer, they unstrung their bows, returned them to ornately embroidered sheaths. They paused in doing this, and though one might take his eyes from her, the other was always watching, as if she were a snake or some other dangerous thing.

Done disarming, they urged their mounts closer to where she stood, and she, not certain how to respond, merely watched them come.

"*Du'unuzho, shigiindeye?*" one asked softly. "Are you all right, cousin?" His accent was strange, not like that of Brother Horse, though she could still understand him. Up close, his face was not as fierce as it appeared from a distance; lean and narrow, it tapered pleasantly. His eyes were not black, as were her own or those of the other Mang she knew, but a light brown, flecked faintly with green. He was quite young, perhaps no more than fifteen. His companion looked the same age, though more thickly built, his face and eyes more typically Mang.

"*Gaashuzho,*" she answered. "I will be."

He nodded, but his face registered the strangeness of her accent. He cast his eyes down for a moment, as if considering how to say what he wanted to say.

"You are not Mang," he settled upon at last.

"No," she answered. "No, I am not. But I am in the care of the South People." Brother Horse had told her to explain that to *any* strangers she met.

"It is *she*," the second rider hissed, but the first held up his hand to silence him.

"My cousins call me Moss, for my eyes," he explained. "My war name is Strums the Bow. You may call me Moss, if you please. My cousin's name is Chuuzek."

"Hey!" Chuuzek grumbled, and Hezhi wondered if he was upset because his name had been given to a stranger or if it was because the name Moss gave meant "He-Continually-Goes-About-Belching."

"My name is Hezhi," she replied, knowing it was polite to give a name when one was offered. "Have you come here for the Ben'cheen?"

"Partly," Moss told her. "We are of the Four Spruces People." He said that as if it should be significant, and Hezhi was sure that it probably was, to other Mang. It meant nothing to her, but she nodded as if it did. Moss regarded her impassively, then cleared his throat. "Well," he said. "I would like to offer you a ride back to the village. It is a long walk from here."

"No, thank you," Hezhi replied. "I have a companion I shall rejoin shortly."

"Ah," Moss replied. Chuuzek looked around the canyon at that, expressing either disbelief or wariness. He grunted something under his breath.

Something isn't right, Hezhi realized. These two were acting oddly, even by Mang standards. It could be because she was not Mang, but there was Chuuzek's blurted "It is *she.*" That worried her immensely, and she wished now that they would go away. Moss seemed pleasant enough, concerned even, but then so had Yen, and *he* had been prepared to kill her.

"I think," Moss said apologetically, "that I should insist. It is not meet that we leave you here, wandering about in the cliffs. Your companion is Mang?"

"He is."

"Then he will find his way home easily enough."

"He will wonder what became of me."

Chuuzek snorted. "If he is Mang, he will read the signs well enough."

Hezhi frowned up at them. She could see the hilts of their swords clearly, protruding from sheaths laced to their saddles. Chuuzek had his hand upon his, but Moss' were folded loosely, casually, at the base of his horse's neck.

"You wear war tassels," she said. "I can't know what your intentions are."

"It is true," Moss said. "We are at war. Not with *you.* But I might take you captive, if that is the only way you will allow me to return you to the village."

"I still prefer to decline."

Chuuzek snarled; Hezhi could see that he was genuinely angry. Moss merely looked uncomfortable.

"I would rather have your permission," he began, but at that moment he was interrupted by the sound of another horse approaching.

Hezhi looked beyond them to the new arrival, saw that it was Brother Horse, mounted, Heen trotting a hundred paces or so behind. For just a moment it all seemed far too much. The stranger she knew or the stranger she did not know?

Surrounded by monsters.

She would watch them. She would pretend that she did not care what happened to her. That was simple enough.

"Well, hello," Brother Horse bellowed as he drew nearer. "How are my nephews from the Four Spruces Clan?"

Moss turned in his saddle and then dismounted, a sign of great respect. Chuuzek dismounted, also, with some hesitation, muttering under his breath.

"We are well enough, Grandfather," Moss replied. "Only trying to convince this little thrush that the snow and open sky are no place for her with sundown approaching."

Brother Horse smiled broadly. "My little niece is a hardheaded thrush," he explained, his eyes focused on Hezhi rather than on the two warriors. "I appreciate the concern, however."

Hezhi shivered. Brother Horse seemed so normal. Suddenly she doubted what she had seen; perhaps the monsters within him were merely some illusion created by the Fire Goddess, by the unevenness of her own vision. Once again, she did not *know* enough. But if, inside, Brother Horse was really a demon, what hope did she have?

Her only hope lay with herself. Not with Perkar, not with Tsem, not with the River. She did not need a butcher or a giant. She strained, for the first time trying to *will* the godsight to happen, to force a vision of the old man.

His form did not waver; he remained as he seemed.

Brother Horse leaned in his saddle and the leather creaked loudly within the red walls of stone around them. "Hezhi," he said. "Will you return with us now? It's too cold for an old man to be out searching for his niece."

"Leave her to us, then," Chuuzek grumbled, but he kept his

eyes firmly on the ground, not willing to challenge the old man directly.

"No," Brother Horse said. "My niece is shy around strangers. She is not very trusting."

Was there more than common emphasis on the last word? Was he accusing her?

But why *should* she trust him?

"I *am* cold," she said rather shortly. "I would like to get back to Tsem now."

"Climb up behind me, then." Brother Horse grunted.

"She may share my horse," Moss offered. "I would consider it an honor."

Of course you would, Hezhi fumed. *What do* you *want of me? To kill me, as Yen did? My skin, to hang in your yekt? Or merely sex, like Wezh?* She was unable to avert her eyes quickly enough to avoid shooting him a poisonous glance; she saw the venom mirror against his eyes, saw what appeared to be dismay.

Be hurt, Hezhi retorted in her mind. *But you want something. You may be smart enough to hide it, but your cousin is not.*

"No, best she ride with me," Brother Horse said good-naturedly. But there was a certainty in the way he said it, a gentle termination of the debate.

"Very well," Moss replied, his voice betraying no ill feelings. "I only offered."

"And I only refused you," Hezhi replied, using the polite "you" to soften her words. To imply that at another time, under other circumstances, she might *not* refuse. Though she would, of course.

Climbing up behind Brother Horse, she felt more comfortable almost instantly. Safe from whatever unknown threat the young warriors represented. The feeling was so much against her will— she wanted to stay wary, alert, and angry—that she wondered if it might not be some form of enchantment. Brother Horse was, after all, a gaan, and she knew nothing of the powers he might wield. Still, nothing seemed amiss or odd about the old man. To the contrary, he was just as he had always been.

* * *

THEY rode back to the Ben'cheen all in a clump. The sun was westering, but not, as Moss had implied, particularly near setting. Hezhi kept her head pressed against Brother Horse's coat, thinking that perhaps she would hear a growl or some other strange sound from within his body. She did not, and so instead she focused on the conversation, idly noting the slight differences in their speech.

"Is it odd that you go about with your helmets so?" Brother Horse asked after a moment.

"It would be odd if we were not at war," Moss replied softly, after a considered pause. "As things stand, it is not odd at all."

"I see. And who are my western relatives at war with?"

"The *Mang*," Moss corrected, "are at war with the Cattle People."

Hezhi felt the muscles of Brother Horse's back tighten.

"War? Not just raiding?" His voice sounded casual, but the tension Hezhi sensed remained. "Why have I not heard of this?"

"News travels slowly on the plains in winter. That is why Chuuzek and I have come; we bring the news that our people will not be at the Ben'cheen this year."

"Tell me more of this," Brother Horse demanded. He kept his horse carefully at a walk, and the younger men were obliged to maintain the same pace, though the colorful cluster of tents was visible in the distance, the sounds of celebration already audible.

Chuuzek spit over his left shoulder. "They have invaded our upland grazing lands, built fortresses to defend them. They sent men to *ask* for them first—*very* polite."

"You told them no."

"We sent their heads back. It is *our* pasture."

Brother Horse sighed. "That is true," he allowed. "It belongs to the western bands."

It was only then that Hezhi understood, that she remembered who the "Cattle People" were: *Perkar's* people.

"Oh, no," she muttered.

It was a small exclamation, not intended to be overheard, but Moss caught it, favored her with brief but intense scrutiny.

"Where is your niece from?" Moss asked quietly.

Hezhi understood, of course, that Moss did not for a moment believe that she was Brother Horse's niece. Though her appearance more resembled the Mang than it did Perkar's strange folk, there were still quite noticeable differences. And Moss had heard her speak, could not help but know her Mang was recently learned. "Niece" was merely the polite way for an older man to speak of a younger woman—particularly one under his protection.

"She is from Nhol," Brother Horse told him in a tone that made it clear that the question, though it had been answered, was not a welcome one. "And she is my niece in all but blood."

"Huh," Chuuzek grunted, but Moss merely nodded acceptance.

"There are two more at my fire right now," Brother Horse went on, "two more who also do not share the blood of the Horse Mother, who have no kin amongst the herds. But they are under my protection, as well. My clan and I would take it hard if anything should happen to them."

He's telling them about Perkar and Ngangata, she thought.

"Also from Nhol?" Moss asked.

"No, not at all," Brother Horse replied.

There was a brief, restless silence, during which Chuuzek became more and more agitated, chewing his lip and bunching the reins in his hands.

"If they are Cattle People, I will *kill* them," he suddenly blurted defiantly.

Brother Horse reined his mount to a full stop and turned in his saddle to face the young man squarely.

"If you kill a man—or a woman—under my protection, in my village, I will consider it murder," he said. His tone remained placid, but the words somehow conveyed the most resolute finality imaginable. Chuuzek made to speak again, but Moss intervened.

"Of course we understand that," he said. "We are Mang. Our mothers taught us well."

"I would hope so," Brother Horse returned. "I would hope it would take more than war to see our ancient ways set easily aside."

"This *is* more than war," Chuuzek growled, but then, at another glance from Moss, he lapsed into sullen silence.

Brother Horse moved his mount forward again, and the silence pooled around the horsemen, threatening to stay with them all until they reached the village. Still, Brother Horse made no move to quicken his pace.

What could Chuuzek have meant, this was more than war? Hezhi barely understood war at all—as the insulated daughter of the emperor, she had rarely had occasion to think about it—but how could a war be *more* than that?

"I see the pennant of the Seven Hoof People," Moss remarked.

"They arrived yesterday," Brother Horse told him.

"Is old Siinch'u with them this year?"

Hezhi felt the cords of her companion's back loosen a bit. He even uttered a little chuckle, and Hezhi was certain, though she could not see his face, that he was grinning. "Oh, yes. I caught him trying to sneak into my granddaughter's tent the other day."

"Still the same then."

"Of course. Gods help lecherous old men."

Yes," Moss replied. "Didn't I hear that you spent several years on an island hiding from the Woodpecker Goddess because you and her daughter—"

"No need to repeat rumors like that," Brother Horse snapped. But it was his mock anger now, a joking kind of disapproval, very different from the low, dangerous tension of a few moments before.

Had she *seen* that danger, that thing with claws and molten eyes?

"Tell me about your granduncle Snatch-the-Pony. I heard he—"

"Yes, it's true," Moss nearly crowed, his face opening into a radiant smile. "He went over to the Fang Hills . . ."

So when they reached the Swollen Tents Brother Horse and Moss were laughing together. But Chuuzek, trailing a bit, kept his face flat and expressionless. Hezhi thought it to be a thin, translucent mask over murder—and perhaps more.

VIII

Tales of the Changeling

Perkar sat staring at the Blackgod for a long while. He noticed and understood Ngangata's occasional glances warning him to be cautious. Perkar felt he hardly needed such a warning, but then again, the record of his life seemed to register one mistake after another. The Blackgod simply gazed at the fire, his lips moving every now and then, as if he were speaking to the Fire Goddess, but otherwise he remained cryptic—as unknown and unfathomable to Perkar as the marks that Hezhi made on her long white leaves.

Good Thief added nothing to the silence. He ate the dried meat they gave him without speaking; he seemed to have expended his energy not only for threats and self-recrimination but for everything else. More than once Perkar thought he had fallen asleep, but his eyes always fluttered back open.

Destroy the Changeling. Perkar had spent months denying to himself that such a thing was within his power. Good people had died when he believed it was. His *king* had died, and a war with the Mang had begun because a single, stupid boy had believed he could slay the unslayable.

Now a god who claimed to have created the world told him it was possible, that it had been a part of things all along.

And he was afraid to ask the vital question—afraid to ask *how*.

Because if Karak told him, he might believe. And if he believed . . .

Across the fire, the Blackgod raised his weird yellow eyes. He smiled, and Perkar saw, in the spooled lights and images of his memory, a great black bird, gripping Apad's shoulders, plunging his beak down into brain and blood, only to come up wearing the grin of a Crow.

"How?" he asked, knowing the question would damn him.

"How?" the Blackgod repeated, blinking at Perkar.

"No," Ngangata stated flatly. "Perkar, let it go. Whatever he plans—whether he tells the truth now or not—it will not go well for *us*."

"You can ride away," Perkar said. "In fact, I beg you to ride away. You have shared enough of my burdens, my friend."

Ngangata worried at the fire with a stick, banked it a bit. "We should both ride away."

Karak softly clucked with his tongue. "There is so much Alwat in you," he said to Ngangata. "Always ready to let things be. Always satisfied with the way things are."

"Things could certainly be worse," Ngangata retorted.

The Blackgod nodded. "Alwat through and through. But your friend, here, is Human—through and through. Better, he is a hero."

"Perkar knows my opinion of heroes," Ngangata replied.

"Enough," Perkar snapped. "Tell me. Explain to me how I can destroy a god who lies across the entire breadth of the world."

"Oh, *you* cannot," Karak said.

Perkar blushed with fury. "Then why did you say that I could?"

"Well, you can certainly help to slay him. It is within your power to bring *about* his destruction."

"Karak—"

"*Blackgod.*"

"Blackgod, then," Perkar snapped. "Perhaps the gods enjoy

such quibbling. Perhaps immortality twists you so. But I want no part of it. Speak to me plainly or do not speak to me at all."

Karak's eyes flashed red and then white hot. A snarl curled his handsome lip, and he bolted to his feet. Perkar, suddenly filled with Harka's sense of danger, reached for the blade, but his hand never reached it.

The Blackgod clapped his hands together and lightning was born. Thunder came in the same instant, to shatter the very air around them. Perkar was flung back roughly, dazed by the blinding light and deafening noise. Both throbbed in his head. He was only dimly aware of being lifted bodily off the ground as someone took a double fistful of his shirt. A great river of flame still ran across his vision, and he was not even certain whether his eyes were open or closed. He fumbled again for Harka, but an iron claw closed around his sword wrist and held it with absolute strength.

He dangled there, held in the air by chest and arm, until the brightness across his eyes faded and he could make out the Blackgod's face, set and grim, inhuman. The brassy roar in his ears lingered.

The Blackgod was now white. His skin was ivory, his hair a cascade of thistledown, his eyes pearly slits with a single blue pinpoint to mark their pupils. His face was still essentially Human, but his nose had become a sharp alabaster beak, a dagger aimed between Perkar's eyes. Ngangata and Good Thief sprawled behind Karak, and Perkar could not tell if they were alive or not.

"Know this," the god hissed, his voice cutting somehow through the crashing in Perkar's injured ears. "There are limits to the insolence I will tolerate from such as you. You will treat me with respect. You will do this, or I will turn your companion inside out. I will flay his skin, and then I will have yours."

With that the god released Perkar. He tumbled roughly to the ground, dizzy, on the verge of violent illness.

"Now," Karak said, in a more reasonable tone. "Now you can let me answer your question or you may politely ask me to

leave. All other options include pain for you and yours. Do
you understand this? Are you now aware of our respective
positions?"

Perkar realized dully that blood was drizzling from his ears and
down his neck. He wiped ineffectually at it.

"Y-yes," he managed to stammer, though he could not hear
even his own voice as well as he could that of the god.

"Fine. Now listen carefully. Long ago, the Brother of the Forest
Lord did not walk long across the land as he does now. Long ago,
he kept to a certain place, kept all of his water about him, contained. He was only *tricked* into releasing it, you see. But once
he was running free, he became hungry. He became insatiable. He
began to grow then, to eat everything.

"Until now, at least he has been lying in one bed, and so he eats
only what he can reach from it. But he tries to throw pieces of
himself out, toss them away but keep hold of them, too. This is so
that he can wander where he does not flow and eat what is there,
as well. He wants it all, you see?"

Perkar nodded, even as he coughed. The pain in his ears was
sharpening, and he could not tell if that was Harka healing him or
just the fading of shock and the return of sensation.

"Well, this girl Hezhi is such a piece of him. But you and I,
Perkar—we took her away from him before she could be whole.
Before she could be him. It was a near thing; you don't even know
how near."

"But now she is safe?"

"Safe? Oh, no, pretty thing. No, now he wants her back. She is
his best hope and his most terrible danger. He is awake now—*you*
awakened him—and he bends his huge will to reclaiming her.
And he knows you, too, of course."

"This Mang gaan, then. He serves the River?"

"Yes, in a sense. The River sends him dreams, shows him
visions of greatness. He is one tool the River wields now."

"There are others?"

"I can't see them well. They are still in his shadow, where my
vision has trouble walking, with him awake. But something waits

there in Nhol, ready to spring out across the plains. When it comes, it will be a whirlwind."

"What then?" Perkar groaned. "What am *I* to do?"

"She can slay him," the Blackgod answered, eyes narrowed to milky slits. "She must be brought to his source, to the spot he was born. There she can slay him."

"Hezhi?"

"Good. You understand. Take her to his source."

"And then?"

"Then she will slay him."

"How?"

"That is not your concern. Suffice to say she will do so."

Perkar opened his mouth to speak again and then thought better of it. He was afraid, and he realized that it was a sensation that bearing Harka had muted for some time. He searched for his earlier disdain, his passionate anger, and found it buried beneath terror.

"Take her to his source," he said, repeating the Blackgod's words. "How shall we find it?"

"You know where it lies—in the mountain at the heart of Balat. And I will leave you roadmarks in any event. But have a care—do not travel upon *him* to reach it. You must go overland."

"Even I know that," Perkar muttered.

Karak squatted before him, so that his beak nearly touched Perkar's nose. The Blackgod smiled fondly, reached over and tousled Perkar's hair, the way one's grandfather might.

"Of course you do, pretty thing, little oak tree. I just remind you."

Before Perkar could reply—or even flinch from the god's touch—Karak suddenly curled in upon himself, knotted into a tight white ball, and bloomed into flame, like a dried rose consumed by fire. He uncurled his body as the heat licked up from him, black again, completely a bird. A Raven larger than any man. The Raven hopped back from Perkar, regarded him with its head cocked.

"Just reminding you," the Raven said, and strutted over to

where Ngangata and Good Thief lay. Both had begun to stir, to watch the exchange between Perkar and Karak with dull eyes.

The Raven stooped over Ngangata, and ice formed in Perkar's chest. He desperately willed his hand to reach for Harka, commanded his legs to bring him erect. He could not govern his limbs; they refused him.

Karak regarded Ngangata for what seemed an eternity, and Ngangata stared back at the god, his expression set and unreadable. Then the god hopped on, to where Good Thief lay.

"Hello, pretty thing," the Blackgod cooed.

Good Thief looked not at Karak but at Perkar. His eyes held a desperate mixture of fear and anger.

"My horse," he shouted. "His name is Sharp Tiger. Look after my horse, Cattle-Man."

It was not a command, it was a plea. It was the last thing Good Thief said; Karak's talons dug into his belly, black wings opened and boomed, and the god was rising up, the Mang dangling helplessly, his eyes still fixed on Perkar.

He watched the god and his prey until they dwindled to a speck, were gone.

PERKAR barely had enough energy to help Ngangata into the tent—the fire was scattered, the night chill sinking into their bones. The tent was warmer but still uncomfortably cool, and the two huddled together, not speaking. Perkar thought of talking to Harka, but that seemed useless, somehow, and instead he lay there, remembering Good Thief's face growing smaller. He certainly did not believe he would sleep, but suddenly it was morning, light glowing in through the tent skin.

Ngangata was still asleep, and Perkar did not disturb him. Instead he got up and pushed as quietly as he could through the tent flap. The sun was already well up, feathering the rolling clouds above with shades of gold, pink, and gray. Blue sky peered through cheerfully.

Perkar—not cheerful at all—gathered wood and started a fire.

He found the corpse of the dead archer, his back open in long stripes, his eyes wide and uncomprehending. He dragged the stiff body to where its companion lay, and there he sang a song for the dead, offering what little wine he had to them. He did not know their names, of course, except for Good Thief, but there was an appropriate song for dead enemies, and he sang all of it. After that, he began to search for stones to cover the bodies.

After a long search, he found only a few fist-size stones. He looked down at the horse and the man, wondering how best to deal with them. Not far away, Sharp Tiger whickered, further reminding Perkar of his obligations.

"Let the sky have them," a voice croaked from behind him. Perkar turned to see Ngangata, bleary-eyed, standing near the tent.

"They were valiant enemies," Perkar told him. "They deserve some consideration."

"Let the sky have them," Ngangata repeated. "They are Mang; that is their custom."

Perkar puffed out a long, steaming breath. "You mean leave them here for the wolves?"

"Yes."

"There should be something more we can do than that."

"For dead bodies? No. Offer to their ghosts later, if you still feel guilty. Now we should leave this place before their kinsmen arrive."

"How did they know to come *here*, in the first place?"

"Their gaan saw us, no doubt."

"Then he will see us wherever we go."

Ngangata shrugged. "If we are moving, there will be no place to see."

Perkar nodded reluctantly. "I have to take Good Thief's horse."

Ngangata gave Perkar a somewhat painful flash of a grin.

"That is a Mang war horse. No one but his rider may approach him."

"Good Thief asked me to. It was his last request."

Ngangata raised his hands in a gesture of helplessness. "I will pack the tent," he said.

Perkar stared at his fallen enemy for a few more heartbeats, then turned his attention to Sharp Tiger.

The stallion eyed him dubiously as he approached. Sharp Tiger seemed a fitting name; though most Mang horses bore stripes upon their flanks and hindquarters, his were pronounced and black, laid upon a tawny field. His mane was jet. Of course, his name would have nothing to do with his appearance. Mang horses were named after dead Mang warriors, just as Mang warriors were named after dead horses. Perkar wondered, as he approached the beast, whether a man or a mount had first borne the name in the long ago.

Sharp Tiger watched him draw closer, eyes flaring; he dipped his head up and down restlessly.

"*Shununechen,*" Perkar said gently, as he had heard Mang say to mounts not belonging to them. "Smell me, cousin."

Sharp Tiger allowed him closer, until he could place his cupped hand near the animal's nostrils. The beast sniffed him uncertainly.

He was still saddled, the bit still in his mouth. Perkar sadly realized that he hadn't even unsaddled T'esh for the night; he could see him grazing some distance away, nearer the stream. This was no way to treat such beautiful mounts.

But then, neither was cutting the legs out from under one, he reflected, gritting his teeth.

"Are you going to let me on, cousin?" he asked Sharp Tiger. His plan had been merely to lead the horse behind T'esh, but now he had an inexplicable urge to ride him. Ngangata, of course, was right. This horse would never let anyone but Good Thief upon his back. Still . . .

He put his foot in the stirrup, and Sharp Tiger stood there, passively. It wasn't until he tried to swing his other leg over that the beast reacted.

Perkar was suddenly in the air, propelled upward by Sharp Tiger's explosion of movement. He thudded to the ground and rolled. Sharp Tiger came after, lashing down with his forehooves. Only Harka's preternatural sense of danger saved Perkar from the stallion's hard, sharp weapons; he was only lightly grazed on one arm before he fought clear and returned to his feet. Sharp Tiger ceased his attack as abruptly as he began it and watched Perkar with clear, dark eyes.

Perkar smiled wryly at his own stupidity.

"Very well," he said. "Then will you let me lead you?"

Sharp Tiger stood, quiet now. When Perkar cautiously took his reins, he followed without complaint.

Not much later, with the tent packed and Ngangata mounted, they set out toward Brother Horse's village. Perkar rode with his thoughts, and one eye on the cloudswept sky, the fear and memory of black wings clear in his mind.

IX

The Reader of Bones

HE took himself down to the docks to think.

Almost, he feared the sunlight. Tatters of stories remained in his mind, fantasies spun in the dark alleys of his youth by the poor and the fearful in Southtown. Creatures like himself stalked those tales, ghouls who fed on the lifeblood of the living, who shunned the bright eye of the sky lest it wither them away, reduce them to droplets of polluted and stained River water. In the daylight, such things remained in their deep crypts below the city, in the bottomless depths of the River . . .

But the sunlight did him no harm. In fact, it cheered him, as did the brightly clothed merchants bustling about the quays, the pungent stink of fish, the sweet incense of fortune-tellers, the savory scent of meat grilling on the charcoal braziers of food vendors. He stopped at one of the last, paid a dark young girl with a pox-scarred face a copper soldier for two skewers of garlic lamb and a thick, spongy roll of *tsag'* bread. He sat on a dock with his legs dangling out over the River, eating his meal and watching the gulls worry about the barges, the thick-armed men unloading cargo from the Swamp Kingdoms, from up-River and from far-off Lhe.

Beneath him, he could feel the River, like a father, proud of his presence.

"You are mighty," he said, addressing the limitless waters wonderingly.

Only reluctantly did he bend his mind to his worries.

His time in Nhol was limited; that much was clear. He could not kill every man and woman who recognized him. Already the priesthood must be investigating the disappearances, especially of the slain Jik. And it was surely urgent, in any case, that he leave soon to find Hezhi.

But the world was vast, and he knew not where to look. Only Ghan could tell him that, and Ghan had made it plain that he would say nothing. Given time, Ghe felt certain that he could win the old man's confidence—he cared deeply for Hezhi, and that was a lever which could be worked until the man's stone heart was prized up, lifted so that Ghe could make out what was underneath. But he needed *time* for that.

Time, also, to learn a few things. Even with the powers of his rebirth, he would face enemies he only vaguely understood—the white-skinned barbarian who would not die, for instance. Was he like Ghe, some sort of ghoul? Was he more powerful? And in Ghe's mind were vague shadows of other powers, out beyond where the River could reach. He must know something of them, as well.

He let his gaze settle over the city, wondering where he might find the answers he sought. In the library, perhaps, where Hezhi had found *her* secrets. But Nhol had many dark places, where old knowledge slept.

The foremost of these towered behind the dockside taverns and markets, as pristine and monumental as they were squalid and ordinary; the Great Water Temple. It was a stepped pyramid formed of white stone, water geysering from its sun-crowned summit, a fist of the River shaking aloft toward the heavens. He had been inside the building, seen the perfect column of water drawn up through the very core of the structure, and wondered, awestruck at the rush and power of it. From where he sat now, he could see two of the broken slopes where the water cascaded down, four streams for four directions rushing to rejoin their source in the canals that surrounded the priesthood's most holy building. To him, also, it had once been holy, a symbol of the great power he served and of the order that had raised him from sleeping with dogs to a position of respect and honor.

Now, with the River's perspective, he saw it much differently. Within its white shell, he now sensed a heart of mystery, a labyrinth of falsehood and deceit. From its caverns the priesthood spun their spidery webs, shaped the bonds that held the Rivergod in place. It held libraries, too, vast dusty rooms of forbidden knowledge, chants and formulae of terrific power. He had but glimpsed such things when he was initiated as a Jik, but now he had some sense of what was hidden there, beneath the falling water, the great hill of rock.

He turned his gaze back to his feet, to the god flowing below them. "You want me to go *there*," he whispered.

That would be dangerous, even for him. The priesthood had the power to shackle a god—and what animated Ghe was less than a finger of the River's power. But the priests had taught him, made him from a common thief and cutthroat into a finely wrought weapon. A weapon could be turned upon its smith as easily as upon anyone else.

The food was not as good as he had anticipated. The smell had been wonderful, tantalizing—but in his mouth it had no flavor. As if, along with so many things, he had forgotten how to taste. Discouraged, he tossed what remained of his meal into the water. "Eat well, my lord," he said, before rising and resuming his walk.

He went next to Southtown, though he was in no way certain why. He knew that he had been born there, but the nets in that part of his mind were the most torn and tangled; they held the fewest clear images. Walking down Red Gar Street, the place he remembered best, was like hearing only snatches of a song. Here a shop sign was as well remembered as his name; but blocks would go by that seemed as alien as the depths of the palace. Still, it brought something of a return of his earlier good cheer; his nose and his skin seemed to recognize the street as his eyes did not. A sort of melancholy happiness walked with him, the ghost of recollection.

And then, when he stopped on a corner to watch a boy pick a minor noble's pocket, someone spoke his name.

"Ghe!" An old woman's voice, one he utterly failed to recognize.

He turned in surprise, fingers knitting into deadly shapes. It *was* an old woman—an *ancient* woman—dressed as a fortune-teller. Her clothes were faded, shabby, but she wore a steepled hat with golden moons and stars embossed upon it that looked both new and expensive. Before her was spread a velvet mat for her fortune-bones. Her face was split in a half-toothless grin, and her eyes sparkled with an odd mixture of lights—happiness, wariness, and concern.

He knew her face. Images of it lay about his mind like shards of a shattered pot. But no name was attached to it, no past conversations, nothing. Nothing save for a faint, pleasant sensation.

"Ghe? Haven't you come to sit with an old woman?" The old eyes had sharpened with suspicion. He hesitated, searching his mind, thinking desperately. He smiled and knelt by her mat.

"Hello," he said, managing to sound cheerful. "It has been a long while."

"And whose fault is that? Ah, little *Duh*, what has the priest-hood made of you? I scarcely recognize you in that collar. You look tired, too."

She knew about the priesthood. Who *was* this woman?

"It is a busy life," he muttered, wishing he at least had a name to call her by. Was she some relative of his? Not his mother, surely. She was far too old for that.

The puzzled, suspicious look was still clear on her face. He had to—do what? He should run, leave, that was what he *should* do.

"Read the bones for me," he said instead, gesturing at the inscribed, polished slats that lay on the mat.

"You put store in that now? The priesthood teach you to respect old women properly?"

"Yes."

She shrugged, picked the bones up, and rattled them around in her hands.

"Whatever happened to that girl?" she asked casually. "The one you liked, that they set you after?"

His dismay must have been as clear to her as the call of gulls above. Her own eyes widened. "What have you *done*, little one? What is this about?"

Ghe felt a little tremor walk up his spine. He had to do something. He reached out for the little, fluttering knot of strands that made up her life. She knew it all, this old woman. That he was a Jik, about Hezhi, everything. Best to kill her now, quickly.

But he could not. He knew not why. The moment passed, and he shrank back from the strands, though now he felt a bit of hunger—completely unabated by the bread and meat he consumed earlier.

"Listen," he hissed. "Listen to me." He took a deep breath. "I don't know who you are."

Her eyes widened and then flattened. "What do you mean by that? Life in the palace made you too good to talk to old Li?"

Li. He had heard that name in his vision, when he was reborn. Then it meant nothing, just a sound. Now . . .

Now it still meant nothing, save that it was this old woman's name.

"No. No, that isn't what I mean at all. *You* clearly know me, know my name, know much about me. But I do not know you."

Her face cleared then, blanked like a perfect, featureless mask: the inscrutable fortune-teller.

"What *do* you remember?"

"Bits of things. I know I grew up around here somewhere. I remember this street. I remember your face—but I didn't know your name until just now."

Her face remained expressionless. "Perhaps some sort of Forbidding," she muttered slowly. "But why would they cripple you so? This makes no sense, Ghe."

"Perhaps," he began, "perhaps if you were to *tell* me, remind me. Perhaps the memories are only sleeping."

Li nodded slowly. "That could be. But again, why? You are still a Jik?"

"Still," he said. "Always."

"Last I heard from you, you had been set to watch one of the River Blessed. A young girl. Did something happen?"

"I don't remember," he lied. "I don't remember that, either."

The old woman pursed her lips.

"I should read the bones, then," she said. "Maybe the bones will show something. Sit with me here a bit."

She rummaged in a small cloth bag and began taking things out.

"You gave me this, you know," she said, as she laid a little cone of incense out on her velvet mat.

"I did?"

"Yes. When you were initiated. This cloth and this hat. Be a dear, little Duh, and go light this on the flame of old Shehwad over there." She waved her hand at a man cooking skewered meats a few tens of paces away. He nodded, rose, and walked over to the stand.

"Li asked me to light this here," he told the person—who, despite the fact that Li referred to him as "old," was certainly younger than she.

The man's sharp features began a scowl, but then suddenly transfigured. "Why, it's little Ghe, isn't it? We haven't seen you about here in an age."

"No?"

"No, not since . . . well, I can't remember when. Since before the priests came asking about you."

"The priests came asking about me?" Ghe asked, straining to control his voice, to sound casual.

"Months ago. There's some flame for you." He presented Ghe with a burning splinter of black willow from his cook fire.

"Thank you." He couldn't ask more; it would seem too suspicious. Why would they have sent anyone here?

Because, of course, his body had never been found. The Jik he had killed in the palace had indicated that someone had seen him dead—and then he had disappeared. They had *looked* for him.

Did the priesthood suspect? *Could* they suspect? That was worrisome. He had been trained to kill, but his knowledge of priestly magic was not great. Was there some way of *seeing* what had happened to him? Some magical trail or signature?

He turned back to the old woman. *She* must know that the priests had been here, but she hadn't mentioned it.

"Light the incense, silly boy," Li said, when she glanced up from arranging the bones. He complied, touching the brand to the cone until it sputtered. A thick, pungent scent drifted up from the cone.

"Now, just sit here. I'll cast the bones, and we'll read them, just like we used to."

Like we used to. Ghe grimaced. Who had she been to him? She was so familiar, in some ways. And he had confided in her, told her of the vast empty places in his mind. That had been stupid, but what other choice had there been?

Watching the people moving up and down Red Gar Street, he knew the answer to that. He watched them; the wealthy and the poor, the noble and the mean—none of them saw an old woman and a man clad to his neck in rough silks. They were unnoticeable, invisible. Every person that passed had some pressing business, some private thought, some destination, known or unknown. If he were to reach into Li, take her life . . .

He still didn't want to do that. She had meant something to him once, that much was clear. The only person who meant anything to him now was Hezhi . . .

That brought a frown. The priests might have been looking for *him*, but it must have been her they wanted to know about. To what lengths would the priesthood go to retrieve her? Had they already sent an expedition after her? Ghe knew that thought should have troubled him, stung him to action, but for the first time since his rebirth, he felt a heaviness, a pleasant weight across his forehead and eyes. The sun was warm, relaxing, and Li's voice floated soothingly as from far away.

"Now I cast the dice. Oh, see, they've fallen in the 'telling' pattern, the eye of the clouds . . ."

There was more, but he lost it, his eyes fluttering shut just for an instant.

When he opened them again blearily a moment later, the old woman was glaring at him, livid. He shook his head, uncomprehending. Why was he so tired? Why was the old woman so angry?

"You are not Ghe," she hissed flatly. "I *knew* that you were not. You are nothing more than some ghoul who has swallowed him."

No! Ghe wanted to say. *No, see my neck? It is my body, my head, not some ghostly simulacrum. It is me* ... But he couldn't say it. He couldn't speak at all; his mouth and throat were numb, as were his extremities and his senses.

The incense! He should have recognized it, should have known. He sharpened his sight, and everything changed. Li faded to her little bundle of life, as did those on the street, vibrant strands in a transparent world. The incense was a spot of nothingness, of black beyond darkness, a hole sucking his strength into it. Snarling, he swept at it clumsily.

"No!" the old woman managed to choke out. She had clearly believed him weaker. She began muttering under her breath.

This time Ghe did not hesitate. He reached out, around the vacuum of the smoke, took hold of her life, and ate it.

It took only an instant; she writhed a moment, then was part of him. Gasping, he stumbled up, away from the burning cone, and the instant its fumes were no longer brushing him, feeling rushed back with a fierce, insistent tingling, as if his limbs had been momentarily deprived of blood.

Around him, the street continued to bustle, people hurrying hither and back. He struggled into the pedestrian stream and let it sweep him along. He glanced back once, saw Li lying as if asleep, her hat with its moon and stars fallen and lying across her bones.

"It's beautiful," he suddenly, sharply, remembered her saying once, long ago, of that hat. *"The moons and stars seem to shimmer. Is the thread gold?"*

"I don't know," he had replied. *"I only knew that you would like it."*

And though he remembered nothing more than that, he began to weep.

THAT night, he slept for the first time in seven days—since his rebirth. He slept and he dreamed.

Dreams were not as he remembered them. They were not vague, strange reiterations of his little fears or of days gone by, not shadow plays with little sense or substance. They were strong, clear, and simple. The colors were not right; they were too sharp, too bright, and without shading. Everything that was green was the same hue of viridian; all red was sanguine. These dreams had meaning, however, meaning that blared like the din of a cracked horn, rattled the frames of his dream images. The messages were loud, but they were not clear. Ghe imagined they were the sorts of things insects might hear if a man stooped and spoke to them.

He dreamed of being whole, knotted perfectly together, a vast and content serpent gnawing his own tail. It was an ancient feeling, barely remembered.

He remembered the Bright God coming, taunting him, cajoling him. In his dream, the Bright God was like a little sun, golden-feathered, light incarnate. He dreamed shame then, and anger, as the Bright God tricked him into uncoiling, into stretching himself out. Shame at being tricked, at being opened up. In revenge, he ate the Bright God's light, nearly killed him, but his foe escaped, though without his brilliance and beauty.

Now he rushed across the world, and his fear and shame began to fade; he coursed out for leagues, taking it all beneath him, cutting himself a bed, a comfortable place. And for a short time, he knew another kind of contentment, a wonderful hurtling joy. Time passed, and the earth changed, his bed shifting now and again, and he started to feel a hunger. At first it was merely discontent at no longer being whole. He was not a circle anymore, not a thing unto himself. The sky drank from him, plants took him up into their long, narrow bodies, and in the end he poured into a great emptiness, a gulf too vast for him to fill. He had become all motion, and nothing about him was still, nothing all his own. So the hunger began, a desire to take in the world about him, devour it, make it of himself until there was nothing without. Until, once again, he was within himself, a tightly coiled snake eating his tail. After a time, this hunger was all that mattered to him.

As ages passed, he found the limits of his reach. The other gods could see what he was about. His brother, the Forest Lord, sent the Bright God and the Huntress about, and boundaries were made. He paid them no mind, but his reach faltered nevertheless. He had dug himself into the world, and it would not let him out again.

Ages, again, and Ghe felt himself ache with need greater than he had ever known. He grew angrier with each decade.

At the height of his anger, Human Beings came to his banks. They were like the gods, in certain respects, though without the same sort of fire within them. Still, they were inventive, and in some ways they had great strength. He realized that these people were like vessels he might fill, feet that he might walk within, to leave his channel and devour the enemy gods.

So he set about filling them up. They were small, they could contain only a bit of him—but over time, he knew, the vessels of their bodies would be slowly perfected. That was another good thing about Humans; they were malleable rather than fixed, as gods were. All gods but himself, that is, for *he* could change. That was his chief strength, the thing that set him apart. It was also his agony.

He sent the little bits of himself out, patiently, and to his surprise the people built a city. They went out from his banks, and they slew the gods of the borderland, pushed his boundaries farther than ever he could have himself. This was good, and he continued to wait as generations passed and his people grew stronger and stronger, became more and more capable of carrying him in their bones and veins.

But then torpor overcame him, and he slept. He awoke only briefly after that, and thus it was a long time before he realized that something had been done to him, was *making* him sleep, robbing him of his sentience. It was a dull, muted frustration. He still did not know what had happened to him, though he could sense a dark well in the heart of his city, bleeding him, binding him somehow. He still had his children, born stronger with each generation, but they were distant from him. One was finally born who could contain him.

Now she was gone.

GHE woke then. He woke and sat up on the pallet he had arranged. His little room was dark, but he could nevertheless see the spare walls, the small bundle of clothes and weapons that were his only possessions.

Hezhi, he thought. She was the one the River had waited for. He shuddered briefly. The thoughts and feelings in his dream were not *human*; he understood that they only seemed so because they had bent through *his* mind.

What the River felt for Hezhi, however, would not bend, would not settle upon any emotion Ghe had ever experienced, though it resembled lust in some ways. The old Ghe would not have understood it at all, but *he* was beginning to. That was why he shuddered.

Ghe understood something else now that he had not before.

The River did not know about the priesthood, did not even know they existed. To him, they were blank spaces, nothing. And the center of his pain—the dark vortex that bled his power, drew him relentlessly into slumber—*Ghe* knew what that was. He had been there, many times.

It was the Great Water Temple itself.

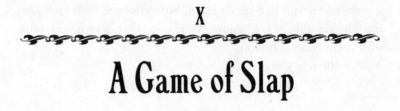

X

A Game of Slap

Tsem met them near the edge of the camp. He was perched on an old house foundation, fending off a swarm of curious children. When Hezhi saw him, she slid down from behind Brother Horse and flew across the intervening distance to him.

"Princess," Tsem growled, "where have you been?"

"I'll tell you later," Hezhi said. "Right now, stay close to me. Please."

"Of course, Princess." The Giant turned wary eyes on the newcomers and said—loudly enough for the horsemen to hear, in his broken Mang: "They not *hurt* Princess, do they?"

"No," she answered. "They only escorted me back here."

"Princess, this is not the palace," Tsem said more quietly in their own language. "You can't go running off alone whenever you want."

"I know," she said. "I know that."

Brother Horse spoke to Tsem, also in Nholish. "Giant, take your mistress back to my yekt. Keep close watch on her. Things are happening I must attend to, and I need for you to keep her safe. I will send Yuu'han around, as well."

"What?" Tsem asked. "What is happening?"

"I am not sure," the old man replied. "I will come tell you when I know." Hezhi noticed that Moss—and Chuuzek, of course—seemed restless.

Chuuzek confirmed that by growling to his cousin, "What is this babbling? What are they saying?" Moss shrugged, conveying his own puzzlement.

Ignoring them, Brother Horse turned to Hezhi and continued in her language. "Please do not fear me, child. I know what you saw, and it is nothing for you to fear. I should have explained more before asking you to *see*, that is all. Accept my apology, and I will come speak with you as soon as I can. In the yekt, with your Giant present." He smiled, and she could not help believing him; his sincerity, for the moment, was more real than the strangeness she remembered.

Brother Horse switched back to Mang to speak to the other horsemen. "I am sorry to have been impolite," he said. "The Giant knows but little of our speech."

"I could teach him a word or two," Chuuzek snapped. Moss only nodded.

"It was my honor to meet you, cousin," Moss said to Hezhi, emphasizing "cousin." "I hope to speak to you of your homeland soon. I have many questions about the great city, and I have never seen it for myself."

Hezhi nodded politely but did not answer aloud. With Tsem's massive hand on her shoulder, the two of them made their way through the crowd. Behind them, whoops went up as horsemen rode up to meet the newcomers.

"What is this all about, Princess?" Tsem asked again, as they moved toward the yekt they were staying in.

"I wish I knew," Hezhi told him glumly.

HEZHI noticed that Yuu'han appeared not long afterward, subtly. He sat near the fire outside of the yekt, talking with animation about something with a warrior near his own age. Hezhi noticed, however, that his eyes wandered the camp, fastening more than occasionally on the yekt.

"Is he trying to keep us in or keep someone else out?" she wondered, and Tsem's brow ridges bunched deeper. He did not repeat his earlier question, but Hezhi explained her meeting with Moss and Chuuzek. She skirted around the issue of why she had run off into the desert in the first place; she did not want to talk about that until she understood more. Tsem seemed content enough with that; after all, he had spent countless hours in Nhol following her at a discreet distance when she sought privacy by wandering the labyrinthine ways of the abandoned and ancient sections of the palace.

"I wonder what this means, this war?" Tsem asked.

"I don't know. I think that at the least, it means Perkar and Ngangata will receive a poor welcome when they return."

"But what does that mean to us? To you?"

"I hope Brother Horse will tell us when he returns." She paused. "I think Brother Horse believes me to be in some sort of danger."

"That seems obvious," Tsem replied. "But what sort of danger? What would these Mang want with you?"

Hezhi spread her hands to acknowledge her ignorance.

Tsem sighed. "I understood things in the palace. There I could protect you. Here . . . here I know nothing. We should leave this place, Princess."

"And go where? There is nowhere we will understand better. And of course we cannot go back to Nhol."

"Another city perhaps. Lhe, Hui . . ."

"Those are very far away, Tsem. How would we get there, just you and I? And when we got there, what would we do? They would not accept me as royalty there. We would have to live in their Southtowns."

"Where do *you* say, then?"

Hezhi thought about that for a moment. "Here may be as good a place as any. Or . . ."

"Yes?"

"Perhaps with Perkar's people."

Tsem grimaced at that. "His people are no better than *these*. Barbarians."

"Well, then," Hezhi grunted, dismissing the whole question with the back of her hand.

"You once said we might seek out my mother's people," Tsem put in, unwilling to let the matter drop.

"Yes, I did, didn't I?" Hezhi said. "But where do they live? How would we find them? The two of us cannot travel alone. Can you build a fire, or kill game, or set a snare? *I* can't." She looked up at Tsem squarely. "Back then, Tsem, it seemed as if the whole world was open to us. Now I see things in a different light." She hesitated for just an instant before going on. "Yet there *is* something I can do, something to give us some choice, I think."

"That being?" Tsem grunted, rolling his massive head back on his shoulders.

"Brother Horse says I have a gift for sorcery. It is the only thing I have, it seems."

"You have *me*, Princess."

Hezhi softened her voice and patted the Giant's arm. "And never doubt how much I value that, Tsem. You are my only true friend. But here, in this place, value is counted in terms of kin, and we have none. It is counted in horses, and we have none. It is counted in yekts and war honors and hunting trophies, and we have none. Nor are we likely to acquire any of those things."

The Giant nodded ruefully. "Yes, I can see that."

"But they also reckon worth in power, and *that*, perhaps, I have."

"Witchery is dangerous, Princess."

"Yes. Yes, but it is the only thing I have to make a place for us. And if we are ever to go where we will, we must have people willing to help us. We must have some way to pay them."

"Or coerce them."

"Yes," Hezhi admitted softly. "I had thought of that, too."

THE village was not as Perkar and Ngangata had left it: it had bled out over the plain, filled it with color and life, horses pounding around makeshift racetracks, riotous noise. It was wild, barbaric, exciting—and not altogether unfamiliar. It had the quality of a homecoming or a hay gathering, though it was bigger, brighter, and more boisterous.

Where he and Ngangata rode, however, faces pinched tight in suspicion, even faces they knew, and by that Perkar understood that the news of the war had already come to Brother Horse's village. How could it not, with clans from the entire Mang world attending?

"It might have been best not to come here at all," Ngangata gritted from the corner of his mouth.

"We have no choice," Perkar muttered back, wondering how many warriors he and Harka could take before all of his heart-strands were severed. His sword made him much more powerful than mortal, but it did not make him invincible; the Blackgod had made that more than clear to him.

"If they attack me, I won't have you fighting with me. The war between their people and mine is not your concern."

Ngangata shot him a scathing, raw look. "You may have forgotten this, Cattle-Man, but though I have no kin or clan amongst your people, it was still there that I was raised, and it was to your king that I swore my allegiance. Your people never gave me much, but what I got you will *not* take from me."

Perkar stared for a moment, then nodded, blushing. "I'm sorry," he said. "Feel free to die with me, then."

"Thank you."

It was almost as if that agreement were a signal for a handful of riders to rush up to them, shrieking. Perkar snarled and snatched for Harka.

"They are not attacking," Harka said. *"Not yet. Keep me ready."*

Perkar eased his breath out then, and the riders parted around him, shouting, brandishing axes and thick curved swords. Perkar knew none of these, but like the riders at the stream, they had their war plumes on. Each wore a Human skin as a cloak, the empty arms and hands flapping like the wings of spirits.

He and Ngangata sat their horses as the riders circled them, enduring the Mang curses. At last, one of them parted out and brought his stallion stamping and gasping to relative stillness. He was a young man, thickly muscular.

"You!" he shouted at Perkar. "Cattle-Man. We will fight."

Perkar avoided the man's eyes: meeting them squarely was considered an affront by the Mang. Instead he gazed up at the sky, as if wondering where the clouds were. "I have no wish to fight you, man," he replied.

"We are here on the invitation of Brother Horse," Ngangata added. "We are not here to fight."

"I am not speaking to you, Brush-Man," the warrior said. "And I do not care whose protection you are under."

"It's true," Perkar heard someone say. "They were hunting with us in the high country." A few others echoed the sentiment.

"Hunting in the high country. Is that where he got my cousin, there?" He jabbed his thick fingers toward Sharp Tiger, and Perkar realized that if things could get worse, they had. They were *Mang*. Of *course* they would recognize the horse and wonder where its rider was.

Perkar was spared having to answer when a second man rode up beside the first. He was quite young, and his eyes were a peculiar color for a Mang—almost green. "Be still, Chuuzek. Brother Horse told us of these two."

"Someone get Brother Horse," someone else called from the side. "Bring him here quickly!" Perkar did not turn to see who it was, but thought he recognized Huu'leg, with whom he had hunted and shared beer.

"As I said," Perkar repeated, "I have no desire to fight."

The man who had been called Chuuzek glared at him. The crowd seemed split on the matter of their fighting; Perkar could hear many urging Chuuzek on, but others were as loudly proclaiming that such a breach of hospitality could not be tolerated. "What is your quarrel with me?"

"You are the pale man and the Brush-Man. You began this war," Chuuzek proclaimed loudly, matter-of-factly.

Perkar could only stare, openmouthed. It was Ngangata who answered the charge. "Who told you this?"

"The gaan. The *prophet*."

And at that, there was silence for a moment, before Brother Horse's voice rose up.

"Well, my nephews are back!" he said dryly, not loudly at all. But in the quiet after Chuuzek's assertion he was more than audible.

"A Mang's nephews are *Mang*," Chuuzek spat.

"Well, so they are," Brother Horse agreed. "And so *they* are—in *this* camp, at this moment." The old man pushed through the crowd, two younger clansmen trailing closely. He glared up at Chuuzek. "*Mang* know how to behave properly in a relative's camp."

"Yes," the green-eyed boy assented. "Yes, they do."

Chuuzek, whose face had been set in a fierce scowl, suddenly grinned broadly. He turned to Brother Horse. "You misunderstand, Shutsebe. This is the time of the Ben'cheen, of feasting and games. I was only asking your nephew if he wanted to go at the bech'iinesh."

"He does *not*," Brother Horse snapped.

Perkar pursed his lips, trying desperately to place the word. He had heard it before, and it meant something like "flat" . . . No. It meant "they slap." It *was* a game, and a rough one.

Chuuzek shrugged off Brother Horse's pronouncement.

"He can tell me himself," Chuuzek said, "if he is too small and soft for a Mang pastime."

"Well," Perkar said softly, "I have no wish to fight you. But if it is only a *game* you wish to play . . ."

Brother Horse was frowning and shaking his head *no*, and the lift in Ngangata's brow also told him that he was agreeing to a bad thing. But if he did not do *something*, he would not know peace long enough even to *get* Hezhi. And if he did, there was nothing to stop a party of these men from following him from the village and attacking him in the open desert, away from Brother Horse and his hospitality. No, it was time for him to do something. And Chuuzek was looking at him expectantly.

He had five hundred leagues of Mang territory to ride through to reach his home. Best get this over with—or a least begin it—now.

"Of course. I accept your invitation," he said, and the crowd burst into a hoarse cheer. Chuuzek bared his teeth in satisfaction.

"Fine," Brother Horse said. "But let my nephew get a bite to eat, something to drink. There is plenty enough time for Slapping today."

"No," Perkar said. "No, I feel well enough to play now." As he said this, he stared fully into Chuuzek's eyes and saw the malicious light there.

Brother Horse sighed. "Perkar has no paddle. I will loan him mine." He turned and strode off.

For an instant, no one spoke, but then the crowd surged around them, and it almost seemed as if they lifted up Perkar and his mount and carried them to the track around the camp. Still shouting, they parted about the hoof-beaten path and lined the sides of it. Perkar wasn't certain, but many of them seemed to be taking bets.

Presently Brother Horse returned, bearing a wooden paddle as long as a man's arm and a hand's breadth wide. It looked to be hardwood wrapped with leather over some sort of padding. Brother Horse handed it up to him, and he took the felt-wrapped grip. It weighed almost as much as a sword.

Chuuzek was nowhere in sight.

"What do I do?" Perkar asked.

Brother Horse shook his head. "Tell me what you want buried with you. Chuuzek is going to kill you."

Perkar smiled and nodded. "Yes, yes. What do I *do*?"

The old man pointed around the track. "He's around on the other side of the village. In a moment, someone will blow a horn. You ride toward each other. You hit each other with the paddles."

"How is the winner known?"

Brother Horse spit. "Oh, you'll know," he said. "You just keep going until someone can't or won't. My advice to you is to fall off right away. Very dishonorable, but then again, it will give Chuuzek only one chance to break your neck."

"Can I parry his paddle?"

"You can do whatever you want. It won't matter."

"You've never seen me fight."

Brother Horse laid a hand on his leg and looked up frankly. "You bear a godsword; I know that. No doubt with it in your hands you are a great warrior. But today you are just a man on a horse with a wooden paddle, facing a Mang who was in the saddle nine months before he was born."

"Oh."

"Yes. Normally, people are careful enough when they play this game. Accidents happen, though, and if it looks like an accident, people won't call it murder. With you, it won't even have to look good."

Perkar nodded grimly. "Well," he muttered. "Let's go, then."

Brother Horse nodded. "When someone blows a horn, ride *that* way." He pointed north.

Perkar tightened his grip on the paddle, swung it experimentally a few times.

And someone blew a horn, two sharp notes. The crowd cheered raggedly, and Perkar dug his heels into T'esh. His mount leapt forward almost without that, as if it knew the significance of the horn. Perkar flexed his hand on the grip, then tightened.

"You can still help me, Harka?" he snarled into the wind.

"*Some. Not much. Draw me and I can help you much more.*"

Perkar gritted his teeth but did not answer. T'esh had fallen into a fluid gallop, what Ngangata called an "archer's gait." Where was Chuuzek?

The howling of the crowd, already deafening, rose in pitch. Chuuzek and his mount appeared in the curving track. For an instant, Perkar felt a dismay so powerful and shocking he nearly bolted his steed from the course. Chuuzek resembled a bear, his eyes glinting like obsidian with a feral ferocity that smote Perkar with nearly physical force. Mang avoided eye contact normally, but for Chuuzek, only Perkar existed. There was no wavering there, no second thoughts, only murder.

Perkar bit his lip furiously and dismissed his fear. He was Perkar of the Clan Barku. He had faced the goddess of the Hunt on her lion, felt the steel of her lance in his throat. No Human horseman could match the terror of that, or sway him.

So he narrowed his eyes, counted hoofbeats, and when the time came, he swung. The moment seemed to slow, as the hurtling mounts converged, eyes rolling but no hesitation in their strides. Chuuzek struck simply, hammering his weapon in a flat, sidewise arc designed to catch Perkar in the face. He was passing on Perkar's right, and there was little he could do save block the furious swing, so Perkar cut around at his enemy's paddle.

The boards clapped together, and a staggering shock raced up Perkar's arm and jarred his teeth. The blow lifted him up and out of his saddle, and it was only luck that one of his feet stayed in its stirrup. Brother Horse's paddle went spinning from his grip, and his head banged against his horse's rump. For a moment, Perkar couldn't grasp what was happening; then he had fallen, slammed into the dusty ground. His foot still in the stirrup, the ground cut and burned him as T'esh thundered on another ten paces before slowing, realizing that his rider was no longer mounted.

Perkar twisted out of the stirrup and spat the sudden taste of iron from his mouth. His lungs were burning and the air seemed like a rain of golden fire that threatened to drown his senses. The hooting of the crowd was distant, like a faraway flock of black-birds chattering. Chuuzek, paddle held high, vanished around the edge of the track.

Grimly Perkar fought to his feet. A boy of perhaps ten was hurrying toward him, bearing the paddle, and he lurched forward to take it, stumbled back to T'esh, and remounted. For a dizzy moment, he wasn't sure which direction to ride in, but T'esh seemed to know, and he crouched in the saddle as the great beast beneath him returned to a full charge.

Chuuzek reappeared, a happy snarl on his face. Perkar felt

anger, white hot, surge through him, and suddenly all he cared to do was to shatter those smiling teeth into the big man's throat. He heard a hoarse cry and realized that it was himself. Bouncing in the stirrups, leaning forward, he struck straight overhand. Chuuzek's blow was arcing out as before, but Perkar ignored it; Chuuzek's face, his stupid leering face, was his target, and he cared for nothing else. At the last instant, he stood as tall as he could and felt his blow land, even as Chuuzek's paddle cracked into his sternum. Something in his chest shattered, and he saw sky, earth, sky reel around him for what seemed a long time before the dust claimed him once more.

XI

The Codex Obsidian

GHAN looked up wearily at the boy Yen.

"If you want help finding a book," he muttered, "then I will help you. If you've come merely to bother me, leave before you waste any of my time."

"No, in fact," Yen said, "I *have* come for help in finding a book. My order has set me to work on a repair of the ducts in the Great Water Temple."

"And they sent you here to find a book concerning such repairs?"

The young man looked suddenly uncomfortable, fingering his unfashionably high collar nervously.

"Well, to tell the truth, Master Ghan, they did not specifically tell me to look here, and I was afraid to ask them. They were impressed enough by my earlier work, and I think that they believe me more capable than I am."

"You had excellent help before," Ghan reminded the young man.

"Indeed, Master Ghan, I did. When I was in here last, you kindly offered—"

"I know what I offered," Ghan snapped. He did not like Yen. He had not liked him when he was so transparently courting Hezhi, but the fact that he insisted on reminding him of her was intolerable. Though, to be fair, the young man had been discreet enough not to bring her up this time. So far. And *Hezhi* liked him, would help him if she were here.

"I can help you rather simply," Ghan said. "There are no books concerning the Great Water Temple in this library. Not of the sort that you might want, anyway."

"What do you mean?"

"I mean that the priesthood is exceedingly jealous of its secrets. The construction and content of the temple is their most ancient secret."

"Nothing here at all?"

Ghan readied a surly reply but paused. "What is it you want to know?" he asked slowly.

"Well, if there is nothing here on its construction, I will surely be supplied with plans of what I am to work on. But . . . is there nothing of its history here? Of its dedication?"

"Why would that interest you?"

"If I am to have the honor of working upon something sacred, I think I would like to know more about it." He blushed. "I suppose I am merely curious."

Ghan regarded the young man steadily. What was his hidden motive? Everyone in the palace had one. He had seen that in Hezhi instantly, though it had taken many months for him to untangle *her* secret. It was important to understand that no one told you what they really wanted and that sometimes they themselves did not know. Now here was this merchant's son, a member of the Royal Engineers but a junior one, just in his first year of service. He wanted to know about the temple, and the assertion that he was to work upon it was clearly a lie. But why did he want to know?

But the answer was clear enough to Ghan. He wanted to know because of Hezhi. He was clearly obsessed with her, frantic to discover her whereabouts. He had heard something or seen something that made him certain she was not dead.

Ghan realized that his mind had wandered far enough afield that the boy had noticed.

He will think me a senile old man, Ghan thought.

"I can help you with that, perhaps," he said. "Wait here while I consult the index."

Yen nodded as Ghan unfolded his legs and stood; he winced inwardly as his stiff joints popped and complained at the shift in position. Moving into the adjoining chamber where he kept the index, he took the huge volume down and carefully spread it open.

He flipped through the subject headings until he came to *Wun Su'ta,* "temples," and scanned through the lists, trying to remember which ones were most suitable. As he recalled, Yen could read only the syllabary, not the ancient glyphs, so he excluded many right away.

He felt a little catch in his throat as he noticed the last few entries. They were nicely formed, very distinctive characters. Hezhi's writing.

"Such a bright girl," he muttered, and wondered what she was doing at the moment. Sitting in some Mang hut, bored to tears, or riding about the world, seeing things he himself had only read about?

He paused and faced the dread he had been avoiding. There were other possibilities. Only the word of a few Mang horsemen —certainly men of less than untouchable repute—evidenced that she had escaped the city at all. He had received no reply from the letter he sent with the horsemen, though he had not expected one soon. The simple facts were that Hezhi could be dead, or below the Darkness Stair with her monstrous relatives, or . . .

Why did Yen want to know about the Water Temple? What did he know, or suspect? Was she *there,* for some incredible reason?

He noticed that his hand was trembling, and he frowned. *Weak old man,* he chastened himself. *Weak. Stupid. She is safe and far from here.*

What had he been thinking, though? Entrusting her to that pale-skinned foreigner on no more substance than a dream? He had given her hope, and he desperately wanted to believe that her hope had been rewarded. But he was an old man, long familiar with failure and disappointment. Things never worked out as one hoped.

If he could only know what Yen hoped, and why.

With a heavy sigh he noted down the references. Best that he watch, for the moment. Yen was an engineer, whose organization rested somewhere between the priesthood and the emperor. It could well be that he knew something that Ghan did not, especially now, since he had been cautious of late. There were many in the palace who disliked him—hated him even—and rumors that he might have had something to do with Hezhi's escape were not lacking. Not common, either, but certainly not lacking. If he were to show the slightest interest in her whereabouts, the Ahw'en investigators would take note with their hidden eyes, and then he must kill himself, ere they could torture Hezhi's whereabouts from him.

But perhaps this Yen could look *for* him.

And so, sighing heavily, Ghan noted down the best reference he could find by shelf and location.

He took it out and handed it to Yen.

"You remember how to find things from an index reference?" he asked.

"I look for this number on the shelves."

"Yes. The volume you are looking for is entitled *Notes on the Codex Obsidian*."

"I don't understand. This tells of the Great Water Temple?"

Ghan smiled thinly. "If it said as much in its title, the priesthood would have taken it from me long ago. This is a modern translation of the *Codex Obsidian*, a book written in the ancient hand. But the *Codex Obsidian* itself contains a long citation from the *Song and Consecration of the Temple*, the holy text that describes the origin and building of the temple and its associated fanes."

Yen shook his head in wonder. "Amazing. Books within books within books. I see now why she . . ." He paused, embarrassed. "Why some spend so much of their time here," he finished lamely.

"Indeed," Ghan intoned flatly. "Now, if you please, I have much to be about."

"Yes, yes of course. Thank you, Master Ghan."

"I accept your thanks," Ghan muttered, waving, returning his gaze to the work he had been transcribing.

But he watched Yen from beneath his brows as the young man ventured into the labyrinth of books.

I have given you what I can of the temple, he thought. *Now let me see where that takes you next.* Tonight, when everyone was gone, he would retrieve the same book, read what Yen had read. He would keep pace with him, each step.

The old, he reflected, should be good at that, at least: watching, waiting.

He returned his hands to their work, but his mind haunted the world, the steppes of the Mang, the expanse of the River, the black depths of the Water Temple, searching. Searching for a young woman with a heart-shaped face and wonder in her eyes.

GHE found the volume easily enough, high on a shelf and weighty. Still, with his strength he had little difficulty in lifting it down.

He paused in midreach as a vivid memory flashed through him, brighter and more insistent than most that remained to him. It was of himself, looking at the girl, Hezhi, her black eyes with his features reflected in them. The look of delight on her face as he handed her the bronze statuette, his own sudden, unexpected reaction.

He would have killed her, he knew, despite that. He would have killed anyone, if the priesthood had asked him to.

But how much better now that he did not ever have to think of killing her again. That was not—had never been—the River's plan for her. So much better that he be her savior, especially now, now that he knew he loved her.

Loved her? Ghe felt a sudden trembling deep in his bones. When had he decided *that*? Back in the sewers as his head fell off? In the depths, in the death before his rebirth?

Had *he* decided it at all?

But, of course, he had. The River knew no more of Human love than it did of Human hatred. It could not make him feel thus. And so it must be he, Ghe, who loved Hezhi.

He shivered again and shook his head. What had he been about? He glanced down dully at the book clenched in his white-knuckled hands and remembered, though he did not recall actually lifting the volume down. *The temple.*

He took the tome over to a reading bench of polished teak and laid it flat. He admired the spine of white ivory, the ivory pins that riveted it together. The cover was a sort of leather unknown to him, black and densely wrinkled. Some kind of lizard or alligator, perhaps, or one of the great tusked beasts he had heard of.

Inside, the supple white pages were tattooed in blue and black, the sometimes curving, often choppy lines of the syllabary. That was a relief; he had no facility with the ancient hand. Rebirth had made him no better at such things; the River had many powers to offer, but apparently the River could not read, not even books about itself.

The Codex Obsidian read the title page. Ghe began prowling through it, searching for what he was not certain. But the center of his lord's frustration and torpor—the place he could not even *see*—Ghe knew, instinctively, that it was the temple. When he looked out over Nhol from the roof of the palace, he could see all of the city; the wings of the palace sprawling crookedly along the crests of the hill, the docks and merchant quarter, the thickly cluttered Southtown, and the temple rising high above it all. But when he closed his eyes and *pictured* that same scene, he saw only darkness where the temple should be. The god that pulsed the blood in his veins simply could not perceive it.

The temple, he remembered hearing, had created the priests the way an oven creates bread. Ordinary men had walked into it, when first it was formed, and the first priests had walked out. Priests were *still* made thus, though the process took many years. But whence had come the temple itself? That seemed an important story, and there was a sort of itch in his brain that suggested, maddeningly, that he had once *known* it. Surely he had been indoctrinated into the lesser mysteries in the time he had been trained for killing.

It galled him that he must search so for something he had once known.

And after a time he found it, in spidery characters that were written differently from the rest of the book, so old in style he must furrow his brow to puzzle through them, whisper the words aloud.

We read that in the fiftieth year of the ascension of Water to the throne of Nhol, the last of the monsters were killed, and the surface of the Lake was forever broken. There was rejoicing, there was feasting. The Chakunge thought, then, that it would be good to have a palace, and a keep, and walls to protect the city. It would be good to have canals to carry his Father's waters into the dry land, it would be good to have letters to record his thoughts and the thoughts of his Father.

And so he loosed some of his blood back to his Father, and he prayed.

A season passed, and then came a stranger. He rode in a boat of ebon wood, and likewise his clothing was jet, likewise his skin and hair.

"The River, thy Father, has sent me," said he. "For though your king is of his blood, a son should not serve his Father. Servants are needed, and I am midwife to all servants."

A faint memory awoke in Ghe. The passage referred to Ghun Zhweng, the Ebon Priest, about whom the priesthood told many tales. It was he who brought the planting of crops, the knowledge to build canals, the sciences of architecture and engineering. It was he who established the temple. Ghe read on, impatient with the dry history, hopeful that he would find something of use. A bit later, his attention became more focused.

Then Ghun Zhweng drew for them a plan. "The River must be honored in a Great Temple, where his waters will flow, fourfold. It should be made in the shape of She'leng, the mountain from which the great god flows; it should have places, hidden and deep. It must

*have a belly of crystal, wherein the treasures are kept and the
bones laid to rest. It should be measured to the following height
and width . . ."*

Something turned in Ghe, twisted, and the bright images of his
Riverdream seeped from his eyes onto the very page. A mountain,
cone-shaped, steepling high into the clouds and capped with daz-
zling brightness, where he had once been contained, content: the
mountain that was his home, his cradle, his source.

His shuddering became bright fury, inhuman fury so great that
he felt the pulsing of his blood threaten to burst forth from his
heart and break his mortal body. *Who did this? Who is this Ebon
Priest, who made these shackles, this priesthood, this temple?
Who is he, for I shall shatter him, harrow and eat his soul!*

His teeth began to chatter, and his fingers clutched spastically
at the pages of the book. The colors from his dream filled the
room, a vortex of nightmare light, and for an instant he knew that
he lay once again on the surface of oblivion, a greedy darkness
eager to drown him forever. But then, by degrees, the anger
retreated, diminished to mortal stature, and then less than even
that, so that he was left wondering what he had felt, and why. He
was dizzy and weak; sweat slicked his skin and matted his hair.
Dazed, he wondered if the terrible lights he had seen had been
only in his own eyes or if they had truly filled the library, and he
looked around him carefully; no one was about, there in the most
jumbled recesses of the archives, and so far as he could tell, no
one had come to investigate. Still, to the senses of the Waterborn,
or of a priest, it must have seemed as if a fire had burned briefly or
a claxon sounded. Ghe swiftly stood, wiped his brow, and
arranged his hair as best he could. He replaced the book on its
shelf and, with a hasty word of thanks to Ghan, exited the library.

As he hurried toward his room in the abandoned wing, his sense
of urgency sharpened with each step until it became a razor
carving at the inner dome of his skull. His time in the palace was

drawing to an end, one way or the other. As a Jik, he had been the stinging end of the wasp, not its brains. The brains were the Ahw'en, and he vaguely recalled that they commanded intelligence and sorcery in no small measure. By now they certainly knew that something fell was loose in the royal halls. His experience with the old woman on Red Gar Street had reminded him to respect witchery. Whatever the River had made of him, it had not made him unstoppable; he was susceptible to the same measures used against ghosts and the Waterborn themselves. The incense that had stunned him was the same used to banish ghosts and to stupefy the Blessed; priests routinely swept the halls of the palace to chase its hundreds of specters back into the darkness below its cobbled courtyards, and incense was the least potent power the priests wielded; even the lowliest acolyte could be taught to use a spirit-broom. What secret weapons did they keep against demon wraiths, against ghouls such as himself? It was a shame that he could remember so little of his learning as a Jik beyond the reflexes of killing; he might have once known how to track, trap, and destroy such a thing, an eater of life. Instead he had only the vague knowledge that it could be done.

Probably he had capabilities he did not yet recognize; but the time to discover those things was in short supply. Yet he ground his teeth at the very thought of leaving the palace. The River had *chosen* him in a way that it chose no one else. It had given him life and power to serve him as the Waterborn could not and the priesthood *would* not. Who had more right to live in the palace than he? But it was foolish to risk himself in this way. He could hide in Southtown and feed on as many *scorps* and *gung* as he wished; the Ahw'en would not find him there—would probably not even bother to try.

He entered an abandoned courtyard and surveyed the cracked and weed-rampant walk through it. Not for the first time, he wondered why this part of the palace was empty, falling into dust. Once when he was a child someone had shown him a chambered shell from deep in the River. It was a straight cone, like a horn, and inside it was partitioned, the largest spaces toward the widest end. Trumpet-cuttlefish, someone had named it, and he had listened in wonder at how the creature, as its life progressed, added greater and grander chambers to its home while abandoning those it had outgrown. It had been a thing of water, of the River. Were the Waterborn of the same nature? No one had ever said such a thing—not that he could recall, of course.

In the center of the court was a sink, a well down which unwanted things and dirty water had been passed. He lifted the grate and lowered himself into darkness. Passing a short distance— about twenty paces—he reached a second grate, clambered up and through it, thus entering his apartments.

His courtyard was bare of any life at all. When he had found it, it had been infested with weeds, as well, but a wave of his hand had withered them, given their water and life to him. Now the stone was clean and cold, simple and pure.

This suite of rooms was actually sealed off from the rest of the palace, the doors to the outside halls not only bolted but plastered over, like the backmost chamber of that strange creature.

He paused before entering the room he slept in adjoining the courtyard. *Who* had told him those things, shown him that shell? A seaman, at the docks? But that seemed wrong. It might have been a woman . . . He remembered, then, the old woman on Red Gar Street, and he felt a catch in his throat. Perhaps it *had* been she. He could not remember.

He crawled into his room, trying to ignore the hunger that gnawed in him. Soon enough he would have to feed again; it seemed that he needed to kill more and more often as time went on. It might, indeed, be best to retreat to Southtown, where monsters could live with impunity.

He curled up on his stolen sleeping mat like a spider, thinking, planning, and waiting for the darkness.

Almost he slept; his body sank into a torpor, though his mind remained active, peering at the strange fragments of knowledge he had attained.

He understood for certain now that he must invade the temple, though he knew not why. There his lord, the River, was no guide, for in that parody of some far-off mountain, *he* could not see. That was why Ghe was needed; to go where the god could not go.

Had that not always been his role, as a Jik, as a ruffian on the street? Always Ghe went where others were not willing to. As a child for pay and loot, as a Jik for pride and the priesthood. What reward would the River give him, one day?

But of course, he knew the answer to that, too: Hezhi. Hezhi would be his reward.

Thus he thought, and thus he was still thinking when the wall began to shudder beneath the weight of mallets, accompanied by the high, shrill keen of priests chanting.

XII

The Breath Feasting

HEZHI heard the roaring of the crowd outside, but she had been hearing such for several days, and in her pensive, withdrawn state she certainly thought nothing of it. Nothing, that is, until Yuu'han and Ngangata dragged Perkar's still body into the yekt. His eyes were closed and a bright string of blood ran from one corner of his mouth. His nostrils, also, bore red stains. He was pallid, and she could not see if he breathed or not.

She stared, unable to think of anything to say.

Tsem, however, easily found his voice. "Is he dead?" the Giant grunted.

Hezhi frowned at Tsem, still trying to understand what she was seeing. Yuu'han had stripped off Perkar's shirt, and beneath it his chest was livid, purple and red, as if he had been stepped on by a Giant twice Tsem's size. No, not stepped on; *stomped*. But how could he be dead? She had seen Perkar alive after being stabbed in the heart. She had seen the blade appear from the front of his chest, a red needle with Yen behind it, laughing at her, at her stupidity. What could kill Perkar, if not that?

No one answered Tsem, and finally Hezhi, more irritated at that than Tsem's blurted question, finally asked, "What happened to him?"

Yuu'han met her gaze levelly, for just an instant, before looking off into some middle distance the way Mang were wont to do. "He played Slap," the young man said. "He won't play again, I think."

"Then he *is*—"

Perkar interrupted them by coughing. It was actually more of a gurgle than a cough, but he blew a clot of blood from his mouth. His eyes did not open, though his face pinched tight with pain. Yuu'han stared aghast, made a hurried sign with his hand in the air.

"*Naka'bush!*" he hissed. In Mang it meant an evil ghost.

"No," Ngangata told Yuu'han. "No, he is alive."

"He was dead," Yuu'han grunted, watching Perkar's chest begin to rise and fall, hearing his wheezing, rasping breath.

"No. It is that sword he bears. It heals him."

"The godblade?"

The Alwa-Man nodded. "Tell Brother Horse but no one else."

Yuu'han looked uncertain, but after considering he nodded and then left the yekt.

"He will heal, then?" Hezhi asked, her voice still dull with shock.

"I believe he will," Ngangata answered, "considering that he was *dead* before and is now breathing again. That would seem to me to be the biggest step toward recovery." His alien face remained expressionless, and Hezhi wondered what the strange man was thinking. Were he and Perkar friends or just traveling companions, forced together by circumstance? Did Perkar really *have* any friends? In the past months, she had begun to regard him as such. There were moments when he made her feel better than anyone else did, happier anyway. And she believed that, unlike Tsem or Ghan or D'en, Perkar could not be taken from her by death. It seemed *safe* to care for him. Now even that illusion was shattered.

"I hope so," Hezhi replied, still unable to think of much to say.

Ngangata rubbed his forehead tiredly and selected one of the yekt's large, colorfully felted pillows to slump down upon. He looked very tired. "I have to know what you have heard," he said after a moment.

Tsem crossed the room bearing a pitcher and bowl.

"Drink something," he told Ngangata. Hezhi felt blood rise into her face with a wave of shame. She should be *doing* something. Ngangata took the water from Tsem.

"Fetch me a rag, Tsem," she said quietly. "A rag and some more water. We should clean him up, at least." Perkar's breath was still coming erratically, labored, but at least he was breathing. Tsem nodded and went to search for a rag.

Ngangata watched her expectantly.

"I don't know," she said at last. "I'm not sure what is going on."

"You've heard about the war?"

She nodded. "Yes, just today. Some men came in earlier. They found me out in the desert—"

"Found you?"

Hezhi helplessly realized that she was only making things more confused. "I was walking over in the cliffs," she explained. "Two Mang men from the west found me."

"Found you in the cliffs? What were they doing over there?"

"I don't . . ." She didn't know. "That's a good question," she finished. "It isn't on their way, is it?"

"Leave that for a moment," Ngangata said. "What have you heard about the war?"

"Not much. Just that there *is* one, Perkar's people and the Mang. There was an argument between those men and Brother Horse. He told them they were not to attack the two of you. I guess he doesn't have much authority over them."

"It's too bad he didn't have even less," Ngangata said wryly. "If they had simply attacked Perkar, he would have killed them with his sword; that much is a fact. As it was, they challenged him to a 'game'—you see the outcome."

"I don't know," Hezhi said. "You know more about bar—about these people than I do. If there were a real fight, with swords and everything, wouldn't others join in?"

Ngangata nodded. "Probably. It might have even turned into a little war, with Brother Horse's closest kin trying to protect his hospitality. All in all it was probably best this way. His sword will still heal him."

Tsem returned with a damp cloth and a basin. She reached for it, but he gently held her away and began sponging Perkar's chest himself. Hezhi started to protest, but realized that Tsem probably knew more of what he was about than she did.

"I've seen him with worse wounds and still capable of walking and talking," she commented. "Worse looking, anyway."

"As have I," Ngangata agreed, and Hezhi thought she caught a deep worry in his burring voice. He did not, however, offer anything further.

Tsem wiped Perkar's face, and the young man hacked again, moaning a bit.

"Did he find what he went looking for?" she asked.

"I suppose. I think he learned much. We learned about the war, at any rate."

"From this goddess of his?"

"And from another god. From Karak, the Raven."

Hezhi pursed her lips. "Perkar told me of that one. It was he who set you and Brother Horse to watching for us, when we were fleeing the city."

"Yes. It was also he who tricked Perkar and his friends into betraying our king. He is a strange, willful god."

Hezhi sighed and shook her head. "I know nothing of these gods. They are *all* strange to me." *Monsters,* she finished inwardly.

"I don't know everything he learned from Karak," Ngangata went on. He seemed to want to tell her something, but was trying to work to it carefully.

"Weren't you there?"

"I didn't hear the conversation. But afterward, Perkar was

eager to return here, to find you. I think Karak told him something about you, something important."

"Oh?"

Tsem growled low in his throat. "I like this not at all, Princess," he muttered. "Too much, happening too fast. Too many people wanting you again."

"I know, Tsem."

"What do you mean?" Ngangata queried. "What is this?"

"Those Mang who met me in the desert. They acted as if they wanted something from me, too."

"And they found you in the cliffs, though no trail from the west passes near. That means they were looking for you."

Hezhi tried to deny that with a little shake of her head. "They might have seen me run into the cliffs." But they hadn't. She knew that, somehow. "No, you're right, Ngangata. They were looking for me. And Brother Horse put me in this yekt, as soon as we returned, and set his nephews to guard me. He could tell something was wrong." She did not add that she was worried even about Brother Horse's intentions. No one who could not *see* into him would understand, would merely think she had become mad with paranoia.

Ngangata nodded slowly. "Something with big feet is walking," he muttered. "We were attacked by Mang, as well, up at the stream. They were looking for *us*. They said that a prophet had seen us in a vision. Perhaps he saw you, too."

"But Perkar knows more."

"He does, but he was tight-lipped with me. Whatever he learned worried him." Ngangata chewed his lip, and then went on. "I did hear Karak say that there was some connection between this gaan and the Changeling."

Hezhi shuddered at a sudden bright chill crawling along her spine. "The Changeling? The *River*."

"Call him what you will."

"I thought he could not reach this far."

"Not with his own fingers, perhaps," Ngangata answered. "But perhaps with the hands of a Mang shaman he can."

Hezhi heard her voice tremble. "He wants me back, doesn't he? He will have me back." And she realized that, once again, the scale on her arm was itching dully. She reached to touch it.

And gasped; the room seemed to turn around, sidewise, so that she could see it all from a different angle. Tsem and Ngangata appeared hollowed out, skeletal, and the fire in its hearth was a dancing blade with laughing eyes. Perkar . . .

Perkar was hardly there at all. His skin glowed translucent, and at his side there lay a god. She could not look at it, at that nightmare jumble of wings and claws and keen, sharp edges. It hurt her, scratched at her inside as if there were a man in her head with a sword, swinging it. She lifted up her sight, tried to tear it away entirely, but Perkar himself riveted her attention.

On his chest crouched a blackness, a crawling, shuddering blackness. As she watched, long hairs as thick as wheatstraw grew from it, wrapped sluggishly around Perkar, and reached inside of him to seize his bones.

The blackness opened a yellow eye and stared at her, and she screamed. She screamed and ran, tripped, sprawled, and scrambled back up. Even when Tsem caught her she kept trying to run, kicking at his shins and wailing, eyes closed, shuddering.

When finally she opened them again, the room was as it had been before.

But she knew now. She had seen it.

"Tsem, go get Brother Horse," she choked out. "Go and hurry. And let me sit outside."

SHE flinched away from Brother Horse when he arrived, fearful that her sight would return and reveal him for what he was. She should not trust him with Perkar—she knew that—but she could think of no alternative. *She* did not know what to do for him, and something was wrong, terribly wrong. Brother Horse regarded her sadly for an instant and then entered the yekt. Hezhi remained on the stoop, and Tsem joined her.

"That's a big fire," he noticed, after a moment.

Hezhi regarded the enormous bonfire from the corner of her eye, unwilling even to risk seeing the Fire Goddess. For some time, the Mang had been carrying in fuel from all directions, and flames and black smoke rose in a thick column skyward.

"I wonder where they found all of the wood," Tsem went on when she did not answer.

Hezhi shrugged to let him know she had no idea. "I think it's for the Horse God Homesending. A ceremony they perform tonight."

"What sort of ceremony? Have you written of it in your letter to Ghan?"

Good old Tsem, trying to distract her. "I think Ghan will never get any letter from me. Whatever we thought, these people are not our friends."

"They needn't be our enemies, either," Tsem pointed out. "They are like everyone, concerned for themselves and their kin before all else. You and I don't threaten them; Perkar does."

"Does he? Perhaps his people do. I don't know. We are lost here, Tsem."

"I know, Princess," he replied softly. "Tell me about this ceremony."

She hesitated a moment, closing her eyes. The village did not vanish as she hoped it might; it was still there in the vivid scent of burning wood, in the shouts of children and the wild cries of adults, the yapping of dogs. It would not go away merely because she willed it thus.

"They believe that they and their mounts are kin," she began. Who had told her that, so long ago? Yen, of course, when he gave her the statuette. He had told her something like that anyway, and it had not been—like everything else he told her—a lie. Yen, who at least had taught her the folly of trusting anyone.

Tsem's silence suggested that he was waiting for her to finish. "You know that by now," she murmured apologetically. "They believe that they and their mounts are descended from a single goddess, the Horse Mother. Now and then the Horse Mother herself is born into one of these horses. More often one of her immediate children is, a sort of minor god or goddess. When this happens, the Mang shamans can tell, and the horse is treated with added respect."

"That would be hard to imagine," Tsem noted. "They already treat their mounts with more kindness than any servant in the palace is shown."

"The horse is never ridden. It is fed only the best grains. And then they kill it."

"Kill it?" Tsem muttered. "That doesn't sound like a very good thing to do to a god."

"They kill it to send it home, to be with its mother. They treat it well, and when it goes home it tells the other gods that the Mang still treat their brothers and sisters—the other horses—well."

"That is very strange," Tsem said.

"No stranger than putting the children of nobility beneath the Darkness Stair," she countered.

"I suppose not." Tsem sighed. "It's just that everything these people do seems to involve blood and killing. Even worshipping their gods."

"Perhaps they recognize that life is *about* blood and killing."

Tsem touched her shoulder lightly with his thick fingers. "Qey used to say that life was about birth and eating. And sex."

"Qey said something about sex?" Hezhi could simply not associate the concept with the servant woman who had raised her.

Tsem chuckled. "She is, after all, a Human Being," he reminded her.

"But *sex*? When? With whom?"

Tsem squeezed her shoulder. "Not often, I suppose, and with an old friend of hers in the palace. She would have been married to him, I suppose, if it had been allowed."

"*Who?*"

"Oh, I shouldn't tell you that," Tsem said, mischief creeping into his voice.

"I think you *should*," she rejoined.

"Well, perhaps if you were a princess and I your slave, I would obey that command. However, since you insist that such is no longer the case . . ."

"Tsem." She sighed, opening her eyes and arching her brows dangerously.

Tsem rolled his eyes and put on an exaggerated air of secrecy. He leaned very near, as if confiding a bit of court gossip. "You remember old J'ehl?"

Hezhi's mouth dropped open. "J'ehl? Qey and J'ehl? Why, he was a wrinkled little old man! He looked just like one of those turtles with soft shells and thin long noses! How could she—"

"Perhaps he had more use for such a nose than you might imagine," Tsem remarked.

"Oh!" Hezhi cried. "No! Darken your mouth! I won't hear any more of this. You're inventing this because no one can call you a liar out here. Except me! Qey and J'ehl indeed. Qey and *anyone*. She was too old, too dignified—"

"Oh, yes," Tsem said. "Do you remember that time when J'ehl came to deliver flour, and I took you into your room and sang very loudly to you, the same song, over and over?"

"The only song you knew!" Hezhi exploded. "I kept telling you to sing a different song, but you wouldn't. After a while it got to be fun, though, me trying to put a pillow over your face, and you just singing and singing . . ." She stopped. "What are you saying?"

"Qey *made* me do that. So you wouldn't hear."

"No!" Hezhi almost shrieked, but she was laughing. *Laughing.* It was shocking, horrible even to think of Qey and that little man making love as Tsem roared and she squealed, but somehow it was funny. And she realized that Tsem had tricked her, tricked her into an instant of happiness, despite everything.

"Those were good days," she told him as her laughter trailed off. "How old was I?"

"Six years old, I think."

"Before D'en vanished."

"Yes, Princess."

"And how did that song go?"

"You don't really want me to sing it!"

"I think perhaps I do!" she commanded.

Tsem sighed hugely and squared his shoulders.

> "Look at me.
> A giant mon-key
> Live in a tree
> A giant mon-key!"

His deep voice bellowed out into the evening air, and three dozen Mang heads turned in their direction. Though they could not understand his words, most smiled and a few laughed, for off-key is off-key in any language.

> "A big mon-key!
> Him love Hezhi!"

Tsem shouted on, until Hezhi was wiping tears of mirth from her eyes.

"Stop, stop," she said. "We've too many serious things to worry about."

"*You* told me to sing," Tsem answered.

"You haven't sung that to me in a long while."

"Well, you haven't asked me to, and when you got a bit older and started wandering about with D'en so much, Qey and J'ehl had little trouble finding time for their passions."

"I *still* refuse to credit that!"

"Believe it, little Princess. I could not imagine such a thing myself were it not true."

"I think you imagine sex all of the time!"

"Yes, but not with Qey!"

She chuckled at that, too, but her brief happiness was already waning. It amazed her that she could have forgotten her troubles for even such a trivial moment, but Tsem had always been good at that.

"You *are* a big monkey," she told him. "And I love *you*."

Tsem blushed but read her sobering mood, and from long experience he made no attempt to keep her laughing.

"I know, Princess, and thank you. Out here it is good to have someone who loves you."

Hezhi turned her face back to the bonfire. She felt braver, and dared to look at it full on. "You've never said anything truer than that," she said.

There was a small cough behind them. Hezhi turned to see Brother Horse regarding them.

"I need to speak to you, Granddaughter."

"Call me Hezhi," she said, frowning.

He sighed. "Hezhi."

"Tsem will stay with us," she informed him.

"Very well. An old man will sit, if you don't mind."

"I don't mind."

Brother Horse shook his head. "Look at that. They don't need to make the fire that big! They must have burned everything for a hundred leagues."

Hezhi frowned over at the old man to let him know that today she had no patience for the Mang propensity to chitchat before getting down to the business at hand. He caught the hint.

"Perkar is very ill," he announced, the playfulness suddenly gone from his voice and replaced by an almost shocking weariness. "He has been witched."

"Witched?"

"You saw the thing on his chest."

"I saw it."

"You *are* strong, or you would be mad now. What you saw was a sort of spirit—something like a ghost, or god—perhaps the offspring of a ghost and a god. We call them 'Breath Feasting,' because they eat the life in a person. Usually they eat it right away, but Perkar's sword continues to heal him."

"I don't understand. I thought Perkar was hit with a Slap paddle."

"It must have been a witched paddle. Such things have been known to happen."

"You mean someone *did* this to him."

Brother Horse nodded. "Of course. It would have to be a gaan, someone with the power to bind spirits."

"Like yourself, you mean."

The old man grunted. "No. Someone with much more power than I ever possessed. Someone who could put the Breath Feasting in a Slap paddle and command it to wait." He turned a frank gaze on her. "I know you were frightened by what you saw in me. I know you do not trust me now, and I should have explained before you *saw*. But I never believed that you could see into *me* so easily. That is one of the hardest things to do, to see a gaan. Gods are often disguised by mortal flesh, even from the keenest gazes. You must forgive me, you see, for I never thought that even if you *did* see into me, it would frighten you. I forget, sometimes, what it means to be from Nhol, where there is no god but the Changeling."

Hezhi pursed her lips in aggravation and thrust out her jaw, trying to retain her bravery of a moment before. Tsem, beside her, was a presence of enormous comfort. "Are you telling me you are some sort of god?"

"What? Oh, no. No. But there are gods *in* me. Very small ones, very minor ones."

"In you? I don't understand that."

"There are many kinds of god," Brother Horse began, after a moment's pause to collect his thoughts. "There are those that live in things—like trees and rocks—and there are those that govern certain places, certain areas of land. There are also the Mountain Gods, whom we call the *Yai*, and they are different yet again; they are the ancestors of the animals, as Horse Mother is the begetter of all horses, as Blackgod is the father of all crows, and so forth. Those are the most powerful gods, the gods of the mountain."

"Yes, this had been explained to me," Hezhi said, uncomfortably.

He nodded. "The Mountain Gods have younger relatives who walk about. Small gods cloaked in the flesh of animals—such as those we select for the Horse God Homesending that we hold tonight."

"I know that, as well."

"Such gods dwell in flesh, sometimes in places, and those places are like their homes, their houses. But when their house is destroyed—when their bodies are killed or their place ruined—

then they are without homes. They must return to the great
mountain in the west to be reclothed in skin. However, it is
possible to offer them—or sometimes compel them—to make
another home, here." He tapped his chest with a forefinger.
"That's why we call this *yekchag tse'en*, 'Mansion of Bone.' You
saw the *dwellers* in my mansion, child. Two spirits live within me
and serve me, though they have, like myself, grown old and
weak."

Hezhi took that in doubtfully. "And what do these gods *do*,
living in your chest?"

"First and foremost, they dim the *vision*," the old man said
gently. "They toughen you so that the sight of a god does not
enter you like a blade, to cut out your sense. Once you have a
single familiar, no matter how weak, then you can resist."

She suddenly understood what Brother Horse was getting at,
and her eyes widened in horror. "You aren't saying *I* have to do
that? Have one of those *things* inside of me."

Brother Horse examined his feet rather closely. "It isn't
bad," he said. "Most of the time you never need them or notice
them."

"*No!*"

He shrugged. "It is the only way. And *I* can do nothing for
Perkar. You can trust no other Mang healer, for we do not know
who did this. You are his only hope, and you are your own only
hope. You have been lucky and strong thus far, but you will
weaken, and when you do, your Giant friend will not be able to
help you, nor will I. I know you don't like it, but you must face
this, Hezhi. I am trying to *help* you."

"Brother Horse, I *can't!*" She worked her mouth helplessly,
hoping it would fill with more words of its own accord, explain to
the old man her horror of *losing* herself, of becoming something
not Hezhi. That fear had been a strength when the River threatened to fill her up with himself, make her into a goddess. Now . . .
one of those things, those monsters, living *in* her? How could she
be the same, ever?

But if she did not, what would Perkar do? And what would she and Tsem do? Her talk to Tsem of using her power to help them survive—would she pretend she had never said it?

"How is it done?" She sighed weakly.

"Princess, *no*," Tsem gasped. *He* at least understood her, knew her fears.

"I don't say I will *do* it," she muttered. "Only that I want to know how it is to be done."

Brother Horse nodded. "I have a few moments, and then I must return to my responsibilities. This is a bad time, such a bad time for all of this." He reached around and pulled up the bag he had carried before, when they went into the desert. From it, he produced a small drum, thin and flat like the tambors played for jugglers in her father's court.

"I made this for you," he said. "It is called a *bun*."

"Bun," Hezhi repeated. "Like 'lake.' "

"Exactly. A drum is a lake."

"That's nonsense," Hezhi snapped. "What do you mean?"

Brother Horse continued patiently. "The surface of a lake is the surface of another world. Beat upon its surface, and ripples are formed. The things that live beneath that surface will see the ripples, feel the beating. Some may come to investigate. The skin of this drum—" He touched it gingerly but did not sound it. "—is the surface of another world, as well, or at least to a part of this one that only you and I—and others like us—occasionally see. And if you beat upon it . . ."

"Something will hear," she whispered, for suddenly she remembered another time, in the library, a book in the old script. Two days before, Ghan had shown her the key to understanding the ancient hand, how the ten thousand glyphs were ultimately composed of just a few. She was reading of her ancestor, the Chakunge, the Waterborn, and how he slew the monsters. When he banished the last of them, the text said he "broke the surface of the lake." At least that was how she had read it, though the character was just a little circle that she did not think resembled a lake very much. But she remembered the *word*: *wun*. Bun, wun. He had banished the monsters and broken the surface of that other world, and even in the ancient language of Nhol the name for that surface was drum.

"Something will hear," Brother Horse acknowledged, and his voice brought her back to the dusty desert and the shouting celebrants. "Or feel. And if it pokes its head through the drum, you can speak with it and strike your bargain."

"That simple?"

"It is not simple," Brother Horse said. "There are songs to be sung—you can send your words through the surface of the lake. But ultimately, yes, that is the essence of it."

"I hear drums beating now," Hezhi said. "Are they attracting gods and ghosts?"

"Perhaps," Brother Horse said. "But their drums are not like this one, or like this one will be when you have made it yours."

"And how do I do that?"

"As I told you before, it begins with blood. You must wipe a bit of your blood on the surface of the lake, and it will be yours. The lake's surface will open into *you* rather than into the empty air. Your familiar can climb right out of the spirit world and into your body."

"Then I cannot pass through the drum, into that other world myself?"

Brother Horse smiled ruefully. "You understand quickly. Yes, you may. But you don't want to do that, Hezhi. Not yet, not until you have many gods on friendly terms with you, or in your power."

Hezhi regarded the old man for a moment. She was still afraid, terribly afraid. And yet, with that drum she could have power. Like being the keeper of an important doorway, through which anything might come. It was weirdly compelling, and briefly, her curiosity nearly matched her fear. She reached over and touched the drum skin; it felt ordinary, not at all unusual. But then, Brother Horse had not seemed unusual either, until she suddenly saw *inside* of him.

"I'll take the drum," she said. "But anything else—"

"Take the drum," Brother Horse confirmed. "Think on this,

and in the morning, after the Horse God has returned home, we will talk again."

Hezhi nodded and took the tight disk in her hand. Its tautness felt suddenly to her like something straining, pulling. But it was straining to stay together, of one piece.

Much like Hezhi herself.

XIII

Becoming Legion

THE wall shuddered again, and Ghe knew for certain that it was no hallucination. Impossibly, he could faintly smell incense, seeping through some unseen crack.

Found out. How stupid he had been! But he never imagined that it would be so soon, so sudden.

Ghe was not accustomed to panic, and panic he did not. Instead he quickly surveyed his meager possessions, choosing what to keep and what to leave. Nothing to assure them of his identity; they probably knew, but perhaps they did not.

He poked his head around the door into the courtyard. It was black as pitch, a moonless and overcast night, but that meant nothing to him; his vision was better than an owl's, able to pierce the deepest darkness with ease. Thus he saw the shadow shapes ranged along the palace roof, awaiting him.

Of course. Pound on the wall to flush me out, catch me in the courtyard. They are not stupid, my old comrades.

What of the sewers? But the duct from his courtyard's sink led only to one place—the sink in the other courtyard. Beyond *that* he might find liberty, but the chance was far too great that they had stationed incense-burners there. His best chance, he realized, was the roof, despite the six Jik he counted on it. None of them seemed to be burning spirit-brooms; he could not see the spots, like holes in the air, that he had come to identify with them.

He hesitated only an instant longer, for the door to the apartment had begun to splinter. Choosing what he judged to be the most thinly guarded wall, he sprang, darting across the court and leaping like some nocturnal predator for the second-floor balcony.

Instantly, light flared above him, soft witch-light that caused the air itself to incandesce, a burning cloud like swamp fire. Not bright enough to blind his enemies, but enough for them to see him by. An arrow whirred near, and another, and to him they seemed almost to hang in the air as his senses raced furiously ahead of their motion, the River in him flowing as swiftly as a mountain stream.

His leap brought him to the balcony, clutching at the wrought-iron railing. He hissed as the bolts that held it to the rotten stone protested and then tore, and for an instant he hung in space, sagging backward over the cold stone below. It was an instant the Jik on the roof did not waste; an arrow sank joyfully into his back, just missing his heart, puncturing his lung. The pain was astonishing; it was like being pinned with a lightning bolt, and a deafening roar filled his ears like the thunder following.

The railing held long enough for him to vault over and onto the stone floor of the balcony; two more arrows skittered by him. The one piercing him began to writhe like a snake in the wound it had made.

Ghe still did not hesitate; he could have run out into the second-story apartment, but he knew that it, too, was sealed and that he would be cornered there like a sewer rat. Despite the unnerving pain, despite the sudden loss of strength and speed he felt, he crouched and leapt again, this time for the very edge of the roof. A shaft skinned across his knuckles as he gripped the plastered edge, and then, with the strength of his fingers alone, he levered himself up onto the flat roof.

A Jik waited there, of course. Ghe lunged immediately; power was bleeding out along the squirming shaft of the arrow that was surely more than an arrow. He was still faster and stronger than a man, but only just so. A blade, a pale ribbon in the witch-light, cut just over his head, and then he was inside the swordsman's guard. He jabbed stiffened fingers into the soft flesh of his opponent's throat, felt cartilage crush as the man lifted from the ground with the force of the blow. Two more assassins converged from the sides, and Ghe now saw the bloom of flame that was a broom igniting.

A roll gained him the sword and saved him from two more arrows, but a third impaled his thigh and, like the first, began to work some killing magic. It might be that he was already doomed; he could not tell, knowing as little as he did about the priesthood's witchery.

It suddenly struck him as stupid to rely on the sword; his old instincts as a Jik were betraying him. Instead, he reached out and snatched at the nearest man's heartstrands and tore them brutally, gasping as the sweet reward of stolen life pulsed into his veins, replacing what the arrows were taking. Turning, more swiftly now, he blocked a single stroke from his second tormentor, slid his own stolen blade neatly through solar plexus and spleen, bathed in the sudden release of energy as the man's spirit gushed out. Another arrow grazed him, and he ran, burning his newly gained strength, dodging erratically, hoping to outguess the archers. Missiles flew from unlikely places, and he realized that he had not yet seen all of his attackers, but that mattered not, so long as he ran fast and well. Night was his ally, and though new witch-lights bloomed here and there, there were not enough Jiks to be everywhere. The single man who managed to place himself in Ghe's path died without succeeding in loosing his shaft or swinging his sword; Ghe tore his life out from thirty paces away.

I am a blade of silver, a sickle of ice. Ghe sighed, intoning his old assassin's mantra, hurtling across the space between two rooftops. He bounded up and over a ridgebeam, fell un-controlled down the steep, opposite side as new fire entered his wounds. Fetching up against a parapet, he grasped the shaft protruding from his chest and yanked it out. The arrow squirmed in his hand, and he saw it as a line of darkness, like burning incense. Just holding it stung his hand, and he tossed it away, wondering if he had ever known of such weapons before this day.

He ran on across the rooftops, feet slapping on roof tiles, the black scales of the sleeping night dragon. When he was certain his pursuit was outdistanced, he stopped to withdraw the second dart from his leg; this was easy enough, for the missile had somehow eaten a nearly fist-size hole in his thigh.

He continued to weaken, even with the arrows removed. By the time he reached the wall surrounding the palace, he was dizzy, stumbling. He heard a surprised shout from one of the imperial sentinels, and then he was over, plummeting toward the street. He struck it clumsily, one leg twisting horribly beneath him. Had he been merely Human, he knew he would never have survived the fall at all, but even so, he felt things tearing.

Sobbing in frustration, he struggled to hands and knees and began to crawl.

No! he snarled inwardly, and then "No!" forced from his pant-ing mouth. "No crawling." He staggered up again and sagged against a wall. There were several shouts from atop the looming darkness of the palace, and so, gritting, he stumbled off down the street.

On the next corner, he met a woman, perhaps sixteen, and he took her life immediately, greedily. Her eyes never even registered shock, glazing over whatever thoughts she had been entertaining, the faint smile on her lips frozen as well. Ghe proceeded across the city like that, feeding as he went, leaving a score of dead behind him. It was like trying to fill a cracked pot; the new strength leaked from him as soon as it entered, and he knew he was leaving a trail of corpses any fool could follow.

Worse, he realized that he didn't know where he was. He had allowed some animal part of him to rule, and that was stupid, stupid, for any animal, no matter how strong, could be hunted and killed by the weakest man, so long as he was clever. The Ahw'en and the Jik were more than clever. He reeled about on the night-dark street, searching for some clue to his whereabouts. His wounds ached, and the life of his latest victim leaked from his yawning mouth. He leaned against a stoop to gather in his breath.

"What is wrong with you?" a small voice asked. Ghe turned in surprise, and his hunger urged him to reach to where the voice was and take sustenance. Ghe fought the impulse, focusing his sharp eyes instead. A child sat on the stoop, gazing at him with large, ebony eyes.

"Hezhi?" he gasped.

"No," the child answered. "That isn't my name."

It wasn't she, of course. In fact, it was a boy, and some years younger than Hezhi.

"Boy," he whispered, "how can you see me in this darkness?"

"I can't see *anything*," the boy replied. "I've never seen anything. But I can hear you."

"Oh." It was difficult, fighting the urge to kill. But he had questions to ask. "Perhaps you can tell me," he managed. "Where am I?"

"You sound hurt," the boy said. "You smell funny."

"Please. Just tell me."

"This is Southtown, just along Levee Way. The River is behind me. Can't you smell him?"

Ghe closed eyes. He could. Of course he could.

"*I* can smell him. I can hear him, too."

"Hear him?"

"He sings to me. He woke me up tonight."

"Did he?" Ghe was growing impatient, but something stayed his hand yet.

"And I dreamed. I dreamed of vision. I dreamed I could see."

"What?"

"Yes," the boy went on. "I dreamed some beast ate me, but he did not chew me up. He just swallowed me whole, and I could see through his animal eyes."

Ghe had heard enough. He could no longer concentrate on the boy's words. He reached out hungrily, tore the pulsing strands of light from their fragile moorings. The boy gave a little cry, a shudder, and fell forward into the street.

He did not chew me up, the boy's words seemed to repeat themselves, and Ghe, despite his furious need, paused.

What would happen to these little bundles if he did not devour them? He remembered the Jik he had killed, days ago, how the heartstrands had drifted off, a seed that might become a ghost, but which more likely the River devoured. As he considered this, the boy's life began to tug toward the River, and Ghe followed.

It wasn't long before he could feel the water, his lord. This part of Southtown was mostly abandoned because the marsh had invaded it, and the mud streets were filled with standing water. He sloshed through the quagmire and instantly felt strength returning, hunger abating somewhat. His thoughts sharpened, cut from his brain through the flesh of the beast.

The little ghost was still tugging at its leash, trying to bleed into the River water, but Ghe kept hold, considering. The River had sent him this child; for what purpose? Experimentally, he pulled the knot of spirit into him, but not to the furnace in his heart. Instead he discovered a sort of empty space, one that he had not known existed. The ghost settled in there, tied itself to his own strands and, though it faded, remained. Ghe felt, then, a new sort of strength. Incremental, to be sure, but it was a strength he knew would not fade. The boy's memories were there, too, for him to use. He leafed through them as through a book, the years of darkness in Southtown, a hunger of its own sort. Memories to replace his own lost ones. And he felt the fear, the surprise of death, though it was retreating, replaced by awe and wonder. For what was left of the boy was part of Ghe, and Ghe could *see.*

Ghe reached the levee and strode over it, found the vastness of his lord beyond, waded in until he was submerged. In the water of the River, he had no need of breath, and as his wounds finally healed, he considered what he had done, what it meant.

What if he had not eaten that first monster, there beneath the Darkness Stair? Would its strength be slave to him now, bound to him as this boy was? How stupid he had been! The River meant for him to *bind*, not merely to feed. He could be not one, but legion, fill himself with a whole court, and he would be their emperor. *That* was where his real strength lay. Still he would be cautious, still the priesthood might find some way to kill him. But now he was more than he had been, and he would be much more still. Content for the moment, he rested, knowing his lord would hide him, even from those who followed.

BEFORE dawn he found an abandoned house, nearly consumed by the fringe of the Yellow-Haired Swamp. He watched the dawn flush the waving, waist-high grasses that spread out south for as far as he could see, bordered only by the River on his left and a string of huts trailing its western fringe. Someone had told him—he could not, of course, remember who—that before he was born, this part of the swamp had been a checkered expanse of rice paddies, and in those days Southtown had enjoyed a certain mild prosperity, its inhabitants working the fields and keeping some measure of the crop for themselves. The River had flooded, however, not hugely but enough to silt up the fine network of paddies, and whatever lord owned it had decided the rice wasn't worth his trouble, not with cheaper rice coming upriver by the ton on barges from the Swamp Kingdoms. The swamp had been allowed to have the fields.

The house that now sheltered him reflected that earlier, more affluent year. It had been raised on sturdy cypress posts, and its floor had once been polished, traces of smooth sheen still noticeable in a few places. It had two stories, though now the roof was gone and birds nested in the upper story, whose rafters were gently collapsing in like the ribs of a corpse. The posts had now shifted and begun to sink, and the floor sloped at a noticeable angle, bird droppings covering most of the once beautiful planks. Such, in sum, was Southtown.

Even this early in the morning, Ghe could make out a few bobbing heads scaring up the cranes and blackbirds; men and women wading through the muck with gigs and nets, searching for the almost inedible mudfish, salamanders, and eels that lived beneath the grasses. More than one would probably cut his feet or calves on the spines of the mudfish. He could remember an old man he once knew, his foot and finally his whole leg distended, blue and purple, rotting even while he was still alive. The boy he had gathered remembered more, his father dying from such an infection, the unbearable sweet scent of it. Terrible grief.

There was food in the Yellow-Haired Swamp, but there was more danger. Most in Southtown preferred a life of begging or thievery to the dangers of the mud, though a few still cultivated pitiful patches of rice here and there.

Wading in the swamp had never been for him, he was certain, though he remembered hunting frogs at its edge, recalled the stink of it more than well enough. As a Jik, he had learned the reason for the stink he had been accustomed to for most of his life: the central sewage ducts from the palace emptied there.

Still, the swamp had a certain beauty, he could see that now, and with the wind blowing at his back, bending the grass away from Nhol, the stench wasn't so bad. He found himself wishing the fishers luck, when before he had only thought them stupid.

He could afford to be generous with such sentiments; he was strong now, his injuries entirely healed. Only the oldest wound, the ridged scar encircling his neck, tingled a bit uncomfortably, and he suspected that he knew the meaning of that. The River was becoming, in his way, impatient. Things must be happening elsewhere, with Hezhi, with her demon swordsman. Now that he understood what kind of strength he had, it was time to put it to use; before the Ahw'en and the Jik found him once more and made a better job of ending his existence.

He fingered the scar and wondered, absently, when it had ceased to repel him, when he had ceased to be at least inwardly horrified at his state. His lack of memories still troubled him, but now he had those of the boy—smell, touch, and taste anyway—to fill in the blank spaces of his childhood. An odd comfort, and he knew he would once have been disgusted by that, as well, but that had been a different, somewhat stupider Ghe.

And what would the smarter, stronger Ghe do today? He would invade the Great Water Temple, though on the surface that hardly testified to intelligence. But it was now or not at all, he felt sure of that.

And so, after watching the sunrise, Ghe rose up from the floor that creaked beneath him, and he thought of how he might best enter the most holy place of the priesthood, the sanctum of those who hunted him so persistently.

The answer gurgled and spluttered no more than a stone's throw from the dilapidated hut: a sewer duct, emptying into the swamp. Wide enough to crawl through, but only just barely. Ghe allowed himself a bit of a smile. *Hezhi* would have crawled into such a tube, if she thought knowledge lay through it. Could he do any less?

He found the sewer firmly sealed by a heavy iron grate, but for him, at the peak of his power, that was no deterrent. The pins that held it in place were newer—*much* newer—than the rotten ones that had torn beneath his weight back at "his" apartments, but they protested no longer when he exerted himself. He peered up into the darkness, aware of the almost unbelievable stench but unconcerned by it. Even the old Ghe would have been able to deal with that, and he, the ghoul, cared far less about such temporary discomforts. He paused only a moment before entering, to check his weapons, a reflex so thoroughly ingrained in him from his training as an assassin that it was not a matter of thought. When he realized what he was doing, he chuckled aloud, for, of course, he had no weapons of steel. But still he had the *jwed*, the way of darting hands, and he had his power. They had nearly failed him back in the palace, but a weapon would have helped him not at all. His hands, his power, his cunning must serve him, or nothing would.

And so he crawled into the tube.

Only the faintest tingle of claustrophobia and a hint of boredom betrayed his Human origins; otherwise he slithered up the tube like a snake. When the sediment on the floor of the duct had settled too thickly, he could not move forward at all, and he would stop to patiently claw at the offending matter until he could squeeze through. When the tube dipped and filled with water for a time, he was just as unconcerned.

How long this took, he could not say and only vaguely cared. After some interminable period, he reached another grate, this one of steel, and though it resisted him a bit longer, it soon opened before him, too, allowing him to enter into a larger way, one that he could stand in, albeit hunched.

He twisted through the labyrinth, the complex overlapping of sewers, flood drains, and, finally, sacred water tubes that he knew Hezhi had mapped. He, however, did not have need of such a map, for in him was the River's strange awareness of flowing, his own expertise with the underways, and even an added tactile sense from the ghost of the boy that was tethered to his heart. The River's unspecified "map" of himself was somehow filtered through the boy's sense of space without sight, and though Ghe would not have *needed* this added advantage to find the temple, it helped. And when he reached the temple itself, the River in him would be blind, would it not? He wondered, then, how much of his power he would retain, in those dark precincts below the great fountains and the alabaster steps. Perhaps, once again, his head would merely roll from his shoulders, and he would be undone, a corpse made puppet and then corpse again as its strings were severed.

He did not believe that would happen, but no matter. This was the path to serving the River, and it was the way that led, finally, to Hezhi. And he was no mere puppet, not some silly creature on a string.

And that was what he was thinking when his vision blurred, grayed, and doubt renewed itself as, at last, he crouched beneath the Great Water Temple.

XIV

Horse God Homesending

HEZHI sat on the stoop, contemplating her drum, as Brother Horse, with a pat meant to be reassuring, rose and went back to his duties. The sun set and stars scattered across the dome of the sky, obscured only by a few tatters of indigo velvet clouds that quickly faded to mist. The Mang kept up their chanting, and the very air seemed to hum with some secret presence.

Tsem went in to get some more water, and when he returned, he said in a worried voice, "Something is happening to him."

Hezhi turned fearfully back to the yekt, reluctantly stood, and walked inside.

Ngangata watched Perkar, his thick features cast in a worried mold. His forehead—what little there was of it—bunched like columns of caterpillars, his eyebrows their furry sovereigns.

Perkar moaned, then thrashed a bit. He opened his mouth and a few syllables bubbled forth, nothing she understood. Ngangata, however, nodded. "Here," he answered in Mang, then switched to another language. With his right hand he beckoned her.

To her horror, Perkar's eyes slitted open, and the orbs beneath were glazed a peculiar blue, like those of a fish several days dead.

"Hezhi," he muttered, barely audible.

"I am here," she answered. She thought of taking his hand from Ngangata, but the idea repelled her; she knew what was crouched on his chest, what she would touch if she touched him.

"You must . . . *shikena kadakatita* . . ." His tongue stuttered off into something she didn't understand, as if his River-given command of Nholish were failing. She looked to Ngangata.

"You have to go to the mountain," Ngangata translated reluctantly.

"*Balatata.*" Perkar gasped.

"Yes, I know," Ngangata assured him.

"What? What does he mean?"

"He is perhaps delirious."

"Tell me what he said," Hezhi insisted, and then to Perkar, in Nholish: "Perkar! Tell me."

Perkar's eyes opened wider, but his voice dropped away.

"He seeks you," the faint breath from his mouth said. "The River seeks you. You must go to She'leng, the mountain. Look for signs . . ." His mouth kept working, but even the semblance of sound failed.

"His body seems a bit stronger," Ngangata remarked after a moment. "But he should be well now. What did Brother Horse tell you?"

"That he has had a witching placed on him."

"No more?"

"More," Hezhi admitted, "but I must think on it."

"Think quickly, then," the half man urged, "if there is anything you can do."

Behind her, Tsem growled. "Have a care, creature," he said, the Mang thudding clumsily, like stones from his mouth.

Ngangata frowned but did not reply. Nor did he relinquish the hold of his gaze on her for several more heartbeats.

"I will think quickly," she said, and left the tent. Tsem followed her, but not without casting a hard glance back.

"Thank you, Tsem," she told him once they were outside, "but Ngangata is right. I can't let him die."

"You could. It might save us a lot of trouble."

"No, Tsem, you know I can't."

He grumbled incoherently and shrugged a bit.

"Ngangata is like you, you know."

"His mother a Giant? I think not."

"You know what I mean."

Tsem nodded sadly down at his feet. "Yes, Princess, I know what you mean. You mean we are alike in what we are not, not in what we *are*."

"Oh." She hadn't thought of it that way, but that was exactly what she had meant. Each was half Human and half . . . something else. What they were *not* was fully Human.

"Tsem, I—" But there was nothing right to say about that now. Instead she threw up her hands in frustration. "Leave me alone for a bit," she said at last.

"Princess, that would be unwise."

"Stay near the door. If anything happens, I will cry out."

She thought, briefly, that he would disobey her, but he did not, and brushed open the doorflap with his enormous palm.

Alone on the stoop, she once more contemplated the drum.

It seemed alive; larger drums had begun thundering, out where the Mang were holding their ceremony, and the small hand drum shivered in sympathy with its brother instruments.

She remembered Perkar, the rides they had taken together, the brightening in his eyes when he spoke of his homeland. She recalled only a few days before, when he had shown her the wild cattle, the sudden intense affection that had seized her. How could she let some black creature eat all of that, if she had the choice? Perkar said he had done terrible things—and she believed him. But she had also done terrible things. And some feeling for Perkar rested in her, she knew that now, for it had glowed hot with pain when he left her to go to see the Stream Goddess, and it lay chill in her now like a frozen bone. She had denied that it was love—and it wasn't, not the sort of love that made you want to marry someone—but it was a fragile thing, a part of her that existed only because she knew him. And when it was not hot or chill, it was warm and pleasant. Not comfortable, but more like the itchy moment before laughing or crying with joy.

And, even all of that aside, Perkar *knew* something, something important about her.

So there was no question of letting him die; she must admit that now to herself as she had to Tsem earlier. There were few paths open to her, and that admission closed all but one for now. Tomorrow she would ask Brother Horse to instruct her. She did not really trust him, not anymore, and the other Mang were clearly less trustworthy even than he. Their treatment of Perkar, even after months of companionship, testified to where strangers stood among these people.

But Perkar was dying and the River was after her. Perkar had said so, said that she must go to She'leng. She'leng, the mythical mountain from which he issued. If the River sought her, why should she fly to his very head? It made no sense to her, but Perkar had spoken to one of his gods, one that had aided their escape from Nhol, one who seemed inclined to help them. But what did it mean, and why? "Look for signs," Perkar had whispered, but she didn't know what *that* meant, either. Perhaps none of it meant anything, as sick as he was, but she had to know, had to do something. Once again she was being tossed about by forces she did not understand, and *that* she could not tolerate. She needed information; she needed *power*. All of that lay in the little drum.

"How fares your friend?" a quiet voice asked, interrupting her thoughts. She turned, startled.

It was the strange Mang, Moss, the one who had found her in the desert. He had come up, apparently, from behind the yekt. Sneaking up on her? She prepared to call for Tsem.

"I mean you no harm," the young man assured her quietly. "Really. I only meant to inquire after the stranger."

"What business is that of yours? He is not *kin* to you." She emphasized the word in a sudden disgust for the whole concept.

Her "kin" back in Nhol had never cared for her; for her worth as
a bride perhaps, but never for Hezhi. They would have placed her
below the Darkness Stair and forgotten her. Family were people
who never earned your respect or love but demanded it nevertheless. These Mang took that to such a ridiculous extreme she
wanted to shout with laughter and disdain.

Moss did not flinch from her words *or* her rude, direct gaze. He
only bowed slightly. "That is true, and to be honest, I will neither
be happy nor sad if he dies. I will only be disappointed that the
hospitality of this camp was violated."

"That means nothing to me. You Mang make much of your
laws and traditions, but like everyone else in the world, you compromise them the moment they seem encumbering."

"Some do, that is true, when the danger seems great enough,
when temper flares. That is not to say we ever discount our
ways."

"Words," Hezhi scoffed. "What do you want of me?"

Moss' face held nothing but concern, but Hezhi had seen that
before, on the face of another young and handsome man, and she
would not be fooled twice in the same lifetime in the same way.

"I wanted only to explain."

"Why do you owe me any explanation?"

"I do not," Moss replied, and for the barest flicker his green-
tinted eyes lit with some powerful emotion, then became carefully
neutral. He was not, Hezhi reminded herself, more than two or
three years older than she was herself.

"I do not," he repeated, "and yet I want to speak to you."

"Speak, then, but don't bother to try to fool me with any false
concern. It only makes me angry."

"Very well," he said. He glanced back toward the western
quarter of the camp; the drums were beating frantically as the fire
threw new stars at the night sky.

"Soon the Horse God goes home. *That* you should see, if you
care to understand my people."

"I don't care to understand them," Hezhi replied. "Get to your
point."

Moss frowned, showing irritation for the first time. "I will. You know of the war between my people and those of your friend?"

"I know of it. It was *you* who brought the news, remember?"

He nodded. "Just so. But this war is more than a war between mortals, Lady of Nhol. It is a war of gods, unlike anything the world has seen in several ages. Among my people, there are visionaries, shamans who see things in the future, who barter and truck in the world of Dream, and they have seen many ill things coming with this war."

She noticed then that his gaze had fastened upon her drum, and she deliberately placed it on the other side of her. "Go on," she said.

"It is only this," Moss said, chewing his lower lip for a moment. "There can be war, and many men and horses and perhaps even gods will die. They are *already* dying, you know. I don't know if you understand what that means."

"I have seen men die," Hezhi told him. "I know death."

"These are my kinsmen dying," Moss said.

"For whom I care exactly as much as they care for *me*, for Perkar," she retorted.

Moss breathed deeply. "You wish to anger me, but my people have charged me with something to say, and I will say it. You have been seen, Hezhi, in dream. A great man has seen you, a powerful gaan who would avert the worst of this war, bring peace. But what he has seen is that only *you* can bring this peace."

"Me?" Hezhi narrowed her eyes to slits.

Moss nodded. "You. That is what was seen. You are the only hope for peace, and the Cattle-Man, Perkar, is the bringer of death. You must go from him, come with me. I can take you to the gaan and together we can stop all of this. If you remain by the side of this man—" He gestured at the yekt. "—then it will be as a rain of fire, sweeping over the land and burning all before it."

"Me? Bring peace? How?"

"I know not. I have only been told this, but the one who told me is beyond trust and deceit. It is the truth, I promise you."

"And of course I believe you," Hezhi replied. She wanted to, of course. She had been the cause of so many deaths that the image of her as a peace-bringer was like a beautiful flower in a wasteland. She held on to that image wistfully but knew it had to be false. *Must* be false.

"How dare you?" she said slowly. "How *dare* you? For twelve years no one cared what happened to me, whether I was happy or sad, whether I lived or died. Now the whole world seems to want me, to use me like some workman's tool. I gave up the few things I loved to escape that, but I loved those things dearly. Do you understand me? I fled my home to live with you stinking barbarians to *escape*. I have given everything I'm going to give, do you hear me? How *dare* you say this to me?" She was trembling, and her voice had risen to a shriek. Words were spilling from her mouth without any consent from her, but she did not care. The fierceness in her heart might have been panic or fury or both, it was impossible to tell, as tightly bound up and volatile as it was. "Get *away* from me, you hear me? If I had any of the power you people think, do you honestly believe I would *help* you? I would strike you down, burn you to blackened bones, scatter your ashes from here to the ends of the earth!"

She wanted to go on then but finally caught herself, panting, reason overtaking anger. But she wanted to hurt Moss, sear that mild expression from his face, and she arrowed her remaining anger at him, as she had done in Nhol. There men had fallen, twitching and dying. Here Moss merely smiled a bit sadly.

"I'm sorry to have upset you. I thought you would be honored to save two peoples and perhaps the world itself from so much pain and suffering. I suppose I have misjudged you."

"Your *gods* have misjudged me," Hezhi snapped. "The very universe has misjudged me. I only want to be left alone."

"That is not your fate," Moss answered placidly.

"*I* will determine my fate," Hezhi said, over the rising furor of the drums.

Moss stepped back, his condescending little smile still in place. "I must go," he said. "The ceremony nears completion."

"I have *told* you to go," Hezhi retorted.

"Just so.. But I would speak of this later, when you have thought upon it."

"I have thought upon it," she said. "I have thought upon it all that I will."

Moss shrugged, bowed, and backed away for a few paces before turning back to the fire. Hezhi watched him go, aware that her entire body was trembling uncontrollably. She heaved in several deep breaths, attempting to steady herself. After a moment she glanced around her.

The yekt flap bulged slightly outward.

"It's okay, Tsem, he's gone," she said, and the flap relaxed.

"And thank you, Tsem," she finished. He, at least, was always there for *her*, because he loved her, and not for some mysterious thing she might be able to do.

She took the drum back up and stared at it, her fingers still trembling. She looked out toward the fire, where the Horse God was going home.

"Tsem, come on out here," she called back into the yekt.

Tsem's huge head emerged immediately. "Yes, Princess?"

"Do you think that the roof of this yekt will bear our weight?"

He considered that. "I have seen many people sitting on them before. You weigh nothing, and I weigh as much as three men, but I think they can bear more weight than that."

Hezhi nodded, remembering the thick beams that held up the roofs.

"Help me up onto the roof, then," she said. "I want to watch this."

"As you command, O Princess," Tsem said, "if you will explain your conversation with that barbarian to me. I could not follow all of it."

"I will explain, I promise," she said. "But later."

Tsem nodded and came outside. Together they walked around to the back of the house, where the outside beams formed a rough ladder. Tsem boosted her up and then followed, more laboriously. Hezhi expected the roof to at least creak beneath the half Giant's weight, but it held firm without protest.

She stood and peered out toward the assembled Mang.

She could indeed see better. The huge bonfire lit an encircling inner ring of excited faces, more dimly the next, until the crowd became a jumble of shadows and then darkness. The space cleared about the fire was perhaps twelve or thirteen paces in any direction. Seven drummers hammered away on drums from the size of her own to one monstrous instrument that stood as tall as the man striking it; it seemed, as well, that everyone in the crowd had some kind of noisemaker, a rattle, a string of bells, *something*. The drums, however, washed over these and engulfed them with thunder.

In the circle, masked dancers capered, wearing hoods or carved wooden masks that reminded her eerily of the masks the priests had worn when they came to test her. She shivered a bit, glad that they were distant from her. One dancer stood out, a madly prancing figure in bright colors who seemed to be making fun of the other dancers, like a clown or jester in her father's court. He wore a gaudy green shirt of Nholish satin, pantaloon breeks of some bright red cloth. His mask bore a ridiculous grin puckered out almost into a beak, and rather than hair the mask was furnished with a ruff of black feathers. The oddest thing about this dancer was his feet, which Hezhi could just make out; he wore shoes that somehow created the precise illusion that he danced upon a bird's three-clawed feet.

The Horse God stood nearby, and in Hezhi's vision she shimmered, a striking mare of the rare sort the Mang named *w'uzdas*, the gray of a thunderstorm streaked with jagged white bolts of lightning. Bedecked in fine harness, silver and gold bells, plumes of feather and long strips of ermine woven into her tail, she coursed in and among the dancers proudly but nervously, shying from the crowd.

"Barbaric," Tsem muttered.

Hezhi agreed but thought that there was a strange beauty to the spectacle, as well.

The capering clown suddenly leapt at the mare, landed astride her, and in an instant she arched her spine, pawing at the sky with silver-shod front hooves and then reversing, planting front feet solidly and bucking her rump high into the air. The momentary rider was pitched head over heels, struck the ground, and rolled smoothly to his feet, to the appreciative roar of the crowd. The mare, furious, began to snap and paw at the other dancers and the crowd; she tore into one part of the circle, and Hezhi saw at least one person fall beneath the flashing hooves before the clown distracted her by swatting her rump. She turned to pursue him but stopped, puzzled by all of the sound and motion.

Now four women with spears emerged from the crowd, and Hezhi felt her throat tighten; but they did not move toward the mare, instead joining in the dance.

Hezhi glanced at Tsem, noticed that he was rapt, riveted by the spectacle. For no reason she could explain, she removed her own drum from its case. In watching the ceremony, in not thinking, she had completed her decision. From her skinning kit, a little leather purse dangling at her side, she removed a bone awl.

The dancing was becoming more furious, the thrumming of the drums joining into a kind of breathless rushing with no space between their beats. Hezhi gripped the awl in her right hand and pressed it to her finger, felt the sharp point and tried to force it forward.

It hurt, and the thought of drawing her own blood suddenly sickened her; she bit her lip in frustration, wishing she had more courage. *Why can't I do it?* She pressed a bit harder, still not hard enough to draw blood.

Then the night seemed to rupture; the drums and beaters crashed with a terrible furor and then died away; Hezhi gasped and started in surprise, pricking the bone awl into her finger. Her gasp turned into a little hiss of pain, as, in the same instant, the women plunged their spears into the mare.

The horse shrieked, screamed in a thoroughly inhuman and yet horribly Human way. She seemed almost to fly forward and flail at one of her attackers, catching one of the women in the shoulder with a sharp hoof, and Human blood joined the spectacle. The other spearwomen scrambled away, and the crowd was hushed as the mare started after one of them, stumbled, blood pouring from four wounds, three of the spears remaining in her. Her front legs buckled and she sank as if bowing, worked for a moment to regain all four feet, and then, as if suddenly resigned, slumped to the dark earth, rolling onto one side, flank heaving.

The dancers ran to her. One took the dying beast's head in her lap, another laid one hand on the mare's breast and stretched the other high. Hezhi watched, her own pricked finger forgotten.

The kneeling woman began moving her raised hand, beating a slow rhythm in the firelight. Tentatively the smallest drum began taking up that beat, and then the others joined, a slow, faltering rhythm, *throoom, throoom, throoom, throoom.*

"It's her heartbeat!" Hezhi told Tsem, and he but nodded. In her hand, Hezhi's drum was shivering again, shaken by the very air. People began emerging from the crowd, laying presents about the dying horse, gifts of food, incense, beer and fermented mare's milk, jewelry. Brother Horse had told Hezhi of this part; each Mang was whispering prayers for the Horse God to take home, back to the mountain. The mountain? She'leng!

Hezhi was dizzied by the sudden revelation. The River and the greatest gods of the Mang issued from the same place! It had to be true. There could be only one such place, one such mountain.

The drumbeat slowed, faltered under the direction of the woman pressing near the mare's heart. A final beat shuddered into the night, and then profound silence. Hezhi took in a quivering breath, wishing she understood. The pain in her finger reminded her of what she had done, and she glanced down. She dully realized that several drops of her blood had found their way into the rawhide drumhead.

Well, that is done, she thought. Perhaps doing it at such an auspicious moment would lend her more power later, though she doubted it.

The drums boomed, shivered the earth, and Hezhi looked up, startled. They struck again and again, irregular at first, then gaining speed. Hezhi stared wildly, not understanding, and a peculiar panic seized her. She felt the hammering of her own heart, wildly fast, out of time with the increasing frequency of the percussion. If the drums had been the mare's dying heartbeats, then what was this? The quickening life of the god, the ghost, the spirit?

And, all of a sudden, the drumming matched her own thudding heartbeat, and the little instrument in her hand suddenly came alive, not merely humming in harmony with the ceremony but awake, speaking in the same tones as her heartbeat as if actually drummed by the blood in her veins. The itch of her scale became a searing, livid pain and Hezhi turned into fire, a cyclone. The drum opened up a doorway into utter nothingness. Tsem was reaching for her, mouth agape, but he seemed to move slowly, so very slowly, as, like a storm seeking a vacuum to fill, she rushed through the doorway, screaming.

XV

❧❧❧❧❧❧❧❧❧❧❧❧❧❧❧❧❧

Beneath the Temple

THE sudden weakness did not pass, but neither did it worsen, and Ghe smiled grimly. He had been reborn to go where the River could not, and it seemed that this held true, even here, in the heart of his impotency. His vision remained viable, but only just so, and he relied more heavily than ever on the ghost of the dead boy, straining for sound, the touch of air moving on his skin—the senses of the blind.

The tunnel he traveled in debouched into a large chamber, devoid of furnishings but thrumming faintly, faintly. Ghe knew that he must be feeling the water being drawn up the great central well of the temple, further evidence that he approached his destination. By feel and faint sight he found a passageway, cemented shut with bricks. Though he was weak, still he was not as weak as a mere Human Being, and the ancient bricks were rotten, returning to the mud from which they were formed. Wishing now that he had at least a blade or bar of metal, he set to work pushing, tearing, prizing them apart. When the first hole appeared, an appalling staleness breathed through the aperture; whatever space he was digging into was sealed, as well.

He widened the hole enough to crawl through and slithered in, lubricated by the coating of muck on his body. He lowered himself gently to the stone floor, having already made more sound than he wished, wondering what wards this place held, if he had already triggered some alarm.

He had dug into a hall, its floor marbled, but with a low, vaulted roof. He could stand upright in it, but reaching fingers could touch the ceiling. The hall was wide, however, twenty paces or more, and the walls were stuccoed with faint images. He approached and tried to make them out, but his vision was too dim, his sense of color gone entirely. Shrugging, he passed on, removing his shoes, for they squeaked and squished with the moisture in them. The stone beneath his toes was smooth, cool, and still he could feel the hum of rushing water somewhere ahead.

The hall soon widened and deepened, the floor sloping away from him, and he saw that he was entering a chamber filled with water; at least its paths were, for what he saw resembled a city of canals, each building isolated from the others by a trail of water less than a full step wide. These miniature buildings were also of stone—most seemed to be composed of marble, granite, or striated sandstone. Ghe had learned each of these and their properties as a Jik, that he might know how each might be climbed, which were easiest to drive spikes into, and so forth. Puzzled, he moved on, until his toes encountered the still water, and then a sudden tingle rushed up his leg, much like what he felt bathing in the River, but somehow stronger, more forceful. He bent and touched the surface, and his fingers came away dry.

Smokewater, he thought. *The Ghost of the River.*

He recalled the hall where he had been reborn, the sunken place where the Blessed were placed. The smokewater contained them there, but it had not contained him, only given him puissance. He felt the raw power thicken in him as he waded into the dry fluid, but his vision improved only a fraction. The River's *power* was here but not his sentience.

If smokewater was a prison for the Blessed, then what was

imprisoned *here*? But he believed he knew, both from memory and from hints in the *Codex Obsidian*. He approached one of the islanded structures and took the handle of its brass door.

The door opened easily, never protesting, and Ghe peered inside.

A man rested in the small space, or, at least, what remained of one. His bones lay jutting through rotten finery, a rusted iron scepter ringed by the disarticulated finger joints that had once held it. Ghe stared at the remains curiously. What king was this? Hezhi might know, would probably be able to read the ancient glyphs that patterned the tomb, recount some of the man's deeds. None of this really mattered to *him*, however, and with a small bow, he stepped back to close the door.

The bones shivered, blurred, and he realized suddenly that a nearly invisible shroud lay over the skeleton, a translucent film. This was now oscillating, wavering like the air above a stove or a fire. A tendril reached out tentatively to touch him, and he let it, wondering what it would do. A thin pain, a burning, started on his flesh where it touched him, and the shroud suddenly scintillated, glowed, tremors of color running through it. The bones themselves remained still.

He stepped farther back, brushing away the mist that touched him, and when that did not work, he disengaged it with his power. He could now see the simply knotted heartstrings, glowing above the dead king, the sort he had come to associate with ghosts. It had been clear, drained, and yet now with just a hint of his own power, it lived faintly.

These are not tombs for their bodies, he understood suddenly, *but for their ghosts.*

To trap them. To keep them from wandering or returning to their source. If the River could give *him* such power, what might it not do with a body and soul *made* to contain his will, the body of an emperor? This was the priesthood's way of making certain that such would never occur. The River's anger at that was distant from him, and so he did not fly into a rage as he had in the library. But what he saw confirmed his growing certainty that the priesthood worked against the River, not for him, and that they had been doing so for a *very* long time.

Staring at the fading ghost, it occurred to him that *it* could be tethered to him, just as the boy was. He could take the knowledge of an ancient king with him on this quest, use it to read the old hand and thus the enigmatic inscriptions all around him. Indeed, perhaps the solutions to all of the mysteries he sought to unravel lay here, in these tombs. But a strong instinct argued against that. The smokewater had so weakened these souls that to bring one to full sentience might drain *him* of power. Its touch had been so supremely hungry—what if *it* became the master of his body? A runner could usually gauge how far he could run, a jumper how far he could jump, and the same sense of ability made Ghe suspect that devouring the ghosts of these ancient Waterborn might be more than he was presently capable of.

So he moved on, brushing the tombs of kings with his hands, wading thigh-deep in water that did not dampen him. All here were dead: men, ghosts, River. As he advanced, he wondered what had brought him to this place. Understanding, surely, but understanding of what? What exactly did he seek? He hoped that the answer would be evident when he found it, that it did not lie in one of the many tombs. If it did, how would he discover it, by searching each and every one?

Perhaps he sought the priestly library, but he was certain most of *those* books were in hands he could not decipher easily or quickly. Of course, *Ghan* could, if he took one away. But how would he even know which one to take? In the end, he might have to gamble with a dead king anyway.

Perhaps he sought something more basic than books. The River wanted Hezhi back, but more, he wanted free of his shackles. Was there some way for him to overthrow the temple itself, compromise its power? *That* would be worth seeking, if he only knew what that might be, what valve he might adjust. It seemed unlikely that such a thing existed; more probably the entire structuration of the temple was responsible for its function; the bits of architecture he had read in preparing to converse with Hezhi had suggested as much. Certainly the fountain was involved, the flow of water up and into the temple, cascading down its stepped façade. And the *Codex* had suggested that the temple was in some way like She'leng, whence the River flowed. No, this was all too complicated for him. Still, he had to know what was *here*. Perhaps the River could sort some sense into it when he left the stultifying effects of the temple.

The hall of the dead ended at last, steep steps rising from the smokewater, and he set foot to their treads, padding upward carefully. He could hear the water now, not merely feel it and, at last, a few moments later, see it as he emerged into a grand hall, lit by a dim phosphorescence. As feeble as the light was, however, the walls and high ceiling picked up every bit of it and turned it back to his eye; for every surface of the room was mirrored with cut glass. The mere presence of his form awoke a million eyes that fluttered and blinked, his reflection passing through each facet.

And of course, the water. It rushed in a solid column from floor to ceiling, and he knew that it continued up through the many tiers of the temple until at last it emerged from its summit and streamed down the four sides like the water at the four corners of the world. He stared awestruck, despite himself. It had the appearance of a column of jet and silver; there was no spray, no spume; each drop went where directed, up and farther up still, like blood pumping through an artery. If he could *sever* such an artery—

"Who is this?" came a voice, but Ghe could not see from what throat it issued; he knotted his muscles, prepared to spring in any direction, but a long moment passed and still he saw nothing, scanning what he could see of the room again and again. It was a high voice, the voice of a priest, certainly. Slowly, very cautiously, Ghe sidestepped to his left, moving around the room's fountain core, until he saw the speaker at last. It was a boy, perhaps thirteen, perhaps younger or older by a year. He wore a black robe and his head was shaven. In his hand, limply, he held a golden chain, and a shadow was bunched at the end of it, a quivering murkiness.

"Who is this?" the boy repeated. Ghe pinched his mouth, wondering what to do: strike instantly or stay his hand, see what he might learn? Reluctantly he decided on the latter. It would give him a chance to close the intervening space, and surely there was more here than it seemed. He trod carefully, wary about placing his weight without first testing for a pit or some other trap; he had heard stories of the many ways in which the priesthood guarded its treasures. The Jik would plan such traps, and when it came to death, the Jik were inventive.

"I am no one," Ghe replied softly. "Just a mouse scurrying in these corners. I mean no harm."

The boy looked amused. He settled down on the edge of the dais on which he stood. Ghe could see more clearly now, could make out that the dais held all manner of objects: weapons, books, a rack of painted skulls, chests and boxes. The light was coming from there, as well; a wrought-iron lantern that burned quite dimly, with no flickering, as if its glow did not issue from any flame. Perhaps, like everything here, it was only the ghost of flame.

"Sit, be comfortable," the boy enjoined. "I rarely have anyone to speak to, and thou must have questions, if thou comest here."

"I have questions," Ghe acknowledged. "But I would not bother *you* with them."

"Thou bother me not at all," the boy answered, as Ghe peered more intently at what crouched, leashed, at the boy's feet. The dark shape confounded him, refused to resolve into any recognizable form. The boy's accent was more than old-fashioned; it was nearly another language, and Ghe had to concentrate intently to understand him. He moved closer, since he seemed to have been invited to.

When he was ten paces away, the boy waved him back. "It would be well if thou approached no closer," he said. "Mine dog is known to bite."

Ghe nodded to show that he understood, but he did not sit, as instructed, preferring to stand so that he might quickly respond to a threat, if need be.

"Thou came in through the crypts," the boy observed. "I have the right of it, have I not?"

Ghe saw no point in denying this and so nodded.

"Here, give me something to call thee. It need not be thy name."

"You may call me Yen," Ghe answered, wondering too late if the boy might not know of that identity.

"Art thou unsighted, Yen? I sense a blindness about thee."

"I am blind." It dawned upon Ghe that the boy himself was without sight, his pearly orbs never focusing on anything. If the boy thought him blind—perhaps sensing his ghostly thrall—then why argue?

"It seemed that it should be so. They say that *only* the blind can come here."

"Why is that?" Ghe asked.

"My father made it so," the young man replied, smiling.

"Your father, the River?"

The boy chortled. "Thou does not know where thee beest? No, my father is not the River. Not he."

"Do you guard this place?"

"Thou lack persistence," the boy said. "Thou wouldst know of my father."

"I have no wish to be rude."

"Trespassing is always rude, thou, but mind that not. I am the *keeper* of this place, and its guardian in that sense."

"What do you guard?" Ghe asked, eyeing the treasure behind the boy but playing his role as a blind man.

"Baubles, bangles. Mostly this *place*, as I said."

"But who do you guard it from?"

"Thee, I suppose."

"I don't want anything here," Ghe lied.

"No, I suppose thou merely took a wrong turning. It is a common mistake, and many make it," the boy mocked.

"I was curious, nothing more."

"Come," the boy said, a bit of anger creeping into his voice. "Tell me why thou art here. It matters not what thou sayest, save that I am bored and wish to speak with someone."

It matters not what thou sayest. Ghe caught the threat in that. Was this boy merely delaying him, as more priests came? But he had heard no alarm, felt no odd play of power. Though it was like peering through a mist, he had occasional glimpses of the guardian's heartstrands, and they looked strong and strange, and he seemed confident, as if understanding that he *needed* no aid. And then there was the shadow at his feet, pulsing with malevolent force. If he could feed on them, or better, capture them, what might he not learn?

"Very well," he relented. "I have come seeking the secret of the temple, I suppose. Seeking how it holds the River senseless here."

"And dost thou have thine answer now?"

"No. This place was mentioned in a book that was read to me, but now that I have reached it, I know no more than I did."

"Fortunate that thou hast encountered me, then. I know this place well."

Ghe hesitated barely an instant. "The book speaks of a mountain far away."

"Su'leng, the source of the Changeling."

"Changeling?"

"Another name for the River. Yes, there is such a mountain, which thou namest Su'leng. And what dost thou think that has to do with *this* place?"

"It was built to resemble that mountain," Ghe answered, once again wondering at the antiquity of the boy's speech. No priest he knew spoke in such a manner, save in incantations, and never did it flow so smoothly from their lips.

"Very good. And thou wouldst know why?"

"Yes, of course."

"Imagine," the boy said, clasping one knee between his hands, leaning back and staring sightlessly up at the ceiling, "Imagine . . . Wert thou *ever* sighted? But of course thou wert; I can sense it. Imagine then, in thy sighted days, standing before a mirror.

Imagine now, another mirror behind thee, just precisely behind thee. What is it thou seest?"

"Myself, I suppose, reflected into infinity."

"Indeed. Now suppose thou art stupid, like a blue jay or some other noisy bird. Hast thou ever seen them fly against glass, accosting their own reflection?"

"No, but I can imagine it."

"A truly stupid bird might batter itself into senselessness against a mirror. Caught between two, it would be a virtual certainty."

"You say that the River is such a stupid bird? That the mountain and this temple are like mirrors, facing one another?"

"Well, I only offer a little story. The truth is much more complicated, I suppose. The River flows on past this temple, is aware beyond it. But in a sense, a part of him is fooled into thinking this place is his point of origination, his womb, and that—though he knows it not—is what he truly seeks: return to his ancient home. He cannot see this temple because he confuses it with the mountain, and for him the distance between is somewhat meaningless."

Ghe remembered his dream, the dream of completeness long ago, when the River was an endless circle, content. He was aware that he sought his ancient state but thought to reachieve it by growing larger. But if part of him were fooled into a dream of contentment . . .

"So he feels the water rushing through the temple—"

"And believes that it is himself, flowing out from his source. It confuses him, but the nature of the wyrd is that he does not know he is confused."

Ghe nodded his head. "That may be so. But there is more."

"Oh, certainly. A thousand ancient songs—lullabies, if thou wilt—are pooled here, and over time such songs lie upon one another and gather strength. A thousand blocks of incense are burned, and priests are made so that the River cannot see them, either. But those things are just ornament, paint, gilding. I have given thee the very essence."

"And this was all done by the Ebon Priest?"

The boy laughed. "The Ebon Priest is actually quite lazy, but he knows how to set others at a task. Thou wilt not see him here now in the midst of this drudgery he created for us all. I suppose he laid out the plan but left others to refine the details. What thou seest is more my creation than his, in many ways."

Ghe narrowed his eyes. Was this man lying? He seemed only a boy, and yet Ghe already knew better than that.

"You are the Ebon Priest's son?"

"His bastard, yes. Thou—*you* knew that."

"I do now, I suppose. Then you have been here for some time."

"You have an engaging talent for understatement."

As they had been speaking, the boy's strange speech had gradually altered, until now he spoke with Ghe's own soft dialect. That was somehow much more unnerving than hearing him speak in the ancient, incantive tongue.

"You have been here since the First Dynasty?"

The boy shrugged. "Now and then I sleep. I was sleeping when you arrived, but my pet, here, awakened me." He tugged playfully on the golden leash, and the darkness quivered a bit.

Ghe did not ask about the pet, remembering that he was supposed to be unsighted, nor did he ask about the books, the weapons, the skulls.

"Are those all of your questions?"

"I don't know what else to ask."

"Perhaps you would prefer to speak to someone else?"

"Someone else?"

"Why, yes. One of my companions, perhaps."

Ghe studied the room carefully. He saw no "companions" save for the "pet"—whatever it was.

"I listen for the Sound of Falling Water," he said, the standard acceptance of a master's wisdom by the pupil. He realized, even before the boy had uttered his short, barking laugh, how ludicrous the phrase now seemed.

"Well, then, who shall we speak to?" The boy stood and walked over to the skulls, rubbed their smooth craniums with his palms.

"Su'ta'znata? Nungeznata? No! You would want to speak to

Lengnata. Here." He lifted up one of the skulls and brought it over, sat with it on his lap.

"There, Lengnata. Speak to your loyal subject Yen."

The boy was certainly mad, Ghe thought. Quite mad indeed.

"Thou mockest me," Ghe heard himself say suddenly, harshly. He clutched at his throat. "Leave me to sleep. I have no subjects, nor ever did I." He heard himself go on. His voice, speaking from his throat, without his command.

"No! Stop! Make it stop!" Ghe cried, this time of his own volition. He could feel nothing, no intruding presence. It was not as if someone were forcing him to speak; it just . . . happened.

The boy tittered, as Ghe answered himself. "Slay him, if thou canst, and if not, escape from here. If thou ever wert a subject of the Zhakunge . . ." Ghe concentrated furiously, trying to make it *stop*, but it would not; the words kept vomiting from his mouth. He barely noticed how, at the mention of the Chakunge, the boy nearly doubled over in laughter.

Stop, stop, Ghe thought, as Lengnata muttered on madly in Ghe's voice. Desperately he reached out with the tendril of his power, searching for a way to make the babbling cease, to kill the source of the utterances. He felt into the skull and found it there, the ghost knot, and frantically seized it, closed the fist of his mind on it, and *squeezed*. The babbling suddenly did cease then, and almost instinctively Ghe pulled the ghost of Lengnata into himself and tethered it with the blind boy. It was a weak, starved creature, easier to manage than he had guessed.

He realized suddenly that his knees must have given up holding him; he was on his hands and knees facing the floor, shuddering heavily.

"Give that back," the boy said slowly, deliberately. He no longer seemed amused at all.

"No," Ghe managed. "No, I don't think I will." And he struck like a snake, reached for the bunched strings of the guardian's life.

Fire hollowed Ghe out, burst from his eyes and mouth, and, as if physically struck, his body arched back and slammed to the stone floor, writhing. He kicked away madly, aware of his own shrieking but unable to do anything to stop it. A small part of his mind remained intact, trying to ride the crest of the agony, understand what had happened to him. He had reached out toward the boy and encountered something, a venom that struck up through him like a sword. He waited for the next blow, the one that would finish him, but something stayed it. Surely not *him*, though he felt a hard kernel of power in him, still untouched. He kept that near as, trembling, he turned back to the boy.

The boy had a nasty grin on his face. His "pet" had risen up, and Ghe saw that it now wore Human form; a tall, striking man with enormous, fishlike eyes, a nose almost beaklike in its angularity. He wore armor made of some gigantic crustacean, and he carried an aquamarine blade. Within his bulging eyes were empty hollows in which danced darkness and white sparks. His hair hung long, jet, lank, bound by the golden circlet of a king.

"Bow down, Yen," the boy spat. "Rise, but only to your knees so that thy emperor may receive you."

Ghe still felt on fire, but the pain seemed to have been mostly illusion, or at least nonphysical. It had been as if his eyes and flesh actually melted, but he was still whole . . .

What was the guardian talking about? The apparition whose chain he held was *not* the emperor; he had seen the August One many times. No, this was some ghost, or demon.

"I see you do not recognize him, the First Emperor, the Riverson."

Ghe parted his lips to retort but could not find the air. It couldn't be, he knew. Couldn't be not *a* Chakunge but *the* Chakunge. If such were true, the power of this boy must be *hideous* . . . But now he could see the boy's power revealed, the fire and lightning raging in his heart, a cyclone of light. What had he done, what had he wakened?

"Now. Give me back what you took."

I return to death regardless, Ghe understood. And so he ran, striking out with the force in him rather than reaching to take. Four steps he flew and felt his blow deflected, drained away, but then he was leaping, hurtling through the air. The boy shrieked in fury when he saw Ghe's target, and Ghe felt a thousand hot needles of brass piercing his spine. The ghost of the Chakunge moved as quickly as a dark lightning crackling across the floor, chips spalling from the stone where his feet touched. In the same instant Ghe struck the roaring column of water and it struck him, a giant's fist with no mercy or care. Light and thought vanished into thunder and then void.

XVI

Gaan

THE sound of drums faded, replaced by an enveloping silence that included not even her heartbeat. Hezhi had a sense of rushing, of rapid movement, but there was no confirming wind on her face. The terrible fear that gripped her faded, however, receding like the drums and her own heartbeat, and with some startlement she understood that her eyes were shut tightly. She opened them.

Something was hurtling by beneath her, a broad, endless something that could only be landscape, seen from high in the air. It was a dark landscape, the bunched masses of hills indigo, the plains mauve, wriggling strips of ebony that must be streams or rivers. The brightest color seemed to surround her; she was wreathed in clouds of sparks, exactly like the sky-seeking flashes from the bonfire, and with a shock she realized that the sparks were not merely following her but emitting from her; her body glowed like a red-hot brand.

What have I become? she wondered. But she still *felt* like herself. Ahead of her, matching the pace of her flight, was a second brand, trailing flame like the comets she had read of, nearly white at its center, nimbused in orange and yellow, the faintest tail of the torch swirling away into turquoise, jade, and at last, violet. It was more than merely astonishing but beautiful, and she found that while her fear seemed to have been cut from her like a lock of hair, her wonder had not.

What had happened? She struggled to understand as her speed increased, the weird landscape sheeting beneath like an inconstantly choppy sea.

She had passed through the drum, the bun. She must be in that otherworld Brother Horse described, and she realized that she had never believed him, despite her experience with things arcane. Ghosts and the power of the River made sense to her; this land of gods and demons and worlds within worlds did not, and deep down she had always thought it to be some Mang superstition. That assumption had led her to be incautious, to meddle with something she understood not at all. It could be that she was dead, she thought. She must resemble a ghost quite strongly, a ghost such as the one that had attacked her in the Hall of Moments. Had her body been stripped from her like the peel of a fruit? Was Tsem even now holding her lifeless corpse, weeping?

She turned back, attempting to see more of her "body," but only flame was revealed to her, a coruscating skirt billowing into nothingness.

If she were a ghost, then what flew ahead of her? But she thought she knew that, too. It must be the spirit of the horse, running back to its mother, the Horse Goddess. *It* was certainly dead, and that led Hezhi to suspect that she was, as well.

The land below grew rougher, and her flight swooped and climbed to follow the rising contours of it. She wondered, vaguely, if there was any way to control her flight, but after a certain amount of experimentation—willing herself to turn, waving her ethereal arms—she gave up. It was as if she were borne along on a swift stream, perhaps one that the Mang ritual had created to send the horse home. She was going farther and farther from her drum, then, which was probably her only way back to the world of the living—if that world even existed for her now.

Ahead, something bright shone, a brilliant eye with lids of rainbow arcing about it. It grew larger and nearer with immeasurable rapidity. She felt certain that this was their destination, for the shooting star ahead of her turned subtly to intersect it, weaving through the sawtooth silhouettes of mountain peaks, and she followed. The whiteness grew, expanded to fill the horizon. She had a sense of enormity, of a mountain larger than any mountain in the world and a tree with branches in the nether stars before the light enveloped her, and, shuddering, she came to a halt.

SHE first became aware of voices, muttering in a tongue she did not understand. She could pick out four, possibly five distinct speakers: two women, two men, what might be a girl or young boy. Around her, the light was fading, becoming red spots on her eyes.

Finally, magnificence replaced the spots.

She stood in the grandest hall she had ever known; no court in Nhol could even begin to match it for size. Its splendor was stunning, as well, but it was of an alien sort to Hezhi, resembling more the natural beauty of the cliffs and mountains than it did the refined—though often decadent—architecture of the palace. Still, in its vastness there was a simplicity that matched certain Nholish ideals.

The walls—those that she could see—were curtains of basalt, flowing to the floor and rising beyond vision above, though the hall was well lit by the barbaric guttering of perhaps a hundred torches. The floor was polished red marble, and by that she knew that some hand had crafted this place; otherwise she might have thought it a purely natural cavity. The floor was mostly empty, like a vast dance theater, and by comparison the part of it she stood upon was cluttered, for nearby were a throne, carved from a column of basalt, the dais that it sat upon, a vast table, and its attendant benches. None of these was occupied.

The other occupants of the room stood on the open floor,

some forty paces from her, and they held her attention much more than the room. Foremost was a creature completely beyond her identification, a vast monster that resembled a bear but also resembled Tsem. He?—*it* had a single eye, a black orb filmed with faint rainbow. Perched on his shoulder was a raven the size of a goat, and still the bird seemed insignificant, so large was the bear-thing. A pace from both of these was a woman, naked, her flesh cloaked only in soft black fur. That and her pointed teeth reminded Hezhi of some sort of cat, save that horns grew from her head and tangled hair fell in a mass almost to her waist. A second woman seemed most familiar of them all; matronly, strong-limbed with thick, long straight hair, she appeared to be a Mang—or even a Nholish—woman. In fact, Hezhi was reminded of Qey.

Kneeling before them was the wavering, ghostly apparition of a horse. Hezhi held her own hands out before her and saw only bones swathed in shifting patterns of light and smoke.

"Well, well," the cat-woman said, her voice barely a sigh and yet perfectly audible in the great hall. "And who have we here?"

"You know her," the Raven clattered harshly, *his* voice just slightly more intelligible than the cawing of one of his smaller brethren.

"I don't," the Mang woman said, stepping up to stroke her hand upon the horse's fiery mane. "How has this child come with *my* child?"

"I would say she did something very foolish," the cat-woman said, walking toward Hezhi with fluid, padding steps. "You may speak to us, girl."

"I . . . I don't know what—" These were gods. They must be. What could she tell them?

"You haven't come here to be clothed in flesh, that much is certain, for you still have the stink of flesh about you. You are no goddess, though you think yourself one, and you are no beast."

"She smells of my brother," the giant rumbled, in tones so low that Hezhi first mistook them for mere growling.

"Why, we should eat her, then," the cat-woman opined,

flashing her smile full of needle-teeth. "Yes, we have not dined on mortal flesh in some time."

"Hush," the Raven croaked. "You know what becomes of you when you dine on Human flesh."

"Do I? I can never remember."

"Exactly. *Exactly!*" the Raven cackled.

"What about you, girl? Do you wish to be eaten?"

"No," Hezhi said, anger beginning to slice through her awe. "No, not at all. I only want to understand what has happened."

"Well, you flew through a lake, I suppose, and came to the mountain. That would mean either that you are dead—which you are not—or that you are a great shaman . . ."

"Which she is *not*," the black bird finished.

"No," Hezhi agreed. "I don't think I am either of those."

"You followed my child," the other woman—who could only be the Horse Mother—said. "What do you want of my child?"

"Nothing!" Hezhi cried. "I only want to go back. I made a mistake."

"Imagine that," the Raven said. "But I say when one visits the mountain, one never goes away the same. Look at her, my kindred. A girl who flies about like a shaman, and yet she has no servants in her mansion." He tapped his breast with his beak.

"What concern is that to us?" the cat-woman asked. "What does it concern us that this Changeling brat has no helpmates?" She looked suspiciously at the bird. "Is this some trickery of yours, Karak? Some part of your silly machinations?"

"I know her only by reputation," the Raven said. "She caused something of a stir down the Brother's course."

"I cannot see there," the monster with one eye rumbled. "He has closed that to me."

"Then it might not hurt to have an ally there, even a mortal one. Give the child what she came for." The bird winked at Hezhi.

"I didn't *come* for anything," Hezhi insisted.

"Everyone who travels to the mountain comes for something," the cat-woman snarled. "I'll give her none of mine; she hasn't earned them."

"Be reasonable, Huntress. *I* could only give her a crow, not really the sort of helper that would do her much good."

The "Huntress" snorted. "No, I should think not. Silly, willful creatures, always cawing in alarm at the slightest scent of danger."

"I won't argue," Karak said agreeably. "That is why I suggest *you* give her something. A tiger, perhaps, or even a ferret."

"A tiger? No, I think not. I'll have none of this."

The Horse Mother looked up from her child. "Did you come for a helper? You must know it was foolish to come to the *mountain* for such a thing. Without one, you can never return."

"I didn't mean to come here," Hezhi said, helplessness—and thus anger—swelling in her.

"Life often ends with a mistake," the Huntress remarked.

"Huntress—" the Raven began.

"No! Enough of you, Karak. Balati, judge!"

The giant blinked his eye slowly. "Hold her until her body dies," he said. "Then we will reclothe her in something. You decide, Huntress."

"Lord—" the bird began, but then his beak seemed to seal shut; and though he struggled to speak further, only muffled grunts escaped him.

"Fine," the Huntress said, smiling. She waved toward Hezhi, and she lost consciousness.

SHE awoke in a chamber of obsidian, if "awoke" was the right word to describe her passage back to consciousness. Her "body" no longer sparked and flashed; it had faded to a faint translucence through which she could see the shadows of her bones, her organs, the faintly pulsing lines of her heart. The scale on her arm showed as a searing white spot, however, and from it whirls of color traced up her nonexistent arm, making it seem much more real than the rest of her.

"Hello!" she shrieked, but she expected no reply and got none. She wondered, dully, if the altered appearance of her ghost meant that her body had died or if it reflected some other change in quality about which she knew absolutely nothing.

She had met gods now, not just the little gods in Brother Horse and the landscape, but the Emperor of Gods, Balati, the Huntress, Karak the Raven, and the Horse Mother. Perkar had described all of them save the Horse Mother. It still seemed worse than unreal to Hezhi; it seemed like the cusp of nightmare and waking, her mind insisting that it was all illusion and night terror, assuring her that she need only keep hold of her fear until morning. How could this be real?

But the Blessed beneath the palace were real; the River was real. In a world that held *those* things, why not gods with antlers? Because she thought they were silly, or barbaric, or unlikely? They would kill her, no matter what she thought.

She set about exploring her prison. It was less a chamber than a glassy tube, traveling roughly upward. She wondered if she could fly, as she had before, travel up along it. She tried, but nothing happened. She attempted climbing and had better success. Her ghost body seemed to have little if any weight. The slightest purchase of her fingers was enough. Unfortunately, there was little enough purchase of any kind in her prison, and she never gained more than thrice her own height, climbing.

She was still trying, however, when a voice spoke from behind her.

"Such a determined child. The Changeling chose well when he chose you."

She turned, lost her tenuous hold on the wall, and plummeted. She fell with a normal sort of speed, but the impact hurt her not at all.

"Who are you?"

"You should know me. Perhaps Perkar has spoken of me."

She peered into the darkness, made out a pair of yellow eyes. "Karak?" she asked, the alien name croaking clumsily from her mouth.

"In the well-wrought flesh," the voice answered.

"Perhaps you have come to taunt me, then," she said. "Perkar speaks of you as a malicious god."

"Perkar seeks to assuage his own guilt by blaming others. No matter; I am fond of Perkar, though he maligns me. Tell me, did he return to the camp yet?"

"Yes."

"And what did he tell you of his journey?"

"Nothing. He was injured."

The Raven stepped forward, or perhaps became somehow more visible. "What injury could prevent him from talking? He carries Harka."

"He is ill; some sort of spirit is eating his life. That is one reason I attempted the drum."

"To save him?"

"Yes."

"How delightful!" Karak cackled. "But don't speak of that to anyone else here; his name is not particularly distinguished in these halls."

"I know."

"Well. This brings me, I think, to the point of my visit. I have decided to aid you."

"You have?" Hezhi asked, hope kindling but kept carefully low. She did not ask *why*.

"Yes, as I said, I am fond of Perkar and, by extension, his friends. Actually, what you just told me clinches my decision. If he is ill in the way that you say, it will take a shaman to save him." He changed then, went from being a bird to a tall, handsome man, though his eyes remained yellow. "Grasp my cloak and follow."

Hezhi stared at him helplessly for a moment, but whatever he had planned for her could be no worse than remaining in this glass room for eternity. Karak had helped her once, in the past, or at least she had been told he had. Reluctantly she took hold of his long, black-feathered cape. Karak gave a little *grak*, became once again a bird, but this time the size of a horse, and she, she was knitted like a feather to his back. He rose effortlessly up the tube, spiraling higher and higher, until at last she saw a glimmer of light.

Karak emerged from the hole and alighted on a mountain peak, became a man again, and Hezhi was able to step away from him. If she had had breath, she would have been without it, for she had never been upon a mountain, never gazed down from the roof of the world onto it. Clouds lay out below her, like tattered carpets on a far vaster floor; they hardly obscured her vision of the surrounding peaks, marching away to the edge of the world, snowcapped, clothed in verdure elsewhere, revealing their handsome granite bones now and then. Farther down still, blue with mist, were the bowls and gashes of valleys.

She saw no streams save one: a bright, silver strand winding from the base of the mountain.

"Your kin," Karak said, gesturing at the River.

"Then this *is* She'leng," Hezhi breathed. "Where he flows from."

"Indeed, your people call it that. We merely call it home."

"You keep calling him your brother. Are you kin to him, as well?"

"Indeed. I suppose that would make you a sort of niece, wouldn't it?"

"I—" But Karak was laughing, not taking himself seriously at all.

"What are those?" Hezhi asked, waving her hand.

Small lights, like fireflies, were drifting up from the valleys. From most places there were only a few, but from one direction— she was not sure of her cardinal points here—a thick stream of them wound.

"Ghosts, like yourself, coming to be reclothed. Some Human, some beast, some other sorts of gods."

"That thick stream? Where do they come from?"

"Ah! That is the war, of course. Many are losing their clothing there."

Losing their clothing. Hezhi had seen men die; they never seemed to her as if they were merely undressing.

"Can't you stop the war?"

"Who, me?"

"The gods," Hezhi clarified.

"I don't know," Karak said thoughtfully. "I doubt it. I suppose the Huntress could come down from the mountain with her beasts and her *wotiru* bear-men and join one side or the other; that would, I think, bring the war to an end more quickly. But I can't think of anything that would prompt her to do that—nor, I suspect, is that solution the one you were suggesting."

"No," Hezhi replied. "It wasn't."

"Well, then, you have your answer."

Hezhi nodded out at the vastness. "What of me, then? You said you were going to help me."

"Yes, and I will. But I want you to remember something."

"What?"

"Trust Perkar. He knows what should be done."

"He said that I should come to the mountain. I am here."

Karak cocked his head speculatively. "This is not what he meant. You must come here in the flesh."

"Why?"

"I may not say, here and now. Perkar knows."

"Perkar is very ill."

"Ah, but you will save him, shamaness."

"I am no—" Hezhi broke off and turned at a sound behind them. The Horse Mother stood there, and the ghost of the horse.

"Is this the only way, Karak?" the Horse Mother asked. Hezhi could hear the suspicion in her voice.

Karak—huge crow once more—ruffed his feathers, picked with his beak at them. "Can you think of another?"

"No. But I am loath to give my child like this."

"You have many children, clothed in flesh. And it is only for a time."

Horse Mother nodded. "I know. Still, if I discover there is some trick here . . ."

"All of these years, and you still cannot tell the Crow from the Raven."

She snorted, and it sounded like a horse. "No one can."

Hezhi followed the exchange in puzzlement. She wanted to ask what they meant, but felt she had already been too bold around such strange and powerful creatures.

The Horse Mother turned to her. "Swear that you will care for my child."

"What do you mean?"

The woman glanced hard at Karak. "She doesn't understand."

Karak stared at Hezhi with both yellow eyes. "To return, you must have a spirit helper. The Horse Mother proposes to give you her child, since the Huntress will part with none, nor will Balati. Your only other choice is to wait here until you die and then be reclothed in the body of some man or beast, bereft of your memories, your power."

Hezhi frowned down at the stone of the mountain. "I might be the better without those."

"Your choice," the Horse Mother told her. "But if you choose life now, you must do so quickly, before the others discover us. And you must swear to treat my child kindly." Her face hardened. "And your companion, Perkar—*he* has offended me, tortured one of my daughters. When the time comes, he must pay a price, and you must not stand in my way."

Hezhi turned her startled glance back to the goddess. "Perkar? What do you mean?"

"A trivial thing—" Karak muttered.

"*Not* trivial. Her spirit arrived here lately, told me how shamefully he treated her. I will remember."

"Perkar is my friend," Hezhi said. "He saved me from a terrible fate. I cannot knowingly allow harm to come to him."

"Not necessarily harm," the Horse Goddess said, "but he must certainly pay a price. Tell him that."

"I will tell him. But if you seek to harm him, I must stand between you, no matter how grateful I am."

The goddess eyed her steadily for a long moment before finally inclining her head slightly. "I give you my child freely, with only the single condition. I understand loyalty, no matter how misguided."

"I swear to care for your child," Hezhi said. "But—"

Karak vented an exasperated squawk. "*What* now?" he croaked.

"I don't know if I want some creature living within me. I hadn't decided when all of this—"

Karak cut her off. "Your time for making such decisions is spent. Either you take the child, go back, live, save Perkar, and fulfill your destiny, or you expire and spend your days here, first as a ghost and then eventually as a salmon or some such. It should be an easy choice."

"None of my choices is easy," Hezhi burst out. "I should be choosing which dress to wear to court, which suitor to allow to kiss me, what kind of bread I want for breakfast!"

"What is this nonsense? What are you babbling about? You were never destined for such humdrum choices! You walk between gods and men. Your choices are only between despair and hope!"

"Karak is a poet," Horse Mother grunted. "Who would have known *that*?"

"Not I!" Karak answered, spreading his wings and contracting them.

"He is right, little one, though he knows more of you than I do," the woman continued, her dark eyes kind. "You will have my child. I will watch over you."

Perkar would die without her. *She* would die and be lost, a ghost, as pathetic as the apparition that once inhabited her apartments.

"I agree," she said then. "I will be as kind as I know how to be."

"Fine, fine," Karak snarled. "Quickly, now."

Horse Mother stroked the horse. Like Hezhi, she had cooled from her flight and now had the appearance of a gray skeleton filmed with gauzy flesh. Still, Hezhi could sense the creature's confusion, *its* fear. "Hush, my sweet," the woman said. "This is Hezhi, and she will return with you to the land of the living, to the pastures and the plains."

"Now?" Karak snapped.

"Now," the goddess replied, reluctance still clear in her voice.

"Good," Karak answered. He pointed to Hezhi. "Cut to pieces."

Hezhi just stared at him, wondering what he meant, and then

pain was all that she could comprehend. Something chopped her to bits, dismembered her violently; she felt each bone wrench apart, and each individual piece ached on its own, so that even severance added layers of agony so profound that, though she did not lose consciousness, she quickly lost the ability to interpret anything. How long her ordeal lasted, she had not the slightest inkling; she was only aware of trying to scream and scream without lungs, tongue, or breath.

She had no awareness when the bits came back together, knitted solid. The Horse Mother and Karak spoke, but she understood absolutely nothing of what they said. After that, she had only flashes of the purple and black landscape beyond the drum and a persistent pounding that seemed like hoofbeats. And inside, a frightened voice, as confused as she.

WHEN sense truly returned, it was to those same hoofbeats. She was still high in the air above the otherworld, but rather than being swept along, as she had been before, she was running, her own hooves carrying her through the empty spaces between the clouds.

Hooves? She glanced at herself. As before, she was glowing like a coal, striking sparks from the very air, but this time she had more of a form. She could see her own arms, her hands, her naked upper body. But below . . .

Hooves, the thick, layered muscles of a horse's forepart. Turning back she could see rump and a flying tail of lightning.

I have become the statuette! she thought. *The half-horse woman.*

But she was still herself. She could feel the Horse in her—that was who ran, who flexed the great muscles that carried them through space. But the spirit in her was not invasive, not seeking to seduce her as the River had or bludgeon her like the gods she had seen since escaping Nhol. Instead, she was there, tentative, but a companion willing to learn.

"Thank you," Hezhi said. *"Thank you for coming with me."*

The Horse did not answer in words, but Hezhi understood her response, her welcome. Together they struck lightning across the sky, and soon enough, Hezhi knew that they had reached the village of Brother Horse, the yekt where her body lay without her. Nearly laughing with the pleasure of thunderous flight, ecstasy replacing their fears, Hezhi and the Horse raced thrice about the village, above the racetrack. She could not see the people, save as flickers of rainbow, and she wondered if any of them could see her.

It was actually with reluctance that she approached the yekt, lit upon its roof. She saw no one there and so descended into the house along its central pole, whose shadow in the otherworld resembled a tall and thickly branching tree.

The tent was the belly of a shadow, the people in it less than specters. She saw them as frames of dark bone, cages that enclosed furnaces of yellow light.

One of the figures lay prone—Perkar, of course—and something squatted upon him. Something real.

As soon as she saw it, Hezhi steeled herself for the sickening stab she had felt before, but it did not come. It was as if a strong wind parted around her, and she suddenly remembered what Brother Horse had told her about spirit helpers. About how she could *see* now without the vision *clutching* her.

So she examined the thing carefully, though even so it was terrible to behold. At first, there was no sense to what she perceived, only a jumble of coiled, glittering sinew, scales, and polished black ivory. But then the Horse moved in her, just a bit, and her perspective changed. It was like a snake, or more, like a centipede, jointed and sheened as if with oil. It nestled a cone-shaped skull into Perkar's chest, and a thousand smaller worms wriggled from every part of the creature. The radiance in Perkar's breast was dim, though a stream of orange light fed into it from the sleeping, birdlike form at his side she guessed to be his sword.

Every now and then, the worm—or perhaps mass of worms—shuddered, rippled, and broke into crawling parts that then re-formed. Two yellow eyes opened on the base of its "skull."

"Leave. He is mine," a voice told her. It was a clattery voice, like bones snapping.

Hezhi had no reply. She just stared at the thing.

"If you have come to fight for him, shamaness, you will surely fail. Go back to your bright world, leave this dying man to me in mine."

The monster did not gesture, but she felt her eyes drawn beyond it, as if somehow it had directed her to look. There lay a circle of light. Through it she saw the interior of the yekt—part of a support pillar, a rug, and a hand. *Her* hand. The image wavered a bit, as if it were a pool into which grains of sand were dropping.

Hezhi hesitated. She could see plainly enough now that the thing on Perkar was killing him. But as of the moment, she had not the faintest idea what to do about it.

"I'll go," she muttered to the thing. *But I will return.* Then she edged up to the drum and stepped through.

In a swirl of dizziness and disorientation, she bolted up, gasping. The horse body was gone, and she felt her own flesh upon her, suddenly so familiar, so well fitted that she would have burst into melancholy tears at being reunited with it.

Save that at the same moment, the body of a man slapped into the ground only an arm's length from her; she saw his eyes widen in surprise as the impact shattered his spine. All around her was shouting and the harsh grating and hammering of steel on steel.

INTERLUDE

The Emperor and the Ghoul

THE great door creaked faintly as the emperor pushed it open, startling the orange-speckled house lizard on the wall into frantic though short-lived flight. It ran only a few spans before crouching against the edge of a tapestry, watching him with its cat-pupiled eyes. She'lu felt a brief amusement, considered flicking the tiny beast with his power. What audacity it had, a common house lizard, entering the court of an emperor!

He let it go. It was told that the spotted ones were good luck, and even an emperor needed that. Especially now, with the increased Dehshe raids on the border garrisons, the icy relations with once-friendly Lhe, and Dangul, at the limits of the Swamp Kingdoms, pressing to levy a tariff—a *tariff*—on goods shipped through their territory. It was a modest tax, of course, easily paid, but a subject did not—*could* not—tax its *emperor*. Even the backward Swamp Kingdoms knew that, which could only mean that Dangul was testing the waters, hoping to gain greater, if not complete, independence.

In the morning he would dispatch a company of soldiers and

Jik under the command of his nephew Nen She' to deal with the governor of Dangul, but there was no telling how well prepared the governor was, how good his spies were. Another reason to send Nen She'; he would be a capable enough ruler if the governor bowed to him without resistance, but if the mission failed and he was killed, no one would miss him, either—at least, not much. But then, of course, She'lu would have to send *real* troops, and that he did not relish doing at all. Wars cost money, and it seemed the Nhol had fought many wars of late. All small, all mere nuisances, but costly nevertheless.

He walked out onto the polished, bloodred stone of the court, enjoying the measured, solitary clapping of his wooden soles upon the floor. Seldom enough was he alone; even now, guards were near, but he had laid a minor Forbidding on them, preventing them from approaching him unless he requested their aid or called out. So now, in the hour past midnight, he could pace, sleepless and finally, finally alone in this, his favorite of courts, the Court of the Ibis-Throated. It was small, much too small for grand ceremonies, not severe enough to convene the everyday matters of the empire. Indeed, since his father's day, the court had seen no official use. But after She'lu's accession—when his father had begun the *withering*, as often happened to the Waterborn when they passed their seventieth year—his father had brought him *here*, with Nyas, the vizier, and the three of them had stayed, long into the night, drinking plum wine and speaking of things they had never spoken of. There were many such things; after all, She'lu had barely *seen* his father until after his fifteenth year, and even when he moved down the Hall of Moments to join the family after passing the priestly tests, his father was distant, cold, the emperor. It was only after, when the crown came off, that the old man spoke of love, of his pride in his son, of his grief over the loss of his other son, L'ekezh. Even that last had touched She'lu; he had always been jealous of L'ekezh, but when they took his twin off, shrieking, to the depths below the Darkness Stair and left *him* to inherit the throne unchallenged—well, after that he could afford to be generous, to pity his brother.

He had often met with his father and Nyas, secretly, the guards away and Forbidden, learning from the two of them how to be an emperor. Two years only, but he remembered them as the best years of his life. Young, excited by his role as lord of Nhol and its empire, touched by his father's long-hidden care. Then the old man withered and died, and his corpse was taken off by the priests while it was still warm, to be joined back into the River, and he had become emperor in earnest, learning the eternal, wearying drudgery that mingled with and eventually over-whelmed the excitement.

He stroked his hand on a yellowed column, slender as the legs of a crane, gazed up at the stars showing faintly through the eye-shaped aperture in the domed roof.

He had thought, someday, to bring a son of his *own* here. *He* would not have waited so long, until he stepped down and had only months to live. *He* would have shown a son affection the moment he ascended to the Hall of Moments, left childhood and its terrible possibilities behind. But the seed of the River had never produced for him a son. Of late he had turned his mind toward daughters—*someone* of his blood to share his stories, his secret thoughts, who would adore him as he had adored his own father. But with the two who had ascended, he had waited too long. Both were married, and like their mother they enjoyed the cloudlike wonder and oblivion induced by Nende'ng, the black snuff from Lhe, more than they did conversation. Hezhinata, who had been the youngest, was now slain by the Jik, but that had been neces-sary, and privately he would have rather had her slain then sent down to where L'ekezh still dwelt.

She'lu paused in front of the throne but did not sit on its sable cushion. Instead, he lowered himself to the steps, as he had when his father was still alive. He had refused to let the old man sit below *him*; even though She'lu was emperor in fact, in the Court of the Ibis-Throated, he gave his father the throne. Yes, it was a shame he had never brought any of his children here, when they were young enough, even though they were daughters. He could at least have told them about their grandfather. Hezhi—if not the others—would have probably liked that. Though he knew little enough of the child, he did know that she had spent her last months in the library, that she had apparently enjoyed reading, relished learning of the past. He smiled; secretly—*very* secretly— he was proud of his daughter. She must have had *power*, power rivaling his own. Her sisters had shown no sign of such. Hezhinata had killed priests, *many* priests, and a Jik. Of course, her bodyguard had killed some of those, but still . . .

She'lu frowned. Certainly he felt pride, had felt it since the day Hezhinata was killed. But what he felt now was almost a *glow*, a silly sentimentality. He realized that *all* of his thoughts had been flavored with nearly lachrymose emotion, and a faint suspicion stole over him. Why had he awakened? Not that it was an *uncommon* experience for him to lack sleep. But it seemed to him that a dream had brought him out of bed, one of the simple-colored dreams the River sent now and then. More and more of those dreams had come of late, but rarely did they reveal anything to him that was of help in his policies. When he could remember them, he would discuss them with Nyas, and together they would try to sort them out, but this was different. He could not remember the dream itself, but it had left him thinking maudlin thoughts about his father and his daughters. No, not his daughters, but his *daughter*, Hezhinata, the only child of his to be born with power.

Thinking of this now, he recognized the signs. The River wanted him to think of her—something he was not in the habit of doing. Certainly the thought of bringing her here had *passed* briefly, whimsically, through him, as had the fleeting joy that one of his seed had so frustrated and wounded the priesthood. But these feelings of *love* came from the River. At least, most of them did. He sighed. Should he wake Nyas?

At that moment he felt something, the equivalent of a footscrape or a loud breath, but it was not sound. Someone was here, in this room, with power. She'lu pursed his lips. Not power like the priests, that annoying power of *not* that got progressively stronger with the rank of the priest. No, this had "sounded" more familiar.

He flooded the room with force, filling it so quickly with his puissance that it would be impossible for the intruder to slip away undetected. If the intruder were Human, he would be dead or mindless in an instant, but She'lu already knew the hidden one was more than that.

"Show yourself," he snapped, as the air rippled with killing magics.

Someone stepped from the shadows. He seemed to be shrugging off the attack, maintaining an admirable calm as he did so. She'lu could sense a sort of raw power that might be as great as his own, but it was artless, and he knew that his attack must be causing some pain. Despite this, his visitor walked out into the center of the floor, bent to one knee, and bowed deeply.

More puzzled than ever, She'lu withdrew the spears and nets of his strength and laid them into a dike about himself, securing his person but still prepared to lash out if need be. Who was this man? Even the most powerful of the royal family would have been at least stunned by his show of force, and yet this man retained the ability to walk and kneel.

"Thank you, my lord," the man said, and so showed he could speak as well.

"Who are you? Step closer."

The intruder did so, rising and moving close enough for She'lu to make him out. He was a well-built fellow with a thin, ascetic face. He was clothed simply in a black tunic and kilt, the signature dress of the Jik.

"You are an assassin," She'lu said flatly.

"I am an assassin," the man acknowledged. "But I am no longer a Jik. I do not serve a priesthood that does not serve the River."

She'lu stared at the man, more perplexed than ever. What was occurring here?

"I recognize you," he realized. "You were the one assigned to my daughter. The young one."

"My name is Ghe, Majesty, and I am your servant."

"You were killed, or so I heard, along with my daughter."

The man paused for just an instant, and in that flicker his guard descended a bit, and She'lu could suddenly make out more than one web of heartstrands in the man. A sudden fear knifed into She'lu. He had heard, as a child, of such creatures, been informed of them as an emperor.

"It is true that I was killed, Majesty. But your daughter was not. Of that, I pray to speak to you."

"My daugh—" *No*, damn him. First things first. "You say you died," She'lu hissed. "But I see no ghost before me. You are a ghoul, or something very like one."

The man cast down his eyes and reached to his throat. He unwrapped the black sash that obscured it. She'lu could not make out what was thus revealed until he conjured a pale yellow glow to illumine the court. Then he could see plainly enough the thick ridge of scar encircling Ghe's throat.

"A ghoul, I think," Ghe said, "though I know little of such things."

"The River sends them," She'lu said softly, wondering if it would do any good at all to call the guards. "When an emperor goes against the will of the River, he sends them to kill him."

The ghoul stroked his chin with his thumb, a remarkably Human gesture for someone who must have been decapitated and then given new, unholy life.

"I cannot speak for other ghouls, my lord, but that is not the case with me. I think that you should consider what you have heard to be yet another lie of the priesthood."

"My spies have told me of a ghoul in the palace. The priests drove it from here."

"And I have returned, at great peril to my existence. It is true that the River gave me new life, but it was not to harm you. You are the Chakunge, the Riverson. Why should he wish to harm you?" The ghoul paced slowly across the floor, and She'lu opened his mouth to speak before he realized that he was bereft of anything to say.

"It is the priesthood, my lord," the man continued. "They keep your power in check, do they not?"

"They are a nuisance," She'lu admitted.

"I have discovered that they are much more than that," the ghoul told him. "They and their temple bind all but the tenth part of the River's power, and *you* are the most of that tenth part, you and your kin. Hezhi was his greatest hope."

"Hezhinata," She'lu corrected.

"No, Lord, *Hezhi*. She lives yet. She escaped with a barbarian and her Giant bodyguard. Think on it and you will know that you never saw her body."

"The Waterborn must be given back to the River in the crypts."

"Another lie. I have been to the crypts. They are prisons for your ancestors, dungeons where their ghosts are kept to fade into eternity, *never* rejoining the god. But that aside, even if they did take Hezhi there, what of her bodyguard, the barbarian? Were *their* bodies seen by anyone you trust?"

"They were left in the desert to rot."

"But I repeat, did this information come from a source that you trust?"

She'lu's head was awhirl. The things this man spoke of were incredible, but they were not preposterous; they were all things that he himself had considered, at one time or another. His own father had warned him of the priesthood, as had Nyas, countless times. They had always been a scratch in his eye, but to hear these things said, all at once—and of *course* he had been suspicious of the strange stories surrounding Hezhinata. Seven of his elite guard, killed by some "barbarian" at the docks? She'lu had always suspected the hand of the priesthood in that. In fact, the barbarian was said to have been nearly impossible to kill, bleeding from mortal wounds and yet still standing. Was that not a property ghouls were said to possess? How many ghouls did the priesthood control?

"Enough of this," She'lu snapped. "Babble no more. If you have come to kill me, do your best. If you come for aught else, tell me what you *want*."

The ghoul scratched his chin again, a gesture that She'lu was beginning to find annoying. "I want to find Hezhi and bring her back to Nhol. I want you to help me."

She'lu could not speak for several moments, but the ghoul did not go on. The emperor vaguely realized that this "Ghe" had done what he commanded: told him only what he wanted and then stopped.

"What?" he whispered.

"I told my lord that—"

"Yes, yes, I understood you. She *really* is alive?"

"My lord, I cannot be certain. But *I* did not kill her, nor did the priests or the soldiers. She escaped into the desert, where the River has no power to see, and she may have been killed there, though, knowing her, I doubt it. But she is in danger; I know that to be true. The priesthood knows she is alive, and they will not rest until she breathes no more. There may be others." The ghoul's voice dropped lower, and She'lu heard the deep sincerity in it. "My lord, the River brought me to life for this purpose, and this purpose alone: to find your daughter and return her to the River, so that she may fulfill the destiny of you and all your family. Can't you see how carefully the priests control you? They keep you from your children, slay or bind captive all but a few who have power . . ."

"My brother was one so bound," She'lu interrupted. "He was insane, and would have destroyed all. There is good reason for that binding."

"In *some* cases. I do not doubt that the power drives many to madness. But Hezhi was his chosen, as you are, and yet they would have disposed of *her*. You, they keep tranquil with lies."

"Have a care how you speak of me!" The ghoul seemed to be getting bolder, less respectful by the moment. She'lu tensed, expecting attack but unwilling to launch his own. Despite its insolence, this creature was making a sort of sense. And the River had prepared him for this, he realized, sent ahead thoughts of his daughter, fond memories. Behind all of that lurked his ever-present knowledge that the empire was losing its form at the edges, the persistent nagging feeling that power was somehow slipping past him, that his reach was not what an emperor's *should* be.

"I'm sorry, Lord," the ghoul amended, "but I believe it to be the case. The priesthood has labored for centuries to check your power in a thousand subtle ways. Even your ghosts are kept chained."

"You mentioned this before. What do you mean?"

The ghoul suddenly began shivering, power tightening around him like a cocoon, and She'lu raised his hands reflexively. But no thrust of potence came, no claws stretched to strike at his heart. Instead, the ghoul spoke again, but in a very different voice. Not merely in timbre and intonation; the very language was different, the ancient tongue of his ancestors.

"Thou knowest this be the truth, Chakunge my descendant. We are trapped in the tombs, starved to nothing, until such time as we amuse them. Then they may take us out, command us to speak, to sing, to blaspheme. We are their library, their drama stage. They play with us, grandson of my grandsons."

"What?" She'lu sputtered. "What?"

"They keep us there, in their temple. *The Chakunge himself, the First Emperor, they keep on a leash like a dog!*"

She'lu knew that this was no trick; he could see the soul image, and it was not the ghoul's. Though he could not tell who it was, this was certainly one of his ancestors. His skin crawled like a bed of ants.

"Who are you, Lord?" he asked.

"I am Lengnata, fourth to the throne of the Nas Dynasty. Your ancestor."

"The First Emperor is in chains?"

"As I said. You, too, will be chained when you die. Only a few escape, and them the priests destroy. I myself departed only in the heart of this ghoul, and now I am slave to him. But it is better, better. For through the ghoul, I see the River has a plan to destroy the priesthood, and that is good."

"Lord Ancestor, I . . ." But the ghoul was the ghoul again.

"Pardon, my lord, but I have only recently entered into this power of mine. My control over it is growing but still imperfect."

"You admit your weakness to me?"

"If I had no weakness, I would not beg for your aid. I was made to go where the River cannot go, Lord, and where the power of his true children thus cannot go. I cannot bear his strength as you can, cannot *become* him as Hezhi can; he has given me the strength to find my power as I go along, that is all. But to go where Hezhi is, I need help. *Your* help."

"If this is all true . . ." He grimaced. "I must speak to Nyas."

The ghoul shook his head. "My lord, the Ahw'en and the Jik seek for me everywhere now. I have killed many of them and invaded their temple. I have their secrets and I have stolen one of your ancestors back from them. I have seen the Chakunge of our most sacred legends on a leash like a dog. I have power, but the priesthood can kill me. If you do not ally yourself with me, help me, all will be lost. *All.* And it must be now, quickly—*this night.*"

"Why did you not approach me sooner?"

"I did not know. We are taught that the emperor and the priesthood are warp and weft in the same cloth. Only as a ghoul have I found the truth."

She'lu drew a deep breath. This was very sudden, but if it were true, if Hezhi still lived, if she could bring back the real power and glory of the throne . . . if even an emperor must eventually suffer a fate like that of the Blessed, a fate he believed he had escaped . . .

"What do you want of me?"

The ghoul knelt again. "A fast ship, to sail up-River. Horsemen and swordsmen, as many as you can spare. But most, most of all, I need the librarian from the archives."

"Ghan? The old man?"

"He knows where Hezhi is. I *know* he does."

"How do you know this?"

"I just feel it, Lord. They were very close, he and your daughter. He helped her escape, though none knew that but me. He knows where she has gone."

"You may have him, then. And the ship, thirty mounted men, fifty foot. Will this suffice?"

"That will suffice," the ghoul answered, and She'lu could hear the surge of victory in the voice.

"But tell me," She'lu asked. "Why drag this old man out into the desert? We can torture the information from him, or merely snatch it from his brain."

The ghoul smiled thinly. "I considered that. In fact, I could swallow his soul and keep it with me, open his memories like a book. Three things stop me: first, I believe he may be canny enough to prevent it somehow; you would almost certainly never torture him, for he would kill himself in some clever way rather than be the instrument of Hezhi's capture. The second is that I believe he will be wiser alive. Those I bind to me lose much of their essence, their ability to think. They are, really, just parts of me. This Ghan is worth ten counselors if he is on your side."

"Three reasons?"

"Hezhi loves him and hates me. If Ghan is with me, she will trust us."

"But you say the librarian helped her escape. You were a Jik at the time. Why should he trust you?"

"He never knew my identity. Still, he will be suspicious, and so a series of lies must be told him . . ."

She'lu scrunched forward, forgetting for the moment that he was an emperor and this man a ghoul. Something was happening, something that might make his reign a memorable one. He could not launch an assault on the Water Temple; such had been tried in the past and only resulted in the worst sort of bloodshed. But if this creature was right, he could free not only the River but himself. Of course, he would make some provision for his own interests; he could not *trust* this stranger—all the more reason to surround him with eighty of his handpicked men. That would be a thousand times better than having him skulking about the palace. Could he keep the priesthood from finding out? Maybe. But in the palace, at least in his own section of it, the emperor was supreme.

Yes. A barge could be spared, and men. These were cheap; and if the expedition failed, he would be no worse off than before. But if it succeeded . . .

He was aware that the promise of majesty he felt was only

partly his own, that most of it surged into him from the River. The god had never, in his memory, been this strong or wakeful. Some of his ancestors might have been glad of that, happier to rule without the intervention of the divine, but She'lu did not share their sentiments. He would see Nhol strong again. Perhaps, if all went well, he would see the priesthood spitted on stakes for his pleasure. He smiled then at the ghoul.

"Come with me. Tell me what else you require."

PART TWO

UPSTREAM PASSAGES

(c) Chevot '96

XVII

Kinship

Tsem roared and swung a stool at one of the swordsmen, caught the bright edge of slicing metal on the wood. The sword snapped with a metallic cry and the Mang echoed it as the half Giant's makeshift weapon thudded into his chest. He joined his fellow on the floor of the yekt, wheezing.

For an instant there was calm, in which Hezhi desperately tried to assess the situation.

"Princess!" Tsem growled, glancing toward her, but only for an instant, for another warrior stood in the yekt, menacing them. Ngangata, his face spattered with blood, held a throwing axe in each hand, his expression that of a caged predator, driven to fury. All told, three Mang lay on the floor, two unmoving, one clutching his chest and grimly working to regain an upright stance. A fourth warrior stood just inside the doorway of the yekt, and Hezhi could see several more just outside. She recognized two of them; the one whom Tsem had just battered with the stool was Chuuzek, the surly tribesman who had met her the day before; one of the men outside was his companion, Moss.

The interior of the yekt was in total disarray; only Perkar seemed unchanged, still pale with unnatural sleep.

"Tsem, what is happening?"

"Treachery," Ngangata snapped, loudly enough for those outside to hear. "Though Brother Horse promised us hospitality, his kin seem bent on dishonoring his name."

"There is no honor in harboring monsters," Chuuzek gasped, already up on one knee. Tsem stepped quickly forward and slapped the man's broad face with the half-curled back of his hand, and Chuuzek sprawled back, spitting blood. A cloth bandage on his head, caked with old blood, began to dampen with new wet redness as well.

Moss stepped into the doorway. "Chuuzek! Stop!" he shouted, the first time Hezhi had heard the young man raise his voice. Chuuzek, fumbling for a knife at his belt, ceased, and instead scooted back against the wall of the yekt.

Moss took another step in, eyes intent on Hezhi. "There is no need for this," he asserted. "These friends of yours need not die."

"So far we aren't the ones dying," Ngangata remarked. Hezhi had never seen *him* in such a state, either. He was normally so mild, deflecting insults or ignoring them.

"It's not to you that I am speaking, Brush-Man," Moss replied.

"I don't understand any of this," Hezhi groaned, and then more firmly, "Get out of this house. *All* of you, go away!"

Moss frowned. "I would not have chosen this," he said. "My cousin acted hastily, but his motives were pure. You *must* come with us."

"I *must* do nothing," Hezhi snarled. "Yesterday you spoke of hospitality. What did you say? 'I'm only sorry the hospitality of this camp was violated.' Fine words, but I see now which hole they issued from. Not from your mouth, *that* much is certain."

Chuuzek stirred again angrily.

"Stand back up, little man," Tsem growled. "I will break your neck."

"You cannot break *all* of our necks," Chuuzek returned.

"He does not have to!" came an angry voice from outside. "Move out of my way, all of you, you worthless carrion dogs!"

Hezhi saw the look of consternation, quickly mastered, flash over Moss' face. Reluctantly he stepped back as a burst of shouting from outside was followed by sudden silence. Brother Horse came shouldering into the tent, swept furious eyes over the scene. His short, spindly legs and wizened body no longer seemed in the least comical or kindly; the old man bore his rage in every angle of his stance, spat it in each terse syllable. The wolf she had seen inside of him now shone out like a candle through a red paper lantern.

"Get out of here," he said to Chuuzek softly. "Get out of my house, and take these piles of buzzard dung with you." He kicked one of the dead or unconscious men with the toe of his boot.

"Now we see," Chuuzek said. "We see the great man cares more for his dun'cheen friends than he does for his own people."

"I care," Brother Horse gritted, "more for the ways of the *Mang*—the *Mang*, you whelp of a cur and a turd—than I do for your insolent disregard of all we know. I promised these people hospitality, and you steal that from me, you thief. You *horse* thief!"

Which was about the worst thing one Mang could call another. Raiding and robbing others was war—and acceptable—but stealing from one who gave you hospitality was one of the worst offenses conceivable.

"Perhaps you want her for yourself, old man."

Brother Horse ignored Chuuzek. He swept his gaze over Tsem, Ngangata, Perkar, and Hezhi. "Are you injured, child? Has any one of you been hurt?"

"I'm fine," Hezhi answered. "I don't know about Tsem and Ngangata. I just . . . awoke."

"We are not injured," Ngangata answered. "No true harm has been done . . . yet."

"No *harm*?" Chuuzek roared. "My cousins lie there thus, and you say no harm has been done?"

"They *begged* for their fate," Brother Horse answered venomously. "Were they—and you—not protected by the same hospitality that protects these others, I would have you all on the frame, screaming for days on end."

"I would spit in your face."

"Brave talk," Brother Horse answered him. "You have never been on the frame; *I* have." He turned to Moss. "You had my answer yesterday. You may seek to turn all of this on your rock-brained cousin, but I know better."

"I warned you," Moss said quietly. "I respect you greatly, and I understand your position. If you had let us take her, you would not have been dishonored; the onus would have been shouldered only by Chuuzek and myself. You need only have been too long engaged elsewhere. As it is . . ." He signed with his hand and four more warriors crowded up to the doorway.

Brother Horse shook his head. "You would slay *me*, in my own house, during the Ben'cheen? You are not Mang."

"We do what must be done," Moss answered. "We will bear the dishonor. Please don't make us bear the responsibility of your death as well, honored one."

"The warriors of my clan are just behind you. Make another move, and you shall wear a coat of arrows."

Moss smiled grimly. "You mistake your own family. These warriors have agreed to stand aside. They will not aid me, but neither will they aid you. I have spoken with them all."

"Yes, well, I have spoken with them all, as well, and I *told* them to answer you thus. I wanted to see how far down this wrong, waterless trail you would stumble. Now I know."

Hezhi wished she could have laughed at the sudden understanding on Moss' face, but her heart was still thudding too painfully in her chest. Too much happening, too much. First the mountain and then, with no letup, this.

The green-eyed man seemed to sag slightly, but then he recovered himself.

"You will regret this," he said sincerely. Not with heat, but with a kind of sadness.

"I regret much in my life," Brother Horse murmured. "This will not greatly add to my burden, I'm sure."

"In that you are mistaken," Moss assured him.

Brother Horse merely shrugged and slapped his hands. Men came from behind and seized Moss and his kin roughly.

"Watch them," Brother Horse called to his men. "Disarm them but do them no harm. They *are* protected by my word, and I will not break that word."

Two men came in to get the bodies. Chuuzek managed to leave under his own power. Brother Horse grimly watched them go before turning to examine those he protected.

"I'm sorry," he said. "I didn't think things would go this far."

"You knew," Hezhi stated.

"Yes. I knew when I saw you with them in the desert. They *meant* to take you then, would have if I had not been present. Moss is honorable at heart, and thought to persuade me rather than slay me. It was a very near thing, though. Did you notice the way Chuuzek kept fondling his sword-grip?"

"No," Hezhi admitted. "But I knew something was wrong."

"Something is *very* wrong," Brother Horse agreed.

"Thank you for your help," Tsem said. "Thank you for protecting Hezhi."

Brother Horse eyed the half Giant. "I had no choice, so there is no need to thank me."

"I think you *did* have a choice," Ngangata disagreed. "Moss was right; had you turned your back, they could have taken us and no one would have faulted you."

Brother Horse grinned tightly. "We work to keep the good opinion of our elders, but none here is my elder. That leaves me in the unfortunate position of having to stay clean in my own eyes."

"They would have killed Perkar," Ngangata answered, his tone still conveying thanks.

"They would have killed you all, all but me," Hezhi added.

Tsem nodded. "They must have known you were ill and come to take you while you lay asleep."

"Ill?"

"Princess, you have lain as dead for a day."

That long? But it had seemed even longer.

"She was not dead," Brother Horse said. "You bled into the lake, didn't you."

"Yes."

He sighed. "Yes. I wish I could have been with you, to help you."

Hezhi held her hands up. "You were here when we needed you most, I think. What should we do now?" She surveyed her companions helplessly.

"Princess, that is your decision," Tsem quietly responded.

She thought that Brother Horse or Ngangata would disagree—hoped they would—but to her surprise they did not, only watched her expectantly.

"I . . ." She stared back at them. "*I* don't know what to do. We can't stay here anymore, though, can we?"

Brother Horse pursed his lips. "I never anticipated any of this. I offered you a life in this village, with my people, and yet . . ."

"We've been nothing but trouble to you," Hezhi finished.

The old Mang grimaced. "It's this war, and something else, something Moss wouldn't explain to me completely."

"He said I could bring peace."

"Yes, he told me that, as well, but wouldn't explain how. I don't think he knows."

"In any event, we have to leave," Ngangata said. "We have to get Hezhi and Perkar away from here. They seem almost as bent upon killing *him* as upon snatching her."

"What do you mean?" Hezhi asked.

"We were set upon by warriors out on the plains. They came to kill Perkar."

Brother Horse waved his hand. "They are Mang, he is a Cattle-Man, and we are at war."

"No, it was more than that. They were seeking *him* specifically, and no other."

"It's because Perkar knows where we should go," Hezhi broke in suddenly. "Karak told him."

Brother Horse stretched a grim smile. "What do you mean, 'where you should go'?"

"I . . . I don't know," Hezhi realized. "There is something I'm supposed to do, but I don't know what."

"You learned this on the other side of the drum?"

Hezhi nodded thoughtfully.

"Well, let me warn you that if you have only the word of the Blackgod, then you have little worth trusting."

"He has only aided *me*," Hezhi said.

"When he set me to watch for you at Nhol?"

"No, since then."

Brother Horse raised his eyebrows in surprise but did not inquire further.

"He works for his own purposes, that much is certain," Ngangata said. "But he helped us against the warriors on the plains, too. He seems to have cultivated a liking for our little family."

"How quickly do we have to leave?" Hezhi asked, mustering as much determination to put in her voice as she could.

"Tonight would be best," Brother Horse admitted sadly. "We can hold Moss and Chuuzek and the rest for a few days, give you an escort and a head start to wherever you are going. Beyond that, my own people will begin to rebel at the thought of holding their cousins captive. Young people these days don't respect the old as they should."

Hezhi nodded solemnly. "Ngangata, can Perkar travel?"

"Can you heal him?" the halfling countered.

"I don't know how."

"Well," the half man considered. "We can tie him to a horse, but that will slow us. It would be better if he could ride."

"Put some distance between yourselves and the village first," Brother Horse advised. "Then I believe I can show Hezhi what to do. She has the power now."

He was looking at her strangely, deeply, and Hezhi understood that the old man could see what the others could not, the change in her.

"You will go with us?" she asked him.

"I will accompany you long enough to help with that. Afterward . . . well, there look to be many affairs that need my attention."

Hezhi took a deep breath. "Running again. Always running."

Tsem moved up to stroke her hair, and his tenderness awoke

buried tears. She did not shed them, but they crowded into her throat and threatened to cut off her air.

"Well," she gasped, "where shall we run? I know nothing of these lands." Her pleading gaze fastened first on Brother Horse and then on Ngangata.

"North, perhaps," Brother Horse muttered. "North, across the Changeling, or perhaps east. Away from all of this."

Hezhi sat on her mat. "Away. At first it seemed that just leaving Nhol was 'away.' Now . . . what lies north and east?"

"Ah . . . plains, forests, mountains. North, Human Beings are scarce. East are the Stone Leggings and other tribes. Giants northeast eventually. Beyond that I don't know."

"We can't cross the Changeling," Ngangata stated, his voice solid with certainty.

"No. No, of course." Images of distant lands where no one knew or cared about Hezhi faded as soon as they formed. Was there such a place, anyway? A place where her blood would merely lie quiet and the River was not even a legend? Probably not.

"We'll go where Perkar said to," Hezhi mumbled. "Where the Blackgod said to."

"Where?"

"We'll go to the mountain."

Ngangata frowned. "Princess, I—"

Hezhi stared at him, suddenly angry. "I know. I know he flows from there. But that is the only compass we have at the moment. If any of you has a better suggestion, tell me or decide for me. But if you want *me* to decide . . ."

Ngangata shifted uncomfortably. "The war is there. We would only be plunging into the heart of things."

Brother Horse cleared his throat. "I know of a camp, up in the White Crown Mountains. It should be far from any such troubles."

"If you know of it," Hezhi retorted, "it is certain that other Mang know of it. Besides, this gaan seems to be able to smell me wherever I am. He knew to send Moss and Chuuzek here."

"*That* could be coincidental, Princess," Tsem pointed out.

"No. They came straight to where I was, in the cliffs. I was in a closed-off canyon, wasn't I, Brother Horse? What reason would they have for going in there?"

"They might have seen you on the plain, wondered who you were," the old man muttered.

"You don't believe that," Hezhi answered.

He shrugged his bony shoulders. "No."

"If we go out into the desert and hide, they find us without you and your kin to protect us. If we go back to Nhol, the same fate that I fled awaits me. The same, too, if I try to cross the River. Twice now I have been told to go the mountain. That would at least put us in Perkar's homeland, where *his* people might protect us, would it not?"

Ngangata nodded wearily. "Yes. But that is a hard journey, by land, and we have to cross the country where the war is being fought."

"One of you decide, then," she said.

Tsem snorted. "You great men, you horsemen, you hunters. My princess has lived in these lands for half a year, you for your whole lives. Can't either of you think of anything?"

Brother Horse scratched his chin. "Only that she is right," he admitted.

"That's all?" Tsem snapped—audibly, as his nut-size teeth cracked together on his last syllable.

"Listen, Giant," Brother Horse suddenly blazed. "She is not a princess here. There are no armies waiting to march at her command. There are no kings on the huugau. Would that there were and I were one. I would surround her with my soldiers and a wall of stone and *make* her safe. But this is Mang country, do you understand? I have no soldiers, only kinfolk, and I have to spend as much time trying to please them as they to please me. And if I tell them to do something they are set hard enough against, they *will* ignore me. Then I lose face and power, and the next time listen to me even less. Those men you killed today have relatives in my own clan. They will not forget you, or *her*, or *me*, for not giving you up. I have few enough years left to live, and I had hoped to live them in comfort, but that dream withers in the sun now. So don't you upbraid me for not being able to do what no man can do!"

Tsem's eyes widened with startlement, but his face stayed set. "I'll kill anyone else who tries to touch her, too," he said. "So you better help us get away from here, before I have to break more of your precious kinsmen and make your old age even *more* uncomfortable."

"Tsem," Hezhi said softly. "Hush. He has already helped us, don't you understand?"

"No. I don't understand why they can't let you be. You've already . . . we've already . . ." Tsem suddenly bent and ground his face into the wall, shuddering.

Hezhi's gut wrenched. "Tsem!"

The Giant moaned and thrust his hand back, motioning her away.

"He must have been wounded," Ngangata muttered. "I didn't see—"

"No," Tsem croaked. "Not wounded."

Hezhi understood then. The half Giant was crying.

"Please," she said to Ngangata and Brother Horse. "Please get the horses together, or whatever. If we have to leave, we have to leave. But could the two of you make the arrangements?"

The old Mang nodded, but Ngangata hung back stubbornly.

"I will watch Perkar," she assured him. "I'll watch him."

After a moment the half man nodded curtly and followed Brother Horse from the yekt.

Hezhi approached Tsem and laid her hand on his massive ribs.

"I've never seen you cry," she whispered.

"I don't mean to," he wheezed. "It's just that . . . why can't they leave you *alone*?"

"Shh."

"I saw how the priests hurt you, in Nhol, and I could do nothing. I saw the horror that never left your face, after you went down into that place, that place under the sewers. And then I could do nothing. Finally—"

"Finally you helped me escape the most terrible fate anyone could imagine."

"Yes, and had to be carried away from Nhol on my back. *I* know who saved *whom* back in Nhol, Princess."

She knelt, and hot tears were starting in her own eyes. "Listen to me, Tsem. You *did* save me, just not the way you think. I almost . . ." Became a goddess? Razed Nhol to its foundations? Would that have been so bad, looking back?

"I almost became something terrible," she finished. "You saved me."

"I don't remember that. How could I have done that?"

"Just by being Tsem. By loving me."

"Ah. I thought you wanted me to *stop* crying."

"I don't care if you cry," she soothed. But she *did*. Even wounded, Tsem had not seemed so feeble to her. He had always been her wall, her strength. Wounded, he had merely been awaiting repair, being rebuilt to be her tower again. But this struck her down to the bone, all the way down. She was really alone here, in this place. She had to be her own strength, and even Giants couldn't protect her now.

She hated herself, but she wished he hadn't cried. She wished he had kept it in, wept to the wind later. But he hadn't, and now she knew, and she loved him enough not to tell him what he had done: that he had made it all worse.

"Come on," she whispered. "We have to get ready to go. The world awaits us."

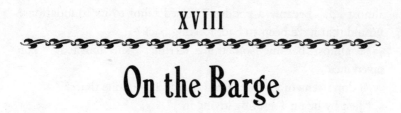

XVIII

On the Barge

A bright clattering of gulls blew through the door as the old man stepped into the darkened cabin. He stood for a moment, silhouetted in a rectangle of sunlight, a breeze that smelled like water and iron seeping past his body. Ghe motioned him in.

"You," Ghan grunted. "What do *you* have to do with all of this?"

"My father has more influence than I ever told anyone," Ghe answered, secretly amused by his joke. In his heart of hearts, his father was the River.

"Enough to command the use of a royal barge? Don't lie to me, boy."

Ghe sighed and stood politely, smoothing the hem of his dark green robe. He motioned for the librarian to sit on the pillows heaped about the cabin. Ghan ignored the motion, stubbornly continuing to stand on the slowly rocking deck.

"Yes, then, you've seen through me," Ghe admitted. "Please sit down. Have a measure of coffee."

"I don't intend to stay."

Ghe shook his head. "As you imply, you and I are in the grip of powers greater than ourselves. The emperor's soldiers are still outside, and I doubt that I can persuade them to leave." Ghe was amazed at the strength of the old man. He could sense the cloud of fear and uncertainty about him, and yet his face and manner betrayed no such sentiments. A worthy opponent and a needed ally.

"But you know what this is all about?" Ghan asked, eyeing him critically.

"Indeed. As do you, I expect."

"Hezhi," the old man said dully, reaching to pinch the folds of his brow with one hand.

"Hezhi? Not 'Hezhinata'?"

Ghan's only answer was a glare.

"She is in danger, you know. Master Ghan, she is in deadly danger."

Ghan folded his thin arms across his chest like a hedge of bone, protecting him. "Danger."

"Please sit down, Master Ghan. I tire of standing myself."

Ghan pursed his lips in undisguised frustration and then, with a slight nod, settled onto one of the felted pillows. He appeared uncomfortable, sitting without a desk in his lap, a book splayed open before him. Ghe smiled reassuringly, bent, and poured coffee from a silver urn into twin porcelain cups. He offered one to Ghan, who took it almost without seeming to notice. His attention was focused entirely on Ghe, as if he were trying to peer through his clothing to the lies they hid, through the scarf about his throat to the impossible scar.

"Tell me what danger," Ghan demanded.

"From whom else? From the priesthood."

"The priesthood?"

"It has come to the attention of the emperor that the priesthood plans an expedition to search for her."

"Search for her? Why?"

"Who knows what purposes hide behind their robes and masks? But the emperor believes that it has to do with the Royal Blood."

"Away from the River, she is no danger to them."

"I know little of these matters, Master Ghan. I am only the son of a merchant, an engineer at best. What I do know is that what is true or false is of no consequence to the priesthood. Set in motion, they are like a stone falling. What remains beneath them is crushed. For whatever reason, we know they seek her. Furthermore, we believe that they know where she is."

"They could not."

"Couldn't they? They have been sending out spies for the better part of a year. They have been working their sorcery, watching the stars."

"All of this the emperor told you."

Ghe held out his hands. "I did not, of course, have an audience with the Chakunge himself. But his minister spoke to me, after I made my concerns known."

"Your concerns?"

Ghe nodded vigorously. "Oh, yes. The priests talk, and the careful ear ensnares their words. I have heard things."

"Why were you researching the temple?"

"A false trail. I believed that they actually had her captive in their sanctum."

"They do not."

"You seem certain of that," Ghe observed.

Ghan tightened his mouth, realizing that he had said too much.

Ghe leaned over the coffee urn and spoke intently. "The emperor knows, Master Ghan, that you helped his daughter escape the city. He has been watching you, hoping for some sign that you know her whereabouts."

"And you were the spy?"

"One of them, Master. Please understand, it was from my concern for *her*."

Ghan frowned sharply. "What is this all about? If you wish me to confess some crime, I will not. I have no patience for these courtly games."

"This is no game, Master. In the morning, this barge swims upstream to search for the daughter of our emperor. Unlike the priesthood, we have no idea of where she is, save north and away. You can help us."

"I do not know where she is."

"You do. Assuredly, Master Ghan, you do."

"Torture it from me, then."

"The emperor won't do that. At least, he said he would not. He wants your cooperation and your loyalty. You are dear to Hezhi, and it is important that she believe in our good intentions when we do find her."

"You aren't—" Ghan's face registered shock for the first time. His mouth actually dropped open. "You aren't *really* suggesting that I go *with* you on this mad search?"

"But that is *precisely* what I am saying."

"Out of the question! The library—"

"The emperor has actually been considering *sealing* the library. It has been the center of much trouble, of late."

"*Sealing* the library?"

Ghe sipped his coffee, let the implicit threat sink in. A mask of fury settled on Ghan's face and then quickly vanished.

"I see," he clipped.

"Perhaps only temporarily, until you return." He regarded his coffee cup once more. "There has also been talk of restoring certain names in the capital, of ending certain exiles."

Ghan was nodding his head now. The sweetmeat and the rotten pear were both on the plate before him. Ghan's family was in exile and had been for decades; only his intense love of the library kept him in Nhol. The simultaneous threat to close the library and promise to reinstate his clan had to be a powerful combination.

"No purse is large enough to make me a whore," the old man declared almost inaudibly, eyes nearly shuttered by his angry lids.

"Those were the emperor's words, *his* promises and threats," Ghe whispered. "*These* are mine. I love Hezhi, Master Ghan, and I know you do, as well. You helped her once, at gravest risk to your own life and everything you hold close and dear. Help me help her. When we find her, I promise you—I swear to you—that whatever pleases her, we shall do. The emperor wants her back here, but *I* want what is best for her. And she must be warned, at the very least, about the determination of the priesthood. At the *least*."

"You are mad. This entire city is mad, the nightmare of a brutish, sleeping god."

"What does that mean? Do you mean to wish away the world as it is and replace it with one you imagine? If so, you must cease merely reading your books and *do* something. Come with me, Master Ghan."

For the first time, Ghan raised his coffee to his lips, and in an instant—like the batting of an eye—Ghe sensed his fear and hesitation vanish. Replaced by . . . Ghe's new senses were like smell. Fear he had scented often enough to know it. This was something he did not know.

"I must have certain books. I must have maps."

"You are free to return with the soldiers to the library. They will help you carry anything you need. You accept, then? I can relay that to the emperor?"

"You may tell him I will accompany you."

"I will tell the captain, when he boards."

"You are not the commander here?"

"As you say, Lord Ghan, one so lowly as I cannot command a royal expedition. A noble will be placed in command. But you and I will lead them, will we not?"

Ghan did not answer. Instead, he stood shakily. "I wish to gather my things now."

"Very well. The emperor thanks you."

"I'm sure."

"And I thank you." Ghe was surprised to find that his voice rang sincere, even in his own jaded ears.

SUNLIGHT sheathed the streets in molten copper, beat them bright and hot as Ghan trod across cobbles worn smooth by a hundred generations of feet. Last time he had walked this path, it had also been to board a boat, to arrange passage for Hezhi to his kindred in the Swamp Kingdoms and thence to far-off Lhe.

In hindsight, that had been a poor plan. Not only because it had not succeeded—the boat had been attacked by members of the same royal elite who now escorted him—but because in Lhe the priesthood would have found Hezhi easily, had they cared to look. In the Mang Wastes, finding *anyone* would be no easy task.

For weeks and then months he had awaited the writ of the executioner, sure that in the chaos of Hezhi's escape he had been found out. If the arrangements at the docks were known to the emperor, then surely the *arranger* was known, as well. But the writ had never come, and his old head remained where it had been for sixty-three earthly years, bobbing about on a neck that sometimes seemed too thin to support its weight. Now was such a time.

If he weren't in such terrible danger, he might be amused that the emperor and his servants could so deeply underestimate him. They believed that their courtly intrigues were so complex, so deeply cunning, that they could shift Human Beings about like the markers in a game of *Na*. Perhaps they shifted each other around so, but *he* was a scholar. He could see through their pitiful, dull machinations as if they were sheerest silk. Not every detail, perhaps, not yet, but he could see the shape of something beneath that thin skirt, and it was not the curved courtesan he was *expected* to see.

Who was Yen? That he did not know, but he was no merchant's son. His accent, while passable, was all wrong. His manner, his pretense of submissive cooperation was poorly acted indeed; they hoped to disguise a deeper haughtiness. None of this had mattered before now, and thus he had simply not expended the mental energy to make these connections. But since Yen's reappearance, his questions about Hezhi, his research on the Great Water Temple, Ghan was forced to reevaluate everything about the young man. Now that he set his mind to it—a finely tuned instrument, even now—it was clear to him that Yen had pretended from the first moment. His intention had always been to be near Hezhi. That made it likely—almost certain, in fact—that it had been *Yen* set to watch her, *Yen* who betrayed her, and who now sought to redress his error in allowing her to escape. And so Hezhi *was* in danger. Yen's suggestion that her peril came from the priesthood was probably a lie—unless the expedition the man was assembling was created by the priesthood. That was a logical conclusion—after all, those set to watch royal children were usually Jik assassins and therefore of the priestly order. Yet these were unquestionably the emperor's elite escorting him, and it seemed improbable that the emperor and the priesthood would work together on anything.

Anything, that is, save perhaps in the containment of one of the Waterborn. The priesthood and the emperor were of one mind on that, and only that. And perhaps they knew something Ghan did not, something about Hezhi's power or potential that moved both parties to cooperate above and beyond the norm.

So, Ghan thought as he passed the ever-grander house walls lining the street, *best assume it is both of them. The emperor and the priesthood, but only I know where Hezhi might be.*

And so this elaborate tale to convince him. Well, he *was* convinced. If he resisted, they might find some way to force him to tell. If he pretended to be duped by their moronic ruse, then he could do something. *Something.*

But what?

AFTER Ghan departed, Ghe sat brooding in the cabin. He wished to leave the narrow confines of the living quarters, to pace the proud decks of the barge, meet the sailing men who would carry him up-River. But by now, surely, the priesthood had gotten wind of *something*. He knew well how deeply the palace was penetrated by the eyes of the temple, and this movement of men and supplies to one of the barges must have raised at least a few suspicious hackles. If *he* were seen, they would know for certain what was afoot, and whatever story was being circulated about the purpose of the expedition would be known as false. He was commanded by the emperor to remain cloistered until the barge was well away from Nhol.

It was a wise command, and therefore he heeded it. And so, instead of following his desires, he explored the world he was allowed, for the moment. That meant the little cluster of rooms at the rear of the barge which, from *off* of the boat, resembled an elegant, spacious mansion.

Inside, that apparent grandeur was seen as illusion, though the design of the cabins was essentially the same as a suite of rooms in the palace. His cabin opened directly onto the central deck, but it also had an entrance into a courtyard, of sorts. It was a small, narrow imitation of the ones in the palace, but it served the same purpose, allowing fresh air into the cabins arranged about it, especially those that crowded to the edges of the barge and could not thus open onto the deck. In all, four cabins similar to his own opened into the yard—relatively capacious rooms, furnished with colorful rugs and pillows, beds of down-stuffed linen. There were two much larger spaces, but those stacked sleeping shelves so that ten men could room in each. The whole complex was sunken into the deck on the rear end of the ship, and Ghe knew that there was another such cluster of rooms forward, but all of those were crowded ones, built to accommodate sailors and soldiers. The floor of the cabins was the bottom hull of the barge; the surface of the deck set a half a man's length higher to provide protected space for cargo.

Ghe wandered through the various rooms, noting their furnishings, access, and escape routes. He always preferred to know every way by which a room could be exited. One of the larger cabins, he discovered, had a latched access to the cramped cargo space that ran the length of the barge between the two "houses" at each end. After a moment's pause, he shucked his expensive robe—it had come with the cabin—and entered the dark space, clad in only the brief cotton cloth that wrapped twice around his waist and once to cover his crotch and in the scarf tied about his neck. Unused as he was to fine clothing like the robe, he did not want to soil it in his explorations.

In a deep crouch, he wandered curiously about the hold. Light streamed through a pair of open hatches and through the occasional perforations in the bulwarks at floor level that would drain rainwater or any other inundation that might tend to flood the barge or stand in the hold. Several sailors stood in the hatches, shuttling a few remaining items into storage. Though there was no particular need to, Ghe avoided them, padding through the shadowed crates and bags, identifying them by their markings: food, rope, assorted trade goods if they needed them. In addition, Ghe knew, there were sealed packs of arrows, spare edged weapons, extra boots and clothing for cooler climates. Finally, wrapped carefully and stored separately, a number of the head-size pitch balls that the catapult mounted abovedeck could fling at any vessel that might oppose them.

The horses were not on board yet, but Ghe found and wandered through the maze of stalls, wondering how such large beasts would be able to stand imprisonment that scarcely allowed them a pace to move in. This part of the hold was also open to the sky, though canopied in good weather with an elevated tarp. He wound through the stalls in the suffuse light that bled through the canvas, and though the deck was clean to a polish, he smelled the faint, musky odor of beasts. He found where the bulwark could be opened to let the animals on and off and marked it in his memory for his own possible use.

It seemed, to Ghe, a well-equipped expedition. Fifty footmen—most of them elite—thirty horse, himself, an engineer, the captain, whoever he was—and Ghan. Yes, it seemed a force to be reckoned with, but then, what did *he* know of that? What sort of dangers might they meet? He would have to talk—to Ghan, to the sailors who had been up-River before. Despite the tales he had told Hezhi, Ghe himself had never been more than a league beyond the walls of the city.

He could summon the ancient lord living in his belly to his lips, he supposed, ask *him* a thing or two. He could reach vague understandings with his ghosts without empowering them. But to deal with them specifically, he had to give them his voice to speak in.

Though he could now summon and banish them at will, still he disliked hearing his voice chattering without his leave. No, he would save that summoning for later, when he had learned what he could from the living.

There was some change above him; the faint cadence of work songs, the thudding of feet on the heavy planks died away into silence, and replacing that, the faint tones of a single voice.

This must be my captain, Ghe thought wryly. He considered once more that this might all be some elaborate trick, that the emperor had merely devised a ruse to rid himself of a dangerous ghoul. It would make more sense, in many ways, than the scenario he seemed to find himself in. Hiding like a spider in the rich cabin of one of the emperor's own barges, the elite guard obeying his orders? Much since his rebirth had been painted with the gray and blue of nightmare. Even moments of success and joy would suddenly flatten into something akin to terror when he remembered that he was, after all, dead. Here was one such moment, mocking even this achievement. A gutter scorp from Southtown on a royal barge . . .

He had taken the risk, and he believed he had won. *Had* to believe it, for the nightmare reached its nadir in the Water Temple. Returning again from oblivion, awakening in a canal with priests and Jik swarming in search of him, he had known that without powerful help his mission was doomed. He would fail against whatever that *thing* was that held the first emperor himself on a leash. Ghe was not the only inhuman creature walking in Nhol, nor the most powerful. Only the emperor himself was an ally worthy of that thing, and Ghe had known, then, that it was his to win the emperor or win nothing at all.

But the Chakunge was a man as well as a god, a *living* man, and as such had a natural abhorrence for Ghe and what *he* was. Perhaps the expedition was meant to go on, but *he* was not.

If so, however, the emperor should have had him extinguished in the palace, for here, floating on the very skin of the River, Ghe was in the flower of his strength. Even the gnawings of hunger stayed distant, an occasional irritation, but nothing he need feed.

This was fortunate, since on a ship with only eighty people, he could not sate his hunger without being noticed.

So, with the barest hesitation, he threaded softly back to the entrance to the cabin, lifted the board aside, and entered.

"What sort of ship's rat is this?" a voice purred softly. A woman's voice. Ghe whirled, wondering how he could have been so preoccupied.

She stood there, regarding his condition of undress with obvious amusement. Thick, sensual lips bowed faintly at the corners of a narrow, tapered face. Opalescent eyes shimmered with amusement, curiosity—perhaps cruelty, as well. Her hair, bound up with a comb, was black, but unlike that of most of the nobility, it was not straight but instead slightly wavy, like his own—usually a sign of lower-than-noble birth.

Her clothing carried a message quite different from her features and hair, however. Though not ostentatious, her dress was of *jeh*, a fiber much like silk but rarer yet, available *only* to Blood Royal.

"Well?" she asked, and he realized he had not answered her. "What cause have you to skulk in my quarters? And what sort of apparel is this, loincloth and neck-wrap? Some new fashion in the court I haven't learned of yet?"

"A-ah," Ghe replied, all but successfully avoiding a stammer. "You must pardon me, Lady. If you will hand me my robe, I will don it."

"*Your* robe?"

"Yes. I did not wish to stain it inspecting the cargo."

"I see." Her gaze fastened on his scarf, and the amusement faded a bit, replaced by . . . fascination? An odd gleam in her eye, anyway. "You are Yen."

"I am he."

Only the emperor and perhaps Nyas, his advisor, knew Ghe's real name. Easiest to hide his identity from Ghan if *he* were the only one avoiding mistakes.

"Well, I think we expected you to be dressed to receive us. I do not stand on such formalities—with men, anyway—but Lord Bone Eel *shall*, I think." She stooped and handed him the robe, which he stepped into immediately. She was slight though not particularly short. Young.

"I was expecting only Bone Eel," Ghe said, frowning, trying to understand the faint buzz of emotion emanating from her, and failing.

"*Lord* Bone Eel is my husband. I am the Lady Qwen Shen."

"Oh. I was not informed." He stopped and bowed what he thought to be the appropriate bow, and she did not laugh outright.

"You will be accompanying us?" he asked when he straightened.

"Yes, of course. I could not let my husband stray far from my sight. Servants will be along soon with my clothes. I only wanted to see my quarters."

"Well, then," Ghe answered. "I hope that you approve."

"Oh, I don't," she said. "They are drab and cramped, and I detest them already."

"Except when it rains, a pavilion will be erected for you on deck," Ghe informed her. "I have seen such pavilions, and they are much more comfortable than these rooms." Though he thought his cabin was very nice indeed, compared to anywhere *he* had ever lived, or to the crowded common rooms the soldiers must make do with.

"Well, it isn't raining now. Come up on deck and greet my husband."

"Unfortunately, I am under direct orders from the emperor himself to remain here until the voyage begins. I regret the inconvenience, but the lord must come below to meet me."

"He won't like that, even though he must come down here anyway. He prefers for his men to greet him on the deck."

"Once again," Ghe said, "I must apologize. But I must also do the emperor's bidding."

"Yes, you must, I suppose," she replied indifferently. Her mood had changed; whatever interest and amusement she might have found in him earlier departed. "Well." She brightened. "Perhaps I will go see about having that pavilion erected."

There came a clumping behind them, as someone descended

from the upper deck. "I have seen to it already," a man's voice assured her. Ghe turned, not caught unaware this time.

"Lord Bone Eel," he replied, bowing a degree or so lower than he had for Qwen Shen.

"Yes, yes, enough bowing. We are shipmates, and you will find that on board ship there is less of that *stifling* formality we have in the city."

"Yes, Lord," Ghe replied, trying to get the captain's measure.

He already knew a thing or two, of course. The highest nobility, those in the immediate family of the Chakunge, were all named so that water was actually mentioned in their names. It was the next tier down, the secondary nobility, who tended to be named for creatures *of* the water. He thus knew Bone Eel to be well removed from the line to the throne, but not as far removed as the most minor nobility, who were named for creatures that lived *around* but not *in* the River, such as the little whelp who had courted Hezhi. Wezh, whose name meant "gull."

Bone Eel *looked* like a captain. He was tall and striking, his profile hewn from a strong stone but polished to perfection. His hair was straight, glossy black, and worn cropped like a helmet at his ears. He was dressed in a simply cut but elegant yellow sarong and a sailor's loose shirt, umber with bluish turtles batiked upon it. A scabbarded sword hung casually from a broad leather belt.

"You are Yen, the diplomat of whom the emperor informed me?"

Diplomat? "Yes," he answered cautiously. "I am Yen."

"And who do we wait for now? This scholar, Ghem?"

"Ah, *Ghan*, my lord," he corrected. "And he will join us sometime hence."

"Well, let's hope he arrives soon. I wish to be under way before nightfall."

"Nightfall? I thought we were to leave by morning."

"As did I," Bone Eel replied, his mouth flattening into a grim line. "But the emperor said that we were to take no priests on this journey, you see?" By his look he clearly took for granted that Ghe *did* see.

"No, Lord, I'm sorry, I don't." Ghe was beginning to feel a certain irritation with the man. He let his gaze wander inside the captain's chest, thought idly about just *stroking* the strands there, the way one might stroke a harp. But the time for that would probably come soon enough, not now. He must have patience, for there was much he did not know. If he had learned anything at all in the past days, it was that impulsive actions were not always wise ones.

"No? Well, ships are *supposed* to carry at least one priest, and they are raising a mighty hue and cry about this barge leaving without one. We must be under way before things become too noisy."

"Oh." Ghe wondered if the Ahw'en were behind this—if they suspected—or if it was just the usual petty political war waged daily in the palace courts.

"In any event, I am ready to go!" Bone Eel exclaimed, his deep voice tinged with enthusiasm. "Too long have I been a prisoner of land. I'm ready to feel the River beneath my feet again."

"And how long has it been since your last voyage?" Ghe inquired.

"Oh, it's been—well, let me see . . ." He ticked off one finger, then the next, frowning.

"It's been five years," Qwen Shen put in sweetly. She beamed at Ghe, but he thought perhaps there was a hidden glare in the expression.

"*That* long?" Bone Eel muttered. "Yes, too long indeed."

Bone Eel continued to agree with himself as he went back above.

XIX

Drum Battle

A wind slanted out of the east with the dawn, and Hezhi leaned into it, let it relieve her weary muscles of some small part of the task of supporting her. She was listing in the saddle anyway, worn out in more ways than she knew, and she could almost imagine that the wind, fragrant with its scent of sage and juniper, was a pillow, nestling against her, welcoming her to sleep.

Her body may have lain as *if* asleep while she traveled the skies, but it had apparently received no rest. After the fight and the discussion—after her decision—they had wasted little time, slipping from the camp while the sky was still an inky beast with a thousand eyes. Now they were more than a league from the Mang camp, the most immediate danger behind them, and events, unbroken by oblivion, crowded together in Hezhi's brain until they were a senseless litany of colors and shapes. Her eyes read the sky and the landscape only from habit, without much comprehension.

Of the night's watchful eyes, only one remained, the rest having fled or fluttered shut beneath sky-colored lids at the graying of the horizon, and that only made her sleepier, made her wish that *she* were a cold, distant, *sleeping* star. The holdout still flamed, defiant, defending his domain in the vault of heaven even though his was the easternmost portion, where the sun's birth was heralded by servants of copper and gold.

"What star is that?" Hezhi asked wearily, in an attempt to keep awake.

Brother Horse cracked the barest grin in the gray light. Hezhi noticed not so much the show of humor as how *old* he looked, with the stubble of beard on his chin.

"We call him *Yuchagaage*, the 'Hunter.'"

"What does he hunt?"

Brother Horse waved the back of his hand at the star, winking dimmer each moment to their right. "He has hunted many things. Right now he hunts the sun."

"Will he *catch* the sun?"

"Well, watch for yourself. The Bright King will kill him, sure enough, before even he has risen."

"The Hunter is not the most intelligent of gods," Raincaster added from up ahead of them, next to Tsem. Hezhi had been staring east in the first place to avoid watching the tail of Raincaster's horse, which threatened to mesmerize her as it switched back and forth.

"True," Brother Horse said. "He lies in wait for the sun, each morning getting closer. Always he is slain; he never succeeds—nor learns, apparently."

"But he is still here, when the other stars have fled," Hezhi noted. "He lives longer in defiance than in retreat."

"The other stars are smarter," Raincaster answered, but Hezhi thought she heard a faint contempt in the young man's tone—or had her ears added that?

"But not braver," Hezhi retorted sourly. "And he isn't always *running*."

"I won't play this word game," Tsem said, turning to speak but not so much that she could see his face. These were the first words he had spoken since crying the night before. "It was you who decided we should leave."

"I never *decide*, Tsem," Hezhi replied. "It always *happens*, but I never decide."

"Well, you are not a *star*, Princess, and if you are blown out like a candle one morning, you will not return to light the world again. I don't know much about these ghosts that people out here call gods—you know much more than I, as always. But they seem to me, from what I have heard, to be poor creatures to model your actions after."

"Well put," Brother Horse agreed, "though I must admit that as a young warrior I carried the likeness of the Hunter on my shield. Many young Mang do so still. He is a rash god, but then, young men value rashness."

"What do *old* men value?" Raincaster asked.

"Young women," Brother Horse answered. "If I carried a shield now, I would paint one on it."

Ngangata—riding slightly ahead of Raincaster—turned, his face a weird rose color in the light of the rising sun. "Perkar is like the Hunter," he put in glumly. "Always. And you see where it gets him."

The wind picked up, clean and cool, and for an instant it swept the rooms of Hezhi's mind of the broken bits of thought that cluttered them. She had to raise her voice a bit for Brother Horse to understand her.

"Yes, Perkar," she said. "You told us we would speak of him."

"Later, when you have had some rest."

"I should rest soon, then. When I returned—well, just before I awoke, in your yekt—I saw the monster again, the one feeding upon him. I think it may be winning. If I do have the power to help him now—as you say—I may not in a few days."

"That's probably true," the old Mang conceded. "But first tell me everything. How you went through the drum, what happened— *everything*. We have time enough for that."

Hezhi nodded and told him, trying to leave nothing out, though even the wind failed to keep her mind clear and the droning of her own voice threatened to put her to sleep. Her story became a patchwork of digressions, and she feared that what little sense it had ever made was now lost. The sky continued to brighten, as the sun puddled red on the horizon, and then, finding its spherical shape, rose up. At Brother Horse's direction, they put the rising light to their backs, bearing nearly due west. The land rolled and then flattened out like a pan, rimmed at the limits of their sight by hills on the south and north. Ahead, Hezhi could make out the purple contours of distant mountains. The sky was as clear as blue glass, and the last traces of snow were gone from the ground.

The end of Hezhi's story whipped off with the wind across the endless plain, and Brother Horse rocked silently in his saddle for some time without commenting on it. Hezhi did not rush him, instead looking about her once more.

Tsem sat a horse nearly twice as massive as the one she rode, and he was still too large for it, though the horse bore his weight without complaint. Tsem himself remained glum, his visage hidden from her as she recounted her journey to the mountain. It was just as well, for she feared what her words might have written on his face. Ngangata now rode well in front of the rest of them, ever the scout, and Heen had paced ahead with him. Yuu'han led Perkar's horse, and Perkar dragged and bumped along behind on a travois. At Ngangata's insistence, they were also accompanied by Sharp Tiger, the mount that Perkar had been leading when he reached the Ben'cheen. Raincaster, after their conversation, had dropped back to rear guard, his hawklike features clouded with exhaustion. Two additional horses carried their provisions and tents.

Seven people and nine horses. *We make no more impression on this plain than a line of ants,* Hezhi thought. *Dust in the eye of the sky.*

Brother Horse broke the silence, clearing his throat. "You have had an unusual experience," he said. "Unusual, I mean, even for a gaan."

"It seemed unusual to me," Hezhi admitted. "But I know nothing of these things."

"You were caught up in the wake of the sacrifice. Traditionally we must make certain that the Horse God returns home without delay when she is slain. We must make sure she does not lose her way. So we sing her a path to follow."

"It was more like being caught in a stream," Hezhi said.

The old man nodded. "I have never flown in such a manner. Few gaans ever purposely risk the mountain. It is too dangerous by far."

"Then perhaps," Tsem exploded, turning in his saddle and unwittingly yanking his poor mount's head about, as well, "perhaps you should have *warned* her before giving her the means to *do* so. Or did you *hope* that she would do what she did?"

"I did not *think*," Brother Horse admitted, more to Hezhi than to Tsem. "I did not think. I honestly never believed you would open the lake without my help . . . without my urging, even. You seemed so reluctant."

"Whatever else she is," Tsem said, "she is still a very *young* woman. Impulsive."

"Tsem—"

"Princess, I have served you for many years. Until quite recently, it was not enemies I protected you from but yourself. You have the mind of a scholar—I know you are smarter than me—but you have no *sense* sometimes."

Hezhi opened her mouth to frame an angry retort, but she let it die unsaid, for Tsem was right, of course. Sometimes she became so lost in thought, she could not see where she was walking. At other times, it seemed as if she acted without any thought at all and had to spend her wakeful hours making up stories about *why* she did things. Anyway, it was the same old Tsem litany. He didn't really understand.

Instead of replying, she nodded wearily.

"In any event," Brother Horse said, "with some rest, you should be adequate to the task of helping Perkar."

*   *   *

Hezhi awoke, cold, though she was well bundled in blankets. The embers of a nearby fire gave out a dull heat, as well, but the air quickly sucked it away. Hezhi could not remember stopping; she must have fallen asleep in the saddle. She still felt tired, but it was a manageable weariness, not the soul-numbing shroud of exhaustion she had worn earlier. Most everyone else seemed to be asleep, as well, scattered here and there about the floor of some sort of cave or rock shelter. Outside the gaping entrance, moonlight drizzled onto the plain when swift-flying clouds allowed; she watched several of the dark forms pass before the Bright Queen, dress briefly in silver, then rush on to their nameless destinations. The air smelled wet.

"It will rain soon," a voice raspily whispered. Hezhi turned from the tableau to Ngangata. She could see only bits of his face in the dim glow. It seemed very inhuman, and she suddenly remembered the dreams she once had of a deep, ancient forest, of trees so huge and thick that light never fell, undiffused, to the earth. And though she had never dreamed of Ngangata—only Perkar—in the bits of his face she somehow sensed those trees.

"You can tell?"

"Yes. It is no difficult thing, really."

"How is Perkar?"

"Breathing a bit more shallowly, I think," he answered.

"Well," she chuffed, rubbing her eyes, "would you go wake Brother Horse for me?"

"Do you have the strength for this? I know I urged you earlier, but . . ."

"I won't let him die, Ngangata. Not if I have a choice in the matter."

He nodded and rose lithely, with no sound, and padded off on cat's feet.

Nearby, Tsem stirred. "Princess?"

"I'm here." She rummaged through her things—they were in a pile near the blanket she had been wrapped in—and withdrew her drum.

"Can't that wait?" the half Giant asked.

"Wait forever, you mean? Tsem, try to understand."

"Tsem always *try* to understand, Princess. Tsem just not very bright."

Hezhi could not tell if Tsem was trying to make her smile or rebuke her with his "dumb act," the one he had used in the palace so often.

"You'll be right beside me."

"I was right beside you before, when your spirit left your body for two days. You almost fell off the roof and broke your neck."

"I was foolish. I didn't know what I was doing."

"And now you do," he replied sarcastically.

She didn't answer. Ngangata was returning with Brother Horse. The old Mang man knelt and touched Perkar's brow.

"Yes," he muttered. "We should do this now."

"How?"

"I will do it. *You* will lend me the strength I need."

"I don't understand. You told me you couldn't heal him."

"I can't—not without you. I don't have the strength. On the other hand, you don't have the knowledge, and I don't have time to teach it to you; that would take months of apprenticeship."

"What do I do, then?"

"Tap your drum; follow me and watch what I do."

"What will you do?"

He spread his hands expressively. "We must fight and defeat the Breath Feasting. We will use our spirit helpers. Watch how I call mine forth, and then call yours forth in the same manner."

"The Horse, you mean—the spirit of the Horse."

"Yes, of course."

"Of course," Hezhi repeated, not at all certain things were as obvious as Brother Horse seemed to think them. "I'm ready."

"The rest of you be silent and do not touch us," the old man warned. "Do you understand? Giant, do *you* understand?"

"If anything ill befalls her, I will break your neck."

Brother Horse sighed and shook his head slowly at the cave floor. "If, when we get started here, you interfere, you may have no need to break either of our necks. The Breath Feasting may do it for you."

Tsem glowered but protested no more.

They sat and after a still, silent moment, Brother Horse began scratching the surface of his drum with his nails, faintly, faintly. Soon he began to tap it, and Hezhi joined in, also tapping with the nail of her index finger. The effect was nearly immediate; though almost negligible, the vibration of the taut rawhide tremored up her finger and into her bones and blood, filled it with rhythm. She moved to a pulse not her own, pumped not by her heart but by the skin head, by the scale on her arm. She was only remotely aware when Brother Horse began to chant, a wordless incantation at first, a droned note repeated over and over and an occasional odd rise in pitch. But in time, the meaningless syllables resolved into words, and these she caught as they drifted by.

> Wake up, my guest
> You have slept long
> In the house of my ribs,
> The house of my heart
> Wake up now,
> See through my eyes,
> Walk with my feet,
> *Yush*, my old friend

As he sang, Brother Horse began to shiver, wavering like flame in high wind. In that uncertainty of form, his face was the face of a wolf and his own at once, and she gathered from his limbs a sense of lean gaunt grayness that was not wholly Human. He chanted on, speaking to the spirit in him, and the air about Hezhi began to dream, to fill with the colors from behind closed eyelids. Tsem, Ngangata, and the others became shadowed, dimmed away as the real and the unreal traded their substance. Brother Horse continued to spread, became two shapes, wolf and man, though they were not entirely separate.

"Now," the old man told her, though he still chanted when he said it, "sing as I sang. Call up your helper."

Hezhi closed her eyes, rocking. It no longer seemed as if her finger moved the cadence of the drum; rather, it seemed to move itself. Hezhi's sight turned inward, and there she saw the horse-child, waiting for her call. She appeared as she had in life, iron gray with blazing white stripes, mane whipped by a fierce wind, racing upon a limitless, grassy field.

This is in me, Hezhi realized. The Horse's world nested within her, a world of hooves pounding and strong, willful blood.

Come on out. Come out and help me, she thought. Her lips formed the same chant that Brother Horse had recited, but this inner speech seemed more important than the formal words. It was her wish that the mare responded to, not the syllables in Mang. The mare came gladly, the thunder of her hooves shaking the drum so violently that Hezhi very nearly dropped it.

Hezhi opened her eyes. Brother Horse was talking again, perhaps to her. He seemed to be speaking urgently, but in her dreamlike state she felt sluggish, too lazy to puzzle at his meaning. She was more interested in the spirit emerging from her; it was almost as if she were giving birth—or at least, the way she had imagined giving birth might be. Far away, she heard a dog barking frantically. Heen? He was never frantic about *anything*.

Then she noticed Perkar standing, facing her, bending toward her. The almond molds of his eyes were entirely black, seething, bubbling like boiling tar. He grinned oddly, and his teeth were black, too. His sword squirmed in a white-knuckled grip, now a blade, now an eagle, now a single long beak or claw.

"I told you," Perkar said. "I *warned* you." He lifted the sword to point at her throat slowly, as if it were heavy and he was having trouble raising it.

A feral swirl of gray and teeth and claws smacked into Perkar and his black grin turned to a snarl. He staggered beneath the onslaught, swiping clumsily about him with his weapon. Brother Horse still sat, hands tapping the drum, as the wolf that had emerged from him tore with white teeth at Perkar.

Hezhi stared, gaping. Were they to kill Perkar? If the price of evicting the Breath Feasting from his body was to *kill* him, what was the point? But Perkar did not seem in danger of losing. One hand gripped the wolf by the throat now, and though it squirmed and shifted shapes from wolf to serpent to man, still he held it and brought the godsword around. The wolf split nearly in half, and its yowl was deafening. Perkar tossed it aside and advanced upon Brother Horse.

"Old man, you should have stayed away from this. He has been given to me by one much stronger than you."

"By whom?" Brother Horse asked. His eyes remained on Hezhi, however.

"I will take your ghost to him, and he will have some use for it, I think."

"I regret that I cannot accompany you."

Hezhi noticed that the two halves of the wolf were still joined by a thread of life, and the doglike creature was obstinately dragging itself across the cave floor toward Perkar. It would never reach him before the Perkar-thing reached Brother Horse, however. Only Heen stood, teeth bared, between the old gaan and death—but if a wolf god fell so quickly, how long could an ordinary dog stand?

Hezhi hesitated just an instant longer. What if Brother Horse *was* the enemy, and this all a trick to kill Perkar once and for all? She still, despite all of her experience, had only *his* word that he was on her side. But watching him sit there, calmly, facing something that looked like Perkar but was not, not really—

"*Come, Goddess,*" she cried. "There is your enemy!"

And the spirit bolted from her chest, like a heartbeat escaping, heart and all. It was not unlike the feeling of terrible sadness or joy, tightened beneath the tiny bones of her breast, suddenly bursting out, and of the two, more like joy. The gates of her heart swung open, and the Horse God sprang out.

Perkar turned at the sound, gaping wider than humanly possible. In fact, his whole head hinged open, almost comically. Black flame coiled out from an open mouth framing sharklike teeth. He brought his blade up, but he was too late. The mare erupted into existence, fury and passion rolling in her eyes, and her hooves slashed with more speed and force than summer lightning. They caught Perkar in the head and his skull split, burst into shards like a shattered pot. He swayed on his feet for an instant, as the Breath Feasting pulled free of the stump of his neck. The demon leapt out, coiled sinew and scales scratching at the air, spinning out rays like a thousand-legged spider, each leg a segmented worm tipped with a sting. It wheeled toward the Horse God, who reared to meet it, teeth bared and snapping. Hezhi braced for their impact, but it never came; something suddenly settled about the demon, a hoop of shivering light, and Hezhi realized that she had not seen Brother Horse approaching the duel, though now she felt how insistent his drumbeat had become. He swept the circumference of his instrument—which seemed now much larger than before—over the Breath Feasting, and as the beast passed through, it came apart. It literally burst through the skin head of the drum, a fountain of worms rotting into shreds of moldy black cheese and finally smoke. The only sound was faint, something between a snap and a gasp.

The old man made a few more passes with the drum, making certain that all of the fragments had become vapor, but no darkness was left, no visible remains of the demon; even the smoke was gone now. Then he bowed to the mare and knelt by the wounded wolf-spirit. He drew the creature to him, and in a gentle shudder they became one again. When he came back to his feet, there was a new shuffle and limp in his gait, pain etched plainly on his brow. He approached Hezhi and gently took her hand. It seemed as if her fingers were farther away than Nhol, not part of herself at all, but when he took them, the sound of drumming ceased, and she realized that she had never stopped tapping her instrument. The Horse whickered, pranced widdershins around them both, and then leapt back into her; Hezhi felt only a vague shock, smelled horse hair and sweat.

Fear smote her. The world beyond the drum was stark and, in its way, simple, and Human emotions were dim things there. But now, afterward, the reaction set in as wonder realized that it should have been terror. And Perkar had been *killed*, not saved. His head had burst apart, destroyed by her own hand—or by the hoof of her spirit helper.

She blinked. Perkar lay on the cave floor, as he had before. His head was whole, and as Brother Horse and Ngangata bent over him, he moaned once.

"What happened?" Tsem demanded. "Why are you shaking?"

Hezhi looked up into the Giant's puzzled face.

"The fight? Didn't you see?"

"See? I saw you and the old man tapping your drums and singing nonsense. Heen there started howling and growling, and then Brother Horse stood up and waved his drum around. There was some smoke or something; that's all I saw."

"Truly?"

"Princess, that's all that happened."

Frowning, Hezhi turned back to Perkar and the two men with him.

"Well? Is he better?"

Brother Horse shook his head solemnly. "He is still ill. It will take time for Harka to heal him entirely. But the Breath Feasting is gone."

"Thanks to you."

"Thank the Horse Goddess, or yourself."

"*You* slew it."

Brother Horse spread his hands. "It is not really slain, but it will be many years before its substance knits back together."

"You drew it through the drum."

"Yes. It is a dweller in the lake. Cast out of its waters, without flesh about it, it suffocates, in a sense. It comes unbound."

"Are all gods thus?"

"No. The Breath Feasting is delicate, in some ways. But any passage through the drum—from one side of the 'lake' to the other—must be prepared for, by spirit, god, or Human. The transition is always dangerous."

"What are you talking about? What lake?" Tsem asked.

"I'll explain later," Hezhi said, patting his arm. "I promise I'll explain later."

"Good. Because right now, the two of you sound quite mad."

Brother Horse did not grin, but his old humor seemed to flicker in his eyes as he shook his head and said, "Indeed. Madness is a prerequisite for becoming a gaan." He reached down and gave his dog a scratch between the ears.

Tsem rolled his eyes. "Then everyone out here but me must be one."

Yuu'han chose that moment to interrupt.

"Out on the plain," he said. "Look."

Hezhi followed the pointing finger, but all she saw was moonlight and clouds. Ngangata and Brother Horse, however, had a different reaction.

"I thought they would hold them longer," the old man remarked.

"Perhaps it is someone else."

"Perhaps."

"What? What is it?" Hezhi asked.

"See there?" Ngangata pointed.

Hezhi followed the imaginary line described by his finger, but still she saw nothing. "No."

"It's a campfire. Someone following us, between a day and half a day behind."

Brother Horse groaned. "I had hoped to rest before sunup."

"We can rest in the saddle," Ngangata answered. "At least our tracks will be covered."

"What do you mean?" Hezhi asked. But then she understood, as the first patter of rain came from outside. A distant thunder tremored, and a line of blue fire walked around the far horizon.

"I told you it would rain," Ngangata said. But he was looking at Perkar, who moaned once more, and Hezhi thought she caught the hint of a smile on his wide, strange lips, a whisper of thanks from his halfling eyes.

XX

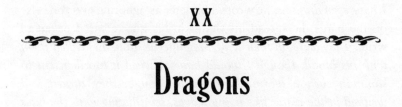

Dragons

G HAN paused at the threshold of the library and turned back, scrutinizing each block of visible shelving as the soldiers with him coughed impatiently.

"Wait," Ghan grumbled. He could see a volume, lying on a table, out of place. He moved stiffly across the room to retrieve it.

"Now, where do you go?" he asked rhetorically, checking the notation on the book, which told him exactly that. It belonged in the labyrinthine rear stacks—the ones Hezhi had named "the Tangle." He motioned to the soldiers to indicate he would return shortly and took the book to its shelf. Alone, he rested his head against leather-bound spines.

"I've spent my whole life among you," he muttered to the books. "What will you do without me?"

The tomes did not answer him, of course, but as he walked heavily back to the waiting guards, to his surprise, he answered himself. He rested his fingers on *Grimoire Tertiary*, the last in the row before he again crossed the reading area.

"Good-bye," he whispered. "Someone will always come who cares for you. Someone."

And then he left, not looking back again, turning his mind stubbornly outward to what must be.

I *have seen dragons,* he wrote a bit later as, ignoring everyone else on the barge, he spread his things in his quarters and began to write. *They were, in their way, magnificent. Bone Eel called them with his blood, though I would have believed it too deficient to summon even a worm. But it was enough; they turned and writhed in the water like living waves, scintillating with the hues of a green rainbow. Quite beautiful. When they slid into their moorings, down beneath the barge, the first tug showed their power, for in one moment we were still and in the next the boat was in motion. Soon we will not give them a second thought, but they must work tirelessly, pulling us up the River that gives them life.*

He set the pen aside then, folded down onto his bed, and closed his eyes. The day had been long and wrought much upon him, and even writing gave him little solace.

GHE emerged into the light before dawn, and Nhol was gone. Even with his enhanced vision, the River was almost all that he could see; on the nearest side he could make out the artificial horizon of the levee, willow, cottonwood, and bamboo rambling at its base. The other bank was so distant that it showed only as a thin green line. He took in a breath and thought it clean, new. They were in motion! The expedition—*his* expedition—had begun. And they would find her, he was sure of that. It was a vast certainty, inhuman in scope, but it still gave him joy.

Footsteps approached; the ghost of the blind boy identified them instantly, knew the cadence of walking like a name from first introduction, and so Ghe did not turn but called out, instead, a soft greeting, enjoying the sigh of air across the moving barge. "Lady Qwen Shen," he remarked. "You stir at an odd hour."

"As do you, Lord Yen."

He half turned his face toward her so that she could discern his sardonic grin. "No lord I, Lady."

"Is that so? I wonder, then, why the emperor gave this expedition into your hands."

"Your husband is the captain, madam."

"Oh, yes." She sighed. "My husband. Perhaps we should speak of him."

"Speak, Lady?"

The corners of her mouth turned up, and he noticed, once again, her great beauty, the slightly . . . *exotic* air about her.

"The emperor told you that he would furnish you with a barge to pursue your quest—and the trappings to go with the barge. A crew, a captain. My husband, Bone Eel, is just such a trapping."

Ghe scratched at the scar on his chin. "Then who gives these soldiers their orders?"

"Bone Eel does. But he gives the orders *I* suggest, and I suggest what you tell me to. That is how command works on this vessel."

"That seems needlessly elaborate," Ghe observed. "Is Bone Eel *aware* of this arrangement?"

"Aware?" Ghe turned so that he could see the lady's eyes sparkle as she spoke. "He is barely aware that breath passes in and out of his lungs. He is quite *unaware* that he never conceives an idea of his own. The emperor has given him a charter to sail up-River to 'Wun and parts beyond' as the emperor's ambassador. It is up to you and me to determine to what 'parts beyond' we shall navigate."

"No offense, Lady Qwen Shen, but wouldn't it have been simpler to put Bone Eel—or some other captain—directly under my command?"

"Of course not," she said, turning her face to catch a zephyr sighing across the water. "No lord would suffer to be commanded by a commoner—and a commoner cannot command a royal barge. Believe me, this is the best arrangement that can be made. Your directives will be carried out, never fear."

He simply nodded at that. "The emperor explained our true mission?"

She solemnly returned his nod, and her voice husked lower still. "His daughter," she all but mouthed.

Ghe nodded. "You've said enough." But his brow stayed bunched in consternation.

"Don't worry," Qwen Shen soothed. "This is a charade I am accustomed to. You and I will captain this vessel quite efficiently."

"An honor," Ghe said, but what he thought was that he was at this woman's mercy and a bit of his earlier elation faded. A gull cried in the darkness, and far out across the River's supine majesty, Ghe could see another, smaller barge moving with the current. He wondered if it, too, had dragons leashed beneath its bow—or if it moved at the behest of more mundane forces.

"Bone Eel does not know?"

"As I told you," she answered. "Nor anyone else save the old man. You must tell him to watch his tongue."

Ghe flashed her an evil little smile. "No one has to tell him to keep *his* mouth darkened. He usually only opens it to insult or argue. But I will make certain he understands our situation, anyway. Just so long as *you* understand that he is not to know I have any real role in this expedition. He believes me to be an engineer with some love for Hezhi, that is all."

He was aware of her regard spidering about him as they spoke, walking delicately here and there. Often it touched lightly on his throat. He kept his own gaze studiously out and away. When he did glance at her, the intensity of her inspection disturbed him.

"What of you, Lady? What do *you* think me to be?"

She was silent, and the boat glided on for a time, before she turned to him frankly and answered that question by asking her own.

"May I touch your flesh?"

"What?"

"Your hand. I wish to touch your hand."

"Why?"

"I want to see if it is cold."

"It is not," he assured her. "It is the temperature of flesh."

"But I want to touch it," she insisted. "I want to know . . ."

"You want to know how the flesh of a ghoul feels?" he hissed.

She did not flinch from him. "Yes."

He darted his hand out, swiftly, so that she would understand that he was *more* than Human as well as less, and he gripped her hand in his with enough strength to hurt her. She gasped but, other than that, did not complain.

"*That* is how my flesh feels." He grinned savagely.

She closed her eyes but did not jerk away as he thought she might. "You were wrong," she told him instead, and he suddenly felt her other hand, the free one, tracing along his knuckles. "Your flesh is warmer than that of a man."

He released her hand with a dismissive thrust. "Does that satisfy your curiosity, madam?"

She rubbed her abused hand absently with her other. "No," she said. "Oh, no. My curiosity is just beginning to awaken."

And she favored him with her own sardonic smile as she retraced her path to the colorful pavilion beneath which her husband slept.

Ghe, for his part, stood rooted where he was long after sunup, nursing his astonishment into anger, the anger into rage. If Qwen Shen were going to play games with him, she would regret it. He planned a number of inventive ways to make her do so, and then, as more sailors began to move about the deck, checking the depth with long poles, casting out nets, or merely watching the River and shore for dangers, Ghe went below to speak with Ghan.

"She is not near the River, you can be certain of that," Ghan told him—a bit warily, Ghe thought.

"Why is that?"

"I am Forbidden, so I will not delve in great detail into the subject. Suffice to say that she fled not Nhol so much as she fled the *River*, and to return to him would thwart all of her hopes."

"Then we shall not return her," Ghe assured him. "We will find her and warn her of the priesthood and its plans."

"I don't see how the priesthood can find her."

"They have ways."

"And you know that the temple's expedition goes up-River rather than overland? That is why the emperor outfitted a barge for *our* journey?"

In fact, Ghe had not thought much about why he requested a barge; it had seemed the natural thing, at the time. Now he realized that he might have let the Rivergod betray himself; the River could only *conceive* of up-River and down-River, and so naturally Hezhi *must* be in one of those directions. Ghe's sense was that she was up-River, but now it dawned on him that the River's belief in this matter—even filtered through him—was not trustworthy. The River did not *know* where she was.

His only clues were visions the River had been sending him in the past few days. Unlike the first—which had been about the River himself—these pictured a man, a dark, wild man on a striped horse who rode with companions dressed, like himself, in barbaric costumes. It seemed to Ghe—in this dream—that the wild man knew where Hezhi was, was somehow like himself: an extension of the River's purpose into places where he could not flow. But the River gave him precious little information otherwise. And he needed information, something to make Ghan think he knew more than he did.

The man on the horse reminded him, almost against his will, of the little statuette he had given Hezhi, the half-woman, half-horse creature from Mang fantasy. If the man in his dreams was Mang, then perhaps—but all barbarians looked alike.

No, *that* wasn't true. Some of them were as white as albinos with eyes like pale gray glass. Mang, at least, looked like *people*.

If he did not take the chance now, before Ghan said something, then Ghan would control all of the information. The old man could tell him *anything*, and Ghe's arcane senses were not keen enough to identify subtle falsehoods. Ghan had to *believe* in the fictitious temple expedition, had to believe that the *priesthood* knew where she was.

And so, mustering all of his confidence, he asserted the only thing he could think of. "We—and the priesthood—know only that she is among the Mang." Then he fought to suppress a triumphant smile, for he smelled Ghan's chagrin, a bitter, salty scent. He had been right! Or partly right. Now Ghan would have to be careful what he *said* when he lied, for he could no longer be certain of what Ghe did and did not know. He could see the struggle in the old man, the hope of formulating a lie, the desire to fashion one as close to the truth as it needed to be to be believed. He nodded inwardly; yes, Ghan would deceive him, if he thought he could get away with it. Where would the scholar have led them, if he no longer believed the priesthood to be a threat to Hezhi? Then he would conclude that the only possible threat was from *this* expedition. But now he had *evidence* that the priests knew where she was, and *that* would motivate him to tell at least part of the truth.

"She is among the Mang," Ghan finally agreed, and Ghe clenched his fists in victory. "That much is true. The priesthood must have been watching me more closely than I thought, must have known when I got word from her."

"I have seen maps," Ghe said. "The Mang Wastes are enormous. Knowing she is in them does not narrow our search significantly."

"Yes," Ghan said quietly. "But I know where she is to a much finer degree."

"Must we travel overland? What is our course?"

Ghan sighed and lifted up a tube of bamboo and brass from beside his desk. He pulled a chart from it and spread it across the flat surface.

"Here is Nhol," he explained, and Ghe recognized the spot easily enough. The River was represented by three waving lines, parallel to one another. Nhol was a drawing of the Water Temple, a stepped pyramid. Ghe felt a bit of familiar anger at that—that the city of the River should be represented by his nemesis.

"These are the wastes," Ghan went on, gesturing at a vast area that lacked any real detail—save for the figure of a man on horseback, sword raised. The River cut right along the edge of those lands. The other side of the River was labeled "Dehshe," which Ghe knew to be another barbarian tribe.

"We might as well stay on the River until we reach this point here," Ghan said, indicating a single waving line that intersected the River.

"What's that?"

"Another, smaller watercourse. It may be that we can take the barge up it some distance. Then we will have to debark and go overland."

"To where?"

Ghan glanced up at him frankly. "Understand me," Ghan said. "I think I have little use to you or the emperor other than my knowledge of where Hezhi is. I wish to preserve that usefulness as long as I may. For now, I will say only that you should sail to the mouth of that stream and then up it, if possible."

Ghe nodded. There was nothing stupid about the old man. Indeed, he reminded Ghe of someone. For an instant, he knew who it was; the old woman on Red Gar Street, whom he had murdered. He felt a sudden flush of emotion at the thought, a shadow of the sadness that overtook him after she died. Why should this old man remind him of her?

They were both old, both ugly, both hard and unforgiving, that was what. Both dangerous, added to the list. But there was something more fundamental he could not remember.

"Well, then," he said, to interrupt his own thought. "I shall take this news to Bone Eel, unless you wish to advise him yourself."

"Please." Ghan snorted. "I have spoken to him once; that shall suffice until such time as I die and he summons my ghost and *compels* me to speak to him again. I have avoided his sort for many years, and now I am crowded shipboard with one."

Ghe nodded. "I understand you. The priesthood and engineers are full of his kind. I believe that it is actually Qwen Shen who leads this expedition."

"Yes, Qwen Shen. Lady Fire, Lady Ice."

"What?"

"That is the meaning of her name, you idiot," Ghan said. "Fire, ice."

"Oh."

"Go. I have much reading to do."

"Master Ghan, do you never do other than read?"

"What do you mean?"

"I know that you have never been north of Nhol on the River. And yet, here you sit, closeted away, rather then beholding the world as it unfolds."

"Yes, well, as of now I can pretend I am not *on* this mad journey. I can keep my mind on important things. Soon enough— when you have me marching overland on these ancient legs—I will not have that luxury. Besides, what can one see 'unfolding' out there?"

"Well . . . water and distant levees, I suppose, another boat now and then. I see your point."

"Indeed. And a person of normal intelligence would have seen my point long ago and thus spared me wind that I cannot afford. I am old; there is not that much left in me."

"Once again I apologize, Master Ghan, and I will leave you to your work."

He bowed briefly and exited the room. He went back above and thought that he did *not* see Ghan's point. As he stepped out onto the polished planks, the world seemed wondrous and entirely new. The sun cast a cheerful yellow light on the world, and clouds meandered good-naturedly across a sky that, like the sun, was as simple and unshaded as the colors in his dreams. Some thirty or so of the soldiers stood along the railings, still in their aquamarine-and-gold kilts and burnished steel armor. *His* soldiers, really, here because *he* asked the emperor for them. Men who would fight and die at his command.

Best of all, the enterprise was not the wan hope it had once been. Ghan knew where Hezhi was, knew *exactly* where she was. Soon he would find her, protect her from her enemies, embrace her once again. He would bring her back to her father—not the poor flesh-and-blood one in the palace, but the one she truly belonged with. She fled him only because she did not understand him, and that because of the priesthood filling her from childhood with the wrong notions, notions that came from that dark place beneath, where a terrible creature masqueraded as Human while

toying with the First Emperor on a *chain*. She had learned to
fear the God, equate him with the perversions of the priests—
perversions and fears that he himself had once embraced before
death awoke him. But the River—the truth of him—was this he
saw now, vastness, the sky come to live upon the earth, life, the
cycle of rain. Joy. In that instant, he felt his head and his feet as a
world apart, and between them crawfish, gar, flatfish, crabs, catfish, eels—all of the living things in the waters, the vast brakes of
reed and cane, the thick cypress and mangrove stands of the
Swamp Kingdoms. No trace of hunger pained him, and the nightmare verity that he was dead seemed far distant, a misplaced
worry. Only one unquiet thought lay in him, and it was annoying
because he could not find its heart at all. In it was something
of the temple and its weird master, but that was not the seed of
his . . . worry? Fear?

Whatever it was, he would deal with it when it came, and now,
for the first time since his rebirth, he felt—bizarrely—almost like
singing. He would not let one skewed thought pull him away
from this rare sensation. Nor would he *sing*; that would be too
much, and others on the boat would think him addled—but he
would watch the River gliding past and worship it, know it for his
destiny, and that would be *like* singing.

IN his cabin, Ghan studied the map carefully, and another that
held more detail. He cross-referenced it against the geography he
had brought with him.

He trod a tightrope now, with razors on either side. If only he
were absolutely certain that the priesthood had not sent a mission. But if they had, it was far ahead of them, and Hezhi and
Tsem would have already escaped or been captured.

He did not see how the latter could happen unless the Mang
sold her to them, and he could not imagine what a priest might
offer or wield that would buy or intimidate the Mang.

His plan was still only half shaped, still coming together. Too
much of it hinged upon Yen, who continually surprised him.

There was something about Yen he did not understand, a part of the tapestry unwoven or out of sight, at least.

Meanwhile, he had his maps and his geography. He would learn what he could from them.

Thus, as Ghe walked abovedecks, wondering what prickled at his happiness, Ghan turned back to the first map and absently ticked his finger upon the conical drawing of a mountain labeled "She'leng," whence the wiggly line signifying the River began. It was odd, he thought, how much it resembled the drawing that marked Nhol, half a world away.

XXI

The Shadow Man

W*AKE up.*

Perkar opened his eyes to a sky that shuddered and bumped so that he feared the clouds would shake loose from it and fall upon him. In fact, it seemed that some of them already had, for he was soaked to the bone. He raised his hand feebly in a vain attempt to brush the water from his clothing, and the world wobbled even more dangerously.

Someone chattered in a language that he didn't immediately understand—and then recognized as Mang. He jerked up, realizing suddenly how weak his body felt, how limp. His last real memory was of playing Slap with a big Mang warrior—and losing. What had they done with him?

He couldn't sit up, because he was tied down, strapped to a travois.

"Hey!" he tried to roar, but instead issued only a weak cough. Still, someone else heard it, and the scratching progress of the travois suddenly stopped.

A thick, half-Human face blotted the sky, and quick fingers pulled at straps on his chest.

"Ngangata," Perkar croaked.

"How do you feel?"

"The way I felt after the Huntress was done with me. What happened?"

"Well, that is a *very* long story, and—"

"Perkar!" A rustling of cloth and soft boots on sand accompanied an excited shout. He turned his head and saw Hezhi scrambling across desert toward him.

"Brother Horse said you would wake up soon! I thought the rain would do it!"

"Hello, Princess. I hope someone can explain *something* to me soon."

Thank her for saving your life, Harka muttered in his ear, faintly—as if the sword, too, were ill.

"Saved my life?" Perkar paraphrased. What was going on here? Surely he had broken his neck in the game of Slap and had taken some time to heal. But Hezhi stood wringing her hands, a variety of emotions playing across her face, and Ngangata looked *happy,* and perhaps surprised—as if neither ever expected to hear him speak again.

"What do you remember?" Hezhi asked, biting her lip.

"Nothing, I only—" But then Hezhi had buried her face in his shoulder, kneeling down to do so.

"I'm glad you're back," she gasped, and her throat caught once, as if she would cry. Perkar was so startled that he had no reply, and by the time he thought to raise his own arms and return the embrace, she had already pulled away again. Her face was dry, and moreover, she suddenly seemed a bit embarrassed.

Ngangata had finished untying the straps. "Don't try to stand yet," the Alwa-Man cautioned, but Perkar ignored him, trying to swing his feet around and ending by tumbling into the wet sand. Distant thunder rolled across the hills, probably one of the gods laughing at him.

"Well, alive again," a gruff voice barked. It was Brother Horse. "Remember what I told you about the Mang being the only race to survive out here, in the time of creation? Remember that next time you think to play one of *our* games."

"I will try to remember."

"I will help," Ngangata said. "Next time I will remind you by rendering you unconscious. You would suffer less damage that way, you *idiot*."

"Nice to be back," Perkar said, wobbling—*finally*—to his feet.

"Stay in the travois a bit longer, until you are stronger," Brother Horse suggested. "We have to be moving."

"Why?"

"We are being pursued. We will explain that later, too."

"I can ride alongside," Hezhi offered.

"Give me a few moments to think," Perkar said, "to speak with Harka. Then tell me." He lay back into the rough construction of hide and poles, then bolted back up as a sudden thought occurred to him.

"Sharp Tiger? Did you think to bring Sharp Tiger?"

Ngangata gestured with the back of his hand. "There he is. Now lie back."

Perkar strained his neck to follow Ngangata's gesture, but he could see Sharp Tiger there, staring at him with what was probably horse-ish disdain.

He lay back and soon the sky began to rattle again. A gray cloud was winging over, and against it the tiny but brilliant form of some sort of bird—perhaps a crane.

"You seem to know what has happened to me, Harka."

"Indeed, what has not happened to you? At some points I was nearly as ill as you, so my own memories are shaky through some of it."

"You were ill? What does that mean?"

"Our heartstrings are paired. Anything that brings you close enough to death weakens me, as well."

"But if I died, you would be set free."

"Normally. Not in this instance, however."

Perkar shook his head in amazement. "Impossible for me to believe any of this. Tell me all, then, Harka. And tell me why I have Hezhi to thank for my life."

Harka told him then, and afterward, Hezhi rode alongside to

explain the occurrences in the world outside of his body. The fight, their flight from the Mang village, the battle of spirits for his life, the pursuit that they could see in the distance. Through all of this, Perkar felt steadily stronger. Without a supernatural entity to battle, Harka was healing him at the usual rapid pace. By the end of her story, Perkar was ready to try riding.

"Good," Hezhi said. "Ngangata says we will be harder to track without the travois."

"Probably. A travois leaves pretty deep and unmistakable prints. Even a hard rain might leave traces. How hard *did* it rain?"

"Not hard enough."

The party regarded him silently, nervously, as he placed one boot into T'esh's stirrup and then heaved his belly onto the stallion's back. Grunting, he pulled his other leg over.

They resumed, and though he felt faintly dizzy and still very weak, Perkar was able to stay in the saddle for the rest of the day, refining his questions as they went along.

THAT afternoon they entered a hillier country, and their path tended generally to be upward as the land itself rose away from the lower steppe. In the distance, the mountains ceased to be faint purple clouds and had become worlds unto themselves, with forests, deserts, snowfields—close, it seemed, yet still far away and above them. It made Perkar feel easier, more at home, and a sudden realization struck him.

"Hezhi, where are we going? Other than fleeing from pursuit?"

"We are going to the mountain," she stated, simply.

"The mountain." There it was, lurking. He had been so concerned with the events during his days of forgetfulness that he had not put the days *before* it into perspective. Though he had not forgotten it, he had delayed thinking about his meeting with Karak— or the Blackgod, or whatever the fickle deity insisted on being called. Karak had told him to make certain that Hezhi reached the mountain.

"Why? Who made that decision?" he asked.

Hezhi pursed her lips. "You don't remember telling me to go there?"

"No."

"Was it just your madness then? Did the Raven not instruct you to escort me to the mountain?"

Perkar felt a wave of irritation. "Did Ngangata tell you that?"

Hezhi frowned further, and her voice frosted a bit. "*No*. He told me that you spoke with the Blackgod, but he knew little of the substance of what you said to each other."

Perkar took a deep breath, using it to cool his growing angst. What was upsetting him? "I'm sorry, Hezhi," he said. "What I told to you—though I don't remember telling it—is true. Karak says we are to go to the mountain in the heart of Balat."

"He told me the same thing."

"*You* spoke with Karak? Where?"

Hezhi couldn't suppress a grin when she answered.

"Another story I need to hear," Perkar said, dazed. He felt as if he had awakened sliding down the slick side of a mountain of ice with only one foot under him. After the meeting with Karak, he thought he knew what to do, but the world had moved on without him as he lay among the dead.

"After," Hezhi insisted a bit forcefully. "First you tell me: *why* must we go to the mountain?"

If she had spoken to Karak, why hadn't the Crow God told her *that*? Perkar brushed at T'esh's mane thoughtfully. She deserved to know. Particularly she deserved to know after saving his life from the Breath Feasting. But his people—possibly his father and his brother—were dead and dying. It was his fault, and he must weigh that into all of his decisions. Piraku insisted that he put the higher cause first. At least, he thought it did.

"Karak was vague," Perkar answered carefully. "But he said that if we went to the mountain, to the very headwaters of the River, we could slay him."

"Slay him? Slay the River?" Hezhi's voice was thick with incredulity. "Haven't you already stumbled drunkenly down that path? Haven't I heard this story?"

"It sounds insane," Perkar admitted. "I abandoned that ambition long ago. But Karak—Karak tells me we can do it, and moreover that we *must*." *That you can do it,* he thought guiltily. But she had to be convinced a bit at a time.

"And Karak is trustworthy?" Hezhi asked.

"No, but Karak is a god of the same sort as the River, one of the ancient gods who created the world. And he has no love for the River—"

"You used to scoff at that. When you tried to explain about all of the gods out here, you were skeptical of their claims."

"I am less skeptical now," Perkar admitted. Deep down, he knew that he was overstating the case. He still doubted Karak rather deeply, but he *believed* his assertion that they could slay the River. He believed it because of Hezhi and the power he had seen her gathering about her, back at Nhol.

"I will not go near the River, Perkar," Hezhi insisted quietly.

"It may not be necessary that *you* go," Perkar lied. "But please, hear me out. I don't know the entirety of Karak's plan. It may be that it will make more sense as we near the mountain. It will be a long journey, and Karak promised to leave signs. In the meantime, where else should we go?"

"He told me, too," Hezhi muttered. "He told *me* to go there."

"Tell me of that. Of *your* conversation with the Crow God. Perhaps we can piece more together from both stories than from either."

HEZHI agreed, and told of her improbable journey. In telling it, she realized how ridiculous it sounded and for the first time really began to doubt the truth of it. It might, she realized, have been some sort of vivid dream.

Save for the goddess living in her chest. She could hardly doubt *that* anymore.

Perkar's recovery had loosened some of the despair in her heart, and with a little time she thought she might cough some of it up and spit it out. She understood that much of her depression came from powerlessness, from being swept along by events, with no part in shaping her own fate. The reality of her new powers cast all of that in a different light. That new light filtered through a shattered crystal, producing more than one image and color— she was in many ways as terrified of what she had done as she was elated. But she remained *herself* and yet wielded power—in the end, the direction of the journey had been *her* decision, and that felt good. The power she had been offered before—the power of the River—would have been immeasurably greater, but such puissance would mean the end of *her*, Hezhi. She understood now that though the world of the "lake" was strange and terrifying— still, the spirit that moved there was her own. The Mountain Gods had trapped her, they would have killed her—but even they had no wish to *transform* her.

Brother Horse, Ngangata, Yuu'han, and Raincaster all looked at her with more respect now, she was certain of that. And Perkar was back, alive, and best of all, *she* had played a major role in saving him. Now perhaps the debt he pretended she did not owe him would be mitigated, at least somewhat. Perhaps without that between them, they could really become friends. When he understood her part in saving him—and she thought she had minimized her role—he had thanked her, humbly and sincerely. She captured that moment like a butterfly, enjoying the motion of its wings while it lived. Knowing Perkar, she thought a bit sourly, it was not likely to live long. He was too preoccupied with his own worries, his own guilt—what, together, he called "destiny."

Did he really believe he could slay the god of the River, merely because some self-styled Crow God told him so? Well, perhaps it was true. Perhaps that was the only way she could ever be truly safe from the River God. But she knew his power, knew it the way a child knows the fists of a father who beats her, and she did not believe he could die. If there was anything in the universe that was eternal, it was the River.

But perhaps *nothing* in the universe was eternal. She had read cogent arguments in several books to that effect.

For the moment, it seemed reasonable—insomuch as *anything* seemed reasonable—to pursue the course that, after all, *she* had chosen: to go on to She'leng. But unless she learned much about this plan of the Blackgod, particularly its execution and its likely aftereffects, she would not actually commit to approaching the source. The scale upon her arm told her just how dangerous that could be.

Perhaps her new gaan powers could help, however. She would have to ask Brother Horse, then consider *all* of the information available.

That night they had no choice but to sleep in the open, so they camped in the lowest spot they could find and ranged the horses about so that they might serve as sentinels. There was no sunset, for the sky had gone leaden, and the day faded pitifully away. Hezhi felt cheated; each sunset and sunrise usually seemed more spectacular than the last in the Mang Wastes, as if there must be some compensation for the lack of splendid palaces, gold filigree, and *books*.

As she closed her eyes, she wondered what Ghan was doing right then. She speculated, briefly, whether she could send her spirit abroad to Nhol, but the answer to that seemed obvious. If she went near him—or sent the Horse—they would be eaten. Brother Horse had done nothing in the lands of the River but *watch*, with his vision, if she remembered his story. He had never loosed his wolf or sent his senses out. She added that to her list of things to ask him about.

But she could *picture* Ghan, bent over a book by flickering lamplight, tracing the sublime curves of the ancient hand, certain of each stroke. She missed him.

I shall have to write him another letter soon. Though, of course, she had never managed to send the last. In fact, she realized with considerable chagrin, the earlier one was still in the yekt at the Mang camp.

Mentally composing its replacement, she drifted into sleep.

IN her sleep came a hurricane. Wind shrieked across a darkling plain, the colors of which were indigo, black, and beetle green.

Rainbow lightning brightened the sky so that it resembled the stained glass Hall of Moments, back in the palace, save that here the glass shattered and re-formed in every instant. Images formed and died in the trails the light burned on her eyes.

She did not stand but sat a horse, and she understood that it was her mare, her spirit. Dust devils birthed and died about them, danced like the ladies of the court, stunned into a simulacrum of carefree behavior by Nende'ng and wine, seeking only the sensation of movement and the promise of oblivion.

Across the vast courtyard—for such it was, she understood suddenly—a shadow man came walking. She saw him enter from a hall on the horizon, as tall as the great Water Temple, stalking toward her, lightning pattering upon his head and shoulders like fiery rain. From most of these obvious attacks he did not flinch, and she watched him approach in growing terror that even the nature of the otherworld could not entirely suppress. Beneath her, the mare whickered, stamped, and rolled her eyes. Hooves rang like bells on the polished marble.

Suddenly the sky sleeted white, however, a bright, furious light that blinded her, stilled the wind, and rocked the earth the mare stood upon. When the blaze faded, she saw only the giant's court, darker than before. The hulking shadow giant was gone. Above, she thought she saw vast wings vanish amongst the lofty unlit regions of the roof-sky.

"I had hoped to impress you," a voice sighed from nearby, breaking the new stillness. "Now I am fortunate merely to be alive."

She peered toward the voice. It was Shadow Man, but grown much smaller. Smaller than she, even, and curled into a ball like a fist.

"Who are you?"

"I am the gaan, the one who sent Moss and Chuuzek to find you."

Hezhi opened her mouth to speak, but he quickly went on.

"I know you have been told I am your enemy. I know it must seem that way to you. But you have many enemies, Hezhi, and only a few who love you."

"You do not *love* me," Hezhi snapped scornfully.

"No. But I know who does. I know he is coming. I can take you to him."

"What? What do you mean?"

"Your old teacher, Ghan." The shadow paused and clucked. "Gaan—Ghan. Have you ever noticed that?"

"Ghan is in Nhol," she snapped, ignoring his linguistic observation. "I can never go there again."

"Both of those statements are untrue," the Shadow Man contradicted. "They are both lies, though you know not why you tell them. Ghan is coming here. Your father has sent him to make you understand."

"Ghan sent me from Nhol in the first place," Hezhi whispered, feeling as if she would fall from the mare. "He would not come to get me back."

"I know what I know. Even Ghan can come to understand he was wrong. Hezhi, listen to me. Before, the River—your ancestor—was asleep. I do not know what transpired between you, exactly, but I know that it frightened you. Imagine him as a great creature, who, while asleep, did not recognize even his own daughter. In that state, he may have frightened you, and you would have been right to worry, perhaps even to flee him. But he knows you now. He feels remorse. Hezhi, you are the most important child he has ever produced. Karak knows that, that's why he plots with Perkar. Karak and Perkar will do you harm, Princess, though I cannot see of what sort."

"Perkar is my friend."

"Oh, no, Princess, he is not. Neither is the Blackgod. It was he who attacked me just now."

"So you say. And even if he did, that would only mean he was helping *me*. Before you were a monster filling the horizon. Now you are a somewhat pitiful thing."

"As I said before, I only endeavored to impress you. Even the greatest gaan is no match for a god like Karak, and Karak and all his brethren are no match for the Changeling. You are the Changeling's daughter, Hezhi, and they are no match for you, either, not if you don't want them to be. This tinkering about with little spirits and little victories—that is what *I* do, what *I* am capable of. You are destined to change the face of the world, not dirty yourself with such paltry forces."

"What do you propose I do?" Hezhi snapped, making no effort to hide her irritation.

"Separate yourself from those you ride with. Find Moss and Chuuzek, who follow you. They will take you to Ghan. He will explain to your satisfaction the rest."

"Leave me alone."

"*Listen* to me," the shadow hissed, rising up, growing to Human size as it did so.

Hezhi clapped the flanks of her mount, and the mare leapt forward, hooves flashing. Shadow Man leapt back, kept leaping back, growing more distant in a series of bounds that eventually carried him beyond the horizon and out of the hall. His voice, however, stayed near.

"You must learn who your friends really are. You have been mistaken about such things before," he said. "Watch Perkar. Especially watch the Crow God."

Then the plain went dark, as if it were a room in which all of the candles had been blown out. Real sleep swallowed her up, and no more dreams came until dawn.

PERKAR sat gazing at the fire, knowing he should feel elated, wondering why he did not. He felt weary—unbelievably weary, considering that he had only been awake for half a day at best—and yet the thought of sleep unaccountably sickened him.

"They say there is a man at this fire in need of some wine," a soft voice asserted from just behind him. It was Raincaster, returned from rubbing down the horses for the night. Yuu'han was only a score of steps behind him, bearing a wineskin.

"I should have helped you with the horses," Perkar murmured. "I feel well enough."

"You don't *look* well enough," Raincaster said. "And it insults a horse to treat her halfheartedly."

"I would *not* have been half—"

"Raincaster meant no insult," Yuu'han intervened. "You are not as strong yet as you would like to think, that is all. Have some wine." He proffered the skin.

Perkar sighed. "Very well. I'm sorry, Raincaster."

Raincaster wiped his forehead, a Mang gesture that dismissed all blame. "You have been fighting for your life against demons," he reminded everyone. "No reason to think such an experience would sweeten your mood."

Perkar returned the smile, though he did not feel like doing so. He *liked* Raincaster. He liked Yuu'han, as well, but with Yuu'han there was always the sense that his cordiality to Perkar arose out of duty—duty to Brother Horse and the responsibilities of hospitality. Raincaster seemed to genuinely *like* him—and to have an interest in the ways of the Cattle People. "Perhaps I *do* need some wine," he said, by way of further, though indirect, apology. Perkar accepted the proffered skin, tilting it back and catching a mouthful of its contents—though with some misgivings. He quickly discovered his misgivings were justified; the wine was *kbena*, a strong drink made from some sort of desert plant, sweet and tainted by an unpleasant aftertaste that reminded Perkar of rotten pears. It was certainly nothing at all like woti, the prized drink of warriors in his home country—save that it *did* warm his belly. He also knew from experience that the first mouthful was the worst, and so quickly swallowed another before passing the skin on to Raincaster. The three of them drank in silence for a while, watching the Fire Goddess consume withered juniper scraps. The night sky lay heavy above, revealing no light.

Perkar quickly realized that he did not want to get drunk any more than he wanted to sleep. The fifth time the skin came around, he shook his head and passed it on. Yuu'han shrugged and took a long draft.

The wine stirred something in Perkar, something he might ordinarily not have brought up.

"I know it was hard for you," he mumbled, addressing both of the Mang.

Yuu'han nodded, understanding him and already accepting the implied thanks, but Raincaster's expression demanded that Perkar express himself more fully.

"To leave your kin to help us. With the war and everything." Even a mere five drinks of the potent kbena was enough to thicken his tongue and make him feel more stupid than usual. He wished for eloquence rather than the gruff, clumsy, apologetic statement he had just uttered—but, as usual, it was too late to correct.

Raincaster shrugged, apprehending the spirit of the comment. "Our uncle is right, and the others are wrong. Anyway, I've never cared much for those Four Spruces People. They've always had delusions of grandeur."

Yuu'han's somewhat bleak expression softened at that. "Remember Mane Gatherer?" he said.

"I've heard the story," Raincaster replied.

"*I* haven't."

"Mane Gatherer told us the sun had spoken to him. He wanted us all to band up behind him and invade the Southlands—conquer Nhol, the Fisherfolk, the whole world, he said."

"Oh."

"Yes." Yuu'han gulped down another mouthful. "He said it was the destiny of the Mang to rule the cities."

"What happened?"

Yuu'han cracked a cryptic grin. "You've seen a city. Would *you* want to try to *rule* one?"

Perkar stared at the two Mang for only an instant, considering, before swearing, "*No*. By the *gods*, no."

Raincaster clapped his cousin on the shoulder. "Our reaction exactly," he proclaimed.

NOT much later, Yuu'han took the watch and Raincaster retired. Two tents had been erected: one for Tsem, Brother Horse, Heen, and Hezhi, the second for the two younger Mang, Ngangata, and Perkar. Perkar sought his blanket near Raincaster, after making

Yuu'han promise that Raincaster—who had the next watch—would wake him for the last, or dawn, quarter. He could tell by Yuu'han's answer that he would *not* be trusted to stand watch, not in his present condition.

He lay awake long, unable to understand what was growing in him, gnawing at him. He dozed fitfully once and awoke sweating, heart pounding. Raincaster was gone from his blanket, and Yuu'han was in his place. Ngangata was curled in his blanket, snoring faintly. The brief nap had not rested Perkar in the least, but it had tightened something in his mind, so that he knew what dark disquiet had replaced the demon Hezhi and Brother Horse had driven from him. It gathered itself together and shouted him its name.

Fear.

A mere spark before, it had caught in him now and burned furiously. In the past year, he had seen more bloodshed than he dreamed possible. He had murdered and fought fairly. More to the point, he had been disemboweled, been lanced through the throat, and stabbed numerous times—once through the heart. He still dreamed of each of those wounds; the pain of each was written clearly on his body and in his mind. When he thought about it much, it revolted him. Despite all of that, still he had developed the illusion that he was invulnerable, unstoppable, because keeping grasp of that belief was the only thing that kept all of his terrors at bay. When he was a child lying in bed with the terrible nighttime understanding that death would claim him one day, he had faced *that* by pushing it away, insisting that it was many, many years before he would have to face such an unfair reality. The child in him had used Harka to do that again, to place death in a far-off place and time he need not think about.

But now he had experienced the pain of death several times over and no *small* taste of her oblivion. He owed his beating heart to Harka, but now he understood that even Harka could not protect him. Not against Karak, who had brushed him aside as if he were a child—not against Chuuzek, either, who had flicked him almost casually from his saddle.

He did not consciously remember the past several days, but *something* in him did. He felt as if he had been lying in a grave with spiders crawling in and out of his mouth, with worms chewing at his eyes. A simple warrior—a *boy*—was not fit to deal with such things. He was in a struggle meant for shamans, wizards, and godlings. Useless, even if he had his heart, whole and full of bravery, but his heart was *not* whole; it was deeply scarred, and not just metaphorically. Now . . . Now what he wanted most to do was ride away, leave Hezhi and Ngangata and all of his responsibilities, and *hide*—hide from gods, from wars, from the sky itself.

HEZHI awoke with the dawn. Ngangata was cursing and saddling his horse, as were all three Mang.

"Stupid. I should have watched him. We should never . . . *whose* watch was it?"

"Mine," Raincaster answered, voice carefully neutral. "He said that he was going back a bit, to see where our pursuit was when the sun rose."

"I'm sure," Ngangata snarled. Hezhi sat up, fully alarmed now. "What's happening?"

"Perkar," Tsem told her. "He's gone."

XXII

The Dreamsnare

GHE felt a flash of pain and smelled life leaking into the air. He turned, puzzled, to see that one of the soldiers had thrust an arrow into his own eye and was working it deeper even as Ghe watched.

No. He had been *shot* in the eye and was merely grasping at the shaft as he died. Even as Ghe realized that, two more soldiers swore at arrows sprouting in the deck next to them.

The mist had hidden them, but now Ghe could see a half-dozen canoes ranged upstream on the River. All were converging on the barge furiously, each paddled by ten or fifteen barbarians.

The soldiers knew their jobs and did not remain surprised for more than an instant or two. Within heartbeats, twenty of them were at the bow, a wall of spears and swords, bows twanging behind them. Three men loaded and cranked the catapult. Ghe was just wondering what he should do when his better-than-Human ears detected a clamor aft. Grimly he raced toward the rear of the boat, springing up upon the cabin roofs and crossing them in great strides.

A boatload of the barbarians swarmed over the brass railing onto the afterdeck; three Nholish soldiers lay beneath their feet, pumping red life onto the planks. Other than barbarians and dead men, there was none to witness Ghe snarl and leap from the roof; two of the invaders managed to shoot him before he was amongst them, but neither shaft gave him pause. He was a panther among dogs.

The trip up-River had lulled them all. The people in the villages nearest Nhol had been coolly cooperative when they docked for supplies, but the farther away they voyaged from the great city, the more eager were people to see them. At Wun, the governor had thrown them a magnificent banquet, and though Bone Eel seemed bored by it—it was perhaps not sufficient for his jaded standards—Ghe thought it a grand show of hospitality, as did the soldiers. That had been a day ago. The governor had warned them that the Dehshe tribes on the east bank of the River were troublesome, but Ghe had gathered that most real attacks were on the outposts farther south and east.

But here they were. The impact of his body hurled several of them back, and then he was amongst them, carving at their hearts and lungs with the icicle point of his knife. He used the blade for two reasons. The first was that the soldiers on board the ship did not know his nature, and he did not *want* them to know. Let them think him a superb fighter—which, in fact, he was and could easily demonstrate. A more salient justification was that he *enjoyed* the feel of his blade in flesh, the exquisite geometry of cut-and-thrust, and though he could draw their lives from them more easily than he could stab them to death, the latter gave him greater pleasure. It recalled the joy of learning the ways of the Jik, and with that memory came a vague inkling of why he had ever been loyal to the priesthood, though they were so clearly monstrous. They gave him a thing of beauty; the discipline to kill with *elegance*, with art.

Of course, he did have the unfair advantage of already being dead. His wounds closed almost as quickly as his enemies made them, for this near the River, the flow of energy through his body was continuous.

He shattered an instep with a staccato stamp of his foot, plunged his blade through the gaping mouth of the ankle's owner, spun to parry—again, more for pleasure than anything else—a descending blade.

A flash of metal from his blind spot, and suddenly steel bit into his neck. His *neck*.

Ghe's shriek turned gurgle as his head flopped onto one shoulder. The blade had cut almost halfway through. He felt, rather than saw, the enemy arm cock back for a second blow.

Ghe blew the rest of the barbarians out like candles, reaching frantically for his head. It was already straightening, a weird, familiar tingling setting in. Ghe bit down on another shriek when the halves of his windpipe knitted back; then he nearly collapsed in a fit of trembling. He saw again the face of Hezhi's white barbarian, the demon, cleaving his head off, his life, his remembrance, blowing away on dark winds. Sagging against the rail, he shook like an ancient, palsied man.

And then his heart exploded. It was more reflex and gravity than design that toppled him from the barge and into the furrow of water behind it. *Li, think kindly of my ghost,* he thought, for the second time in two lives.

GHAN heard the sudden explosion of shouts, the twang of bows. He put his writing brush down carefully and approached the door to his cabin. He latched it. It was clear enough to him that the barge was under attack or that some sort of dispute involving most of the crew was coming to a violent resolution. He suspected the former rather than the latter. Though Bone Eel commanded no real respect from the men—he was *such* a fool—no one seriously questioned his station. And Qwen Shen did a fine job of seeing that he made the correct decisions, anyway, and so kept the men on his side. These were also imperial elite troops, not likely to mutiny under any circumstances—and thus far the voyage had been rather pleasant. Surprisingly so.

So they were likely being attacked, and likely by Dehshe barbarians—though also he considered that it could be the doing of the governor at Wun. The man, while affable enough on the surface, had a devious countenance when he thought no one was looking, and he seemed more than passing curious about the barge and its purpose. He had certainly not believed their stated reason for going up-River, which from the lips of Bone Eel amounted to no reason at all. What if the governor were in league with the barbarians, hoping to set Wun up as some sort of independent state? Ghan was familiar enough with the history of Nhol and other empires to understand that when an empire was weak—as Nhol was now—such things tended to happen. Or perhaps it was even simpler than that; perhaps the governor had turned pirate.

Ghan heard the clatter of a door opening and footsteps outside his door. Crouching slowly, so as to make as little sound as possible, he crouched to peer through the keyhole. He saw a figure just crossing from the sunlit hall into the shadow by the door that opened onto the narrow rear deck. That door suddenly swung wide, and a blaze of light flooded through, burned the person into a black silhouette bearing the arcing sliver of a bow in his hand. Through the door, Ghan could just make out another figure on the sunlit deck, leaning heavily against the rail. He thought it was Yen but could not be certain. The first figure raised his bow and fired. Yen—if it was Yen—tumbled over the rail.

The bowman stepped out onto the deck.

In the sunlight, Ghan could see that the man was not a barbarian or one of the governor's troops; he was one of the emperor's elite soldiers. Ghan had seen him several times standing watch. His scalp prickled. What was going on? He suddenly reassessed the possibility of mutiny and stepped gently back from the keyhole, realizing that he was holding his breath.

There came the sound of the outer door closing, then more footsteps, approaching his room. There they paused, and the door strained slightly against the latch.

By now Ghan was sitting on his bed. He looked up at the ceiling, an exaggerated expression of concern on his face. If the assassin looked through his keyhole, he did not want to be seen studying the door. Rather let him think him an old man, cowering until the battle was over.

Which, of course, was exactly what he was.

The footsteps went on. He heard the door to the main deck open. By then, the clamor of battle seemed to have mostly ceased. He heard soldiers barking orders, but no more frantic shouting or screams of pain.

Ghan's hands were shaking a few moments later when he screwed up the courage to open his door. There was no one in sight, but he could hear several soldiers talking on the rear deck. They must have catwalked around the side of the cabins or across the roof; Ghan had heard much trampling up there since the fighting began.

As he opened the portal, the entrance to the outer deck swung wide, as well, and for a terrible instant, Ghan thought it was the killer. But, though it was a soldier, it was certainly not the same man.

"Are you all right?" the man asked hurriedly. "Did any of them get in here?"

"No," Ghan replied. "Any of *whom*?"

"Barbarians, either Dehshe or Mang. I don't know the difference."

"Are they gone?"

"Yes, or dead." The man smiled a bit wolfishly. "Took on more than they bargained for, I'd say."

Ghan nodded absently. The soldier moved around the cabins, the rest of which were empty. Ghan followed him onto the rear deck.

"Great River, what happened back here?" the soldier muttered.

Ghan counted eleven dead men. Three were soldiers, but the rest were barbarians of some sort, dark-skinned, clad in rude leather and felts. He thought that the thick, lacquered wood and leather jackets they wore were probably intended to be armor. Most of them were heavily tattooed with blue lines and circles.

"Dehshe, I think," he told the soldier. "I've read that they tattoo their faces—and that the Mang don't."

"Well, Dehshe or Mang, they're as dead as dogmeat," the

soldier observed unnecessarily. He rolled one over. "This one's not even cut." The corpse in question stared at Ghan with vast surprise and horror.

Ghan realized that he was going to be sick an instant before he actually was, and so he made it to the rail in time not to add more noisome fluids than blood to the deck. The soldier, probably embarrassed for him, left. The other three, having completed their inspection, moved on, too, leaving him mercifully alone. After he was done heaving, Ghan stayed crumpled on his knees, unwilling to turn back to the corpses, afraid that he would choke out his very stomach if he did. His chest ached from the unusual action of the muscles there, and he took deep breaths, hoping thus to soothe himself. Watching the boiling gash of wake, he tried to pretend that the whole nightmare would be over soon.

Though, of course, he knew it was just beginning.

It was as he rose to leave that he saw a hand emerge from the water and reach weakly for the barge. It clawed at the side, failed to find purchase, and fell away again. Ghan furrowed his brow; a mooring rope lay no more than an armspan from him, already knotted through an eye on deck. But was this friend or foe? As if he *had* any friends on this ship. Fingers showed again, grasping more weakly.

Ghan fumbled for the heavy rope. A corpse lay half upon it, and he had to shove the still-warm body aside. He pushed the coil beneath the rail, and it unspooled into the River with a muted splash. Ghan then picked up one of the fallen swords, thinking that if the man in the water were an enemy, he would merely sever the rope. He realized—too late—that the sword was so heavy, he might have real trouble doing that.

It was the first time he had ever held a sword in his life.

The rope tightened. A face emerged from the water, and Ghan let the blade relax when he saw it was Yen. The boy had an expression of dumbfounded pain on his face. He looked up vaguely at Ghan.

"Li . . . ?" he gasped. It was both a question and an imprecation.

"Come on, boy," Ghan urged. "I don't have the strength to help you. But you've done the hardest part." He remembered the archer, certain now that it was Yen who had been shot. He felt a sinking in the pit of his stomach as he realized that this was probably all for nothing, that the young man would die regardless. How had he kept up with the barge?

Yen managed to pull himself to the rail, and Ghan took hold of the man's shirt and leaned back, felt how appallingly weak his grip was. He was not certain that this helped in the slightest, but the younger man flopped up, under the lowest rail, and dragged himself stubbornly onto the deck. Ghan could see the arrow wound now, though the arrow itself was gone. It oozed blood, or some fluid that resembled blood but was darker. He darted his head about, but there was no one aft.

"Come on. Can you walk? We have to get you to my cabin." Because the assassin was somewhere on the ship and, when he learned that his job was not complete, would probably wish to finish what he began.

Yen managed to get to his knees and, by clawing at Ghan's proffered shoulder, to his feet, though he leaned rather heavily. Puffing, Ghan steered him toward the open door of his cabin. He tried to lower him to the floor gently, but the result was that both of them collapsed. Ghan fell awkwardly, his hip slapping painfully against the hardwood floor. The hurt was mind-numbing, and for an instant he believed that he had cracked the bone.

Outside, he heard several men enter the corridor between cabins. Groaning, he disentangled himself from Yen, crawled on all fours toward the door, and pushed it closed before anyone could come in sight. Then, back to the door, tears of pain in his eyes, he waited for the inevitable shove against it. What story would he tell? He tried to think; the pain was subsiding to a warm numbness. No one tried his door.

Yen, for his part, coughed. A few flecks of blood came up, and Ghan knew that to be a bad sign. It was thus strange when the boy rose unsteadily to his feet, went to the door, and latched it. When he looked down at Ghan, this time, there was a sharp sense of recognition, and something unreadable flashed across his face.

"No," Yen muttered—clearly to himself. "No, I won't."

For the first time, Ghan stopped to wonder why he had rescued Yen at all, despite his basic distrust of the man. But the boy was the only one on the barge he really knew. And Hezhi liked him, which surely meant something.

Yen reached down for him and lifted him off the floor as if he weighed no more than a feather, cradling him like a baby. Ghan tried to protest, but the pain and his exertions had left him without a voice. The bed was soft, wonderful, when Yen laid him in it.

"Thanks," he managed to breathe.

"No, thank *you*," Yen answered. "I . . . may I stay in your cabin for a time?"

"I think you should," Ghan replied. "Someone up there is trying to kill you."

Yen raised an eyebrow. "You know who it is?"

"I saw him. I don't know his name."

"Really? That's good. That you saw him, I mean." He sat down and drew his knees up to his chest. His breathing seemed to have evened out.

"It might be Li, I suppose," Ghan offered.

Yen looked startled—no, he was *shocked*. "What? Why do you say that?"

"It's the first thing you said, when you came up out of the water."

"Oh. No, I . . . Li was someone I used to know, when I was a boy. I thought you were her for a moment."

"She must have been hideously ugly," Ghan remarked.

Yen chuckled. "Most found her so," he said, "though I did not. Funny." He looked at Ghan with clear eyes. "I believed I had forgotten her. And yet there she is."

"Memory is strange," Ghan said. "There are moments from my boyhood sixty years ago that I recall more vividly than yesterday. As you grow older, you become accustomed to that."

"There is no 'older' for me," Yen mumbled, and Ghan caught the glitter of tears in the dim lantern light.

Ghan swung his legs toward the edge of the bed, still worried about the ache in his hip, but certain he could walk now.

"I'll find Lady Qwen Shen. There must be someone on board who has medical knowledge."

Yen shook his head vigorously. "No, let it be. I'm growing stronger each moment."

"Let me see your wound, then."

"You won't see much."

"What do you mean?" But Ghan felt a sharp jab of premonition. It turned into a pain in the center of his chest, and he clutched at it, astonished by the sudden force beneath his sternum. The room shuddered. Somewhere, inside the maelstrom of pain and fear, he knew he was about to die.

But then Yen quietly said "No," as he had before, and the ball of pain in his chest was released. A sweet breath surged into his lungs, and another.

"I'm sorry," Yen said. "You didn't deserve that. I—"

"What are you *jabbering* about?" Ghan snarled, pain and relief suddenly churning into anger.

"Listen to me, Ghan. I wasn't lying when I said you and I were Hezhi's only hope. We are, and that is more certain to me now than ever. The emperor gave this expedition into *my* hands, do you understand? Not Bone Eel's."

"Yes, yes. That much is clear. You and Qwen Shen control this expedition."

Yen nodded grimly. "So I am betrayed by the emperor or more likely the priesthood. Possibly *both*."

"I don't understand."

Yen sighed. "I'm not certain I do, either. Have you explained to anyone else about our destination? Does anyone else but myself know even generally where we are bound?"

"The Lady Qwen Shen knows as much as you do. No one knows more."

"Then they must feel certain they can get the information from you. They don't want to risk me because they can't control me."

Ghan realized that Yen no longer seemed as if he was in pain at all. He had risen, begun pacing furiously about the cabin, though he kept his voice low, raspy.

"I saw your wound," Ghan said, articulating each word with great care.

"You are the greatest scholar I know," Yen said. He stopped pacing, and Ghan could see that his face was nearly drained of color. "Probably the greatest scholar in Nhol. And so you must tell me what I am, Ghan." He reached to his throat and unbraided the silly-looking scarf he always wore, let it drift to the deck. Ghan stared, frowning for an instant, before what he saw made itself understood. Yen turned slowly, to help him.

Another shudder touched his chest, just a light caress, but Ghan thought he knew now where the pain came from, what it threatened.

"L-let me think," he gasped, stammering for the first time since his eleventh birthday, eyes fixed on the impossible scar.

"Take your time," Yen said.

THERE was a rap at the door. Ghan, deep in furious thought, looked up at Yen. Yen placidly replaced the scarf on his horribly scarred neck and went to the door.

Their visitor was Bone Eel, dressed handsomely in blue turban and matching robe. Ghan caught the gleam of steel beneath the robe, however. Bone Eel had apparently been moved to don a cuirass, at least.

"Ah, there you *both* are," he said, sounding delighted. "I only wanted to make certain you had both weathered our recent bit of trouble. Very exciting, wouldn't you say?"

"Oh, indeed," Yen answered.

"Master Yen, your clothes are wet."

"True. Unfortunately, as I rushed to defend the barge, I stumbled and fell overboard."

"No! That's dreadful."

"It was. Happily, one of the mooring lines hadn't been tied up properly, and I managed to get hold of it. Otherwise, the boat might have left me behind with those barbarians."

Bone Eel smiled happily. "There wouldn't have been many to

bother about, I assure you. We killed most of them, I'm happy to report, and the others will think long and hard about ever attacking an imperial vessel again."

"That's good to hear."

"Master Ghan? All is well with you?"

Ghan tried to focus his thoughts on the lord's demented patter. It was difficult. It was very much like sitting near a fantastically poisonous viper; the viper had struck, playfully, once, just to show him its speed, leaving him to wonder whether the viper would strike him, or Bone Eel—or not at all.

"Well enough," Ghan tried to snap. "Though I would be better—*far* better—if I had never been included in this ridiculous mission." His tension loosened, just a bit, as he warmed to playing himself. "I think your charter has been well satisfied. We have sailed to Wun and 'points beyond,' and I think it's time we pointed the nose of this scow back down-River, to civilization."

"Now, Master Ghan," Bone Eel soothed. "One day up-River of Wun is *hardly* 'points beyond.' I think young Yen here would agree with that."

"I do," Yen confirmed.

"I never *asked* to be included on this trip, however," Ghan acidly retorted. "If I had—"

"Master Ghan, I've heard this objection from you before, several times, and I say what I said then. It is the emperor's wish that you chronicle this voyage, and so chronicle it you will. Now, I'm sorry for all of this unpleasantness, but the barge was never in any serious danger. We repelled all boarders and lost only seven men in doing so. Those are remarkably small losses, as I'm sure you know. Now, I must see to things, and knowing you are well, I do so without concerns for your health." He made as if to leave and then stuck his head back in and said, "Try to be more *cheerful*, Master Ghan. It is good for digestion." Then the noble left, closing the door behind him.

"Yes," Yen repeated. "Try to be more cheerful."

Ghan turned to face him. His speech about going back was

contrived, but the outrage he had discovered was real. "You ask me what you are? Don't you know?"

Yen's show of tears was over; his face was placid, his eyes frozen jewels, cold and without feeling. But though his lips formed a faint smirk, Ghan thought they lay there uneasily. He had a brief ridiculous thought that Yen had *pressed* them into shape with his fingers while Ghan's own attention was on Bone Eel. In any event, Yen did not answer except to gesture with his hand for Ghan to go on.

Ghan shook his head stubbornly. "No. You can kill me if you wish—that much is clear to me—"

"I can do far *worse* than kill you," Yen interposed, sending a chill down the knotted bone of the old man's back.

Ghan drew on all of his obstinance to continue. "*But* if you want my help, you must help *me*. What do *you* think you are?"

Yen stared at him poisonously for a moment, and Ghan wondered how this could be the same boy who had seemed so grateful a moment ago, who had so thoroughly charmed Hezhi a year before. But, of course, they probably were *not* the same.

"Very well," Yen snapped. "I call myself a ghoul. That was what we called creatures such as myself when I was a child."

"You have been a ghoul since childhood?" Ghan asked, his accustomed sarcasm reasserting itself finally. It was an old friend, comforting to have around, especially in the face of *this*.

"Very clever. I am not asking you to be clever in *that* way, Master Ghan."

Ghan was impressed by the gentle force behind the threat, but he had found himself now and wasn't about to retreat to that younger, fearful self. He was Ghan, and Ghan would not cringe.

"When did you become this?"

"The day that Hezhi escaped from Nhol. Her white-skinned demon—"

"Perkar."

Yen stopped, and a look of utter hatred crossed his face. "Perkar. He has a name. I knew I should have consulted you long ago."

"What did Perkar do?"

"Cut my stinking *head* off, that's what."

"You were in the River?"

"In River water, in the sewers. Something else was happening, too, but I don't remember. There was a sort of fountain of colors . . . no, I don't know what it was. It was next to Hezhi."

Ghan pursed his lips. "I have heard of creatures like you, yes. The old texts call them different things. Names aren't important, though. It's what you *are*, what properties you possess, that matters, and you know that better than I. Are you still Yen at all?"

"I was never Yen," the man admitted. "I was . . . my name is Ghe. I was a Jik."

"Set to watch Hezhi."

"Yes."

Fury brighter than any that Ghan had ever known jolted through him then, and before he knew what he was doing, he had stepped up and slapped the Yen-thing, once, twice. The creature looked at him in real astonishment, but as he pulled back to strike again, anger danced across the young features. Ghan never saw Yen—Ghe?—move at all, but suddenly an iron grip closed on his wrist.

"Sit down," Yen hissed. "I deserve that, but sit down before you make me angry. I have much to tell you. Then I must decide whether to kill you or not." He pushed back, and Ghan was suddenly sitting on the bed again.

"Now listen, and then counsel me if you can. Because despite it all, *our goal is the same*. That you must believe. If you don't— well, there is a way I can kill you and keep your memories. But I would rather have you alive."

"Why?"

"Because Hezhi loves you. Because you helped me just now. Because you remind me of someone."

Ghan measured his breaths. Would things ever start getting simpler? He understood more about what Ghe must be than he let on. He had a few ideas about how such creatures *might* be destroyed. So did someone else on the boat, for they seemed to have almost done it. And yet, ultimately, Ghan thought, whatever this thing was, it had been cobbled together from a man. The pieces of it were Human, though perhaps glued together with something both more crude and more powerful than humanity. But Ghe had feelings that could be known, understood. And understanding was a weapon greater than a sword. Especially in this case, when a sword was likely to be completely ineffectual.

But he had to live. He could not let the Life-Eater swallow him. He had read of *that* ability, as well.

"Tell me then," he said. "If what you say is true—if you really want only to help Hezhi—then I will help you. But you must convince me."

"I will," Ghe returned grimly. "One way or the other."

W HEN he finally left Ghan's cabin, Ghe felt more powerful than ever, strong enough to rend the barge in two. Now his power was tripled; the holy strength of the River in his veins, the tethered ghosts at his beck and call—and Ghan, as an ally. He could never fully trust the old man, he knew, but he wasn't without his senses. He could *feel* that the scholar would cooperate. Certainly he would not go to Bone Eel or Qwen Shen—though little would be lost there, since Qwen Shen already knew what he was. And Qwen Shen had tried to kill him, of that he was certain. Not herself, by her own hand, but she had arranged it nevertheless. Why? Of that he wasn't certain, and he needed to know. Was she a tool of the priesthood or the emperor? He thought the former, or else the attempt on his life would have been far less subtle. He went to his cabin, sponged off, and changed into fresh clothing.

He found Qwen Shen on deck. She smiled when she saw him coming. "Master Yen. I am happy to see you survived the skirmish."

"I am happy to have survived it," he acknowledged. "Overjoyed that *you* were not injured."

"Well, how very kind of you, Yen. Perhaps I am winning you over, after all."

He smiled thinly. "Perhaps."

"They say there were many dead barbarians on the afterdeck," she said. "Many with no apparent injuries. No one claims to have killed them, even the ones so expertly carved by knife."

Ghe bowed slightly. "It would be better that it remain a mystery. But if rumors develop, it might be hinted that I have been trained to kill with the force of my hands, without need of a knife. Such killing may leave no obvious marks."

She sidled toward him. "This is true?" she asked, reaching to touch the callused ridges of his hand. "You can kill with these?"

"You like that?" Ghe breathed. "That intrigues you?"

"It exhilarates," Qwen Shen replied. "It makes me wonder what else such hands are capable of."

"Such things may be discovered," he remarked.

"*Can* they?"

"They can." He bowed again. "And now I return to my cabin."

Qwen Shen bowed back, but her eyes remained fixed on him. He felt her scrutiny return to the cabins with him. It felt, to him, like an archer sighting along a shaft.

Qwen Shen did not wait long to accept his invitation. He had barely enough time to sit down before someone rapped on his door. Trying to anticipate almost any sort of attack, he swung his door wide, but no darts or flashing blades threatened, no incense or mysterious vapors. Just Qwen Shen. She glided through the door when he opened it, then stopped a few steps inside.

"Close the door," she said, and he did, latching it. "Now, then. What shall we *do*?"

"I have some questions for you. If you do not answer them, I will be forced to—"

"Hurt me? Will you *hurt* me, Yen?"

"What?" He stopped in midsentence.

"Why not hurt me *first*?" she cooed, reaching for the scarf at his neck. He reached to stop her, but she shook her head.

"If you want me to answer your questions, you must cooperate with *me*—at least a little."

Ghe had not expected precisely this, he was certain. If she had been responsible for the attempt on his life, there should be some fear on her part, some worry that he suspected her. After all, he had rebuffed her advances since the voyage began. Why should he extend his own now?

Perhaps she had some weapon, concealed in her clothing.

"No," he said. "You take off your clothes first."

She stepped back from him, her grin broadening.

"Very well," she whispered. She shuffled farther back and undid the sash on her kilt, then the kilt itself. They crumpled into a pile about her ankles, revealing slim, brown legs, a thick dark scorch of pubic hair, a sensuous curve of belly. With the same enigmatic grin she shucked off her shirt in a single motion, and then she was entirely, beautifully naked.

But nothing stirred in him, and he knew that it should. *Would*, if he were the man he had once been rather than a ghoul. She walked carefully toward him, as if balancing on a beam.

"And now you, my lord." She pushed him back on the bed, and he numbly allowed her to.

He lay there, watching her undress him, feeling nothing save the stroking of her hands on his flesh—but his flesh seemed like wood. She flicked her tongue along and around his necklace scar, and a spark fluttered, guttered, and died. He *tried* then, suddenly frustrated. Could his body not remember *this*, remember what to do at all? He forgot about what he came here to do, forgot that he had never once desired Qwen Shen. He tried, concentrating on her beauty, her warmth, and the luxuriant softness of her flesh.

"Ah, Lord Yen," she sighed. "You are keeping a dream from me. That is the problem. Don't try, don't worry, my love. Just let me know your dream."

My dream is to be *alive*, he thought, but he knew now, for certain, that he was dead. He wondered, dully, if when he was fully certain—when every corner of his brain accepted the truth—he would return to oblivion.

"I believe I know your dream," she said softly, coyly. "You

dream of a little girl, a little heart-shaped face, a little girl named Hezhi."

Anger stirred, if nothing else. What was this woman doing? Besides touching him, that is, here, *there* . . .

"Yes, Hezhi. You can say the name of your dream, can't you?"

"Shut up!" It exploded out of him before he knew what was happening. She sat astraddle him, and he struck her across the face. Her head snapped back, and she gasped, but instead of shrieking, she laughed. She gazed down at him with a broad, bloody grin.

"Say it," she repeated.

"Hezhi!" he snarled, and struck her again.

And suddenly he came alive. A jagged bolt of sensation was born in his belly and roared out into his limbs, his groin. In that instant, Qwen Shen ceased to be Qwen Shen, and he recognized who she *actually* was.

She was Hezhi. Not the little girl he had known but the woman she would grow to be. She still had the same face, and he was amazed that he hadn't noticed before. The same pointed chin and bottomless black eyes. The breasts pressed so passionately against his own bare skin had been barely hinted at before, the curve of her hip deepened, thickened appropriately with the passage into womanhood. The legs were longer, almost as lean, but had more shape. It was Hezhi as she would be, his lover, his queen. Her flesh met his in ardent rhythm, and in rhythm he passed from passion into forgetfulness. He remembered Hezhi, gripping her lip in her teeth, a look of adoration in her eyes. Then he forgot that, too.

Qwen Shen was dressing as he awoke. He brushed at the fog that seemed to hang about his brow.

"What?" he sighed.

"Shhh. Quiet. You made enough noise earlier."

"I don't . . ." He was naked, his body and the sheets drenched in sweat. Qwen Shen grinned faintly at him around her swollen lip.

"There, my sweet ghost. You rest." She fingered her injury. "Next time you should not hit my face. I can explain it this once, but if you continue to leave marks, even Bone Eel may come to the obvious conclusion." She bent, playfully nipped at his nose, then kissed him more fully on the lips. It seemed a distant thing, but his body still hummed with remembered passion. He could even recall the surge of volcanic pleasure . . .

He just couldn't remember *doing* it.

"Thank you," he told her as she approached his door.

"Save your thanks for later," she whispered. "There will be another time." Then she was gone, a patter of footsteps outside of his room.

With her going, he continued to cool. An image hung tenaciously at the edge of his vision, a young woman's face, one he almost knew . . .

But he could not summon it in detail, could not call it into recognition. He felt a slight frustration. It was probably some old lover, called back to his mind by making love with Qwen Shen.

He had to have made love with her. It was the only thing that made sense. But he couldn't *remember*, and that meant that the River must still be making him forget things.

He felt—not quite resentment, but puzzlement at that. He had assumed all along that the memories he lost were parts of him that died before the River salvaged what was left of him and made him into a ghoul. He still felt certain that such was the case, because many of the things he had once known would have aided him in his mission. Not knowing the Jik back in Nhol, for instance; the necessity of killing him brought on by his forgetfulness had hastened the Ahw'en finding him. But if he could *still* forget things, *new* things . . . He shivered at that thought. How much of what he knew was real?

And floating around that memory was the one he had finally recalled. He knew who Li was, knew that he had loved her and trusted her more than any mortal creature. And in his ignorance, he had slain her. Why would the River allow that?

The pain of remembering who Li was had come closer to

killing him than the sorcerous arrow that impaled his heart, but the remorse, like his passion, was cooled in him now. He wondered if it had cooled on its own, or if that, too, had been forgotten *for* him.

In the end it did not matter; all that mattered was finding Hezhi, the rest was mere distraction. His longing for her was almost frantic now, though he was not certain why. He must have her, his daughter, his bride . . .

This time, the strangeness of that thought troubled him not at all.

XXIII

Deep Wounds

COWARD, *coward, coward,* T'esh's hooves seemed to beat on the sand of the gorge. Perkar bit down on his lip until he tasted blood.

"Where are we going?" Harka asked.

"To get something that was stolen from me. To kill a thief."

"That's a riddle, not an answer."

"You're my sword. I don't *owe* you any answers."

"You just spent five days sleeping on the threshold of Death's damakuta. Whatever you are about, you should wait until your head is clearer."

"I don't think my head is likely to get any clearer," he snarled. "It's too much for me. I just want to be home, with my father, with my mother, tending cows. Why *me?* What did I do?"

"Loosed your blood in the Stream Goddess. Swore an oath. Killed Esharu, who guarded me. Betrayed the Kapaka and your people—"

"Stop, stop," Perkar cried. Tears coursed down his face and streamed back toward his ears. "I know all that. I only meant . . ."

He kicked T'esh harder, and the horse stumbled violently. Perkar's stiff legs almost failed to maintain their grip, as they jolted to a confused halt on recovery.

"*Easy,*" Harka cautioned. "*I can help you see in the dark, but not your horse.*"

"She had a *name?*" Perkar gasped.

"*Of course she had a name.*"

"And you know it?"

"*She was my guardian.*"

"You never told me."

"*You didn't want to know. You still don't.*"

"That's right," Perkar whispered furiously. "I don't. Don't ever tell me anything else about her."

Reluctantly, Perkar returned T'esh to a walk, at least until they were back to more open, level ground. Soon. The eastern sky was pinkening, as well, and so, shortly, T'esh would be able to see.

"*Where are we going?*"

Perkar collected himself before he answered. "I'm on some sort of edge," he answered at last. "If I fall one way, I become an animal, hiding from the sun, afraid of everything. I have to fall the other way."

"*Where do you fall if you fall the other way?*"

"I don't know. But if I let my terror overtake me, I'll be worthless for anything."

"*So, where are we going?*"

"It's death I'm terrified of. The last men to hurt me so, to defeat me, are down there following us. If I defeat them, I defeat my fear."

"*I doubt that. Many who bore me thought that by killing, they themselves could conquer Death. As if Death would be so pleased at them for feeding her that she would never swallow them.*"

"I didn't say I would defeat Death, only my fear of her."

"*This is not a rational decision. And you should know, because you made this same decision before, when you charged down upon the Huntress. You build up so much debt in your heart— and then try to discharge it by dying. But I won't let you die, and*"

*so it just builds up again. Anyway, you know that when a man
die in debt, his family must pay the balance.*"

"Shut up. Shut *up*."

"*Not rational.*"

"Listen," he said savagely, "it *is*. First of all, this is not the
Huntress and an army of gods. These are five Human Beings,
nothing more, and you and I have defeated twice that number.
We have a long way to go to reach the mountain, and we can't
worry about pursuit the whole way. We don't have enough horses
to keep the pace ahead of them. Better to deal with them now
before they come upon us one night."

"*But if you happen to die in the endeavor, you will die a hero,
and no one will blame you for not solving the larger problems you
have created.*"

Perkar did not answer, nor did he respond to any more of Harka's
overtures, until the sword—glumly, it seemed—warned him.

"*There.*"

Without Harka Perkar might not have seen them, camped in a
wash and shadowed by cottonwoods. Now, however, he caught
the motion of horses and men. Probably they heard him already,
and he had no intention of being coy. If he did, if he hesitated, he
would never do it. Terror beat in his breast, a black bat with
clawed wings, and for a moment his fingers were entirely nerveless. He drew Harka anyway.

I'm going to die, he suddenly knew.

"No!" he shrieked, and rode down into the wash in dim but
waxing light. An arrow and then another flew by, and his fingers
ached to tug on the reins, to ride out and away. But the arrows
were terribly wide of their mark, and his shriek became a whoop
that *pretended*, at least, to sound brave.

"*Something wrong here,*" Harka said.

Perkar sensed it, too. He counted five Mang bodies, sure
enough, but only one of them was moving. That one was Chuuzek, leaning heavily against the bole of a tree, bow raised awkwardly. Perkar leapt from his horse and rushed toward the
thickset warrior, splashing through the shallow water of the

wash. He suspected that at least some of the bodies he saw were merely bundles of clothes and the other Mang were hiding in ambush.

Chuuzek fired once more, missed, and drew his sword barely in time to meet Perkar's attack. It was a weak parry; the Mang weapon was flung back by the force of the blow, and Harka plunged into the warrior's lower chest. Perkar withdrew the sanguine blade and quickly stepped back.

"That for our game of Slap," he snarled.

"You be damned." Chuuzek coughed raggedly. His knees folded, but oddly, he did not fall. He seemed to balance on his toes, one arm draped against the cottonwood. Perkar searched for other attackers.

"No others," Harka assured him.

"What?"

"He was the only one, the only danger to you."

Chuuzek was trying to gasp something else out. The sword fell from his fingers, and he tried to reach for it. His hand seemed to be stopped by some invisible barrier that would only allow him to reach down so far. With a sudden shock, Perkar realized that Chuuzek was lashed to the tree. He could see the cords now.

He could also see that the man had numerous wounds other than the one Perkar had just given him. They were crudely bandaged, but the blood soaking them seemed fresh.

"Chuuzek?" Perkar asked. "What happened here?" He moved up to cut the man's bonds.

"No!" Chuuzek roared. He almost seemed on the verge of tears. Blood flowed freely and formed the largest pool amongst several already in the sand. "No. I deserve to die on my feet, you hear me? I *deserve* it."

"What happened?" Perkar repeated. "Are the others all dead?"

"All dead, all but me. Knew you would come. Go away, let me die among my own, without some shez around."

"Why do you call me that?"

"You are an abomination," Chuuzek whispered. "You are the doom of us all."

"Who told you this? This gaan I have heard about?"

"A drink of water. A drink of water and I will tell you."

Perkar found a waterskin near the remains of a fire that had not been fed in several hours. He brought the skin over to the dying man.

Harka warned him, but he did not move quickly enough. Chuuzek's knife slid in, cold as an icicle. He felt it scrape his ribs. Perkar sucked for air and fell back onto the sand, clawing at the offending steel. He got it out with considerable pain, then lay there gasping as the day came fully to life around them.

"*We are still weak, both of us,*" Harka apologized. "*I should have known more quickly.*"

The wound had stopped bleeding, though it still hurt mightily.

"Chuuzek . . ." He rolled over, so that he could see the other man. Chuuzek's eyes were already glazed. The knife, coated in Perkar's blood, stood point first in the sand.

I murdered him, Perkar thought grimly.

He had just managed, shakily, to stand, when he heard horses arriving. He retrieved Harka, lying an armspan from where he fell.

"*Not enemies,*" the sword soothed him. His hand was shaking.

Harka, of course, was right. The riders who came down into the wash were Ngangata and Yuu'han.

PERKAR was not greatly surprised to find that Chuuzek had either lied or been wrong. Three of the other Mang were dead, their throats torn open. One remained alive, however; the young man, Moss. He wasn't even bleeding, though there was a nasty bruise just beginning to purple on his forehead. He was spattered with a black fluid that Perkar recognized.

"That's godblood," he told Ngangata. "Godblood is either black or gold, in my experience."

"*Something* attacked them," Yuu'han muttered. He was staring suspiciously at Chuuzek.

"I killed him," Perkar admitted. "He had a bow. I didn't know he was wounded already."

Yuu'han shrugged. "He was brave, but his notions of honor were twisted. And at least he got to stab you."

Perkar almost retorted, but then he took Yuu'han's meaning. When he stabbed Chuuzek, it had been murder, plain and straight. The Mang had been in no condition to fight him. But he probably would have died anyway; he had strapped himself to the tree so that he would die standing up, with some slight chance to kill another enemy. Perkar—unintentionally—had given him that last opportunity. Perhaps Chuuzek had even died believing he had *killed* Perkar. Perkar felt a brief smile play on his lips.

His humor was short-lived. He had proved nothing to himself. There had been no battle, no real test of his courage. Indeed, he had killed an already dying man and then been duped into being stabbed. If the knife had been witched as the Slap paddle had been, he might be dead now despite it all.

Ngangata shot Yuu'han an irritated glance but did not speak to the Mang's comment. Instead, the half man followed the speckles of black blood across the wash.

"They wounded *this*, too, whatever it was. Perhaps that explains why two of them survived."

"Chuuzek must have wounded it before it could kill Moss. The others died in their sleep, I think."

Perkar joined Ngangata and stared intently at the trail himself. "What sort of footprints?"

"They look Human."

Perkar nodded. "That's no surprise. Gods take their mortal forms from the blood and bone of mortal beings. Most are said to appear Human, more or less."

"Should we follow?"

It took Perkar a moment to register that Ngangata was actually asking him what to do. "Maybe," he answered. "It could be the Blackgod, couldn't it? 'Helping' us?"

"It could," Ngangata replied, his voice empty of inflection.

Perkar followed the trail of dark fluid with his gaze, thinking. He remembered the hideous strength of the Crow God, the casually summoned lightning. He remembered Good Thief's doom, and how easily the fickle Blackgod might have chosen Ngangata instead. "Whatever it was—the Blackgod or some local spirit—it has done us a favor," Perkar finally said, trying to keep his voice even. It felt shaky, and he seemed to have trouble backing it with breath. "I think we should leave here now, before whatever it is turns on us."

"Good," Ngangata replied, heat creeping into his voice. "I wanted to see if you had even *that* much sense. If you had chosen otherwise, I would have clubbed you unconscious, magic sword or no. What kind of stupid idea came into your head and sent you down here alone? Playing the *hero* again? Haven't you learned your lesson by now?"

Perkar knew he couldn't explain to his friend, but he owed him something. He raised his hands—almost as if in defense—and tried to think of something to say.

"No," Ngangata snapped. "I don't want to hear it. You always think you're right, think you know *exactly* what you should do. Challenge me to a fistfight because I didn't know my place. Attack the Huntress. Leave me on the island with Brother Horse, because you *knew* it would be better for me—"

"You were *dying*," Perkar said, faltering beneath the rush of Ngangata's words.

"Always you know what to do, and always you are wrong. Then you say 'I surely was wrong that time, but now I know better, and next time I'll be *right*.' You stupid cowherd."

Perkar flushed with shame. He wanted to tell Ngangata that it wasn't at all like that this time, that he hadn't thought he was right, he had just wanted not to be *terrified*. He had needed to *do* something. But he couldn't say that. What came out instead was quavering, uncertain sounding.

"I just . . . you've all been fighting my fights for me while I lay on my back. I wanted to do something myself." Not a lie, not as unspeakable as the truth. He *might* have been able to tell Ngangata, but Yuu'han was there, judging him with that hard Mang judgment, and he simply could not.

Ngangata just frowned and started for his horse, his ration of words apparently spent for the day.

"Wait," Perkar said. "I wasn't wrong about leaving you on the island. I was *right* about that. You would have died on the River. If you hadn't, you would have died when the soldiers attacked me in Nhol. I didn't want you dead."

"*You don't want,*" Ngangata snarled, spinning on his heel. "You don't want this, you don't want that. Maybe *I* don't want to see *you* killed doing some damn stupid thing like this, did you ever, *ever* consider that? And maybe Hezhi and Brother Horse don't want you killed, or they wouldn't have risked their lives in the otherworld to get your stupid ass back."

He strode violently over to Perkar and, quick as a snake striking, slapped him so hard that he rocked back on his heels and sat down, violently, his teeth snapping with the impact.

"Now get on your damn horse and ride back up the hill with us and start using your head for more than a battering ram."

So saying, he leapt upon his stallion, gave heel to it, and in a flurry of dust was gone, leaving Perkar, blinking, on the ground watching him depart.

Yuu'han regarded him placidly, then offered him a hand up.

"If it's any comfort," Yuu'han confided, "I don't much care if you live or die. I say you should feel free to ride down on our enemies anytime the mood strikes you."

"Thanks," Perkar said, spitting blood onto the warming sand.

"We should take Moss with us," Yuu'han added. "Could you help me tie him to one of these horses?"

"Yes, of course." Perkar went to get one of the horses standing about.

"You didn't warn me that he was going to hit me," Perkar complained to Harka.

"*No, I most certainly did not,*" the sword replied.

THEY broke camp when Ngangata and Yuu'han returned with Perkar and Moss. The latter was unconscious, tied unceremoniously across the saddle of a horse Hezhi had never seen before. When she saw this, she expected to behold Perkar strutting about, full of his brave deed, and she was prepared to give him the tongue-lashing he deserved. Instead, she saw him looking more ashamed and uncertain than ever.

He wouldn't speak to her, other than to mumble a few apologies and to make *certain* she understood he was thankful to her for saving him from the Breath Feasting. After a few moments of strained silence, she kneed her horse up ahead to where Ngangata rode vanguard. There she pried the story from the half man, who doled it out in short, clipped phrases.

"What's *wrong* with him, though?" Hezhi asked. "Wasn't it better that he didn't have to fight?"

Ngangata lifted his odd, square shoulders. "I don't know. Sometimes I despair of ever understanding him."

"You've known him for a long time."

"No. Only just over a year."

"Really?" Hezhi thought she understood the general outline of Perkar's story—what Ngangata jokingly called the "Song of Perkar." But this part of the tale she did not know.

"How did you meet?"

"We were both members of the expedition to Balat. Of the five of us, only we two survived."

"It must have made you close. You seem like brothers."

That seemed to amuse Ngangata. "The first time we met we insulted each other. It may have been my fault. Later on we fought—with our fists, not with swords. That was *his* fault. After that . . ." He trailed off, but after a moment's thought picked up the thread and sewed it a bit further. "There is some good in him, you know, of a peculiar kind. Being as I am, I act as a sort of sieve that most people flow through, if you know what I mean. Perkar nearly went through, but in the end, he stayed. Whenever that happens, I count the person a friend, because it happens so rarely that I can't afford to ignore it."

"You mean most people are repelled by your appearance."

He shrugged. "*I* am repelled by it. There is nothing I hate more than a mirror or a clear pool of water. Well . . . maybe there are things I hate more, but I dislike seeing myself."

"I don't find you ugly," Hezhi said.

"You stopped in a different sieve long ago—your friend Tsem. So I would count you a friend, were we to know each other better. But you would never marry me, or bear my children."

That startled her. "I haven't—"

He waved with the back of his hand. "I only wanted to show you how alien the thought is to you. I have never given any thought to courting you."

Hezhi bit her lip. "Or anyone, I guess."

"Or anyone," he confirmed.

"Then you should, because I think someone would marry you, Ngangata. You are a good man, thoughtful. There must be a woman who wouldn't fall through the sieve."

He smiled. "Show me this woman and I will court her," he allowed. "I am not as fatalistic as Perkar. I take what opportunities come my way and do not spend time regretting those that do not. Show me such a woman, and I will take my opportunity."

"I'll keep my eyes open," Hezhi said. "But you should, too." She glanced at him and then away to the increasingly hilly land. "We haven't spoken very often," she said.

"No."

"I must ask you a question. I must ask you to answer it truly or not at all."

Ngangata raised his thick brows and waited.

"Can I trust Perkar?"

The half man pursed his lips and rode silently for so long that Hezhi believed he had taken the offered option not to answer at all. But finally he nodded.

"It depends on what you mean. You can trust Perkar to always try to do the right thing. That doesn't mean that you yourself can trust him. In the end perhaps you can, because the people he knows are dearer to him than Perkar himself comprehends. He believes, for instance, that it is the failure of the expedition to Balat that gnaws most at him—the fact that he let his people down. And he does feel that. But what strikes him most deeply is that the actual people who trusted him died: Apad, Eruka, his king. Now he struggles to right those wrongs, and it may blind him to certain things. Do you understand the distinction? Perkar believes in the pursuit of higher causes. That is why I call him a 'hero.' But when he focuses his vision too narrowly on saving the world, he can make terrible mistakes, and it is usually those close to him who suffer for it. In that way he is very dangerous, Hezhi. You should be careful of Perkar. He means no harm, but people die in his wake, nevertheless."

"I think I knew that. His rescue of me was for some 'higher purpose.' "

"Yes."

Hezhi shifted uncomfortably in her saddle. That seemed to be the end of the discussion about Perkar, though it only served to confirm what she already suspected. Unexpectedly, she found that she enjoyed speaking with the halfling—and was not yet ready to end their conversation. "What do you know about dreams?" she was surprised to hear herself ask.

"Not much. I do not have them. If I do, I do not remember them."

"How odd. I thought everyone dreamed."

"I have had hallucinations, when I was fevered. But I've never had a dream or a vision."

"My father has dreams," Hezhi said. "All of those of Royal Blood have them. The River sends them so that we may know his will."

"Have you had such a dream?"

"Something like that," she replied cautiously.

"You should speak to Brother Horse. He knows more of this than anyone here—as I'm sure you are aware."

"Yes, and I'll speak to him eventually. But I want you to know, too. In time it may become important."

"I'm flattered," the half man said, and he did not sound sarcastic.

"First of all, I don't think I got the dream *from* the River—not directly. I believe that if he could send me a dream, he would do more than that. I believe that I really am beyond his reach. But I think he sent his message through someone else."

"Who?"

"This Mang gaan the Blackgod told you about, the one who sent Moss and Chuuzek, whose men attacked you and Perkar earlier. *He* has found a way into my dreams. He tells me lies."

"What lies?"

"That part isn't important. I just thought . . . if he can send dreams to me, he might be able to do more. I know just enough about sorcery to suspect that." She looked down uncomfortably. "What I'm saying is, perhaps I can't be trusted, either. Perkar nearly slew me once, and for good reason. A dreadful power sleeps in me, Ngangata. I just want you to know that I should be watched, that's all."

Ngangata smiled. "I trust very little about the world," he said. "Perkar is perhaps my best—if only—friend, and as you know, I don't trust him. Inside of you, however, there is a—I'm not good with words—a kind of glimmer. Or maybe a truth. Something I trust, anyway." He looked away, plainly embarrassed.

"I hope you're right," Hezhi said.

"Well, I have been wrong before," Ngangata admitted. "And believe me, I never rely entirely upon such instincts. I will watch you—even more closely than I have."

"Thank you."

"No need for that," Ngangata assured her.

THEY traveled steadily until noon, and then the men conferred and called a halt. Brother Horse and the other Mang were essentially convinced that whatever creature had dispatched Chuuzek's party was not following them, guessing that it was a territorial rather than a roaming god. Perkar diffidently agreed. Moss had awakened, and everyone wanted to question him.

But it was Moss who asked the first question. "Chuuzek? What has become of my cousins?"

Moss sat on the ground, weaponless, hands tied in front of him. His feet were hobbled with a length of rope that would not hinder him much walking but that would prove inconvenient if he attempted to run. Brother Horse, Perkar, and Ngangata stood over him.

"Don't you know?"

"I don't remember anything much. Something struck my head as I was waking—" He fingered the bruise tentatively.

"Your cousins are dead. Something bleeding black blood killed them. Do you know what it was?"

"No," he replied, but his eyes flicked to Hezhi, and she saw something there that made her doubt his answer.

"Why were you following us?" Perkar demanded.

"You know," Moss answered sullenly.

"I know only that some shaman sent you to kidnap Hezhi. I don't know any more than that."

"That is the only thing you have need to know."

Brother Horse crouched, creakily, before the boy. "Moss, we want to know this thing your cousins died for. They died well; one tied himself to a tree, and whatever god they battled, they sent it away wounded."

Moss looked a bit triumphant at that but said nothing. Nor did he reply to any of their other questions. Hezhi was afraid they would strike or torture him, but after a time, they merely stopped in frustration; Ngangata, Perkar, and Raincaster went to hunt, Brother Horse retreated to tend the fire, Yuu'han watched Moss from where he whittled at a cottonwood branch. After a moment, Hezhi stood, brushed at her dress, and walked over to the green-eyed Mang. Heen roused himself to accompany her—the old dog seemed to have appointed himself her guardian as well as Brother Horse's.

"May I talk to you, Moss?"

"You may."

"You tried to convince me to go with you before. You said I could bring peace."

"I did tell you that."

She nodded. "I know you believe that to be true. There is much I don't know about you, Moss. I know even less about this gaan who sent you to gather me up. I only know that you aren't much older than I am and you can't be much wiser."

He started to interrupt her, but she held up her hand. "Listen to me, please. I want to say something to you, while I am not too angry to say it."

He subsided then and she continued. "When I was younger than I am now, back in Nhol, my best friend vanished. I looked everywhere for him, but I knew where he was all along. The priests took him away and put him in a dark place. They did this because he bore the blood of the River—the one you call the Changeling—and because that blood had marked him. I understood then that if his blood marked me, I would be taken away, too."

"That would have been a shame," Moss said. "A shame to put such a lovely woman somewhere dark."

Hezhi felt some bitterness creep into her voice and wished she could keep it out somehow. She really wanted Moss to understand her, not to raise his hackles. "Some have called me pretty— some, perhaps, because they thought it, others merely to flatter me. But if the Royal Blood had worked long in me, no one would have thought me pretty. My relatives so marked all became monsters. Do you want to see my mark?"

"Very much."

She pushed up her sleeve and revealed the single iridescent scale. "That was only the beginning. When I knew for sure that the change was coming to me, I ran. All of these people you see around me *helped* me run. They have all suffered for it, and many died because of my selfish desire to live. Now your gaan sends people after me, and more men are dying, and I want it to stop. But I will never go back to the River, because no matter what you have been told, *I* have felt his blood working in me. I know what I would do should he fill me up. He is tricking your shaman, trying to bring me to him. Your shaman in turn tricks you, and he sends me dreams, pretending to offer me my heart's desire. But I know what is best, because the River has been *in* me. People die now, but it is as nothing compared to what will happen if you return me to the Changeling. I will be forced to end my own life, if that happens, and I don't want to do that. But if men like you—good men, I believe, in your hearts—continue to die because of me . . ." Now she was weeping. "Why doesn't it stop? Why don't you all just stop it?"

Moss spoke very gently, and his eyes were kind. "The world can be seen from so many different angles. Each of us is born seeing the world in a different way, and each moment we live shapes our eyes and hearts differently. I believe everything you say, Princess. You have my sympathy, and I am sorry to have caused you pain. But I still must place my duty first, and now I have the blood of my cousins to avenge, as well. I will think on what you told me, but I will not lie to you; my way is clear."

Hezhi felt anger spark, but she pushed an acrimonious retort away.

"I don't expect anything from you," she said evenly. "I just wanted you to *know*."

Moss sighed. "And now I know."

As far as Hezhi could tell, there was nothing left to say. She felt tired, drained. Her vision had robbed her of most of the night's rest, and she wished she could take a nap, at least.

But there were two things she still needed to do. She had to speak to Brother Horse about her dream—but not now. Her talk with Moss had worn her out on that subject. There was something else, a nagging in her heart. She needed to talk to Tsem.

He had been moping for days. It troubled her that they had not spoken, but she was embarrassed, both by the Giant's morose self-pity and by her own reaction to it. Was this what growing up consisted of? Discovering that what you had always believed to be towers of eternal stone were really only shoddy façades? She had believed that her childhood had nurtured few illusions, but the feeling that Tsem was as unbreakable—in spirit, at least—as the iron he was named for had always been with her.

Now it had been swept away in wind, and what was left for her was someone who needed *her* comfort.

In all of her life, she had never been the one to *give* comfort. She had always sought it. It seemed a chore that she was probably not capable of. But she loved Tsem, and she had to try.

Making certain that Yuu'han was still watching Moss, she went to find her old servant, unhappy at how much she dreaded finding him.

XXIV

Sorceress

GHAN emerged into the fresh air and light of the afterdeck reluctantly; he had much reading to do and too little time, he feared, to complete it. But the motion of the boat—imperceptible as it usually was—made him queasy when combined with many hours of reading and writing. And though in Nhol he had considered sunlight about as desirable as poisoned wine, here he found it revived him, soothed him for more work.

Unfortunately, Ghe's sharp ears always heard him emerge and the ghoul almost always joined him, where they sat like a pair of spiders, limbs curled and eyes squinting at the brightness of daylight. This time was no exception; the door soon eased open behind him and Ghe trod noiselessly across the baroque patterns of rust-colored stains that recalled the carnage of a few days before.

"The dream becomes more persistent," the ghoul informed him, with no preamble, as if they were already in the midst of a conversation. Ghan glanced up from his absent study of the bloodstains, but Ghe was not watching him, staring instead at some middle distance.

"The dream about the Mang?" Ghan asked.

"Yes." Ghe drew his legs beneath him cross-style as he sat. "The emperor included you on this expedition for the purpose of counseling me. Use your scholarly wits and tell me what these dreams mean."

"I'm a scholar, not a soothsayer," Ghan snapped. "You need an old woman with casting bones, not me."

"An old woman with casting bones . . ." Ghe's eyes widened in startlement, then went far away—a sign Ghan had come to interpret as a search through his shards of memory. After a moment, he unfurrowed his brow and leveled an enigmatic gaze at Ghan. "Well, there are no casting bones here and no old woman. You must know *something* of dreams."

Ghan rolled his eyes and then tapped the deck, as if he were explaining to a child. "Hezhi had dreams about Perkar, before he came to Nhol. The River linked the two of them with visions, drew them together through them. You understand that much?"

"Have a care, Ghan," the ghoul cautioned him.

"You asked for my help."

"Yes, yes, go on."

"The River sends dreams, especially to the Waterborn. You told me he had sent you other dreams, in the past."

"Yes, to explain my purpose."

"Just so," Ghan agreed. "If you press me for my opinion in the matter, you are being connected to this Mang man by the River. He is an ally or an enemy."

Ghe twisted his mouth ruefully. "But which? *I* can sort *that* much sense into my dreams. Bone *Eel* could have told me *that*."

Ghan snorted. "Please, be my guest in seeking scholarly advice from Bone Eel." He rocked back against the bulkhead. His hip still hurt, and he wondered if he had cracked it. He turned to find Ghe, jaw muscles locked, staring intently at the water.

"You are wrong, you know," Ghan remarked.

"About?"

"I told you what I thought about your dream, and I told you I didn't know the explanation for it. A *fool*—like Bone Eel—would have given you a definitive answer."

Ghe fingered the little scar on his chin. Ghan thought he looked a bit more relaxed. "I see what you mean. Though even if you *had* an answer for me, you might not reveal it to me."

Ghan let that pass. Why deny the obvious? Instead he settled for at least appearing to be helpful. "What do *you* think about this mysterious horseman?" he asked. "What *feeling* do you have?"

Ghe shook his head as if affirming something. "That he is like me, a servant of the River. That he seeks Hezhi as I do." He shifted on the deck, produced a knife from somewhere, and began absently picking at the wood. As he spoke, he kept his gaze focused on the knife point, only occasionally half glancing at Ghan.

Like an embarrassed little boy. For some reason that comparison trotted a little shiver up Ghan's spine and disturbed him more than the moment when he had seen the scar and known what the man *was*.

"The *odd* thing is," he went on, digging a little trench around one of the larger stains, "though I have more frequent dreams of the horseman now, they are more shadowy, as well. His face is less clear than it was the first time I dreamed of him."

Ghan continued to shiver despite the deep warmth of the day and turned to watch an enormous green heron lift from the reeds at the banks of the River. Beyond the reeds and a few willows, short grass extended to the horizon. Two days farther south it was desert.

From the corner of his eye, he noticed Ghe following his gaze— or, more probably, eyeing his back. His shoulder blades felt cold suddenly, like twin hatchets of ice buried in him. But when the ghoul spoke, his voice was tinged with wonder, so that it seemed impossible he could be thinking of killing. "He's out there somewhere, isn't he? *She's* out there."

Ghan nodded and cleared his throat, surprising even himself as he recited:

"With their ship, the Horse,
They ply the sea of grass,
They stalk the walking mountains,
With stones they make their beds."

He trailed off and studied the deck more intently. "Well, you have to imagine it *sung*," he muttered.

"What *was* that?"

"From an old book, *The Mang Wastes*. I sent a copy of it to Hezhi when I learned where she was."

"You've read much about the Mang?"

"Lately. Lately I have."

"Since you discovered her whereabouts."

Ghan nodded in reply, caught the crooked look Ghe sent his way.

"You *do* know where she is. Well enough to send her a book."

"I told you that much before," Ghan replied.

"So you did. But you never showed me how to get there. When will you tell me *that*?"

Ghan answered with some heat in his voice. "You could *take* what you want. I know that. In fact, I wonder why you haven't." He set his chin defiantly, so that it wouldn't quiver.

"Qwen Shen wonders that, also," Ghe said. "I'm not certain what to tell her."

"Qwen Shen?" Ghan snorted. "Is she your advisor, too? Does she help you chart your plans as you take horizontal council with her?" He knew he was straying over the line, and he braced for the fist closing in his chest. But it made him *angry*, when people were stupid.

Ghe did nothing more than frown dangerously. "Have a care, old man," he advised. "Qwen Shen is a loyal servant of the emperor and the River. She deserves your respect."

"Five days ago you suspected her of plotting your destruction," he persisted.

"Five *days* ago I had just been *wounded*. I suspected everyone. Now I conclude that the assassin was a Jik, placed among the guards by the priesthood."

"Have you questioned *him* in this matter—the would-be assassin?"

Ghe raised his palms in a small gesture of helplessness. "He was killed by a Dehshe shaft just after wounding me. Not the death I would have invented for him, but at least he is no longer a danger."

"You don't see the great convenience in that? In his dying before you could question him?"

"Enough of this," Ghe snapped in annoyance. "We were discussing *your* decision to tell me where Hezhi is."

Ghan sighed. "My life has recently taken a turn for the worse, but I'm still selfish enough to value it. I will *take* you to her."

"Old man, if I were going to kill you, I already would have."

"I know that. It isn't *your* killing me that I fear." Which was not entirely true. Ghe inspired both fear and revulsion in him. And something was *different* about him these past few days, unpredictable since he and Qwen Shen had begun their liaison.

Ghe's lip curled, half protest, half snarl. "I told you—"

"I know what you think of her. But *I* am not sleeping with Qwen Shen—and *I* don't trust her. You just as much as said she's trying to convince you to swallow up my soul, or whatever it is you do."

Ghe gazed straight at him then, his eyes like glass, the unwinking regard of a serpent. He clucked thrice with his tongue, as if chastising a baby. "You don't understand about her," he said. He leaned close, and his voice became confidential. "I know we can trust Qwen Shen because she is the River's *gift* to me."

"What?"

"For serving him." Ghe lowered his voice further, and his murderer's eyes focused on the vast horizon. "Since I was reborn, I've never forgotten that I was dead," he explained. "When I was a Jik, I used to say 'I am a blade of silver, I am a sickle of ice.' That was to remind me that I was merely a weapon, something the priesthood might wield against its foes. I was content with that. When I was reborn, I knew that I was still a tool, but this time my lord was higher, my purpose grander. But still a tool, to be dis-carded when the job was finished."

A sickly grin writhed upon his lips. "Do you know what it is to live in nightmare? In my world, Ghan, food has no taste, wine no intoxication. The River has large, but simple appetites, and the small things Human Beings enjoy are beneath his notice. Night-mare, where nothing is as it should be. You bite into the sweet-meat and find it full of maggots. You shake your mother to wake her—and find her dead. *That's* what it's like, if you want to write it down. Yet now, *now*, the River has given me Qwen Shen. You can't possibly comprehend what that means."

"You love this woman?"

"Love her? You understand *nothing*. She is a gateway. She pre-pares me."

"Prepares you for what?"

Ghe stared at him as if he were insane. "Why, for Hezhi, of course."

Ghan bit back a reply, but as it sunk in, he shuddered again at the sheer dementia of that claim. He very much wanted to leave the afterdeck and go somewhere else, but there was nowhere else *to* go. Ghe asked if he understood living with nightmare, and he wanted to reply that he *did*. The entire barge seemed like a floor ankle-deep in broken glass, and him without shoes: no place to tread safely. His hopes of misleading Ghe and the others grew slimmer with each moment; if the self-styled "ghoul" ever suspected that Ghan was lying to him, he would merely devour him. It would probably be best for him to drown himself now, before they got what they wanted from him one way or the other. But even that might be pointless, if Ghe really was linked with some Mang ally of the River. In fact, since the Mang were nomadic, Hezhi was more than likely *not* where Ghan had known her last to be. This dream man of Ghe's probably had more current information on her whereabouts than *Ghan* did.

So killing himself would probably not help Hezhi significantly, and it *would* remove the only *real* ally she had. No, as long as a chance existed for him to help her, he would not remove himself from this game of Na. He might not be an important counter, but he *was* a counter. Even the lowest such could eclipse and remove any other marker on the board.

"Tell me more about the Mang," Ghe said, abruptly interrupting his thoughts.

Ghan motioned at the surrounding plain. "You see where they live. They travel and fight mostly on horseback. They live in skin tents and small houses of stone and wood."

"That passage you quoted, about walking mountains. What did that mean?"

"The plains are home to many large creatures. The Mang hunt them to survive."

"What creature is as large as a mountain?"

Ghan cracked a faint smile. "That was Saffron Court literature. Literature from that court is prone to hyperbole."

"Hyperbole?"

"Exaggeration."

"But what were they exaggerating?"

Ghan shrugged. "We shall see for ourselves, soon enough."

"That's true," Ghe murmured. "I'm looking forward to it." He gestured once again at the alien landscape. "I never understood how big the world was, how strange."

"I would settle for a smaller one at the moment," Ghan admitted. "My own rooms, my library."

"The sooner we find her, the sooner we can get you back there," Ghe reminded him.

"Of course," Ghan muttered. "Of course."

Sleep eluded Ghan for most of the afternoon, but he was near finding it through a dark thicket of half thoughts and full fears when he heard shouting. In that realm of semislumber, it seemed like a bell, clanging, and an image erupted from his sleeping memory into vivid life; the alarm ringing in his clan compound, himself just turned sixteen, the grim-faced soldiers filling his father's court like oddly colored ants, the look of terrible despair on his father's face.

"Hezhi!" The bell rang, and Ghan came entirely awake. The noise was from Ghe's cabin, along with the now-familiar rhythmic thumping of his bed. Ghan's mouth felt dry, and he reached a trembling hand to the stoppered jug near his bed and took a drink. The water was warm, nearly hot, and it failed to soothe him as it might. He wished it were wine.

Twice now he had heard Ghe shout Hezhi's name in the heat of his passion, and he shuddered to think what it meant. He forced himself to, however, because there was something crucial happening to Ghe, something the ghoul himself wasn't aware of— something Qwen Shen was *doing* to him. Ghan could see the consequence, but he didn't understand the cause.

The effect was that Ghe was becoming stupid. In earlier conversations—both as Yen and Ghe—Ghan had not been unimpressed by the young man's native intelligence. Despite a clear lack of formal education, he was still able to comport himself better than most nobles and to discuss topics of which he had no knowledge with fair dexterity once he had been supplied with basic items of information. Now, suddenly, he was unable to make obvious connections. His memory seemed worse than ever, erratic.

The manifest probability was that Qwen Shen had somehow ensorcelled him. That made it likely that Ghe's earlier—now stupidly discarded—guess that she was somehow connected with the priesthood was correct. He had seen but never read the forbidden books in the Water Temple, texts on necromancy and water magic. The references he had found to what lay *inside* those covers suggested that there were ways to turn the power of even a god against itself.

He remembered Ghe's tale of what lay beneath the Water Temple, the things he had learned. Many would have thought that account the insane ravings of a mad beast, but he had always had his own suspicions about the priesthood. How had Ghe explained the power of the temple to stupefy the River? It had to do with the resemblance between the temple and She'leng, the source of the god. The River sought, ultimately, to return to his source, and a part of him was tricked into believing he had found it, into forming a circle.

Ghan sat up in bed, fists clenched on his chin. What if Qwen Shen had somehow done the same thing to Ghe? *His* purpose in existing was to find Hezhi. Whatever Human emotions he confused with that purpose, it came ultimately from the River. What if Qwen Shen somehow convinced a *part* of Ghe that he had found her? Did Ghe somehow suppose he was making love to Hezhi?

Well, clearly he either thought that or fantasized it.

And this was making him stupid. Controllable.

That wasn't necessarily bad. Ghe was a dangerous creature, an eater of life, a ghost in flesh. Whatever motives Qwen Shen had, they were bound to be more *Human* in origin and scope. But what *were* they? Unfortunately, though, he knew little of her motives, but he knew at least *one* of her aims: *his* death. That in itself was incentive enough for him to find some way of freeing Ghe from her influence. If she ever managed to convince him that Ghan was worth more as a ghost than as a man, he was doomed.

He was probably doomed no matter what, he thought, and with that optimistic assessment, he lay back down and sought sleep once more, hoping that his own dreams might provide, if not answers, solace.

"How can we be *assured* this is the right stream?" Ghe demanded, making certain that Ghan caught his suspicious tone.

The old scholar blinked like an owl in the brilliant noonday sun. He pointed vaguely at the River mouth. A sandbar trailed downstream from it, and the banks were verdant with bamboo and other plants whose names were unknown to Ghe.

"It's the first one *wide* enough on this side—since going upstream of Wun," he answered, somehow managing to make those dry facts sound like grumbling, a sharp retort. Ghe considered chastising him, but Bone Eel and Qwen Shen both stood nearby, and appearances had to be maintained.

He turned to Bone Eel, who was gazing at the stream mouth unhappily. "Can we navigate that?" Ghe asked. Bone Eel knew little else, but he did know more about boat travel than Ghe.

Bone Eel waved his arms theatrically. "Not far, I suspect. That sandbar is a bad sign. Makes me think the whole tributary might be fairly silty." He turned to Ghan, hands now balled on his hips. "Does your book make any mention of depth?"

Ghan looked cross and consulted the volume he had reluctantly dragged from his room to the Tiller Pavilion. It lay on a mahogany desk usually reserved for charts.

"Let's see," he muttered. "Thick about with bamboo—the fishing is fair, if one likes trout—here we go. 'The mouth is twelve copper lengths wide, and the channel is five deep. Both the width and the channel maintain themselves for a distance of eight leagues inland, where the River splits into a greater and lesser branch, neither of which will take the hint of a keel. By flat skiff, one may then make one's way.' " The scholar glanced up from the pages. "That's what it says," he noted.

Though he listened to Ghan's words, Ghe found his attention drifting back to the open River mouth. It *appeared*, to his untrained eye, that the barge could easily fit, once beyond the sand and debris that seemed to clutter the entrance. Past that, the small river looked wide and clear.

Ghe narrowed his eyes. *Something* was happening where the tributary met the River. Water swirled into him, and where those waters *met*, Ghe saw a line of turbulence—not just in the liquid, but in the substance behind it. And he felt despair, humming in the air like some familiar song.

Despair and pain, hunger. The first two from the stream flowing in; the last, of course, from the River, for it exactly resembled the hunger he knew when he was away from the water and the living were his bread and meat. The River devoured this smaller watercourse: not just its water, but its spirit. Which meant that there were other spirits than the River in the world. Not *gods*, surely, but creatures *like* gods.

The sudden import of that struck him nearly physically, and he heard not a word of the conversation that continued between Ghan and Bone Eel. Instead, as he gazed at the continuing death of the tributary, he heard again the laughter of that *creature* beneath the Water Temple, its smugness, almost as if it viewed the Rivergod with *condescension*.

He nearly killed Bone Eel when the fool plucked at his arm. He felt the might gather, and behind it a sudden renewal of hunger, perhaps a sympathetic reflection of the River's own hunger. But he caught Qwen Shen's concerned gaze, and he relented. "Really, Master Yen," Bone Eel was saying. "I must insist you pay attention."

"I'm sorry," Ghe said, trying to infuse his voice with interest he did not feel. "I was just taken with the thought of leaving the River. It seems so strange."

"Yes," Bone Eel agreed, "and I wonder why we are doing it. Eight leagues isn't very far. What can we discover in eight leagues? It seems to *me* that we would be better off sailing farther up the River himself."

"Darling," Qwen Shen said sweetly, patting his shoulder. "Don't you remember explaining to me how important it is to chart navigable watercourses and land routes? Master Ghan assures us that both can be found up this stream. You may also remember that you said the crew needed a break to hunt and forage for a time. What better opportunity than now?"

"Oh, that's true," Bone Eel said. "I *was* thinking that."

Inwardly Ghe wondered how such a woman as Qwen Shen could stop herself from smothering this silly fop in the night, but he also knew the answer. For women in Nhol power could be had only through a husband, a son, or a brother. Bone Eel was heir to a fair amount of power but hadn't the wits to use it. Probably everyone at court understood the source of the nobleman's ideas and was relieved that he had a keeper.

"Very well," Bone Eel said. "Haul on the tiller, and I shall command the dragons!" he called to a knot of sailors awaiting his orders. "Soldiers, I want to see bows and fire for the catapult! This is unknown territory, and who can say what we shall find?"

Moments later, their prow nosed carefully through the mouth of the River and entered, by way of water, the lands of the Mang. When they crossed that line—the one no one but he could see—Ghe felt a tremor, a wave of sickness that quickly passed. But it left undefined worry behind it. He noticed Qwen Shen's batted eyes, the invitation they issued. *She* understood his moods and knew just as well what was good for him. After a few moments, he left the deck and went to his cabin to await her.

Ghan was already back in his room, deeply engrossed in yet another tome. How many had the man brought with him? In passing, he noticed a feeling like . . . triumph? Hope? It was hard to tell with Ghan. He must have found something in his book he had been searching for. Hezhi used to light up with that same sort of ebullience when she found something she suspected or hoped for in her research. Though then he had not the power or need to *sense* those feelings; Hezhi *radiated* them, the way the sun produced light.

Hezhi. Soon!

His body stirred, in anticipation of Qwen Shen's arrival.

GHAN heard when Ghe went by; he had learned the ghoul's gait long ago. Desperately he began reciting a poem to himself, over and over, trying to mask his true feelings, his precariously balanced hope and triumph.

Ghe passed, but Ghan kept repeating the verse:

> "Often sweeps Death
> The houses of living,
> A menial task,
> That brings into her fair, dark eyes
> A sparkle of joy
> At the little things she finds there."

Only when he heard Qwen Shen enter and the sounds of pleasure begin in Ghe's room did he return to the book, tracing his finger back to the point he left off, a paragraph or so below the bold caption that read, in the ancient hand:

On the Nature and Composition of Dragons.

XXV

Falling Sky

THE shadow surprised Perkar when it settled upon him. Not because he hadn't heard the methodical progress of someone climbing up the broken, stony face of the mesa; he had known for some time *someone* was coming up, presumably to see him. What amazed him was that the abundant silhouette could be cast only by Tsem, even with the cooperation of the westering light to lengthen it. Tsem, or perhaps some gigantic beast—but then, Harka would warn him of the latter.

Then again, remembering that Harka had been less than perfectly reliable of late, he turned to see from what shoulders the dark umbra fell.

It was, in fact, Tsem. Perkar's face must have registered his amazement, for Tsem held out a hand signaling that, once he ceased wheezing and panting, he would explain what he wanted.

That took a few moments. Despite the coolness of the afternoon, the half Giant was sweating profusely; a faint breeze mingled pungent man-smell with the desiccated tang of juniper, sage, and yarrow.

"My mother's people," the half Giant finally managed to gasp, "Giants must live on soft, flat land. Surely we were not made for climbing up and down mountains."

Perkar stretched his lips in a grin he did not feel. He had volunteered for the watch up on the mesa to be alone; he had much thinking to do, and he knew he was poor company. Still, he had a guarded respect—admiration even—for the half Giant, although time and circumstances had allowed them only the most cursory of relationships. If this were some overture on Tsem's part, it couldn't hurt to *appear* a bit brighter, though he would much prefer to sulk. His father always said that a friendship missed was like an important trail passed by, and Perkar felt that he had already passed by many such trails in his short life. Of late, his friends had shown a tendency to die, and he was left, really, with only Ngangata and perhaps Hezhi, neither of whom seemed to be speaking to him at the moment—with reason. He could *use* another friend.

So he smiled his difficult smile and waved at the mesa edge, and said, to be social, "This isn't much of a mountain, either. Really just a ridge." He turned his gesture beyond, jabbing an index finger toward a high line of peaks to the northeast. "*Those* are mountains. Be happy we skirted around them."

"I am," Tsem assured him, mopping his brow and looking around. "Nice up here, though. It reminds me of a place Hezhi and I used to go."

"It does?" Perkar could hardly imagine that. What he had seen of Nhol had been impressive, and from a sufficient distance its hills and high walls of stone had a certain recondite beauty; but there was nothing of the Nhol *he* had seen that suggested the crumbling stone slope of the plateau they sat upon or the verdant, stream-etched plain five hundred paces below where Hezhi and the others were camped.

"In a *way*," Tsem clarified. "It's like being up on the roof of the palace, looking out over the city. The way the light shines, the smell. And there was a courtyard with flowers like this." He waved a sausage-fingered hand at the white yarrow that blazed over the plateau, blushed pink by the sunset—an ethereal carpet of blossoms ruffling knee-high in an imperceptible breeze. They shone in vivid contrast to the stark black skeletons of ancient hills that bounded the tableland on its south and west.

"I never saw any sights like that in Nhol," Perkar confessed. "My time there was short."

"And spent mostly on the docks. I know." Tsem's massive features crushed themselves into a thoughtful frown. "I came up to ask you a favor," he blurted suddenly.

"Ask," Perkar said. "Although at the moment, I wonder what use I can be to you."

"Oh, but you can," Tsem said. He stopped, grinned. "It is *so* good that you ken my language. Even Hezhi speaks it only when we are alone, and lately not even then. She wants me to learn Mang." He looked embarrassed. "I'm not very good at it."

Perkar nodded understanding. "Neither am I, friend. I speak your language because the River taught it to me somehow. Or maybe Hezhi did, without knowing. But my Mang is at least as bad as yours."

"Me bet we talk to each other good in Mang," Tsem stammered in his broken version of the tongue.

"Yes. We speak good together," Perkar answered in kind, and they both smiled. Perkar felt, once again, a warmness for the Giant that was difficult to explain; Tsem had threatened his life when they first met and had been at best brusque since then. But something about the quality of his loyalty to Hezhi, his genuine selfless love, demanded affection from Perkar. When the River transformed her, only Tsem had prevented Perkar from killing Hezhi, not by stopping him physically but merely by being there, by protecting her with his own wounded body. To kill Hezhi, Perkar would have had to kill Tsem—and he had been unable to do it. Perhaps because, in so many ways, the Giant was like Ngangata. Not just because they were both only half Human, but because they shared fiercely good hearts.

He had never gotten to *know* Tsem, though. Injured in the escape from Nhol, the half Giant had been unable to accompany the Mang to the high country for autumn and winter hunting. And of course Perkar himself had been injured immediately on his return to the lowland camp.

"You almost made me laugh," he said, still grinning from their exchange of garbled Mang. "That's more than anyone else has done for my mood lately. Ask your favor."

"I think you should know something first," Tsem said solemnly, and the smile fled from his face. "Something that shames me. When you were ill, I advised Hezhi to let you be, to give you up for dead."

Perkar nodded slowly, narrowing his eyes, but did not interrupt as Tsem pushed on with his admission, eyes focused firmly on a yarrow plant two handspans away.

"She's already been through so much," he explained. "I understood that she would have to do this thing with the drum—this thing I don't understand, only I understand how *dangerous* it is. I couldn't bear the thought that she would—"

"I understand," Perkar said. "You have nothing to explain. She didn't owe me anything."

"She thinks she does. Maybe she *does*. But that's beside the point, because I owe you. You saved her when I couldn't. You saved us both." He frowned again, chewed his lip. "That really made me mad."

Perkar did chuckle then, though it was a bitter humor. "I think I understand that, too."

"I haven't said the worst," the half Giant growled. "After I got hurt, I just lay there, surrounded by these people speaking nonsense. I guess I had fun with a few of the women—" He shrugged. "That's nothing. But Hezhi *left*, went off with you. I thought 'I can't save her anymore and I can't keep her company.' And I figured you two would get married and that it would only get worse. And I couldn't tell Hezhi *any* of this, you see?"

"Married?" Perkar said, incredulous. "Whatever gave you the idea we were courting?"

Tsem shrugged his mammoth shoulders helplessly. "I don't know. Nothing. But she *cares* for you, the way she has never cared for anyone except me and Qey and Ghan. It scared me. And when I thought she might risk her life for you, that scared me more than anything."

"Because you love her."

"No, that's the worst thing—the very worst. Because I thought 'What will I do out here without *her*?' Not 'What will she do without *me*?' "

Perkar regarded the Giant's agonized face for a long moment. "Does she know any of this?" he asked quietly.

"She knows I'm useless out here. She thinks I'm pathetic. She tries hard to talk her way around it, but she does. She looks to the rest of you for help and strength, but for me she only feels pity. And she's right. I am no use to any of you out here. Anywhere but in Nhol—in the *palace*. Such a little place; it was easy to be strong there, Perkar."

Perkar honestly did not believe he had ever seen such a doleful expression. Like everything about him, the Giant's sorrow was huge.

"And so what can I do for you, my friend?" Perkar asked gently.

"Teach me to fight with something other than my fists. Teach me to be useful again. Teach me about this country."

"What? I don't *know* this country. It isn't my home. And I'm no great warrior."

"I've seen you fight," Tsem said. "If you don't want to help . . ."

"Wait, wait, I just want you to understand. I fight well because I carry a godblade, not because of my own skill."

"I don't understand. It's your hands that carry it."

"True enough. But Harka cuts through ordinary steel, helps me know where to strike—and if I make a mistake and get stabbed, Harka heals me."

"But you know how to use a sword, or none of that would do you much good."

"True enough. I'm not a *bad* swordsman, Tsem, just not as good as you think. And as a teacher . . . well, I've never done *that* at all."

"But you *could* teach me," Tsem persevered.

"Why me?" Perkar asked, suddenly suspicious. "Why me and not Ngangata, Yuu'han, or Raincaster? Because I'm the *killer?* Because Perkar is the one you just point toward the enemy and say 'kill that,' like some kind of *hound?*" He tried to keep his frustration in check, but it was spilling out. Tsem thought of himself as useless. Was that better than being thought of as having only *one* use? And what good to be a killer if one were suddenly afraid of even that?

Tsem didn't answer the outburst, but his brows rose high on his forehead.

"Answer me," Perkar demanded again. "Why me?"

Tsem made a strange face—Perkar could not tell whether it was anger, frustration, or hopelessness—but then the wide lips parted from champed white teeth in what seemed a furious snarl. But it wasn't; Tsem was urgently suppressing a smile. A giggle! Perkar's anger evaporated as quickly as it had come.

"What? What are you laughing at?"

"I shouldn't laugh," Tsem said, hand across his chest, trying to hold in a series of deep, growling snickers. "But you looked so serious . . ."

Perkar watched him in absolute befuddlement, but the Giant's laughter, however inexplicable, made him feel foolish, and more, he found himself smiling, as well. "What?" he demanded again.

"Well, it's only that I chose you because you speak *Nholish,* that's all." And then he interrupted himself with a real guffaw. It sounded ridiculous coming from the man-mountain, and then Perkar could help himself no longer, joining Tsem in his laughter.

"WELL, a sword isn't for you," Perkar said later, when they began discussing the matter again.

"No?"

"No. First of all, we don't have one to spare, certainly not one that would fit your grip. Second, with your strength, you would probably break any blade you used. No, you would be an axe-man."

"My mother carried an axe."

"Your mother was a warrior?"

"She was one of the emperor's guards. He usually has full-blooded Giants in his elite."

"But *you* weren't trained to fight?"

"Just with my hands. Wrestling and boxing. I think they were afraid to teach me to use steel."

"I can see why. I would hate to have a slave three times my size that was armed."

"No, that wasn't it. My mother was larger than I, and the men of her people are larger still. But they aren't . . . they aren't very *bright*. It would never occur to them to try to fight or run away, as long as they are well fed and treated with some respect. But I was an experiment. The emperor ordered my mother to mate with a Human man. I'm told that it had been done fairly often, but that I was the first successful cross. The emperor thought I might be more intelligent than my mother's folk, and so he never had me trained in weapons. He kept me at court for many years, as a curiosity, but then I suppose he grew bored with me and sent me to guard his daughter."

"They crossed your parents like cattle? That's disgusting."

Tsem looked thoughtful. "It's no different from an arranged marriage, is it? Your folk do that, I'm told."

"Well, occasionally, but that's different," Perkar said, taken aback by the comparison.

"Why?"

"Well, because marriages are arranged for property, inheritance, or alliance. Not to create hybrid stock!"

Tsem grunted. "I am *not* as smart as a full-blooded Human, so you will pardon me if I don't see an enormous difference. Anyway, in Nhol, marriages *are* arranged to concentrate the Blood Royal."

"I . . ." Perkar frowned, shook his head. "Anyway, to get back to our *real* problem: we don't have an axe, either. No, I think for someone with your size and strength, and given our situation, we shall have to find a club for you."

"You mean a big stick?"

"I mean a wooden mace. A good, heavy branch or sapling with a solid, hard knot on one end. We can work it down with a knife until it's right." He nodded thoughtfully. "We could make a spear, too. And a shield!"

"Do I really need a shield?"

Perkar reached over and poked him in the ugly scar across his belly, where the assassin's sword had nearly gutted him. "Yes. You can hold the shield in front of you thus—" He hopped to his feet and turned so that only his left side faced Tsem, left arm crooked as if bearing a shield. "—and you strike over it, *thus*." And he cocked an imaginary club back to his shoulder, then swung it down past his ear and over the equally fictitious shield. "With your reach, *no* one could get close enough to you to fight around your shield or through it. With a shield and a club, you will be more than a match for most warriors, even without a lot of training."

"But you will train me?"

Perkar nodded, oddly elated. "Yes."

"Good. I will never counsel Hezhi to leave you for dead again. When do we make my club?"

"First we have to find one. I think I know what to look for."

"Can we look now?"

Perkar shook his head. "Too late. We should either start a fire up here or go down. There are wolves in this country."

"You can start a fire?"

"Sure. Go collect firewood for me. We'll keep watch together."

He watched the Giant lumber off, happy to see him enthusiastic about something—he had never seen that in Tsem before. This development did nothing to solve his own problem, but neither did thinking about it. The distraction was welcome.

"WHO is that singing, Heen?" Hezhi whispered, reaching to scratch the yellow-and-brown mutt where he lay near her feet, nestled against the sprawling cedar she rested upon. Above, a few stars glittered, jewels in a murky sea. Heen nuzzled her hand indifferently. Whatever the chanting was, it did not worry him. Curious, Hezhi smoothed her riding coat and stood. Though the days were warmer now, nights were still murderously cold, and even in the tents they all slept fully clothed—she never took the heavy wool garment off. She felt a fleeting worry for Tsem; she had seen him climbing up the mesa and wondered what business her former servant could have with Perkar. Whatever it was, the two of them were likely to spend the night together up on the plateau—it would soon be too dark and chill to descend safely.

Her soft boots made little sound as she walked around the steep projection of the slope to where she heard the faint music—a man's voice, a lovely tenor lilting in a haunting minor mode. It suddenly occurred to her that she might be going into danger; gaan were also known as *huuneli*, "singers." What if this were her enemy, the Mang shaman, following more closely than any of them realized, even now invoking some god against her?

A hushed padding alerted her that Heen was accompanying her, and though she wasn't certain what such a tired old dog might do in her defense, it gave her the courage she needed to round the prominence.

The singer knelt on a flat stone, eyes closed, face rapt. Nearby stood his mount, a familiar tawny mare. The song itself was in Mang, and she caught the sense of a single verse before the young man opened his eyes and noticed her.

> "Hard Wind
> Sister with iron hooves
> Together we shall travel steppes
> That no man nor mount has seen
> Courage will be my saddle
> And your bridle shall be my faith in you . . ."

That was when Raincaster became aware of her and stopped, his dark blush visible even in the twilight.

"I'm sorry to interrupt you," she apologized. "That was beautiful."

"Ah," he murmured, looking down at the sand. "Thank you."

"I have heard your people sing to their mounts before, but never with such silvery throats."

"You flatter me," Raincaster demured.

Hezhi lifted her hand in farewell. "I will leave you," she said.

"No—please, I was finished."

"I just heard you singing and wondered who it was, that's all."

Raincaster nodded again, and Hezhi hesitantly took that as an invitation to stay for a moment.

"I still do not fully understand the bond between you and your mounts," she went on cautiously. "I love Dark; she is a wonderful horse, but I can't say that I feel she is kin."

"That's because she isn't," Raincaster told her. "She can't be." She knew immediately he meant no offense but was only stating a simple fact. Still, she pursued it.

"Could you explain?"

He shrugged. "In the beginning the Horse Mother gave birth to two children, a horse and a man. Both were Mang, and neither of us ever forgets. Our lines have been separate, of course, but the kinship is always reckoned, always kept track of. We share our souls; in some lives we are born as horses and in others as Humans. But inside we are the same." He looked at her curiously. "Do you not feel kinship with the goddess who dwells within you?"

Hezhi remembered the wild ride back from the mountain, the sensation of being joined to the mare. "Yes," she admitted. "But I still do not think it is the same."

"No," Raincaster said, his voice very soft. "The old people say that when the perfect rider and mount are joined, they are not reborn amongst us. They go on to another place, where they become a single being. That must be more what you feel." His voice had a wistful tone.

"Maybe," Hezhi allowed. "We are as one at times, but mostly I do not notice her."

"It is a rare gift, to be a gaan. You should be proud."

"I am," Hezhi assured him. "Have you never considered—" She paused. "You are such a fine singer. Are you not a gaan?"

Raincaster turned to his mount and began brushing at her coat. "There are two sorts of singers. There are two sorts of songs. I do not have the sort of mansion that gods can live in." He could not hide the disappointment in his tone.

"Oh." She searched for something else to say. "You have the gift to make beauty," she offered finally.

"It is a small gift," he replied, still not facing her.

"No, it isn't. I may have power—I may be a gaan—but it seems that all I ever do is destroy, never create. I could never sing so wonderfully as you." And then she did stop, for she had embarrassed herself.

Raincaster turned toward her then, and a faint smile graced his handsome face. "Songs need not reach the ear to be heard and understood. Such music is not *made*, it simply *is*." Then he turned back to Hard Wind, his horse. Hezhi waited another moment, then turned quietly to leave.

"But thank you for your praise," Raincaster called after her. "It is important to me, though it shames me to show it."

The night was growing colder, so Hezhi made her way back to the fire, though her heart felt warmer already. Finally, she seemed to have said the right thing to someone.

THREE days later, Perkar found Tsem's war club when they stopped to hunt. It was nearly perfect without finishing, a natural cudgel of black gum that rose almost to Perkar's waist when stood on end. That night, around the fire, he showed the half Giant how to shape wood by charring it in the fire and scraping off the burnt part.

"It hardens the wood, as well," Ngangata put in, watching over their shoulders. He had just returned from hunting, and instead of a piece of wood, *he* had returned with an antelope. Tsem nodded at them both. It was just dark, and the wolves Perkar had warned of were singing in the distance, accompanied by the occasional skirl of a tiger owl. The sky was cloudless, the air crisp enough that the fire felt good. A pattering of twin drums a hundred steps or so from camp were Brother Horse and Hezhi, teacher and pupil at their arcane studies. Perkar gathered that Hezhi was making rapid progress in her study of the world of gods—not surprising, since the blood of the most powerful god on earth flowed in her veins.

Tsem scraped enthusiastically at his club. He was clumsy, but the wood and the method of working it were forgiving. A simple but deadly weapon was taking shape in his hands.

"I remember my first sword," Perkar told them. He felt quiet tonight. Not happy, but not crushed by the weight of the world, either. For once, he felt no older than his age. "Oh, I crowed about it. It was such a beautiful thing."

"What became of it?" Tsem inquired.

"I . . . traded it for Harka." He didn't mention that the blade his father gave him, the blade made by the little Steel God Ko, now lay near the corpse of the first person he was responsible for killing. But at least his father's blade had never *itself* been sullied by murder.

Perkar looked up in time to catch the warning glance Ngangata shot Tsem. Ngangata, trying to protect him again. Did they all think him so fragile?

Why shouldn't they? His tantrums and sulking had given them ample cause to think so. He resolved to be stronger, take a more forceful role in the journey. After all, it was *him* the Crow God entrusted with the knowledge of what should be done.

"How much longer, Ngangata? Until we reach the mountain?"

Ngangata considered that. "If we keep this pace, don't lose any horses, and all else goes well—two more months."

"Two *months*?" Tsem asked incredulously, looking up from his work. "Won't we walk off the edge of the world?"

Perkar and Ngangata grinned at that. "No. We could ride another ninety days beyond the mountain and still not find the end of the world."

"What would we find?"

"I don't know. Ngangata?"

"Balat, for many of those days. Balat is a very large forest indeed. Beyond that—Mor, the sweet-water sea. Mountains, forest, plains—finally, I hear, the great ocean. Beyond *that*, perhaps, the edge of the world, I don't know."

"How far have you been that way? I never asked." Perkar drew his knife and began helping Ngangata dress his kill. The hard knot of anger in the half Alwa seemed to have smoothed somewhat. He seemed willing to speak casually to Perkar again, which had not been the case since his "raid" on the Mang camp.

"I've been to Mor, no farther."

"I should like to see that someday," Perkar said.

Ngangata didn't look up from his task; his hands were bloody to the wrist as his knife worked efficiently at the carcass. "I would like to see Mor again," he agreed, and Perkar smiled as the strain between them loosened further.

"Such a large world." Tsem sighed.

"Yes, but two months gives us plenty of time to teach you how to be a warrior in it."

"Two months until *what*?" Tsem asked suspiciously.

Perkar stopped what he was doing, raised his eyes to meet those of the Giant. "I . . . well, until we reach the mountain."

"And we will have to fight there?"

Perkar spread his hands. "I honestly don't know. But probably."

"Why?"

Perkar felt a bit of his old confidence return, so that his words seemed only *somewhat* ridiculous rather than absolutely absurd.

"Well, Tsem, we're going to kill a god, and they rarely take that lightly."

Tsem's enormous jaw worked furiously for a moment before he suddenly threw down the club and gazed fiercely at them. "Why haven't I heard about this? What are you talking about? I thought we were trying to reach your people, Perkar, that we might live with them. I have heard nothing of slaying gods."

Perkar realized his mistake, realized also that he needed badly to speak with Hezhi. Since his illness, he had been so occupied with his own fears and desires he had completely lost touch with the status of the group. Perhaps plans had even changed since he and Hezhi last talked; she was more firmly in charge than he was, more aware in some ways of what was going on. Perhaps the plans *should* change. Trusting Karak was a perilous thing, and though he had been convinced, at first, that what the Raven had laid out for them was possible, he was now skeptical again. Furthermore, what he had *told* no one—not even Ngangata—was that Hezhi was the essential ingredient in the scheme. At the headwaters of the Changeling, *she*—and only *she*—could slay the god: that was all he knew. But Karak had made it seem a simple thing, easily accomplished. All they had to do was get there.

That still wouldn't be easy. The high plateau and mountains were dangerous, prowled by Mang and even more dangerous predators. And ahead of them was the war, where his own people fought and died against those of Brother Horse. How would the old man and his nephews react when they reached *that* point?

And Hezhi was willful. She might not agree to help, once he explained. But the longer he put off his explanation, the angrier she would be that he had kept it from her.

And there was Tsem, glaring at him, the consequence of his talking without thinking, of *another* stupid blunder.

"We haven't talked this over yet, Tsem. Hezhi and I haven't really discussed it, so as far as she knows, what she told you is true."

"No. No, I remember her saying something about a mountain now, back in the yekt. That she chose that destination because of something you said. Yet she told me nothing about *why*."

"She doesn't know, perhaps."

"I think she does," Tsem muttered. "I think she's trying to protect me again."

Before Perkar could protest further, Ngangata softly replied. "Probably. These two have a habit of 'protecting' us, don't they?"

"If you mean leaving us in the dark about their intentions, yes," Tsem agreed. "Though that's never made *me* feel very safe."

Ngangata snorted and coughed a bitter chuckle. "No, me, either. Perkar, maybe you should talk to her. You are, after all, her kind."

Perkar flushed scarlet. "You don't have to remind me of how I once treated you. You know my opinion of the Alwat has changed."

"We aren't talking about that," Tsem said softly. "You are two of a kind because you both think you bear the world on your shoulders."

"You're a fine one to talk about that."

"No, I've never borne the *world* on my shoulders. Only *Hezhi*. That was the only burden I ever wanted, and I want it back."

Ngangata had never looked up from what he was doing. Perkar understood what the Giant was saying—he had heard Ngangata say the same thing in different words. And Ngangata had steered the conversation on this bent. To remind him? Perkar resolved that he would tell Ngangata, at least, the whole truth as he knew it, next time he had a chance.

"I will talk to her," Perkar said. "Together we'll decide what to do."

"I worry about decisions the two of you make."

"By together I meant *all* of us," Perkar clarified. "But I must speak to her first. Meanwhile, finish that club! No matter what we do, trouble seems to find us, and now that you've brought it up, I want to see you armed. Some enemies will flee us just at the *sight* of you, mark my words."

He shot a glance at Moss when he said that and realized with a bare shock that their captive was awake, hearing everything they said. How long had he been awake? Had he heard Perkar's ill-considered remark about godslaying?

Probably. The more reason not to let him go. When they reached the pastures of his people, they could give Moss into the keeping of someone else. Perhaps he could be traded to the Mang for captives. But he must not be allowed to return to the Mang gaan who sought Hezhi and report what he knew. Perkar would kill him first.

Moss smiled thinly, as if he understood that thought. Perhaps he saw something in Perkar's eyes; but rather than fear, the smile held a hint of mockery.

"I'm going on watch," Perkar said softly. "I'll see the two of you in the morning." Then, in Nholish, to Tsem: "Watch this prisoner, Giant. I don't know what Hezhi has told you of him, but he is a terrible threat to her."

"I know he sought her," Tsem growled darkly. "I think I should blood my club on him when I'm done making it."

"No." Perkar sighed. "We've killed more than enough, and we'll probably kill more before it's done. No reason to do so when it isn't really necessary."

"I suppose."

"Good night, Tsem. Be careful not to let the fire eat too deeply."

Tsem looked up, black eyes caging bits of flame. "Just deep enough, I hope," he replied.

PERKAR put off his talk with Hezhi until the next morning. They were ascending onto the high plains the Mang named the Falling Sky, and the going alternated between troublesome and dangerous; not a good time for what might become a heated discussion.

When questioned about the name, Brother Horse explained how legend held that a chunk of heaven had cracked loose and plunged to earth. If so, their horses now climbed the eroded edges of that shard, beveled by time and wind into a stepped slope of banded sandstone. The going was easiest in the trenched furrows dug by long-dead streams, but it was midday before they found one of these broad enough and long enough to ease the constant upward stumbling into some semblance of normal traveling. Brother Horse explained that there were other, more established paths farther north but that they would risk meeting other Mang traveling there, especially now that news of the war was widespread; young, unproven warriors from every part of the Mang country would be streaming to earn honors for themselves in the mountains.

So they clattered up the dry streambed for another few leagues, until it broadened to vanishing, until dense black soil crept to cover the stone again, and they entered onto the spacious back of the Falling Sky.

"We will never be out of the shadows of mountains now," Brother Horse told them, and it was true; they could see mighty ones on the north and west. Behind them a few trailed off, but it was the vastness of the lower steppes that struck Perkar. Though the last few days of their travel had been in hills, distance and scale crushed the most rugged of them into the imperial, awesome flatness that sheeted out and beyond the horizon, where sky and earth met in a confused haze of blue-green and brown.

Brother Horse reined his mount to a halt. "We'll offer at this cairn to the lord of the Falling Sky," he told them. Perkar nodded as he took in the vista they had just arrived upon. Despite the bordering giants, the high plains were, if anything, flatter than anywhere below them. It seemed not so much a piece of the sky as a place where the sky had lain for a time and crushed everything level. In fact, going back over what Brother Horse told him, that might have been what the old man meant. He had not lied to Tsem in claiming his Mang was less than perfect.

Brother Horse began chanting behind him, and pungent incense seasoned the wind. He thought about joining, but he didn't know the song or the gods of this country. But soon! Despite it all, despite the dread he felt at facing his people with his crimes against them, the thought of his father's pasture and the little, unambitious gods he knew—*knew* the songs for, the lineages of— sixty days, and he could be there. He would not be; actually going by his father's damakuta would put them many days later getting to the mountain, days he somehow believed they could not afford. Still, the thought stirred him, not only with trepidation and sadness but also with joy.

He noticed that Hezhi had ridden out away from the rest, had her eye fixed somewhere westward. He urged T'esh toward her. To his vast surprise, Sharp Tiger followed. Since the time Perkar had adopted him, the horse had shown him, at best, disdain. When Yuu'han or Brother Horse led him, he would follow, but *none* was able to get upon his back. But now, as he trotted to join

Hezhi, there was Sharp Tiger, two horse lengths behind—as if he wanted to hear what the two of them would say. Perkar wondered himself.

"What is that?" Hezhi asked, arm thrust out toward where the wind whipped a wall of dust along before it.

"That's wind coming down from the mountains. It may have some rain in it. See the darkness behind?"

"I don't like it," Hezhi murmured. It seems . . ." She trailed off.

"Well. You rode over here for a reason, I know. You haven't spoken to me in days."

"I know. I've been thinking a lot, feeling sorry for myself."

"What a surprise. *You* feeling sorry for yourself."

"You're angry."

She flung her hair back over her shoulder and set her little mouth in a scowl. "*What* do you think you are doing with Tsem?"

"Tsem? He asked me to teach him—"

"How to fight, I know. But you shouldn't have done it without asking *me*."

"And why is that, *Princess*? It seems to me that you told Tsem he was no longer your servant. That he was free."

"Maybe I did. I *did*. But that doesn't mean I shouldn't have anything to say about him. I've known him since I was born. You barely know him at all."

"I'm only doing what *he* asked. He wants to feel useful, Princess. He knows that you pity him, and it eats at his heart. Do you want to stop him from doing the one thing that might give him a sense of worth?"

"He *said* that? He thinks I pity him?"

"You say you have known him since you were born. What do you think? That he is so stupid he can't sense disdain?"

She looked down at her saddle pommel. "I didn't know it was so obvious," she said. "I just don't want him to get killed."

"Out here, he'll get killed a lot faster if he is unarmed than if he has *some* kind of weapon. And you saw him carrying his club today. Couldn't you see the pride in his shoulders?"

"It's false confidence," she hissed. "We both know that branch is nothing more than a toy."

"Princess, that—"

"*Stop* calling me that. You only call me that when you think I'm being stupid."

"That's true, Princess," Perkar snapped. "What do *you* know of fighting? That 'toy' of his is capable of being a very deadly weapon indeed. A weapon doesn't need an edge when it's wielded by a man the size and strength of Tsem. One blow from that thing would crush a man in full armor. Hauberks are made to turn edges, but they are no defense at all against impact. Do you honestly think I would trick him into thinking he had a real weapon when he didn't?"

Hezhi looked away unhappily. He thought she was about to reply when he heard the sudden thuttering of hooves. For a moment he paid them no mind, thinking them to be Yuu'han or Raincaster, stretching his horse's legs on the welcome flat. But then a shout went up from Yuu'han, and it did not sound like a shout of jubilation but instead one of warning. In the same instant, Heen began barking frantically.

Jump! Harka fairly shrieked in his ear, and so he did, rolling from T'esh's back as *something* whistled past his face. He hit the ground and rolled, coming up in time to see the collision of three horses. Sharp Tiger was not one of them; he danced nimbly aside as Moss and his mount barreled into T'esh and Dark. Hezhi shrieked and fell from Dark's back, but Moss, completely in control of his mount, caught her neatly in the crook of his arm. With an earsplitting shriek of triumph, he tore out across the plain toward the fast-approaching wind and its skirt of dust.

Harka was already in his hand. The something that sped by was returning, and he was forced to gaze at it. He had the urge to blink, but Harka wouldn't let him.

It was a black thing, like a bird, larger than most. Even at first glance, he knew it wasn't a raven—or any other normal, living creature. In Harka's vision it was yellowed bones wrapped in a tarry blackness. It whirred past Perkar, who shouted a warning.

Raincaster, just mounting to chase Moss, looked up too late. Caught weaponless and with no time to dismount, he attacked in the only way possible, by punching at the thing. It struck him and he snapped back in the saddle, his face and neck drenched scarlet. The bird banked and began another pass.

An arrow intersected its flight but sailed on, though a second shaft from Ngangata hit something solid—probably a bone—and the thing rolled, missed several beats before recovering, and then dove right at Perkar. He could see a pair of immortal heartstrings, iron-colored, and Harka swept out, eager to meet them.

XXVI

Demons

SLICKED in sweat, Ghe clutched at his damp bedsheets, feeling as if a hundred wasps had entered his lungs, his mouth, his very organs. He gazed at Qwen Shen beside him, knew a momentary pleasure at the faint, satisfied curve of her thick, sensuous lips. But his brain was afire, sputtering and popping like hot grease. He sat up, clutching his skull, but that was no help. Except that he suddenly understood what was wrong.

The agony emanated in stinging threads from the scar on his neck. His heart pulsed sluggishly, haltingly, and the pulling of his lungs became more difficult with each breath. But those pains were spatters of blood near a torn jugular; the source of his illness was hunger.

"Qwen Shen," he gasped. "Get out. Leave, now!"

"What? Why? Bone Eel will be busy for some time." The urgency in his voice seemed to have jolted her from languor but not frightened her yet. He wished she were frightened.

"No!" He struggled to form more words, an explanation, but even if his thick, clay tongue could frame it there was no time—

not if she was going to survive. Within her, he could see life working, hear it, *smell* it.

"Quickly, go, and send someone to my cabin. Someone unimportant."

"But—"

"*Now!*" His voice was actually shaking, and Qwen Shen no longer questioned his urgency. She quickly dressed and left his cabin.

He tried to stand but fell from the bed and lay clawing at the floor. What had happened? He hadn't felt hunger in . . .

He knew what was wrong, but he couldn't form the thoughts. His body kept asking *why why why* without giving his brain time for a reasonable answer. He tried to ignore the enticing fragrance of life from down the hall—Ghan—but after a short time, he simply could not. He could *taste* him anyway, and then do what Qwen Shen had been urging him to, capture his ghost for the information it held. He had resisted that, but now, for the life of him, he couldn't understand *why*.

He was crawling toward the door when there came a knock at it.

"Come in," he gasped. The door opened and the soldier who stood thus framed in it had time only to widen his eyes before Ghe was upon him.

When it was over, moments later, Ghe gazed dully about the room, the arabesque pattern of blood and brains on the floor and bed.

I never did that before, he thought. *Why did I do that?* It had seemed as if just taking the life he needed wasn't enough. The beast in him had become a brute with no reason at all, not understanding that it could eat without *eating*. Revolted now, Ghe spat out the taste of iron that remained in his mouth, approaching nausea but never quite arriving there.

"And I will have to clean this up myself," he muttered, irate, blinking owlishly at the mess. After another pause, he went about the task of doing just that, before the blood had time to saturate and stain any more than it already had.

His linens were certainly ruined.

* * *

After a bit of careful consideration, Ghan decided that the best
place to be was abovedeck—though his *hope* was that no place
would be particularly safe. He went to the afterdeck, where his
chances of being alone were maximized, taking with him the
journal he kept and brush and ink to add to it. Once settled, he
contemplated the landscape that surrounded him and tried not to
shake—tried not to think about the possibility that *these* could be
his last moments in life.

They had traveled perhaps two leagues up the tributary, and
the vegetation had thickened a bit, at least near the watercourse.
The majority of trees were familiar—cottonwood and juniper—the
former leafless, of course, for the climate was cooler here than it
was in Nhol. Thick, tenacious trees he suspected of being stone
oak shouldered amongst their more elegant cousins. The banks of
the stream rose steeply from the water and went on uphill to the
plains; there were no low, wet lands. That was all for the better,
Ghan speculated. It meant that the water here was not of the
River, was not him backed up into a swampy tributary. This
stream flowed swift and sure down from the mountain valleys of
the west.

Now and then the barge hesitated against a snag, and each time
Ghan closed his eyes, clenched tight the muscles of his belly. After
the first few such incidents he made a deliberate effort to compose
himself by readying his pen and mixing the powdered ink with its
mate, water. It was, for him, an old ritual and usually calming to
his mind.

Predictably, Ghe joined him before he had a chance to write
anything of note. Next to Qwen Shen, he seemed to be the only
member of the expedition Ghe cared to talk to, and Ghan certainly could not discourage that. The more Ghe told him, the
more clues he had to work with. He might still need such clues, if
his current suppositions were wrong. Another worry struck him
as he glanced at Ghe's handsome but pallid face. How would
being away from the waters of the River affect a ghoul?

Probably not in any *positive* way.

Ghe settled near Ghan on crossed legs, reminding Ghe again of a large spider curling about a meal. As usual, Ghe began their conversation with a question.

"What do you know of gods and ghosts beyond the River?" the ghoul asked him. Odd, Ghan thought, how they had settled into a sort of pupil-teacher dialogue—with Ghe at least pretending to be the pupil. Was this some tactic of his to make Ghan feel at ease, afford him some illusory measure of control?

"*Beyond* the River? What do you mean?"

"I mean outside of the River's influence," Ghe snapped. "Where he is powerless. You have mentioned them before, as did the governor at Wun. Remember? He spoke of the 'gods of the Mang.' As if there *are* gods, other than the River."

"Ah. Well, some, I suppose, though what I have to go on is mostly superstitions gathered from the people who live out here, like the Mang."

"What about that barbarian, Perkar? Did he tell you nothing about his gods?"

Ghan shook his head. "He and I had scant time for pleasantries."

"You told me once that his folk live near the headwaters of the River."

"Yes."

"But they do not worship him?"

"Not from what I have read." Ghan furrowed his brow. He had to make this *interesting*, stay on this tangent of thought, on the oddities of foreign gods. "Actually, as I understand it, they do not 'worship' gods at all. They treat with them, strike deals with them, even develop friendships and *mate* with them. But they don't *worship* them, build temples dedicated to them, and so forth."

"Neither do we in Nhol," Ghe muttered. "Our temples are not to worship him but to *chain* him."

"Ah," Ghan remarked, "but that was not originally true. And despite what you say, most people in Nhol *do* worship the River, make offerings to him. It is only—if I am to understand what *you* have told me—the priesthood that doesn't worship him. The temple, whatever its *true* function, is a symbol of that worship."

"Agreed," Ghe conceded, obviously restless on the topic. "True enough. But we've strayed from the subject. Out here, beyond his reach—"

"Do we know that we are beyond his reach?" Ghan interrupted.

Ghe nodded slightly but intensely. "I assure you," he whispered, "I can tell."

"I suppose you can," Ghan responded, wishing to pursue *how* Ghe knew that but aware that he shouldn't. "Please go on with what you were saying."

"You say that here in the hinterlands there are many gods, but they are not worshipped. They sound like petty, powerless creatures."

"Compared to the River, I'm certain they are."

"More like ghosts," Ghe speculated. "Or myself."

Ghan took a controlled breath. This was *not* where he wished for the conversation to go.

"I suppose," Ghan allowed, hoping that a half truth would not ring in Ghe's dead senses as a lie. "I suppose," he went on, "that they are something like that, save that they did not start out as people."

"Where *did* they come from, then?"

"I don't know," Ghan replied. "Where did anything come from?"

Ghe stared at him in surprise. "What a strange thing for you to say. You, who always seek to know the cause of everything."

"Only when there is some evidence to support speculation," Ghan answered. "On this topic there is naught but frail imaginings and millennia-old rumors."

"Well, then," Ghe accused, "your assertion that they do not begin as Human is without foundation, as well. Why *couldn't* they be ghosts? Without the River nearby to absorb them when they died, might not they continue to exist and finally claim godhood, when all who knew them in life had passed on?"

"That's possible," Ghan admitted, but what he thought was *How can you not see? See that ghosts, like you, are created by the River? Like* . . . No, shove that thought away.

"Why all of this concern about gods that you do not believe are gods?"

Ghe shrugged. "Partly curiosity. That was the wonderful thing about Hezhi; she wanted to know everything, just to *know* it. I think I apprehended a bit of that from her. But more practically, though I may not believe them gods, I admit that there may be powerful and outlandish creatures in these cursed lands beyond the waters of the god. I wish to know the nature of my enemy. I think I may have met *one* of them already, perhaps two."

"Really? Do you care to elaborate?"

"I think your Perkar was a demon or some such. Even you must have heard about his fight at the docks. I myself, with my *living* hands, impaled his heart with a poisoned blade. He merely laughed at me—much as I laugh at those who stab me now."

Ghan's memory stirred. He did know of Perkar's fight; the strange outlander had claimed that his *sword* held a god, but perhaps Ghe was correct, and that was a lie. What sort of creature might he have sent Hezhi off with?

But *she* had dreamed him.

"And the other?" Ghan asked.

Ghe ticked his finger against his palm. "The guardian of the Water Temple."

"Why him?"

"The priests don't have power as such; they are like darknesses *resistant* to light. But he was filled with life and flame, and it was *not* the life and flame of the River."

"You don't *know* that," Ghan interpolated. "He may have some way of siphoning the River's strength through the temple. Perhaps that is why he remains there."

Ghe regarded Ghan with what appeared to be respect. "I see *you* have been thinking about that, too."

"Indeed," Ghan said. "It's an intriguing mystery."

"A *crime*," Ghe corrected.

"If you will, then," Ghan agreed. "A crime, but one committed a thousand years ago, when Nhol was young. When a person the old texts name the Ebon Priest came to our city."

"Yes, I read the record of it, in the book you showed me."

"But that account is a lie, of course," Ghan continued, pausing just an instant for emphasis. "Because it says that the River sent the Ebon Priest, and clearly the River would not send someone to bind him."

"No, wait," Ghe corrected. "*The Codex Obsidian* stated only that the Ebon Priest *claimed* to have been sent by the River."

Ghan wagged his finger. "You should have become a scholar rather than a Jik. You have sense for detail, and that's important."

"Important for a Jik, too," Ghe observed.

"I suppose so," Ghan conceded. "As a Jik then, someone familiar with crime—"

"I did not know I was committing crimes," Ghe snapped. "I believed I was working for the empire."

"Very well," Ghan soothed. "I meant no insult, nor did I mean *that*. But the Jik and the Ahw'en also *solve* crimes, punish criminals. The people you executed, for the most part, were criminals against the state." *Or helpless children, committing no greater crime than continuing to breathe,* intruded bitterly.

"That makes you angry," Ghe said.

"I'm sorry," Ghan lied and, continuing to lie, explained. "My own clan was declared outlaw, you must understand. Exiled. I had to disavow them."

"I knew the first, of course. But disavow them? Why?"

"To remain in the library," Ghan answered. *The library from which you have taken me at last, despite everything.* But let him feel the anger of that; Ghe would confuse it with the fury at injustices done his clan.

"Ah," Ghe said, perhaps sympathetically. "Now I understand why the emperor told me to threaten you with sealing the library. You could have joined your family in exile."

Ghan waved that aside, tried to wave his outrage aside with it. "No matter. The point is only this: when someone commits a crime, how do you discover who committed it?"

"I was a Jik, not an Ahw'en."

"Yes, but you have enough intelligence to know where to begin an investigation."

"With motive, I suppose," Ghe suggested after a moment. "If you know *why* the crime was committed, you might make some guess as to who did it."

"Exactly," Ghan said. "Yet in this case, we *know* the criminal—the so-called Ebon Priest—but we have no idea what his motive was."

"I see," Ghe said thoughtfully. "And you have no possible motive in mind? It seems to me—"

At that moment, the barge bumped into another snag, and Ghan's heart skipped a beat. Ghe glanced at him sharply, opened his mouth to ask what was wrong—

And the barge leapt straight up from the water at least the height of a man, lifted and dropped. Weight left Ghan's body, replaced by a peculiar fluttery sensation in his gut—and then stunning pain as the deck slapped against him. Timbers protested, and from somewhere came a shrieking. Ghan bounced on the hardwood like a stone rattling in a jar, and he wished, belatedly, that he had remained in his cabin, on the bed. Then something kicked again from below, and Ghan fetched against the brass rails as the nose of the barge tilted up to point straight at the noonday sun. It poised thus, the entire mass of the barge above him, Ghan wondering dully why his end hadn't been pushed under by the weight, whether the craft would choose to fall back the way it had come or continue over, to bury him and all of his enemies against the muddy bottom of the stream.

Good-bye, Hezhi, he thought. *I would have liked to have seen you again.*

Ghe scooped up Ghan and leapt as far out into the stream as he could. If the barge flipped over on them . . .

The water felt dead around him, as if he were bathing in a corpse. Rather than *giving* him stamina, the frigid water actually seemed to leach it away. He stroked furiously with his free arm, keeping Ghan's head out of the water. Fortunately the old man did not struggle; he was either unconscious or too smart to fight— probably the latter.

A roar and trembling shook the very water as the barge struck it again, mixed with the sound of splintering wood and the piteous shrieks of men and panicked horses. The great vessel had not capsized but had landed seam down and split up the middle.

Through the wreckage, dragons arose.

They were as Ghe remembered them, quickened water and spirit, slick and scintillating skins like oil lying on water, eel bodies and the heads of flat and whiskered catfish. When Bone Eel had summoned—or created—them, they had seemed powerful but tame, awesome without being terrifying. Now the twin serpents lashed heavenward, their toothless maws gaping trumpets of insentient fury and agony. The life in them shuddered, boiling out of them in such blinding rage and heat that Ghe could sort nothing, understand nothing, but that what died in the dragons was the River's seed in them, his dream that they existed. And even in that moment of understanding, something cracked, and live steam writhed skyward, clouds in search of their place while godstuff shrieked south, thinning and vanishing. The dragons with their color and august dread were gone, leaving no bones but flotsam and no sound save the stillness of a hurricane's heart.

Ghe reached the bank and dragged himself and Ghan onto it. Already small fragments of the wreckage drifted by, seeking downstream toward the River, messengers of failure and destruction. The first lifeless corpse of many washed past, eyes staring sightlessly at the bottom of the stream.

Ghe shook his head, uncomprehending. *What had happened?*

He was not given time to contemplate or theorize. The water before him erupted, a spray of foam that almost instantly thickened. It became a demon, while all he could do was gape like a speared fish.

Her skin was the color of sun-bleached bone, her alien eyes winking fiery gold. Her hair hung dark and lank as that of a drowned corpse. She was naked, magnificent, and terrifying. Leveling an accusing finger at him, the demon strode imperiously across the surface of the water, cracked out words to him as if her tongue were a whip lashing silver chimes.

"How many years have I waited for you to make a blunder of

this sort?" she demanded. "Oh, how many ages? I never dreamed
you would be so stupid as to *give* me something to hurt, to pay
you back in even the smallest way."

She was less than an arm's reach from him now, hating him
with those impossible eyes. He could see the power gathered
about her, how it reached away, up- and downstream, for as far
as vision reached; how her white flesh trembled to contain her
puissance and her fury. Ghe shook, as well, shivered as mad fear
pranced along his bones. This was the second demon he had
known, and the first had killed him. He caught the vaguest
glimpse of Ghan nearby, raising himself to a sitting position.
Behind her lithe form, more wreckage drifted past.

"It is your arrogance," she hissed, sibilant and venomous,
"always your arrogance. You think you may go *anywhere* with
impunity. You think because you devour me day by day, you can
violate me upstream, as well." Her eyes constricted to bare slits,
and her orbs darted beneath the lids, as if searching there for a
lost dream. Then she leaned close, like a sated lover, and sighed
into his ear, "But here, Devourer, *I* am goddess. I fed your silly
snakes to lure you farther in, to see how far your haughtiness
would bring you. And it brought you *too* far."

Ghe opened his mouth to reply—perhaps to ask her what she
meant—but her hand struck for his throat, faster than even he could
move. He gasped as the windpipe crumpled in and she knotted
ivory fingers into his hair, lifted and swung him like a ragdoll
through the air. He plunged into the water, felt again the shock of
its sterility. But now he understood that it was not empty of
power—it had that in plenty—it was simply power that he had
not the slightest claim on. Thrashing, his feet seeking purchase on
the bottom, he desperately fought to ready himself for her next
attack, to chain his overwhelming panic because she was like the
one Ghan named Perkar, his killer. Because *nothing* could be as
powerful as this except the River.

She caught him by the hair again; she seemed to have doubled
in size.

"Swallow me, old man," she snarled. "Swallow!" And he gagged and bit as she forced her hand relentlessly through his mouth, pushing it down his throat into his gut. The flesh at the edges of his mouth tore like the skin of an overripe fruit, but she was doing far worse things inside of him. "Eat me up." She laughed, and then, abruptly, he was beneath the surface of the water, shoved there by monstrously powerful hands.

How can she hate me so? his mind screamed. He tried to draw in a breath and then realized that his ability to survive without air existed only in the waters of the River. Darkness crept over everything, and he knew that he was fading. It was over; Hezhi was lost to him.

As the sights and sensations of the outer world faded, he became more aware of his "guests," the boy and the ancient lord. They both seemed to be shouting at him, but their words made little sense. Perhaps they, too, were remonstrating with him for sins he did not understand or remember committing.

"Reach up," one of them was saying. "Can't you feel it?"

He puzzled at that, but even the voices were fading.

"Reach it for me," he muttered. "I don't know what you're talking about."

"Know you nothing of power? Give me your leave."

"You have it," Ghe said, chuckling at the absurdity of this conversation of ghosts.

That was when flame shrieked through him like a destroying wind. At first, he believed that it was simply the end; Death had returned to claim him, to force him to pay with pain for eluding her the first time. But the flame raced into his heart, and rather than consuming him, it filled him, expanded him, sent his arms and feet and fingers racing up and down the stream. He shuddered and burst from beneath the water, lungs heaving, slapping his demon opponent in the chest with sudden potence. She staggered back from him, arm glistening with gore, her gaze puzzling at him.

"What . . ." she gasped, and then stretched out to wrap him up again.

At first Ghe wished that the lightning channeling into him

would quit, for the pain was nigh-on unbearable, but whatever the ancient lord had done would not stop. He could *see* it now. One of his strands was fused to the core of her, as if one of his veins had been grafted to an artery, and her lifeblood was all pumping into *him* now.

She struck out again, but he deflected her blows, confidence growing even as the pain did, his own nameless fury soaring to match her own. He did not speak at all, but took her lovely throat in his grip and squeezed until her flesh dissolved away into water. Even then he did not, *could* not stop, as the vastness of her body shrank, distilled, burned brighter and fiercer until he found a place, a strongbox in his heart and *locked* her there. Then he staggered to the bank and, after three lurching steps, sank to his knees. Ghan moved to help him, but he did not remain kneeling, for suddenly his body seemed as light as air and he had the unaccountable urge to laugh aloud. And so he did, for not even on the River himself had he felt so powerful, so filled with flame and purpose. The demon was in him now, but he had caught her; she was his, in the same way as the blind boy and the lord. Now he was four, but the emperor was still himself, still Ghe.

He swept his gaze around, at the debris, the nearby plains, and at Ghan's openmouthed gaze.

"What happened?" The old man gaped. "Where did she go? What happened?"

"I believe," Ghe said, grinning at the peals of triumph ringing in his own words, "that I have just eaten a goddess."

And he grinned more widely still at Ghan's lack of an answer of any sort.

GHAN was too numbed by the torrent of events to feel either triumph or despair, though he had good reason to feel both. His unspoken suspicion that the dragons were mere distillations of the River and not "real" had been borne out spectacularly, and all of his subtle and overt urging that the barge be taken up the tributary had, as he intended, crippled the expedition. Of the soldiers, only twenty-five were well enough to travel. The majority of the provisions were ruined or missing, as were all of his own books and maps. Most devastating of all, the horses were all dead. Without them for mounts and pack animals, the future effectiveness of the expedition would be severely limited. And incredibly, he had not spent his own life in achieving this. Yet.

But Ghe was still alive, and neither Qwen Shen nor Bone Eel numbered among the dead. Ghe was more powerful than ever, and his will to find Hezhi was fundamental. Ghan had hoped that as they departed the influence of the River, the ghoul would lose some of his sense of purpose, but the River had built him well, selecting only those parts of him that remembered and liked Hezhi, leaving other parts of him out. He wondered if Ghe understood that, the nature of his poor memory.

They passed the night in crude shelters, cold and damp. Some blankets and tarps had been salvaged but they were soaked through.

They ate horsemeat that night and the next day. Qwen Shen pointed out that the meat would spoil sooner than the retrieved rations. Some of the surviving soldiers argued for burying the dead, but Ghe, Qwen Shen, and Bone Eel dismissed that as a waste of effort. Instead, they moved upstream, away from the stench that would soon pollute the air.

After the move, as the men were working upon new shelters, Ghe came to speak to him for the first time since the catastrophe.

"Well, old man," he began, squatting next to where Ghan slouched against a tree. "Shall I make the coming journey easier by carrying you inside of me?"

"Do what you will," Ghan told him dully. "I care not."

"Maybe you don't," Ghe replied. "But I do. And I think I would rather see you *walk* on those frail old legs."

Ghan shrugged indifferently.

"Because you *knew*," Ghe went on. "You knew that would happen."

"No," Ghan corrected. "I only *hoped* it would."

"Well, you got your wish. But nothing can stop me, old man.

I've eaten one of these 'gods' and I'll eat more. I'll send them out to serve me and bring them back in. If I tire of one, I will feast on him entirely."

Ghan set his jaw stubbornly, about to retort, when a shout went up from the soldier watching the plains. Both men turned at the cry.

The horizon was dark with riders, savagely dressed and bristling with spears, swords, and bows.

"Well," Ghan remarked. "I told you I would bring you to the Mang. Here they are."

XXVII

Stormherd

As Harka struck the bird, violent numbness raced up Perkar's arm, an agonizing tingling that chattered his teeth and jerked his heart weirdly in his breast. He caught a sharp whiff of decay and something burnt as the demon bird shrilled and clacked its cruel beak; Harka had severed one of its immortal strands. It climbed into the air and circled once; Perkar braced to meet the dive, only dimly cognizant of the blood oozing from his scalp.

It did not dive. Instead, it lifted a wing as if to salute the east and flew off toward the approaching storm.

Something in the storm, too, Harka told him. Perkar ignored the sword, scrambling for T'esh. Moss and his captive were already dwindling figures. Raincaster was down, Yuu'han at his side, and Brother Horse was still watching everything with mouth wide open. Ngangata had stayed to shoot at the demon bird, but as Perkar bounded onto T'esh, the halfling was already dug into his saddle, his mount at full gallop.

What did Moss think he was doing? Weighed down like that—fighting Hezhi—he could see her kicking and squirming furiously, even at this distance—how could he hope to outdistance them for long?

Perkar realized that was the least important question. A much more pertinent one was how Moss had managed to free his bonds without anyone noticing. Even more pressing was the matter of the demon bird and *its* origins. Had it been sent to aid Moss, or had he merely noticed it about to attack and snatched his opportunity? If Moss had one supernatural ally, did he have more?

It was obvious that Moss hoped to reach the approaching cloud of obscuring dust, use it to confuse them, and thus escape; but Ngangata was closing the gap at such a rate that it was clear Moss would be caught before entering his hoped-for refuge, though only by moments.

But Harka was buzzing in his ear, frantically trying to tell him something.

"What?" he snarled, over the rush of wind on his face.

"Look. Just look, will you?"

And then he saw, and wished he had not. Behind the dust storm indeed followed rain, boiling black clouds torn by lightning skating over the rims of the mountains. But while it might be the windy edge of the tempest that was swirling the black dust about in the air, it was *hooves* kicking it up. The wonder was that he only now felt the earth tremoring up through T'esh, thunder burrowing underground.

Ahead, Ngangata waved his hand and pointed; he, too, had seen. It was a wall, not of air and dust, but of wild cattle, charging almost shoulder to shoulder. They ran in bleak, eerie silence. Though the ground trembled, there was no bellowing, no chill cries of calves going down, overrun. Perkar redoubled his speed; surely Moss did not intend to fly into the face of that monstrous herd? If so, his hope must be to *kill* Hezhi, even if it meant his own life. The shape of the lead bull emerged as Perkar raced toward the herd, and he suddenly beheld the spectacle with a new, razor-edged lucidity. In his chest, comprehension rapidly gave birth to a nest of stinging worms that immediately attacked his heart.

The gargantuan shoulders of the bull bunched and pulled a tall man's height from his hooves. He was black, blacker than charcoal, but for his eyes, which were hollows of yellow fire. His black horns were bent earthward, and if the bull were to stumble, the twin furrows he dug would be more than a horse length apart. There was no flesh on his skull.

"Harka, what is that? What *is* it?" T'esh fought to turn aside, and though his mount did not outright refuse to continue forward, Perkar knew that soon even this Mang-bred stallion would balk at racing into the horns of *that*.

"*A god. It is certainly a god.*"

"Do you know him, recognize him?"

"*Something familiar . . . not one of the Mountain Gods, like Karak . . .*"

"What can we do?"

"*Ride the other way. Quickly.*"

"Moss is trying to kill her. He's riding straight into them." He realized that they *might* catch Moss in time, but never with enough leisure to escape the hooved death bearing down upon them. All four of them were going to die.

The squirming panic had gnawed deeply into his heart by now; how could Moss do this? And then T'esh suddenly took his own nose, turned sidewise to the beasts. Perkar realized that he had slackened his control without even thinking, as if *hoping* his horse would balk. Grimly he cinched up on the reins. Ngangata hadn't slowed in the least.

His resolve wasn't firm enough, and T'esh knew it. The stallion made a frantic attempt to wheel about at full gallop as Perkar hauled with all of his might on the reins. The result was a sickening lurch as the steed lost his footing, and then both of them slammed to earth. T'esh rolled over him, and Perkar felt his leg twist oddly. The horse was *heavy*.

Somehow he kept hold of the reins and, though his blood hammered so violently in his temples that he feared his skull would burst, he struggled to remount while T'esh reared, his eyes rolling with madness. Across the plain, tiny figures were limned against the unearthly stampede, and though he knew he should be fighting T'esh back into control, he watched them helplessly instead. Ngangata stood in his saddle, bow in hand. Moss was crouched low in his, avoiding the halfling's shafts. Hezhi—where was Hezhi?

He saw her then, a tiny, colorful creature in her red-and-black skirt and yellow blouse. Her black hair streamed with the wind running before the lead bull as she stood to face him. Grimly Perkar doubled his fists into T'esh's reins and yanked down on them.

"Hey!" he shrieked. "Stop it. Stop it!" The stallion quit rearing, but his eyes were still frantic. Perkar took the horse's head into the crook of his arm. "Come on, boy," he whispered. "Never forget that you are Mang! Don't forget that. Your ancestors are watching."

T'esh was still trembling when Perkar remounted. "Come on," he said, and then shouted, the closest approximation of a Mang war cry he could produce. The stallion spurted forward then, and when Perkar shrieked again, he put his heart into the charge, though it took him to the horns of the bull. A Mang horse, Perkar knew in his heart, would never balk if its rider was brave.

He *still* was not brave, but his old fatalism had seized him; his path was set, and to his knowledge there was only one way to go. Without Hezhi, all of his trails came to an end. Without Ngangata . . .

But it was far, far too late. Cowardice had already betrayed hope. His only ambition now was to reach them in time to die with them.

HEZHI looked up dully at the approaching mass of beasts. Her *sight* already told her that they were not what they seemed; stripped of the god who animated them, they were nothing more than bones. That meant nothing to her; bones could crush her as easily as real flesh and blood. She was still stunned from her fall. Moss had never had a secure hold on her, and despite his superior strength, he had also had to concentrate to keep his balking horse pointed into the stampede. The two goals had proven incompatible when Hezhi managed to swing her legs around and kick him in the face. Now she realized that she had been fortunate not to break her neck or shatter her skull in the fall.

Moss wheeled, a look of terrible distress on his face, but two arrow shafts whizzed by him, and he grimly turned instead into the skeletal cattle.

What could she do? Running was pointless. Ngangata would reach her too late, and Perkar was farther back still. If she crouched, might they run around her?

It was amazing how calm she felt. It was as if the coolness of the otherworld, the lake, had come over her. But she did not have her drum, and so that was impossible.

She frowned. Perhaps when the otherworld was *manifest*, already in front of her, she did not *need* a drum. She had a few instants to find out. Searching herself, she found no fear, but there was certainly waking anger, and there was her mare.

Help me, she said, and then she clapped her hands, once, twice, thrice. The lead bull was so close she could make out the cracked nostrils of his skull, the architecture of his skeleton beneath manifested flesh. She could see *him*, inside, a furnace burning gold and black. A web flowed out from him, and she knew in that instant that there were not thousands of beasts bearing down on her but only one, *this* one, whose horns lifted toward her.

Vaguely she saw Moss ride into the herd, uttering a shrill, ululating cry. She expected him to fall instantly, but he did not, miraculously dodging the first few beasts. Then she lost sight of him, and her universe became only one thing: the god before her. The world seemed mired in torpor, captive to inertia. Ngangata had arrived, was leaning from his saddle to scoop her up in one long arm. The bull churned toward them, black dirt spraying up from his hooves, yellow flames waxing in hollow sockets. Hezhi slapped her hands together again, and the air shattered; when she spread them apart, the lake opened between them, and the mare charged through, galloping on the surge of force from her throbbing arm. The Horse God struck the bull in the heart once and he broke stride, stumbled. Twice, and he suddenly fell. At the same instant, Hezhi reached through and tore at the strands supporting the other cattle. They shredded easily. Hezhi shouted, triumphant, as Ngangata swung her up into his lap. He pivoted his mount, and then the wall of bones struck them. Mare and riders fell, but Hezhi was laughing as they hit the earth, darkly delighted.

PERKAR saw through Harka's eyes and through his own, and he understood neither set of senses. He beheld Hezhi, standing directly before the bull, solemnly clapping her hands, as if playing some child's game. He saw the bull, bones articulated by heart-strands of black and gold, a net of such strands cast out from him to the other revenant cattle. Then something erupting from Hezhi's chest like a bolt of lightning, an erratic brilliance that struck into the bull. Ngangata reached her, lifted her up—and the herd came apart. Skulls separated from vertebrae that themselves spun out into falling streams of disks. Legs unjointed, and ribs flew apart like rotten cages. But the bones lost none of their momentum, and so as they collapsed, still they hurtled forward, a crashing wave of black bone and dust. The wave smacked into his two friends, and they went down beneath the leading edge of it. Shouting hoarsely, Perkar bore down on T'esh, urged him ever faster toward the bizarre scene.

In the lake of bones that remained, only one set remained standing: the bull himself, stock-still.

By the time Perkar reached them, it was obvious that Hezhi and Ngangata had survived the impact. They were both on their feet, as was Ngangata's mount. Perkar dismounted, Harka drawn, and with two bounds placed himself between his companions and the Bull God.

Only then did he realize that Hezhi was chuckling. Ngangata looked dazed.

"How are you two?" Perkar asked frantically. "Are either of you hurt?"

"No," Ngangata clipped out.

"I'm fine," Hezhi answered, laughter subsiding. "Leave the bull to me."

"What do you mean?"

"It's mine now," she replied. She walked around him toward the thing. It stood shorn of the illusion of flesh, a beast of black bones and fire.

"Hezhi, don't," Perkar commanded, moving to keep himself between the girl and the monster.

"She knows what she's doing," Harka said. *"Though I would never have believed this."*

"Believed what?"

Hezhi walked confidently up to the thing. She tapped it in the center of its skull, the horns reaching around her like the gathering arms of some handless giant. The skeleton collapsed, and the air shivered with flame which was quickly gone.

"What happened?" he asked Harka softly.

"She swallowed him," the blade answered. *"Took him in. She has two gods in her damakuta now."*

Hezhi turned to them, an insuppressible grin of triumph on her face. Behind her, the river of bones stretched off, empty of life.

Ngangata was the first to break that strange and uncomfortable moment with words.

"Where is Moss?" he asked.

RAINCASTER was dead, an artery in his neck severed by the wicked curve of the demon bird's beak. They left him on a natural table of stone for the predators to find, as was the Mang way.

Of Moss they never found any trace.

"He got away," Perkar finally admitted. "How?"

Hezhi crinkled her forehead in thought. "I saw him ride into them and not fall."

"It's clear enough," Brother Horse said. "The bird, that herd— they must have been sent by the gaan, the one who dreams for the Changeling. Probably he sent Moss a dream last night, telling him what to do." He shook his head. "This is a powerful man, with powerful spirits at his beck."

"One of them is now at *mine*," Hezhi reminded him. Brother Horse could not cloak the wonder from his eyes. He plainly believed her. A worry awoke in Perkar. He remembered her, back in Nhol, filled with power. She had laughed then, too. It had sounded much like her laugh earlier today, when she stopped the god and his ghost herd. Wasn't her power supposed to be diminished, away from the River? Was it diminished, or merely no longer under the Changeling's command? He would have to watch her even more closely than before.

But after that moment of sardonic glee, she seemed to return to being Hezhi.

"I don't see any point in tracking him," Ngangata said, apparently in response to a suggestion by Yuu'han that Perkar had missed. "He'll be returning to the gaan, probably, and probably with more aid of the sort we just saw."

Perkar nodded. "Right. We have to go on."

"He knows where we're going," Hezhi said. "He heard our talk about the mountain. He may not know why, but he knows that is our destination."

"Is it?" Tsem asked. "I heard of this only recently, Princess."

Hezhi shrugged. "Perkar and the Blackgod both insist we should go. I'm not afraid to now."

Brother Horse cocked his head at that. "Princess," he said, "what we have just seen is astonishing. You stopped and tamed a powerful god. But as powerful as he is, he is still nothing compared to the gods of the mountain, less still to the Changeling. The Changeling could swallow both of your guardians like small morsels and still have plenty of hunger for us."

"Nevertheless, I won't spend the rest of my life being chased and hounded by the likes of Moss. Perkar is right; whether we like this or not, he and I must see this through to the end."

"Raincaster won't be seeing it through to the end," Tsem observed.

Perkar felt a familiar lump rise in his throat, and Hezhi's face twisted in anguish. In an odd way, that was comforting, to see this girl who had just defeated a god mourn a Human Being. To know that, at least to that extent, she was what she appeared to be—a thirteen-year-old girl. Perkar cleared his throat into the silence following Tsem's remark. "You all see what faces us now," he said. "The skein of this destiny was wound from Hezhi and myself. The rest of you may have entered the tapestry knowingly or unknowingly. Either way, none of you needs face another god, another gaan, or another battle. Raincaster died for us, and others have done the same. I wouldn't blame any of you or think you lacking in Piraku if you were to leave us now. In fact, I even ask that of you." He glanced at Hezhi, and she nodded in agreement, her little mouth set and certain. In that instant, he wanted to place his arm about her, stand with her as if they were a single tree. But he did not—or could not.

The others watched them blankly for a moment, all but Tsem, who looked as if he would erupt at any time. It was Brother Horse who answered Perkar, however. Except that he spoke not to Perkar but to Ngangata. "How long do you think these two would last on their own, halfling?" He cleared some dust from his throat and spat it out on the dry earth.

Ngangata seemed to consider that. "Well, let's see," he considered heavily. "Between them they have a godsword, a shaman's drum, and two guardian godlets—have I left anything out?"

"Three Mang horses, including Sharp Tiger," Brother Horse added.

"Yes, I should have mentioned them. I don't know; they might make it seven or eight days with all of that."

Brother Horse shook his head in disagreement. "No. I think they would either be so busy arguing or avoiding each other or just prancing along in self-satisfaction that they would ride right off a cliff without noticing—in the first day or so."

Ngangata nodded thoughtfully. "Yes. I withdraw my estimate."

After that, both men sat their horses and just smiled thinly at Hezhi and him.

Perkar glanced over at the girl. "This ought to make us mad," he said.

"It *does* make *me* mad," she snapped. "But I suppose they've made their point?" She balled her fists on her hips and stared up at the others expectantly.

Tsem finally sighed hollowly. "If we're going, shouldn't we go? Before Moss can go tell every other monster or god or whatever where we are?"

"I have to sing a dirge for Raincaster," Yuu'han insisted softly. "Then we can go."

"Yuu'han . . ." Brother Horse began, but his nephew flashed dagger-eyes at him.

"*We* can go," Yuu'han repeated, and then walked over to the corpse of his cousin. Presently they heard singing, and Hezhi began to weep. Perkar felt salt sting his own eyes.

Soon after that, they started out across the high plains.

INTERLUDE

A Letter to Ghan

Ghan, it has been long since I have written. Two moons have waxed and waned as we travel across the wildlands, since we were driven from the village of the Mang. Too much has happened for a pen to capture, and I must be brief, for one cannot write in the saddle, and that is where the most of my days are spent.

The world is stranger and more varied than I ever believed possible. Living in the palace, I knew that I was confined, that my world was small—cut off from even the city—but a part of me never really understood what a tiny universe that was. It may be that the part of me that is River—that can only comprehend himself and never understand what lies beyond his banks—was stronger in me than I thought.

Now I have traveled far from the palace, far from Nhol, mercifully far from the River. Fifty days I have ridden with my companions across vast plains, through jagged mountains, through forests that I am told are green even in the harshest weather. In leaving Nhol, I have lost my greatest love—the library—but here, in a sense, I find compensation: discovery, at least, and as one of my friends put it, mystery.

My new calling is shrouded in both of these, and it terrifies me as often as it elates me, I must admit, but I am coming to accept it. I have become what the Mang call a gaan, a person who talks with ghosts and gods, who cajoles them into doing favors and occasionally whips them to it. It is power, and until recently I thought I was happy to leave power back with the River. The strength that he offered was infinitely more potent than what I have acquired on the shaman's path, but the price that came along with the River's strength was more than I will ever be willing to pay. The cost of becoming a gaan is much lower, and one I believe I can afford. I strike bargains, most often, with my servants; all but one of them serves me because they wish, rather than because they must. Three gods dwell with me now—I acquired my latest tenant only a half-score of days ago. The first who came to live in my "mansion"— this is what they call the place within us where the gods rest—was the ghost of a horse, and the story of that is too long to tell here, and not very typical of how a gaan normally works. The second case is even more extraordinary: that one was a strong, passionate spirit sent to attack us, and him I took by force. When I did that, Ghan, my power did feel like that moment by the River, for it gave me the ability to command. I liked it; when that dread god knelt before me and sullenly entered into my service it made me feel like the princess I should have been. However, I shall not use force again, for now that he is there, within me, I fear him. I do not fear him so much as the things he offers; he coaxes me, promising that with his aid, no spirit can escape my power to bind, swears that I can become a shaman such as the world has not seen in a thousand years. I feel that this is true—I believe him—and so am tempted, for with enough power I could crush all of my enemies and the dangers to my friends, as well. I am tired of running, of battles, of death. And so when Hukwosha—that is the name of the Bull God—when he offers me such power, I want it. But I fear it, because it is merely another path back to what I avoided when I left the River. Ultimately my power comes from him, even this power I have to be a gaan; it is not my wish to become like him, an eater of gods. It is not my desire to become lost in dreams of conquest. I only want to live, to be free, to be left alone.

Forgive me when I digress, but writing of my feelings helps me to comprehend them.

This last god I have acquired as a companion is—according to my teacher, Brother Horse—a more typical shaman's helper than the other two. This one I call Swan, because that is how she appeared to me. I found her in a lonely valley of ghosts, guarding their tombs. How long ago she was set there to ward them, I cannot say, and she had little sense of passing time; but all of the ghosts had departed, and Swan had nothing left to do—and yet could not herself depart. In this case there was no battle, no danger, and no desperation—only a lonely god. I offered her a place in my mansion, explaining what sort of service I would expect from her, and she agreed more than readily. After the capture of the bull, it was a great relief, and though the swan is not a powerful or ferocious helper, she comforts me in a way the others do not.

Tsem became a warrior three days ago; he is very proud. Perkar and the others have fashioned him an enormous wooden mace and a shield with a wooden frame covered in elkhide. We were set upon by creatures Perkar names Lemeyi, which are half god and half something else. These three had the appearance of long-legged wolves. They paced us for a day before attacking, shouting with Human speech. I could have taken one—as I did the bull—but the thought repelled me. Instead I sent out the mare to attack, and she dispensed with one. Perkar dispatched a second, but it was Tsem who broke the spine of the third. It writhed and cursed at him in Nholish, scored deep claw marks into his shield, but he hit it again and again, until it did not move.

I protested when Perkar began teaching Tsem to fight with weapons, but now I admit that he was right to do so. The Lemeyi was trying to reach me, and Tsem would have interposed himself in any case, armed or not. These creatures had claws like sickles and fangs like daggers. He would have died. As it is, he came to my rescue. He knows it, too, and walks more proudly, makes jokes readily for the first time since leaving Nhol.

The encounter with the Lemeyi affected Perkar more than the rest of us. He has brooded almost without words since that fight. Ngangata says that Perkar was once tricked by the Blackgod in the guise of a Lemeyi. This is yet another instance that makes me wonder how much I can trust either Perkar or the Blackgod whom he names Karak.

We began this journey in the southern Mang country, a place where only the skeletons of mountains remain. Now we are in places where mountains are in the prime of life, mountains such as I never dreamed could be. It astonishes me that a peak more magnificent than those I have seen can exist, and yet I know that it can, for ahead of us, in a forest Perkar calls Balat, She'leng awaits. I have seen it before, in the otherworld of the lake, but the memory of that place fades like a dream; the colors and shapes are difficult to remember—exactly like a dream, in fact, since Brother Horse calls dreaming "floating on the surface of the lake." We shamans do not merely float—we dive—but those deeper dreams are often as nonsensical as the ones at the water's edge.

My fourteenth birthday is four moons away, and I wonder often if I shall ever see it. I think that I won't. Just as my blood moved the River to pull Perkar and me together, something is moving us all again. It seems as if, instead of a mountain, She'leng must be a vast pit—an ant-lion trap. For months we have been skittering down the widest, least sloping part of that funnel, digging in our heels sometimes, now rushing down in great leaps. The Blackgod told Perkar that what awaits us at that bottom place is the death of the River, the end of a war. Perkar believes that the war which will end will be that of his father's people against the Mang. That may be. But it seems to me that a larger conflict rages, and neither side much cares about us save in how we might be used.

I wish you were here. An enemy lately taunted me with the possibility of your presence. It was the only thing he offered that held temptation for me. It may be that he was telling the truth about you, and in that case I am sorry, for you have been drawn into this deepening pit with us. Perhaps we will have a chance to meet again and talk, before we reach the bottom.

PART THREE

THE GODS OF SHE'LENG

© Cherry '96

XXVIII

~~~~~~~~~~~~~~~~~~~~~~~~~~~~~~~~~~~~~

The Drum Scout

A few ravens took to the air as Ngangata led the way into the field, but most remained where they were, glutting themselves on the corpses that lay broken on the rough ground.

"Harka?" Perkar murmured.

"All dead. No one hiding in the woods."

Nevertheless, Perkar joined the others in scanning the far tree line. It kept his gaze from touching the hollow regard of the dead, and, in any event, survivors of the battle could not be far distant, for the ruins of two yekts still smoldered nearby.

Brother Horse and Yuu'han rode out impatiently, studying the dead and muttering to one another the names of their clans.

Two bodies belonged to no Mang clan at all. They were clad in hauberk and helms like his own folk, and from beneath their steel caps bushed hair the color of wheatstraw. Perkar sighed heavily and dismounted.

Studying their ruined faces, he felt a selfish relief in not knowing either of the men, though the bloodied embroidery on their shirts identified them as being of the Kar Herita or some closely affiliated clan.

How often had he imagined this moment, when he would first see one of his own people again? From before the start of the journey home, of course, but in the last few days his every waking moment seemed plagued by visions of this first encounter. In his dreams—sleeping *and* waking—it was the broken body of his father or his younger brother he found first. For once, at least, his imaginings were more painful than the reality.

"Six dead in all," Ngangata told him, after making a circuit of the meadow.

"The rest Mang?"

"Yes." Ngangata nodded. "Four Mang and two Cattle People."

"This is much deeper into Mang territory than I thought my people would ever come," Perkar muttered, kicking at a stone. "This is such poor pasture for men to fight and die over." He glanced up at the half man. "How are Brother Horse and Yuu'han taking this?"

The two Mang were riding over to inspect the ravaged yekts. Ngangata followed them with his gaze. "We all knew that it would come to this eventually."

"I've tried to talk them into turning back."

"Yes. But this war concerns them, too. They wish to see it ended as much as we."

"What if we come upon a battle in *progress*, Ngangata? I won't be able to watch my people fight without helping them, and neither will they."

"Then we must avoid any such battles."

"How?" Perkar asked irritably, aware that Hezhi and Tsem were approaching. Tsem's eyes were watchful, darting here and there, and his massive club was cocked back on one shoulder, ready.

"I can help, I think," Hezhi offered.

"What do you mean?"

"Well, I didn't think of this before because I didn't really understand what you meant by *war*. I didn't expect it to be like this."

"What *did* you expect?"

"Well, the only wars I've read about were those fought by the empire. I always had the impression of enormous numbers of men all lined up and marching toward one another."

Perkar nodded. "That happens sometimes."

"I mean thousands and thousands of men," Hezhi clarified.

"Oh. I see what you mean," Perkar said. "I have heard tales of armies that numbered as high as a thousand, but that was long ago."

"Exactly. And so I imagined that when we reached the borders of your country we would encounter a sort of line of soldiers, going on for miles, fighting each other. That probably sounds silly to you."

"It does," Perkar admitted. "You might find a damakuta like that, surrounded by men fighting or under siege. But our country is much too large for the Mang to encircle. Most of the battles will be like this, fights over homesteads or damakutat. The heaviest fighting is probably in the Ekasagata Valley, where the best land is. There we probably *would* see camped armies. But that is the way we have *avoided* all along."

"Then it should be simple to avoid battles like this."

"No. The country is vast, but as you see, from here on it's a land of valleys and passes, narrow places. Raiding parties like the one that came here must be wandering around everywhere, seeking revenge, looking for some likely settlement to attack. We can never know where they will be."

"Of course we can. I can send out some of my spirits to check our path ahead."

"You can do that?"

"I'm certain Brother Horse *has* been doing it. Remember when he counseled this trail over the last at the fork a day ago? I think he saw a battle ahead of us."

Perkar mulled that over. "If you can do that, at no danger to yourself, it would be best. I'd hate to have to put our friendship with those two to the test. I usually fare poorly in tests like that."

"Well and truly said," Ngangata remarked, dryly but with no apparent malice.

Perkar took a heavy breath. "Still, if we manage to get through the frontier unscathed, it will actually be more difficult to proceed through the pastures unnoticed. My people are watching carefully, I'm certain, and the thought of skulking about in my own country pains me." He thought secretly, too, how desperately he longed to hear his own language spoken, taste woti again, see a face familiar from childhood.

"Why must we take such care there?" Hezhi asked.

"Because I cannot guarantee how any of us would be treated," Perkar muttered. "Not by any but my own close kin. Passions are probably high against the Mang—which they will assume *you* to be, as well, Princess."

"But it's *they* who have invaded Mang lands, not the other way around," Hezhi protested, indicating the burned yekts where Brother Horse and Yuu'han had begun chanting.

"I know," Perkar said. "But people die on both sides, and if a relative of yours is slain, it matters not to you who began the battle. It matters only that you avenge him." He gestured at the dead men. "You can be sure that this man's clan will not remember that he led a raid into land not his own. They will only remember that he was slain by the Mang, and for that reason it is good to slay Mang in turn."

THE party traveled sullenly for the remainder of the day, the two Mang riding somewhat apart with their grief from the rest. They camped for the night in a small, high valley, the sort that made poor pasture for horses *or* cattle and was thus generally unsettled by both Mang and Perkar's folk. Perkar also hoped that it would give them a good view of the trail they hoped to pursue the next day.

Before sundown, Hezhi followed Perkar up a narrow trail in the hillside; Tsem was convinced with some difficulty to stay behind, but he could see as plainly as anyone else what a difficult way it would be for someone of his size to tread.

Hezhi admired the ease with which Perkar negotiated the ascent, which often became a climb, requiring the use of hands as well as feet. She always seemed to be just a *bit* too short to reach the next handhold with ease, her fingers a little too small to grip the same knob of stone with as much tenacity as Perkar did. And he was much stronger and tired less quickly. He often glanced back at her, a tacit question about her well-being in his eyes that both annoyed her by its implicit condescension and warmed her with its concern. It was a melange of feeling she had come to associate with Perkar: irritation and fondness.

At last they reached a high point, the balded peak of a ridge, and from there the folded, crumpled land spread out and away in all directions. There was no distance anywhere unserrated by mountains, and for an instant, Hezhi felt that she stood on the same mountain as she had with Karak, watching the souls of the dead drift skyward to She'leng.

But here she saw no ghosts, only deep troughs filled with shadow and bloody sunset.

Perkar edged toward the sheer western face of the ridge and extended his finger northwest. "There," he said. "Can you see up this vale? Is there battle there tomorrow?"

Hezhi considered the vista for a moment. "Where does your country begin?" she asked.

"I'm not sure," he answered. "Not far, surely. Here in the Spines there are few people of any sort, only mountain people of no nation, wild creatures." He turned to her. "How long will this take?"

"I'm not certain," she answered.

"Be quick if you can. I misjudged the distance and the light. Soon it may be too dark to go back down."

She nodded and removed her drum from its bag and, after just a moment of preparation, began a measured tapping, as Brother Horse had shown her. The drumming of the skin head quickly became ripples upon the surface of the otherworld, and she turned her vision inward and saw her companions. The mare welcomed her with a shake of her head; the bull lowered his deadly horns sullenly. The most recently acquired god—now in the appearance of a white swan—regarded her solemnly.

"Which of you will go?" she inquired of them.

The bull gazed up at her. In here, he was no skeletal creature animated by flame; he was magnificent, auburn with great shoulders cloaked in darker, longer hair, the eyes between his gleaming horns huge and brown, full of intelligence.

"*Take me,*" he said. "*We shall thunder across the plains, we shall gore the lion, and trample the wolf pack. Too long have you kept me in this peaceful place.*"

Hezhi's fear of the beast, as well as the passion and power he offered, clung to her even beneath the cold waters of the lake, but she shook her head. "Not today, not now. I only need a messenger, not a warrior. I send you, Swan."

She sent the swan out through the doorway, her vision carried in her eyes.

Perkar sat impatiently, watching as Hezhi's eyes glazed over and she tapped away on her drum. She was *gone,* not in her body at all, and that woke in him a faintly sick feeling, perhaps a buried memory of his own time in the otherworld.

"It's still not settled," he told Harka, while he waited. "I still don't know what will happen when I face combat again."

"*It will be fine,*" the sword answered. "*You are braver than you think.*"

"I flinched in the face of the bull. If it hadn't been for Hezhi, we would all be dead."

"*That would be true whether you flinched or not. Learn from your mistake, don't dwell on it.*"

"A mistake is something you do on purpose that turns out to be wrong. That's not what happened with the bull. I was *afraid.* I didn't do that on purpose."

"*You've been afraid before.*"

"This is different."

"*I know. But courage exists only if fear does, too. The greater the fear overcome, the greater the courage. Fearlessness is only another name for stupidity.*"

"Has no one ever carried you who was fearless?"

"*Of course. And he was as stupid as a stone.*"

"What was his name?"

"*One of them was named Perkar.*"

Perkar furrowed his brow in annoyance and refused to provoke any more conversation from the sword. Instead, he set about gathering scraps of juniper and twist pine; it was clear that night would settle down before Hezhi was done, and it would be cold, this high.

Sparks were dancing up when the drumming ceased; the only remnant of the day was a languid red rim on the western peaks.

Hezhi shook her head sluggishly as her eyes seemed to awaken to him and the rest of her surroundings.

"It's cold," she sighed.

"Come over here, let the Fire Goddess warm you," he said. She nodded, picked up her drum, and padded along the ridge to sit across the flames from him. She rubbed her hands, working the fire's heat into her chilled flesh. Perkar fought his impatience, knowing she would speak eventually.

And eventually she did.

"Men are dying up there," she said. "I'm sorry."

Cold fingers reached out of the night and prodded at his heart. "Many?"

"I think so. More than fifty, more than I could count. They've stopped for the night, but I believe that in the morning they will begin again."

Perkar's lips drew into a thin line.

"My father could be among them," he muttered. "My brother."

"I'm sorry."

Perkar saw that she really *was* sorry. Her eyes were rimmed with wetness.

"It's hard to cry over there," she said. "Everything I feel is different, flatter. But now—" Her little shoulders began to quake. "They were just *dying*. Arrows in their throats, big holes in them—" She stuttered off, wiping at her face.

"Perkar . . ." she began, but he stood stiffly and walked around the fire, feeling foolish. He settled next to her and drew her against him, expecting her to stiffen, fearing she would.

She didn't. Instead she seemed to melt into his side, her head nestling against his chest, where she sobbed quietly for a while. Her tears were contagious, and a salty trickle began from the corner of his own eyes. Almost unconsciously, he rocked back and forth, stroking her thick black hair.

After a time, he had to rise and add wood to the fire, and he realized how reluctant he was to release her. When he returned, he felt awkward, uncertain whether he should hold her again or not. He finally reached for her tentatively.

"I'm all right now," she said. He withdrew his arm, embarrassed, and they sat there for a few moments in an uncomfortable silence.

"What I mean is," Hezhi began again, "you don't *have* to do that. You don't have to feel sorry for me."

Perkar snorted softly. "You know me well enough to know that I only feel sorry for myself," he answered.

"I don't believe that," she said. "Ngangata thinks you ache for the whole world."

"Ngangata is the kindest man I've ever known. He flatters me. Still, *he* has never been shy about numbering my faults, especially my selfishness. Nor have *you*, for that matter."

"I'm sorry," she said.

Perkar glanced at her in surprise. "That's the third time you've said that tonight," he remarked.

"No, I am. A few months ago, when we were in the hills with the Mang, before all of this started, I thought we were going to be friends. But since then, I've been terrible to you. To everyone, really, and especially to Tsem. You think *you're* selfish—"

Perkar smiled and began tossing twigs into the flames, where they stirred little cyclones of sparks to life. "The fact is," he told her, "Brother Horse and Ngangata are right about us. We both see the world wheeling around our noses. We both think that the rising of the sun and the Pale Queen hinges upon us."

"It's hard not to," Hezhi muttered. "So many people fighting and dying, and even the *gods* say we are the cause."

"No. Make no mistake, Hezhi. The gods are the ones who began this. You and I—"

"I don't want to talk about this tonight," Hezhi said suddenly. "It's all I think about, all *you* think about."

Perkar hesitated. He had been about to tell her, was right on the verge of telling her *all* of what Karak said—that *she* was the one who had the power to slay the Changeling. But he could tell her that later, tomorrow. There was time enough, now that he had decided to do it.

"Well, then, what *do* you want to talk about?"

"I don't know. I don't *know*!" she lamented, helplessly frustrated. "What would we talk about, if we were just two people, with no godswords, no spirit drums, no mission, no war?"

"*Nothing*. We would never have met."

"I'm *serious*. What would we talk about? What would you tell me if I were one of *your* people and we were alone here?"

He chuckled. "I don't know, either."

"Well, *try*," she demanded, crossly.

"Yes, Princess."

"And *don't* call me that. Not now."

Perkar reached out, without thinking really, and stroked her hair again. "Now *I'm* sorry," he said. "I really am." He realized what he was doing suddenly and pulled his hand away as if her head were a hot stone. She rolled her eyes at that, reached up with her tiny fingers and took hold of his, draped his arm back around her.

"I changed my mind," she grumbled. "I'm cold."

"Ah . . ." Perkar felt his face burning, but he pulled her close again. After a moment's thought, he unrolled a blanket and settled it over both of their shoulders. He took her hand in his and was gratified when she squeezed back.

"Thanks again for saving my life," he murmured.

"Shut up. This is exactly what I'm talking about," she cried, beating his chest with her palm. "Just tell me *something*, something of no importance at all."

Perkar thought for a long moment before he finally said, "I know a story about a cow with two heads."

"What?"

"A head on each end. My mother used to tell me that story. There was a fox who owned a cow with two heads—"

"*Tell* it, don't summarize it," Hezhi insisted.

"It's a silly story."

"Tell it, I command thee."

"Your wish I grant, Princ—Lady Hezhi," Perkar amended. "It seems that in the long ago, in the days when people and animals often spoke, and the cooking pots had opinions, and the fence-rails often complained of boredom, there was a fox who had no cows. And he asked himself, 'Now, how might I gather a fine herd and Piraku—' "

"Is this a long story?" she interrupted.

"Yes."

"Good."

And for a time they pushed away death and destiny, and Hezhi grinned at the antics of the fox and his magical cow, and in the end they fell asleep, curled together.

HEZHI awoke first, uncertain of where she was. Her arm was asleep, and something warm was next to her.

She remembered then and extricated her arm with great care from where it lay beneath Perkar's back. He was still sleeping, and she gazed at his face, astonished and confused by her feelings.

It was nice, the way sleep smoothed away his pains so that she could see the face of the boy he had been, once, before their destinies became bound. The boy he *might* have been. How old was he? Twenty at most.

And what did he feel for her? Pity? Protectiveness?

She wasn't certain, but there was something in the way he held her, after she stopped crying, that seemed like neither of those things. It had seemed somehow desperate. And the oddest thing was that she *understood* that desperation, felt something akin to it. It was as if she had been growing a skin of stone, as if her face and fingers could no longer feel, any more than a piece of wood could. It was deeper than numbness. How long had it been since anyone held her, touched her? Even Tsem had been distant from her since the night they fled from Brother Horse's camp. She had not even realized how much she missed her contact with the Giant. She was hungry for *any* touch.

But Perkar's touch was something else again, something special. It was more akin to what she felt when Yen held her, but it wasn't even that. Yen's touch had been exciting, forbidden, and sweet. *This* was something that caught in her throat, and usually it came out as anger or spite. But last night it manifested as something else entirely, something with deeper roots. She wondered what she would have done had he kissed her. Had he even thought about it? She had feared that he *would* kiss her, last night, force her to decide what she felt or retreat from it. Now she wished the decision had been forced, for the one thing she did *not* need right now was this powerful new uncertainty.

What would she do when he woke? How should she react? She lay back and closed her eyes again, a mischievous smile on her face. Let *him* make that decision.

XXIX

Forward-Falling Ghost

The first day, Ghan was sure that he would die. By the second, he wished he would. No torturer of the Ahw'en could have developed a more fiendish device for torment than the hard Mang saddle and the horse beneath it. Trotting rubbed his thighs and calves raw; the middle pace shook pain into his entire frame. It was only the extremes—walking and full gallop—that did not immediately pain him, but in the next day he realized that the death grip he kept on the beast when it ran had to be paid for with cramping muscles and febrile pain along his bones. Thrice the meat and tendons of his leg knotting into a bunch near his ankle had sent him sliding to the ground, cursing and shedding tears of pain.

They did not stop for sleep, and as he had never been on a horse before, Ghan was entirely unable to doze in the saddle as did the rough barbarians around him. When he did drift off, it was only to awake, heartbeats later, in terror of falling. By the end of the second day he was haggard and speechless.

He did not understand the Mang language, though it contained vague echoes of the ancient tongue of Nhol, and many words were similar. But Ghe could speak with them somehow, perhaps through the same agency by which Perkar had "learned" the speech of Nhol.

Ghan gathered, before he became unable to take in new information, that the troop of horsemen had been *searching* for them, apparently at the behest of the man Ghe dreamed about, who was some sort of chief.

The only other thing that Ghan knew was that they were riding to meet this dream man. And, of course, that he would never live to do so.

To distract himself, he made an attempt to observe the men around him—if such creatures deserved to be called men. It did not help much. They all looked much the same, with their red-plumed helms, lacquered armor, and long black or brown coats. They all smelled much the same: like horses. They all jabbered tersely in an ugly language, and they all laughed at *him*, an old man who couldn't even sit a horse without considerable aid. His only comfort came from one of the surviving Nholish soldiers, a young fellow named Kanzhu, who stayed near him, caught him when he was near falling, and gave him water. Kanzhu was a cavalryman himself and knew well how to ride.

Ghe did not speak to him at all, but rode ahead with Qwen Shen and Bone Eel, both of whom seemed to have at least some facility with horses.

On the third day, he awoke to find himself lying in short grass. Someone was spattering water in his face, and a large locust sat on his chest.

"Master Ghan? Can you move?" It was Kanzhu. Ghan sipped gratefully at the water.

"I guess I fell asleep," he conceded.

"Come on. You will ride with me for a while."

"They won't allow that."

"They'll have to, or leave you, and then they'll have to leave me. I won't abandon a subject of the emperor alone in these lands."

A few of the Mang jabbered something at Kanzhu when he got Ghan up behind him in his saddle, but they eventually relented. The main body of riders was far ahead anyway, and they did not want to be left behind arguing.

"Don't they ever sleep?" Ghan growled weakly into the boy's back. The hard young muscles felt firm, secure, as if his arms were wrapped around a tree trunk. Had *he* ever been thus?

Probably not.

"This is some kind of forced march," Kanzhu explained. "Lord Bone Eel, Lady Qwen Shen, and Master Yen seem to have struck a bargain with the leader of these barbarians, though no word has come back to us about where we are going—but I've heard a few of these men mention someplace named Tseba. If that's where we're going, they mean to get there *fast*. Even the Mang would never push their horses like this unless there was some dire need."

"How do you know Tseba is a place, and not a person or a thing? Do you speak any of their language?" Ghan asked.

The boy nodded uncertainly. "Not much. I was stationed at Getshan, on their border, for a few months. I learned how to say 'hello' and a few other things. That's about all. But a lot of their places start with 'tse.' I think it means 'rock,' like in Nholish."

"Can you ask how many more days to this place?"

"I can try," Kanzhu answered. He thought for a moment and then hollered at the nearest Mang, *"Duhan zhben Tseba?"*

The barbarian screwed up his face in puzzlement. Kanzhu rephrased the question in slightly different syllables. After a moment, comprehension dawned on the man's face, and he grimly held up three fingers.

"Three more days?" Ghan groaned. But then he gritted his teeth. He wouldn't complain anymore; barbarians and soldiers hated the weak, and while he could do nothing about the infirmity of his body, he could certainly stop whining.

"Three days then," he restated, trying to sound positive.

* * *

Miraculously, the next day was not quite as bad. Ghan speculated that most of his body had resigned itself to death and so no longer troubled him with pain.

Kanzhu trotted up that morning. He looked worried. "Something happened to Wat last night."

"Who?"

"One of the soldiers, a friend of mine."

"What happened to him?"

"He died," Kanzhu stated simply.

Ghan nodded dumbly. Of course. What else but death would rate notice here, now?

After a few moments, Kanzhu cut his eyes back toward Ghan furtively.

"He wasn't stabbed or anything; I saw his corpse. He was just *dead*."

"Oh." Ghan lifted his brows but offered nothing. What good would it do Kanzhu to know? It would only put him in danger.

Two more soldiers vanished that night. Kanzhu said their bodies weren't found and confided to Ghan that he hoped they had deserted, though it was clear that he didn't believe they had. Ghan offered his sympathy, but his own worries were growing. This was a bad sign; Ghe was losing control. Though he had consistently avoided Ghan since the Mang had found them, he had ridden near lately, his face a frozen mask, his eyes like hard, black iron. It was as if the humanity in him were sleeping, or strained beyond reason.

Ghan tried to think it through, to understand what was happening to the ghoul. Though terrible pain still housed itself in his shoulders, his thighs—and weirdly enough, the muscles of his abdomen—it was no longer *agony*, and he had managed to drop into sleep during periods of walking, which were signaled, like the other paces, by a horn trumpet. This meant it was actually possible for him to *think* again.

Ghe was a dead man animated by the River. His body had the signs of life, it *was* alive in most ways—save one. The spirit, the ghost inside his skin was not that of a man, was not held together by the same stuff of life that held a man together. It was not self-contained. Neither was a living person self-contained; it needed food and water, and in time despite it all, the essence of a person's life came unmoored from its flesh. But whatever Ghe was, his life came always from outside. Near the River, where the flow of vital energy was constant, what left through his eyes and mouth and every action was merely replaced. Out here—life had to be found elsewhere. And he had more mouths to feed than his own, if Ghan understood his nature correctly. One of them was a goddess.

The old texts had called creatures like Ghe Life-Eaters, but in the ancient tongue they had also been named "forward-falling ghosts." That name made sense to Ghan now; Ghe must be like a man trying to run down a hill when his head is moving more quickly than his feet. He cannot stop, for he would fall. He can only run faster and in the end *fall* faster.

This was the creature who hungered for Hezhi. He had to be stopped, but Ghan was out of ideas. He was tired, and he wanted real sleep.

He cast a hopeful look at Kanzhu. Maybe *something* more could be done. Maybe he could convince Kanzhu to help him flee.

But that night Kanzhu vanished, and Ghan never saw him again.

THE next day brought a wonder that cut briefly through all of Ghan's pain and trepidation. The horn to trot had just sounded, and the horses stepped down from running. Ghan was disappointed; now that he was *able* to stay on the back of his mount without straining every muscle, running was the gait he most preferred—next to walking, of course—because it was the smoothest. Kanzhu had taught him how to survive trotting, as well, but it involved bouncing in the stirrups, using his frail, worn-out legs to absorb the constant jolts. It was more work.

After only a moment of trotting, however, the signal came to slow to a walk, which was unusual; the shifts in speed were not usually done in such brief intervals. Soon, however, the reason for slowing became obvious. Mountains walked on the horizon.

The Mang named them *nunetuk*, but that word seemed somehow too short—or too long—to capture them in sound. Four legs built like the pillars of a hall supported their impossibly massive frames. From their heads snakelike appendages protruded, and to either side of that, sabers of bone—no, it must be ivory—curved up menacingly. They were shaggy, hair ranging from reddish brown to black. Fifteen or so stood in a clump, near a distant line of spruce, grazing in the tall grass. At first there were only the trees to give them scale; but with a sudden chorus of shrieks, a detachment of seven Mang tore off across the prairie toward the monsters and put them in firmer perspective: even mounted, the men scarcely reached to the bellies of the monsters.

"What are they doing?" Ghan asked incredulously. But none of the Mang answered him—and Kanzhu was gone.

Still shrieking, the warriors raced up to the now-wary beasts. Some of the larger nunetuk had formed a defensive ring about the smaller ones and the *very* small ones—only about the size of a horse—which Ghan took to be calves. The men had drawn swords and brandished them in the faces of the beasts; they appeared to be attempting to get close enough to cut them.

Wouldn't lances be better? he thought, but then he understood that the Mang were not trying to *kill* the huge animals; they were merely trying to *touch* them.

Though that seemed insane, the longer Ghan watched, the more apparent it became that it was true. Deftly avoiding the lunges of the beasts, the massive white tusks that slashed at them and their mounts, the Mang were leaning in to *spank* the gigantic creatures. The Mang who were still in ranks cheered and shrieked, and for the first time in several days the whole troop clopped to a halt for something other than water or to graze the horses.

It was a short break; apparently satisfied, the seven men came hurtling back through the grass, waving their weapons. Another group detached and seemed ready to go, but someone ahead barked a string of orders, and, after some brief argument, the seven fell back into line, grumbling. Ghan was watching *them*, rather than the returning riders, when the yelling and screaming of the Mang redoubled and took on another, more frantic pitch.

Ghan jerked his face back around toward the approaching horsemen, wondering what had happened. Six of them were wheeling about in confusion and one could not be seen, apparently down in the chest-high growth. His horse's head bobbed up, however, shrilling a sound that Ghan was unaware horses could make, a chilling scream that grated along the bones of his back. The horse disappeared again, hidden by the grass.

Two of the six riders had lost control of their mounts; one, a handsome beast that was nearly solid black, pawed wildly at the air. Something rose from the grass swiftly, implacably. It disemboweled the horse with a single blow of its huge, blood-soaked paw and lunged for the next rider.

From the corner of his eye, Ghan saw someone converging on the bloody scene. It was Ghe.

G HE sensed the beast in the grass before the riders were attacked by it, and with a snarl he urged his mount forward. The mare was used to a more practiced rider, but it responded to his inexpert touch promptly, and he left Qwen Shen and the Mang headman, Chuk, behind him, with only a bemused chuckle from the headman, probably at his poor riding form.

Ghe cared not for the men who were about to die, but he was *hungry*, and it was inconvenient to take soldiers during the day. Since noon, he had been able to think about little but feeding, and to be surrounded by the Mang and their horses was like sitting starving in a banquet hall. A smaller part of him also knew that it could not hurt to earn the respect of these wild men. Riding over to the huge nunetuk would have only seemed silly, and it would have been suspicious beyond belief if one of the giant beasts folded up with death as he approached. The Nholish soldiers would certainly guess what had become of their dead comrades then.

But this thing in the grass, he could pretend to kill.

By the time he reached it, three men and two horses were already dead or dying. He snatched what he could of their essences, but it wasn't much. The demon he had swallowed gave him great power, but it took much energy to control her, as well. Since taking her, he was always hungry.

His horse panicked, reared, and threw him, but it seemed to happen incredibly slowly, his senses racing far ahead of motion, and so he easily turned in the air, landed cat-deft on the prairie, and like a cat, he leapt low and fast. Knife in hand, Ghe met the thing in its element, beneath the waving tufts of the grass.

In that surreal quickening of his senses, he had leisure to inspect the creature in detail. It seemed low and thick, but that was an illusion of its proportions; it would actually stand well clear of the grass if it were not crouching. More than anything else, it resembled a mastiff, a savage dog with an almost square skull and very little snout. Its gore-covered paws, however, were short and thicker than his leg, supporting at least as much mass as a horse, if not more. It was tawny with coffee-brown stripes. Muscles bunched in an ugly hump behind its head.

Its open maw could easily receive Ghe's head, and that was clearly the intention to be read in the monster's beady black eyes. Were it not for his own power, the thing would be blindingly swift, *much* faster than a horse, at least in short spurts.

Ghe hardened himself, sank roots of power into the prairie, pulled density and substance to himself the way the demon had from her river.

Beast and ghoul cracked together. Despite all of his strength, the impact was staggering, but the monster was more surprised than he. Having just batted a horse from its path like a flea, it had not expected this slight man-creature to withstand. Still, he toppled beneath the claws, at the same time thrusting his knife up through the beast's lower jaw. With the maw open before his face, Ghe saw his bloody steel erupt through the tongue, pass into the upper skull, and emerge in the center of the head. That didn't kill it, he knew; if he were an ordinary warrior, the dog-thing would certainly have enough life and anger to finish him before succumbing to a cloven brain; but in the same instant Ghe took its ghost, drank it down in great, satisfying gulps. For good measure he kept the remnants of its spirit, as well, joined it to the others in his heart.

So now I am five, he thought as the stinking body collapsed upon him. He let it, smiling at the impacts that shook the great body thereafter as the warriors, belatedly, attacked its corpse.

He let them pull him from beneath the thing, drenched in its blood, and the cheer that went up then was more than gratifying. He waved his bloody knife in the air, and the cheer redoubled. Walking back to the column of horses, he let one of the warriors chase down his mount, knowing he would appear more dignified on foot than in the saddle.

The headman rode out and dismounted, which Ghe knew to be an honor, and clapped his bloody hand savagely.

"I have *never* seen such a feat," he said, clearly trying to restrain his admiration a bit and failing. "The gaan was right about you. He said you would be a lion, and only a lion could have hoped to match a shezhnes."

"Shezhnes?" Ghe repeated, inquiring.

"A grass bear. He must have been stalking the nunetuk when our warriors had the bad fortune to ride upon him." He shook his head in disbelief. "Is that a godblade?" he asked, indicating his poignard.

Ghe frowned in puzzlement. "A what?"

The Mang slapped him on the back. "That answers my question, I think."

"But it doesn't answer mine," Ghe said. "What is a *godblade*?"

The headman looked bemused. "A weapon with a god in it. I've heard of them but know little enough about them. I'll be happy to tell you what I do know, though."

"I would appreciate that," he said. In his mind he traced the bitter image of Perkar's sword arcing toward his, how his own

River-blessed blade had shivered and nearly shattered when the strange green metal met it. *Godblade.*

"The gaan can tell you more."

"When will I meet him?" Ghe asked a bit distractedly, waving to the still-shouting crowd.

"He meets us tomorrow, at White Rock," the headman said. Ghe nodded, turned to wink at Qwen Shen, whose own eyes held an interesting mixture of fear and relief. He felt renewed affection for her; she was an amazing woman and had given him much. When he was at last rejoined with Hezhi, his *true* love, he would be as gentle as possible in ending her life.

TSEBA, Ghan discovered, meant "White Rock," and the place seemed aptly named, a low-walled canyon of chalky stone that led more or less north into a range of high country. In the last day of the journey, they had been joined by more and more riders; over a hundred sets of hooves clattered into Tseba.

A single rider awaited them there.

Ghan wasn't sure what he expected of a Mang chief, but he certainly thought the man would have at least a few retainers, perhaps musicians to herald his coming. The rider was some distance away, but from what Ghan could make out, he wore no regalia—indeed, he seemed worn and bedraggled, as if he had ridden harder and longer than they. He would have doubted this man's identity, save that every Mang present dismounted before him, as did he and most of the Nholish soldiers when they realized what was going on.

Ghe, Qwen Shen, and Bone Eel were led before the chief by the headman, and the group of them began speaking. Voices carried far in the canyon, but so did the whickering of horses and the stamping of restless hooves, and even though Ghan could hear them speaking, he could make out none of what they said.

But after a moment, Ghe left and strode back into the army of men and horses. He came like a titan, men moving deferentially from his path, and it was clear he came for Ghan. Ghan gathered his strength and awaited him.

"Hello, Ghan," Ghe said when he arrived. "I see that you fared well enough on our journey."

"Well enough."

"Would you come with me?"

Ghan quirked a faint half smile. "Do I have a choice?"

"No."

"Why, then, I will be more than happy to come." He dusted the horse hair from his legs, and when he took his first steps they nearly wobbled from under him.

"Let me help you, there," Ghe said, and took a firm—even painful—grip beneath his arm and began escorting him toward the fore of the party.

"I must admit, Ghan, I've been angry with you," Ghe confided as they walked along. "Though that isn't precisely why I have avoided you these past days."

"Oh? Have you avoided me?"

Ghe tsked. "You betrayed me, Ghan, and betrayed Hezhi, too, though I'm sure you pigheadedly thought you were helping her. I have avoided you to save your life, however. Every time I look at you, I desire to empty your withered shell of its spirit. And yet I thought some use might still exist for you. And, as it proves out, there is."

They were almost to the other leaders now, and Ghe slowed a bit—perhaps so that he would not appear to be *dragging* him. Ghan opened his mouth to ask Ghe what *use* he might have, but then they were there, the Mang chieftain watching him with bright eyes.

He *was* weary-looking, clad in the same manner as any of the Mang around him: long black coat, breeks. The only marked difference was that he wore no helmet. The *most* astonishing thing was his age; he couldn't be more than sixteen.

"You are the one named Ghan," he said in heavily accented but comprehensible Nholish.

"That is what I am called."

"You and I have much to talk about, along with these others," he said, indicating Ghe and the rest. "You may be happy to know that Hezhi is still alive and well."

Ghan blinked as the words sorted into sense, and with comprehension came a flood of sudden emotion, cracking the levees which had so long held it in place.

"How do you know?" Ghan asked.

The chieftain tapped his chest. "I see her, in here. Not long ago I rode with her." He placed his hand on Ghan's shoulder. "Allow me to introduce myself. I am shaman and war prophet of the Four Spruces Clan, and also by the will of the River and heaven, the chieftain of the three northwestern bands." He swept his hands to encompass all of the men and horses who stood dismounted in the valley, awaiting his command.

"But you, my friend, may call me Moss."

XXX

The Roadmark

PERKAR drew a sharp breath and stiffened when Harka suddenly hailed.

"What?"

"*Fifteen men at least in the rocks ahead,*" the weapon replied.

"Within earshot?" he whispered.

"*Shouting, I would think.*"

"Mang?"

"*How should I know? I only know they haven't certainly decided to attack you. They are waiting for someone or perhaps guarding something.*"

Perkar noticed Hezhi staring at him. He flashed her a little smile.

"Just pretend we're talking about something innocuous," he said softly.

"I thought we *were*," Hezhi answered, recalling the conversation Harka had interrupted, about the merits of red cattle as opposed to brown ones.

"There are warriors up ahead of us."

"They weren't there last night," she assured him.

"Well, now they are. Ngangata, do you hear all of this?"

"Yes. I say we go back the way we came."

"Too late for that," Perkar said. "They surely know we're here. When I give the word, all of you bolt for the cover of those trees. I don't think we're in line-of-sight for bows yet, anyway—"

"You aren't going to fight them all by yourself," Hezhi hissed.

Perkar smiled weakly and reached over to touch her hand. "I don't intend to fight them at *all*, unless I have no choice. These are most likely my people, considering where we are. But in times of war, rash, unplanned things can happen. If they shoot too hastily at one of you, it might kill you. If they make the same mistake with me . . ."

He said this with confidence he certainly did not feel. They rode in a gorge so narrow that only the merest sliver of sky lay above them. Would he heal if a boulder were pushed onto him? What if his legs were broken by some snare and they simply hacked him to pieces?

"If they make the same mistake with *me*," he went on, "the results won't be as dire. If they attack me, you can all feel free to come to my aid, though some of you should stay back to protect Hezhi."

"I'm not helpless," she reminded him, not quite sharply but with considerable insistence.

Since their time alone on the peak five days before, the two of them had gotten along well. *Very well*, in fact. And so he answered that with a little smile, leaning close, so that only she could easily hear him. "Is that the only stupid thing I've said lately?"

"More or less," she replied. "In the last few days, at least."

"Then you should be proud of me."

"Oh, I am. And be careful."

He nodded assurance of that, then looked over his shoulder at the others in time to catch Ngangata rolling his eyes.

"What?" he called back at the half man.

"They could decide to come this way at any moment. You two had better save your courting for some other time."

Perkar clamped his mouth on an indignant protest and dismounted. Trying not to think about what he was doing, he strode forward. The others clopped quickly into the trees.

Despite his efforts, he felt as if he were walking through quicksand. Only the gentle pressure of his friends' surely watchful gazes kept the appearance of confidence and spring in his step.

Fifty paces he went before a rock clattered nearby. He slowed up.

"I've come to talk, not to fight," he shouted.

A pause then, and he heard some whispering in the rocks above and to his right.

"Name yourself," someone shouted—in his own language.

"I am Perkar of the Clan Barku," he returned.

More scrambling then, and suddenly a stocky, auburn-haired man emerged from the fallen pile of rubble that leaned against the cliff face.

"Well, then, you've got some explaining to do, for you *ought* to be a ghost, from what I hear." He shook his nearly round head, and it opened into a broad grin. "Instead you've turned Mang, it seems."

"You have the advantage on me," Perkar answered. "Do I know you?"

"No, but I've heard tell of you. My name is Morama, of the Clan Kwereshkan."

Perkar lifted his brows in amazement. "My mother's clan."

"Indeed, if you are who you say you are. And even if you aren't—" He shrugged. "—you are certainly a Cattle Person, despite those clothes, so we will welcome you."

"I have companions," Perkar said.

"Them, too, then."

"Two of them are Mang; the others are from farther off still."

To his surprise, the man nodded easily. "If you are Perkar—and I believe you to be—then we were told to expect that. You have my word and Piraku that they will not be harmed unless they attack us first."

"I'll bring your promise back to them, then." He started to go but suddenly understood the full import of the man's remarks.

"What do you mean, you were 'told to expect that'? *Who* told you?"

"My lord. He said to tell you, 'I am a roadmark.' "

Perkar did turn back then, a faint chill troubling his spine.

Karak.

Hᴇᴢʜɪ lifted her small shoulders in a helpless shrug. "I'm not sure what I pictured," she told Perkar. "Something like this. It looks very nice."

Perkar chewed his lip. She knew he was probably trying to suppress a scowl with a show of good humor. "I know it isn't your palace in Nhol. But it *has* to be better than a Mang yekt." He said this last low enough that Brother Horse and Yuu'han wouldn't hear; the two warriors were nervously walking about the bare dirt of the compound.

"That is certainly true," Hezhi said. "I'm anxious to see the inside."

"That will be soon enough," Perkar told her, dismounting. "Here comes the lord."

The "lord" was a rough-seeming man, tall almost to the point of being gangly, dark-haired, and as fair-skinned as Perkar. Nothing in the way he dressed signified his station to Hezhi, but she reminded herself that these were strange people with strange ways.

Perkar's people. It was the weirdest thing to see so many men— and women—who *looked* like him. Though she had always understood that somewhere there were whole villages and towns full of his tribe, she had always imagined that Perkar himself was somehow extreme, the strangest of even his kind. The Mang, after all, were the only other foreign people she had met, and aside from their odd dress, they much resembled the people she had grown up among. Unconsciously, she had thought of Perkar as she thought of Tsem and Ngangata—as another singular aberration.

These implicit notions of hers now vanished. Amongst the people of this damakuta she saw hair the light brown of Perkar's and some as black as her own. But two people had hair the same shocking white color as Ngangata's, and another had strands of what looked to be spun copper growing from his scalp. Eyes could be blue, green, or even amber in the case of the "lord" and two others she noted.

The damakuta—well, Perkar was right; she was disappointed. When he spoke of it in Nholish, he called it a "hall." And so she had imagined something like a *hall*, or a court, like the ones in the palace. But this damakuta—first of all, it was *wooden*. For a wooden structure it was undoubtedly grand, and it certainly had a primitive charm with its peaked roof, hand-hewn shingles, and weirdly carved posts. To be fair, she realized that Perkar had described all of this—her mind had merely translated it into her own conceptions.

Of course, he had *never* mentioned the red-gold and black chickens poking about the yard, the dogs sleeping on the threshold of the damakuta, the curious and dirt-smudged children who played, more or less naked, amongst the chickens.

But Perkar was right; for all of that, it was certainly grander than a Mang yekt.

The "lord" approached and said something to Perkar that Hezhi did not understand. Perkar looked tired; the seams on his brow were deep with trouble, and whatever response he gave to the other man seemed uneasily given. He added something, as an afterthought, and then waved her and the rest to his side. Hezhi complied with a reluctance she didn't entirely understand. There was some quality about the tall man's eyes she found disquieting. When they arrived, however, he bowed to them slightly.

"Pardon the thickness of Mang speech on my tongue," he told them. "It has been more than a day since I have spoken it."

To Hezhi's ear there was nothing wrong with his Mang at all. Probably Brother Horse and Yuu'han could tell he was no native speaker, but *she* could not.

"In any event, I am known as *Sheldu Kar Kwereshkan*, and

welcome to my damakuta. Its rooms, its wine, its food are yours
for the taking, and if aught else calls a need to you, do not hesitate
to pass that request on to me or mine." He turned to her.
"Princess, I am told you have traveled far and far to be here. Be
welcome." His amber eyes lingered on her uncomfortably, but
Hezhi smiled and nodded. It was probably, after all, only the alien
color of his orbs that distracted her.

"Brother Horse, once known as Yushnene, your name is well
known to my family. You and your nephew understand that you
are under our protection here, and no harm shall come to you."

"Very generous," Brother Horse replied, perhaps a bit stiffly.

The tall lord greeted everyone else. Hezhi gazed back around
the compound, wondering what the building might be like inside.
She wondered if there might be a *bath*.

SHE sighed, ladling more water onto the steaming rocks. The
liquid danced frenetically on the porous, glowing stones, and the
next breath she drew was almost unbearably hot, though delicious. Heat gripped through her muscles to her bone, and soreness seemed to ooze out of her with her sweat.

It was like no bath *she* had ever known, but it would certainly
serve.

Several other women shared the sauna with her; unclothed they
were more ghostly than ever, white as alabaster tinged here and
there with *pink*. They were polite, but Hezhi suspected that they
were inspecting her with the same bemused regard. Men used a
separate steamhouse, she was told, and likely that was where
Tsem and the rest were. Perkar and the lord had gone off to talk
alone; Hezhi suspected that he would ask for more men to escort
them to the mountain.

The mountain. She'leng. She closed her eyes against the heat as
another steam tornado writhed into the air. She drew up the
images of her journey through the lake to that *other* She'leng,
which she understood was in most ways the same as the one she
was moving so steadily toward.

Why must she go there corporeally? She had already been there as a spirit, but Karak insisted that she must make the journey in the flesh. She ran her finger over her scale absently. It was quiet, untroubled, and yet still it had the power to trouble *her*. *Someone* was not telling her *something*. She hoped it was not Perkar, and even at that thought her heart sank, a tightening in otherwise relaxed muscles. Perkar had been so good to her these past few days. She still did not know what she felt for him, exactly, but his arms around her that night had been *good*, comfortable. Not disgusting as with Wezh, not full of trembling, silly excitement as with Yen, but quiet, and warm, and good. If Perkar were betraying her, too . . .

Unfortunately, she was forced to admit, he might be—if he thought his reason was good enough. She remembered her conversation with Ngangata. But that was before—well, she *knew* Perkar had some sort of feelings for her.

Or he wanted something, very badly indeed.

She frowned and threw more water on the rocks, reveling this time more in the sting of pain from the cloudy effervescence than in its more soothing results. No, she wouldn't think that way. She would trust Perkar, as much as she could. She *had* to trust someone.

And if Perkar were plotting against her what chance did she have?

What a silly thought that was, she admonished herself. As if she were without power. She had never been in the habit of trusting those around her with her life; why should she start now, when she had more resources within her than ever before? Had refusing her heritage from the River broken some self-reliant part of her? These past months she had *counted* on people more than she ever had in her life. Yet back in Nhol, when her very existence had been in danger, it had been *she* who found the answers in the library, in the tunnels beneath the city. Ghan and Tsem had helped, but it been her own initiative and hunger that saved her. Her only moment of weakness had been in summoning Perkar, in wishing for a hero. She had not known that her blood would mingle with the River and bring that about. She had not consciously been at fault. But her sin had been in wishing for someone else to help her, when real experience proved again and again that she could rely only on herself, in the end.

But Perkar *had* saved her then. Without him, Yen would have murdered her.

She tried to relax back into the steam, reclaim her peace in long-deserved luxury, but it was gone. Once again, she did not know enough about her own destiny. In Nhol, the library had given her the key to surviving, a golden key of information better than any lockpick.

Here books were of no use to her, but tonight she would invoke other ways of learning. She would have some *answers* before taking another step toward She'leng.

WHEN they were alone, Perkar waited an instant, clenching and unclenching his fist—to calm down, to manage his temper, to let memory counsel him rather than stir him to useless stupidity.

"I know you, Karak," he snapped at last. "You cannot fool me, hiding behind the skin of a relative."

The seeming of Sheldu Kar Kwereshkan merely smiled and gestured for him to sit. Nearby, a jar of woti sat in a warm pot of water; for the first time in over a year, Perkar's nostrils and lungs were pleasured by its sweet scent, and his throat ached to feel the warm drink coursing down it. He almost salivated when his host poured two cups and handed one to him.

"Piraku," the man said simply, raising his cup. Perkar raised his own, brought the fuming drink below his nostrils, and let the warm scent of fermented barley linger there. It was *woti kera*, black woti, the finest and most expensive form of the beverage.

"Please, drink," his host insisted. "Why do you only inhale it? Drink!"

Perkar regarded the dark fluid once more and then carefully put the cup on the floor. "I am like a ghost, Karak," he said. "You have made me like a ghost. The things of my people are no longer real to me, only shadows that I do not deserve. Woti is the drink of a man and a warrior, and I deserve only what a ghost enjoys of woti; its vapor. Only that for the man I might have been. I will never drink woti again, not until I have corrected my past mistakes."

The man sighed, sipped his own woti, and sighed again. "It is a *drink*, Perkar," he said. "A thing to be savored, enjoyed—not *agonized* over."

"It is a drink for those with Piraku, and I have none. Nor, I suspect, have you."

"Pretty thing, I was winging through the skies above this mountain long before any thought had been given to Piraku—or to your kind at all. I probably *invented* woti, though I don't remember for certain."

"You *are* Karak."

The man took another sip of woti before answering. "If you accused the *real* Sheldu of having no Piraku, the two of you would be stabbing at one another with swords by now. Yes, yes, I have come to point your way. It is more than I thought would be allowed, but less than I had hoped for."

Perkar sucked in a retort, and when he had the control, asked, as humbly as he could, "Will you tell me now how the Changeling can be destroyed by Hezhi?"

Karak cocked his head appraisingly. "You are *learning*, pretty thing. Perhaps my despair over you has been unwarranted. What an irony that would be, since it has kept me sleepless."

Perkar worried that *he* would grit his teeth into grains of salt. His anger was dissolving—or at least mixing with a bottomless terror as he remembered that Raven gone white, holding him helpless off the ground. He wanted to retort, to singe the god with his words, but he could not. And he knew—as Karak seemed to know, from the mocking sarcasm in his tone—that it was fear and not wisdom that stayed his hand and tongue.

"Please," he said. "We have come too far to fail. If you don't tell me what we should do—"

"Never fear, Perkar. Some of the burden I have lifted from your shoulders. The thing I foresaw marching out from Nhol has come, and it gathers power and terror about it. It is a demon of sorts, what your folk call a *Tiskawa*."

"Life-Devourer," Perkar muttered. "That lifts no burden from me, Karak. If such a thing stalks us—"

"Well, you trade for this and you get that," Karak allowed. "When the time comes, I am confident that you and Harka can stand against such a creature. What *eases* your load is that because of this thing and the stink of Changeling about it, its *power*—I may now escort you to the mountain. With such a blemish crawling through Balat, the Forest Lord will scarce take notice of *us*, unless we give him excessive cause to. So you see, your fears that you will not know what to do once we reach his source are unfounded. I will be along, in this guise, to help you." He leaned up, and his voice became lighter in tone but heavier with threat. "And only you and I are to know this, of course. The others need only know that a distant kinsman of yours and thirty of his men will ride with you on your quest. But you had thought of it yourself, hadn't you?"

"What of Hezhi? She does not know that *she* is the crucial one. What if she refuses to go, fearing the Changeling as she does?"

"She will go," Karak assured him.

"And what of my feelings on this matter?" he snarled, forcing strength into his voice despite the quivering in his limbs. "Suppose I will not help you lead her there without her consent?"

"You have had many months to tell her if you were going to. You have not; you will not. You, too, desperately wish to have your lost Piraku back, to end the war with the Mang, to set your part in your people's affairs to rights. And if that isn't enough—" He smiled. "Draw out your blade."

Perkar hung his head. "I have made no move to do so. I have not threatened you."

"You misunderstand me," Karak said softly. "I said *draw—out—your—blade*." His command was like knife thrusts through a silk shirt.

Numbly, Perkar took Harka out. *He doesn't need me now to get her to the mountain*, he realized. *He can take my form. No one will know.* He held his weapon up, saw with dismay the way the firelight quivered upon the metal—or, rather, the way the blade shivered in his grip.

Karak reached out laconically and pressed his palm against Harka's tip. He pressed until a faint, golden drop of blood started. Perkar felt sweat beading on his brow. What was the Blackgod doing?

"Close your eyes," Karak intoned.

"If you are to kill me, I wish to die with them open," he answered.

Karak rolled his own yellow orbs. "Stop being so melodramatic, you fool, and close your eyes. I only want to show you something."

Perkar breathed deeply, captured a breath, and held it for an instant. As he released it, he allowed his lids to meet.

He saw a boat, broken by dying dragons. His vision was odd, as if he stood far away and high above the things he observed; yet they were all clear to him. There was no doubt of what he saw. But what was happening? He watched in confusion as the great serpents became steam and vanished, as countless men and horses died in the water, from impact, from boiling alive.

Now he saw two men he knew. One was Ghan, the old man who had contracted with him to rescue Hezhi, back in Nhol. The other was familiar, sharply so, and yet he could not precisely place from where he knew that face. And where they were seemed familiar, as well, a small river. . .

Then she emerged. And as he watched what transpired then, he shrieked and he wept, and that night he did not sleep at all, but rode round and round on that same black nightmare, a mount with no mercy, that squeezed and squeezed his heart until anger crushed into fear, despair into hope, joy into pain. Crushed together until they became, at last, something different from all of those emotions, something that gleamed like the fangs of a beast or the edge of a butcher's blade.

* * *

HEZHI lay awake in bed, muffled in the lush folds of a down-batted quilt, surrounded by the faint gleam of polished wood in moonlight from a half-slatted window. She felt, now, that she had misjudged the damakuta. It was, indeed, a place of comfort and, more to the point, a place of warmth. She shared her room with three other girls, all within a few years of her own age. Though they spoke no common language, they had been kind enough to her, saw that she had plenty to eat and warm covers, and gave her a long thick woolen shirt that, though it itched and scratched, kept away the mountain chill. The food was odd: bread boiled into dumplings, a thick stew of curd and pungent cheese, some kind of roasted bird—but it was cooked and filling and warm.

That and the sauna almost convinced her to put away her fears and sleep, and when she struggled out of the nightshirt and slipped into the enveloping softness of quilt and mattress, she very nearly surrendered. Almost asleep, drifting languidly from one terrace of cloud to the next . . .

And then she awoke, to a falling terror, to the call of some nightbird strange to her.

After that, her heart would not stop thudding, but instead picked up her earlier worries, pumped them round and round her body so that they pulsed in her throat, at her wrists, until finally she could bear it no longer and slipped from the bed into the cool night air. She paused at her shadow, cast by moonlight, turned slowly so that the Queen of Night could cast more angles of her on the floor. Her body had changed since leaving the River. Grown more . . . *awkward*, somehow. She could see the same thing in her roommates, before they fell asleep. Sisters, they were like images of each other at different ages—and in her own mind, of herself. The youngest was all smallness, limbs smooth and uniform, balanced and beautiful. The eldest girl—Numa? Perhaps fifteen years old, she looked like a woman; sweetly curved hips, breasts, symmetry. The middle girl, though, that was her. Feet, like a puppy's, too big for her body. Bumps that could not yet be called breasts but that ruined the younger harmony of her body.

And all of that happening without any interference from gods or spirits or anything else. She shook her head at the clumsy outline on the floor and wished she had a mirror.

And then she smiled at that. What a silly time to discover vanity.

She found her discarded nightshirt and donned it. Unpacking her drum, she took it by the rim and, with its beater, stepped softly through the wide vertical slats of the window onto the slope of the roof. There she took in her bearings with a breath of night breeze and turned to absorb the high beauty of moonlit mountain slopes and silver-chased clouds. She padded slowly and carefully up to the roofbeam, thinking how much the cedar shingles, in this darkness, resembled the baked clay tiles she had trod so often in Nhol. Except that they smelled better, like the sauna, like the woods.

The nightbird called again, sounding less alien now—Perkar had named it for her, a few nights ago: some sort of owl.

Sitting on the roofbeam, she tapped softly on her drum, on the rippling surface of the lake, and ripples parted upon darkness and night as she went first into the otherworld of her heart.

There they all awaited her: the mare, the swan, and the bull.

"This time, you all come with me," she said. And the bull stamped and rolled his eyes.

TOGETHER they rushed beneath the surface of the lake, sometimes three and sometimes four figures limned in flame bruising the otherearth with the thunder of their passage. She rode with the mare, half horse as before, and she flew on the wings of the swan, and finally, when he offered for a third time, she joined the bull, felt the uncanny furnace that raged in his chest fill her with fury and unholy joy. She cackled with glee as stone shattered beneath their hooves, as they reached the edge of a precipice and flung out into space to write a line of lightning across the mauve sky.

The instinct of the beasts drove them toward She'leng; they

were born there and returned there to be reclothed, and this near they were always able to find it. In the shadows of the air, Hezhi saw what she had not seen before: the dark forms like serpents and wolves that lay in wait for the unwary, for the weak; the thousand thousand jaws and eyes of the otherworld that dared not open to her and her companions. Beyond fear and worry, she knew only fierce elation at such power, at such untouchability. She only barely remembered the concerns that had driven her to seek the mountain with her ghost self, but they all seemed unimportant now.

Perhaps she would visit the River himself and see how *he* lay here. Perhaps she would challenge him here and now and have an ending to it all.

She understood, distantly, that these were the sentiments of the bull, but she did not care; it did not trouble her.

They struck back to earth from the sky, for solidity gave more pleasure to run upon; the mountain loomed and the lands rose, but it caused them no pause; there was no fatigue here.

But in the midst of seeming omnipotence, something shattered the earth; it twisted beneath them and dashed them, scattered them. A sharp jolt of ecstatic fear burnt through the quicksilver joy, and Hezhi scrambled back to her feet, the bull, mare, and swan forming a rank of protection before her as something dark rose looming.

A black lion, she was, whose mouth parted to reveal the shadows of dagger-teeth against the red soul that burned in her shell, that illumined her eyes from behind, as well, slits of flame with no pupils. A black lion the size of the bull. He lowered his horns to meet her.

"Call back your beast," the lioness said. "The others will not aid you."

Indeed, Hezhi saw with a thrill of dismay that the mare and the swan were kneeling, after their fashion. The bull himself trembled, trepidation mixed with fury.

"Who are you?" Hezhi asked, her godlike confidence quickly evaporating.

"We have met, you and I," the lioness said, and she seemed to grin—at least she showed the full range of her teeth and switched her great tail behind. She spoke then, to the bull.

"Kneel down, Hukwosha. I know you, and you know me. You know I cannot be challenged here. Be wise for your new mistress."

The bull regarded the lioness steadily, but Hezhi sensed a frustrated easing of muscles, as if the bull agreed, however reluctantly, with the pronouncement of the great clawed beast.

As easily as that, I am without protectors, she thought.

"You should remember me, and it pains me that you do not," the lioness growled, padding closer, pausing to run her tongue on the fur of the mare—whether grooming or tasting, Hezhi could not tell. She advanced until the twin coals of her eyes were inches from Hezhi's own.

"Let me introduce myself," the lioness went on. "I am Paker, Apa, Bari—I have many names, but most often I am called Huntress."

XXXI

The Lady of Bones

SENSATION *crept along Ghe's skin, pleasure and darkling pain, and he bit into his lip until he found the iron tang of blood. A fountain of flame seemed to erupt from him, and white-hot stars fluoresced and faded in the heavens behind his eyelids. The woman caressing him stroked his face, and he looked up into her features. And remembered.*

Hezhi's older face, Qwen Shen—both stared down at him. Fury and futility surged in the wake of gratification. How many times had she done this to him? How many times had he forgotten? Somehow he understood that he always forgot, remembered the passion but not the details, the woman but not the witchery. What was Qwen Shen doing to him? A wave of humiliation coursed through him as he answered himself: she controlled him. She held him taut on a leash, and he did not even realize that, save in these lucid instants after . . .

After what? What had he been thinking? Something annoying, but slipping from him. Something about Qwen Shen's face, glowing above him, lips curled in a gentle, teasing expression.

And then, of a sudden, she was no longer Qwen Shen. He was suddenly straddled by a corpse, bones of black ice, the withered face of a mummy leering down at him. And then that horror was replaced by yet another woman, beautiful and dark, whom he had never seen before.

"Ah, sweet Ghe," she sighed as she stroked his face with a finger that was both a yellowed bone and supple, black skin. "Thy mother gave you unto me with thy birth. It is my womb you return to, and it aches for you. You and this godling cause me pain with this delay, sweet one."

"You," he gasped, frozen by terror or glamour, he knew not which. In his mind he suddenly beheld the little bone statuette that Li once kept, the forbidden image of a goddess the priests said did not exist. But the accursed of Southtown believed, down deep, in their ancient goddess—though he never had; for him the only god was River, and the Lady just another tale to frighten children.

"Yes, of course you know me," the Lady said, and where she touched him, worms sprang from his flesh. "Come with me now, before you cause yourself more pain. He only tricks you, you know. You will never live beyond his wish. Much of you is already with me, if you would like to see it."

"What?" he asked.

"Everything you have lost—the most of you, sweet Ghe, lies corrupting in my house. It is all there, your childhood, memories of Li—whom you took from me, by the way."

"I did not—I never . . ."

She smiled, and her smile split back to her ears, as her black almond eyes were suddenly Hezhi's. "All men are surprised by me," she assured him. "But few wish to resist."

"I will not go," Ghe snarled suddenly. "Not yet."

She looked down at him sadly, an old woman—Li, in fact. "Why torment yourself?"

Ghe reached out, then, intent on swallowing her—after all, a goddess was a goddess, and he had already swallowed one such. But what was in her eluded him; nothing was there to devour, only emptiness. She laughed.

"*Even gods are living,*" she cackled. "*But I am death.*"

"*I will defeat you then,*" Ghe snarled. "*I have taken many gods into myself these past days. I have dined on great powers, and they will sustain me until nothing lives or moves on the earth.*"

"*For me,*" she replied sweetly, "*even that space of time is nothing—save perhaps annoying. You don't want me to be annoyed when you come to suckle at my breast at last.*"

"*Take me if you can,*" Ghe shot back. "*And if you cannot, then leave me.*"

She nodded distantly. "*Very well,*" she told him. "*I gave you the chance, for Li, who loved me, who burned incense for me. I will not offer this again.*"

"*You offer me only death.*"

"*Death is sweeter than anything you will know now,*" she answered, and was gone.

He awoke shuddering. Qwen Shen stroked him, consoled him with little words, with small kisses. She looked worried. He reached to touch her face, and for just an instant, a bare instant, he saw not her face but Hezhi's, and a sudden rage filled him, but try as he might, he could find no reason for the emotion. So, bit by bit, he allowed himself to be soothed, knowing that given time, he would discern his vision of the Lady to be only a lying dream, perhaps a false vision given him by one of his more willful vassals—for a few still fought for freedom. But now he was far too strong to be escaped or troubled by dreams; since meeting the Mang shaman, Moss, at White Rock, he had found the land rich in these so-called gods and now he was swollen with them, distended. Perhaps it was merely a sort of heartburn that plagued him.

"You are well now?" Qwen Shen asked, the first words she had spoken.

He nodded.

"Good, then. What was wrong?"

"Nothing," he answered. "A sort of night terror."

She clucked softly. "But you do not sleep, my love."

"No, but it is always night to me, and even for me there is

sometimes terror in the darkness." He stopped, angry. Why would he show even Qwen Shen his weakness? No longer.

"I'm sorry for that," she soothed. "But I must tell you something, something that terrifies *me*."

"What is that?"

"I fear this shaman, this Moss. I worry that he plots against you."

Ghe levered up on one elbow. Outside of the tent, cicadas sawed their shrill tunes, frogs croaked imprecations at the moon. It was the first night they had spent together since leaving the ruined barge—indeed, the first night not spent on horseback. Moss insisted that they must make great speed if Hezhi was to be found in time, before the demon Perkar and his conspirators harmed her. But the pace they kept had killed many horses, something the Mang loathed to do, so now they camped in a broad meadow while fresh horses could be found to replace bone-weary ones and new provisions could be hunted. A delay of a single day presented an opportunity Qwen Shen made certain he took—to "relax."

"Why do you say this of Moss?"

"I mistrust him. I believe that he leads us to our doom. I have heard him speak of it to his men. He and the Mang are in league with this white demon of yours."

"Moss is a servant of the River."

Qwen Shen's eyes narrowed dramatically. "*I* am a servant of the River, *you* are a servant of the River. Bone Eel carries his blood, though he is too insensible truly to serve. But these are barbarians, not people of Nhol. You cannot trust them."

He sat up and rested his chin on his knees. "What have you heard? What have you heard the men saying?"

"They fear you. They will be glad to be quit of you. And they think that Moss is very clever in his plan to dispose of you."

Ghe frowned. He knew the first two things, of course. His senses were keener than men thought; he could make out even distant conversations, if he cared to listen. They feared him because they suspected the men who disappeared were his prey—which, of course, they were. Since his killing of the grass-bear, his reputation had grown, but it was the reputation, he saw now, that one might credit to a feral beast, not to a man. He was respected because he was feared, and the Mang believed that their shaman could keep him in control.

They were wrong. Moss was indeed powerful; he kept many souls within him, as well, but his control over them was of a different nature, and he did not draw his sustenance from life the way Ghe did. *His* hunger was not a weapon. In a contest between Moss and Ghe, Moss would lose.

"I must think on this," he muttered, arising and donning an elkskin robe. He pulled it so as to cover his naked body, drawing it up high around his neck and holding it bunched there with one hand. Without a backward glance at Qwen Shen he brushed through the tent flap and out onto the meadow. He stalked toward the tree line, a lean wraith in the night.

The "Lady" could have been sent to him by Moss. He knew Moss could send dreams, because he admitted sending them to him and to Hezhi, as well. But what purpose would such a dream serve the shaman, unless Qwen Shen were right, and Moss was trying to frighten or weaken him?

He thought back over the shaman's story; how he had been captured by Perkar and escaped by summoning one of his familiar demons, how he had held Hezhi in his very grasp and then lost her, fled here to meet him, and organized this forced march by contacting his captains in their dreams. His hope, he said, was to stop Hezhi before she reached the source of the River, where Perkar and some barbarian "god" were leading her. But now that he scrutinized that story, it made little sense. Perkar's aim had always been to keep Hezhi *away* from the River, deny her heritage to her, probably to father some litter of white whelps on her in some squalid wilderness cottage. Why would he take her to the River's very source?

Maybe Moss *was* lying. Qwen Shen had a keen, incisive mind; the emperor had chosen her well for this expedition, and the River had chosen her well for his lover. She came thus highly recommended, and her advice until now had been good, very good. If he had listened more carefully to her all along, and less to Ghan, things would be very different now. And now that he thought of it, Moss treated Ghan well, brought him to ride beside him, lavished attention on the old man, as if they were old friends. He *claimed* that this was to honor Ghan because Hezhi loved him, but what if, somehow, the old man and the young Mang shaman were in league?

That made *perfect* sense. Ghan had led them into the trap of sailing upstream, knowing the dragons would not survive it. Ghan had made contact with the Mang before, even sent things to Hezhi through them. And when his plan to wreck the barge succeeded, was it not a suspicious coincidence for the Mang to be there, at that very spot, *awaiting* them? As if they had been informed of the scholar's plan? And to what purpose? *Not* to lead him *to* Hezhi, but to lead him as far from Hezhi as possible. While *he* journeyed to She'leng, *she* was racing away, farther away each moment.

He had reached the tree line now. He shuddered with self-fury at his stupidity. It was difficult to *think* sometimes, this far from the River. But that could be no excuse; he was Hezhi's only hope, the River's only hope. He could not betray them through weakness of mind, not when he was this strong otherwise.

Moss had been sent to confuse him and had done a good job. He could not outthink Moss in this state, and if he confronted him, challenged him to tell the truth, the Mang would merely spin some plausible web of lies—and *he*, dulled by distance from his lord, might succumb to deceptive, honeyed words. Better not to give him the chance; better to confront him only with death and be done with him. *Then* he could torture the truth from the shaman's soul, once he had captured it.

That decided, he stepped from his robe and gathered darkness to him instead, sheathed himself in armor made of night; it was a simple trick, one he knew from devouring an odd little god in the form of an owl. He gathered a second armor of wind about himself and lifted into the air, and in that instant, Death and her embrace seemed a distant, impossible thing. He pulled the strands of wind like reins, commanding them to take him to Moss' tent.

"Eat more," Moss told Ghan. "You'll need your strength in the high country."

"No I won't," Ghan stated flatly. "I shall never reach the high country. Your new ally, Ghe, will devour me before ever we get there."

Moss considered the chunk of venison between his fingers, licked a bit of grease from it. "I think not. His tastes are for gods now, not for men."

Ghan gazed up at him dully. "Then why do soldiers still disappear each day?"

"Some are deserting," Moss pointed out.

"Yes. Because they know that their fate is to be evening repast for a monster." Ghan shot the younger man a pointed look.

Moss sighed. "I have protected you thus far, Grandfather."

"I'm no one's grandfather," Ghan snapped.

Moss crinkled his brow in frustration. "It is considered mannerly to address an elder so."

"Is it also considered mannerly to march me across these foreign lands against my will? To force me to aid you in a cause I want nothing to do with? Why put fair paint over rotten wood by *addressing* me courteously?"

Moss finished his meat and followed it with a sip of wine. "As you wish, old man. In any case, what I was saying is that I have protected you thus far and I will continue to."

Ghan snorted. "You are a fool, then. Don't you know what he *is*? You cannot protect me from him."

"But I shall, you have my word."

"How relieved I am," Ghan sneered.

Moss grinned. "You really should eat something. I don't want Hezhi to think I starved you when we find her." He paused and then lifted his wine cup again. "She loves you, you know. I think if I could have really convinced her that I would reunite the two of you, she would have joined me."

"What do you care about this?" Ghan exploded suddenly. "I have held my peace, hearing you talk about her, but what is it that you want? Ghe is a mindless sort of thing, and I *know* what the River wants of her, but *you* . . ."

"I want only peace," Moss replied mildly. "I want my relatives to stop dying. And I want my people to have the blessing of the River as yours do."

"It is no blessing," Ghan snarled. "It is a curse. It is a curse for those who bear his blood and it is a curse for those his children rule. This is a misguided desire you have."

"So it may seem to you," Moss answered shortly. "But I know better."

"Of course—" Ghan began, but Moss' eyes suddenly blazed, and he jabbed his finger at Ghan.

"I *know* better," he repeated.

Ghan slowly closed his mouth on his unfinished retort. There would plainly be no fruit from a conversation that branched from *that* tree. He slowly gazed around the meager furnishings of the tent, gathering energy for another try.

"Will you kill her?" he asked dully. "Will she die?"

"Old man, she will die only if the Blackgod has his way. If *I* win this race and this battle, she will live to be the queen she was destined to be. She will unite all of the people of the River in a single kingdom. *That* I have seen."

"With you at her side?" Ghan asked, carefully this time.

Moss shrugged. "It matters not where I am then. My work will be done. When she is queen, the sort of power I command will mean nothing. The little gods will be swept away and the world will be clean of them. The mountains and plains will be home to men and only men. And there will be peace, without the likes of the Blackgod meddling in our affairs."

There, Ghan thought. *There is a tender spot.* What experiences had shaped this boy? He was beginning to see the glimmer, the veiled shape of his motives. If he could understand *those,* perhaps he could talk real sense to him. For the moment, however, he lowered his voice to nearly a whisper.

"But I ask again, why do you ally yourself with the Life-Eater, this ghoul?"

"Because only he has the power to see us to the mountain. The gods will resist us each inch of the way. We have already been attacked thrice, did you know that? Each time Ghe disposed of the sendings. I might have done so, but only after terrible struggle. And when we meet the Blackgod himself—"

Ghan held up his hand. "You keep saying 'Blackgod,' " Ghan muttered. "But this word? In my language, 'god' is used only for the River. What do you call him in your tongue?"

"Many things. Mostly we call him 'Blackgod.' "

"No," Ghan snapped. "*Say* it in your language."

"*Yaizhbeen,*" he complied, clearly puzzled.

Ghan chewed his lip. "Wait, wait," he muttered. "*Zhbeen* means 'black.' "

"So it does," Moss replied, bemused.

"In the old language of Nhol, *zhweng* was the word for black."

"I have noticed our tongues are similar," Moss said. "Your name, for instance, and my profession, 'Ghan' and 'gaan.' "

"It is not my name," Ghan said. "It means 'teacher.' But there is another word in the old tongue: *ghun*. That means 'priest.' " He mused, clenching his fist before his face, all other thought forgotten, save the puzzle. "*Ghun Zhweng.*" He whirled on Moss. "What if I were to say *gaanzhbeen* in your language? What would that mean?"

"It would mean 'black invoker, black shaman.' It is merely another name for the Blackgod, for he is a wizard, as well."

"How stupid." Ghan scowled. "How very stupid of me. When Ghe told me about the temple, I should have seen it. But what exactly does it mean?"

"What are you talking about?"

Ghan snorted. "Our priesthood was founded by a person known as *Ghun Zhweng*, the Ebon Priest. Do you see?"

Moss stared at him, openmouthed. "Your priesthood was founded by the Blackgod?"

"So it would seem."

"Tell me this tale. How can this be?"

"Ghe visited the Water Temple. Beneath it he found—"

Moss wasn't listening to him anymore. His eyes had glazed. "This will have to wait," he whispered. "It may be that you should leave."

"Why?"

"Something comes for me."

"Something?"

Moss looked back at him, eyes hardening. "Yes, perhaps you were right. I don't understand why, but Ghe is coming for me. He just slew my outer ring of guardians."

I know, Ghan thought frantically. *I know why he is coming for you. Because Qwen Shen holds his leash, and Qwen Shen is from the priesthood, and the priesthood* . . . was a creation of the Blackgod. And whatever else this Blackgod was, it was an enemy of the River and of all of his blood. He was Moss' enemy—he was *Hezhi's* enemy, though she knew it not.

"Leave," Moss repeated.

"N-no," Ghan stuttered. "I think I can help you."

"Why would you help me?" Moss asked, rising, facing the tent-flap. Outside a wind was rising.

Ghan started to answer him, but Moss dismissed him with a simple wave. "Go. I have no more time to speak to you." His body had begun to blur faintly. At first Ghan thought something was wrong with his eyes; then he understood. He had seen the emperor thus resonate with power. Moss stepped outside. Ghan followed quickly, as far as the tent opening, to watch.

Something roughly Human in shape and size hovered perhaps ten feet off of the ground; wind gyred about him, sparks from a nearby cooking fire dancing madly in his cyclonic path. The figure itself was darker than the surrounding night, a nothingness.

"Why do you come to me thus?" Moss demanded somewhat

mildly. "Why do you slay my guardians when you have only to ask to pass them?"

"You have tricked me," the shadow said, and it was Ghe's voice, of that Ghan was certain.

"I have not, and I know not why you think I have, but we should talk."

But Ghe was apparently in no mood to talk. Light gouted from the sky as if the substance of the heavens somehow had been slit open. It ruptured into a million starlike fragments that cooled from white to violet and finally to a sullen red, all in the briefest instant, and then, like a swarm of bees, the summoning fell upon Moss. Moss himself sprang back, and Ghan saw that he had produced a drum. He struck its head and shouted, and the fiery hornets were seized by pandemonium, flying everywhere. Many struck the tent, which instantly burst into flame.

Meanwhile, something huge and dark was forming beneath Ghe.

"Ghe, you idiot!" Ghan shrieked in the brief, pregnant silence. "You fool!"

Whatever was coalescing suddenly blazed yellow as a vaguely tigerlike thing leapt from Moss' drum and shattered itself upon the small cyclone around Ghe. Ghan saw a skeleton of something snakelike sublimating and then nothing at all. The shadow cloaking Ghe burned away like a tissue, revealing him naked, grinning, still above them, his outstretched hand against the sky. But in the next moment he languidly brought both arms down in front of him. He held up a single finger as if for their inspection, and Ghan could see that it terminated in a lethal-looking talon.

Moss had stumbled, his drumbeat faltered, but now he had regained his feet and begun a frantic chant. But Ghan was only faintly aware of him. What caught his attention was Ghe, drawing his own talon along his wrist. Blood drooled out, and Ghe dropped his hand; the black liquid trickled down his fingers, and he flicked droplets out and away from him.

They fell on the earth, and in each spot they struck, something erupted. The air was suddenly thick and sweet with the smell of blood, earth, and corruption, with the storm-scent of lightning striking.

Ten grass-bears arose, shook their great, flat heads, and attacked Moss.

Ghe turned then, to Ghan. "And now for *you*," he said, and advanced, walking down to him as if upon invisible stairs.

XXXII

Beauty

"I remember you now," Hezhi said, her voice small. "But before you were—"

"Yes, I have many suits of armor, many forms I may wear. Not as many as Karak, perhaps, but sufficient," the Huntress answered.

"You wanted to eat me before," Hezhi said, trying to summon some bravery to calm her voice.

"Yes. Perhaps I will yet, sweetmeat, but not at the moment. Karak's silly plan has finally come to my attention, and when I saw you coming, I thought to speak to you."

"Oh?" She felt a faint relief wash over her, but kept a firm grip on her skepticism. Could she fly faster than the Huntress? Perhaps she and the bull could, but she did not want to lose the mare and the swan.

"Yes. I have some things to show you. We will travel together."

As she said this, the mare and swan shook themselves as if waking. "Come." The Huntress turned from them and began loping across the land. "Stay in my prints," she called back over her feline shoulders. That commandment was simple enough to keep—the pawprints of the lion blazed the earth, blurred together into a trail of heatless flame. Hezhi rode with the bull, the swan on her shoulder, the mare just behind them so that they were really one, an eight-legged chimera with wings. Surrounded by her beasts, Hezhi felt confident again, but now she knew how illusory that confidence was, and she did not allow it to overwhelm her.

Running in the footsteps of the Huntress, their speed increased fivefold. The otherworld blurred into a void of transmuting shapes and colors.

When at last they stopped, it was upon the edge of a precipice; below stretched a plain.

"Here," the Huntress purred. "This is as close as we dare approach—for the moment."

"Approach *what*?" Hezhi asked, wondering what the Huntress could possibly fear.

"There," the Huntress answered. "Take your swan through the lake, there, and look—but only from a distance."

"Can I *do* that?" Hezhi asked doubtfully.

"Yes. I will guide you."

Hezhi cast another uncertain glance at the plain, and her keen eyes caught something, strange even in the otherworld. It looked something like a spider, or perhaps a spider and its web somehow become a single thing; a mass of tangled black strands and faintly multicolored bulbs that writhed aimlessly as they crept across the earth. "What is *that*?" Hezhi asked, pointing.

The Huntress growled, deep in her chest, before replying.

"That is what the Changeling sends to reclaim you," she answered. "I have watched him grow from a seed of death into that mockery of gods and men that crawls where no such thing should crawl. Long have we tolerated the Changeling, for his power was so great, and, after all, he lay quiet in his bed most of the time. Now he sends things like *this* out and about. For that affront I have chosen to help Karak kill him."

Hezhi turned to face the lioness. Crouching on the stone, she had changed a bit in appearance. Her fierce feline visage had crushed itself flat, so that the brilliant points of her teeth now gleamed from a face that somewhat resembled that of Ngangata or Tsem, but harsher, more brutal. The cords of leonine muscle had altered subtly so as to be more Human in appearance, as well, though Hezhi counted, with startlement, eight breasts on her tawny chest and belly.

"Why do you need *us*?" she asked. "I have a little power, it is true, but it is as nothing compared to yours. Perkar is handy with his enchanted weapon, but he told me of encountering you once before and how easily you dispensed with him. And yet every step of our journey has been planned by you gods. You cajole us and order us—I suspect one of you attacked Moss and the other Mang who followed us."

"That last was one of Karak's pets," the Huntress confessed. "But as to the other questions . . ." She leaned close, until the stink of rotten meat steamed in Hezhi's face. "I am not wont to answer questions. But you have been brave, and you command Hukwosha. And who knows, if all goes well you will have more power yet, before it is over, and perhaps I will ask favors of *you*. But listen, for I will not tell you a second time." She glanced— almost furtively—back at the spidery thing on the plain and then continued. "In the mountain, you met us all. Balati the One-Eyed Lord, Karak the Raven, Ekama the Horse Mother, and myself. But we are not separate things, and at times we do not exist at all. In all of the mountain, there is really only one god, and that is Balati. But Balati is vast, and ancient, and his tendency is to let *this* part of himself go this way and *that* part of himself go another. Karak is the one who is the most unfettered, the least like the rest of us in will and in purpose. Balati, he of the single eye, is where our true home resides—much as your spirits now reside in your heart—but he is a slow god, moving to the cycles of the earth and sky, not to the little moments and heartbeats that living things cherish. That *I* cherish.

"Now, this god you call the River, *we* call the Changeling, but we also call him 'Brother,' for he is that to us. Indeed—" Her brow bunched and played as she considered her words. "—it may be that he was once a part of us, just as I am. If so, he escaped entirely. And now Balati is slow to understand peril; he is still reluctant to act against his brother. He is angry, yes, but he cannot see the danger. Until recently, I was of the same mind. Only Karak knew better; Karak has labored long and secretly against the Changeling."

"Why? Why secretly?"

The Huntress grinned a sharp, malicious grin. "If Balati is so moved, he can extinguish any one of us. Karak as Karak could cease to be, and of all of us, Karak most loves *being*."

"I still don't understand."

"It's simple enough; the irony is delicious. Were it not for Karak, there would *be* no Changeling. *That* is the secret he has worked so long to keep hidden. That is why he strives so mightily and so stealthily to destroy the Brother."

"Karak's fault? I don't understand."

"It was a prank, at first, some joke of his that got out of hand. It is too long to tell, here and now. Suffice to say that once the Changeling was just a god like other gods, content and contained within the mountain. Karak tricked him into releasing himself, into becoming the River you know. That was long, long ages ago, but for Balati it was an eyeblink. He will not let us cut out the Changeling like the cancer he is. *That* is why we need you mortals. He does not notice you. When your enemies—" She waved a pawlike hand at the plain. "—when they invade Balat, the great forest, he will not object to my attacking them. When you enter into the mountain and find the River's source, he will not be aware of you, for Karak and I will cloak you. There you can do what must be done."

"And what is that?" Hezhi demanded.

The Huntress raised her hand to her face and ran a large, black tongue over her fur.

"That I don't know," she admitted. "Karak knows; he is the trickster, the sorcerer, the bringer of newness. He knows, and he will tell you. Trust that."

"Do we have a choice in this?" Hezhi asked, not wanting to, but knowing she must.

The Huntress considered that for only an instant. "Of course. You can choose to die. Little thing, the River made you to pour himself into. The Life-Stealer down there wishes to return you to him, and if he is successful, you will show him to be the shadow that he really is. You will be much like him, but if he is a blade of grass, you will be a forest. You will devour all of the world, including all of my children, and *that* I will not allow. I will kill you myself, if I can."

"If the danger is that great, I probably *should* die. When I come to his source, won't he take me then?"

"Not if you are strong; he can no more see himself at his source than you can see your own brain. And you have resisted him before."

"It was too hard," she whispered. "I nearly failed. Perhaps I should die."

The Huntress crooned a long *"noooo,"* and to Hezhi's vast surprise, she laid a now fully Human—if still furred—hand upon her shoulder. "He will only make another, in time. It may be a thousand years, but he will make another. And it is a paradox—at least this is what Karak says—that only one suited to hold him can destroy him. I don't know that this is true, but if it is, then his opportunity is also ours. Karak has apparently had his eye on this situation for many years. I despise trusting him, but here even I have no choice." She turned a slit-pupiled eye on Hezhi. "Nor do you. *Now*, look."

Hezhi felt the swan settle up higher on her head. She closed her own eyes and, when she saw again, it was through those of the bird. And in a single blink, she beheld blue sky and green grass, as those eyes slipped through the surface of the otherworld and into the more familiar colors and sounds of her own.

On the plain, where the spider-thing sat beneath the lake, an army rode, an army of Mang. She glided over them, buoyed up by the heat rising in lazy spirals from the earth. Another bird flew with her, she saw, a keen-beaked falcon with the Huntress' twinkle in her eye.

She followed the falcon down, until she could easily pick out the weary faces of the men, see the perspiration on their brows.

And so, at last, with a braided mixture of joy and horror, she saw Ghan. On a horse! He rode listlessly, but in his face she could see mirrored the blaze of thought that must burn behind his weariness.

Near Ghan, she made out another familiar face—Moss. And now she could see what he had hidden from her before: the spirits crowded within him. No wonder the bull had found them so easily, no wonder Moss had ridden through the herd unscathed! *He* was the gaan, the great shaman.

And with them rode another figure, one that even in mortal vision shimmered with such power and elicited such fear that she could not mistake him: he was the Life-Eater, the web of blackness.

He was Yen.

SHE came back to herself on the roof, her drum still held in nerveless fingers, her face salty and wet. All of her fear and horror bloomed when she pierced back through the drum into the living world, and nearly it was too much to bear. For a long time she shuddered, and each tear seemed to empty her heart, to hollow her, until soon enough she feared that her skin would collapse in upon nothing. Before that could happen, she clambered back into the damakuta, still weeping. She padded into its halls and into another room, until she found the sleeper she searched for. There she curled against him, until he woke, snuffled in confusion and then, without comment, wrapped the immense bands of his arms around her and rocked her gently. She slept the rest of the night in Tsem's arms, as if she were five years old—desperately wishing she were.

AT breakfast, Perkar wondered at how drawn and weary Hezhi looked. Dark circles lay below her eyes, and her face seemed pinched. She only picked at the food they were served, though it was the best breakfast any of them had enjoyed in some time—

wheatcakes, sausage, and fresh eggs. Of course, his own meal tasted like wood in his mouth, for he had not slept at all until the very break of day, then only dozing into nightmare images of the same waking dream he had suffered all night: the Stream Goddess, his love, devoured.

He wondered, briefly, if Hezhi had been shown some similar vision, if she, too, were filled with a wintry resolve. He had cried as much as he would; now there would only be killing and dying. His death or that of the Tiskawa, he cared not which.

The irony was that the goddess had spurned his love because she did not want to see *him* grow old and die. It was an irony that would drive his sword arm, he was certain.

After the meal, he confronted Hezhi. He tried to find some warmth in his voice if only for her sake. Part of him wanted to ask what was troubling *her*, to comfort her with a hug, but it seemed like too much trouble, and in her mood she might reject him anyway. He added this to his coldness; whatever tender feelings had developed between the two of them were doomed, and he knew it. He had never been honest with her about all he knew, and now he never would be. The destruction of the Changeling was too important to rest on the whims of a thirteen-year-old girl, even one he cared for. In the end, he might have to use *force* to get her to the River source. He did not want to do that, but he would. *Now* he would.

"We ride out by noon," he told her. "Sheldu and his men will go with us."

"That's good," Hezhi murmured. "We may need more warriors."

"Why do you say that?" he asked, aware of the frost in his voice but unable to do anything about it.

Hezhi's face reflected his tone; hurt and then anger passed over it, ultimately replaced by weariness.

"Never mind," she whispered. "I'll get ready to ride." She turned away, and Perkar realized for the first time that she had traded her Mang clothing for the embroidered yellow riding skirt and woolen shirt of a woman of his own people. It looked wrong on her somehow; the Mang attire suited her better.

"Yes," he said to no one. "I'll get ready to ride, too."

From the corner of his eye, he caught Ngangata's reproving and concerned gaze, but he shook it off, striding with purpose to the stables.

In the stables, he eyed Sharp Tiger, wondering if the beast would yet accept him on his back. His last try at riding the fierce stallion had been two days after Moss escaped them, and that had ended with a nasty bite that Harka had taken three days in healing, "to teach him a lesson." He decided there was no point in trying, and for the hundredth time he regretted his vow to the doomed Good Thief to watch after his mount. Still, Sharp Tiger did not object to packs, and a packhorse was valuable on journeys such as this one. It was just a shame for such a fine warhorse to go unridden, and his own mount, T'esh, was showing increasing signs of rebellion, perhaps having been exposed to one or two too many strange sights and smells. He packed Sharp Tiger and was cinching on T'esh's saddle when Ngangata arrived. He nodded at his friend.

"Two days' hard riding and we'll be in Balat again," the halfling observed. "We'll have come full circle."

"Not quite," Perkar said.

"No? This is how we met, equipping an expedition to ride into the realm of the Forest Lord. Now we are back to that point."

"I suppose. For you and me, this is full circle. Full circle for *me* will be when we reach the mountain. That's where my mistakes began."

"Oh, no," Ngangata said. "Your mistakes began here, too, listening to Apad and Eruka—allowing their prejudices and fears to become your own—and hiding your agenda. The Kapaka would never have taken you along had he known you were in love with a goddess."

"Is that what this is about? Are you here to dissuade me?"

"Yes. Your last quest to slay the Changeling brought all to ruin. Surely you remember."

Perkar kneed T'esh roughly in the side; the stallion was blowing out so that the saddle would be loose, and today Perkar was having none of that.

"As usual, Ngangata, you know best. I even agree with you. Deep down, I no longer even *believe* in this quest. I do not think the Changeling can be slain, and I do not think I can put all my mistakes back the way they were. But I no longer have any choice in the matter."

"You always have a choice."

"Remember your diatribe against heroes, Ngangata? About how they are merely fools who have been glorified in song, how they are death to their companions?"

"I remember."

"Then for the last time, ride away, because I think that soon I will die. And if I am a hero, we both know what will happen to my companions."

Ngangata turned to his own mount. "I know this," he said. "But does *she*?"

"Hezhi? No. Truth to tell, I don't think I am the hero this time at all, Ngangata. I think she is. Maybe she always was. And that means we are to die in her service. What point in telling her that? Perhaps she *can* slay the Changeling, as Karak says. Maybe I'll live long enough to see that. Gods granting, I'll take my revenge on his instrument, at least."

Ngangata shook his broad head and waved away a horsefly. "You are intimately familiar with several gods, Perkar. Do you think them likely to grant you anything?"

"If it serves *them*, yes."

"Very well," he conceded. "But listen to me." He turned his dark, Alwa eyes upon Perkar, eyes Perkar had once found so intimidating. Time and friendship had taught him to see the deep expressiveness of them, the concern there—but they still gave him pause. "I will not leave you, Perkar. I will not allow you to throw your life from you like a worn bowstave. Whatever else you may be, you are my friend, and I can say that of very few. So when you ride to meet death, think of me by your side."

"I don't want that responsibility," Perkar sighed.

"You don't have it," Ngangata grunted, in answer. "But if I force you to think of me—or anyone—before yourself, I've done a good thing."

Perkar watched as Ngangata finished saddling his mount and then led his horse from the stall. "Will we win, Ngangata? *Can* we defeat the Changeling?"

Ngangata uttered an odd little laugh. "Of course," he answered. "Why not?"

Perkar smiled thinly in response. "Indeed," he agreed. "Why not?"

Together they rode out to join the company of warriors.

Perkar wondered idly if "Sheldu's" bondsmen knew who their lord really was, but decided that it did not matter. They were a brave company, well armed, and they seemed fit for anything. Thirty men now, plus his original six. Would the Forest Lord notice them and stop them? Perkar understood from experience that against the Huntress and her host, they would be as nothing. Then again, Karak rode with them, though disguised. Perkar hated to admit it, but it was a huge relief; with a god riding at their fore, he no longer had to worry about whether he was making the right decisions, leading them down the correct path. As when he had been caught on the River, he had nothing to say about where he was going—only about what he did when he got there.

"Why haven't you traveled with us since the beginning?" he wondered to Karak aloud.

"I had things to do and I would have been noticed" was the reply—not explaining *who* would notice, of course, or *what* things he had to do. "Now—well, we are about to enter my home. Even now, however, I must remain disguised. Do not expect much overt help from me. I am your guide, not your protector, though the closer we get to Erikwer, the more help I can be."

"Erikwer?"

"His source; the place in the mountain from which he flows," Karak answered. After that, the Crow God rode up front to talk to one of his men.

So Perkar allowed T'esh to lag back. The stallion's coat gleamed, and Perkar himself had bathed, been dressed in fine new clothes, and a shining steel hauberk rode packed on Sharp Tiger. He should feel new and refreshed.

But two days before, riding and laughing next to Hezhi, smiling at her wonder at the mountains, he had felt a hundred times better. He realized, with some astonishment, that he had actually been happy. Odd that happiness was something one only identified when it was entirely absent.

The sun cast gold on bright new leaves and the upturned faces of wildflowers, but each moment only brought him closer to despair and doom.

He tried to brighten when Hezhi rode up but failed utterly.

"What's the matter?" she asked. For an instant he almost explained; it hung at his tongue. But the chill remained in him, and when he shrugged instead of answering her he could almost palpably feel her pulling back from him, retreating behind her own walls against hurt and closeness.

"Well, then," she said awkwardly. "I came over because I need to tell you some things." Her eyes wandered from her skirt briefly to his face and back down before she went on. "I journeyed last night. I saw an army of Mang riding to meet us. An army much larger than this one."

"Oh?" he said. Karak had not shown him an army, though now that he thought of it, he had alluded to one.

"Yes. They are led by Moss."

"Moss?"

"Moss is the gaan—though I suppose we should have known that. I should have seen it."

"Brother Horse says that gaan can hide their natures, even from one another."

"Yes. Still; when he came to me, in that dream, he was attacked by something I never saw—something commanding lightning. The next day you found Moss, wounded. I never made the obvious connection."

Perkar held up one hand helplessly, not sure what to say. Moss was just a *boy*—who would expect him to be the leader of hosts of Mang warriors? But then, he was older than Hezhi, and not much younger than Perkar himself.

"This army also has someone else with it," Hezhi said. "Someone impossible."

"Impossible?"

He listened intently as she outlined her vision, and when he understood that she had seen the destroyer who had murdered the Stream Goddess, his chest tightened until he thought it might rip itself apart. But then she explained *who* he was, and he remembered.

"I chopped his *head* off," Perkar said incredulously. *"Off."*

"This is the River at work," she replied dully. "I'll fight you no more about going to She'leng, Perkar. I just want you to know that. You need not coax me any longer."

"I was never—"

"Don't lie," she answered, and with chagrin he saw real anguish in her eyes. "Yen lied to me, and now . . . now he's coming for me again. He may not have *ever* been human. All I understand is this: when one of you comes close to me, holds my hand, kisses me, it's only because he wants something besides *me.* Maybe if I live long enough, I can learn whatever secret it is, whatever magic exists that will let me survive that, but for now I've had enough of it. You and I will see this through; we will slay the River or die trying. But I don't trust you, Perkar, because I know you've lied to me. I am certain, at least, that there are things the Blackgod told you that you haven't chosen to share. So I'm not doing this because I trust you, Perkar, but because it is the only thing I can see to do. And I don't know that I like you very much, either."

He listened to all of that helplessly, desperate to respond, but without anything to say. Because it was all true—all, save the implication that their recent closeness was no more than a ploy on his part. But he could see that it seemed that way, and besides, he didn't have the energy to argue. If she wanted it this way, it would only make things easier should they reach an impasse later on.

So instead of arguing, he only lowered his head, knowing that she would take that as a sign that everything she said was true. And after a moment she rode off to where Tsem, Brother Horse, and Yuu'han traveled in a little clump.

In two days they entered the dark majesty of Balat. Hezhi was awestruck by the trees, for though she had seen them in dreams long ago in Nhol, the dreams failed to do justice to their sheer, overwhelming majesty. Some were two horse-lengths in diameter, and the canopy those gargantuan columns supported was like distant green stained glass, the occasional real rays of sunlight that actually fell through that imperial ceiling shining like diamonds amongst the ferns and dead leaves of the forest floor.

Her godsight showed her many things skulking just beyond the edge of vision: ghosts, and gods of a hundred descriptions. Balat was alive in a way that she had never imagined. Despite her resentment—despite having been herself threatened—she began to understand why the Huntress strove so implacably to protect this place. She saw now that Nhol and its empire rested on merely the *corpse* of a land. The only things that thrived there were Human Beings and the plants and animals thralled to them—as the Humans were thralled to the River. Balat was as the whole world had been, once—alive. The "monsters" her ancestors had destroyed lived here still, and they gave breath to the world.

Though to be fair to her ancestors, being rid of such creatures as the Blackgod and the Huntress could at times seem desirable.

Five evenings later they capped a hill and she saw She'leng. She realized, with a start, that she had seen it earlier that day and believed it to be nothing more than a remote cloud, for it was so distant that it was only *just* darker than the sky. Nothing could be that far away and yet fill so much of the sky except a cloud. But when the sun touched it, and red-gold blood quickened on the outline of the peak, it stood revealed, like a ghost suddenly reimbued with life and substance. It was still so far distant as to only be a shadow, but what a shadow! Its perfect cone filled the western quarter of the horizon. Truly such a place might give birth to gods, might humble even the likes of the River.

Throughout the journey, Perkar had become more and more distant, and though Hezhi wept about it once, secretly, she hardened her heart against him. She had given him the opportunity to dispute her, to tell her she was wrong, that he felt something more than some offensive mixture of anger and duty regarding her. He had refused the opportunity, and she would not give him the chance to hurt her again.

Besides, as the mountain waxed in the following days, recognition of the sheer audacity of what they were about grew proportionally, and that brought with it not only fear but a thriving excitement that she hadn't expected. Once she had stood on the edge of the palace, proposing her own death. Now she proposed to kill a god, the god of her ancestors—*her* ancestor.

Feeling an awkward need to express such feelings, she reluctantly guided her mount to where Brother Horse rode. He greeted her cheerfully, though since Raincaster's death his face more often fell in solemn lines.

"Hello, *shizhbee*," he said.

"It is well," she answered, in Mang—her acceptance of his calling her granddaughter once again. He understood and smiled more broadly.

"I *did* have hopes of making a Mang out of you," he remarked.

"I had hopes of being one," she returned, a little more harshly than she intended. *They wouldn't let me,* she finished silently. But Brother Horse knew that, caught the implication, and an uneasy silence followed.

"I'm sorry," Hezhi went on, before the quiet could entirely cocoon them. "You've been good to me, Brother Horse, better than I could have ever expected."

"I've done no more than any other old man would do, to keep the company of a beautiful young girl."

She actually blushed. "That's very—"

"It's *true*," Brother Horse insisted. "I'm like an old fisherman, come to sit down by the lake for a final time. I rest here with my feet in the water, and I know in my bones I won't be taking my catch home, not this time. Old men spend *so* much time thinking about the lake, about the dark journey that awaits us. The sight of beauty becomes precious—better than food, beer, or sex. And you have a glorious beauty in you, child, one that only someone with sight like mine can appreciate."

"You aren't going to die," Hezhi whispered.

"Of course I am." Brother Horse snorted. "If not today, tomorrow, and if not tomorrow, the next day. But it doesn't matter, you see? There's nothing to be done about that. And this is fine company to die in."

"I was worried that you came only because you thought you *had* to."

"What difference does that make?" Brother Horse asked.

"It's just that . . . I'm sorry about . . ." She remembered just in time that it was considered rude to name the dead until that name was passed on to another. "About your nephew," she finished lamely.

His face did cloud then. "*He* was beautiful, too," he murmured. "What is comforting about beauty is that we know we will leave it behind us—that it goes on. When it *precedes* us, that's tragedy."

He turned his face from her, and she heard a suspicious quaver in his voice when he spoke down to Heen, who trotted dolefully along the other side of his horse. "Heen says that's the problem with being as old as we are," he muttered gruffly. "Too much goes before you."

He reached over and ran his rough hand on her head, and she *did* catch a glint of moisture in his eyes. "But *you* won't," he muttered. "I'll *see* to that." He straightened in the saddle and coughed. "Now. What did you *really* ride over here to talk about?"

"It's not important."

"I think it is. You've been silent as a turtle for three days, and now you choose to speak. What's on your mind?"

She sighed and tried to collect the fragments of what she had been thinking. "I was wondering how I should be feeling, going to slay my own ancestor. It should seem like murder, like patricide. Like killing my own father."

Brother Horse looked at her oddly. "But you *don't* feel that way."

"No . . . a little maybe. I was brought up to *worship* him. But then I remember my cousin, D'en, and the others below the Darkness Stair. I remember him filling me up, being *inside* of me, and I don't feel very daughterly at all. I *want* him to die. With so many gods in the world, *he* will hardly be missed."

"Not true," Brother Horse said. "His absence will be felt, but gladly. The world will be better without him. Are you afraid?"

"I was. I have been. But now I only feel excited."

The old man smiled. "Felt that way myself, on my first raid. Just kept seeing that trophy skin in my hand, decorating my yekt. I was scared, too, but I didn't know it. The two feelings were all braided up."

"It's like that," she affirmed. "It's just like that. It's frustrating because I can't *picture* what will happen when we get there. I can't rehearse it in my mind, you see? Because I don't *know* what I am to do!"

"I rehearsed my first battle a hundred times," Brother Horse said, "and it still went completely *wrong*. Nothing I imagined prepared me for it. You might be better off this way."

"But why is this kept from me? Why shouldn't I know?"

"I can't guess. Maybe so no one learns it from *you*. Moss might be able to do that."

"Oh." They traveled on silently for a bit, but this time it was a comfortable pause. In that interval she reached over and touched the old man's hand. He gripped hers in return.

"If we succeed—if we slay *him*—I wonder, will the little gods like those who live *here* return to Nhol? Will the empire become like Balat?"

"No place is like Balat," the old Mang assured her. "But I take your meaning, and yes, I think so. When he is no longer there to devour them, the gods will return."

"That's good, then," she said.

Two days later they reached She'leng. Its lower slopes were folded into increasingly higher ridges, and they wound up and down these, torturously seeking the place whose name she had begun to hear muttered amongst Sheldu's men. Erikwer. Her heart seemed to beat faster with each moment and passing league, filling her with frenetic energy. She could sense the fear that Brother Horse spoke of, but it could not match the growing apprehension of danger, which—rather than fear—kindled a precarious joy.

The fact that Perkar only seemed more sullen and drawn each day scarcely had meaning for her anymore. Four times before her life had changed forever: first when she discovered the library and Ghan; again when she understood the nature of her Royal Blood, its power and its curse. Thrice when she fled Nhol to live among the Mang, and again when she had stepped through the drum into the world of the lake and become a shamaness. But none of these had brought peace to her, or happiness, or even a modicum of security.

Tomorrow would. In Erikwer she would find release in one way or the other, release from the very blood in her veins by slaying or dying. And with that thought, tentative elation waxed fierce, and she remembered the statuette Yen had given her—so long ago it seemed. The statuette of a woman's torso on a horse's body, a representation of the Mang belief that mount and rider were joined together in the afterlife. She had become that statuette now. She was mare, bull, swan—but above all she was Hezhi, and she would live or die as herself. That could never be taken from her again.

Though everyone else trotted, she urged Dark into a gallop, stirring a small storm of leaves in the obscure light. The others watched her go, perhaps amused; she did not care. She wanted to *run*, to feel hooves pound in time with her heart. Tree branches whipped at her as the trail narrowed and steepened, but Dark was surefooted. Whooping, suddenly, she rounded a turn that plunged her down along a hillside—

And nearly collided with another rider. The horses shuddered to a halt as the other person—one of Sheldu's outriders—shot her a look that contained both anger and fear. She opened her mouth to apologize, but he interrupted.

"Mang," he gasped. "We can't go that way."

"What?"

"In the valley," he insisted, waving his arms. "A whole army." He frowned at her and then urged his mount past, disappearing up the slope.

Hezhi hesitated, her reckless courage evaporating—but not so fast as to take curiosity with it. The trail bent in a single sharp curve ahead, and through the trees bordering the trail she could see the distant slopes of another valley, far below. She coaxed Dark around that curve—hoping for just a glance of the army the outrider spoke of.

Beyond, the trees opened, and she faced down a valley furrowed so perfectly it might have been cut with a giant plow. On her right was only open air. To her left, the trail became no more than a track reluctantly clinging to the nearly sheer valley wall. So steep and narrow it was, she could hardly imagine a horse walking it without tumbling off; there were no trees on the precipitous slope to break such a fall before reaching the lower valley where the grade lessened and trees grew. Nevertheless, a group of Sheldu's men stood, dismounted, farther down the trail, and far below them *another* knot of men and horses struggled *up* the track. Below *them*, through the gaps in spruce and birch, sunlight blazed on steel in a thousand places, as if a swarm of metallic ants were searching the narrow valley for food.

But they were not ants; they were men and horses: Mang.

Yes, it was time to return to the group. She wondered how long it would take the army to climb the trail, and if the riders already coming up the slope were friend or foe. They were dark, like

Mang, but even with her god-enhanced sight they were difficult to make out, though one seemed familiar.

That was when her name reached her ears, borne by wind, funneled up to her by the valley walls.

"Hezhi!" Very faintly, but she recognized the voice. And then it came again. Gaping, she turned Dark back toward the approaching army.

XXXIII

The Steepening Trail

GHE'S fingers tightened around his throat, and Ghan felt that his eyes were about to pop from his skull. Fighting for the merest sip of breath, he scarcely had leisure to understand that all around him, men were dying, throwing themselves between Moss and the demons Ghe had summoned from his veins. Ghan wondered, inanely, if the men could really fight and die in such grim silence, or if it was the roaring of blood in his ears that kept him from hearing them.

He clawed at the talons biting into his windpipe, but he might as well have pried at steel bolts set in marble.

"Now, what lie were you about to tell me, old man?" the ghoul snapped at him. "Why were you calling me a fool? Or shall I just find out by opening you up and peering inside?"

Ghan answered him the only way he could: by beating feebly against his attacker's chest. Ghe looked puzzled for an instant and then roughly pushed him back. Blood and breath roared back into his head, and he fell, ears full of ocean sound.

He probably had only instants, but his throat was still closed up. Ghe had paused to examine his self-inflicted wound, the one the grass-bears had sprung from; it had stopped bleeding.

"I remember now," Ghe told him, eyes suddenly mild.

Ghan grunted; it was the best he could do.

"When I died. Hezhi's mouth was bleeding, and her blood was turning into something." He settled his feet onto the ground. "Blood, you see, gives spirit shape. Did you know the stream-demon I took in? She had Human form because a Human girl bled to death in her. And my blood is so *many* things now."

"She's driven you mad," Ghan shouted urgently. "Qwen Shen has you on a rope, like a *dog*, Ghe. Like a mongrel cur from Southtown."

"Shut up, old man," Ghe gritted. "No more lies from you."

"It's true. Did you know you call *Hezhi's* name when you sleep with Qwen Shen? She owns you, bends your soul to her devices."

Snake-quick, Ghe was there, slapping him with an open palm. The earth rippled like a sheet waving in the wind. Another slap, and Ghan saw only night.

WHEN he awoke, Ghe was daubing his mouth with a wet rag. He spluttered, raising his arms reflexively to defend himself. Ghe shook his head, a silent *no* that served only to deepen Ghan's confusion.

Moss stood behind Ghe. He looked weary, and one arm hung in a sling.

"What?"

Ghe shrugged. "I nearly killed you. That would have been a mistake. Like the River, I have trouble seeing myself; I need others, outside of me, to watch me. How do you feel?"

"Confused. I thought you and Moss were fighting to the death."

"We were," Moss interposed. "To *my* death, very certainly. You saved me, Ghan, gave me the information I was missing. I wish you had told me earlier about Qwen Shen's hold on Ghe. If I had known a day ago, many of my warriors would still be alive. It is fortunate for us both that you blurted it out at last."

"I trust none of you," Ghan muttered. "I've made no secret of that. I keep what I know close. If you want it, *he* knows how to get it." He jerked his chin defiantly at Ghe.

The ghoul shook his head. "No. Your knowledge would have been bound up inside of me with everything else, if I had taken you in before. I remember now why I wanted you on this expedition alive: because even hostile to me, you are more useful as you are." His eyes narrowed. "But I will have no more betrayal. You have balanced the old debt; do not incur new ones."

"I still don't understand what happened."

Moss smiled faintly. "I showed him his—what did you call it? Leash. I showed him the trap Qwen Shen had laid for him. Once I knew it was there, it was simple enough to see and reveal." He rubbed his hurt arm. "She is powerful, that one. Dangerous."

"What has become of her?" Ghan asked.

Ghe's visage furrowed in wrath. "Gone, she and Bone Eel both. Gone I know not where. I will search for them."

Ghan drew a deep breath. "Give me a moment to think," he said. "Because I have something to tell you both. And some questions, as well."

Now his senses could make out a cricket chirping half a league away, see a nut hanging on a tree at the same distance, scent the distinctive odor of a soul from even farther. Yet he found not the faintest trace of Qwen Shen or Bone Eel. It was as if they had wrapped a vanishing about themselves, the way powerful priests were able to—the way the temple itself did.

Out of sight of the camp, he raged. Trees splintered beneath his claws, small creatures of wood and field shriveled into skeletons in the tempest of his anger. He wanted to hurt himself, to pound his knuckles until bone cracked and blood covered him. He wanted desperately to feel *pain* once again, to purify himself through it.

But his skin no longer registered such sensations, and his flesh was no more susceptible to tearing than his bones to shattering.

At last he gave up. He had failed the River, but that failure could still be redressed. Especially if he could puzzle out what Qwen Shen had been doing, and why. He remembered their lovemaking sessions now, and part of it at least was plain. She had labored to twist his fundamental desire to find Hezhi into some buried desire for her. She had not failed; he still trembled when he thought of her, her flesh, her eyes. But now he could remember the betrayals, the illusion of Hezhi in the throes of passion, the whispered conversations he forgot, the subtle suggestions that made such perfect sense from *her* lips. . .

Ah, when he found her it would be such a sweet thing. No passion she had ever brought him would be as great as unraveling the threads of her life, one by one, as he also unraveled the flesh and blood surrounding her.

He forced himself to think on the things she had made him forget; memories crowded for recognition, but he had no way of sorting them out. Moss could help him do that, and so could Ghan, though the latter would do so reluctantly. He rubbed his knuckles, again chagrined at their lack of soreness. They seemed odd, as he rubbed them, unyielding, and he realized with a start that some sort of bony plate was present beneath the skin. Puzzled, he continued to inspect his body. Broad sheets of hard substance lay beneath his chest, abdomen, thighs—a massive plate lay across his shoulders, and he realized that the skin there was actually colored by the armor pressing up from beneath, a dull aquatic gray, slightly blemished, like the back of a Rivercrab.

He didn't know whether to be amused or horrified; removed from the protecting waters of the River, his body had begun growing a shell to defend itself. Qwen Shen had hidden that from him, too. Why had she done that?

To maintain in him the illusion that he was Human, of course. To keep him from the persuasions of Lady Death and his own common sense which told him that as much as he might believe himself to be Ghe, he was not.

He couldn't think about that. It didn't matter. It didn't matter, because he was *someone*, and he had the memories of a legion now to draw from, and he had his desire, his purpose, though Qwen Shen may have tainted it. And he would still have Hezhi, if not for himself, then at least for the River and for *her*, so that she might be the empress Moss told him she would be: Hezhi, empress of the world. And in such a world, ruled by the River and his children, might there not be *some* place for such as he?

Furious and bewildered, he stalked back to the rapidly breaking camp. The urge to fly ahead, alone, and confront his enemies by himself was nearly overwhelming. But he must listen to Moss now, who knew this world of magic and many gods better than he. Moss could throw his vision from him, see things far away—something Ghe found himself unable to do; when he tried, the spirit carrying his sight inevitably tried to escape, and he was usually forced to devour it entire. Moss controlled his familiars in a different way, by cajoling them, by bargaining with them; they came and went willingly. The shaman's personal power was as nothing compared to Ghe's, but it gave him some advantages. Moss knew where Hezhi and her captors were, knew that in a few days the paths of their forces would converge, at the base of the mountain looming west. Moss had urged Ghe to wait until then to strike. The waiting was hard, hard. Yet one thing he understood, now that Qwen Shen's hold on him was released: he himself was a *weapon*, not a warrior. The River had made him thus, for it could not give him the wisdom or knowledge to know how he should strike or where. That was Moss' task. Moss knew best how to wield him.

So perhaps—as a weapon—he spent too much time thinking. Thinking only served to confuse him, in the end.

He entered the camp, wondering what Ghan had to tell him.

GHAN stumbled to the stream, sought up it until the current was unsullied by the hooves of horses. Kneeling, he brought handfuls of the clear and incredibly cold liquid to his face, gingerly probed the cuts and bruises on his throat. So close, so close, and yet now he wondered if he had done the right thing. It might have been *better* if Moss were destroyed.

Well, he shouldn't hold himself accountable for what he shrieked when Ghe had a grasp on him. Never in all of his years could he have ever imagined the forces at play, here beyond the simple and sterile world of the River. It was a terrifying world, and he feared for Hezhi. Everything seemed to hinge upon her, and a hinge swung too many times could weaken and break.

But, water take him, he was beginning to fear this unknown, unseen "Blackgod" even more than he feared Ghe. Here was a creature who had plotted and planned against this day for at least a thousand years. Such a creature might be resistant to attempts to alter its plans, and it would surely not take into account the feelings, desires, and wishes of a twelve-, no, *thirteen*-year-old girl. Whatever designs were laid down in the dark places of the world in the past millennia could not account *specifically* for Hezhi. One could not plan *her*—only a child *like* her. Hezhi had her own desires and motivations, and they might not coincide with what the gods wanted from her.

He closed his eyes, trying to imagine her face once more: chewing her lip, bent over an open book. . .

He opened his eyes and was startled to indeed see a woman's reflection on the stream.

"If you cry out," she whispered, "if you make the faintest of sounds, you will die. Do you understand that?"

Ghan turned to Qwen Shen and nodded. Bone Eel stood a small distance behind her. He looked grim.

"You will come back to the horses with me, and you will mount, and you will offer no resistance. If you do those things, you will not only live, but you will see your darling pupil again."

Ghan shrugged, though he found it impossible to conceal his expression of anger. He followed her to the horses.

Surely Moss or Ghe would sense them somehow, find them.

But half a day later, as their horses lathered and panted beneath them, and they entered the bosom of the enormous forest, he was forced to admit that perhaps he was mistaken about that. About midday, Bone Eel called them to a walk, so that their mounts might not die beneath them.

"You are a fool," Bone Eel told him casually.

Ghan turned sharply in his saddle. There was something in Bone Eel's voice that sounded different, somehow.

"Am I?"

"You revealed us. We had the ghoul under our control, and you gave him the means to slip. You cannot imagine what you have released."

"I think I can. I wonder if *you* can?"

Qwen Shen uttered a harsh laugh. "My husband has endured much," she said. "He has pranced and played for your amusement, so that you would focus all of your attention upon me and never watch *him*. But do not be deceived. I have witchery enough, but—"

"Hush, beloved," Bone Eel said, a cord of command strung through the words. "Giving this one knowledge is like giving an assassin weapons. Or perhaps like giving broken glass to a small child, I am not certain which. In any case, he needs to know little enough."

"I know that you are servant of the Blackgod, who in Nhol we name the Ebon Priest," Ghan snapped.

"Do you?" Bone Eel said easily. "Well, I must admit I would be sorely disappointed in you if you had not reasoned at least *that* much. Tell me more, prince of words and books."

"The whole priesthood serves this Blackgod. But *you* are not priests. She is a woman and you are not castrated."

"Right again. You are indeed clever, Master Ghan. Perhaps we were wrong in urging Ghe to swallow you up."

"No," Qwen Shen snapped. "We would still control the ghoul if we had persuaded *that*. What I *endured* from him, and then you render it all for naught!"

"Now, *beloved*," Bone Eel sighed, wagging his finger at her. "You know that you enjoyed him well. Lie not to *me*."

Qwen Shen opened her mouth to protest but when she met her husband's gaze, a devilish look flashed upon her features. "Well, after all, my lord, on the River you were less than your usual self."

"*Hush*, I said," Bone Eel snapped, and this time Ghan caught real anger in his tone.

Qwen Shen obeyed, and the three rode in sullen silence for a bit.

"May I ask where we are going?" Ghan asked.

"You may, and I may even answer," Bone Eel replied.

"Well?"

"We go to rendezvous with Hezhi and her retinue," he answered.

"At best, you can only hope to reach them hours before Ghe and Moss. Less, if Ghe takes to the air. He can fly now, you know."

"I know. Well, you can thank yourself for this mess. The balance was easily tipped in our favor when we had *some* control of Ghe. Now we have none, and the outcome of this shall be messy, at best. I seek the advice of someone wiser and more powerful than myself. Leaving Nhol, I left much of my power and wisdom behind," Bone Eel confided.

"You seek Perkar, who rides with Hezhi?"

"Perkar? The barbarian dolt? No. Actually, you will be pleased to meet him in person, since you have thought so hard upon him."

"The Blackgod?" Ghan grunted. "You're telling me that Hezhi rides in the company of a god?"

"Perhaps, perhaps not. I can only barely see them. But I would bet my last copper soldier that he is near if he is not among them." He shrugged. "Either way, in a day or so you will witness a battle such as this world has not seen in many, many ages. The rotten stump has been kicked, and termites pour out!" He laughed, genuinely and loudly, and the peals of it rang weirdly in the vast roof of the forest.

By the afternoon, he was no longer laughing. They entered a high, narrow valley and began hurrying their exhausted mounts up one slope of it. It was steep, very steep, and none of them was an accomplished horseman. Below, the lean shapes of mounted Mang began to appear, outriders or actual pursuit, it did not matter, for they clearly understood who rode ahead of them—whoops of discovery and triumph echoed through the vale. Perhaps Qwen Shen and Bone Eel had some priestly trick for muddling Ghe's and Moss' supernatural senses, but they could not fool the keen eyes of born hunters and warriors.

Cursing, Bone Eel brayed at his horse for more speed as Ghan noticed a strange hissing sound.

Something brushed through the forest to his right, moving much faster than a bird, and a black shaft appeared in a tree trunk.

"They're shooting at us," Ghan shouted.

"I know that, you fool," Bone Eel snapped back.

"*He* is coming. He is near," Qwen Shen added.

"I know that, too. The two of you darken your mouths and ride, if you've nothing useful to say."

A few more arrows hissed by, but they must be at extreme range—or the Mang would not be missing them.

It took all of Ghan's strength and recently acquired riding skills to remain in the saddle; the way twined tortuously through trees, rising and falling, though in the main it rose. He kept his hands clenched in his mount's mane and his head buried there, as well, above the heaving neck, and more often than not his eyes were clenched shut, too. They were closed when the angle of flight changed sickeningly, as if his beast's head were pointed straight at the sky. A different horse—not his own—suddenly shrieked. He opened his eyes to find that they were scrambling up an incline so steep that Qwen Shen and her mount had fallen and were sliding. Cursing, she managed to remount. Bone Eel paid her no mind, but urged his own beast the more.

These are horses, not mountain goats, Ghan thought, heart thudding madly. But then the trail became just less steep enough that the horse could find a gait, a tortured trot often broken by stumbles. The trees around them thinned and were gone, unable to find purchase on the rocky slope.

When he looked down, a few moments later, he wished he hadn't. The path his horse continued to slip upon seemed less

than a handspan wide, and it wound up the side of a mountain—
the mountain, he supposed—so that to the right was a nearly
sheer cliff rising to greet the sky and to the left—to the left was a
steep plunge that left him dizzy. Below that, the valley was filling
with Mang, and from them lifted scores of black missiles, clattering into the hillside around them.

"There!" he heard Bone Eel shout furiously. Ghan looked
about wildly and then saw them: a trio of horsemen above,
blocking the way up.

"Surrender," Ghan hissed. "We're doomed otherwise."

"No! Look!" And Bone Eel pointed again at the men above.

Ghan did see, then. They were not Mang; beneath their helms,
pallid faces gleamed, and the cut of their clothing and armor was
strange. They were—*had* to be—Perkar's people.

His horse slipped, and a stone flew from beneath its hooves,
out and down. Ghan hoped it struck one of their pursuers on his
helmeted head. He glanced up again. Would they make it? It was
so steep, so far . . .

Beyond the three riders was a fourth, very small, not dressed in
armor at all but in some sort of yellow skirt. The distance was too
great for him to make out any features, only the delicate brown
wedge of her face. But he knew. He *knew*!

"Hezhi!" he shouted with all of the strength in his lungs, and
he heard his voice repeating in the hollows of the mountain. The
rider paused, but as her name began to come back to him, she
suddenly spurred back into action, plunging dangerously down
the trail toward them. "Hezhi!" he shouted again, clapping his
beast's flanks with real force now, his old heart suddenly new
with fierce determination. He was here now, she was alive, and
even with an army below them there was hope; he knew it as
surely as he knew her.

He felt a twinge of pain in his back, wondered why his old
joints had protested no more than this up until now. He could
make out her eyes now, though the light seemed to be fading.
Were there clouds blocking the sun?

The pain in his back was worse, and an odd numbness spread

through his limbs, dizziness. He reached back and felt the stickiness of blood, the wooden shaft sunken into his kidneys.

"Bone Eel . . ." he began. He wanted to tell *someone* how surprising it was, to have something *in* you. He had always imagined the pain would be greater.

The mountain wheeled around him, as if his mount had begun to fly and roll about in the air. It seemed to him that he should cling tightly to something, but his hands had lost their ability to grip. The whirling became floating, and he watched, astonished, as his horse, Bone Eel, Qwen Shen, and the other riders seemed to fly away from him, and only then did he guess that he had fallen, that he was plummeting down the mountainside.

Then he struck something unyielding, and light vanished. Oddly he could still hear a sort of grinding and snapping, a vague and distant pummeling, and then that faded away, as well.

XXXIV

The Teeth of the Host

"GHAN isn't dead," Hezhi explained to herself in a hushed voice. "Ghan is in the library, with his books. Nothing could ever compel him to leave them."

Then who was it she had seen? Whose toylike figure had pitched almost comically off of the trail, bounced thrice on the rough slope before vanishing into the growth of the lower valley?

Not Ghan, that was certain, though she heard someone mention his name—one of the newcomers, dressed in Nholish fashion—gibbering like everyone else in some incoherent tongue.

Why don't you all learn to speak? she thought bitterly. They probably weren't even saying *Ghan*. It was probably *gan* or *gaan* or *kan* or *ghun*. Who cared, anyway? They kept saying "Mang" a lot, too, but that was unambiguous; she saw Mang warriors clustering at the base of the slope, heard their far-off whoops of challenge.

One of the white men took her gently from her horse and placed her up on his. She let him; she was too busy thinking to ride, and it seemed that they were in a hurry. Thinking about who that could have been, who so resembled her teacher. Because *he* was safe in Nhol.

"Is she wounded? What's wrong?" Perkar shouted, when he saw Hezhi's blank expression, and that she was mounted not on Dark but up behind one of Karak's people.

"No," the warrior replied. "She isn't hurt. She just saw someone die."

Perkar had already dismounted and was rushing toward her, but Tsem beat him to it, plucking her from the back of the mare. She was mumbling something to the half Giant, as if trying to explain to him the most important thing in the world. Tsem only looked puzzled.

Two strangers came behind Hezhi, a man and a woman. Both were striking, beautiful even, and both—as far as he could discern, from his limited experience—were dressed in the fashion of Nhol: colorful kilts and blouses. The man wore a cloth wrapped upon his head, though it was so disheveled that it hung nearly off one side. When that man saw Karak, he quickly dismounted and knelt.

"Get up, you fool," Karak—still, of course, in the guise of Sheldu—commanded.

Looking a bit confused, the man straightened and waved up the woman who had also begun to bow.

A man and woman from Nhol who recognized and bowed before Karak. What did *that* mean?

He was tempted not to care, and it seemed he had little time for it anyway.

"Mang, blocking the valley. I'm sure some will come up for us."

"Single file," Karak said. "They can be slaughtered easily."

"Until the rest of them work up the more charitable slope behind us," Ngangata shouted as he rode over. "They can be here before the sun has moved another span."

"This is the quickest way," Karak insisted.

"Only if we get there. How many Mang? A few hundred? Thirty-five of us, Sheldu. We must go over the spine and ride to our destination through another valley."

"Ridiculous."

"Ngangata knows these lands, Sheldu," Perkar interrupted.

"As do I!" Karak roared, his eyes flashing dangerously yellow.

"Yes," Perkar hissed meaningfully, striding close. "But Ngangata knows these lands from *horseback*!"

"Oh." Karak blinked. "Oh."

Perkar turned to see Ngangata smirking at the exchange. He was certain the half man knew by now who their "guide" was.

"Over the spine," Perkar grunted. He turned to Karak. "Unless you are ready to be more than guide."

The Crow God slowly shook his Human-seeming head. "Not yet. Not until we are too close for him to stop us."

"Then Ngangata and I lead; the place you describe can be reached other ways than the one we are going. If the way is longer, then we must go *now* rather than argue. Leave a few of your men here with plenty of arrows to stop the Mang from coming up that trail. Tell them to give us a good head start and then leave, before they can be surrounded."

Karak pursed his lips, annoyance plain enough on his face, but then he nodded brusquely and shouted the orders, moving off to choose his men.

"Well," Ngangata appraised, "I wondered if you had left us again."

"Soon enough, friend," Perkar told him. "But not just yet."

A moment later they were back on the move, their mounts scrambling across the trackless ridge. Mang war whoops seemed to be everywhere, and Perkar watched the tightness gather in Brother Horse's face. Difficult as it was, moving in and amongst trees, Perkar maneuvered close enough to the old man to hold a shouted conversation.

"You've done more than anyone can expect of you," Perkar shouted. "I urge you to leave us now. No one should have to fight his own people."

"I know what I am about," Brother Horse snapped back at him, though he was plainly agitated. "Save your concern. I will not turn on you; I have cast my lot. If I am fortunate, I will not have to slay any of my kinsmen. But what goes on here is more important than any claims on blood."

"I never thought to hear a Mang say that," Perkar admitted.

Brother Horse set his face in a deep scowl. "If you search for an enemy among us," the old man growled, "best to start in your own heart."

"What do you mean by that?" Perkar shouted.

Brother Horse lifted one hand in a gesture of dismissal. "I don't know," he answered. "But the last few leagues have brought me uneasiness about you."

Perkar urged his mount ahead, angry and confused. How dare the old fool question *him*, when it was *Mang* who rode for the Changeling—the enemy of them all?

Ngangata was pacing close behind; their horses broke from run to canter and back as the leaves slapped at them. Perkar was vividly reminded of the last time he had ridden these ridges, fleeing the Huntress. Then, of course, they had been fighting to *escape* Balat and its mysteries; now they strove to reach its heart.

"Our pursuit is gaining more quickly than I thought they could," Ngangata yelled over to him. "I think they split even before we saw them."

"How many, can you tell?"

"Many. Hundreds, coming from possibly three directions."

"How far do we have to go?"

"Too far, from Karak's description."

Perkar smiled savagely. "How long have you known who our friend 'Sheldu' really is?"

Ngangata laughed coarsely. "Almost since you have. I read it on your face. And you've gone fey again." He stabbed his finger at Perkar. "You *aren't* thinking of riding back against them?"

Perkar shook his head. "No. I mean, I *did* think about it, but what would be the point? Most would just go around me. If there were a narrow pass to hold, or if I could reach their head—Moss, or that—*thing* . . ." He turned fiercely in his saddle. "I will warn you of this, my friend. If I see an opportunity to slay the creature from Nhol, I will take it. Do you understand that?"

"No," Ngangata replied frankly, "but I can accept it."

"Good."

Perkar spent the next hundred heartbeats fighting his way to the front of the column. Hezhi still looked dazed, but Tsem's horse could not bear even her tiny additional weight, and so she rode up behind Yuu'han. In fact, the Giant's massive charger quivered so that Perkar feared it would collapse any moment. Then what would Tsem do? Of course, soon *all* of the horses would be useless enough to any of them; even T'esh was near exhausted. And Sharp Tiger, pacing placidly and stubbornly behind him, would be no help to anyone.

The howls behind him were drawing nearer.

Even Karak seemed concerned, glancing nervously around.

"You could stop them," Perkar pointed out.

"That isn't my place," the Raven answered testily. "We are too close to our goal now. I can almost taste our victory. If I reveal my power, if I uncloak myself here, now, Balati might notice all of this going on. Who knows what he would then do? I don't."

"If we are all slain—" Perkar began.

But Karak interrupted. "You and the rest could purchase some time for me and Hezhi," he said. "*She* is the crucial one. Only she matters."

"There aren't enough of us," Perkar snapped. "They would flow around us like the River they serve. My companions and your men together would slow them down not at all."

"It will come to it soon enough. Then I may have to reveal myself," Karak said. "But I won't until I must."

"You mean until the rest of us are dead and you *fly* with Hezhi from here."

"Yes, now that you mention it, that *is* what I mean. But let us hope it doesn't come to that."

At that moment, Ngangata raised his bow and shrieked, and

his cry was echoed by a half score of Karak's men. For a moment, Perkar feared that the Mang had caught up with them, but then he saw the truth; ahead of them, the trees bristled with spears and bows. The dark, lean forms of wolves coursed between the great trunks restlessly, and more warriors than could easily be counted. They stretched out along the ridge as far as Perkar could see, utterly blocking their way.

GHE dug his talons into his palms, calling on all that remained of his self-control. The outriders had discovered Qwen Shen and Bone Eel. He could be upon them in instants, if he wished, take himself up on pinions of wind. Yet Moss warned him not to, and with greatest reluctance he conceded the young shaman's expertise. Though he felt that nothing could resist his power, Moss assured him that such was not the case—and indeed, whatever black arts Qwen Shen and her doltish husband controlled had not only concealed *them* and allowed them to steal Ghan away, but it had also made them exceedingly difficult to follow. Even now he could not sense where they were, though Moss assured him that they were not far, that before the day was done his army of Mang would encircle the whole lot of them, Hezhi and her pet demon included. *Then* there would be fighting enough.

"What we cannot do," Moss had insisted, "is allow our eagerness and anger to separate us. My spirits and I have woven a hundred spells to keep from awaking the Forest Lord and to protect us from the other things that haunt this wood. If you go off alone, you will only have your power to protect you. You have much raw strength, but there are gods here who have more, gods you will not easily dispense with. Together we have a chance, you and I."

So even though Hezhi was so near, he must cultivate patience.

Death came to him on the breeze: Mang warriors, bravely daring the winding trail up which Qwen Shen, Bone Eel, and Ghan had fled. At the top, someone was defending the precarious pathway. He felt their lives flicker and go out, and amongst them—someone else dying—someone familiar.

"Worry not, Moss," he told his companion. "I'll go no farther than the outriders. But there is something ahead I must see."

"Have a care," Moss cautioned. "Whatever you sense, it could well be a trap."

"I know. But somehow I don't think so." He dismounted and, like a hound following a familiar scent, raced off into the scrubby, evergreen foliage of the slope. Whatever it was was fading, fading, and almost it was gone before he reached it. Yet it was stubborn, and when he found the source he knew he should have recognized it by that alone.

Ghan's broken body lay curled around a tree in a sort of reverse fetal position, his back bent completely the wrong way. One eye stared open and empty and the other was closed by the crushing of one side of his skull. Only within him was there any sign of his life, the filaments of his ghost even now fading and detaching from his ruined flesh. Ghe stared, wondering that he could feel any sorrow at all for such an annoying, dangerous old man, but he did. It was a sight that made little sense, the dignified scholar whose pen formed such esoteric and beautiful characters lying *here*, hundreds of leagues from any writing desk, in a forest, broken and arrow pierced.

Gingerly he reached out and tugged at the strands, pulled them free of a body that would serve now only to feed beasts and the black soil. He took the ghost and settled it into its own place amongst the august company of gods, an emperor, and a blind boy.

There, old man. At last I have you.

What? the spirit feebly replied. *What has happened? Where is Hezhi? I just saw her . . .*

Hush, Ghe told him. *Rest there, and I will explain all to you later.* Then he closed up the doors on Ghan, for the fear and panic of the newly captured wore poorly on him, and he could not afford now to be distracted. But it would please Hezhi, he knew, that he had saved the old man. For her, he would even let the scholar speak to her through his mouth. Yes, she would be happy and grateful when he did that.

He turned; Moss had come up behind him.

"I'm sorry, old man," the shaman told the corpse. "If you had only told me of them sooner . . ."

Ghe smiled sardonically. "He kept one secret too many, and now he has none at all."

Moss shrugged, and then his eyes cleared and he gestured up the ridge with his chin. "My spirits have slain those who held the trail, and a third of my force is approaching the ridge from another direction. We'll have them soon, unless something else goes awry."

"When we *do* capture them, Qwen Shen is mine," Ghe stated flatly.

"Well enough," Moss answered, a slight edge in his voice.

"What's wrong?" Ghe asked.

The shaman shook his head uneasily. "It seems too simple. The Blackgod must have planned more elaborately than this. I will trust nothing until we have Hezhi and have reached the River."

"And how far is that?" Ghe asked.

"The Changeling? We are near his source, and he emerges into his upper gorge less than a league from here." He closed his fist. "Once we have her, nothing must hinder us. If we but reach his waters, no god or power on earth will be strong enough to take her back from him."

"They seek his headwaters," Ghe said. "Why not simply let them reach them?"

"No, they must not go to his source. That they must not be allowed to do at any cost. And they will not. Fifty of my swiftest warriors went ahead, weeks ago, and I have but lately seen them with my eyes that travel. Should we fail here, they still stand between them and his source."

"How did you know that was what they sought?" Ghe asked.

The gaan shook his head. "I *did* not. I gambled. I still could be wrong, but I don't think so, not anymore."

"Then let us go," Ghe said softly. "Hezhi awaits us."

* * *

THE host in the forest regarded them but did not advance, and for fifty heartbeats, no words were spoken or moves made. Karak sat his horse impassively, and Perkar had no sense of what his reaction was. A wind sighed across the hill, and in the distance the calls of the Mang came closer with each moment.

Perkar drew Harka. He knew whose horde *this* was, having been once slain by it.

"Can you see the Huntress?" he asked the weapon.

"No. But that is her host. And yet I sense no danger from them."

"No danger?"

"I do not believe they are hunting you."

"Who then, the Mang?"

"Wait," Harka said, and then, *"there."*

Perkar let his eyes be drawn, and then he saw her, emerging from the massed might of her Hunt. When last he saw the Huntress, she had been in the aspect of a black-furred Alwa woman with antlers and the teeth of a cat. She had ridden a lioness, which he had managed to slay before she speared him.

Her aspect had changed, but there was no mistaking her. The Goddess of the Stream had once explained to him that the gods took their appearance from contact with Human Beings, especially from their blood. The Huntress, Perkar knew, had tasted much blood, Human, Alwa, and otherwise. Her present guise was Human, more or less, a pale, lithe woman with thick black hair in a single braid that fell to the backs of her knees. Her eyes were slivers of deep brown with no whites, which gave her the appearance of a statue rather than a living creature. She was naked, and in her hand bore the same spear that he had once felt pierce his throat. As before, antlers grew from her proudly held head, these backswept like those of a fallow deer.

"Well, what a pretty host," she sighed, and it was the same voice, the same cruel set of the mouth that Perkar remembered. She gazed on him and her smile broadened. "Few there are who escape me," she told him. "You will not do so again, if I hunt you. I know Harka now, recall his virtue. Remember that, little one." She walked farther from her beasts and wolf-warriors, her eyes straying to Karak and a silver laugh coming up from her throat. But she said nothing to him, instead advancing toward where Hezhi sat behind Yuu'han, watching her dully.

"Well, child, are you ready? The final race is at hand now."

"They killed Ghan," Hezhi said, and even as she spoke, Perkar could hear her voice awaking, transforming from shocked to fierce. "They killed my teacher."

Tsem dismounted and interposed himself between the Huntress and Hezhi, but the goddess merely stood there, nodding at Hezhi's answer.

"There will be no final moment," Karak said, agitated, "if we are not on our way."

"As you say, Lord—*Sheldu*, is it? As you say."

"I did not expect you," Karak went on.

"I'm hurt," she replied. "Hurt to think you would not invite me to such a hunt as this."

Karak did not reply. What was going on? What sort of games were these gods playing at? But then the goddess was approaching him again, and his skin prickled, remembering the languid glee with which she had once slaughtered him.

"Well, sweet boy," she asked, when he was close enough to see that she bore fangs like a cat and that her tongue was black, "will you ride with me or not?"

"Ride with you?"

"Against *them*," she said, indicating the sounds of the Mang approaching behind them. "Someone must stop them, or your friends will never reach the source of the Changeling. But I will need help, I think—and I seem to remember your love for the hue and cry of the charge."

"I have never cared for it," he muttered back.

"You rode against me once, and you killed my mount, whom I loved. Now I give you a chance to ride *with* the Hunt. Few mortal men are accorded that pleasure—fewer still have ridden on both ends of the spear."

Perkar gazed around at his companions. Ngangata's eyes clearly warned him *no*, but Karak was nodding urgently. Hezhi— he saw many things in her eyes, but was sure of none of them.

"Very well," he said. "Yes, very well. If you promise me the Tiskawa."

"You will find him no easy foe," the Huntress replied. "But as you wish."

"Wait, then, just a moment," Perkar said. He urged T'esh over to Hezhi and gazed levelly into her eyes. She met his regard fully, and he saw that she was indeed past her shock, eyes clear and intelligent.

"If I don't see you again," he said, "I'm sorry."

"Don't go," she said faintly. "Stay with me."

He shook his head. "I can't. I have to do this. But, Hezhi—" He sidled T'esh closer and leaned in until his lips were nearly on her ear. "Watch Sheldu," he breathed. "He is Karak, under a glamour. He knows what must be done to destroy the Change- ling—but don't trust him. And be careful." And then he lightly kissed her cheek and rode to join the Huntress.

"Come," Karak grated, and the company started off as the host of the Huntress began to move, parting around them, opening their ranks so that the Raven and those who followed him could pass through. Only Ngangata remained with Perkar.

"You have to go with them," Perkar said. "You are the only one I can trust to watch after Hezhi. Only you know enough about gods and Balat to guess what must be done."

"That may be," Ngangata said, "but I don't want you to die alone."

"I have no intention of dying," Perkar replied. "I've outgrown that. And I ride with the Huntress! What can stop us?"

"Then you will not mind me joining you," Ngangata per- sisted.

Perkar laid his hand on his friend's shoulder. "I *want* you with me," he admitted. "I've never told you this, because I'm ashamed of the way I treated you at first. But there is no one I would rather have at my side than you, no friend or brother I could value more.

But what I said was true. I fear for Hezhi, and I need you there, with her. Believe it or not, I somehow feel you will be in more danger there than here. I'm sorry. But I'm begging you to go with Hezhi."

Ngangata's normally placid face twisted in frustration, and Perkar thought that the halfling was going to shout at him again, as he had done back on the plains. But instead he reached his hand out.

Perkar gripped it in his own. "Piraku with you, below you, about you," he told his strange, pale friend.

Ngangata smiled thinly. "You know my kind accumulate no Piraku," he replied.

"Then no one does," Perkar said. "No one."

The Huntress—far ahead now—sounded her horn, and Perkar released his grip on Ngangata's hand and turned T'esh to ride with the host.

"And afterward, you must take me to see the lands beyond Balat!" he shouted back. Ngangata raised his hand in salute, but he only nodded, and then he, too, turned and rode to join Hezhi and the rest.

Perkar urged T'esh to a gallop. Wolves paced him, great black beasts the size of horses, as did fierce packs of *rutkirul*, bear gods wearing the shapes of feral men. A few moments at full gallop brought him beside the Huntress, who was now mounted upon a dagger-toothed panther. She nodded imperiously and then grinned a fierce, delighted grin. Despite himself—despite all of his doubts and fears—Perkar felt a bit of her joy, and the boy in him—the boy he had thought to be dead—that boy wondered what songs might be sung of this, of riding with the Goddess of the Hunt.

And as the sounds of the foe drew nearer, he surrendered himself to a whoop to match the howls rising from all around him. They breasted one hill and then the next—and the air was suddenly thick with black Mang shafts. One glanced from his hauberk, and his belly clenched; but then he saw, in the fore of the vast array of Mang, the face of his enemy, the one who had slain his love, and a red veil descended over his eyes, fury washed away his doubts and most of his humanity.

For the second time, Perkar Kar Barku raised Harka against the creature who had once been called Ghe, and pounding hooves closed the gap between them.

XXXV

~~~~~~~~~~~~~~~~~~~~~~~~~~~~~~~~~~~

Shamans

HEZHI gritted her teeth as the horses hurtled madly down the hillside. The sounds behind them were lost—the Huntress and her Hunt, the Mang, and Perkar—swallowed by the forest and the gorge they were descending into. All that existed now were rocks skittering down sharp, sometimes vertical slopes as their mounts struggled to retain footing. Even as Dark recovered from a stumble, one of Sheldu's men shouted as his stallion fell, rolling over him twice before smashing into a tree. The rider, hopelessly tangled in his stirrups, cried out again, more weakly as he and his mount reached a steeper gradient and vanished down it.

"Tsem!" Hezhi called back over her shoulder. "You dismount and walk!" The Giant was well behind them, his overlarge beast clearly unwilling to negotiate the vertiginous path. Tsem nodded reluctantly and got off, stroking the mare's massive head. He reached to unstrap his packs.

"Leave them!" Sheldu shouted. "We are near enough now as to have no need of that!"

Tsem, looking relieved, pulled out his club, threw his shield onto his back, and started down the hillside, puffing and panting.

"How much farther?" Hezhi snapped at the strange man who had somehow—she failed to understand *how*—become the leader of *her* expedition. Mindful of Perkar's assertion about him, she watched him carefully.

"No distance at all, as the crow flies," Sheldu replied bitterly. "On foot, however—it will take some little while. But when we reach the bottom of this gorge, we can ride more freely."

"Tsem cannot."

"He can keep up; we won't be able to run, and even if we could, the horses would never manage it."

Hezhi nodded, but her heart sank; she knew how quickly Tsem's massive bulk tired him.

True to Sheldu's promise, however, they soon reached the narrow bottom of the gorge. A stream coursed swiftly down it, and the air itself seemed cool and wet, *smelled* of stream. It raised her spirits somewhat, and Tsem, though round-eyed with exertion, seemed able enough to keep up with them on the soft, level earth. Hezhi let Dark lag so that she could stay beside him.

"Will you make it?" she asked worriedly.

"I will," Tsem vowed.

"If you can't—"

"I'm fine, Princess. I know what you think of me, but I'm done complaining about how useless I am."

"You were never useless, Tsem."

He shrugged. "It doesn't matter. Now I *know* that I can contribute to this battle. Even if my strength to run fails I can turn and defend you against any enemies that might follow us."

"Tsem, Ghan is already dead."

"You don't know that, Princess. It couldn't have been Ghan. It must have been someone who resembled him."

"I'm going to find out. Do you recognize either of those two?" She gestured at the man and woman who rode beside Sheldu.

"Yes. The woman is named Qwen-something-or-other. The man is a minor lord, Bone Eel."

"A lord and lady from Nhol, *here*. Then it *was* Ghan, wasn't it?"
Tsem nodded reluctantly, but they discussed it no further.

Not much later, Sheldu called a halt when another horse collapsed. They stopped and let the animals drink.

"Perkar and the Huntress are doing their work, I hope," Sheldu said. "I don't hear any pursuit."

"You won't," Ngangata pointed out. "This gorge seals out sound from beyond itself. We won't hear them until almost they are upon us."

"We have to rest, if just for a moment," Brother Horse said. "Sheldu is right about that."

Hezhi made certain that Tsem drank some water, and then she walked across the thick carpet of leaves to where Qwen Shen and Bone Eel sat against a tree bole.

When she approached, both quickly came to their feet and bowed.

"Princess," Bone Eel said. "We are your humble servants. Forgive us for not introducing ourselves until now."

"I have two questions, and no time for courtly protocol," Hezhi snapped. "The first question is, why are you here?"

Qwen Shen bowed again. "Your father sent us, Princess, to save you from the agents of the priesthood."

"My father? The priesthood?"

"Yes, Lady."

Hezhi blew out a puff of air. "You can tell me more of that later. When you joined us, another man rode with you, a man who tumbled from his horse. Who was he?"

Bone Eel lowered his head. "I believe you knew him," he said. "That was Ghan, the librarian. It was he who convinced the emperor of the need for our expedition. He was—we shall miss him. I'm sorry."

Qwen Shen was nodding, and Hezhi thought she caught the sparkle of a tear in the woman's eye. She swallowed the tightness in her own throat.

"Ghan himself—why?"

"He learned of a plot to find you and kill you, or return you to the River. It was commanded by a young Jik, whom I believe you also knew."

"I knew him in Nhol, and I have seen him more recently in a vision," Hezhi muttered. "But he is dead. I saw him killed."

"The priesthood has great power," Bone Eel told her. "They can create sorcerous creatures. This 'Ghe' is not the man you knew."

"The man I knew is not the man I knew," she nearly snarled.

"Mount up!" Sheldu shouted. "We must continue."

Hezhi leveled a cold gaze at the two. "I will hear more of this later, and I will know, too, how you came to be acquainted with this man Sheldu."

"Ah," Bone Eel began. "He is well traveled, an agent of sorts—"

"Later," she repeated sharply. "I'm confused enough as it is. Much of what you say makes no sense. Just tell me this, quickly. You know what our mission is, here?"

Bone Eel nodded solemnly. "You seek to slay the River."

"If you interfere, my friends will slay *you*, do you understand?"

"Indeed, Princess. We have no wish to interfere. It is what Ghan and the emperor agreed upon."

Hezhi tried to keep her face neutral as she returned to Dark. They were lying, lying, lying, and she knew it. But how *much* of their talk was false?

Once back in the saddle, she leaned over to Tsem. "If those two do anything even slightly suspicious when we reach this place we are going," she said softly, "I want you to kill them. Can you pass that along to Brother Horse and Yuu'han?"

Tsem's eyes widened in surprise. "Princess?"

"I mean it, Tsem. We've been through too much to allow agents of my father—or whomever they work for—to interfere. I don't trust them; they act as if they were friends of Ghan, but he would never be friends with such as they." She paused and almost told him of Perkar's warning about Sheldu, but then she decided that it was best to give Tsem only one thing at a time to worry over.

They resumed, beneath a sky that had begun to don a cloak of dusky clouds. She thought that the rest had done the horses scant good, but the Mang and "Sheldu" probably had greater understanding of the needs of the beasts. Dark's flanks heaved and white foam matted her hair, and Hezhi worried; Dark was her first horse, a beautiful creature, and she did not want to see her die.

She regarded Sheldu as they rode along, searching for some sign of Karak in him. Could Perkar have been right? Was that what he was hiding from her? She tried to think back to what he said, but it was all confusion—at the time, her mind had been trying to understand about Ghan falling.

It *had* been he. She ground her teeth on the thought. She *couldn't* dwell on that. Couldn't. She need only keep it back, away from her heart, for another day before allowing it to overwhelm her. She could do that. Now she had pressing things to puzzle over, important things.

She had glanced back up at "Sheldu," intent on understanding what connection could exist between a Crow God and two nobles from Nhol, when the stream before them suddenly erupted into a fountain of sludge and spray. The nearest riders—Sheldu's vanguard—were bowled over by the explosion, and Sheldu himself was thrown from his rearing mount. Hezhi simply watched, gapemouthed, at what took form.

Its upper part was salamander, thickly wrinkled, grayish black, with knobby little eyes and branching gills sweeping back from the sides of its head like feathery antlers. But it sprang forward on hind legs not unlike a man's, though the forelimbs were the stubby-fingered paws of an amphibian. Its toothless maw gaped open, easily wide enough to swallow a person.

GHE saw the Huntress first, felt the pulsing of power from the bizarre woman-thing. Her host was resonant with energy, too, and he realized now that Moss had not lied to him. Defeating this woman and her creatures would be no easy task. He gathered his own host within him, slashed his palm to release his black blood and potence, but even as it trailed along the ground and monsters of his making sprang up to challenge the wolves and savagely dressed men, he saw the demon descending on him.

Perkar, Ghan had called him, but to Ghe that meant only death. Shrieking, his features set in a grimly insane mask, the bone-faced man charged toward him.

Ghe wrapped himself in a cloak of wind, strengthened his living armor, knitted a shield of invisible fire for himself, and, devouring the flame of life in his horse, leapt from its back, flinging out his blood so that it formed into grass-bears and long-legged stalking things he had no name for. Let *them* deal with that blade, those iron-colored eyes. He himself flew like a spear toward the Huntress, certain that if he could devour her, nothing on earth could possibly stop him—not even his old death.

PERKAR screamed in frustration as the beasts spurted up around him and surrendered his rage to the song Harka sang as the sword directed his arm. He snarled with brutal satisfaction as a bear's head sprang from its massive shoulders and a gout of hot black blood struck him across the face even as Harka turned and swept like a scythe through a thin, skeletal abomination that resembled a praying mantis.

Around him, the armies came together, and the forest was suddenly a garden of death, the Mang skirling and the gods of the host venting unrecognizable sounds. From the corners of his eyes he noticed a rider and horse go down beneath the fangs and claws of a wolf; he saw a bear-man, blinded by two arrow shafts, wander into the decapitating edge of a curved Mang sword.

Claws raked against his hauberk and rings snapped with the force, and suddenly T'esh was shrieking and down; he leapt clear, and though he sought with Harka's edge to dispatch his foes, he searched with each free instant his eyes had for the Life-Eater. He finally saw him, as he stepped from the path of a dying bear; the Nholish man was a blur of flame and motion near the Huntress. Her spear had pierced him, but he strove up it, sliding the shaft through his own belly, and something like lightning cracked between them. His throat nearly raw with shouting, Perkar fought that way, and whatever came between him and the Tiskawa died.

Ghe reached the Huntress before Perkar fought his way through, however, and something like sunlight bloomed where they touched. The Huntress screamed, shrill and carrying. Perkar continued to fight, half blind, as his foes redoubled in number and ferocity, and when he again saw clearly, it was to behold the Tiskawa fight savagely from beneath a pile of rutkirul and wolves. As Perkar watched, however, these minions of the Huntress fell away, twitching, and the Tiskawa stood amongst their corpses.

Perkar recognized him now, though his glimpse of the man—when he still *was* a man—had been brief, in the shadows beneath the streets of Nhol. He had been a worthy enough swordsman—without Harka, in fact, Perkar would never have beaten him.

His face aside, there was much about the Tiskawa that no longer seemed Human. Most of his clothing hung in shreds upon him, so the weird colors of his flesh and the bony unnatural lines of his torso and shoulders were revealed. His eyes held a kind of black fire as he pushed up through the slain beasts and gods to confront him. Perkar wondered where the Huntress was, and then forgot worry as he remembered this *thing* devouring the Stream Goddess. He howled and leapt.

Much faster moved the Tiskawa, fading away from the blow, even though he rose from an awkward position.

"You!" it snarled. "This time you cannot have my head."

Perkar didn't answer. He kept Harka in a guard position. When the monster suddenly lunged, darting forward and slashing down with hooked talons, even Harka had difficulty moving his arm quickly enough. He struck for the neck, but an upflung arm interposed itself. Unbelievably, the godblade did not bite but slid instead down the forearm, skinning the flesh from it and revealing the yellow plate beneath. He twisted Harka and stumbled back, carried the blow on into the ribs of the Life-Eater, and there the edge finally parted flesh and bone, cut from the lowest rib through the spine, down to the pelvis. Then the claws swiped across his face and he felt sudden numbness at the same moment that a furious heat seemed to consume him. Like a child burnt by a coal, he shrieked and leapt backward. The Tiskawa tried to follow, but its body sagged crazily as the legs understood the spine that animated them was severed.

Scrambling back farther, Perkar put his hand to his *own* neck and felt a jet of warm fluid, realized that one of the arteries there had been torn, but even as he did so, the flow diminished as Harka closed his wound.

That was nearly it, the blade said. *He dug into our heart-strings, too.*

Snarling, Perkar started forward again, but at that moment a horse slammed into him, battering him to the ground, and he had to raise Harka quickly to meet a Mang warrior's attack. The godblade flicked out deftly and impaled the man as he leapt down. When Perkar returned to his feet, he saw the earth itself rise in a column, form quickly into the Huntress, now massive, bearing the black antlers of an elk on the snarling head of a lion. The Tiskawa had just risen into the air, wind rushing furiously about him, his lower body hanging limp, when she gored him on her horns. The Life-Eater shrieked, but he also reached around her neck with both arms, and—incredibly—lifted the Huntress off the ground. Together they flew into the air, blown up like leaves in the curled fist of an autumn wind. Perkar saw the Huntress transform again into some sort of dark-pinioned bird, and then the two of them disappeared into the dense opaque vastness of the canopy, gone.

Gripping Harka even more tightly, he thought to follow—somehow—but at that moment his body sprouted a pair of arrows; his hauberk stopped their heads, but Harka drew him relentlessly to face his mortal opponents.

"You cannot kill the Tiskawa if you let these Mang hack you into pieces."

Grimly Perkar turned to his work, ashamed that, in his heart of hearts, he was relieved.

For the Tiskawa, he knew, would have killed him, and he wondered if he could face it again. Something that could give the Huntress such a battle . . .

Then there was no more time to think.

Sheldu's men attacked the thing, but Hezhi did not need to see the first of them die to understand that what they faced was a god of no mean strength; she had *seen* him instantly, knew that he formed from the water and dirt rather than emerged from it. She did not even reach for her drum, but as when she had captured the bull, Hukwosha, she merely slapped her palms together and opened the lake.

This time she did not hesitate; she called on Hukwosha, and the bull bolted gleefully to the task.

But we must manifest, the bull said. *We cannot fight only beneath the lake.*

"I don't know how to do that," Hezhi told him.

Give me your leave.

She hesitated only a moment; Tsem was rushing forward with his club, certainly to his death—despite his size, strength, and recently acquired skills. "You have it!" she cried. Might surged into her limbs, and she took in a breath that went on and on. Blood surged in her as her body thickened and distorted with agony that was so exquisite as almost to be pleasure; even before the change was done she was pounding across the earth on four cloven hooves. The colors of the world had faded to shadow, but her nostrils brought a new realm of sensation that she had never imagined and had little time to appreciate. She could smell Tsem, the acrid taint of his fear nearly masked by a sour anger. One of Sheldu's men had soiled himself, and Sheldu himself had no scent whatsoever. The leaf mold and the crisp freshness of the forest faded before the corruption of the attacking god and its sudden fear, stinking like a rotten corpse. Then he was on her horn, and she tossed him, gored him again, and slammed him into a tree. The dull salamander eyes glared at her feebly.

"Hezhi," it groaned—not from its froglike mouth, but from somewhere inside. "Hezhi, listen to me."

Hukwosha stepped back and hooked the monster anew on his horns and began to run joyfully.

"Listen!" Its eyes were fading.

"Talk, then," Hezhi bellowed. "You haven't long."

"Beware the Blackgod, he—"

Hezhi suddenly recognized the voice. "Moss? Moss, is that you?"

"Yes," the voice answered feebly.

"Hukwosha, stop," she commanded, but the bull continued to run, and sudden panic mingled with her elation.

Free, Hukwosha roared. *Free me.*

"No!" She wrenched at him then, grappled him back into her mansion, though it felt as if her body had burst into flame. She knew her body was changing again, and as that happened she sank into the unreal haze of the lake. The dying god shimmered, and she saw him—whoever he was. But linked to him she saw Moss, and he was impaled as plainly as the Salamander God.

"You've killed me," Moss sighed. "I was only trying to . . . I wouldn't have hurt *you.*"

"I'm sorry," she answered, and even in the flat cold of the otherworld she was.

"No matter," he gritted out. "I—" Then his eyes widened, and he vanished as if he had never been. An instant later she blinked and the sight was gone. She was Hezhi, a little girl, lying on the leafy floor of the forest. Nearby, the corpse of the Salamander God blubbered out a final breath, and then its spirit departed.

Through the woods she could hear Sheldu and the others approaching.

* * *

AFTER a tense moment, the task became simple butchery. The unholy creatures summoned by the Tiskawa were all dispatched, and the Mang, though indeed brave and fierce, were no match for the host of the Huntress, as Perkar well knew. The horsemen fell to lion and wolf, to the gods who were sometimes bears, to eagles and hawks that swooped upon them—and to Harka, of course.

Before it was over, Perkar wept for them.

Among the dead he found Moss, who was not dead, though his gut was torn open. The young shaman's eyes followed him, pleading.

"Listen to me, swordsman," he bubbled through a mouthful of blood. Perkar approached cautiously, mindful of what Chuuzek had managed in such a state.

"Listen," Moss repeated. "I have no way of knowing whether you are the Blackgod's dupe or willing ally. But I am slain now, and I saw Ghe carried off by the Huntress. You may be Hezhi's only hope."

"What nonsense is this?" Perkar growled.

Moss closed his eyes. "The lake comes to swallow me," he muttered. "I can't—" He opened his eyes again, and they held a peculiar blankness. "Perkar, are you still there?"

Perkar crouched down beside his foe. "I'm here," he said.

"I think I know what the Blackgod intends," the dying man whispered. "I think I understand now."

He whispered another sentence, and Perkar felt a profound chill. It was a sensation that gathered strength.

"Oh, no," he muttered, because he knew it was true. There could be no doubt.

"Karak must have conspired with the Huntress to separate me from her," he snarled. Moss nodded faintly.

"Does it hurt?" Perkar asked. "Are you in pain?"

"No. It's a sort of fading. Let me fade, if you will—it will prepare me. Many vengeful things await the ghosts of shamans, and we must have what advantages we can."

"Can I help?"

But Moss didn't answer. He was not yet dead, but it was clear that he had spoken for the last time. With Harka's vision Perkar could see the last thread of life unraveling.

Trembling, he stood, Moss' revelation repeating itself in his brain, and grimly he began to run back the way he had come. T'esh was dead, and the last of the Mang horses either fled or devoured. He had no chance of reaching his destination in time, but he also had no choice but to try; once again, it was all his fault.

XXXVI

~~~~~~

Erikwer

GHE tumbled through space, the treetops a nightmare blur that they sometimes hurtled over and sometimes crashed among. They fought with claws and teeth and with the energies burning within them, and almost as soon as they began, Ghe understood that he would lose. The Huntress was the most powerful being he had ever faced save the River himself. Her existence seemed to extend all about him, into the earth and the trees—this form he fought was only a *finger* of her. His sole satisfaction was knowing she was not toying with him; he was giving her a good fight, drawing power from her to hold himself together—but he was losing, for she was both more powerful and more experienced than he. For the first time, Ghe truly understood the sheer desperation of the River in creating him, the minusculity of his chances of success.

Nevertheless, he clung to her as she disemboweled him again and again.

"You hurt me," she admitted in a feral, growling voice. "Few have done that, so feel proud."

He didn't answer, for at that moment one of his arms tore free of his body. Again he was surprised at the lack of pain, and he wondered if there would be pain when she finally bit his head off. Shuddering, he called up all of the gods he had swallowed; he began to burn them for strength. The stream demon was strongest, would burn longest. He did not bother with the feeble fuel of his Human ghosts, though they shouted at him.

One shouted at him more loudly than the others.

River! he shouted. *Ghan* shouted.

Ghe understood in a blaze, but there was no triumph in that comprehension, for it came too late. He could scent him, his Maker, and he realized that their aerial battle had brought them very near his waters. So it *was* worth a try.

Using what strength he could, he tore himself from the Huntress and flew. For an instant he was free of her, and sprawling below him he could see trees, the rising flanks of mountains—and a gorge that pulsed with salvation. How could he have forgotten that his lord lay so near?

"No, you don't," the Huntress shrieked as sharp talons dug into what remained of his spine. "Oh, no, my sweet."

For an instant he went limp with despair, but then Ghan spoke again within him, a single word.

Hezhi.

Ghe snarled and struck his talons into the Huntress, reached for the beating heart of her power. He touched it and it surged through, burning him, tearing at him, far too much energy for him to absorb; his extremities charred and his vision blazed away with his eyes, and then they were falling, the Huntress shrieking and beating about him, but they were *still* falling. She had not recovered.

"No," she snarled, and then they hit something that broke them both.

"I'm fine," Hezhi said, stumbling toward Dark. But she *wasn't* fine. She had killed Moss, and though the man had been her enemy—or had he? She barely knew that anymore. The effort of fighting Hukwosha back into her heart had sapped her of strength, and she could barely stand.

"I've never seen anything like that," Sheldu muttered. "Not in a Human shaman. Surely—" He bit off his remark, seemed almost ready to chortle. "Come. Our success is certain now. In ridding us of that menace yourself, you have removed the last chance that we might be stopped."

"You mean because *you* wouldn't have to reveal yourself, Blackgod?" Hezhi muttered.

The man smiled grimly. "Well. I thought that Perkar might soften, eventually. But it matters not. I would have revealed myself to you—it is to this forest that I dare not show my power—not yet. The actions of a Human shaman such as yourself—"

"I don't understand what you're talking about," Hezhi groaned. "But shouldn't we get going?"

"Indeed."

As they continued their ride up the valley, Ngangata flanked her on one side and Tsem on the other.

"So you know," Ngangata said, his voice low.

She nodded. "Perkar told me."

"Give the word and we flee," the halfling said. "With your familiars and Tsem and me to stand for you, chances are good you can escape."

"Why? Why should I want to do that?" Hezhi asked. "This is what I want. I want to be rid of this malevolent thing our people call Lord. The thing that brought Ghan here to his death—that—that—" She stuttered off, realizing that she was dangerously near crying. She must not weaken now; the end of all of this, one way or the other, was nigh, she could feel that. She took a deep breath and continued. "I care not what designs your Crow God has, what hidden agenda his scheming covers. The truth is that compared to the River he is but a flea."

"A flea who believes he can slay the dog," Tsem muttered.

"And I believe he can, with my help," Hezhi said. "But he is still a flea."

"Do you imagine yourself more, Princess?" Tsem asked softly.

She looked at him, shocked, but then reflected on her words and smiled.

"It sounds like I do, doesn't it? It's just that I know what it feels like, the power in the River. Just now, when I was the bull, I felt I could do anything, and that takes more than a moment to forget."

Tsem bridled. "I wish *I* could forget it in a moment, Princess. If you could have seen yourself—"

"Hush, Tsem. I'm fine: I don't want to be a goddess. That is exactly what I want to be free of. Only the River can poison me with such might—the Blackgod and his kin cannot, will not do it. They have the same desire I do, to end the threat I pose."

"They could do that simply by killing you," Ngangata argued.

"True, which is why I do not fear the Blackgod. He has had ample opportunity to *slay* me and he has not. Why? In another generation the River can produce another like me, perhaps one more receptive to his will. As long as *he* exists, the threat I represent exists."

Ngangata shrugged. "Still, it is never wise to trust the Blackgod completely."

"Or *any* god. Or any person!" Hezhi answered. As she did so, Yuu'han drew abreast.

"An instant of your time, please," he asked of Hezhi.

"Of course." Hezhi was taken aback by the man's tight, formal tone.

"I have tried to dissuade Brother Horse from this trip many times," Yuu'han admitted. "He is an old man, and I fear for him."

"I have tried to turn him back, as well," Hezhi told him.

"I know. I thank you for that."

Hezhi regarded the young man. Since Raincaster's death, Yuu'han—always somewhat dour—had withdrawn from almost everyone but Brother Horse. "If you wish to try again . . ."

"I have done that, thank you. He will stay with you, and because he does, I do, as well."

"Your uncle means much to you."

Yuu'han raised his enigmatic gaze to lock fully on her own,

something the Mang were reluctant to do unless angry—or very, very sincere. "I call him uncle," Yuu'han said, quite softly. "I call him that because he was never married to my mother, and thus I have no right to call him 'father.' Nevertheless, he is the one who begat me. And when my mother died and her clan refused her orphan, Brother Horse drew me into his clan. Few would have done that; most would have let the mother's clan dispose of the child."

"Dispose?"

"The custom is to leave an unwanted child in the desert for the gods to take their mercy on." He glanced away at last, having impressed upon her what he wanted to.

Hezhi looked to Tsem and Ngangata for support; the halfling nodded to himself, but Tsem appeared confused, perhaps not following the entire conversation. Neither of them gave her any clue as to how she should respond to Yuu'han. "Why do you tell me this now?" she finally asked.

"So that if my unc—" Yuu'han paused and began again. "So that if Brother Horse and I are both slain, you will know how to sing to our ghosts. In death I may be spoken of as his son." He smiled wryly. "Understand me, this is no demand. My sword is yours, because Brother Horse is with you. I merely request this of you."

"I would rather promise that you will not be slain," Hezhi remarked.

"Do not promise me what is not in your power," Yuu'han warned. "Do not insult me."

"I will not insult you, cousin," Hezhi assured him. "If you are both slain, I shall do as you ask—provided I survive."

"I say the same," Ngangata assured him.

"Thank you. It is good." Seemingly content, Yuu'han dropped back to where Brother Horse rode.

Shortly they began climbing again, but it was to be a brief ascent. They mounted up out of the valley, and Hezhi realized then just how high they were; She'leng walled off most of the sky—they had scarcely begun ascending *it*—but even the valley they rode in was lofty, overlooking the folded layers of forest marching off from them.

Karak stood in his saddle. "Follow now," he said. "I grow impatient, and one more obstacle remains."

"What's that?"

"Some fifty Mang warriors await at the entrance to Erikwer, the place we seek."

"Fifty Mang?" Ngangata said, taking in the remaining warriors. "That is no small threat."

"For you, perhaps. For me, if I try to maintain my disguise. But my Lord Balat is slow to waken, and I am certain now that he sleeps." He turned to them, and his eyes were blazing now. Many of the men who followed him seemed taken a bit aback, uncertain.

"Know all of you who did not that I am Karak, the Raven, who made the earth and stole the sun to light it. This and many other things have I done for Humankind, for you are my adopted children. Many malign my intentions—" He paused and looked significantly at Ngangata. "—but you will find no tale of me that does not ultimately speak of my love and service to your kind, even in defiance of my Lord. You have all ridden with me, some knowing me, some not, to this place. You have fought and died so that I might preserve my identity until the time came to strike; that time is now, but we must hurry. I fly ahead to dispose of the brave but misguided warriors who yet stand before us; no more of you need die. But when I uncloak, when my power stands revealed, my Lord Balati will begin to wake from slumber. We must slay his Brother before that happens. Slaying him we free the land from a terrible burden and an even more terrible threat."

"And you from a great guilt!" Brother Horse shouted.

Karak leveled his yellow gaze at the Mang. "I freely admit my fault in the matter. Even such as I can make a mistake."

"It was no mistake," Brother Horse shouted heatedly. "It was caprice, like most of what you do."

Karak regarded the old man silently for a long moment.

"Were you there?" he asked softly. "Were *any* of you there, when the Changeling was unleashed, or do you just repeat the rumors my enemies have circulated for five millennia?" He glared around at them. "Well?"

"Enough!" Hezhi shouted. "Do what you must, Blackgod, and I will follow. Do you need any of the rest of them?"

Karak was still glaring angrily. "No," he answered.

"Then go."

For an instant longer, he remained Sheldu; and then, like a cloak turned inside out, he was suddenly a bird. At that instant, the wind rose. He beat his black wings up to a heaven now thick with gray clouds. When he was a speck, the trees began to shudder with the force of the wind.

Some hesitated, but when Hezhi kneed Dark forward, Ngangata and Tsem came after. Qwen Shen and Bone Eel followed closely, and after a moment's hesitation, all the rest.

In the middle distance, lightning began to strike and thunder to sound, a noise like the air itself shearing in halves. First one strike, then another, and then a crashing and flickering of blue light that raged continuously.

When they broke from the forest into the vast meadow, the thunder had ceased. They found the great black bird standing on a blackened corpse, pecking at its eyes. The meadow was littered with burnt and broken men. A few horses raced about aimlessly, eyes rolling.

As horrific as the sight was, Hezhi had become numb to death; what drew her attention and held it was not the corpses but the *hole*. It gaped in the center of the meadow like the very mouth of the earth itself, a nearly perfectly round pit that even a powerful bowshot might not cross the diameter of.

The Raven became a man, a black-cloaked man with pale skin. "That is Erikwer," he said. "That is the source of the Changeling, his birth—and his death." His birdlike eyes sparkled with unconcealed glee.

"What do we do?" Hezhi asked, her heart suddenly thumping despite all of her earlier bluster and confidence.

"Why, we must descend, of course," Karak said.

* * *

Perkar ran desperately, Harka flapping in a sheath on his back. Without the Huntress to direct them, the host was slowly dispersing, returning to whatever haunts or fell places they issued from. They didn't bother him; she must have set some sign upon him they recognized.

But he would never reach Hezhi and the others in time, and that drove him madder each moment, each heartbeat he had to understand what Moss told him.

"Can you give me more strength, help me run faster?" he asked Harka.

"No. *That is not the nature of my glamour, as you should know by now.*"

"Yes. You only keep me alive so that I can properly appreciate my mistakes."

"*What you run toward now could very well end that little problem of yours.*"

"So be it."

"*I thought you had learned fear.*"

"I have. Learned it and relearned it. It makes no difference now."

"*The Blackgod will do you no harm unless you attack him.*"

"It's moot, Harka, if we don't get there in time."

A movement caught his attention in the wood, something large and four-legged coming toward him. He whirled, blade bared in an instant.

"*Not an enemy,*" Harka said.

Perkar saw that it was not. It was a stallion, and more precisely, it was Sharp Tiger.

The stallion paced up to him and stopped, an arm's length away.

"Hello, brother," Perkar said softly. "Let me make you a deal. You let me ride you, and I will slay he who killed your cousin."

The horse stared at him impassively. Perkar approached, sheathed Harka, and took a deep breath. The beast was unsaddled; Perkar had long ago given up trying to ride him. Neither, in fact, did he have a bridle, but if the animal would accept him on its back, he could find a bridle and saddle from one of the dead beasts being devoured by the Hunt.

He blew out the breath and leapt upon Sharp Tiger's back, knotted his fist into the thick hair of the stallion's mane.

Nothing happened. Sharp Tiger didn't react.

"Good, my cousin," Perkar said, after a few instants went by. "You understand. Then let me find a bridle—"

Sharp Tiger reared and pawed the air, and Perkar hung on with his legs and fists with all of the strength in him, preparing for the inevitable, bracing for being thrown. But when the forehooves drove to earth, the Mang horse plunged straight into a gallop so swift that the wind sang in Perkar's ears, racing in amongst the trees and cornering so tightly that Perkar lay on the stallion's neck and wrapped his arms to keep from falling.

As the horse hurtled down a steep grade, leaping and stamping hooves, slipping but almost never slowing, Perkar gasped. "I hope you know where you are going, Sharp Tiger!"

For he had not the slightest control over the beast.

THE path into Erikwer wound down the side of the hole, a vast helix carved into the living basalt of the mountainside. Hezhi tried to imagine why such a hole might exist, a black tunnel bored straight down into the bosom of the world. She traced her gaze back up the way she had come; traveling single file, the entire party still did not complete the circumference of the pit. They had been once around, and in that time the steep path had dropped them into shadow. Sunlight still dappled the walls a bit above her, and bushes and scraggly juniper trees clung in crevasses and along the side of the trail, feeding on the light. At the rim a few Human heads were limned against the sky—Karak had left most of his men to guard against any remnants of the Mang who might yet arrive. Down, she could see nothing, save a vague glimmer in her godsight, the feel and smell of water rising to greet her.

Even here, even after all this time, she could recognize the River. Images danced before her on the black rock, on Tsem's back as he strode in front of her, and behind her lids when she blinked. The sun-drenched rooftops of Nhol, the Water Temple shining as if cut from white cloud, and beyond them the River, all majesty and puissance. In her heart she had never really feared him, but only herself. In her heart, he was still Lord, still Father, still Grandfather.

But there were other images, other sensations. The monstrous ghost chasing her in the Hall of Moments, seeking the blood signaling her womanhood. Soldiers fighting and dying to stop it. D'en, her beloved cousin, twisted and mindless and imprisoned beneath the deep labyrinth of the underpalace. The scale on her arm pulsing. She *knew* what she must do, but entering into the place of his beginning, she could not feel outrage or anger—and only faintly could she feel purpose. What she did feel was what a daughter might, entering the bedroom where her father slept, scissors tight in her hands and murder in her heart, despite what that father had done and would continue to do.

It was more of a relief than anything else to know that matters were out of her hands. The strange and alien presence of the Blackgod was now a comfort. Back in the yekt, she had first felt the burden of guiding herself and her friends, of choosing one path of many, all dangerous. For months she had shouldered that burden, until Perkar came out of his depression and began making decisions—and now, finally, with Perkar gone, someone had stepped in to fill his place. It was good, for she had no strength for it. It was not something she was *meant* for; a princess did not make decisions; she only married well and then let her husband serve those needs. Ghan had tried to bring her up to it, but that had turned out badly all around, especially for Ghan. No, she only wanted to be alone again, by herself, with no one wanting her or needing her, no decisions to make beyond when and what to eat.

After such furious action, it was odd that the very last leg of their journey should be so slow, so measured. They had left their mounts above; even the most trustworthy steed would be a danger here, and their horses were ridden nearly to death, could barely stand. All those climbing down were silent, as if the majesty and presence of Erikwer physically forbade speech. She had leisure—for the first time—to realize that Perkar might be dead, to remember the few moments of tenderness that had passed between them since they met. It was a strange, braided thing they felt for one another, she thought; so like love, so like hate, implacable and fragile at the same time. She tried to summon some anger at Perkar for his deception, for drawing her close and then coldly thrusting her away, but she could not find it; not when he might already be a wraith, winging up to the mountain summit and the merciless gods who dwelt there. Whether he lived or died, he and the Huntress had done what they set out to do, played their part in *her* destiny: stopped Moss and Ghe and the army of Mang who sought to return her to the bosom of the River.

Instead she would go to his head and stab a spike into his brain. But how? Only Karak knew.

And as they descended, the air sank past them in a faint breeze, as if the hole were eternally inhaling. The breeze grew cooler as the light dimmed, as eventually the hole above them shrank and dimmed as night fell over it as well, at which point Karak's men—the ten who accompanied them down—lit torches. The god's breath fattened the flames and caused them to lick downward now and then. Before it was entirely dark, she heard water, a sort of shushing that increased in volume. Soon it filled everything, hummed gently both inside and outside of her skull. Water.

And then, with no ceremony whatsoever, the shaft opened into a vaster place on all sides save the one the path continued on. That descended to a shingle of a black beach, and the yellow flowers of the torches were caught and reflected by a vast, restless sea that stretched out into the darkness. A roof of stone hung over it, vaulting up but always low, and the feeling was an eerie combination of claustrophobia and infinity. The last of them—some of Karak's men—stepped onto the shingle, where the underground sea lapped up and down against the rounded black pebbles that stretched out from the mounds of talus fallen from above. Hezhi gazed up, hoping to see a star, but there was nothing—save for perhaps a vague clattering, high above.

"Now, come here, child," Karak breathed. He still wore Human shape, but his nose was thin and beaklike, and in the torchlight his eyes gleamed with fierce triumph and anticipation.

"Come here, and we shall slay him."

Trembling, Hezhi moved to comply.

XXXVII

Changeling Blood

WATER again, his comfort and womb. Life again, too, but this time he did not emerge into light and air. The River took Ghe and dragged him through the cold and dark.

He was different. The parts of him charred and torn by the Huntress had grown back, but not as Human flesh. Bony plates compassed him, and he propelled himself with limbs more like flippers or fins than arms, kicked something—*not* legs—that he feared even to think about.

His eyes saw the River bottom and the rippling mirror of the surface, and the bare, sterile stone over which he flowed. But another eye—a deeper one—saw something far, far ahead of him.

He searched through his servants and found a few still there. The stream demon, the stalker, and the ghosts of Ghan and the blind boy. The old lord—Lengnata—was there, too, though he was weakened or perhaps terrified into an almost unthinking state. Others—the many that he had bound on the journey across the plain with Moss—were part of him no longer, destroyed or released in his battle with the Huntress. As for *that* one—the

Beast Goddess—the *River* had eaten her. She was *gone*, utterly and without a trace.

And now he was no longer Ghe the ghoul, but Ghe the *fish*, the serpent, the *thing*. Not Ghe at all, though he knew he had never been *that*, not since Perkar took his head. If only he had, at least, the satisfaction of knowing for certain that the pale man was dead, too. . .

You are Ghe, Ghan disagreed, a disembodied voice sharing his prison of plates, stings, and spines. *Despite all that the River has done, part of you is Ghe. I know that now.*

Shut up, old man, Ghe thought. He did not need the scholar's lies and advice anymore. His only reason for existence was to serve the River's will.

If he could enforce his will himself, he would, Ghan insisted. *You saw what he did to the Huntress, how invincible he is in his own domain. If he resorts to making ghouls of dead men, it is to go places where he cannot go himself. But that means that in those places, he does not control you. You can do what is right rather than what he wills.*

"What he wills *is* what is right," Ghe answered angrily. "I am not capable of doubting that. You should understand by now. If you cut up a tree, and make it from a tree into a boat, it is a *boat*, whether you are there to sail it or not. The River made me to find Hezhi. It is the only thing I am capable of!"

If a ghost could vent an exasperated, impatient sigh, Ghan's did. *I'll give you a different metaphor, my friend. If a smith makes a sword, he has no assurance that the weapon he has forged cannot be turned back upon him. You have my memories and knowledge, but I can see yours, as well. I believe you can be turned,* Ghan pressed. *Not by me, but by yourself. I know what I know.*

"You know that the Blackgod and the Ebon Priest are the same. I never saw that." It was too hard to think the way Ghan was asking him to think.

I was going to tell you. Qwen Shen and Bone Eel took me before I could.

"I know that, too," Ghe replied. Overhead, the light filtering through the water abruptly darkened. *We are underground now,* he suddenly understood.

I think Bone Eel may be the dangerous one, Ghan persisted.

"I agree," Ghe returned. "And I think I know who he may be. But what will they do with Hezhi? What is their plan? How can the *River* be killed?"

I don't know, Ghan answered. *But I believe Hezhi is in great danger, or I would never willingly aid you.*

I know that, too.

It grew even darker, and as it did so, his other sight began to fade. It was like being beneath the Water Temple, his senses fading as his potence grew. His surety and his direction vanished, and to his enormous frustration, he felt himself becoming confused. *Again.*

He finally stopped swimming; the water about him was barely moving.

What do I do now? But neither Ghan nor any other part of him knew the answer to that.

And then, in the darkness, a beacon flared, one that seared him with pain, one that struck like a bolt into the River himself. Ghe turned and strained his body to swim as fast as he could, gathering his strength as he went.

THE Blackgod took her gently by the hand and led her to the edge of the water. Her trembling worsened, for suddenly she could feel the power there, latent in the pool. It lay quietly, stupidly, unlike the River she knew, but it was he, without doubt. If she wanted the power she need only reach for it, but it would not enter her against her will, not like before. She would become a goddess only by choice and if she had not chosen it before, she would certainly not choose it *now.*

"What do I do?" she whispered. They had moved far from the torches, though Tsem and Ngangata kept edging after them.

"What are you doing, Karak?" Ngangata snarled.

"What I told you," he answered. "What we came here for."

"What—" Hezhi began again, but then something cold slid through the flesh of her ribs, and though she tried to shout with pain, her breath sucked in and closed on itself. She gazed down in shocked astonishment and saw Karak's hand gripping the hilt of a knife. As she watched, he twisted it.

Then several things happened at once. Tsem repeated Ngangata's question, stepping even closer. Ngangata suddenly exploded into action, whipping an arrow from the sheath on his back and setting it to his bow in a single motion. As the pain from the twisting knife hazed her vision, Brother Horse and Yuu'han drew swords and swung at Bone Eel, who was in the act of pointing a white tube of some sort at Ngangata. Hezhi saw all of this in an incredible blaze of light and lucidity as a single drop of her blood squirted from off Karak's blade and struck the surface of the water; a column of white flame leapt up and ignited the very air.

Then the pain truly caught her, and she realized that there was steel *in* her, and without a single thought she lashed at Karak.

What happened then wasn't clear to her, save that the knife wrenched out and she was shoving her fist into the hole in her side. Karak stumbled away from her, sheeted in blue flame—while *she* was hurled back onto the shingle. She hit and slid, able to think only about the blood that soaked her dress with preposterous speed. She had done something to Karak; he was clutching his eyes—

Her heart reached hummingbird pitch, and the motion around her seemed to slow, so that she could almost leisurely pick out the details of the strange dance being performed for her benefit, there in a stygian courtyard that only a god could imagine. But she could *do* nothing, *say* nothing, because her thoughts were all gushing from her side with the waters of her life.

Tsem hit the Blackgod with his club, and the god pitched back, an arrow appearing in him at almost the same moment. Qwen Shen shrieked as Yuu'han hewed into her, the sorcerous flowers of energy gathering on her fingertips suddenly withering. Brother Horse struck his sword through Bone Eel, but Hezhi could see a coiled serpent of power in the nobleman, revealed as it was unleashed. All of his strands surged into the pointed bone tube he held. As Brother Horse stepped back to gather for a second swing, Bone Eel turned faster than a snake, and the tube he was holding suddenly telescoped, shot out like an improbably fast-growing stalk of grass; it passed all the way through Brother Horse, who stood transfixed for a moment before dropping his sword. Heen, worrying at Bone Eel's leg, went flying, yelping, through the air.

Hezhi choked on a scream, kicking away from it all, crawling back over the black stones, life leaking out of the *hole* in her.

The light from the burning blood was fading, but she could see perfectly well as Tsem hit the Blackgod again, and again, and again, until his club broke. Ngangata rushed toward her, but Bone Eel turned and the weird thing he held suddenly lanced out again, passed through the halfling's shoulder. He gasped and collapsed, bow clattering to the ground.

He's killing my friends, she realized. *Why?*

Hukwosha answered her. *Does it matter? Release me. I shall deal with him.*

"Release you?" Hezhi muttered. The scene was wavering. She felt very weak. "Very well."

And she did.

HUKWOSHA sprang into the frail and wounded body with a terrible shout of triumph, a bellow to shake the heavens. Too long had he been bound by first this godling and then that, and finally, humiliation upon humiliation, by mortal Man and Woman! But wounded and half out of her mind, *this* one had released him, and he did not intend to pass the opportunity by. Before him lay an entire world, as it had in the beginning, in the darkling plain even before Karak brought the sun. What cared he for these scheming gods and their demented brother?

But it nagged him to run. Hezhi wanted him to stop the man with the tube—he had killed Brother Horse and Ngangata! No, he saw that that wasn't true; the old man was fumbling with his drum, albeit feebly. Yet what did *he*, Hukwosha, care for the old man, for Hezhi's desires? He bunched his muscles and prepared to go—as an *attack* struck him, the point of Bone Eel's jumping spear-bone turning on his hide. His fierceness overwhelmed his reason then. He turned on the man—ah! not a man, but a Lemeyi, one of those silly half-god sorcerers. He lowered his horns. *Little creature,* Hukwosha thought, *you've made a singular mistake.*

His first charge lifted the puny thing from its feet, rammed him into the stone wall. Fierce energies rained upon him, attacks gnawed at his heart, and given time they might have succeeded; but he twisted the immortal heartstrands on his horns and snapped them, sent all of Bone Eel's potence out into the air to fade. Then he shook the impudent, broken thing from him.

When he turned, there was Karak, rising up over the body of Tsem like the shadow of the carrion bird he was. Karak appeared unhappy.

"Hezhi," he snarled. "You fool. You are wasting your blood, don't you know that? It is the only thing that can slay him!"

"My blood?" Hukwosha snarled.

"You will slay him and take his *place*, Hezhi. You will not die, you will become a goddess. But you must stop fighting me." Then his face hardened further. "Or fight me, it matters not."

Hukwosha lowered his horns to charge again, but sudden weakness jolted through him. He became aware of the gash in his side, shifted his hand in it in the vague hope that the blood would stop pouring out, wondering where his horns and hooves and *might* had all run off to.

"Hukwosha—" Hezhi began, but Karak reached out with an impossibly long talon and ripped Hukwosha from her, tore the great bull into shards of light, scattered them on the water. He fixed what remained—*her*—with the suddenly argent orb of one eye.

"Now, child, your blood. It is for the best. There *must* be a River, you know. It just need not be *him.*"

Hezhi stumbled back, but all of the bull's strength was gone. "I don't want to be a goddess," she murmured, as if trying to explain something *simple* to a child.

"You have no choice. Only his blood can slay him—and *you* we can control. We will not make the same mistake we made with him. Perhaps Balati need never know at all, once you wear the Changeling's clothing."

He stepped forward.

"Not just yet," shouted *something* as it arose from the water.

P ERKAR'S fingers tingled as he loosened his death grip on Sharp Tiger's mane. That wasn't easy to do, for the Mang stallion continued down the narrow spiral trail, if not at a *full* gallop, well beyond a canter. No horse could be so surefooted, but Sharp Tiger seemed either unaware of or unconcerned about that simple fact. Still, Perkar knew he would need feeling in his hands soon, feeling enough to wield Harka one last time, and so he unknotted his fingers from the thick black hair and let his legs hold him on, allowed himself a moment of reluctant humor at the memory of the expressions on the faces of Karak's men as he and the stallion crashed from the woods, through their ranks, and into the pit.

He wondered how much farther down he had to travel; night had fallen, and he could no longer make out the opening to the sky, nor tell how fast and far he had already descended.

He remembered the last time he had entered Balat, what seemed like centuries ago. Could he really have been so proud, so arrogant, so absolutely sure of himself? It didn't seem possible. When he entered the mountain, he had been a boy, full of dreams and ideals and hopes higher than the stars. When he left he had felt old, used, and worn. Scores of days had passed before the first *glimmer* of light had entered back into his soul. One such glimmer had been Brother Horse, when he met the old man, hiding on an island in the Changeling. Another had been Ghaj, the widow near

Nhol who taught him that he could find pleasure with other than a goddess. But in the end, in the aftermath, it had been Hezhi who brought real joy back to him.

Why hadn't he ever admitted that? Because he would rather force her to share blame for his crimes than enjoy her company? Because he feared she could never care for a killer and a fool?

His scalp prickled and he urged Sharp Tiger on for the first time since mounting him. Incredibly, the stallion *did* increase his speed in response, though Perkar would not have believed that possible. He recalled, with a sudden chill wonder, part of a song Raincaster once sang—*tried* to sing, anyway, in Perkar's own tongue, so that he would understand it. In Mang it had flowed glissando, one syllable to the next. In Perkar's language it had rung stilted but still powerful—wounded but not crippled.

> And whosoever should kill you
> Bright steed, blood-girded brother
> Let him beware, let him fear
> *My* life, become a weapon
> Such that vengeance itself will
> Appear a small, whimpering thing.
> This I swear to you as I live
> And when buzzards pick my bones
> And when my bones are dust
> Four-hooved brother.

A man would avenge his steed as he would a relative, according to the ancient word and blood of the Horse Mother. Would a horse do the same for its rider? Would the Horse Goddess aid such a purpose?

He would find out soon enough, he was sure—if he wasn't too late. Had the Blackgod already slain Hezhi? Had her blood already destroyed the Changeling and replaced him? The sick feeling in his gut told him that deep down, he must have always known that Karak's solution would be this. What had he pictured, some sort of battle royal, them flailing at the water with their swords? A jar of the god's essence that they could simply crack? No, this was the only way that made sense. Human blood had such a powerful effect on gods, and Hezhi's blood was both Human and Changeling. It would flow down him like hemlock, numbing him as it went so that he wouldn't even know he was dead until the last drop of him reached the sea. And in his place would be Hezhi, or whatever it was that Hezhi had become—a goddess, but perhaps one that Karak and his kin could exert more influence over. A weaker River Goddess with less ambitious aims.

But *Hezhi* would be dead. The woman just waking in her child's face would never come fully alive; she would never read another book or see another herd of wild cattle. And she would be lost to him.

It always comes back to me, he thought angrily.

If only he weren't too late.

Ghe rose from the water, trembling with power and rage at what he saw. Hezhi lay before him, her blood and life leaking out of her like a flower cut off at the stalk. Others lay about, dead or dying, and a clump of soldiers who emanated only confusion but were now turning toward him. Qwen Shen was among the dead—he regretted that bitterly, for he would have preferred to dispense her punishment himself—and Bone Eel was among the mortally wounded. Bone Eel's Human guise had been stripped bare, however, and the fading life Ghe saw was that of the guardian of the Water Temple, the foul creature who had made *pets* of emperors. Another regret; but Bone Eel—or whatever the thing was really named—was still fading, so perhaps there would be time to punish *him*.

Presiding over the massacre was what could only be the Blackgod, a maelstrom of power, standing above Hezhi like her executioner. He turned angrily at Ghe's challenge, his aura sharpening into a threat of power greater than even that of the Huntress. But he had defeated the Huntress, had he not? And the cold expanse of water below him would absorb any amount of energy he cared to take. Still, before attacking, he reached out and ate the approaching warriors as a first course.

He sprang with the speed and force of a javelin, and the Blackgod fell back. Desperately he plunged stinger and claw— both physical and arcane—through the weird flesh of the being, hoping to quickly find the artery of his strength. If the discharge burnt him, so be it.

Lightning speared him, burnt a hole in the tough plates of his belly large enough for a cat to crawl through. Every muscle in his body clenched into knots so tight that some pulled loose of the bone. Another bolt flashed, lit the underground lake with violet light, and he was torn loose from the Bird God, thrown roughly to the shingle, twitching.

The Blackgod laughed as Ghe struggled to regain control of his inhuman limbs, his strength ebbing with each instant. The water was near, but it was as if a wall had been erected between him and that source of life. Feebly he tried to crawl.

"So this is the best Brother can send against me," the Blackgod mocked, shaking his head and clucking. "Let me introduce myself, Ghe of Nhol. I am Karak, sun-bringer, storm lord, master of rain and thunder, the Raven, the Crow."

"You are a corrupt demon," Ghe snarled, "and you must die."

"Oh, indeed?" Karak asked, and lightning lit the cavern once again in a hideous similitude of twilight.

Perkar beheld the tableau below, long before the lightning; Harka gave him vision in the darkness. And so it was with a sense of unbelievable helplessness that he watched the tiny figures meet and fall, not certain who any of them were. A monster rose from the water and attacked one of the shapes, and then came the lightning, and from that he knew which participant was Karak.

He and Sharp Tiger were a single turn of the spiral path from the cavern floor—perhaps the height of fifteen men from the stones—when a third peal of thunder roared up through the pit; Perkar saw, almost precisely below him, the shadowy form of the

Blackgod and the blasted carcass of some fishlike monster. To his horror, he also saw Hezhi crumpled nearby, an unmistakable pool of blood spreading beneath her. Brother Horse, Yuu'han, Ngangata, and Tsem all lay immobile on the black stones. *All* of the warriors who came with Karak lay still. He knew he should be angry, but all he could summon was a vague denial and a rising wind of fear. Too far, too long to complete the last turn as Karak, the clear victor, turned to Hezhi's body.

Perkar suddenly stiffened as the air rang like an iron bell, and through saddle, flesh, and bone Perkar suddenly saw Sharp Tiger's heart glow like a red-hot anvil, heard the stallion scream, felt him leap into space. It was no slip, no mistake; the horse laid back his ears and jumped. Perkar's mind—already staggered—simply refused to accept what had happened for an instant, but as the fall took his weight and filled his stomach with feathers, a sudden wild elation stifled a nascent yelp. "Brave boy, Tiger," he had time to say instead, before he and the vengeful mount of Good Thief crashed into the black-cloaked figure.

The impact robbed him briefly of his senses, but Harka would not let him plunge into true unconsciousness, shrieking alarm in his ears. It was a good thing; he regained his feet at the same moment as Karak. Sharp Tiger, unbelievably, was still alive, struggling to rise on four broken legs. With a snarl, Karak reached and slapped the stallion's skull; it split open, and the beast died. Perkar hoped—in the brief instant he *had* to hope—that Mang legend was true, that Sharp Tiger and Good Thief would be reunited as one on some far-off steppe. Then he had no time for thoughts of that sort or otherwise as he fell upon Karak with Harka.

The first five or so blows landed, and Karak tripped back, golden blood glistening from several wounds. Perkar howled, swinging the blade savagely, not so much like a sword as like an axe, as if he were hewing deadwood. Karak's daunting yellow eyes stayed steady on him, but he knew that he must just keep his attack going, not give the god a single pause, keep the fear from gathering tight in his chest to slow his arms.

A black fist leapt past his guard and smote him with such force that he felt bones crack in his jaw. He slapped into the ground, rolled, and came back up with his blade ready.

Karak loomed over him, still with Human form and face but glossy black save for the orbs of his eyes. He shook his head *no*. "Pretty thing, is this how you repay me? I am only doing what I said I would do. Stand aside and let me finish what we began together."

"I won't let you kill her," Perkar shouted. "Not even to slay the Changeling."

"She won't *die*," Karak returned. "Only her flesh will die. She will become mightier than she ever dreamed. Otherwise, she is dead already. Her body is beyond saving."

Perkar glanced again at Hezhi's feebly moving form, heart sinking at the sight of her pale face and the huge pool of blood. Could such a tiny creature contain so much blood? It didn't seem possible.

"Her death will be meaningless unless she bleeds her last into the Changeling," Karak hissed urgently. "She will have died for *nothing*, when she needn't die at all. But we must hurry!"

Perkar turned slowly back to the Crow God, knowing that he had already done his best and failed. But the storm of dread in his belly, instead of rising to a cyclone, began to *break*, diminish. "Between the two of us, Karak, we have brought about the deaths of everyone I hold dear," he said measuredly, wishing he had something more profound to offer as last words. "I have lost my Piraku and betrayed my people, and you were behind it all. So let one or both of us die today—and I hope for the sake of the world it is *both*. And if it is me, you may do as you will." He raised Harka.

Karak sighed and reached to a sheath at his own side. "Very kind of you, to give me your leave. I could deal with you as I did *him*," he said, indicating the fish-thing. With a horrible start, Perkar saw that it had a man's face—the face of the Tiskawa, in fact. "But *you* I will give a chance to die with Piraku, for you have served me well, Perkar Kar Barku." He drew his blade. "Do you recognize this sword?"

Perkar stared, his mouth suddenly dry. "Yes," he admitted unwillingly, haltingly. "It is *my* sword. The one my father gave me."

"*Is* it? I found it in a pool of red blood, here in this very mountain. I had it retempered to suit me. But I must correct you in one particular; since you threw it away, it is *my* sword now."

"*Something very strange about that blade,*" Harka warned him, but Perkar was beyond reason. The sudden fury that filled him was greater than any he had ever known, a tenebrous joy that could not distinguish between killing and dying. He flung himself at the Blackgod, Harka curving out and down.

"HEZHI," a voice muttered from very near. She turned to see Brother Horse, clutching a drum in one hand.

"Grandfather," she whispered back.

"Can you see it? Can you see what you need?"

"Brother Horse, I'm dying."

"Listen to me," he snarled angrily. "I told you I wouldn't let you do that. Won't let you die! Listen to me . . ." But his eyes fluttered and he spat blood.

"What?" she asked, though she hardly felt concerned anymore—instead she felt strangely serene, light-headed.

"There." He pointed at the thing that might have once been Ghe. "See, beneath the lake. Look beneath the lake."

She looked. It was easy, for death was dragging her beneath anyway. She first saw Brother Horse, a fading warmth, his ghost already coming unmoored.

I can take him in, she thought. *Like a god, keep him in my breast.* She reached to do so.

But above the lake, his hand clutched hers. "No," he barely whispered. "You don't have the strength for that. You need me like *this*." His eyes gleamed with laughter, love, and comfort as he gripped her hand more tightly. "Tell Heen I said farewell," he murmured. "Heen tells me he loves you . . ." Then his eyes lost their light as a flame surged into her, filled her with new strength.

And Brother Horse was gone, his hand already cooling, no trace of his heartstrands remaining.

Look beneath the lake, he had said, and, trembling, she did so, afraid to waste his last gift on anguish.

The "waters" closed over her. *I am dying,* she realized again. *The Blackgod stabbed me.* And, finally, she understood Karak's words, saw the use her blood would be put to, the results it would bring. She had to stop that somehow—and Brother Horse had seen how she could do it, seen some weapon she might use. He had pointed at Ghe.

She saw Karak still—a black thing of feathers and blue fire in the otherworld. She saw Ghe, too, knew him instantly. He still resembled some sort of inky net, with the scintillating bulbs of stolen souls bound to him like jeweled weights. But the net was rent, the pattern of his body in disarray. A few souls still glimmered there, however, and she reached, featherlight, to touch them.

Her swan and mare were still with her, though injured as she was. The swan guided her and the mare held her up, and together they brushed her fingers through the shattered remains of Ghe. One of the souls responded to her tentative inquiry, produced a voice that floated thinly to her.

"Hezhi?" it said. "Hezhi?"

She paused. She knew that voice. "Ghan?"

"Indeed," he answered, gathering a bit of strength.

"Ghan, how did you—"

"I died. He captured my ghost—a fairly simple matter for him."

"Ghan, I have so much to tell you," she began. An image of him formed in her mind, his parchmentlike face, the knowing twinkle in his black eyes that could so often glare with irritation. She had lost Brother Horse, but here Ghan was back.

He laughed. "No time for that. No time for that at all."

"No time for anything, I think," she said.

"No, you are wrong. Ghe is stronger than the Blackgod knows, and I think if we can win his help, there is yet something we can do. But Hezhi, we must hurry."

"Tell me what to do then."

He told her.

Harka slashed down as Karak's blade rose to meet it, and the two came together in a shower of sparks. In Perkar's ear, Harka shrieked piteously. He had never known the weapon could feel pain or fear, but now both shuddered through him, as if the blade had become his own arm, skin removed and nerves laid bare.

Karak hammered down a second blow, and Perkar raised his blade to meet it.

"*No!*" Harka screamed; then steel clashed and the godblade burst into a thousand bits. The hilt leapt from his hand, and in his ear, Harka's dying cry faded into nothing. Perkar swayed, weaponless, in the following silence.

"Now," Karak said, "that silliness is over with." He bent toward Hezhi's body.

An arrow shaft appeared in his eye. Karak shrilled and straightened, seeking his new attacker. Ngangata stood less than a score of paces away. Half of his body was soaked in red Human blood, but he raised his bow for a second shot. Karak darted forward, faster than a mortal eye could follow, and in that eyeblink his sword plunged into the halfling's chest. Ngangata snarled and yet tried to raise his weapon, but Karak twisted the blade, and Ngangata's eyes turned to Perkar. They brimmed with tears of agony, but his gaze held no self-pity or even fear—it conveyed *apology*. Apology—for having failed him. Perkar leapt once again, shrieking inarticulately, still unarmed, bent upon tearing the Crow God apart with his bare hands. With a flashed look of utter disdain, Karak turned and ran *him* through, as well, the blade sliding into his navel and out his back. He knew no shock at being impaled, because in the past year he had taken more than one such wound. But before, he might have fought up the blade, or at least quickly disengaged himself. Now he merely glared at his murderer, still refusing to admit it was over.

Karak held him up with the blade for an instant, yellow eyes bright with contempt. "See how you like *that* without a magic sword to heal you," he spat.

"Ah," Perkar moaned. Karak released the hilt. Sword still in his belly, Perkar felt his knees wobble and give way, and he sat down roughly.

He almost fell on Ngangata. The halfling was still alive, though just barely so. Karak regarded them for just a moment, then stepped toward Hezhi.

"I-I'm sorry," Ngangata managed to stammer.

"Shut up, you dumb Brush-Man," Perkar whispered. "You didn't do anything wrong."

"I could have ... I could have ..." Ngangata seemed confused, unable to think of what he might have done.

Trembling, Perkar leaned over and kissed him on the forehead. "*I'm* the one who is sorry, brother. Piraku with you and about you." He patted the dying halfling on the shoulder. "I've got just one more thing to do," he said, feeling a little giddy but otherwise surprisingly well, considering. "Then I'll come join you here."

Ngangata nodded but said nothing.

Perkar put both hands on the sword hilt, closed his eyes, and *pulled*.

GHE brushed his lips upon Hezhi's and felt triumph. He, a gutter scorp from Southtown, had kissed a *princess*. He stepped back from her, wanting to see her lovely eyes, *hoping* to see love there.

What he saw instead was urgency.

"Hello, Yen," she said very seriously.

"Princess."

"I need your help."

Ghe noticed for the first time that there were other figures behind Hezhi. They all stood in the little courtyard above Nh l, where Hezhi had taken him once to look down at the ships. But he understood that could not be where they were as his memories—what little remained of them—returned.

"I've failed you," he said, feeling hot, unaccustomed tears start in his eye, remembering the Blackgod carving him with a knife of living thunder.

"Not yet. There is still time," Ghan said from behind Hezhi. The third figure was the stream demon, the woman—she sat sullenly on the bench by the cottonwood tree. Near her, looking old and defeated, stood the ancient Nholish lord he had captured in the Water Temple. Lengnata was fat, his eyes piggish little dots.

"Where are we, really?" he asked Hezhi.

"In your mansion. The place where you keep the souls you capture."

"How did you get here?"

"I came to see you, Ghe. Because there is something you can do to save me."

"Anything."

"You must slay the River to do it."

Ghe's limbs began to quake. He shuddered violently. "I can't do that. You have to know I can't do that. Even if I had the power—"

Anger wrote itself on her features. "You owe me," she declared. "You made me think you liked me, maybe *more* than liked me. You owe me."

"I *love* you," he whispered.

"I don't know what that means," she retorted, but softening. "But I know that I need your help."

"I cannot slay the River!"

Ghan interrupted him. "Have you forgotten Li again, Ghe? We found bits of her in you, in your memory, hidden away and dimmed from your waking mind. The River tried to clean them out of you. He made you *kill* her, Ghe, because he would not give you what few memories you cherished."

Hezhi held something out to him—not something physical,

but fragments of his mind, like a shattered mirror. Images of an old woman, her love for him, the care that only she had ever lavished upon him. A day long ago, on the levee of the River . . .

"He did steal her from me, didn't he? Why did he do that?"

Hezhi reached up and brushed the hair from his eyes. "To keep you from being distracted. A real man—one with his own thoughts and motives and loves—a real man makes a poor weapon for the River. The River hates us because he will never really understand us, no matter that he wants our bodies as vessels. He *hates* you, Ghe, hates me, simply *because* he needs us. I know what it's like, to have him in me. I do." She laid her hand on his shoulder. "But Ghe, he made you *from* a man. Part of you is still a man. And despite what you did to me, you don't deserve what *he* has done to you. Neither of us deserves it. I am *dying*, Ghe. Only you can save me."

An inchoate anger was growing in him, but still he persisted. "I . . . He made me *so*. I cannot but serve him."

"No," Hezhi said. "No, if you love me, you can serve *me*. You once told Ghan that whatever *I* wanted—"

"I lied! Ghan knows that."

"You thought you lied," Ghan said. "But I believed you because it was a deeper truth than you knew. It was the man in you, rather than the Riverghost."

Ghe stilled his trembling, braiding his anger and his love. He reached into the secret, cold place that had helped him kill, back when he had been merely Human, when a misstep meant his own death, when compassion was a deadly thing. He wove that into the fibers, too, a warp to lay the weft through. *I am a blade of silver, I am a sickle of ice,* he whispered, and finally, once again, he *was*.

"What must I do?" he heard himself say.

Hezhi leaned up and kissed the scar on his chin, the first wound he ever received. "I'm sorry," she said. "But what you have to do is die. But we will help you." And she gestured to the stream demon.

"Die," he considered. "I have to die." He focused on her again, on the exquisite shape of her face. "Will you forgive me then?"

"I already forgive you, Ghe."

"Call me Yen."

She smiled. "Yen."

IT took three pulls to remove the sword, each more painful than the last, and the final heave was followed by a gout of blood that he knew must surely have drained him. Nevertheless, though his legs felt like wood, he struggled to stand.

Nearby, another *huge* figure stood over Hezhi, which Perkar recognized as Tsem. The Giant interposed himself between the girl and the god.

"This is getting tiresome," Karak said. "Perkar, lay down and die. Tsem . . . oh, never mind." He raised his hand.

A scorpion stinger as thick as a Human leg struck the god as a nightmare jumble of limbs and plates suddenly crawled back into motion. Karak rolled his eyes—not in pain but in irritation—and struck the thing away with his hand. "And you!" he snapped. The monster with the face of the assassin from Nhol rose unsteadily on several spiderlike legs. It should have been dead—Perkar could see the hole in it, how burnt and charred it was. Only its head remained Human, and it was the Human eyes that held Perkar, not the monstrous body.

"Perkar," the thing croaked.

He was *so* weak. His knees shook. He didn't even know what he imagined he would do with the sword he had just pulled from himself. Strike Karak one more useless blow? But here was this thing, the thing that had eaten the Stream Goddess. . .

He raised his sword, though the earth sought to drag it from his hand.

He carried his weight into the swing, knowing that if he missed it wouldn't matter anyway, he would never stand to attack again. He wondered dully why the Tiskawa tilted its head back, as if *inviting* the blow.

The Blackgod was perhaps more injured than he let on, for though he lunged to place himself between Perkar and the River-thing, he was too slow to avoid Tsem's broken club, which struck him in the shoulder blade and caused him to stumble. Then it was too late, and the sword Perkar's father had given him—the sword forged by the little Steel God Ko—bit deeply.

For the second time, Perkar watched Ghe's head leave its body. It was strange that the final expression to grace the assassin's face seemed to reflect victory rather than defeat.

XXXVIII

Horse Mother

Blood geysered into the cavern, spewing from the stump of the River-thing's neck. It fell toward the lake and gouted liquid into the water, and the water *burned*. It caught like dry leaves in high autumn, like pitch. Glorious light of many colors gyred and capered madly in the cavern, and Perkar sank back to his knees beneath the rainbow dance of the River's death—and his own. And though wonder should have been shocked out of him, he still laughed and wept tears of joy when he saw, amongst those flames, a lithe form he had once loved, the Goddess of the Stream, hair coursing opalescent as she skated across the surface of the dying god.

"What have you done?" Karak shrieked. "What have you done?"

"Slain the River, I think," Perkar answered, dropping his blade so he could lower himself to the floor with one hand and clutch his belly with the other. It was starting to hurt now, a slow burning that he knew would consume him for a long time before finally killing him.

"Not as *I* planned, pretty thing," Karak snarled.

"Nevertheless, I think he is dead."

"Perhaps," Karak said. "I don't see how, but—"

"It is true; you know it. I have done it for you."

"It is not as I wished it to be," Karak complained, his voice becoming a trifle petty.

"Karak, please. I know you can heal Hezhi and Ngangata, if they are not dead. Please. We did what you wanted. The Changeling is no more."

"But what is in his place?" Karak snarled. "That I do not know. Perhaps he will be as bad as the Brother."

That seemed wrong to Perkar, but it was just a feeling. And it was too much trouble to argue. "Save them," he repeated instead.

"What of *you*, pretty thing? *You* don't want to die, do you?"

"No," he answered, knowing at last that it was the truth. "No, I don't. But they should come first."

"How sweet. But seeing as how you acted contrary to my wishes, I will heal *none* of you."

"As if *you* ever acted in accord with anyone's wishes," a voice boomed, shuddering the very stone beneath their feet. "As if *you* ever accomplished the goal without twisting the intent."

Karak and Perkar turned as one at the low, grating voice, a voice nearly below Perkar's hearing.

"Balati," Karak said, almost a groan, almost an imprecation.

It was, indeed, the Forest Lord. His single black eye reflected the glimmering flames upon the water, but the rest of him seemed to drink in the light, a mass of fur and shadow and antlers that were really, Perkar could see now, trees that reached up and up, never ceasing to rise and branch. Near him stood a mare with a coat of gold and rust, the most magnificent mare Perkar had ever beheld. As Balati spoke again, the horse turned and sniffed first at the still form of Sharp Tiger, then at Hezhi.

"You have played a merry prank on me, Crow," Balati muttered, his voice as solid and unyielding as stone. "You have killed my Brother."

"He was dangerous," Karak hissed. "In another thousand

years—when it was far too late, and he was eating *you*—you would have understood that yourself."

"That is what *you* are for, Karak," Balati said. "That is my use for you, and you have performed it well. My Brother was ill—dead even. He was the ghost of a god, envying the living."

"Ah!" Karak brightened. "It is well then—you *do* understand. In that case, perhaps I should fly and see precisely what *has* been wrought here. The new Rivergod, like the old, has no sentience in Erikwer, but when he emerges from the cavern—"

"Oh, no, I think not," Balati said, almost gently. "You need humbling, I believe, and I need you *with* me for a time, so that I can quicken enough to understand all of this."

"Lord," Karak said, "there is much I need to be about, much to be done in the world as it shall become."

"Yes, I'm sure. But we will let mortals do it for a while, and the little gods of the land."

Karak suddenly transformed into a crow and took wing, but as he flew, he shrank, and the Forest Lord reached out a massive paw and closed it upon him. Perkar heard a single, pitiful *grawk* and then saw no more of the Raven.

"L-Lord Balati—" Perkar stammered.

"I know you," Balati said. "You slew my guardian, stole my things."

"Yes," he admitted. "But I—and I alone of these here, and of my people—" Perkar groaned through thickening pain. "I was to blame, no one else."

Balati cocked his head slowly to one side. Unlike the Raven, unlike the Huntress or indeed any other god Perkar had known, there was nothing Human in the gaze of Balati. He was the world before men or Alwat, the forest and the land before the forest came alive. There was no mercy, no compassion—nor hatred nor envy nor greed—to be understood in that nebulous single orb. "You wanted something before," he rumbled. "What was it?"

Perkar blinked. "Before . . . ?"

"When you stole my things."

A year ago, Perkar realized, when Apad and Eruka and the Kapaka and the Alwat all died. "We . . . we came to request more land for pasture, so that we need not fight the Mang."

Balati gazed down at him for some time. "That is reasonable," he said. "You may have them."

"Have them?"

"Two valleys, the two which lie along west of the rim of Agiruluta. You know the place?"

"Yes, Lord," Perkar muttered faintly. "I know it. Thank you."

But the Forest Lord no longer stood before him.

Now only the mare remained, stood near where Tsem crouched, weeping, beside Hezhi. The mare walked toward him, and as she did so, she became a woman, Mang-seeming, handsome. She looked angry.

"The girl Hezhi still has some life in her, and since she is the house my little colt lives in, I have healed her. Your friend will live."

"Thank you," Perkar murmured.

"Do not thank me yet." She knelt nearby and put her hand to Ngangata's throat. Then she turned to him again. "You slew one of my children in a foul and vicious way. You cut her legs from under her and left her to suffer."

"I did," Perkar admitted. "I have no excuse."

"No, you don't. And so as punishment, I will give you a choice. I will either heal the halfling or you, but not both."

Perkar closed his eyes. He *did* want to live. His goal was accomplished, and suddenly he could imagine a life that might have Piraku and perhaps even joy in it. He might once again sip woti, own cattle—and with Hezhi alive, he might even find a companion. And he was *afraid*; afraid of the hours of torture that lay before him, of the oblivion to come . . .

"You *are* cruel," he said. "Of course you must save my friend."

The Horse Mother hesitated. "Perhaps I should do the contrary then. If you really want this one to live, then he shall die."

His mouth worked, but he couldn't manage an objection, realizing the mistake he had made. After all, hadn't he used the same logic against the River long ago? Tried to guess his desire and then frustrate it?

But then the Horse Mother laid her hands on Ngangata. "No," she said. "I haven't the heart for that sort of cruelty. I was just taunting you. Ngangata will live. But I will not help you—I will not go so far."

"Thank you," he managed.

And then she, like the Forest Lord, was gone.

He lay there for a moment, watched the now steady rise and fall of Ngangata's chest.

"Tsem," Perkar whispered. Perhaps the half Giant could be persuaded to kill him quickly. But before he could utter another word, a sudden, sharper pain took him into oblivion.

Iᴛ took everything he had to stand still while the white-faced demon swung his sword *again*. But this time the pain and the shock meant very little to him. He was almost thankful to Perkar. To Hezhi and Ghan, he *was* thankful. "Good-bye, Hezhi," he sighed, as shade descended.

He was a little boy, walking along the levee, looking for a dead fish, *anything* to eat. His feet were cut and bleeding from fleeing across broken shards of pottery; the soldiers had seen him taking a merchant's purse of gold, and of course he had dropped it in the pursuit.

Ahead on the levee he saw an old woman, basking in the sunshine. She had an apple and a salted catfish before her on a red cloth. And *bread*, warm black bread that he could smell, even on the fetid breeze from the marsh. He felt about in his pocket again—but his knife was really gone. He walked toward the old woman anyway, thinking *hard*.

She saw him and frowned—but then she waved him over.

"I saw you looking at my food," she said. He nodded sullenly.

"I've seen you before, on Red Gar Street."

He shrugged, unable to take his eyes from the fish.

"We'll play a game," the old woman said. She reached into a

little bag and withdrew three clay cups and a copper soldier. She lined the cups up, placed the copper under one of them, and then moved them about quickly.

"Keep your eye on the copper," she said. "Now, tell which cup the coin is under, and I'll give you my bread."

"It isn't under a cup," he said. "It's in your hand."

She opened her hand, and there it was. "How did you know that?" she asked.

"I've seen *you* on Red Gar Street, too."

She laughed. "Take the fish *and* the bread."

"What? Why?"

"Because I like you," she answered.

"That's no reason to *give* me something," he said, but he took the food anyway, as she watched through narrowed eyes.

"My name is Li," she told him, as he swallowed a huge hunk of the bread.

He stopped chewing then. "Really? Are you really Li?"

The old woman smiled thinly and shook her head. "No, child, not really, no more than there was a soldier under those cups. But I can take you to where she is."

"You're the *Lady*."

"Yes."

"Shouldn't I be afraid of you?"

"Yes and no. Are you?"

Ghe shrugged. "A little. Will I disappear?"

The Lady smiled. "Now *that* would be telling. Why don't we go see?"

Ghe nodded. "May I finish the bread first? I'm still hungry."

"Of course, child. Finish the fish, too."

HEZHI awoke, cradled in Tsem's arms. The pain in her side was still present, but when she felt for the wound, *that* was gone, though her clothes were sticky—in some places stiff—with dried blood. She remembered—knew—that it was her own.

Tsem stirred, tilting his coarse features down to look at her.

They also were smeared with dried blood—a cut marked the summit of a huge gray lump above one massive brow—and caked further with dirt. Below his eyes, tears had cut runnels through blood *and* dirt, but he was dry-eyed now.

"I'm tired," she muttered. "Thirsty. Tsem, are you all right?"

"I have a headache, and I was worried about you. The Blackgod knocked me down and I hit my head. I guess he was too busy to bother with killing me."

"Where is the Blackgod now?"

"Gone."

She tried to look around. "Is anyone dead?"

Tsem nodded his head sadly. "You almost were, but a horse healed you. I know that sounds stupid."

"No, it makes sense," she told him. "Who is dead?"

"Brother Horse. Bone Eel, Qwen Shen. Lots of soldiers."

"Perkar? Ngangata?"

"Ngangata is fine. He's doing what he can for Perkar."

"Perkar? Is he badly hurt?"

"Very badly, Princess. He will probably die."

"I should—maybe I can help him." But she knew that she could not. Brother Horse had never taught her how to mend a torn body, only how to cast off possession. And neither of her remaining familiars had such arts. And they, too, were weak. But Perkar! Added to Brother Horse and Ghan . . .

"Take me to him," she pleaded.

Tsem nodded, lifted her up, and carried her to where Perkar lay.

He was near death, she could see that. Ngangata had bound up his belly, but blood still leaked through the bandage, and he must be bleeding inside, for she could see his spirit ebb.

"She healed *me* but not him," Ngangata muttered when they arrived.

"Who?"

"The Horse Mother."

Hezhi took a deep breath, fighting back tears. "She said he offended her—" she began.

Ngangata laughed harshly. "Yes, he did. That's Perkar, always offending some god or other." He tried to smile, with small success.

"But his sword. Can't his sword heal him?"

"The Blackgod destroyed Harka," Ngangata explained.

"What do we do?" Tsem asked quietly.

"Wait, I suppose," Ngangata replied stiffly.

Hezhi nodded and took one of Perkar's cool, bloody hands in hers. The smell of iron and water was strong, but the cavern was quiet now, and the last of the flames on the water had dwindled to a pale glow. Hezhi began, at long last, to cry—for Ghan, for Perkar, for Brother Horse—even for Ghe. She cried until a light appeared, high above them, a disk of gray and then blue; beyond Erikwer, the sun had risen.

EVEN in Perkar's dream, the pain remained—a nest of ants burrowing in his intestines—but it was, at least, muted. He lay in a grassy meadow, high in the mountains. Nearby, cattle lowed softly. It was an unusually vivid dream; he smelled the sweetness of the grass and the resin of spruce needles, even the almost-forgotten scent of cows. Wishing fervently that it were real, he knew it wasn't. Only the pain was real, the hole in his body. The rest was just his mind trying to ease his death.

"Oh, no, it's real," a voice assured him. He turned at the words and smiled, despite the pain. There, perched on a branch, as regal as any lord of the air, sat the most magnificent eagle he had ever seen. It was a bluebolt, body feathered in black and white with a crown of almost velvety indigo feathers. Its eyes were fierce, the eyes of a warrior, a predator.

"Harka," he said. "I must say you are more attractive in that form than as a sword."

"It's been long and long since I enjoyed a form like this, felt the wind in my pinions," the eagle answered in precisely Harka's voice. "I had actually forgotten, you know, what I *was* until that day you asked my name. I had forgotten having ever been anything but a sword."

"And now?"

"Now the Forest Lord will clothe me like *this*. I can spend a few years in a mortal skin and then perhaps take up residence in the mountain. It will be good, feasting on rabbit and fox again!"

"I'm happy for you. I thought the Blackgod destroyed you entirely."

"Not at all, though I admit I *thought* I was dead; having my body broken like that really hurt. But in the end he did me a favor, freeing me. Though I hated to abandon you, Perkar— believe it or not, I developed a real fondness for you."

Perkar regarded the huge bird. "As I said," he finally said, "I'm happy for you. But I wonder . . ."

"Yes?" Harka sounded almost eager.

"Can you tell me what happened? Exactly? It all went so fast."

"Oh." The god's voice fell a bit, as if disappointed. "Of course." He cocked his head. "Karak believed that only the River's own blood could destroy him, and only at his source. That was probably true enough. But that thing—the Tiskawa the River made to seek Hezhi out—contained many things, many kinds of blood and soul. The ghost of an ancient Nholish lord, your old love the Stream Goddess, other, smaller gods—all were given puissance and life by the River. A potent combination, one that served the same purpose as true Waterborn blood. The death of the Tiskawa performed the same task as Hezhi's own was meant to: killed him deader than a bone."

"You are certain?"

"I am certain. I have flown over him, and I have seen. His death follows him downstream; when these waters reach the sea, nothing will remain of the Changeling."

"And the River will be without a god. What a strange, strange thought."

"Without a god, yes," Harka said. "But not without a *goddess*."

Perkar turned to him so sharply that, even in his dream the pain was suddenly exquisite. "What?" he gasped in both astonishment and agony.

"Well, there was one spirit inside of the Tiskawa uniquely qualified to take over in the capacity of lord of the river."

"The Stream Goddess?"

"None other."

Perkar sank back and stared up at the sky, happy despite the fact that he was dying.

"What a glorious world," he muttered.

"Ah, yes, and that brings up the point of my visit—besides coming to say good-bye. In fact, if you weren't so *thick*, you would *know* why I'm here." The eagle hopped down, flexed its wings, and moved a pace closer. "You are about to *leave* this glorious world—unless you have changed your feelings about me."

"About what?"

"More than once you cursed me for healing you. You asked me to let you die. Do you still want that?"

"You aren't my sword anymore."

The bird lifted its wings to the wind. "No, but I could do one last favor for a friend, if he wanted."

Perkar chuckled. "Fine, Harka. I take it all back. I'm glad you never let me die."

"Does that mean you'll take my help, or would you rather expire as a hero, before you can make another mistake and start things all over again?"

Perkar shook his head ruefully. "I think I will take that chance, if your offer is genuine."

"Of course it is."

"Then I accept, and I wish you well in your travels, Harka. You were my only companion at times, and I was ungrateful more often than not—certainly more than I should have been."

"Indeed you were," Harka said. "Now, close your eyes."

He closed them, and when he opened them, it was to Hezhi and Ngangata kneeling over him, each of his hands held by one of them.

The pain was gone.

"Perkar?" Hezhi asked.

"Hello," he said. He turned to Ngangata. "Hello," he repeated, wanting to say more, to explain to each of them what he felt, but the sheer joy of seeing them both alive and whole—and knowing that he himself would live—was more than he could contain. His words came out as sobs, and when Tsem joined them—he had been only a few paces away—they all clasped in a knot, wordless, gripping hands and shoulders and bloody chests. Behind them, Yuu'han watched—apart, his face expressionless.

It was finally Tsem who stated the obvious, after a few long moments.

"We should all bathe now," he mumbled, and it could hardly be doubted that he was right. Hezhi laughed at that, and they all joined her. It was perhaps not the healthiest of laughter—more than tinged with hysteria—but it served.

When their chuckles faded off into strained silence, Perkar dizzily found his feet, and with Tsem's help struggled over to where Brother Horse lay. Heen licked the old man's face, clearly puzzled as to why his master refused to awaken.

"Brother Horse said to tell you good-bye, Heen," Hezhi explained, from behind Perkar. The dog looked up at his name, but then turned his attention back to the old man.

"Good-bye, Shutsebe," Perkar said.

THE next few hours were something of a blur, and later none of them remembered very much about them. They carried Brother Horse's body up and out of Erikwer and found that Karak's men had vanished, presumably fled. Perkar could hardly blame them, if they had witnessed even the smallest part of what transpired below.

At Yuu'han's direction they laid the body out, and sang the songs, and burned a flame for offerings, though they had little enough to give. Yuu'han had cut an ear from the corpse of Bone Eel, and he offered that to be taken to his uncle by the goddess in the flame. When Yuu'han sang his personal grief, Hezhi happened to hear, though she stayed a respectful distance away. One line stayed with her to the end of her days.

When they number the horses
When they count the sires and foals
Father, we shall know each other . . .

When Yuu'han was done, he departed, and then Hezhi went there. The old man's face had fallen into its most accustomed lines, so that she seemed to read a smile upon it. Heen already lay with him, his head propped on Brother Horse's feet, eyes puzzled. Hezhi knelt down and stroked the ancient dog's coarse, dirty fur.

"He said to tell you," Hezhi murmured to Heen. "But you already know."

But she told him anyway, and Heen licked her hand, and together they sat there for a time.

Night came, and they built a larger fire to huddle about. Unwilling to bathe in Erikwer, they still reeked of blood and sweat and other, more offensive scents. Perkar passed the night restlessly, barely sleeping, suspecting that the others rested at least as poorly.

He napped briefly, before dawn, and when he awoke, he knew why his rest had been so uneasy.

"I don't believe it," he confessed to Hezhi. "I don't believe that the Changeling is dead, even after all of this, all of our sacrifices."

"I felt him die," Hezhi answered, "but I don't believe it either."

"Then there is one more thing we must do, before leaving Balat."

Hezhi nodded reluctantly. "Yes. One last thing."

XXXIX

The Goddess

Perkar placed his feet carefully on the broken red stone, though the way down into the chasm was neither steep nor particularly dangerous seeming. But after all that they had been through—and after searching for the better part of a day for a safe way down the mostly sheer cliffs of the ravine—it would be ridiculous and embarrassing to trip and break his arm or neck.

Below them the river churned spray into the air that the bright sun rendered into a million shattering diamonds and that imparted a wonderful cool dampness to the ordinarily dry atmosphere.

"It's true," Perkar said, speaking up to his companions still perched on the rim. "It *is* true. This is not the same Changeling I once knew."

"Not at all," Ngangata agreed.

Hezhi felt her own trepidation melt away. The scale on her arm reacted to the presence of the river not at all, nor did any part of her. This was just water, flowing through a narrow canyon of red and yellow stone. "It's hard to believe that this narrow stream is really the river," she said.

"This is where I first saw him," Perkar answered. "This is where my journey to you began—*our* journey," he corrected as Ngangata came level to him on the trail. He patted the half Alwa on the shoulder.

"Well," he called back up to Hezhi. "Come on down."

"Wouldn't you rather I stayed up here?" she asked.

"No. I would rather have you with me," he answered, offering his hand to steady her for the next step.

With only a little slipping and sliding, they all reached the bottom of the gorge easily—even Tsem, though Hezhi noticed the half Giant kept casting uneasy glances back *up*, probably dreading the return climb to the top.

"Before you could *feel* his coldness, his hunger," Perkar explained. "Now . . ."

"Now it feels like something living," Ngangata finished for him.

Perkar nodded and shuffled his feet on the narrow stone beach, suddenly nervous. Nevertheless, he reached into a small sack at his waist and produced a handful of flower petals, which he sprinkled into the quieter eddies near shore. He cleared his throat and sang—tentatively, but gradually with more confidence and volume:

> "Stream Goddess I
> Long hair curling down from the hills
> Long arms reaching down the valley
> Reposing in my watery dwelling
> On and on go I
> In the same manner, from year to year . . ."

Perkar sang on, the song of the Stream Goddess as she had taught it to his father's father, many years past. When he had sung it before, it had been to a quiet stream in his clan's pasture, a little stream he could almost leap across. Here, the crash of the rapids almost seemed to add a rhythm to his words, and then new words entirely, so that seamlessly, he was singing verses to the Song of the Stream Goddess that had never been before. And then, almost without him noticing, *he* was not singing at all, but the song continued, and from the nearest eddy, a head rose, long

black hair swirling in the agitated water, ancient, amber eyes in
the face of a young woman gazing up at them with what appeared
to be humor.

"... then came a mortal man," she sang.

> "His mother named him for the oak
> For the spot where his caul was buried
> In the very place I flowed
> He grew like a weed
> And he came to love me—"

Perkar stood, more and more embarrassed as the song continued, but by now it was a story they all knew. She sang of his
foolishness, she sang of her anger, she sang of death. But in the
end she finished:

> "On and on go I
> But not the same now, year to year.
> The Old Man eats me not
> No longer quickens he with my pain
> By foolishness I was saved
> By the love of mortal man I was redeemed
> And on and on go I
> Each year better than the last
> No winter cold to eat me
> Each season a different-colored spring."

And as she sang her final verse, she rose up, more magnificent
than he had ever seen her, and Perkar's knees quaked, and
without even thinking he knelt.

She approached and ran her fingers playfully through his hair.

"Stand up, silly thing," she admonished. "We have been more
familiar than this."

"Yes," he began, "but ..." He shrugged helplessly but then
met her eyes. "I don't deserve this, to be part of your song."

She laughed, the same silvery music he had heard for the first
time what seemed like centuries ago. "Deserving has nothing to
do with it," she replied. "The Changeling is part of my song, and
his name *never* deserved to be sung. But that is how the songs of

gods and goddesses must be. You are a part of my story, Perkar, a part I cherish. After all, it was your love that ended my pain and gave me *this*." She swept her arms wide, indicating the joyful crash of the water.

He kept his gaze frankly on hers. "Long ago, you told me not to be a boy, dreaming of the impossible. But I loved you so much, and I was so stupid. I would have done anything for you—save to heed your warnings. But this thing I have finally accomplished—in your song you say that my love saved you. But I must tell you truthfully, Goddess, I did not do all of this for love of you."

She smiled even wider and swept her gaze across Ngangata, Tsem, Yuu'han, and Hezhi.

"He is *such* a silly thing sometimes, is he not?" She sighed. She turned back to him, her look one of mock despair. Then she gestured to Hezhi.

Tentatively Hezhi stepped forward. The Stream Goddess was the most beautiful woman she had ever seen. Even though she had thought she understood Perkar, she suddenly realized that she had not. She knew, intellectually, that much of what he had done had been motivated by a love for this goddess, but to actually *see* her, hear her voice, made it all different. Hezhi's heart seemed to sag in her chest, as she remembered her own shadowed, ungainly outline on the floor in "Sheldu's" damakuta. Regardless, she approached the goddess and was faintly astonished when the strange woman reached and took her hand. The skin of the goddess was cool and damp, but otherwise felt Human enough.

She was even more astonished when the goddess squeezed her hand and then placed it in Perkar's.

"I never said it was love for *me* that ended the Changeling and set me free," the goddess explained. "Only the love of a mortal man. *Your* love for your *people*, Perkar, your love for these companions, and your love for this girl. Those are the loves of a *man*, sweet thing, and those are what set me free."

"I love you, too," Perkar answered.

"Of course you do. How could you not? But you understand now what I told you so long ago."

"I think so. I no longer dream of you somehow becoming my wife, if that is what you mean."

She only smiled at him and then turned back to Hezhi. "Child, I have a gift for you."

"For me?"

A second column of water rose and became something dimmer, more ghostlike than the very real goddess; but it congealed into a recognizable form nevertheless.

"Ghan!" Hezhi cried.

"More or less," the apparition said curtly—but more than a hint of a smile graced his usually severe features. "Changed but not changed. When you chew up a piece of meat and spit the gristle out—I think I must be *mostly* gristle."

"Ghan!" She was weeping again, though she thought that by now she would have no salt or water left in her body.

"Hush, child. You know how I despise such displays."

"Do you?" Hezhi answered, wiping the lachryma from her cheeks. "I *read* your letter, the one you sent by the Mang. The one in which you said you loved me, that I was like the daughter—"

"Yes, yes," he replied testily. "Old men sometimes write maudlin things." He softened. "And I probably meant them."

"What will become of the library?" Hezhi asked. And then, in a blinding flash of insight, "Of *Nhol*?"

Ghan shrugged. "The library was my life, but I'm oddly glad now that I did not spend my last days in it. The books remain, and there is always *someone*. Someone like you and me, at least every generation or two. They will wait, just as they did for you. As for Nhol, who knows?"

"They will not worship *me*," the goddess said. "I will not *have* it. It causes me more pain than pleasure. But I will not harm them, though it is a city that he built. Human Beings are able to change; that is the most—perhaps the *only*—wonderful thing about your kind. They will be as happy or happier *without* the River as they were with their god, given time."

Ghan smiled. "It will be an interesting time, these next few years. I intend to observe them."

"Observe?"

"The goddess has graciously consented to take this that remains of me downstream with her."

The goddess nodded confirmation. "Unlike the Changeling, I have no desire to flow through a sterile land. I am more comfortable with neighbors, frog gods, heron lords, swampmasters. Perhaps your old teacher can take up residence in one of the many vacant places—a stream, a field, a mountain. I will invite others, too."

"And who . . ." Perkar frowned and began again. "What of the stream that you inhabited of old?"

"Ah, that," she said. "That is already taken care of; a new goddess lives there. Give her flowers as you did me." She smiled oddly, a bit mysteriously, with some sadness, and came closer to him, speaking very softly. "Farewell, love. I have become large indeed, and it is a new thing. I have not yet flowed my length, and part of him still lives, though I slay more of him each instant. But it may be that when I have attained my length I will drowse for a time, and when I waken it may be to your great-grandchildren rather than you. I may never speak to you like this again. But of all mortals I have loved, you were both the sweetest and the most worrisome. You made me less a goddess and more Human than you will ever know. Farewell." She stepped farther from him.

"Good-bye, Goddess," he answered, trying unsuccessfully to keep his voice from shaking.

"Fare *you* well, Hezhi," Ghan said, as the two of them began to collapse back into the water they were formed of. "Perhaps you will burn incense for me someday."

Then he and the goddess were gone. The five mortals silently watched the bright play of the river for a time, before Tsem cleared his throat.

"Ah . . ." he began.

"Yes, Tsem?" Hezhi asked.

"Do you think it would be, ah . . . disrespectful if we were to take a bath, you know—here?"

Perkar, oddly enough, was the first to start laughing. It was more joyful than their nervous tittering back in Erikwer, almost exuberant.

"*I* could use a bath," he replied, when he could. "I'm all for that, and I don't think she would mind at all."

THEY did bathe, then, and climbed back up, and afterward Perkar and Ngangata hunted, returning with a small antelope. They set it to roasting on the flame that Yuu'han, Hezhi, and Tsem had built in their absence. They cooked the meat, and later, licking the grease from their fingers, they watched the sun go down.

"Well, what now?" Tsem sighed. "What do we do now?"

"Now," Perkar said, "we go back to my people. We tell them about the new bargain with the Forest Lord, about the new valleys he has opened for colonization."

"That will end the war?" Yuu'han asked a little harshly.

Perkar turned a concerned gaze on the Mang. "I know a lot of your people have died," he said softly. "Saying I'm sorry means nothing, I know."

"They were warriors," he responded. "They chose their deaths. But I have to know, after all of this, after aiding you even against my own, that it was worth it."

"It was worth it," Ngangata answered. "The war will end. Perkar's people talk a lot about fighting and glory, but they would actually much rather tend their cows in peace. In the lands they have taken from your people, they would *never* know peace."

"*That* is true," Yuu'han conceded. "We would fight for the plains our horses graze upon until none of us were left alive."

"And we know that," Perkar assured him. "Only desperation drove my people to attack yours. Now they can settle peacefully in lands that are more suited to cattle, anyway. You can return to your folk and tell them the war will end, my friend."

"That pleases me. It would please my uncle, as well."

"Your uncle was a good man, a great man," Perkar said. "I'm sorry for what happened to him."

Yuu'han smiled faintly. "He knew he would die. He knew that he would die as soon as he left his island. He had a vision."

"Then why . . ." Hezhi began.

"He was old, but he was still a man," Yuu'han explained. "Still Mang. If he had lived much longer, he might have lost that, might have become another pack for his clan to carry about with them. We would have done that, for he was dear to us. But he would have *hated* it. He saw a path that would bring his death, but also much glory, many songs."

"Piraku," Perkar said.

"As you call it. He died quickly, with little pain, but valiantly. And he cared about you all, was willing to give his life." He looked uncomfortable. "As was I. I only ask that you remember where he died, honor his spirit now and then."

"I don't think we will soon forget Erikwer," Ngangata replied. "And I'm certain your uncle will soon wear other clothes; perhaps those of a stallion or a hawk."

"It may be. Or perhaps he roams with his old mount, Firehoof, in the plains of the Ghostland. Either way, I'm sure he is just the same as he was, a noisy, perverse old man."

"Almost certainly."

"In any event, we will remember him," Perkar promised, "and I will send him plenty of woti and beer, wherever he dwells now. Starting when we get home, and I *have* something to send him. You will join me in some woti, I hope. In a toast to him."

"I think I will return along the river," Yuu'han said, shaking his head. "It will be quicker and easier than traveling through the mountains, and now the Changeling is . . . friendlier."

"When will you leave?"

"In the morning, I think."

"That will be a long journey alone," Ngangata said.

Yuu'han shrugged. "I will not be alone. My cousin will be with me." He jerked his head toward his mount, Huu'yen.

"Of course. But we will miss you," Perkar said.

"And I all of you."

They talked a bit longer, of inconsequential things, watching the red-eyed Fire Goddess in her hearth of stones, and one by one they fell asleep, and though Ngangata stood sentinel, even *he* was blissfully snoring when the new morning dawned.

A Different-Colored Spring

THE warm vapor of black woti carried up into Perkar's nostrils, a delicious scent. The promise of its taste tugged powerfully at him, pulling him back across the years to his first sip of the dark, warm drink, and for an instant he felt anew everything he had known then: pride, joy, love, and above all, *hope*. The promise that his life had just begun, that the great fields of the world were stretched out before him. Had the sunlight really ever seemed so golden, so untarnished?

That had been only five years ago. This was the fifth anniversary of his manhood rite, of the day when his father had trounced him so soundly before his whole family, when he had been given his first sword.

"Drink it, son," his father exhorted. "You have been home for more than a year; time enough has passed. Put away your mourning and drink."

Perkar hesitated, still. The smell was so *fine*. What had he told Karak, a year and some months ago? *You have made me like a ghost, able to appreciate only the smell, never the taste . . .*

Something like that. He smiled thinly, raised the cup to his father. He had never thought of Sherye as old before, but he seemed old now. In the two years Perkar had been gone, his sire looked as if he had aged ten. His hair was more than half gray, his eyes compassed by seams of pain and worry.

"To your Piraku, Father," Perkar said. He lifted the small cup and drank. The wine seemed to rush into his head, filling it with smoke and honey before it burned its way, pleasantly, to his belly.

"To *your* Piraku, my son," his father answered, and drank his own. The older man then poured them both another cup.

"Perhaps I am flesh again now," Perkar murmured, and this time when he smiled, it felt more genuine.

"What do you mean?" his father asked.

"Nothing." Perkar shook his head. "Something best forgotten."

Sherye measured him with iron-gray eyes and smiled ruefully. "My son goes away and returns with a mouthful of cryptic remarks. But at least he returns. And today he is a man for five years." He raised the second cup in salute. Together they drank.

The warmth from the first cup was beginning to reach into Perkar's blood, and finally he felt his shoulders begin to relax. He sagged back a bit on his pillow. They sat alone, his father and he, in the banquet hall of the damakuta where Perkar had been born. Only a handful of candles burnished the walls of polished red cedar, while above, the steep pitch of the ceiling climbed into darkness. The low table before them held only the bowl of hot water, the pitcher of woti it warmed, and their cups.

"I feel that I have been a man for only a year," Perkar admitted. "Two at best. I don't know. I only know that I was not a man when I set out with the Kapaka."

Sherye barked out a short, harsh laugh as he poured yet more woti. "We are never men when we *say* we are, son—it's only later, when we question our worth, that we stand some chance of finding it." He tossed down the third cup, waited for Perkar to do likewise, and then poured a fourth.

"You intend for us to get drunk tonight, don't you, Father?" Perkar asked, already beginning to feel somewhat light-headed.

"Very drunk," his father conceded. "Very."

Six drinks later they were well on their way. Perkar felt his face numbing and softening, and to his horror, tears welled behind his eyes. In his months of self-enforced temperance, he had forgotten the power of woti to draw out the hidden, to release things best bound—to make hardened men bawl like mouseling infants.

His father swayed back and forth when he next spoke, the rustling of his rust-and-black quilted robe the only other sound.

"When will you take the land, son? When will you build your own home? Your younger brother—Henyi—is already gone four months."

Perkar bit his lip. He had tried to remain silent on this issue, keep it in. But suddenly he felt the words bolt past his lips like a willful steed.

"When all have chosen," he cried, louder than he wished. "When all whom I wronged have picked the choicest land for pasture. *Then* I will go."

His father waved his hand impatiently. "Many whom you wronged are dead."

"Their children, then."

"How many generations will you pay, my son? You have redressed your misdeeds—stopped the war with the Mang and haggled new land for the Cattle Folk. Truth to tell, none of us would have known your blame, had you not returned to tell us of what happened. Yours is not the first expedition to go into Balat and not return."

"Yes," Perkar said. "I have heard some accused the Alwat—Akera and his brothers even went to hunt them."

"And found none," his father pointed out. "No harm was done."

It seemed to Perkar that harm *had* been done, if the reputation of the Alwat had been further blemished. And even though the truth of the matter was now widely known, men like Akera would still count the imaginary grudge in a tally against the Alwat. Thus truth was the servant of desire. But the blame against the Alwat was not the worst distortion. "The most embarrassing thing is the way people treat me," Perkar muttered.

"Like a hero? You are that. The songs are already spreading.

How did you want to be treated? As an outcast, a pariah? Would that have made you feel better?" The older man smiled and reached to grip Perkar's shoulder. "The punishment of a hero is that he is treated like one. You will see that soon enough. Go take your land, son. You have waited long enough."

"Perhaps."

"And think about marriage. It's past time for that, as well. Bakume still has a finely dowered daughter . . ." He stopped when he saw the expression on his son's face. He drank another cup of woti. "Ah, well then," he said. "A father might as well try. A man can have *two* wives, you know."

Perkar blinked at his sire. What had the older man seen on his face?

But he thought he knew, and that should be dealt with soon. He had put it off too long.

HEZHI woke with a start, her heart racing. Her blood pulsed chill, like roots of ice digging through her skin, but already the dread images were fading away, her nightmare painted over by the rosy sunlight falling through the higher window onto her bed. She lay there, waiting for the last of the dream to evaporate, wondering if she would ever be entirely free of such sleep terrors. Before last night, it had been almost two weeks. The mare and the swan assured her that they could protect her from her nightmares, but Hezhi felt somehow that such aid would harm her more in the end. With each passing day the horror lessened, just as the tightness of the knife scar in her side lessened under the ministrations of Perkar's mother. The latter required bathing, stretching, and massaging the white lump with tallow; Hezhi had been assured that simply ignoring the scar would result in a stiff, unpleasant pucker that would trouble her for the rest of her days. She suspected that ignoring—or allowing her familiars to suppress—her dreams would have similar results. In the year and more since leaving Balat, the nightmares came fewer and with diminishing intensity. One day they would be all but gone.

Roosters were crowing, so Hezhi rose, dabbed her face at the washbasin, and sought out her robe, the gold-and-brown one she favored. Once dressed she trudged down the stairs to the great hall.

Perkar and his father lay there; Perkar was supine, mouth open, eyes closed. Sherye had nodded his head onto the table and remained there as if bowing to whatever god the wood had been cut from. The shadow of her nightmare was strong enough that a wave of horror washed over her, a fear that they were dead, but she saw the truth quickly enough in the woti bottle on the table, and the relief was so great she laughed. Perkar had relented at last and taken woti with his father. Perkar, too, was healing.

A soft sound caught her attention. Across the hall, Kila—Perkar's mother—gestured for her attention. Hezhi crossed the hardwood floor, treading lightly even in bare feet, wishing to make no sound to rouse the men.

Kila was a tiny woman, smaller even than Hezhi in stature and frame, and yet she *seemed* larger somehow, as if time had lent her eminence. Her face reminded Hezhi of a bird—not some large, beaky bird, but something delicate, like a sparrow. Her hair, worn in three long braids that nearly reached her knees, was that strange red-brown color that Hezhi was slowly becoming accustomed to.

"Thank you," Kila said, whispering. "Best we let them sleep. They would not be pleasant if we awakened them now. Would you come with me to feed the chickens?"

Hezhi nodded and followed the older woman out into the yard.

"Normally Aberra and her daughter feed them," Kila explained as she opened the wooden bin that contained the grain, "but they are away right now."

"I'll help," Hezhi said. She took a handful of the grain and began casting it about the yard in imitation of Kila. The red-and-gold birds appeared from every corner of the walled-in compound, converging on the two women, clucking about their feet like the courtiers who had once surrounded her father. Hezhi smiled at the image, then wondered more seriously what had become of that court, of the palace. With the River dead, did

Nhol still stand? Did her father still rule? Despite herself, she felt again a longing for the city of her birth and, most surprising of all, a faint worry for her father, her mother, her sisters. Though she had barely known them, she understood now that they did matter to her in some small but real measure.

"What's troubling you, child?" Kila asked.

"Thinking of home," Hezhi explained.

"From what Perkar says, I wonder that you miss it."

"As do I," Hezhi admitted. "But I worry about my family. Most of all, I wonder about Qey."

"That's the woman who raised you?"

"Yes."

Kila was silent for a few moments, throwing grain out toward the weaker birds that could not bustle up to her feet. "Will you return?"

Hezhi shrugged. "I don't know. I don't know what I will do."

Kila looked at her frankly. "I hope you don't," she said. "I hope you stay right here. I've never had a daughter—" Her face fell slightly. "—not one who lived, anyway. Having you around has been like having a daughter."

Hezhi smiled. Kila meant well, and she liked the older woman, but she could remember Brother Horse, making her a similar proposition, just after she escaped from Nhol. "You could be Mang," he had told her. And yet, despite the old man's best intentions, that had turned out to be a false promise. She had been with Perkar's people for longer—sixteen months now—but she still had little faith that this could be her home. At least Tsem was happier here; he was much more useful as a cowherd and at building fences than as a Mang hunter. He even seemed to enjoy the hard, outdoor work. Yes, Tsem could live here and be happy. But as more and more time passed, Hezhi wondered what *her* place would be—if there was one for her at all.

Kila sighed. "But even if you stay, I suppose you will marry soon enough. Already we have had two proposals for you."

"What?" Hezhi's head snapped up. "Proposals?"

Kila laughed. "You should have seen your expression! Yes, of course proposals. Look at you! Such a pretty young woman, and well into marrying age."

"But who?"

"Neighbors. Sons headed off to the new lands. Men who care less about a fine dowry and more about having a beautiful bride—and a shamaness, no less."

"I thought no man married an undowered woman."

Kila nodded around at the chickens, satisfied that they had been provided for, and started back across the yard. A gentle morning breeze breathed down from the mountains, cool but invigorating, like a swim in springwater. "Not in normal times," Kila answered. "But these are not normal times. Dowry is usually land and cattle, land being the most important of the two. But right now, there is land to be had for the taking. Anyway—" She shot Hezhi a mischievous grin. "—you *have* a dowry."

"I do?"

"Sherye has dowered you with two bulls and thirteen cows. Did you not know?"

Hezhi was so dumbfounded she literally could not speak for a space of ten heartbeats. "When?" she finally sputtered out.

"Ten days ago, on your fifteenth birthday. Two bulls and thirteen cows. Fifteen, you see?"

"That was very nice," Hezhi said softly, feeling faint.

"I told you that you were like a daughter to us," Kila answered.

Perkar's parents very much wanted her married! Hezhi was wondering just *how* much like a daughter they considered her, and what the greater ramifications of that were. But after more than a year in the Cattle Lands, she thought she knew.

Perkar gave another try at lifting the fence post, lost his balance, and then sat down with a *bump*. He hoped he wasn't going to be sick again.

"Get up and work, Perkar," Ngangata chirped in a cheerful—and thus *evil*—voice. "Sweat it out."

From fifty paces away, Tsem boomed in, "I always wondered if that sword of yours cured hangovers, too, back when you still had it."

"I don't know," Perkar grumbled, holding his head. "I never got drunk when I bore Harka. But I wish I had him back, right now, so I could find out."

"Try this instead." Ngangata smirked, walking over to join him on the crest of the hill. Below, some fifty red cows moved lazily across the pasture. Tsem eclipsed a few of them as he, too, ceased working and labored up the slope to join Perkar and Ngangata.

Perkar eyed suspiciously the skin that Ngangata offered him. "What is it?"

"Water," the halfling replied, inserting a broken stalk of grass between his broad, thin lips.

Perkar drank some of it. It was cool, clear springwater, tasting only of rain and snowmelt. Perkar was sure it would make him vomit. He drank it anyway and discovered that he did indeed feel somewhat better.

"Pass me that," Tsem panted, and Ngangata transferred the skin to the huge man's massive paws.

"We make good time on this fence," Tsem said, his tongue still wrapping thickly around Perkar's language.

"Thanks to you and Ngangata," Perkar muttered. "I've been useless enough today." He glanced up speculatively at Ngangata. "How much longer will you stay?" He hesitated, then rushed on, "I didn't think you would come back at all."

Ngangata straightened his shoulders and gazed off at the forest, as if worried that something might lurk there. "Well, I had to make sure you hadn't already found some new trouble to get into. In any event, I had to come see if the songs were true."

"Songs?"

"Yes," Ngangata answered. "In the songs I heard at Morawta, they speak of the hero Perkar standing as tall as two men together. I had to see if that was true."

Perkar closed his eyes, but that made his head whirl the

worst, and so he cracked them open again. "Tell me not of such songs."

Ngangata sat beside him, touching his shoulder lightly. "I shouldn't taunt you," he admitted. "But you still owe me. Anyway, there *is* one thing I thought you would like to know about the new songs."

"That being?"

"The Changeling. The river who was once the Changeling has a new name."

"A new name for a new river," Perkar said, and despite himself he felt a little thrill. Five years ago he had promised a goddess revenge, and despite everything, he had given her that—and more. "What do they call her?"

Ngangata's smile broadened. "Ah-hah. I *knew* you would want to know *that*." He rubbed his hands together and cracked his knuckles, then lay back to gaze up at the lazy clouds overhead, his alien, dark eyes filmed with blue. "Well, the Mang call her Tu'da'an, the 'River of Springtime,' because she brought new life. Many of your own folk call her simply Itani, 'Flowing Goddess.' But there is another name for her."

The half man lapsed into silence for a moment, as if suddenly listening to the sky.

"Yes?" Perkar grunted testily.

"Ah. Many call her Animiramu."

Perkar had no answer for that, no retort. He only turned to look at the farthest tree line, toward the distant north where she flowed.

"I'm sorry," Tsem interposed after a moment or two, "but what does that mean?"

"It means 'The goddess he loved,' " Ngangata answered softly.

Perkar did not want the subject pursued.

"You didn't answer my question," he rasped, more harshly than he meant to. "How long will you stay this time?"

Ngangata considered for a moment. "I don't know. A few days."

Perkar massaged his head, wondering if he should try to discuss what he wanted when he felt so bad. But Tsem and Ngangata were both here, and no one else around.

"Listen, Ngangata. You, too, Tsem. I think I'm going out to claim some land in the new valleys. I think it's time I did that."

"Good," Ngangata said. "You waited more than long enough."

Perkar considered Ngangata as frankly as he could with his bloodshot eyes. "This is my idea," he began.

"Uh-oh," Ngangata interjected.

Perkar greeted that with a self-deprecating grimace. "Hear me out. I want you two to come with me."

"To do all of the work, I assume," Tsem rumbled.

"To share the land," Perkar countered. "To each take a third of my granting."

Ngangata stared at him silently, weighing those words. *He* understood what Perkar was offering, whether Tsem did or not.

"How could that be?" the halfling softly inquired. "Grantings can be made only to clan members. Tsem and I have no clan."

"I asked a lawkeeper about this," Perkar explained carefully. "My father and I can adopt you. You can share the land with me as if we were siblings. And *your* land would pass on to your sons."

"I could own land? Like this?" Tsem asked. From his tone it was clear that he thought he misunderstood. Perkar repeated his statement in Nholish, to make certain the half Giant comprehended.

"I can have no sons," Tsem said, his voice thick with emotion. "My sort can father no offspring. But . . ."

"That matters not," Perkar said. "Pass it on to whomever you want—it would be *yours*."

"After much hard work," Ngangata added. "This is not cleared pasture we speak of. Perkar, I am a hunter, a guide, not a cattleman."

"For many years, the most of our sustenance will come from hunting, until our herds have strength and many trees have been felled. If you never choose to do aught but hunt it, it would still be your land."

"Yes, but I would be your *brother*, according to those terms,"

Ngangata said, his voice thick with disgust. Perkar looked down in shocked astonishment, certain that after all of this time he and Ngangata were better friends than *that* . . .

But then he saw the halfling was biting back his laughter, and when Ngangata did release his mirth, Perkar understood that it was all right. His offer had been accepted.

"Isn't it beautiful?" Perkar asked, sweeping his arm to encompass the valley. Hezhi thought at first that the question was purely rhetorical, but then he turned his shining gray eyes on her, demanding a response.

"It is," she agreed. And it *was*. The expanse of the valley was breathtaking—not *awesome*, like some of the landscapes she had seen in Balat—but nevertheless lovely, a panorama of rocky meadows and spruce swaying in a breeze easing down a saddle in the surrounding mountains. But it was more wonderful still in Perkar's eyes, that was clear. Like so many things, she could never appreciate it as he did.

"I shall build my damakuta *there*," he stated, indicating a gentle rise in the valley floor, "and *there* shall be my first pasture." He indicated a flatter area nearby, where a stream snaked through a meadow.

"That seems reasonable," Hezhi replied, "though I know little enough about pasture."

He glanced at her again, and she wondered exactly what his gaze held. It looked a bit like fear.

"Come walk with me a bit," Perkar urged, dismounting.

Hezhi watched as he tied his horse to a nearby tree, then reluctantly swung her leg over Dark's mane and head, sliding earthward. "Where have Tsem and Ngangata gotten off to?" she asked. "They were behind us a few moments ago."

"They've—ah—gone off to look at their own allotments, down the ridge," he stammered—and *blushed*.

"Oh." She felt an odd sensation in her stomach, for no reason she could clearly explain. "Where are we walking to?"

"Just walking," Perkar replied. "We have something to discuss."

Something serious, by his tone, and her belly tightened further. What was it he had to drag her four days' travel from his father's damakuta to discuss? It irritated her that Perkar was keeping secrets again. He had kept his offer of land to Tsem from her, for instance. She had been forced to *drag* that out of her old servant. During the journey to this place, he had barely spoken to her, as if his concealments were muzzling him. It was a side of Perkar she knew well and intensely disliked—and yet it was familiar, almost comfortable. Now, as he was about to reveal something to her at last, she was suddenly afraid to know. Could it be that she was more frightened of Perkar's candor than of his evasions?

"You've made Tsem very happy," Hezhi said, to have *something* to say, to delay Perkar's admission or whatever it was.

"Good," Perkar answered. "He deserves happiness."

"Indeed." So why did she feel that Perkar was a thief, stealing her lifelong friend?

"You've made yourself happy, too," she went on. "I've never seen you like this."

"Like what?"

"*Happy*, I said. Excited. All you can talk about is your land and your damakuta. I'm glad you finally decided to come here. Your family is delighted. Why—" She stopped, wondering suddenly what she meant to say.

"Go on," he prompted. They had taken a few steps into the forest, but now he turned to confront her, his eyes frank but nervous.

"Why so far out? Ngangata says this is as far as we could go and still be in the new lands. The closest holding is more than a day away from here."

Perkar shrugged. "Not for long. These lands will fill up soon enough."

"That doesn't answer my question."

He sighed. "The truth is, I'm not at home back there, with my people. Not really, not anymore. And Tsem and Ngangata . . ." He trailed off.

"Will never be at home there? Is that what you mean to say?"

"Yes," he admitted. "But out here we can be. All of us."

"You and Tsem and Ngangata, you mean," she replied, carefully. Just to let him know what he was leaving out.

Perkar's shoulders visibly slumped, and though his mouth worked to say something, no sound emerged. Clearly frustrated, he leaned close, as if he must *whisper* what he had to say . . .

And *kissed* her. It was not what she expected, not then. A year ago, perhaps, but not *now*. Couldn't Perkar get *anything* right?

But the *kiss* seemed right, after an instant, after she fought back the first swell of panic when he leaned in. It seemed careful, and sweet, and when he drew away she was surprised to feel a bit disappointed.

"I—uh—I've wanted to do that for some time," he admitted.

"Then why did you wait until now?" she asked, unable to keep a little of the bitterness out of her voice.

Perkar's eyes lit with surprised chagrin. "I didn't think . . ."

"Oh, no, of course not. Of course you didn't think." She felt some heat rising in her voice. "You didn't think that while your mother was planning my wedding to some cowherd I never met and *everyone* was busily discussing *your* marriage to some cattle princess and Tsem—" She choked off, bit her lip, and went on. "You didn't think to give me *any* sign of what you were thinking or felt—for more than a *year*." She snapped her mouth closed, feeling she had said too much.

Perkar looked down at his feet. "I'm sorry," he whispered. "I thought it was clear."

"The only clear thing to me is that no one cares to see you and me together."

"I just kissed you."

"That could mean a *lot* of things," Hezhi snapped.

"And you kissed me."

"That could mean a lot of things, too," she responded, but her voice wavered, because he was moving closer again.

"What it means to me," he said, his voice barely a breath, "is that I love you."

Hezhi wanted to retort sarcastically to that, too, to tell him it was too late, to *hurt* him just a little.

But what she *said* was "Oh."

He shrugged. "Another reason for being this far out. I love my family, but I want none of their matchmaking. If there is anything that I've realized in all of this, it is that the most precious Piraku is that which you find. And despite everything, I was lucky to find you. It is the only thing I have to thank the Changeling for."

Hezhi clenched her eyelids, but the tears squirted out anyway. "This is a fine time to start this," she murmured, "just when I had resigned myself to leaving."

"Leaving?" He gaped, as if the thought had never occurred to him. "To go where?"

"Perhaps back to Nhol, perhaps to somewhere I've never been. I don't know; just *away*."

"Back to Nhol?"

"Yes, of course. What is there for me here?"

"I've just told you."

"Yes, I guess you have. But I don't know that I'm ready to become a wife. I know I'm fifteen, but for me there was never a childhood, Perkar. How can I become a woman when I was never a child?"

Perkar reached and took her hand. "I haven't asked you to marry me," he replied. "I only told you I love you, something I thought you already knew. You *did* know, didn't you?"

"Yes," she admitted, wiping her tears. "Yes, but you never *said* it."

"Well, we *are* two of a kind then," Perkar rejoined mildly.

"Oh," she snapped, "of course I love you, you idiot."

"Then stay here, with Tsem and Ngangata and me. With your family."

Hezhi drew in a long breath and looked at him, this man she had first seen in dreams, and as she did so, she realized that her tears had stopped. "Well," she said at last. "I *do* want to stay here, with you. I do. But I am *not* ready for marriage. I'm just not, despite my age. I want . . ." She drew her brows together and gazed defiantly up at him. "I want to be courted for a time. I want more stories about two-headed cows. I want to separate what we feel from what we went through together—just a little."

"I remind you that I didn't ask for your hand—" Perkar started, but she shushed him with her finger.

"But you *will*, Perkar Kar Barku. You *will*. And when you do, I want to give the right answer."

Perkar smiled then and took her hand. "Good enough, then. How do I go about this courting business?"

Hezhi wiped what remained of her tears and felt an almost impish grin touch her lips. "Well," she said. "I suppose you can kiss me once more, and then we should really find my chaperone."

Wind rustled the trees and dapples of sunlight streamed through the leaves above. It was a long kiss.

About the Author

Born in Meridian, Mississippi, on April 11, 1963, J. Gregory Keyes spent his early years roaming the forests of his native state as well as the red-rock cliffs of the Navajo Indian reservation in Arizona. Storytelling in his family and on the reservation sparked an interest both in writing and in the ancient. Pursuing the ancient, he obtained a B.A. in anthropology from Mississippi State University. Moving to Athens, Georgia, he worked ironing newspapers and as a night guard to support his wife, Nell, in her metalworking/jewelry degree, and also began seriously pursuing writing in his spare time.

Returning to anthropology, he earned a master's from the University of Georgia, concentrating on mythology and belief systems, long-standing interests that also inspire his fiction. He currently teaches introductory anthropology and a course on reconstructing Southeastern Indian agriculture while pursuing his Ph.D.

In his leisure time, Keyes enjoys ethnic cooking—particularly Central American, Szechuan, and Turkish cuisine—heirloom gardening, and *kapucha toli*, a Choctaw Indian sport involving heavy wooden sticks and few rules.